Dark Side of a Promise

Allan Hudson

Copyright © 2012 Allan Hudson

All rights reserved.

ISBN:
9780988160101

DEDICATION

For Gloria Anne Hudson, the brightest star in my sky

ACKNOWLEDGMENTS

Thank you to my family for their support and encouragement.
An extra special thanks to my two dearest friends, Gracia & Allen Williston for believing this could be done.

Cover design by Manchu Mark Young Designs

Cover model – Nathalie Brun

Thanks to Adam Hudson for explaining guns. Also to Chris & Mireille for the positive vibes.

The following people need to be mentioned for their input, Cynthia Shannon, Carolyn Jardine, Dylan Wright and Ihtisham Kabir

September 21 2004 6:24am

The memory of broken young bodies is still crisp after three long years. They won't leave, they never diminish and they continue to haunt the man standing on the teak deck of his summer home contemplating the rise of the dawning sun over Cocagne Bay. Drake Alexander stands tall against the railing; his strong features are in silhouette to the waking day. An autumn breeze caresses the taut muscles of his sleek torso. Beneath a forceful brow, eyes of the deepest brown stare out at the changing elements. Drake has just finished his predawn swim, a vitalizing ritual that keeps him hardy.

The wafting air is scented with the brine of the sea water that laps gently against the pebbled shore. The horizon burns like hot embers as the sun toasts the scattered clouds a fiery orange. Amidst the cry of frenzied gulls a lone heron silently glides down on open wings, settling lightly into the water. The tide is going out. Soon there will be a hedge of heron dining. Drake is always amazed at this intelligent and adaptive bird that swallows its prey live and whole. He knows of humans with similar dispositions.

Not far from his home a working wharf juts into the water, its curved rocky spine protecting the fishermen and their vessels. A Millennium Marine fishing craft slowly moves away from the pier, taking its owner to another day's wages. Soft ripples from the bow of the boat distort the watery images. The calmness of the bay is inverse to the angst Drake is feeling. He waits for word from his long-time ally and most trusted friend, Williston Payne. Several days ago Williston had alerted Drake that there had been a sighting. Drake waits patiently, sensing his friend was rattled.

Drake knows from his long association with Williston that his information can always be trusted. Information is intangible wealth. Williston's worldwide business interests are legion; his prestigious law firms specializing in international, corporate and tax law are the most influential. With offices spread around the world, his access to information is phenomenal. In their adolescence, Drake had learned from Williston that information is a commodity much like oil or diamonds and that it has to be verified, classified, assimilated, bargained for and traded. Although time makes a lot of material insignificant, the useful intelligence is treasured and filed safely away for future use. Williston stores many secrets in safety deposit boxes in countries that are as disinterested in the contents as the steel that houses them.

Drake is knocked from his reverie by the ringing of his phone – a silly birdsong that his sister Glory, an ornithologist had emailed him. He has assigned it to Williston's cell phone number. He reaches for his cell, which is always nearby.

"Good morning, buddy," Drake said, confidant that Williston is on the other end.

"Good morning to you, too," Williston responds gruffly, then after a troubled pause gets right to the point of his call. "I received notice from Uday last Sunday that he needed to see me urgently, in person. He came to my office earlier today..."

Drake waits for Williston to continue, never having known him to be without words.

"And?"

"Sorry, Drake, but Uday's visit provoked so many miserable memories that I'm still shaken."

"Well, he has been known to stir things up. Isn't that one of the reasons you enjoy associating with him?" asks Drake, knowing that the bond that ties Williston and Uday Saad together is much deeper than their business dealings. The death of Williston's sister Amber and one of her dearest friends, Sakeema Saad - Uday's eldest daughter - three years ago, has cemented the two men in grief and revenge. The pain of absence lingers in their memories but the greatest pain is that that the man responsible – the sadistic and ruthless mercenary Bartolommeo Rizzato - is still at large.

"Uday thinks he knows where Rizzato might be." Williston explained, "And we know that where Rizzato is, something bad will happen. He's a demon willing to carry out anyone else's rancor. Someone with enough money has hired him for his tasteless talents."

"A demon?"

"Well, that's another satisfying and distasteful word I can use to describe the bastard. Regardless, we need to find out if he is indeed there" said Williston.

"Where are you getting your info from Williston? Rizzato is not stupid and like other vermin, knows how to hide and stay alive."

"You remember Uday's nephew, Rafan Bashara, who runs his Bangladeshi offices in Dhaka?"

"Yes I do," replied Drake. "He's the Harvard graduate, a real whiz kid. I met him at his aunt's wedding, when Uday's youngest sister got married last spring."

Williston explains, "On Saturday Rafan sent word to Uday that he overheard Rizzato's name in a conversation at a bar. He then befriended the stranger, who was drunkenly boasting of his acquaintance with Rizzato and the work they were doing south of the city. Rafan tried to get him to divulge more information, but the worker was too far gone to make any sense. Rafan secured him at his apartment with hopes of getting more details from him in the morning, but the man slipped away sometime late in the night."

Again Williston hesitates, sad memories and a bad feeling make him pause before continuing.

"The next day, Rafan found the man's mutilated body in the trunk of his car. It was evident that he had been tortured. Obviously Rafan wasn't the only one to overhear the boastful ramblings and they must have been followed. That's when Rafan notified Uday."

"Yeah... this has Rizzato's stink on it. Where is Rafan now and what is he saying?"

"We don't know. He hasn't been heard from since Saturday, the day he found the body and spoke with Uday. Thinking this incident might lead us to Rizzato, Uday's men left the body where it will eventually be found and disposed of the car so as not to draw any unnecessary attention for the present. We need your help Drake."

Drake was about to respond when Williston adds, "There's more. The body had a crude Z cut into the back shoulder just like Amber's. We both know what that means."

The implication of the three year old clue leaves Drake speechless. Images of Amber in happier times fill some seconds for both men until Williston says, "I'll wrap things up here in Geneva today, keep Uday with me. We'll try to locate Rafan and then fly out first thing tomorrow morning on the company jet. I've got some more digging to do, so meet us on the *Drifter's Dream*. We'll be anchored off the north east coast of Antigua, out past Jumby Bay Island. If you're flying down, I'll have the beacon on – you'll find us."

With a voice of bitter malice, Williston charges Drake, "Find this man for us, Drake, and put him away... or kill him this time!"

"I will, Williston, I promise!"

CHAPTER 1

Drake pockets his phone and reluctantly turns his back on the rising sun. He retains faith that he will return to see it again. Williston's call has given credence to Drake's earlier unease and leaves him feeling restive. He senses he is on the precipice of something significant, something diabolical. It feels like a small insect crawling up the back of his neck, a small segmented creature called *danger*. It isn't fear; fear had abandoned him many years ago.

Drake makes his way across the deck, his bare feet against the warm darkly stained wood, and into the house, calling for his housekeeper, Jemina. The aroma of fresh baking tells him she is in the kitchen, where she is preparing breakfast.

Jemina and her husband, Luis, maintain this large house, giving Drake the freedom to come and go as he pleases. They and their three children have been in Canada for 22 years since Drake's father, Jacob, rescued them from Peruvian poverty and sponsored them as immigrants from South America. The Pisconte's are indebted to the Alexanders, and reward them with undying loyalty and love. After Drake's father died two years ago, the mantle of their continued employment and care had fallen to Drake, who accepted it graciously, knowing that his father would have expected it of him. Drake always reminded himself that this was Jacob's way. Having toiled long hard hours over the years to become the success he was, he always took the time to help others.

Calling out to her, Jemina responds to Drake's summons, hurrying into the great room that faces the bay, her tiny feet shuffling across the wide-board pine floor. "What do you need, Drake," she casually asked, the language escaping melodically from her lips. Still pleasing to the eye at 46, her dark hair falls delicately to her shoulders, framing a shy sweet face. Her diminutive frame is clad in the linen blouse and pants she wears while attending to Drake's needs, the bright hues of her attire redolent of her homeland. Although not much older than Drake, who is 38, she fusses over him like a second mother.

This maternal instinct kicks in as she notices Drake's countenance; she'd seen this before when he left unexpectedly and for reasons unexplained, often for months on end. She rationalizes in her mind that over the two decades she's known him, he has always lived life as if he were on a perpetual dare. She, however, is constantly worried. All she can do is see him off with whatever care he allows her to give, but she never lets him go easily.

"I'm leaving to join Williston for a bit and I'll need you to pack about a week's worth of clothes, please. Some light cottons, several work pants and black tees, raincoat, a light fleece and my usual boots and shoes. Oh, and some deck shoes. We'll be on the *Drifter* and you know how fussy Williston can be," he tells her, trying to act as if an impulsive but casual excursion is in the offing. He figures Jemina is probably on to him, but he doesn't want to cause her concern. If she knew where he'd been and what he'd done over the years, no matter how justified he felt his actions to be, she would probably have him tied up and sedated for the rest of his life to protect him.

"I don't like it when you and Williston get together sometimes, I think you both like trouble too much. You always come back with too many cuts and bruises and sometimes with broken bones," exclaimed Jemina. Looking at him more directly, she places her hand on his arm as if for reassurance and continues, "You always defending somebody, Drake." Fear breaks up her usual faultless diction.

Drake dislikes lying, and the worry he causes her. "You fret too much, Jemina. I'm meeting Williston on his boat and we're going to cruise the Caribbean for a week or two. Eric Clapton is playing in Antigua to raise funds for the Crossroads Centre next week, so we're going to check that out. It's at an intimate venue and by invitation only. Williston is quite the socialite these days. Money and benevolence get him on just about any invitation list he likes. It should be fun. I'll mind my business this time, okay?"

"You are not fooling me, Drake. You be careful. What else do you need?"

Grabbing his shirt from the back of the recliner he proceeds to an antique writing desk. Opening the top drawer he withdraws his passport. Passing it to Jemina, he said, "Please put this with my things for now. I'm taking the Zodiac over to the Island later to get the plane ready and I'll need some help. Do you know where Luis and Alvaro are?"

"Luis left 20 minutes ago to meet with the contractor who's adding the addition to your garage," Jemina replies, leading him toward the kitchen. "Seriously, what are you going to do with all those vehicles you keep buying?" she asks rhetorically, knowing that Drake enjoys his toys. And besides, it keeps Alvaro, her youngest son, busy. "Alvaro will be at the shop in about an hour to start on that engine you wanted changed. Not everyone is an early riser like us, Drake." She points to Drake's usual place at the breakfast nook, with the local newspaper folded neatly on the table, and begins preparing his morning repast. Never having enough food for her or her family many years ago makes Jemina a frugal and practical housekeeper, but she never skimps on anyone with an appetite and she knows that Drake loves to eat.

"After breakfast I'm going to Beth's for a couple of hours and I'd like Luis and Alvaro to get the Skywagon ready, do the pre-flight check, top up the tanks, ," Drake said, seating himself where Jemina has carefully laid out a setting, "I'd like to be away around noon or one o'clock."

"I'll tell them both. Now read your paper and I'll get this ready for you. I'll pack your things when I'm done here."

Both Jemina and Drake fall into a pensive mood. Jemina wondering what Drake is really up to but too polite to ask when he isn't forthcoming with details. She busies herself, a bright red and yellow blur gyrating around the kitchen with efficient silence. Drake watches Jemina fuss reminding him of a humming bird, always busy, always with a purpose. He muses with great affection about how much she and her family mean to him.

The breakfast nook is an annex to the main kitchen area. The nook was architecturally planned to take advantage of the enticing seaside surroundings. Tall glass windows with the lightest, transparent curtains face the water at an angle to the great room they had just come from. Dark brown marble tiles with a rusty colored hue cover the floor. Wood from Italian olive trees with striking burls throughout, lightly stained a matching rust, formed extensive cupboards set against a taupe background. Olive trees were only cut after the tree reached such maturity that it did not bear fruit any longer. While alive, the trees were always trimmed short so that the fruit was easy to reach. Long and wide pieces were rare, making the cabinets markedly impressive and *very* expensive. Stainless steel and black enhancements frame all the appliances. Jemina, with her effervescent presence, would never blend in; she is the exclamation point. The early sun, more yellow now, streams in casting a mellow ambiance. Photos, mementos, keepsakes and memories are tastefully placed about, making the room personal, making it a home.

Jemina presents Drake with his favorite breakfast, a mouth-watering blend of South American and Western cuisine: bacon, cheesy corn cakes called *arepas de queso*, toasted honey quinoa bread and a boiled egg. Neither of them speak, Jemina is contemplative, Drake aflame.

Jemina hastily tidies up, leaving the rest of the kitchen details for later. Pouring Drake another cup of St. Helena coffee, she hesitates at his side. Her lingering quietude stirs Drake to look up and into her direct gaze. Jemina laments, "I don't know where you go at times, Drake, and I don't know what you do, but you remember that I love you like you're part of my family. The many days and months when you are around fill us with delight, and there will never be too many. You come home safe and as soon as you can."

At that very moment an errant beam of pure radiant sunlight reflects from the polished surface of the table causing a faint and delicate tear in the corner of her eye to twinkle. Before he can reply, she turns away, returning the coffee pot to its nest and hastens from the room.

Drake reflects on the moment; then tosses his reluctance to

answer aside. He needs to focus. He doesn't need sentimentality clouding his senses. He'll finish his breakfast and drop by Beth's place to say goodbye, then meet Luis on the island, get his gear packed into the plane, file a flight plan and fly out to meet Williston and Uday.

Drake jumps into his Jeep Wrangler, the top already down and pulls onto Route 535 heading north to Beth's parent's place several miles down the road. Her parents, both doctors who had established a busy and productive practice, and made several shrewd investments, are more than adequately moneyed. They had recently sold their practice and now serve as volunteers with *Doctors without Borders.* Beth maintains their country estate in their absence – a rambling and century-old farm that had been neglected for many years before they bought it. With the aspiration to own a working farm, Beth's parents had recreated the buildings in their original configuration and tenor with solicitous care. The modern, state-of-the-art facilities and equipment that made the farm functional are in some cases obvious, but most are cleverly disguised. It has a Rebecca of Donnybrook exterior with an ultra-modern interior.

Beth could certainly afford her own place, but she has spent most of her life enjoying both the natural landscape and the closeness of the sea just across the road. All four of her sisters have migrated to larger, more urban centers. Drake knows that she genuinely loves living here in rural New Brunswick, just as he also knows that she needs to be near him. They had met when his father had been building the house Drake lives in now.

Drake was born in Massachusetts, near his mother's home, but to a Canadian father who had grown up in this area and had purchased a plot of land shortly after he had inherited his father's jewellery business in 1965. Dominic Alexander, Drake's grandfather had immigrated to Canada from Scotland as a goldsmith apprentice in 1919, his earlier instruction interrupted by the Great War. A little luck, a little money and lots of charming honesty brought him respectful success throughout the '20s. Dominic never bought anything on credit, never sold anything on credit, stayed away from the stock market, banked his cash, invested in his own establishment and survived the crash of '29 in much better shape than his peers. Many businesses failed. The rich still wanted their baubles so Dominic's business on the other hand prospered. As a young man with an astute mind, Jacob joined his father's establishment, and they turned a one-store operation into a thriving four-store family business prior to Dominic's death.

Jacob was embedded in the métier of jewellery, with little time for socializing. In 1950, however, he attended an extravagantly large trade show in New York City that introduces many of the world's finest jewellery pieces and suppliers. There he met Mellissa Wilbraham. Wilbraham's Fine Jewellery was an influential corporation that owned nine stores throughout New England as well as a small manufacturing facility outside of Boston. He wooed her, married her, and united the businesses by setting up offices in both the United States and Canada. They made a winter home in Plymouth, Massachusetts; summers were spent in New Brunswick at their cottage on the old homestead. In 1965, Jacob purchased land in Cormierville that contained a section of wooded land on the west side of Route 535 with five fabulous cleared acres on the east side. Those five acres had over 900 feet of beach frontage that every day either frolicked or did battle with the waters of the Northumberland Strait. That's where he built the grand and fashionable summer home. The one where Drake met Beth. Incredible summers, idyllic romances, crumbled hearts, sun-drenched afternoons, a few bruises – a small collection of the events making those days unforgettable.

Drake slows the Jeep as he approaches the driveway to Beth's place. Turning into the rustic lane, Drake is assailed with the pleasant aroma of cut hay. The gathering season is well under way. As he continues toward the house, he notices the seasonal workers harvesting the bounty so generously produced from the earth. Huge round bales of fodder dot the fields. Drake imagines the generations of farmers before them who had worked the same fields, albeit with differing methods of cultivation, to meet the same demands of their livestock.

Beth must have seen him arriving because she is coming from the back entrance, waving to Drake as he approaches. Bringing his vehicle to a halt, he cut the ignition and jumps from the Jeep. He hollers out, "Glad to see you got that cute ass of yours out of bed so early. I didn't call in because I like surprising you. "

Beth hurries to his side to quickly embrace him with a hearty hug and a quick kiss on the cheek before replying, "Well I'm glad to see that cute ass of yours in my driveway. What brings you around today? I thought you and Alvaro were working on the old truck you bought."

Beth's natural beauty always gave him pause. Her blondish locks are tied back in a classic ponytail, highlighting her pleasing face. Chocolate colored eyes radiate her pleasure at seeing Drake. A square jaw complements her face, portraying an image of unabashed confidence and creating the perfect setting for her audacious and teasing smile. A strict disciplinarian with her habits, she works out daily keeping her body as lithe as a dancer. Clad in white knee-length denim shorts, a red sleeveless top and beige leather sandals she portrays a casual, yet intoxicating image. Drake always joked Beth would look great in a burlap bag.

Eager to share the recent revelation, Drake gets right to the point, "I spoke to Williston earlier. He met with Uday, Sakeema's father. You know him, don't you?"

Beth catches the shift in Drake's demeanor. The delight in their greeting changes to one of grim interest for both of them. She moves toward the cedar gazebo, beckoning Drake to follow and leads him inside. Moving to the compact refrigerator neatly tucked into a kitchenette, she remarks, "Yes, of course, I met him briefly at her funeral. I had an opportunity to talk to him and get to know him better at Williston's birthday party last year when I visited Chrissie." She points to a white wicker chair smothered in cushions, tosses Drake a box of juice then sits opposite him.

Chrissie Alexander, Drake's cousin, is the managing partner of Williston's Geneva law office. As a teenager she became an integral part of Williston's "Gang of 7" – a clique that grew from kids caught between a world of adults and children. They found each other, grew with each other and defended each other. A lifelong trust developed. The girls in the group – Chrissie, Beth and Amber – experienced an affinity cemented by independence and mutual compassion.

Drake shifts in his seat and explains, "The scent of Sakeema and Amber's assassin is strong! Uday has sent word that one of his business managers – also a close member of his family - befriended a local who mentioned Bartolommeo Rizzato's name."

Leaning forward to give his words more emphasis, he continues, "It's been almost two years since that slug slipped away from our last encounter. He only emerges from under some plank when he needs something... Maybe he ran low on cash or maybe he just needs to satisfy his malevolent appetite to maim and ultimately destroy. Powerful people, capable of the same brutality, find him useful. Right now, it seems he's committed to something in Bangladesh, Dhaka more significantly. It's imperative that we hunt him down."

Drake pauses. His words have spewed out in a rush. He too still aches from the girls' demise. The memory is like a knife in his gut; the odor of failure still pungent. Had they connected all the clues just twenty-four hours earlier, the girls would still be alive. Drake remembers too well their discarded bodies, raped and beaten.

Three years ago Drake and his band of confederates, a couple of Canadian Special Ops from Joint Task Force Two, Elijah and Isaac Glass and a former American Ranger, Dakin Rush, had followed leads and clues to the back country in Venezuela. The girls had been on holidays. There Drake and his men had confronted a cadre of mercenaries and miscreants, provoking a shootout. They wiped out everyone until the last man who was seriously wounded. He lived long enough to relinquish the name of the leader – Rizzato – and tell them where the bodies were.

Rizzato was not to be found. There had been no trail to follow. It was as if he had evaporated. At present, the need to find this man weighed heavily on Drake. He stirs from his musings determined that this time he would.

"I get carried away Beth. I let hate obscure my thoughts. I can't rest until Rizzato is behind bars ....or dead." Drake says before pausing to cool down. "Anyway I'm off to meet with Williston and Uday in Antigua to find out what's going on. I'm taking my father's plane."

Beth knows the burden Drake carries. They've been lovers for many years and many nights over the past three years she had offered succor to his crushed heart and fragmented ego. She adores Drake enormously; she always has, always will. If she could shift even some of his pain to herself she would do so gladly. She reaches over and takes Drake's hand in hers. Giving it a gentle squeeze to reassure him that she understands, she replies, "I've said it a thousand times, just as Williston has; it is not your fault, Drake. You are the bravest, most honorable person I know, and you *will* find him. We have the resources to help." Then Beth adds, almost pleadingly, "I'll go with you; I'll cover your back."

"No Beth. You're one of a small group of protectors I would trust as backup, but if anything ever happened to you and I was unable to help, I'd never ever forgive myself for accepting your brave offer. Besides you're an artist now, a singer – a damn fine one, too. Your career is budding; you're working on a new album, you've got that gig in Ottawa coming up, then four nights at the Club Macundo in New York. I'm so proud of you and what you've accomplished. I won't let you endanger your future."

Letting go of Beth's hand, Drake finishes his juice, stands and walks to the one of the windows He leans his shoulder upon the wood separating the windows staring out at the panorama before him. The sun is higher now. The window header causes a shadow to fall across Drake's chest, casting his upper torso in dim light. Minor shadows define and highlight the facets that make up Drake's handsome face. He looks out past the tended lawns, certain sections bearing flora of abundant color and bursting charm, past the road to the inlet beyond and considers what precautions he must take. He gives some thought to taking Beth. Her ability to handle herself is never in question – her dad is an avid hunter and gun fancier. Beth took naturally to weapons and is well able to defend herself. But he will have to insist she remain behind. There isn't a single iota of mercy to be found in these opponents and if they were to capture Beth he might not be able to save her.

Drake spies an osprey gliding aloft, heading out to the bay for sustenance. He's thinking that shortly the wondrous bird will be returning in his direction weighed down with an unlucky Perch. Amazingly the fish's head always seems to face forward, the indomitable hunter striking from behind, embedding its spiked talons along the unguarded spine. Probably while still suffocating from being out of the water, the doomed captive will relinquish his living flesh to a sharp-edged beak and waiting gullet. Feeling sorry for the fish is like apologizing for the rain or cheering when the chipmunk makes it across the road; it wouldn't make any difference. *It was meant to be.* Failure, however, is *never* part of Drake's plan. His resolve to take one step at a time, look around every corner and expect the unexpected, occupies his psyche and he momentarily drifts into deep thought.

Beth remains quiet. She isn't going to pressure Drake to allow her to accompany him; his tone of voice makes it clear it is not an option. She knows he will be prioritizing his movements. Right now he is likely dredging his memory, ferreting for contacts, the people he will need to speak to tomorrow, possibly the day after; people he knows might be able to help him in Dhaka.

Beth is well aware Drake can likely handle any conflict. He craves it! He's been a soldier all his life. As a small boy his favorite toys were weapons and a compass. He always had to be one of the good guys. A natural leader, sometimes getting everyone into trouble but more effective at making them feel like heroes.

Missions with great peril often times would seek volunteers. Drake would be the first in line. The tinge of intrigue, the prospect of endangerment and the notion of honor are what spurs Drake to action. She remembered longing for his furloughs when he was in the Armed Forces, rushing into his arms when he got back, his lean and muscled body enclosing her, knowing only then that he was safe.

Beth shifts in her chair, the mid-morning shadows claiming her body. She glances up at Drake, indulging herself in his good looks. He is wearing a black linen shirt recklessly hanging over khaki jeans, both suitably wrinkled. Drake bears a rugged complexion but his skin is taut from the fresh air, sun and rain. His brazen looks are softened by straight, dark brown hair, which is a little long and doesn`t see a comb too often. She loves the way he subconsciously nods his head to toss the hair from his forehead. She longs... no, she aches, to hold him to her never letting go. To stop him from always running off, taking chances that he might not survive.

Knowing Drake most of her life, she remembers a different man from the past, a man possessing a deep sense of duty. Not the man before her with his desperate need for revenge. Many years before Amber died, action and obligation drove them to numerous adventures. They shared days, months - years in fact – of luxuriant freedom, of risky and unexpected undertakings, of blissful, heady romance when he left the Army. They lived, loved, learned and travelled on every continent for four years with

Drake's trust fund covering all the costs. And then Amber and Sakeema were abducted while they holidayed together. Drake the soldier responded. Gathering his resources and war buddies, he searched for and found them... but too late. Bringing home their bodies was his penance for failing to rescue them.

Many people shared the burden of searching and digging for information on the girls, following trails, finding clues. And many shared the burden of defeat. Drake alone bore the weighty belief that there was more he could have done. Unable to save the sister of his dedicated pal changed him. Williston, of course, saw no fault in Drake's actions and praised him for his efforts. Williston's hurt was deep, for he had great affection for his whole family but Amber had been his favorite. Williston hurt for Drake, too. Drake had never before faced such raw and pure evil. Having been to war was no easy lesson for any man, for few should have to attend that school, but Drake took an oath to defend and did it bravely. Having witnessed the result of killing for pleasure was something he had difficulty in understanding. He vowed then that the villain would be punished.

For 15 months he pursued what seemed a wraith, a shadow called Rizzato. Some of Williston's contacts both above and underground knew of him but not his whereabouts. In May of 2002, Rizzato was spotted in the Netherlands. Drake found him in Amsterdam, in the red light district. Unbearable pleasures injected with high-octane pain is available behind doors that could only be pried open with the smooth grease of money. The patrons are carefully culled and vouched for. With enough money, you can buy anything.

All Drake's adrenalin and pent up need for vengeance clouded his thinking, threw him off balance. He rushed his nemesis. The expiration of his relentless pursuit and anger misguided him, causing him to lose the luxury of surprise. Rizzato, whose lifestyle demanded it, always had an escape plan. But first he had to run. Drawing his firearm from an ankle holster, Drake gave chase along Bloedsraat until some pumped up teenager stealing a car, tore out of a driveway. Drake's full attention was on taking aim at Rizzato's thigh, wanting to bring him down, when he collided with the front fender of the stolen car. The command to shoot had already left the control room of Drake's brain, reaching his finger in nanoseconds. The shot, microseconds later, was thrown high just as Rizzato veered to his right. The bullet, travelling at 1000 metres per second, pulverized the upper portion of Rizzato's ear and took with it a sample of his bushy eyebrow. The unexpected impact of the car threw Drake to the ground. He reached out to protect himself and the force of his momentum broke his shoulder and jarred his head just enough to knock him briefly unconscious. Rizzato, bleeding and terrified, escaped into the night, the darkness engulfing him.

Beth stands quietly moving close to Drake. She reaches her arms around his middle laying her head upon the tense muscles of his upper back. She moulds herself to his hardened body feeling him soften. Her closeness gives him comfort. Still mulling over his options, he responds to her gesture by placing his hand over hers and gratefully squeezing.

She realizes that Drake's commitment to this act of vengeance will take all his time and energy until the evil man is caught. So she will have to take what part of Drake she can get for the present. For the next hour or two she'd help him forget things, however briefly.

Speaking in a soft longing whisper, she says, "Come into the house with me, Drake. For the next short while, take me to the place where only you and I count" Drake acknowledges her request by turning to take her in his arms, her head now resting on his chest. He knows in the coming days that he will be entering a different and incomplete world but for the present he will relinquish his inner core to this magnificent creature. He'll let her transform his thoughts of the coming danger to moments of safe and lofty desire.

Tomorrow Drake will be gone. His return is not given any consideration at this point, just a desired outcome hoped for by both of them.

Chapter 2
April 20 2004 8:10pm

Situated mostly in Durham County, North Carolina, the Research Triangle Park is the largest research park in the United States. It's called the Triangle because of its location amid the three cities of Raleigh, Durham and Chapel Hill. The park has over 130 R&D facilities. More than 150 organizations with as many as 39,000 employees make it one of the most prominent research and development centers anywhere. The largest IBM operation in the world, with 11,000 workers, can be found in the Triangle.

Among the park's 7,000 acres sits a nondescript building of masonry and glass that houses Reactor Chemicals Inc. It is in this building that pesticides are manufactured. Below ground is a 20,000gallon storage tank that holds methyl isocyanides, commonly referred to by chemists as MCI. MCI is a highly toxic material that's been around since 1888. It killed thousands in Bhopal, India, when the Union Carbide gas tragedy occurred in 1984, and continues to cause long-term health issues to this day.

The plant, once a private enterprise owned by a local entrepreneur, has recently been acquired by Crossbow Holdings Limited, an offshore company registered in Belize. The sole reason for the acquisition is so that Crossbow will own the gas stored in the bowels of the property. The gas will become a weapon. To appease the animus of Andrew Stratton, the new owner of Reactor Chemicals, this gas will eventually destroy hundreds of his hated enemies, and continue to curse thousands of their descendants. For his plans, it will be his ultimate manifestation of reprisal. The procurement of the facility is but one step in a carefully prepared plan.

Six months ago Stratton's life changed drastically. The murder of not just one but two of his children caused a formidable awakening that he had not given his children enough of his time while they were alive. It also causes a deep bereavement. Prior to this, work and profit were all that mattered to Stratton. Everything else he had taken for granted, especially his family.

*

In Raleigh the late day rain is ending. The subsiding sun is making a final attempt to show itself from behind steel-grey, roiling clouds while flinging intermittent light over the city. The inferior rays creep into the darkened house on Casey Leigh Lane and clings to the open areas. Andrew Stratton sinks deep into the padded chair as he sits before the door that faces the wooded area to the rear of the safe house, his mood matching the grayness of the evening. The scent of his unwashed body dominates the other smells of this neglected, temporary residence. He is concentrating on a smudge in the top right corner of the patio door and it irritates him. Many things irritate him these days.

He gazes at his reflection in the glass. The face looking back at him is haggard and well beyond the 52 years it should represent. The hair is still plentiful but the grey predominates. Hazel eyes, large and set a bit too far apart, creates a menacing and castrating glare. High cheekbones with a strong chin give his face the dominance it once commanded, but the skin is sagging. He looks tired. Reaching down to the wicker and steel coffee table before him, he picks up his glass of Lagavulin malt whiskey – his fifth of the evening – while scrutinizing the three photos on the table before him.

Pictures of his son Scott and youngest daughter Sarah sit grouped on the right in muted glass frames nestled together just barely touching. Ironically the juxtaposition of the photos reflect the closeness of the real people. Sarah idolized Scott and the two were often inseparable. She had looked to him for guidance, advice and the love that her father failed to provide. He had been missing in their lives. In the end, it didn't matter; they lived their lives without him. Now they were dead. Kidnapped, ransomed and destroyed. Andrew learned much later that the kidnappers had never had any intention of letting Sarah and Scott live. The third frame, sitting by itself on the left as if the separation might keep her from the same destiny, is their sister Sophia.

Andrew drains the last of the amber liquid from his glass. Setting the tumbler down beside the photo of Sophia, he reflects upon his only living child, so unlike the other two. Sophia is more like her mother, Janice: calm, easy going, always thinking things through – her life has a rudder. But there is a mischievous aspect to Sophia's character also. A calm persona that hid a proclivity for intelligent wit.

He picks up the photo, studying the fine features that make his daughter such a beautiful woman. Eyes that twinkle are soft blue, a dimpled smile, short brownish straight hair casually borders her pleasing face. He remembers scoffing at her when she told him of her wish to be a firefighter. He figured this to be another of her amusements, like the time she wanted to back pack through South America, or when she decided to learn Spanish. Well, she proved him wrong by being accepted to wear the three-quarter boots and jacket of the Chicago Fire Department. She was stubborn and persistent with her ideas. She could have chosen so many different avenues, but he knows her to be happy. At least there is a semblance of family with Sophia; she came to his offices on numerous occasions often badgering him for being way from his family so often. As much as he discouraged her visits, she nevertheless cleaved to him like a small prickly burr and he abided her presence. Unfortunately the last time they spoke was over five months ago.

Andrew Stratton was monumentally changed the day he received word that Scott, a freelance investigative journalist, and Sarah, his accompanying photographer had been abducted by the al-Aqsa Martyrs' Brigade in Tel Aviv. He knew his children to be boundless in the search for truth based on their gregarious assumption that the world should know what is happening in every corner. They forged ahead chasing an idea or a rumor until it was either exposed as a fallacy or it became a story.

Andrew shifts in his seat, pulls an annoying cushion from his back to throw it to the floor. He grunts at the idea that they were just like him, two small hurricanes coming over the horizon. Nothing stood between them and their pursuit of answers. That is until they went digging into the Martyrs' Brigade's history. Andrew had known they were off to Palestine.

The 16 year old malt whiskey flows through his body like a euphoric whisper, beguiling him to sleep. His last thought before he nods off was that he hadn't known what they were after then, but he painfully knows now.

*

Scott Stratton was a natural-born snoop. Once, when he was nine years old, kicking around the neighborhood early on a Saturday morning, he came across the lifeless form of a cat near the curb. He assumed it had been stuck by an automobile. A small pool of blood gelled near the shattered jaw. At first he figured it to be a stray, but while bending over the carcass to quench a young boy's instinctive curiosity, he saw a beaded leather collar, much like his sister's bracelets, almost hidden in the fur. There were several beads showing with only the first two readable. They read K, I.

Scott's thinking, *K I is going to be late for lunch and some owner's wondering where their KITTY is.* Well, he doubted KI stood for Kitty so he searched around for something to prod the animal with to get a better look at the tag. He found a dead knotted branch at the base of an aging elm tree, using it to slowly turn the body, exposing the rest of the beads. He also exposed a gaping wound, further evidence that something had struck the animal hard. The beads read KISSY. As he stared at the beads, a sudden inexplicable urge overcame Scott. Finding the owner was important, and would probably be more difficult than he considered. But the idea took hold, much like a pair of locking pliers.

He spent the better part of the day knocking on doors, asking questions. Yes, some people had seen Kissy before, and finally one query led him to the rightful owner, a wrinkled, jovial old man who had one eye that didn't move when he spoke. The owner's delight upon learning of his pet's whereabouts quickly turned sour upon learning of its fate. Scott accompanied the owner to retrieve his feline companion. His earlier feelings of curiosity toward a dead, unfamiliar animal morphed into a sense of loss. As a boy, he didn't understand his first encounter with death. He always remembered, though, the old man's grief that rippled in its wake.

Scott was infused with a sense of accomplishment unlike any he had experienced before in his young life and decided to write down the details. With a little polish the details became a short story. The short story became an essay for his English class. His essay was such a success that his teacher exclaimed to the other students that Scott was one of very few students to be awarded such an exemplary mark in his writing class. He went on and on (much to Scott's embarrassment and delight) about how Scott's cleverly written words generated a variety of emotions in him for he too "had lost a dear and beloved pet." The teacher further explained that Scott's marvelous story revealed to him what it was like to have a free and uninvolved morning turn into a day of jolly adventure through the eyes and thoughts of a nine-year-old. The high recognition for his compelling tale kindled a spark in Scott; an inner drive. Over the next decade and a half Scott would distinguish himself many times with his investigative writings, but he still remained a bitter disappointment to his father, who had hoped to groom Scott as his successor.

A major falling out between them occurred just prior to Scott's 19th birthday in the summer of 1992. Andrew had missed Scott's high school graduation, busy fending off a protracted buyout by a competitor that took him to Washington State during Scott's commencement, but afterwards he convinced his son to join him at their holiday residence on Lake Michigan, about 55 miles from their home in Northbrook, to discuss Scott's future. Andrew naturally assumed that his son would give up his writing for the opportunity to eventually dominate an extremely profitable group of companies. He went into the weekend convinced he could steer his son in the proper direction.

They arrived by car early on a Thursday morning, having passed the last hour in relative silence; Scott still sleepy; Andrew still at work in his mind. They were greeted by a gentle breeze coming off the Lake. Scott loved it here and rushed through the ample backyard to the sweet-tempered shoreline just as he always had upon arriving here since he was small. He was greeted by rolling white froth that bubbled up onto the shore, then gently rolled back upon itself, leaving the sand a darker hue of brown, almost as if it were blushing at being exposed to the dappling sunshine. Scott felt that the fine way the day had begun was, perhaps, an omen – that his father would understand and graciously encourage him to pursue his writing.

Andrew was taking in their luggage and shouted out, "Give me a few minutes and I'll whip us up some breakfast. Your old man still makes the best omelet in town."

A few minutes turned into a few hours. Scott made breakfast. His father's, still on the table, was cold. After cleaning up, Scott ventured down to the edge of the property with a folded deck chair and a new Wilbur Smith novel under his arm. The scent of the neighbors' newly cut lawn commingled with the aroma of steaks cooking on someone's barbeque and provided a familiar, reassuring feeling. Chucking his T-shirt and sandals, he settled into the weathered chair and leaped into Smith's wonderful yarn. He was disturbed about an hour later by his father's presence. Having changed into shorts and a golf shirt, Andrew came striding across the lawn, barefoot, dragging another deck chair.

"Sorry I missed that meal you prepared, Scott. It looks like it was probably quite good."

Scott slipped a bookmark between the pages and shut his book as he straightened in the chair and gave his father a quirky smile, saying, "That's okay Dad. I know you're a busy man running your companies."

Andrew fumbled with his chair for a minute before plopping down next to Scott, facing the water. He commented on Scott's book, and then asked him about graduation, his many girlfriends, being editor of the school paper, and so on for the next half hour or so. An amiable silence fell. Their thoughts were interrupted by the flurry of two gulls fighting over something on the beach. They both spoke at once.

Andrew blurted out, "I think it's time to talk—"

"Dad, you know how—" Scott stopped and curled up with laughter; his father couldn't contain his mirth, either, and broke into a hearty guffaw. It would be the last time they would share a moment of unrestrained laughter together.

Scott took advantage of the light mood and for the next fifteen minutes or so told his father of his plans. "I've already been accepted at Eastern Illinois University. In the fall I'll be studying journalism and living on campus," Scott finished up with a confidant nod to his unusually taciturn father.

Andrew took a few moments before responding, surprised by Scott's ardor and earnest delivery.

"No, I don't think that's going to work Scott. You know I've spoken to you many times about you learning the business. I've created a formidable association of complementary interests, interests that are growing by twenty percent a year – unheard of in my field. You're to become my lieutenant, Scott, and there's a lot to learn"

Andrew rose from his chair, stuck his hands in his pocket and walked several steps to the edge of the sand. He admired a sloop sliding by in the limpid mocking air and remained quiet to allow his revelation to sink in. With his back to Scott, he failed to catch his son's look of astonishment.

Scott came to his feet as well, baffled by his father's instructions. Propelling himself past his father and turning to face him, he questioned him. "Didn't you hear what I just explained to you a moment ago?"

"Of course I heard you, but I don't think you should give up this opportunity. You're only 18. You can't possibly know what you want to do for the rest of your life. That's a long time. At least, we hope it's a long time".

He chuckled at his minor quip, then quickly followed up, "I have an appointment for you next week with Jerome Davies – one of the department heads at Stanford University. They have one of the best business schools in the world, in my opinion. We're friends from our own university days."

Scott took a step closer and stared into his father's dogged eyes. Scott's mind raced with painful thoughts. *We don't even know each other. He never listens to me. He treats me like an employee, ordering me around. I never want to be like him.*

Scott interjected with as much calm as his indignant scorn would allow him, "What makes you think you can decide the rest of my life? You know I've never shown an interest in what you do. If you ever cared, you would know how much writing and books and newspapers fascinate me. All you think about is your company and your profits. You never cared about any of us." The last remark was relayed with a bit of acid.

Andrew had faced many adversaries. Squaring off with his son though, was daunting. He never expected Scott to act so independently. With his feelings momentarily pained, he remarked, "What do you mean, I don't care? Why do you think I work so hard for? I want you all to have the best and that takes work, lots of work. I know my work has been all-consuming, but I do it for you, your sisters and your mother." Somewhat on the offensive, he added, "You didn't seem to mind the profits, as you call it, when you were spinning around the neighborhood in the Mustang I bought you last summer or when you were snowboarding in the French Alps last winter."

In a somber tone, his earlier acrimony overcome by sorrow for his father's blindness Scott admitted, "Yes, you were generous with money, but you've been horribly selfish with your time. Things can't replace a father. Where were *you* my whole life? You never came to any of my baseball games. You never took me fishing. You haven't seen my stamp collection. You probably haven't even read any of my stories."

The pot boiled over and like escaping steam, the condemnations continued. This time they were meant to hurt,

"Did you know that Sarah is gay? Did you know that mother has a thing for delivery men? Did you know that your precious Sophia was sexually accosted by Mr. Finney when she was babysitting for him last year? Probably not, mother did everything she could to keep it hush-hush suggesting Sophia probably brought it on herself, always dressing so provocatively and accusing her of being promiscuous. Why do you think Sophia wanted to go to a private school out of state? Did you know she sees a psychiatrist?" Scott shifted his stance, backed off for a second, then with a hurtful tone that encompassed all his malaise asked, "How could you know any of these things when you were never really a part of our family. We're merely possessions to you, something you use to impress upon your peers that you're not always a bully."

Andrew, mouth agape in disbelief, was stunned by Scott's aplomb. He dropped back into the deck chair and sat silently, the criticism heavy and burdensome. Scott turned his back to his father and waded out into the water, letting the wound fester a bit. The look on Andrew's face confirmed that Scott's condemnation stung him. Years of fatherly neglect confounded Scott. He hadn't meant to confront his father with this cocktail of family mix-ups, but he wanted him to know that everything wasn't all right. There was more to caring than an abundance of possessions. His family had needed him. Scott was more than certain the man had not earned the right or privilege to dictate his future.

A brief moment of repose bolstered Andrew into action. He rushed from the chair and grabbed Scott forcefully by the arm, spinning him to face his wrath, almost causing Scott to lose his balance. He was like a freshly castrated bull, his balls having been ripped off instead of cleanly and skillfully amputated. He raged at Scott, "You little son of a bitch, who do you think you are?" Then stressing each point, he said, "You can't begin to imagine the demanding responsibility of managing over 5000 employees. And do this well enough to generate income beyond your fragile and inexperienced imagination. It gives me outstanding people that respond immediately to my commands and it gives me money to dream bigger dreams. It gives me power."

Andrew backed off, maintained his authoritative pose and glared at his son with contemptuous eyes.

"I know about your mother. I'll deal with that in good time. As for the girls, well... they're complicated little creations and I don't understand them. Your mother knows more about those matters and she'll deal with it. But you! You must bear the yoke of our future. The fruits of my toil, my time and my sacrifices rightfully go to you, and you will look back upon this day as the defining moment of your life. You will do as I command!"

Scott returned his father's insolent stare thinking, *this man is obsessed*. Flashing through his mind was an image of the dinky little ashtray he gave him for father's day long ago with the goofy dialogue about any man can be a father. *He is so naive. This man before him is shallow and ego-driven. Family to him is just a facade.* Scott strode back to the shore, steering clear of his father, grabbed his shirt and sandals, tucked his book angrily under his arm and headed for the street, determined to get as far away from this situation as possible. Andrew watched Scott's retreat with certitude perched smugly upon his face. He muttered after the retreating figure,

"You'll see that I'm right!"

From somewhere in Scott's being, an alien emotion overcame him, a love-hate kind of rush. He turned to his father and the boy-man blurted out with jelled indifference, "Fuck you." Then he walked out of his father's life

After graduating from Eastern's school of journalism, recognition came rapidly after his *expose* on one of the nation's largest and most powerful unions and its connection to organized crime and government. It eerily gave modern-day unionization a 1920's personality. A well-placed figure in the union hierarchy used Scott's pen to come clean. Exhaustive secret meetings took place for several months, in which time Scott gleaned all the details along with the proof required to complete a hell-of-a story. The story linked an alleged gang lord, the union and the then governor of Illinois to a variety of scandals involving millions of union and taxpayer dollars backing illegal undertakings.

The story was known only to Scott and his editor until it went to press. At that moment, the chief of police and one of his nosiest detectives were invited to visit the main office. They were then introduced to Mr. J – the informant. They also met Scott's sister Sarah, whom he had asked to take photos of the accused in secrecy. There, she shot the front page photo of the police chief and detective placing handcuffs on Mr. J to take him into protective custody.

The story broke and dozens of arrests were made that same day. Mr. J testified and went into a witness protection program. The chief of police was promoted. The detective retired in glory and moved to Barcelona. Scott was selected as finalist for the prestigious Goldsmith Prize for Investigative Reporting. He quit his position to become a freelance journalist. Sarah joined forces with him and they became inseparable.

In March 2002, a suicide bomber, in retaliation for Israeli military action in the Palestine refugee camps, strolled casually up to a group of Israelis in the religious area of West Jerusalem. This living stick of dynamite exploded, killing himself and nine others. As many as 60 other people were injured in what has become known as the Beit Yisreal massacre. The militant faction Al-Aqsa Martyrs' Brigade claimed responsibility. That event, coupled with the killing of three Israelis by another bomber in the same month, brought ongoing peace negotiations to a halt. At that juncture in the talks, Israel called off their ceasefire deliberations that were taking place at that time. The United States no longer considered Arafat a colleague. The Brigade was annexed to Yasir Arafat's Fatah faction, which mostly directed its madness toward military installations but too often towards civilians. Therefore it was designated a terrorist group by both the United States and Israel.

Knowledge of this event, in Scott's mind, was something to pay attention to. At that time not much was known about the Brigade. Prior to their last caper, they would briefly make headlines but that would quickly become old. Scott was able to learn that they emerged during the time the Palestinians refer to as the "Second Intifada," around the year 2000.

The uprising would soon become deadly, so miserably unfair in its selfish indiscriminate selection of victims. Roughly a month later, a fervent copycat with the idea of a *blessed eternity* indelibly engraved in his mind entered a marketplace and discharged enough energy to dissolve himself into the already polluted atmosphere, simultaneously executing six civilians and harming 104 others. With no central power, Brigade units acted autonomously and freely. Ergo, intelligence services were often unsuccessful in discovering commanders among their alliance.

The Brigade laid claim to other seemingly random bombings and shootings throughout Jerusalem and northern Israel in the same year. Then in January 2003, with a double bombing in Tel Aviv, the Brigade committed one of the bloodiest onslaughts of the rampant Palestinian uprising. A catastrophic and disturbing pall fell over the Middle East. Western news agencies were clamoring for more news, more photos, and more information on this menacing upstart. What defined Al-Aqsa Martyrs' Brigade?

Scott had not done any major reporting on the Middle East. The preponderance of his work reflected his revulsion for corrupt politicians and there had been enough of that in the Western hemisphere to build a career on. Nevertheless, he felt the itch of a good story, plus he needed a change. He began preparations to visit Israel and gather some facts on the Brigade. Scott contacted Sarah and pulled her from her studio work, and together they flew to Jerusalem. Upon landing there, they took a prearranged chartered flight to Be'er Sheva (formerly Beersheba) where they would meet with Noam Pazy, the head of the Department of Politics and Government at the Ben Gurion University of the Negev. Scott had met Pazy, an elfish man with a monk's tonsure and a boisterous character, at a Harvard sponsored symposium on the Middle East. Pazy's presentation had been on *Force and Corruption in the Middle East*.

Pazy extended them very little time due to the many demands on him but because of his past familiarity with Scott greeted them warmly and offered what assistance he could. They were awarded with very general information. Most of it they could have heard at an Israeli coffee house. He told them what little he knew about the Brigade's doings and how they were affecting the lives of individuals, how they spread fear throughout the cities. He stated more emphatically that his expertise was of a political nature. He shared his thoughts of how recently re-elected Prime Minister Sharon would deal with future threats and how it would bear on his civic future; but as to where they were found or how they could be contacted, he was mute. The police and Mossad were investigating the Brigade, but there was no reason he or his department would be informed of their work. He did, however, suggest they contact a cousin of his, a very distant and not well known cousin, while in Jerusalem. He was a police officer with the *MAGAV* – the Border Police. He could probably find them someone they could talk to. Pazy pleasantly dismissed them and returned to his awaiting tasks, unaware he was sending them to their doom.

They met with Noam's cousin, Jarrah, a strapping individual with a full head of neat dark hair and matching beard. A deep baritone voice confronted them with apprehension. He was curious as to why American journalists were so fascinated by this rebellious faction. He felt an obligation to make himself available at his cousin's request but informed Scott and Sarah he would be no part of any glorification of the Martyrs' Brigade. He shared a policeman's populist view that they were a bunch of cowards who continued to murder innocents. Scott belayed any fears by outlining his story idea. He explained how he wanted to create a story that helped readers understand what would compel a human being to ultimately and decisively forfeit their life while bringing misconstrued honor and infamy to his family; remorseful and penetrating sorrow to families of blameless bystanders whose only common threads were their innocence and geography. He wanted to define this insanity, for his readers, through the eyes of the Brigade or someone close to them. What were they thinking? What was driving them?

The three of them spent an evening of beer and constructive exchange at *Mike's Place*, an uncommon bar cellared among courtly edifices, on Raoul Wallenberg in Ramat Hahayal. Started in 1993 by a retired Canadian photojournalist, it became a popular hangout for a divergent group of patrons. Soldiers, students, Arabs, Jews, travelers, diplomats – all manner of folks, all manner of dress came through the doors. The early evening was dissipating amid the chatter. Mellow mid-evening caught them half a dozen beers later, still exchanging views with Jarrah. He warned them of the trouble their snooping could cause.

Late in the evening, they were introduced to a young Arab boy clad in brownish dull and shabby garb. A bright cinnamon-colored face peered at them from under a traditional dark cotton kufi that sat upon a tangled mass of wicked curls. Jarrah warned Scott that he didn't know the boy well but had known his father for many years. His father had been shamed and disfigured some time ago because he refused martyrdom. He refused to take part in such violence. Beaten, his broken bones were poorly set, leaving him a cripple. And it made him resentful. He informed on his abusers. The father was never trusted by the militants, but anybody listening to the underside of conversations caught what was going on. Secrets here were like leaves in the breeze, fecklessly tossed about.

It was late at night. Unfamiliar shadows from strange dwellings and anomalous figures on unfamiliar streets intrigued and excited Scott. Remembering Jarrah's warnings, Sarah expressed a sense of foreboding as they hurried to keep up with their usher. Leaving the safety of their earlier companions, they followed him through a throng of partiers into a world they were going to regret for the very short remaining extent of their young lives.

Wrongfully trusting their adolescent accomplice, they followed heedlessly into unknown streets. With his sympathies reversed by the cruel hand of a desolate father, the indoctrinated sixteen-year-old, on his first mission for Allah, led them into the clutches of the Brigade. They disappeared from civilization and tumbled into a world of hate, a world of rage, a world of the complicated and viral belief that the destruction of Westerners was tantamount to world peace.

Accused of being Israeli spies, they were bound and victimized somewhere in the bowels of the city. Nothing of use was discovered because there was nothing of use to relay. Their abductors would not or could not accept that they were really journalists. The kidnappers soon discovered that Scott and Sarah's father was a rich and successful businessman. They cut a finger that bore a ring off each of their victims. Having earlier learned of Sarah's sexual preferences, they videotaped her then killed her immediately, taking the finger from a cold body, but Scott's finger they took while he was still alive. The gruesome ordeal was videotaped and packaged to accompany the fingers. As a signal that they knew about the old man that sometimes informed on them, and in a bitter hint of irony, the bundle was dropped on Jarrah's doorstep. Their bodies were never found.

*

Night has firmly settled over Raleigh. The clouds are heavy with water and fill the ebony sky, engulfing the moon and the stars. Accompanying gloom envelopes the house and it stirs with the occupant's depraved intent.

While cocooned in unsettled sleep, Andrew shakes physically, his vile dreams consuming him. Dream like specters disguised as armed, head-covered assailants clamped stout and forceful hands upon his gasping body, after he run fast and far from the very people he hated. It is more than any dream should command. While still dreaming his arm swing out, sweeping his drink onto the marbled floor. The noise from the shattering glass wakes him forcefully from his troubled torpor. He sits up with relief that he is actually here in this darkened house. Relief is quickly foreshadowed by the knocking in his skull. Mr. Hangover has brought his hammer.

He kicks a couple of errant cushions aside and rises from the chair. He groggily seeks out and chucks back some painkillers, following them with a gulp of cold, black coffee left from yesterday morning. He's hoping he'll be dead in a few minutes; he is in so much pain. He props himself up at the kitchen sink, his head hanging down, trying to ignore his stomach's continuing complaints. He curses out loud. He curses his drinking. He curses the Muslims who killed his kids, blaming them for his drinking. He curses the day he was shown the fingers. He curses the day he quarreled with Scott. He curses the money he has paid for nothing. He curses until his voice is just a whisper and his throat is dry as tinder. The painkillers in their powerful glory sideswipe the agony and clear Stratton's convoluted mind. He straightens up, turns and faces the battered box on the table. Inside are two worn and unpolished rings; the authorities wouldn't let him keep the fingers. They thought he was crazy. Andrew Stratton is crazy. But he is also very smart and very rich.

Today he has two things on his mind, to get his shit together, starting with a shower. Later today he is meeting Bartolommeo Rizzato face to face. He needs to look more like a dignified employer than the pathetic sop he's been the last few days feeling sorry for himself. They had talked before on untraceable cell phones. Rizzato suggested an abhorrent price at first. Now money is only a means to an end, so Stratton agreed. Things are being put in place. He isn't sure if he trusts this man, but his lawyer knows these people. Andrew doesn't want to know why. His plan is gaining momentum. He doesn't care that the people who killed his children are a war-like minority. He hates all Muslims. He conspires to execute as many as possible.

Chapter 3

Drake wades out into the water toward the bright red Zodiac sitting obediently between its two mainstays. He pulls in the front anchor and places it in the boat along with his two bags and climbs over the side as the boat stirs in the calm waters. He stows his gear in the stern then grabs the aft anchor line and pulls the craft into deeper water. The cool dampness of the rope is pleasant in his grip. Unfettered, the craft floats indifferently toward the wharf. He sets the motor, steps up to the controls, adjusts the throttle and flips the starter. The Yamaha's 75 horses respond with an impassioned roar. He espies Jemina standing at the edge of the deck, waving a yellow handkerchief, her solicitous way of warning him to be careful. He waves back and gives her thumbs up, opens up the throttle and swings the inflatable out toward the island, which lies half a kilometer off shore.

It is two islands actually, two larger multi-treed bodies connected with an umbilical of sand, saw grass and decades of crushed crustaceans. When the islands became available for purchase, made available by the provincial government divesting itself of unneeded properties, it was sought after by an assemblage of business people with hopes and plans to turn the northern portion into a condo development, with the south island becoming an accompanying golf course. Entrepreneurial hopes were dashed by a stormy protest of locals, ecologists and tree-huggers because the island was the home of a large heronry.

The geography of the island had been mostly unaltered for

centuries, other than by a few locals for camping or bird watchers, the odd hunter. People wanted it to remain that way. Drake settled the issue by outbidding everyone on the provincial government's tender, at twice the assessed value, and an announcement that the southern portion would be donated to the local university for conservation and learning opportunities in honor of his parents, while a ten-acre tract of the northernmost tip would be developed for his own private use, and inaccessible to the general public. The balance of the northern section would be turned into a camp and wilderness area for underprivileged children in conjunction with a local boys and girls club fully financed by Drake's benevolence. It didn't please everybody, but then, was that really possible?

Out past the submerged sand dunes and crossing the channel to the open water, Drake revs up the Zodiac, the hull rising nobly over the water as the boat rips across the shallow waves in the outer fringes of the bay. Tight against the propeller, the agitated water froths and roils into the extended V of the wake as Drake propels himself toward his fate. As he arches the boat out around the northern tip of the island, he passes a small strip of land that points a rough and sandy accusatory finger at him. It causes him to think back of the time he spent with Beth earlier. So much passion! He remembers her as he left her, kneeling naked on the bed. She modestly hugged a pale satin sheet to her chest while one artful breast poked impishly from its folds, her eyes pleading with him not to go. No matter what befalls him, Drake knows being loved so deeply makes leaving difficult, but it makes the inevitable so much more bearable.

Closing in on the east side of the island, he is confronted by the Skywagon secured to the docking pier, keeping time with the undulations of the water. It truly and splendidly gleams in the sunlight. Luis is in love with it, keeping it shined and in pristine condition. It is Jemina's only competition. The sapphire blue of the lower body and tail compliments the beryl and cerulean couplet of water and sky. The wings and upper fuselage beam a solid white, buffed hundreds of times by Luis' devoted hands.

This particular 185 model is a 1964 Cessna, one of 4,400 Skywagons built. Jacob bought it in 1985 with about 10 million hours on her – the very same year they stopped manufacturing them. It was also the last tail dragger Cessna would ever make. Copied after the older WWII type aircraft, with a third wheel mounted under the tail rather than the nose, it had quirky landing and takeoff mannerisms. Tail draggers sometimes have a bad attitude, with their disposition to ground loop. The insurance is crazy.

Jacob had picked the plane up from a down-and-out bush pilot in northern Canada when he'd been up there hunting. Saying it was in bad shape would have been kind. When time allowed, Jacob, Drake, Luis and later Alvaro were forever restoring something, sometimes alone or in pairs but often together as a group. They would remember those experiences as good times, a time to bond, a time of eager learning, of growing trust.

When Luis first came to Canada, working for Jacob he became known for his tinkering. It was soon discovered that he possessed a natural aptitude for anything mechanical. Being exposed to Jacob's extensive collection of tools, housed in a garage so incredible it would flabbergast the most seasoned mechanic, he quickly mastered the intricacies of any engine, transmission, electrical system, whatever skills he needed to repair or reconstruct just about anything, he learned. He ripened into a necessary part of the Alexanders lives, both as an employee and a friend.

The gang had tackled the plane, stripping it to its frame. Over the next 30 months, they had grinded, shaped, filled, sanded, painted, refurbished and rebuilt the bird to its former splendor. They filled any available space with every possible convenience and all the essentials. When the work was done, they held a brief ceremony, hoisting paper cups filled with champagne in toast. Jacob christened the aircraft Mellissa after his wife, then taught them all how to fly.

They later equipped the plane with amphibious floats, giving them the ability to land just about anywhere. They added a 300 HP Continental IO-550 engine that loved to climb, and a removable external fuel tank that kept them gleefully aloft for greater durations. When Drake inherited it, he and Luis installed an aftermarket vortex generator, a stall fence and auxiliary adjustments so that they could pare the stall speed, curtailing the landing and take-off requirements. It was enchanting to operate and a pleasure to own.

Sailing around the aircraft, Drake is confronted by a troublesome scene; Luis, a slight and pacific man, is sprawled upon the stony beach rubbing and shaking his head, an unfamiliar shovel is stabbed into the dormant shoreline close to where he lays. Alvaro, similar to his father in statue but much taller, is farther down the beach engaged in a pushing match with Elmer Furlong, the resident bumpkin. The local joke is that you could use the back of Elmer's neck for a taillight. Elmer's skiff is beached not far from the old Navy zodiac Luis and Alvaro use, its nose buried in dark brown sand that defiantly impeded its advance. In it sits Elmer Furlong Jr. a cheerful twelve-year-old; his cheerfulness is a consequence of a mental impediment, not the result of his forlorn kin. Both of them are clad in mismatched camo, a bold statement.

Drake's Zodiac bore up the beach and stops just short of the jousters. Exhaust fumes catch up to purple the air. Elmer breaks off from Alvaro and positions himself to face Drake. Drake uses the momentum of the checking boat to leap to a defensive stance within a foot of Elmer's homely body. Startled, Elmer recoils.

"What's going on here, Elmer?" Drake demands.

Gesturing toward Luis with a villous and unkempt chin, he says, "Your little monkey there told me I can't dig for clams here. I just needed to persuade him that wasn't any of his business; nobody owns the beach to the high tide mark. I can damn well dig where I like. Then this other nigger here... Alfarto... started to get frisky," Elmer utters in complete ignorance. Anybody he doesn't like is a nigger to him, it's just another swear word.

Elmer is discomforted by Drakes stringent glare, which is all the more penetrating due to Elmer's insensitive dialogue. Alvaro retreats to attend to his father, sitting him up to attend to a superficial wound on the side of Luis' head. He uses his shop towel to staunch the bleeding. He doesn't rise to Elmer's insults.

Drake studies the shabby man before him. Hate and its doting sibling, despair, emanate from his confused raccoon eyes. The dark circles are a result of desolate surroundings and a complicated life. A pinkie-purple bulbous nose takes up most of his face telling of his habitual drinking. So slow of common sense, he remains the only person, to most of the local people's knowledge, who had flunked grade one – twice. He quit school at age ten. No education, crushing insecurities and societal neglect makes him a man bereft of kindness and companionship. Life has not been propitious for Elmer. Instead he is a man who shoulders his way through life, evolving into a contentious tomcat. A true trouble maker!

Drake watches Elmer's eyes, sensing a subtle shift in Elmer's stance. Many opponents have been fooled by Elmer's ragged stoop and over-the-belt bulge, thinking him slow or unstable. It is not so. Having worked at one or the other of the fish processing plants common hereabouts most of his life, he is deft with a boning knife and faster than makes sense. Owning a knife has saved his dirty neck several times. It also saw him off to jail for assault several times. Drake had witnessed a glint in Elmer's eye once before when his clever hand snipped the top button off an antagonist's jacket, coming within an inch of the man's throat, in a defensive and very demotivating move. Drake sees the same glint now.

Drake captures Elmer's attention by briskly stating, "You will watch what you say about my friends. You know very well, Elmer, there are no clams on this side of the island. You also know that Fisheries have restricted shellfish harvesting along here and another 3 miles in either direction. You just want to start trouble. What is it with you, Elmer? We try to be nice to you, but you keep screwing up"

Elmer isn't good with too many questions; he becomes nervous. He is powered up on misguided adrenaline and cheap morning liquor. Elmer flings his right hand towards Drake's upper body, a pint sized boning knife suddenly appearing in his hand. He means to threaten Drake by slashing his life jacket. Drake leans toward the oncoming knife point and, his heart beating fast, seizes upon Elmer's knife wrist on its upward thrust. Drake's places practiced and piercing fingers on delicate nerves and halts the mocking stab. Oppressive pain dances up Elmer's arm, causing him to loosen his grip. It falls unthreateningly to the beach. With an action smoother than wind on glass Drake forces the offending arm behind its owner's back and propels him toward his boat, sending him off with a boot in the pants.

Drake watches Elmer drag his punished ass into his boat while yelling out what he intends to do to them as he motors away from the island. Drake turns his attention to Luis and Alvaro, who are standing off to his right, Luis looking bashful. With much embellishment as to their courage, they recount their run-in with Elmer, sometimes both talking at once or in Spanish or Quechua, both of which Drake is comfortable with. They chat about how Elmer is still sore that the islands are private now. He had been asked repeatedly to halt his excursions to hunt there, especially for trapped deer that walked over in the winter and got stuck after the ice broke up. He had clearly made his displeasure known numerous times. He is always looking for any occasion to be a nuisance.

The three comrades proceed to the hanger that juts out over the water, allowing the 185 to park its lovely wings inside and away from the harsher weather. Drake had the hangar built several years ago, a sister structure to the one he has across the road from his house for the other aircraft he owns. The building was designed and painted to blend in with its natural surroundings. It sits nestled at the base of a small hill, housing a fully furnished bachelor apartment, a man-friendly recluse. The trio sequesters themselves in the open kitchen of the apartment, tending to Luis' wound.

Drake walks to the stereo console in the adjoining living room and opens a side cabinet. While removing a bottle of Hennessy Paradis cognac, knowing well Luis' affection for the angelic fluid, he says, "You could charge Elmer you know, Luis"

"Yeah I know, Drake, but I don't think so. He's a big bully, but mostly I feel sorry for him. You really think I look like a monkey, though?"

Drake passes Luis his drink and hands Alvaro one of the two beers he grabbed from the refrigerator and playfully replies, "Yes, you do a little bit." All three of them laugh at the friendly insult. Drake proposes a toast, "May all the monkeys in my life be so clever"

They touch rims, then Drake and Alvaro gulp their beer while Luis slowly swirls the golden nectar, releasing the delicate aroma from the venerable spirit. Placing it before his nose, he inhales the familiar emanation. With a silly grin, he says to his companions, "Jemina will understand that you found it necessary for me to hasten the pain from my poor head by drinking such splendor."

Alvaro further lightens the situation by adding, "Mother will be responsible for more pain than a rampant shovel if she catches you. Maybe we had better get Drake to write you a soldier's prescription."

 Luis is noncommittal on that point, deciding to savor his drink while he can. Alvaro finishes his beer as he fills Drake in on the preparations for the plane. While he is explaining why he changed one of the fuel injectors, Drake ponders father and son. Luis, a Quechua Indian, sits nursing the cognac, the white bandage on his head incongruous with the dark skin of his Inca ancestors. High cheekbones lend their presence to a handsome middle-aged face. Eyes are dark and knowing. He usually parades about with great vigor, like a man with the world's largest to-do list. At 51, he is showing some wear, the edges aren't as sharp and the wrinkles are winning, but the eyesight and the mind are good. His first 30 years were a nightmare of subsistence, the isolated, marginal life of a farmer cultivating the impoverished earth, barely feeding his young and needy family. Life here by the bay is a dream, deliverance.

Alvaro, gesturing with his long and slender hands to explain the workings of the fuel injector, which atomizes the fuel mixture, is the image of his father. The face longer, the nose narrower and eyes that sing of younger melodies are subtle differences. Plus he has a lot more hair – curly, black and shiny as hot tar. At 21 he is terribly happy and is well liked by other young men. The young ladies fantasize about his lean and athletic frame. Unlike his siblings – Miguel, the oldest, is a priest with his own parish in Ciudad Valles, a city of roughly 100,000, in eastern Mexico, and Theresa is a doctor practicing among the poor in her home country of Peru, having returned there when she was 28 – Alvaro was born in Canada and his *"Eh,"* is true north, strong and free.

The two men know of Drake's endless quest, that it is fraught with peril. They never speak of it with Drake, only in whispers between them. He might be gone for a week or two, maybe months, but his nature would cheerfully linger until he came home once more.

"… You'll feel a more solid resistance in the left rudder, so… Oh, never mind Drake you're not listening. Anyway, you'll feel it," Alvaro remarks, seeing that faraway look in Drakes eyes.

"Sorry Alvaro, I was drifting there. I heard what you said though, and I'll keep those points in mind. I'm going to say goodbye to your dad, then you can explain the rest while we drift out to the plane and unclip it." Alvaro acknowledges Drake's request with a nod of the head as he leaves to ready the boat.

The aroma of fresh coffee lingers in the air; the coffee percolator is farting and gurgling, complaining that it's done. Luis has placed his empty snifter on the counter and is removing the heavy mug he favors from the dishwasher, worrying about Alvaro's reminder of Jemina's resistance to alcohol. Drake approaches and says, "I know we don't talk about it much, Luis, and that you don't agree with my reasoning. But I'm often think of Amber's killer and where he hides. Williston has picked up his trail, and I intend to find him. I won't rest until he pays his morbid debt."

Luis stirs sugar into his coffee while his mind stirs Drake's troubled words. He hesitates before speaking. "Why don't you leave the policing to the police?" he asks, already knowing the truth but hoping the reminder will cause Drake to consider abandoning his quest.

"Dozens of policing authorities have open files on Rizzato, Luis. He's a wanted criminal. He just can't be found. Self-preservation serves him well. He's like a chameleon, able to focus and concentrate in different directions at the same time. He changes color to suit his hiding. When I find him, that lizard's skin will change one last time."

Drake contains his emotion and casually drapes his arm across Luis' sloping shoulders giving him a sideways embrace. "Don't get me going," he jokingly warns. "I'll just rattle your poor brains with my ramblings."

Luis grins and moves away from Drake's reassuring clinch to sit at the table, facing him, deeply concerned. Drake leans back against the cupboards, enticed by his sidekick's seriousness.

"It's not that I disagree with you, Drake, but for the man you seek to escape from the law so freely, he obviously has very powerful friends or a very secure hiding spot. My greatest fear, no matter what you accomplish, is that there are vigilantes who hunt vigilantes. Guns and muscle can be acquired with much ease, as the history of my birth country and many of its neighbors can vouch for."

Luis stands, his bearing erect, walks over to the countertop positioning himself close to Drake in a mimicking stance, his butt against the countertop, his chin lifted, and continues: "You know much of my personal past, Drake, but I haven't spoken much of my Quechua ancestors. Hundreds and hundreds of years even before the mighty Incas, our culture thrived. The Quechua language spread throughout the Andes as it became the voice of trade. Think of that, Drake. We are *Runa*; we are *"the people."* For many generations, we continue to place great importance on *anyi*, our way of saying to help each other. We were a sure and powerful body. But a nation, a people, or a man, no matter how great or how common or how wealthy can always be subdued by a greater force. First the Chancas dominated us, and then the Incas dominated them and us, and then the Spaniards came."

He reflects a moment and returns the earlier affection by reaching up to place his hand upon Drake's shoulder, giving it an understanding squeeze. He looks him in the eyes and says, ``When you leave, beware, there are better hunters than you. Cover your tracks well; don`t strike at anything bigger than you can defeat, and hope to pursue another day. Leave your pride at home."

Drake stoops to embrace the caring man, then straightens and says with equal gravity, "Your wise words are true and well meaning. I'm well aware, Luis, that there will always be better hunters than me. So I don't have to remind you where my will is.

Either you or Beth can retrieve it if you need to."

Eye to eye they stand facing each other, Luis simply nods.

"I'm confident enough, not by pride but in honor of what must be done, that it won't be necessary. As you know, I've dedicated my life to combating evil people. Our "gang of seven" have the money, the resources and the fortitude to bring about what change we may."

He looks the older man in the eyes with that look that reminds Luis of Drake's brave and stubborn ways. Before Drake turns to leave he says, "I'm satisfied that if and when that hunter catches up to me, I will not have squandered my talents nor have strived in vain.``

Chapter 4   April 21 7:04am   Durham, North Carolina

Stratton checks his image in the hall mirror. He stares back at himself with a satisfied smirk, certainly more pleasing than the sleazy image that reflected back from the patio door the previous evening. The transformation is complete, from the razor's call to duty to the navy suit he wears. Tailored expertly to take advantage of his broad shoulders and long legs, as well as hiding his prevailing waistline, it is shaped to fit his frame perfectly. The suit is complimented by a duo of a soft mauve-and-white checked shirt with a purple and navy striped silk tie, all custom made for him by Alan David of Manhattan. As he concentrates on the face in the mirror, for just a moment, the background in the cheval glass wavers and is replaced by a swimming vision of a board room, his minions gathered round, staring at him with overt and feigned admiration. He gloats in this memory until reality taps him and the image refocuses to the drab and impersonal entryway in which he stands.

He misses the business, the control, the manipulation of millions of dollars, the lust for domination. He waits out this moment of craving much like a smoker who has recently quit. Guilt is a much bigger emotion and in mental tugs of war, it always wins, bringing him back to his treacherous intent. He has another hour before he has to leave for the airport, so he sits with his fourth cup of coffee and another handful of headache pills, out on the deck, under the awning where the furniture is still dry. He watches the day break while he waits. His mind goes back in time and he relives some of the events that have brought him this far.

Stratton had spent three agonizing months seeking the safe return of his two children. Three months of building animosity toward their captors, building a hate so violent it blinded him to the specifics of the deadly group he bartered with. His previously structured brain went fuzzy when he recognized the familiar rings on the dried and bloodstained fingers. It shattered when he discovered they were already dead, the money - one million dollars – gone at the expense of indiscriminate deaths.

The money was delivered in a black duffle bag, which the kidnappers had demanded be a specific size and color without any distinguishing markings and with a solid shoulder strap. It was to be delivered by anyone other than Stratton to the base of the statue of the Marechal de Moncey in Place de Clichy, the meeting point of the 8th, 9th, 17th and 18th arrondissements in the northwest quadrant of Paris at precisely 3:15 p.m. local time on a bustling Saturday afternoon. France, mostly Paris, is home to several million Muslims and was often used as a halfway point by the Brigade using local sympathizers. Instructions had been delivered to Stratton through a channel he had established with the kidnappers, circumventing the police authorities who didn't want him to pay. The abductors promised the release of Scott and Sarah after the money was retrieved. Stratton, already frantic by menacing delays and inconsequential instructions had engaged private bodyguards who would scan the crowds for the aggressors and eventually try to capture the person who picked up the money.

At the exact time stated, a short, thick chested man named

Viscossi, hired by Stratton, carried the bag to the base of the statute, avoiding the many vehicles that swarmed the traffic that circled the effigy and its concrete side-walked base. At exactly 3:16 p.m., from nearby points, a dozen or more dark skinned males, dressed in local and touristy garb shouldering identical duffle bags, rushed through the traffic, bringing vehicles to sudden stops, with ensuing snarls, blowing horns and yelling! They quickly surrounded Viscossi. A thirty second melee followed and just as quickly the bunch ran off in all directions with a black bag. Remaining from the confusing tumble was the prone figure of Viscossi; a stiletto deftly buried in his chest. An empty black bag sat at his head. Standing off to the side, close to the base of the statue, was a sweating, trembling, terrified man with an identical black bag over his shoulder. Looking to his accomplices and seeing their backs disappear; he waited until a small crowd gathered near the dead man, then screamed "Allah Akbar" and detonated himself.

The ensuing hysteria defeated any chance of catching the criminals. Panicked searches for Scott and Sarah proved fruitless, their bodies long having been disposed of. At this point, Stratton was dolefully aware that his children would never be coming home. Some suspects were rounded up during the investigation but never connected to the incident, likely as a result of strong, prearranged alibis. Stratton himself, given his grievous loss was being warned not to take anything further into his own hands. He harnessed his grief and redirected his anger.

Several weeks later, with an uncharacteristic calmness, he sold off most of his shares, resigned his many posts, and quit the varied companies he had amassed, relegating full control of those companies to others . He shocked his peers. No one was prepared for his total disappearance. Pay back was driving him to seclusion. Only one thing mattered at this point, revenge!

One evening after tranquilizing his bothered and broken wife, he shared his spiteful reasoning with Sophia as they sat in the dining room eating leftovers late at night, hoping she would appreciate and accommodate his mission. It began as an ardent plea that became an agonizing disagreement. He rationalized that terror should be fought with terror. She swore that if he continued with his foolish ideas, she would never forgive him. Neither of them yielded to their opponent's point of view. When Sarah had seen the derangement in her father's eyes, a frightening shiver scurried along her spine. A silence, pregnant with fear and desperation, overwhelmed their space. Sophia turned her back on her misguided father and quietly, fearfully left the room. Andrew made provisions for his remaining family and went underground.

*

Stratton arranged for all his private wealth to be transferred to the Cayman Islands. All his future legal and immediate business transactions would be handled by Amado Cayetano Herrera y Mendoza, known to Stratton's brother and the select few who require such official and shadowy assistance as Mado Mendoza. A savvy advocate, with offices tucked in a turquoise and white office building off Shedden Road in the center of George Town's banking sector. He was able to create layered offshore companies and holdings, disguising ownership and/or in some instances, completely hiding the principal. His Spanish accent added a reassuring intonation to his educated and articulate speech. He assured Andrew he was able to accommodate most of his clients' normal and sometimes strange requests but his services, while maddeningly discrete, were expensive. All formalities and checks were completed and a satisfying arrangement was realized, Mendoza salivating at the confirmation of Stratton's braggadocio that money was not going to be an issue. He could hardly wait to be of service.

Andrew had holed-up for the fall and winter months on the Islands. He found himself a resident of the Ritz-Carlton Grand Cayman off West Bay Road, renting an ocean view residential master suite at the cost of $4000.00 a month. Mado was handling all transactions; he only needed to bring clothes. The resort, bordered by Australian pines, swaying palms, tanned and luscious bodies, was on Seven Mile Beach. Soothing breezes filtered through the rooms. The only sounds were the heaving ocean and birdsong. It was perfect for Andrew's needs, beneficial to his planning.

There had never been a face to the voice in control of his children, only an aggravating monotone that Andrew came to perceive as the containment of all things Muslim. He couldn't visualize any individuals when he thought of these people, he viewed them as a hive of tormented unrest and a mob bent on death. As he schemed, he thought many times that he would show them what unrest meant! He had searched for a means of revenge, becoming interested in articles and stories of mass destruction. He poured through books and magazines; he searched the Internet for all methods of human extermination. Most so fantastic that Andrew could only compartmentalize the huge numbers involved and he wanted big numbers.

While searching the Internet for large gatherings of Muslims he was rewarded with loads of opportunities. He spent several weeks narrowing down events and times, what they represented and how many people would be there. What was the location and surrounding geography like and when was the event going to reoccur to adjust his timeline. Finally he chose the perfect occasion, a gathering of over 800,000 Muslims in one spot for several days in an easy-to-reach place. It suited Andrew's plans completely and gave him enough time to coordinate his offense.

From his searches, the weapon he favored thus far was gas. A gas that could kill and maim with rapid action and a foolproof delivery vehicle seemed the most likely path to take. An interesting article caught his attention when surfing through disasters, the Union Carbide incident. He settled on methyl isocyanate. It was colorless and acute inhalation was exceptionally toxic to humans, causing immediate damage to lungs and eyes, death and in many of the living, blindness, would ensue. It created long-term effects on the reproductive organs, tormenting anyone exposed throughout their future generations. Splendid, he thought. Andrew toyed with assorted delivery ideas until he awoke from a late morning siesta having dreamt of flying a plane. He knew how he would do it.

He focused his business acumen on the rough sketch of his plot and contacted Mado with his first of many requests. It was the beginning of February and he had ten months to get ready. He arranged to meet Mado at his offices at 8 a.m. on the first Monday of the month. Andrew rose early as usual; four or five in the morning was not a strange time for him to start his day. It was just a little over three miles to the offices so Andrew decided to walk. A temperate breeze came in off the water, making the tepid 70 degree weather sufferable. He marched along West Bay Road at a casual pace, the traffic almost non-existent, the birds cavorting and venting their delight with their crooning. He arrived at Mendoza's office a few minutes early. The walk had proved beneficial, his body was grateful and his mind was made up.

Mado's offices were entombed in a picturesque two storey office building. Tourists and locals gathered in the shops and cafés along the way. The building was white stucco with incandescent turquoise trim. Grand and softly bright colors shaded the surrounding architecture, blending well with the sea, beach and sky crowding the city. Andrew climbed the central stairway inside the main entrance and followed Mado's directions to his collection of rooms. Mendoza met him at the door personally, his staff not being in until nine.

He was a tall man, not particularly handsome. Long wavy hair gave him a rebellious aura. An ancestral olive complexion graced his smiling face. While escorting Andrew to his office, he offered him coffee and nourishment. Andrew accepted while Mado directed him to one of several leather chairs concentrated around an impressive glass desk.

Andrew sat, fatigue from his stroll overtaking him. He selected the chair across from where Mado's seat was and admired the office; it was roomy, restful and pleasing. The wall opposite from where he sat was dedicated to ship models. Glass shelves with hidden hangers displayed boats and ships of yesteryear. Andrew liked boats and had owned several; he found the presentation engaging and recognized a smart replica of the "Santa Maria," a 15th century carrack, the flagship of Columbus's tiny armada. It was centered among four other naus and galleons, all square riggers of that period. Interestingly, the shelving carried four other groupings of five ships, each exclusive to its own time frames.

The exact number per shelf provoked Andrew to scan the room and he noticed the offices were laid out to have five walls, one on a 45 degree angle in the rear right corner. There were five chairs throughout the office. A few other groups of five caught his eye. A family photo on the wall of Mendoza, his wife and three kids – five people. Mendoza had a definite obsession or fascination with the number five. It struck a chord from Andrew's high school poetry classes, which he hated, and he thought the room amusingly decorated in iambic pentameter.

Mado entered the room and placed a carved wooden tray on the table to Andrew's right, the scent of fine coffee escaping from the cups. Stratton took one leaning back in his maroon leather chair.

"When I noticed you from my window, I saw that you were walking. Don't tell me you walked the whole distance from your hotel?"

"Yes, well, my head needed a bit of airing out. I'm not proud to say, I've been under a cloud of concern lately. I've taken to finding solace in my malt whiskey. It's not a habit that I wish to develop" said Andrew as he added cream to his coffee and selected a pecan Danish.

He sat back and swiveled his chair to face Mado directly. This admission was digested by both men as they digested their food. Mado replied,

" I think that most of us at times need a pacifier of some type; I myself have spent too many mornings sorely paying for that privilege. But you seem in good health, walking agrees with you. As well, Andrew, for the hardships you have suffered, you are remarkably resilient."

He meant to placate Andrew, assure him of a supportive partner in his future endeavors. Mado didn't care what Stratton was up to; he would simply grease the wheels and collect his fees, of course.

Andrew replied," Thank you, Mado!"

Not wanting to discuss that portion of the past any longer, Andrew pushed his empty cup and saucer away and reached for the leather-clad portfolio he had brought along. He placed it upon the desk and unzipped the sides, opening it before him. Mado noticed the motion and readied himself for business, the pleasantries over. As Andrew organized his notes, Mado was thinking that while he knew much about Stratton, he did not *know* him at all. There was a darkening in the eyes of the man that sat across from him and it suggested caution. He would not want to get his hands too dirty for this man. He would do only what he knew he could get away with. What Stratton was really up to was not of Mado's concern.

Andrew was relying on his brother's assertion that Mado could be trusted, as long as his fees were paid, which Gregory emphasized must never be neglected, never. Andrew's brother, Gregory Stratton, married into the Irish Mob in Chicago. He owned several "successful car dealerships," laundered money ensuring they were a success. He recommended Mado with the following statement, "Show him your money and don't fall for his charm. He's very discreet. Don't ever compromise him." He would soon see what Mado was made of.

"I trust you have set up several companies that will not identify me as owner and that my retainer has been sufficient?"

"Yes in both cases. By power of attorney, I have created a tiered group sufficient to the needs you expressed. The paperwork is complete. I have a full report here for you."

Mado presented a bound twelve-page document to Andrew, who perused it completely. He complimented Mado on his cleverness and placed the report in his briefcase, knowing he would commit it to memory and destroy it later. Mado continued,

"As to the retainer, as you saw, the report also contains our disbursements, expenses and commissions; another payment would be in order. We very much appreciate your business and know a check will be forthcoming."

Mado sat upright at his desk, pulled a Mont Blanc fountain pen from its holder and drew his writing pad before him.

"You suggested on the phone that you had a more *onerous* request that we should discuss here, in person? What can I do to unburden you?"

Andrew shifted in his seat, pulling a loose page from his binder and passing it to Mado,

"These are a few companies I'm interested in. What will be the deciding factor in helping me choose one, through your investigation and negotiations, will be the plant that owns the largest amount of methyl isocyanate in its manufacturing process. I've highlighted the one that most interests me, but I will rely on your judgment and suggestions. I don't want to be linked to its ownership but will need to have complete control under an alias, which I look to you also to arrange. I've been assured of your extensive knowledge in these matters and I can assure you that you will be very well rewarded for your efforts.

He paused to let that statement take root.

"I want to stop being Andrew Stratton for a short time, known only to you; I'd like to be Jack, Jack Favors. I hope you appreciate the tremendous trust I place upon you. I've been told you are a man of your word. I need a passport, credit cards, access to funds, immediately, anywhere in the world. When we decide on the proper facility to purchase, I will need living accommodations close by, not as grand as my present lodgings, of course, but something suited to what an owner's status would suggest."

Andrew straightened from his hunched position over the desk and leaned back into the luxurious chair, crossed his arms and waited for Mado's response. He wanted to test him as his next request was more crucial.

Mado concentrated on the list while saying, "I can assure you, Andrew, that you have placed yourself in the most capable hands and I will not let you down. There will be no trace of Andrew Stratton. As far as the passports and such, I don't engage in these accommodations myself, but I know those who would be able to help you, for a small fee of course. I'll arrange to meet with them regarding these other matters and charge your account accordingly as we agreed".

Placing the paper on the desk, he added, "I see an interesting similarity in these companies. Why pesticides may I ask?"

"No, you may not ask." Andrew insisted, dismissing the issue, "I must have word on the availability of a property no later than the end of March. Time is important to me, as I expect it is to you."

Mado was chastised by Andrews rebuke. He had swayed from etiquette and asked an inappropriate question. He knew that *why* was not his business, just the what, where, how and when.

"That is not very much time, so I'll proceed at once. I will make this a priority by assigning several of my best team members to your request. I'll have the results for you by the end of the week.

You mentioned there was something else?"

"Actually there are two more things I require," Andrew answered.

He rose from his seat and walked over to the ship-festooned wall, his gaze resting upon the model of a sleek and powerful-looking cigarette boat. The missing link to his plan's triumph was a representative who was noted for heeding instructions more than lacking any conscience. Facets of his gruesome strategy were tasks Andrew found distasteful but that were essential to his quest. He would use his fortune and buy all the muscle he needed. He addressed the fleet before him, saying, "I seek an individual, assuming for now a man but I would not be averse to a woman, who can travel throughout Asia with ease and not leave a trail. There will be some arm twisting, so they should be adept. In some cases they may have to be ruthless. As you know, I have much at my disposal and am willing to share it to further my goals."

He turned back to face his lawyer, his brow furrowed. Mado wonders what propels most of his clients with missions that lay in the shadows of the law.

"I've had similar and certainly more bizarre requests before, Andrew. I have access to such people and as I said before, someone I know, may know someone… Information like this will be expensive, and there will be other fees."

Andrew waved away the mention of fees. To him they were of no matter, but he would expect a detailed explanation of where they went. He returned to the table and as he stood by his chair, he withdrew a check from his portfolio and passed it to Mado, who accepted it casually.

"I'm certain that will cover your immediate needs and commissions."

"That should be more than adequate," Mado said. "I think that there will be one or two people that will want to talk with you in the next several days."

He rose from his glass desk and walked to a heavy walnut cabinet along the angled wall. Opening one of the drawers, he withdrew a padded envelope. Removing the contents, he gave Andrew two untraceable cell phones. The number for each was written on a removable label stuck to the back of each phone.

"They will use one of these numbers so keep them close to you. If you fail to answer either the first one after five rings, then the second after five rings, they will not call back. Use the one marked in red ink as your primary phone. The other is just a backup in case the original is compromised. Remember that your conversation could be overheard. If the information is sensitive then discard the first and use the backup. I'll speak to you again before the end of the week with our progress. I'm certain you will be engrossed in other details. Earlier you said there were two more things you needed Andrew, what is the last one?"

"Oh, that one is quite easy, I need a new will."

*

Andrew awakes from his pensiveness at the ringing of the front doorbell. His drive is waiting. Hazy flashbacks remind him how fruitful the past two months have been and how they have gone by with frightening speed. It's 8:30 a.m. and he is leaving for the airport. A chartered Gulfstream G550 is taking him to meet Bartolommeo Rizzato at Casco Viejo in Panama City. Andrew is aware that Rizzato's movements are limited because of his penchant for trouble, while Andrew is free to travel. Panama is about 1800 or so nautical miles from the Raleigh-Durham International Airport. The G550 cruises at about 500 knots, so with the time difference he will be there early enough to meet Rizzato for lunch. He has been told to be at Restaurante Mostaza just off Av.A and Calle 3 in the old French quarter. Andrew has been informed that area is officially known as Casco Antigua but locals refer to it as Casco Viejo, "Old Quarter" and themselves as "Casquenos." The use of the familiar term used by Rizzato suggests he has spent considerable time among the inhabitants. It is also convenient for Andrew, it's busy and he's not known there. He knows Rizzato is a dangerous man, but he's the man with the cash and, as such, holds the upper hand.

With his raincoat over his arm, Andrew steps out into the day. A heady earth smell remains from the previous day's rain. He follows the driver down to the curb and slides through the opened door into the back seat of a Lincoln Towncar that is available for him twenty-four hours a day. He arranges himself comfortably and waits out the 20 minute drive to the airport. They proceed through an area marked "For Private Aircraft Only." while approaching the designated parking area. Security seems a bit lax. He doesn't worry about being recognized as he travels. His credentials are excellent. He no longer has a moustache, his hair is totally grey, he wears glasses that cover unfamiliar light brown eyes, and he now has more of an overbite. People would know him as Jack Favors now, a wealthy, middle-aged, upper-management executive. Mado's *friends* have performed his transformation exceedingly well.

"Good morning Mr. Favors," says the flight attendant as Andrew enters the aircraft.

A stunning redhead with a bright smile approaches him from the front cabin, pilot's wings emblazoned upon her epaulets and the tight white company shirt suggesting pride and vanity. She extends a hand, saying, "My name is Andrea Layton and I'm doing the flying this morning. My co-pilot, David Achterkamp, is up front doing last minute checks. We have great weather, mild winds, so we should be arriving at Gelabert International Airport in Panama City around eleven o'clock local time. There will be a limousine to greet the plane, as requested. I understand that there will be a two to three hour layover, is that correct Mr. Favors``?

Andrew shakes her hand, liking the confidence he sees.

"I expect it may be less than that, but please prepare for that likelihood. I'd like some breakfast after we are in the air, please. Thank you, Captain Layton."

"Then I'll leave you with John, your flight attendant. He makes a delicious breakfast and I know he keeps the coffee fresh. We'll be taxiing out in about 15 minutes, so if you'd like to get comfortable, I'll finish our preparations."

She leaves off with an informal salute and disappears into the cockpit with a feminine gait.

Andrew stretches out in the luxurious seating. Cabinets, tables and trim trendily finished in bird's eye maple, adorn the cream-colored fuselage. He approves of his surroundings. There are fourteen seats; thirteen are empty. He knows from experience that an aircraft like this, less than a year old, would go for around forty, forty-five million dollars. Chartering it is an extravagance he realizes but he needs to complete this critical juncture in his efforts.

He buckles in. The plane moves cautiously among the trucks and equipment crossing the tarmac, randomly acting like ants with wheels as they move helter-skelter about the planes. His plane falls in line with two other aircraft awaiting takeoff instructions. In a short while, the dynamic thrust from the Rolls Royce engines breaks the suction of rubber and earth and the plane lifts, zooming into the sky. Starting with a wide sweeping turn, with the sun smiling upon the aircraft's long sleek body, it tops out at 35,000 feet and speeds southwest.

Andrew completes his breakfast, the omelet exceptional. After John clears away the table, Andrew draws himself up and opens his ever present portfolio, the worn spine attesting to its frequent use. He separates papers from photos, photos from each other, setting up several distinct piles upon the table. A collection of several sheets are flagged with red tape. He digs them out sitting back in his seat. The documents before him had been dropped off anonymously at the door of his hotel room when he was in the Cayman Islands. A sharp knock was all that told of anyone having been there. Most likely Mado had wanted Andrew to know who and what he was dealing with.

Over the next hour or so Andrew highlights several segments of Rizzato's past that worries him. He realizes he is in no position to judge, but there are crimes quite heinous that are attributed to him. Many countries have issued warrants for his arrest, alleging pathological and cold-blooded killings. Another disturbing issue is the warrants stemming from charges of sexual assault and murder. He wonders, is this man too ruthless? Is there anyone on his tail? Law enforcement agencies don't have budgets to chase bandits all over the world but there are agencies and individuals that could and would.

Along with official documents, no doubt obtained using his considerable retainer, there are two sheets listing Rizzato's capabilities. The notes also contain an inordinate amount of information on Rizzato's background, as they know it, along with a description of his rich and excessive tastes. Money is clearly his deity. The analysis basically comes down to the life of a soldier of fortune. A man so deep into death and crime, his world enclosed by deception and ill will, housed and bolstered with vices. A world inhabited with immoral deeds.

Andrew knows the power of money, but like him it isn't money that drives those that amass wealth, it's the insatiable greed and need to have more, and more; there is never enough. It legitimizes every fantasy, every desire, every longing that can be purchased. It can bring celebrity for those that crave such a life, it buys sycophants and obedience. He also knows money can buy false confidence for its unending use.

Andrew's money supports a crusade that will eventually consume most of his wealth; it already consumes most of his mind. Andrew realizes that Rizzato can have it all if he pulls off this deed.

Their meeting today will be the beginning. No turning back. Andrew drops the sheets to his lap; his eyes glaze over with rapturous delight as he imagines the realization of his wrath. His children's lives may have been wasted on life's sacrificial altar, but Andrew will ensure that hundreds of Muslims will wish they'd never been born.

Chapter 5   5:30pm South of Jumby Bay, Antigua

Drake didn't have to follow the beacon Williston spoke of. Flying south with a bearing on Jumby Bay, Drake spots Williston's yacht idling through the yawning channels twenty nautical miles or so north of Antigua, below the island's horizon. Drake lowers his aircraft to a couple hundred feet off the water, tilts the plane to port to make a sweeping pass circling the boat. He has a splendid view of the top deck and can see people in the whirlpool aft, beneath the radar arch. He speaks into his headset after switching to V HF channel 61, "*Drifter's Dream*, this is Drake in the *Mellissa*, do you copy?" The ship's crew responds, the commanding voice of Bill Berkeley booming, "Loud and clear *Mellissa*. We see you and you're looking mighty fine, Drake."

Captain Berkeley is a brawny man, an expatriate from the Virginia shores of the Chesapeake Bay area, named after an ancient ancestor, some governor or sort he explained to Drake once in a tanked moment they shared. He's been the ship's boss since Williston purchased it five years ago. When Williston's group of companies had busted the twenty million profit forecasts, he had celebrated the milestone by buying the *Dream*. Since then she's been head office. Williston works as much as possible on board. Two staterooms have been converted into a productive office. Williston and an associate, most often his wife, Isabella, can work comfortably. Communications are the root of the layout and every possible source is available: Marine VHF, Internet, cellular and satellite phones, GPS, whatever is needed to stay in touch anywhere in the world, night and day.

"It will be good to see you again, Bill, but I warn you, no more of tequila shooters. I'll grant you they're tasty but the last time you made them I ended up tucked into one of the fire stations in the engine room with nothing on but a pair of flip flops. Of course, nobody remembers how I got there," Drake said with a hearty chuckle, knowing he would certainly be the butt of firemen jokes and reference to hoses soon enough and thought to get the subject out of the way.

"You hold your liquor like the diluted Scotchman you are, you should be hardier than that after all. We only had four bottles of wine and ten or twelve drinks each. Williston and I were fine."

Bill jokes fondly, remembering their night ashore, partying at his condo in St. John's, before ending up in the Jacuzzi aboard the boat. Williston, Isabella, Bill, Drake and two accommodating and lovely young ladies of the island that Drake and Bill had persuaded to join them were celebrating the moon and the stars and life in general, the shooters dabbling with their sensibilities. Drake eventually passed out and slowly slipped below the water of the whirlpool. Quick action by Isabella and Bill saw him hoisted out and on the deck. After making sure he was okay, while he was still unconscious, they had placed him below in the engine room. Drake had crowed all evening of drinking everyone under the table. It didn't happen; he was the first to go. They had awarded him last place by loosely tying him up below decks with an extra fire hose. He was found next morning by one of the crew members checking the boat while it was on layover in harbor. He hastened to his bed, slept another ten hours, emerging too embarrassed to talk about it. Everyone else had talked about it though; they all thought it was dastardly good fun.

"Be that as it may, you remain forewarned. Is Williston aboard?"

asked Drake.

"Actually, he's not, Drake. We're out for Isabella today; she and her clique are having a bridal shower for her best friend. We weren't sure if you would be here today or tomorrow morning so Williston left instructions that if you made contact that we were to tell you to tie up in English Harbor. He's made arrangements for docking your plane at the slipway. These guys are pros and they'll take care of your pride and joy. We'll come about and be there in about two hours; the girls should be tired by then. Williston said there were business details he and Uday wanted to attend to ashore. I gathered he's trying to free some time as he informed me we're in for some serious sailing soon. He says we could be at sea for a while with uncertain destinations. Sounds like Williston, don't you think?" Bill can see Drake circling the ship as he speaks.

 "Yeah, that's him, mysterious and antsy. I'll head out and we'll meet soon, you disreputable old salt." Before he can respond, Drake signs off. "This is *Melissa*, over and out."

The plane circles to a higher altitude and banks into a graceful swing toward the island. Drake's takes one last glance at the yacht and sees her pantomime the same broad turn, the cutting edge of her bow lacerating the aqueous plain, like a solitary wing. With the island in view, Drake checks in with air traffic control, informing them of his intentions. He will be able to clear customs in port. His aircraft will be treated much like a boat and all pertinent documents and fees are applicable. Drake is anxious to meet with the men; he hasn't seen Williston for several months. He had thought long and hard during his flight. He loved the open skies, the aloneness, the clear days, the Lilliputian landscape below, and *JJ Cale* on the Ipod. He concentrated on what he knew of his nemesis, how he operated, what his weaknesses were. He would need to dig into Williston's archives on Rizzato, the soldier's mantra, "Know your enemy," goading him. Soon enough the three men will talk; Williston will know where to go, what the mission is. He's a terrific strategist.

Drake is flying over the long arm of Antigua before looping around to approach English Harbor; the peninsula is cheeked with a blue and sandy complexion. Surrounded by water so clear the bottom is visible for miles. Drake's reflects about his wily friend, remembering when they met.

While every summer was spent in New Brunswick, Drake went to Plymouth North High School in Massachusetts. He was a cocky freshman, bronzed from seaside wind and sun, of a fourteen year old dreaming of being a soldier someday. Williston and his brother, Aloysius, were in the same school. As different as a hen and an umbrella, you would never even guess they were related. Both nerds, though. Both wore heavy, dark-rimmed glasses. Williston was shorter and about 50 pounds heavier. Al, over six feet, blue eyed, dark shorn hair, was always grinning. Williston, never Will or Willis, was the serious one with grey-green eyes and champagne locks who mostly wore a frown. The only iota of similarity was a likable nose the right shape for faces trying to be liked. They usually hung together or with several other Mensa candidates, or smart asses as they called themselves. With their unfashionable dress and unusual minds, they usually attracted the jealous and taunting types.

Early on an October morning, Drake arrived to find three members of the school football team, all of them thick, with IQs the same as their chest sizes, pushing Williston about, back and forth among them. A small crowd had formed, most urging the brutes on; a few though, not brave enough to interrupt the proceedings, were yelling from the back to leave him be. Williston's notebooks were scattered at their feet. Drake found out later that the bullies had ganged up on Williston for embarrassing them in science class, claiming it made them look stupid. Williston spat back that they did that very well on their own. The insult prompted the three boys to resort to what they knew best, physical violence.

Drake knew Williston wouldn't have provoked these guys. He had witnessed their aggressiveness before. Elbowing his way through the crowd he reached in deftly between two of the goofs to haul Williston from their grip. Pushing him aside, he faced the three stooges and said, "You yokels are tough on the field, but you act like cowards in the yard. Always the three of you pitted against one poor guy. Maybe someday that one person you pick on will pick on you right back."

Drake stared at the boys, watching all three at once, his peripheral vision enhanced by the rush of the coming fury. He knew their approach. Gino, the biggest, was in the middle, and he could think a little bit; the two on the sides were stupid and did whatever Gino said. The usual tactic was that the kid on his left, everybody called him Grunt – the teacher was the only one who used his real name, Günter – would charge their opponent, either confronting or chasing them. None of them would ever resort to finesse when brute force was so effective. Then Gino would step in, get his digs. The other one – his name was Sammy, but his football buddies called him Slammy – stood by as backup, coming when whistled for, the obedient St. Bernard.

"Do you think you're the one, Alexander? I don't think so. You're just a scrawny dirty Canuck," said Gino, laughing at his ingenuity.

The other two, as if on cue, joined in.

Drake saw the signal when Gino poked Grunt in the ribs. Grunt grunted and bore down on Drake. With a grin that was mischievous and pleased, Drake assumed a drilled stance. He had earned his black belt in Karate by the time he was twelve, and he figured these goons posed no problems. He probably only needed to ground one, maybe two if they were real dumb.

Seconds before Grunt made contact, Drake stepped deftly aside, placed a foot in his path and flattened the big kid. He hit the ground with a meaty thud, his chin bouncing off the turf. When he came to rest, he shook his baffled head and spat out a bloody piece of tongue. It landed at Lena Jablonski's feet, looking like a little purple slug. It couldn't have landed in front of a more squeamish person. The little Polish girl darted into the crowd screaming, everyone stepping back from the ejected tissue as if it might be dangerous somehow. Grunt meant to push himself up, mouth in pain and tasting of blood, steaming mad. As he rose to all fours, Drake stepped up and hit Grunt's neck with a practiced chop, and down he went again. This time he stayed. A little time out would be good, Drake thought.

He turned to the stunned duo fronting the hushed crowd, and asked quite casually, "Who's next?"

They had just witnessed a scrawny dirty Canuck floor one of the toughest kids in the school and he wasn't even breathing hard, so, bullies that they were, they cowered and gave Drake a wide berth. Grunt stirred and they shuffled him to his feet. Gino dug a towel and some water from his gym bag and wiped the blood from Grunt's mouth. Grunt drank and spit out the crusty reddish water. With a groggy head and an inflamed, severed tongue, he moaned, "Wha' a fuck 'it me?"

"Never mind, we gotta get outta here or we'll be late for class," suggested Slammy.

Grabbing Grunt's bag and their own stuff, his friends pointed him toward the school. The crowd moved on, their chatter and teenage gossip hovering over them like a distended bubble. Drake walked over to Williston's side, whose frown turned north, beaming at his protector. From that point on, they were almost inseparable. Drake's Acadian friends had an apt expression for the two's resultant relationship. They were said to be *"comme deux fesses"* (*like two bum cheeks*), meaning where ever one went, the other would surely be following. They introduced each other to their sphere of interests. Williston became involved in sports and martial arts. The pounds fled. He got rid of the glasses and Drake helped him dress better. The remaining years of high school were fertile ground for an over-hormoned juvenile who had been hiding behind misunderstood intellect and a chubby body for the first fourteen years of his life, who all of a sudden was, "popular." He reveled in Drake's presence and was always beholden to the kid who had changed his life. It was quite natural that they became very best friends.

Drake in turn was tuned into the workings of the mind. It was an academic workout the equivalent of taking his brain around the track for forty laps, every day. He discovered that learning was information: some crappy, some useless, but always some good. Williston's allies weren't total book geeks. They were into science, dungeons and dragons, secret clubs and oaths, reading, more reading, spy stories and sinister gadgets, pirates and other rogues they wished to be. All in all, they were good fun.

Williston was a collector of facts and trivia, folk stories and local lore. He shared his stash of notes, neatly filed and categorized, written in his own unique and neat hand. He also had comments on other students, town officials, school staff, parents and friends to prove he was a nosy and inventive investigator. The one Drake liked the best was the observation of Mr. James, the school principal, patting Yolanda, the school secretary, on the bum. Williston had the date, time of day, how he came to witness the violation and that Yolanda seemed to like it, all written down. It was damning material. Williston was never a person to intentionally hurt people; to him it was just a hobby. He always said that knowing things people intended to hide gave him a sense of importance. He thought it might be useful.

The ensuing friendship and following years cultivated an alliance of seven adolescent members in a bond of teenage bravura. Williston, Drake, Al, Beth, Drake's cousin Chrissie, her brother Ian, and Amber completed the entourage. Some were rich, some were not, but everybody shared. Their cluster soon came to be regarded as the *gang of seven.* Countless yarns grew from their inane and feckless antics. A coming-of-age that soldered their collective souls! Even after high school, the spirit of kinship was a buttress of support. The last time they had been together was during Amber's abduction and the funeral that followed.

Drake's heart still aches with the loss. He focuses on guiding the aircraft into the bay and alights upon the dappled baby blue waters. He glides into the prearranged slot at the Antigua Slipway and is expertly battened down. Customs greets him officially and speeds him through the checks. They ask if he would please remain while they search his plane and check his papers, just routine they assure him. After that he is free to enter the country.

Drake knows of Williston's affection for the Marina Resort which is not far, expecting to find him there. On the walk over he sees dozens of masts stick up like denuded trees around the marina. The display of incredible wealth the flock of boats represent bowls him over. He has money, but these people make him feel like a pauper. They're the crowd Williston runs with.

He introduces himself at the front desk and is informed that Williston is expecting him. The cute, petite blond hands him a key while offering brief directions to the room. When she notices no wedding ban or tell-tale marks of its absence, she comments that there is an intimate and popular jazz bar at the marina, called *Armstrong's*, named after Louis, of course. A Cuban trio are playing that night and *absolutely everybody* will be there. Drake reassures her that if time allows he will perhaps see her there; fully knowing that time will not allow. He enjoys the flirtatious gesture nonetheless.

He takes the stairs to the second floor and finds his room. He enters gay, delightful surroundings with a jaw-dropping view of the bay. Chucking his bag in the entryway he goes in search of the bar; a drink would calm his anxious edge. He locates the vodka, some ice, glasses and tonic and takes them to the covered balcony at the front of the room. Sliding glass doors, activated by a proximity sensor, open quietly in response to Drake's approach. He finds an agreeable lounge chair, settles in and pours himself a drink. He relaxes and scans the bay seeing his plane at the marina. No sight of the *Dreamer* yet, but it's bound to show up soon. Its one hundred and thirty four feet of pulchritude will be clearly observable when she enters the harbor.

Drake sits for an hour or so about to succumb to the smooth blend of cocktail and locale, when he is interrupted by voices hailing him from the entryway. Williston and Uday are engaging in one of their heated discussions; they always sound mad at each other. Drake enters from the balcony and the conversation stops only to quickly continue in good cheer as Williston steps over to give Drake a brotherly embrace. "Drake! Drake! How good it is to see you again my friend!"

Drake responds with a healthy embrace of his own and says, "And you as well, Williston. You're looking fit and trim. You must be working out again."

Williston had been steadily adjusting his belt in sync with an emergent waistline until Drake reproached him one day that should he ever encounter Amber's killer, the man would face a fat, slow and unpracticed enemy. It got him off his butt and the man that stands before him today looks as tough as cast iron. He's larger of frame but stands only a couple of inches shorter than Drake. An ever present hat adds to his bearing. Today it is a white straw fedora. His unmanageable curls, blonder from the sun, outline his stoic face. Even though he greets Drake with true excitement, Drake discerns the burden in his eyes, the grey-green greyer, more wary.

"I feel great, too, Drake, you're an inspiration and I thank you. I'm also able to concentrate much better, and as you can imagine, we have been plotting continuously since we spoke last. Let me get Uday and myself something to drink and we can talk." Williston chucks his hat on the couch and goes to the fridge; he will need a non-alcoholic drink for his companion.

Drake turns to the dark amicable man accompanying Williston. Uday Saad wears a traditional white Thobe. Attesting to his wealth, it is made of silk, and attesting to custom, it flows to his ankles. Attesting to his girth, it is quite large. The Thobe has a mandarin collar burdened by too many chins. It is fastened along the center with tiny white buttons. Polished gold cufflinks, probably 18 or 24 karat, are nested in stiff French cuffs.

A cherub's mug, the color of caramel, grins from beneath a red and white Ghutra held in place by an Igal, a thick double dark band of cord. Most Saudis wear a white Ghutra in the summer months, but Uday prefers the combination. Eyes that are dark and full of vibrant life express his pleasure. Drake greets him with a firm handshake and says, "Assalamu Alaykum."

With a barrel voice, he says, "My dear Drake, I would wish peace upon you too, but I know that where we must go, peace will be a stranger. As grave as our journey is, I am pleased that it brings us as one. I am honored by your presence in the search for my daughter's slayer. I know you to be a courageous warrior. We will unite in our quest, and I feel with certitude that we will apprehend this culprit. I extend all my resources to your search. I look forward to the hostilities with you at our side."

Drake reddens at the praise. He unclenches the handshake and places his hand reassuringly on Uday's forearm and says, "You gentleman get me the information and tools I need and we'll do what we can to bring this criminal in. I've got my back covered; we just need to find Rizzato. But tell me, what of Rafan. Is he okay?"

Uday gives a disquieting nod and says, "Yes and no. Yes in that we found him hiding at a friend's parent's home in the country. No in that he is still quite shaken up. I'm certain he will return to his normal and ebullient self in a short time. Unfortunately I didn't have a chance to talk in detail with him, but I suggest you talk with him when you arrive."

Williston was listening and states, "We're noticing strange goings on around Dhaka besides the dead body Rafan found, and we think we came across another reference to Rizzato. We'll need you to confirm it. We know the trail's thin, but we have a starting point. I'm anxious to give you the details. I'll get my briefcase and we can go out on the balcony."

He passes Uday a concoction of fresh fruit juices he favors. Drake refreshes his drink while Williston goes to the entryway in search of his papers. Rushing back to the room he knocks over a lamp next to the doorway. Offering a muttered curse at its erroneous placement, he straightens it back up and, with his drink in hand, escorts the two men to the deck. Drake says, "Relax Williston, we've got all night. There's no need to be so hasty."

As they arrange themselves on bolstered balau chairs around a wrought iron and glass table, Williston replies, "Actually we don't have all night; you're catching a British Airways flight to Dhaka in about three hours , at 9:40 p.m. exactly. Today's the 8th so you'll arrive on the morning of the 10th, Tuesday, about 8 a.m. local time because of the time difference. I hate to unload all of this on you so quickly, but our time is short and you have a long flight, so let's get at it."

Williston places a dog-eared manila file on the table. He pulls out a police report he has obtained that very day. Isabella is the granddaughter of Sir Wilfred Jacobs, the first Governor–General of Antigua and Barbuda. As such, her contacts in the government meant gracious access to its annals. It is even more propitious that her older brother, Lorimar, is captain of one of the Antiguan coast guard boats. Detective Felix Nettleford and Lorimar have played cricket together on the same team for over 15 years and are good buddies. Nettleford is a gregarious and happy man, very black, very helpful. Friendliness had prospered in time and Felix became a regular at Williston's gatherings.

"We went to the police station earlier today. We shared what we knew with Felix and picked up some interesting information. He contacted the detective division of the Dhaka Metro Police using a story of a missing relative, gave him a phony name and said they were from the Dhanmondi area. He said they should have arrived in Bangladesh yesterday, and asked about any missing persons or homicides. Detective to detective stuff, real friendly. Remember they're eleven hours ahead of us and it's the weekend, but the guy was real helpful. Well anyway we got lucky".

Williston pushes the report across to Drake. Drake picks it up and reads its message. It's a brief summary and identification of three very similar homicides in the last five days. The similarities are itemized. All are young males, 24 to 28 years old. All had been tortured in a similar manner. Two are Dalit – untouchables – found in a ditch that runs through the industrial section of Tongi. The other is Pakistani; fingerprints confirmed a fugitive wanted by Pakistani forces for armed assault in both Faisalabad and Gujranwala. He was found in a dumpster behind the Bangladesh Technical Institute off Mirpur Road. The most unique similarity, the red flag, was that each corpse displayed the letter Z, likely carved with the point of a very sharp knife. It is noted that the shape and texture suggested the cuts were made post-mortem.

Drake looks up at Williston and goose bumps trot up his arms. Each man stares at him with the same intense questioning eyes. Drake confirms what they already know, "It's him. That's Rizzato."

They all reflect on the two women stolen from their lives. Drake had seen the same incision upon their dead chilling torsos. A dark mood befalls them temporarily, but Drake breaks the spell with a burst of hope,

"We have a trail gentlemen and I intend to follow it. We now know he's in the area. Maybe he's working for someone local, which might make tracking easier. I've already been in touch with several of my comrades from my soldiering days. A former American Ranger actually, Dakin Rush will meet me as soon as I relay my location and ETA. I rescued the man from a gruesome death during Desert Storm so we've got good vibes and I trust him. I think you should get back to Felix, see if you can get more on those three stiffs, details on where they were found, time of death, whatever you can. Uday, I'll need a contact in Dhaka, someone who knows their way around, talks the local talk, someone who can take care of themselves."

Uday says, "Yes Drake I have just the person to assist you. They will meet you at the airport upon your arrival, with instructions to follow your every command. I will rejoice when we have terminated this blight in our lives. This terrible man is indeed close, and we must not let him slip away." He lifted his glass in a toast and adds, "To your success Drake."

Williston pulls out several more sheets and hands Drake a small slip of paper. On it a bank's name and address in Dhaka are marked, with an account number. It is accompanied with a safety deposit box key. Drake commits the name and number to memory, and slides the key securely into his wallet.

Drake and Williston had schemed early in their search for Rizzato, knowing his penchant for working all over the world, by providing

Drake with passports, id, credit cards, American and local funds and simple disguises for evasion hidden in other safety deposit boxes in major cities around the globe, much like the one in Dhaka. "I know the power of your memory Drake, but can you still recall the other caches if you should need them?" asked Williston.

"Definitely, Williston, I can even remember all four of your girlfriends from high school. Should I list them?" Drake teases, bringing some levity to their seriousness. Williston senses Drake's assuredness, punctuated by his wit. He likes this side of Drake, cocky and sure of himself.

"That's not necessary, Mr. Alexander," he says sarcastically, and then with typical gravity continues, "Just concentrate on the job at hand. From the dumpster, we know the Pakistani was the man Rafan talked with. It is quite doubtful that one of the untouchables would be at any bar anyway, let alone that one. I think you should start there. The spoor will be cold but you're good, Drake. You can probably dig up something. Maybe concentrate on why they were within Rizzato's influence. What do you think, Uday? Anything to add?"

Uday says," We are only too aware of Rizzato's sick and perverse pleasure in sex, pain, and death. Since the girls were killed, there has been nothing that we can find. I think you need to follow his trail there and we'll follow here with our means. We'll dig deeper, looking for the mark. Maybe there are others. Why is there a mark now, a Zed? Older reports of his alleged assaults and related homicide make no mention of this mark. He has been quiet for some time; his name is not ringing any bells. Why is that relevant now? Bragging maybe? You must check if the deaths in Dhaka had any other similarities to Sakeema and Amber. Other than that, I promise you an experienced guide."

Uday rises from his chair, his enormous girth requiring extensive effort, and suggests to the men," I am going to boil my poor bones in that splendid Jacuzzi in my suite. In there I am almost weightless, can you imagine?" He harrumphs at his bon mot, all chins stirring in agreement. The clever wit doesn't disguise the bittersweet sorrow etched in his eyes.

"I know you have personal things to discuss so I shall leave you two good friends alone. You know how to reach me, Drake. I'll do anything I can to help you catch this man. And when you find him, Drake, be patient. Set a trap and bring him in. I'll leave you with that. Good hunting."

When Uday is gone Williston broaches the subject of defense with Drake. "In that safety deposit box in Dhaka will be your favored weapon, an M1911. I had it modified with the polished double diamond grip you like and the magwell you specified. There are several cartridges, a holster and a knife. I can't think of anything right now to add. Do you have any questions?"

Drake says, "I'm sure the questions will come, but right now I guess I should head for the airport soon. I just want to freshen up and change clothes and I'm good to go."

The men stand taking their glasses to the kitchen. Williston, admonishing Drake, says,

"When you find him Drake, and I know you will, heed Uday's advice and be patient. Don't get blinded by your anger. You're a very courageous man and I'm indeed honored that you've taken on this task. I'm not sure I could do what you do. I always worry for your safety. Please, please be careful, Drake. Now go get ready and I'll arrange your transportation."

Drake stares at his buddy and they fall silent for a moment. There is a faint connection in their minds from years of friendship. They both think of Amber, her radiance and beauty a melancholy murmur. Drake knows as does Williston that there is no escaping the unpredictable fate that lies before them. It is either Rizzato or them.

Drake speaks with an edge in his voice, "Patient I may have to be, but when the time comes, I'll put Rizzato behind bars or I'll kill him. Either that or I won't be coming back. I made you a promise, Williston, and I intend on keeping it.

Chapter 6   April Panama City

Stratton cleared Panamanian customs and walks briskly to the waiting limousine, his name posted on a crisp, bright panel held by a uniformed driver. As he approaches the chauffer, he notices his name tag reads *Juan*. "Good morning Juan. I would like first to go to Banco General on Calle Aquilinio, then to the Mostaza restaurant in Casco Viejo, do you know where that is located?"

Juan Rios is jauntily clad in a bright-red short-sleeved shirt and dark grey trousers. A perfectly knotted charcoal tie, with the company logo centered in red, is wrapped around his skinny neck. A grin so wide it almost conjoins his ears, dominates his copper face. As he is closing the heavy car door, he cheerfully replies, "Certainly Senor Favors. Neither destination is far, so we should be at the Banco in 10 or 15 minutes."

He rushes to the driver's door and while entering the car, he adds," There is fresh coffee in the carafe, as well as cups, sugar and creamers in the center console. The local paper is there also, Senor Favors. Would you like the center shield raised for privacy?"

"No that's fine, Juan; you can leave it down, thank you". Stratton relaxes and loosens his tie, the heat is intense, but the air conditioning is agreeable. A fresh scent of citrus flutters through the car which is probably meant as some silly aromatherapy or the like, thinks Andrew.

As they move away from the airport, Andrew sites the humongous Panamanian flag that surges through the unblemished sky atop Ancon Hill. It's blue and red stars competing for attention with the flag's quartered, matching squares. A carpet of forest waits at its feet. A healthy wind puffs across the hill just then and whips the flag to full extension. It waffles there for a few seconds before collapsing upon itself, as if exhausted from the effort. The view of the flag on the hill is lost to Andrew when the car turns in a different direction. He begins to consider what he must do.

He carries with him, tucked in the side compartment of his briefcase, a folded nylon bag, one that could be picked up at any department store, very generic. At the bank, he will scan his thumb – Mado has forwarded his prints digitally yesterday – and withdraw one million dollars. It had been pre-arranged that there would be one thousand one hundred dollar bills, which will fit perfectly in the nylon bag. The carry-all has a snapping cover that will hide its contents well. Rizzato wanted it that way and Andrew wasn't one to argue with the man. He feels certain that Bartolommeo Rizzato has done this before. As far as the exchange of money and instructions, he will follow the man's lead.

Andrew is leery of this person, as he should be; this man is a killer, something he does just for pleasure on occasion. He pictures Rizzato as a monstrosity, a gross and ugly ogre. He isn't scared; he has the money and he has a cause, a cause that will likely appeal to a man of Rizzato's sensibilities. His every breath is a consummation of the horror he will rain upon his hated enemy. Every action from now on will be to the completion of his avenging efforts. Rizzato is just a tool, an expensive one, but necessary. Rizzato had explained to Andrew that his battery of soldiers was selected for their superb fighting skills, willingness to take orders and aggressive attitudes, but mainly for their cruelty. They all live on the wrong side of the law, hardened people, loyal only to him. There is very little that Rizzato cannot accomplish. He offered that it was a delightful way to earn a living. Andrew could hardly wait to look this man in the eyes to see what kind of darkness they possess.

Andrew's sixth sense tweaks. He immediately realizes he is being a bit naive. He chastises himself for not being more astute, he should have arranged with Mado for a concealable weapon, Andrew is a sport shooter and knows something about guns. It's too late to contact his lawyer now. He glances up at the young man's well groomed head and wonders, "Can I trust him?" He dwells a moment on how to approach the subject with Juan.

Andrew interrupts the hum of silence and says with authority, ""I can see that you are a good and conscious driver, Juan. My businesses are always looking for sharp people like you. If you don't mind me being nosey, how much does the company pay you, young man?"

"Senor Favors, the company does not pay me anything but I am very lucky to have such a good job. If I may be frank Senor, I work only for tips and I hope that my good driving and my desire to see that you are made comfortable will earn your favor. I am also available for any other needs you may have while in Panama City, "says Juan, facing the windshield, eyes steady on the highway. The big car cruises like a wheeled panther.

"So in a good month then Juan, what would your driving earn'" he asks.

"As I said before, I am quite lucky and most months I can earn close to $400.00 in colones or American dollars."

"Juan, it seems to me that I can trust you. I'm having a business meeting with a gentleman who, shall we say, is impatient. I strongly feel that nothing undue will take place, but my confidence would be greatly improved if I could obtain a small handgun. If you could help me find one, very quickly, I'll give you $400.00".

Juan eyeballs the mirror and looks directly into Andrew's eyes. What he sees is not pleasant. His young uneducated mind doesn't have the words for the emptiness they express, but Juan has seen this look before. Strange business brings many dark and brooding strangers to his country. He has had such a request before. Mostly he feigns innocence and a lack of knowledge of such activities. But something about this man, he has the familiar look of family members he drove at funerals, their faces proclaiming their lose. Juan always felt sorry for them, wishing he could say the right words, but he was told during funerals to be quiet, speak only when spoken to and quickly at that.

He averts his gaze back to the road. At an open space he pulls to the curb. The limousine poses obnoxiously in a no-parking zone. When the vehicle comes to a stop, Juan casually puts the automatic in park. He turns, and leaning toward the back, he looks at Stratton directly. "What you ask me could bring very much trouble for both of us. I have an urge to help you. There are people familiar to me that are capable of this request. I need to remind you that if they agree, I will drop you off at a location to be determined and will not be responsible for anything that may happen. These men are a gang that is very dangerous, but like us all, they love American money. I will return to pick you up in the same place exactly fifteen minutes after I leave you. I will wait five minutes *only* .If you aren't there by then, I will be gone." He finishes his challenge with a disarming smile, adding, "Such service would demand a tip of at least $500.00, Senor Favors, nothing less and that will only be the beginning. Do you still want a weapon?"

Andrew frowns at Juan's cockiness. He likes his spunk. He reaches into the breast pocket of his suit and removes his wallet. He extracts three $100 dollar bills.

"Arrange it while I am in the bank and we will do it right after. Get it done right away and get me to the restaurant by 1:00 p.m., and I'll make it another $300 when we get there."

*

The banking was completed with satisfactory assistance. After returning to the car, they are soon rushing through streets that become smaller and smaller, the homes dingier and dingier, Andrew has no idea where they are. His naiveté is perhaps being tested once more. Soon the car slows, stopping on a street corner, the neighborhood abuzz with laughing and yelling kids, the car stirring them like a bunch of amused puppies. They are in front of a decrepit multi-colored building. It doesn't look to Andrew that it could possibly be anyone's home, but it's just a little worse than the rest. The houses sit crouched, crumpled and weary like a bunch of old drunks. Juan leaves the car idling, telling Andrew to go in reconfirming he will be back in exactly fifteen minutes; the sooner they are out of this area the better.

Andrew opens the door and the stench of hot raw humanity punches him in the nose. The air is soiled with the living detritus of poverty. Andrew has never been in such a world, he regards it with contempt. He feels the eyes upon him, his suit and tie are a weird costume making him distinctly out of place. He notices movement in the house. Fear tickles his gut and his heart begins to race. These matters are meant to be done by tougher men with little fear. The kids grow quiet and move away, many running into houses along the streets. Andrew figures strangers usually bring a bouquet of trouble when they visit. He enters the house, wishing fourteen minutes had already gone by and he was on his way back out.

His eyes adjust to the shadows; the room is a poor man's open concept, one room for everything. He notices that there are about ten or eleven teenagers in the house, shuffling about, most with their contemptuous chins stuck up. The common denominator of the group is the black leather pants, some baggy, some ridiculously tight. Some of the boys brandish knives. There seems to be a couple no more than ten years old, apprentices he thinks. A squat adolescent stands in the forefront. His pants are about two sizes too small, and look to be painfully pulling at the crotch. It mustn't do his poor balls any good, Andrew imagines. Taking those off at the end of the day has to be a chore. The adolescent's head, like his body, is squat. Greasy hair and a dirty face make his meanness more intense. The facial scars tell of many scraps. Here is a boy that obviously beat his way to being the boss. Andrew surmises he must be their leader and addresses him with a boldness he hopes disguises his consternation, "Do you have what I came for?"

"Trajo usted su dinero blanco, usted perro Americana," the boy countermands, calling him an American dog. He guffaws at his attempt at swagger in front of his troops. He continues in broken English and Spanish, his voice laden with dislike, wanting to be rid of the man in the suit who will soon be parting with his money one way or the other, "Did you bring money".

"Yes, yes", Andrew said, "show me the gun."

The ringleader gives another teen a distinct nod who upon the signal steps up to Andrew. He is a taller, troubled looking youth wearing a tattered gray vest. Its pockets are stuffed and bulging like a pigeon's chest. He reaches into his left side lower pocket and pulls out a plastic bag. Inside is an object wrapped in a grimy rag. A handful of ammunition is grouped in the bottom of the bag. Stainless steel from the short barrel sticks out of its bed and shines in the dull atmosphere, Andrew ogles the dark killing opening in the barrel. His groin stirs with the thought of its power, his mind clouds with a fog of desire. He reaches for the bag and carefully withdraws the firearm. He unwraps the limp rag and takes the revolver in hand. He recognizes it as a Smith & Wesson 686 with a 2½ inch barrel. It has a 6 round cylinder, which is empty at present. He fondles it with great care, marveling at the few nicks and dents along its rubber grip and yearns to hear their tales.

With his earlier anxiety forgotten momentarily he holds the gun in a shooters stance and swings the gun around the room, the boys jump up, yell and scatter about, some threatening him with their knives and others with their brawn. He laughs and drops the gun to his side saying to his host who is laughing as well, "How much?"

The laughing stops and the young brute steps up to Andrew, their bodies only a foot apart. The odor of poor hygiene follows him. The rest of the young hoodlums crowd around him, almost as close.

With a grimace that bares bad teeth, he says, "All that you are carrying, Senor."

Andrew blanches at the thought of giving this hoodlum the several thousand dollars he has foolishly brought with him. His face darkens and he speaks up with anger, forgetting his circumstances.

"That wasn't the deal. Do you think a brat like you can steal from me at will? I don't think so. I'll make it $1200.00 and we can end this right now. My driver should be here soon and I'm in a hurry."

Andrew is determined that his offer is final and while still holding the gun, he reaches for his wallet. In an instant hands grab him and several honed points cut through his suit nipping at the skin of his back, the balance of the pack closing in like hyenas as if he is already carrion. Brat boy places his hands on his hip and spits at Andrew, "If not for Juan, we would just kill you and take what we want." He strikes the wallet from Andrew's hand, the contents spilling on the filthy brown floor. Andrew impulsively moves to retrieve it but knife points pierce his skin a bit deeper and he freezes in a shocked posture.

The leader reaches for the wallet and gathers up its vomit of plastic and paper. He lifts the soft leather flaps and frees a handful of bills from its burrow. Drooling over the hundred dollar bills, he stuffs them in his trousers, the wad a distinct bump in his contracted pocket. He motions for the gang to back off and they form a half pipe whose end points at the door. He offers Andrew his wallet. Andrew can feel blood running down his back from the aching jabs. Grabbing his belongings, he bends to pick up the bag of bullets that has fallen with his wallet. He shakily stuffs the gun in his back waist band and pockets the bullets. A silence that screams at him to flee reminds Andrew of his ride and he races from the house, the laughter of the boys chasing after him.

Andrew catches Juan just pulling away and yells to get his attention as he runs desperately toward the car. Juan sees him and brakes. Andrew reaches for the door, opens it flinging himself into the car. He loudly exclaims, "Let's go, let's go, get me out of here." Juan floors the powerful engine and a cloud of fine dirt flies from up from the wheels as he fishtails away from the scene. Looking in the mirror he can see that Andrew is seriously shaken. Perspiration adorns Andrew's brow and his mien is fraught with relief. Andrew realizes then that he doesn't want to go through any more instances like that. He is even more aware of how much he will have to rely on Rizzato for this kind of work. Of course, there probably would be dead teenagers if he had been involved.

Neither man speaks as the car heads toward the restaurant. By the time they are entering Casco Viejo, Andrew has gathered himself enough to instruct Juan, even though they are already a bit late, to find him a washroom so he can straighten up. Rizzato must not sense his fear; he might not believe Andrew capable of carrying out his own final role. They stop at a small cafe where Juan's sister works. Andrew and his overnight bag disappear inside. He reappears fifteen minutes later wearing a fresh pale blue shirt and no tie. His silver hair is neatly combed and there is ruddiness to his cheeks. A cracked mirror had been the only witness to the pep talk he had given himself, building up his nerve again.

Getting back in the car he gives Juan a nod to carry on. He dials Rizzato at the number Mado had given him for this meeting. The line connects and a hissy silence follows, shortly comes a raspy "Yes?"

"This is Favors. I apologize but I'm running a bit late. I know your time is valuable Mr. Rizzato and I mean no disrespect in keeping you waiting. The traffic seems somewhat thick today and my driver perhaps is a bit new." Andrew winks at Juan in the rear-view mirror, answering his questioning scrutiny. "We should be there shortly."

Rizzato replies by cutting the connection. Andrew looks at his phone as if it can tell him why the man has hung up. He flips it shut and throws it on the empty seat beside him, disgruntled. He is thinking this day is not going as he had planned. At least he has a gun now, and he knows how to use it. He'd gotten it "just in case," it feels good to tuck a little courage in his belt. Andrew can envisage months of such unpleasant dealings, he had better be more careful and more in control.

Andrew takes deep breaths concentrating on the moment at hand. He exists confusingly, part of him queasy with singular violence and close up death, another part sustained on mass death. His retrograding sanity validates his reasoning. Another man, without the means, would wallow in sustained sorrow at the loss of his children. Andrew has calculated that there will be collateral damage in his venture but didn't think it would affect him. What affects him the most is the thought of dying before he completes his act of vengeance.

Juan pulls up in front of Restaurante Mostaza, a shocking white, three storied building, as neat and charming as a bride's wedding dress. Reaching in the travel bag he withdraws three bills, thinking Rizzato will surely not miss them, and hands them to Juan, who is holding the door for him.

"There was a bit more energy at that meeting than I enjoy, Juan, but I want to thank you for your help. I'd like you to park somewhere close and keep an eye out for me when I'm finished. I probably won't be more than an hour".

He steps from the car and looks up at the arched windows on the highest floor, the arcs softening the square perimeter of the graceful building. Potted plants on wrought iron balconies wreath the upper levels. Contrasting domed doors sit stubbornly in the midst of a carved facade. Andrew enters, reminding himself that from this point on, there is no turning back. Whatever difficulty he encounters now, he will do so with a little more spine.

The natural light from the large windows is complemented with subdued lighting providing the rooms with a healthy glow. Andrew gives his name as Jack Favors to the maître d' and is guided to the third floor, which has been converted to separate rooms for private liaisons. After giving the door a gentle knock, Andrew's chattering young guide leaves him to return to his duties. Andrew stares at the door and feels the same apprehension Alice must have had before she plunged down the rabbit hole.

"Immettere," comes a throaty command. Come in.

Andrew opens the door and the aroma of a Cuban cigar tacks through the air. The room is brightly lit. He enters to find Rizzato, who doesn't bother to get up to greet his affluent guest, seated in a fine fabric chair with a drink in hand, resting on his lap.

Rizzato always behaves with the attitude that these fuckers are coming to him and at no point is he going to kiss their ass. So he greets the world from his self-proffered throne. He points at an antique commode. Its upper doors are open and several bottles of spirits stand in a row, glasses and mixes on a sideboard.

"Help yourself to a drink, Mr. Favors... or should I call you Andy?" Bartolommeo asks, his voice a grating smoker's rasp. He blows a ring of smoke and it lingers as if it doesn't know where to go.

"Yes, I think a drink is in order, thank you. Should I call you Bart?" Andrew says as he moves to the bar. Taking a glass he tongs some ice into it while eyeing the bottle of Royal Lochnager malt scotch. He pours himself a good measure and nods to the owner's good taste.

"I would prefer Bartolo if you don't mind, Jack," he says as he stands facing Andrew's back taking in the man's erect posture and steadiness of hand. He is calmer than most of his clients. These are the dangerous ones, hard to read. Rizzato will watch him.

Andrew swishes the liquid and the ice while turning to face Bartolo. They are a few feet apart and Andrew offers up a toast. "To Jack and Bartolo" he says. They each down their drink while studying each other. Both men cautious.

Andrew wonders about the baby blue safari suit that Rizzato is wearing knowing they haven't been in style for more than thirty years and neither has the dark purple shirt whose pointy collar rests on the lapels of the jacket. A heavy gold chain rests in a hirsute chest visible through the partially unbuttoned shirt.

Andrew didn't even think you can buy those suits anywhere. He can't conceive anyone having one made – the thought makes him shudder. In the seventies you could buy four of those outfits for the price of the shirt he now wears.

When he searches Rizzato's eyes for something that can explain this man, instead of the darkness he expected to find, he is awed by the man's eerie orbs. They are the lightest grey he has ever seen, cornea and eyeball almost one. The ebony center is piercing and direct. A pointy nose gives him a rodent look, hairs growing from the holes. No chin to speak of, but lips full and red. The head is scarred by a mangled ear and one furry eyebrow has lost its tail. A slice, poorly healed, leave a wormlike scar across his neck. The skin is taut and Sicilian dark. A bad comb over, actually a terrible comb over, crowns his head. Slightly taller than Andrew, Rizzato looks to be about 45 years old. He hardly looks dangerous, but a book's cover and all, he thinks.

Bartolo, too, sizes up the man before him and thinks how boring he dresses. He looks much older than Rizzato would have expected of a man of his early fifties. He wears a very pained expression. Andrew's voice in their earlier conversation was bold and bossy; today he sounds worried, his voice unsure, like a resigned man. Bartolo really doesn't give a rat's ass what he looks like anyway, or what his problems are. He had been assured by his own sources that this man is rich, heartbroken and eager for revenge. He needs the money and has been told all expenses will be in cash handled through one of Stratton's empty companies, transacted by Mado.

The brief outline he got from Stratton fascinated him. It is crude and heart-stopping, but he gets butterflies when he thinks of the possible outcome. The old fucker really knows how to drop a bomb, his own Hiroshima. That's why he wanted on board, and the dude is flashing his money anyway. Rizzato has some serious gambling debts chasing him and he's eager to take this gig.

His thinking triggers a smile, which softens up his homely face. "Before we begin, I will forgo the usual frisk that *always* addresses my survival instinct, because my contacts in Chicago speak quite highly of you and your brother. I will expect the same courtesy from you. However, we both know we're each carrying, so I'm telling you right now to watch your ass, old man, and don't fuck with me. I'll do your dirty deeds and help you send hundreds to Allah; I don't like the fuckers anyway, so I think you're doing the world a favor. I'm kind of proud to be part of it actually; I'm sure this event will be historical, knock the dress-wearing pansies flat on their asses." He sits in the big chair again and reaches for his dead cigar as he waits for Andrew's response.

Andrew said, "There's no need to be aggressive Bartolo. I'm the least of your worries. We have a formidable task before us and timing is important. I explained my reasoning to you briefly and what keeps me focused. I need to know that you can handle this and not draw any attention I have to be sure that no one sees this coming. Can I count on you?"

Bartolo waves to the bag by Andrew's feet and says, "Let's see the money and I'll tell you."

Andrew reaches for the bag he set on the floor beside the cabinet with the liquor. Unsnapping the flap he turns the bag upside down over the coffee table. Forty bundles of hundred dollar bills fall onto the polished wooden table, some spilling onto the dark green carpet at Rizzato's feet. One wad lands propped against his boot, an alligator-clad cowboy boot the same blue as his suit. Rizzato stretches down and grasps the bundle with long slender fingers ornamented with several rings. The comb over falls forward to make a hairy fan, it's welded together with gel and fits like a skullcap, sliding back into place when he lifts the notes to his nose.

"I love the smell of money, ink and humans, hundreds of humans. What did this money buy? Can you fucking imagine"? Rizzato flares the bills before chucking the packet back with its sisters.

"I'll assume there is one million dollars there. That will get us through phase one."

"Phase one?" questions Andrew. "There is no phase one in my efforts, there is only one goal. The next several months until the rally is crucial, my props need to be in place. You're on board to see that happens and that there are no traces of our chores. I mean *no traces*. I've been told that you are the man to do this? What can you possibly mean by phase one?"

Rizzato sinks back in his chair, steeples his fingers under his chin and says with an impatient hiss, "I've had more experience at these matters than you could ever conceive of, first timer. There are always more hurdles to maneuver than you would understand. As this plan of yours thickens and uniformed assholes are breathing down our neck, you won't be around. You white collar mother-fuckers run the show from your fancy desks; its grunts like us that put our necks on the chopping block".

Rizzato waits a moment to stop from overheating, thinking this man is like them all, wanting to change the stupid world but not get any dirt on their nice shoes. He stares in Andrew's eyes seeing the revulsion he is accustomed to and carries on.

"We're not organizing a fucking boy scout's jamboree here, you're planning a heavy vengeance. Phase one takes us as far as I think it does. I've given thought to how many hands we are going to need and if you want no traces...well, that's going to be a lot of bodies that we can't leave bobbing in the bay. No, Jack, phase two will start when I say it does and there won't be time for negotiations, you'll pay me what I want."

Rizzato stands and begins to stuff the money back in the bag. Andrew continues to muse over Bartolo's words while watching him handle the cash and thinks, yes he's a grunt and crude but greedy too, I'll fix him with an offer that'll surprise even him,

"Yes Rizzato, I agree that you're accustomed to things like that. I admit that I couldn't do what you do, but terrible, terrible people took my children away forever and only left me these."

He reaches in his suit coat pocket and takes out the rings he constantly carries, horrid mementos he clings to. He shows them to Bartolo. A painful plea consumes his voice and he says, "I don't know who killed my children. I don't know what my kids went through in their last moments. I don't know how much pain they might have experienced. I don't know what the men who murdered them look like. Only one maddening voice was all I heard over and over for days and days. I do know that my kids' lives were wasted by religious zealots who only know terror as a weapon."

Here his voice takes on more brass as it growls, his dialogue aping Rizzato's rough banter,

"I'm the man to show these fucking fanatics what terror is like. I'll show them a terror that they could never imagine, but my destruction will continue for years. The bastards will suffer for a very long time."

He met Rizzato's gaze, "You make this happen and keep me out of the picture so I'll be free when the time comes to personally say goodbye to all these freaks. I'll make you very, very rich. I'll speak with Mado tomorrow and have an account set up for you. I will deposit another million in it and when this deed is done, Mado or I will give you the account location, number and the password. No phase ones or twos as you suggest. This amount is not negotiable, if you're not happy, I'm sure there are other outlaws for hire."

Rizzato rubs his chin as if he is thinking about the proposition, but inside he is already thinking of the villa he covets. He will be able to lead a very gallant life with these kinds of funds. Maybe he could even quit this business. He's getting tired of this shit.

"Very well, Jack. I'll want proof of your generous gesture. So where do we go from here?"

Chapter 7   Aug 10 New Market Dhaka Bangladesh

Saul Morgan is a mulatto of black and Jewish blood who grew up in Soweto. His mingled skin color helps him to blend in with the Bangladeshi going about the bazaar – the main reason Rizzato has sent him to clean up the leak in Dhaka. Morgan knows for certain the first three leaks have already taken care of; Bunker, who is Rizzato's second in command, has already killed them. They just need to grab the business man Raheem had spoken with at the bar. Scare him, make him talk and then eliminate him. This is the kind of work he enjoys.

Morgan has thick straight hair, full on top. A genetic battle had produced a long, flaring nose that centers his face. He's of average height. Prison gyms had sculpted his bulk into a dense mass of muscle; he weighs a lot more than his appearance suggests. An iniquitous smile uncovers gold-capped cuspids, pointy and long. Eyes circumspect and clear take in his surroundings while he concentrates on the apartment building across the street. Earlier today he had stolen a street cart from a vendor at the Naya Bazaar and, with his sidekick, uses it to stake out Rafan Bashara's apartment near to the spot they jostled and threatened for in the New Market Area. Bicycle rickshaws are everywhere, many brightly hued, weaving and flowing through the crowd like a rabble of moths, hampering the view. The apartment entrance is sometimes obscured by foot traffic, but the large doors are mostly visible. Each time they move, Morgan strains to see who uses the doors hoping to see the man they seek soon; Rizzato wants this wrapped up *now*.

Many Bangladeshi men wear Western dress, but to appear more "native," Morgan wears a diverse outfit: a beige short sleeve shirt over a bright blue patterned lungi, beneath which he wears black runner's tights. The lungi is a simple piece of fabric sewn into a tube and tied at the waist to hold it in place; it can be torn away quickly and easily if necessary. It is a great place to hide the knife he carries, an eight and a half inch Vermicellus Simplex medieval-type hunting knife, handmade by Citadel Knives in Cambodia. Such a knife is a magnet to untrained amateurs. In Morgan's hand, it is creatively life-ending. His sidearm, a Walther P99 nine millimeter fitted with a mini-silencer he made himself, is stuffed into a uniquely designed holster inside his rumpled shirt.

His abettor is Malik Hajani, a Pakistani from the Sindh province. His face is nondescript; it looks like hundreds of others in the local crowd. He wears a "poor man's" outfit – a white tank top slacked over a baked brown lungi. Like Saul, he has hiking sandals and runner's pants on too. His lithe frame stands several inches taller than the other man, but he is nowhere near as strong. Instead, an embattled childhood has created a demonic scrapper and a hide as tough as wood. In hand to hand combat, he is fast and dirty. As a shooter though, he is calmly flawless. He is gun obsessed. His weapon sits at his feet, folded into a dented and scratched-up black anodized aluminum case that cradles its contents like a newborn. In the band of his lungi he wears a soft leather belt that holsters his collection of throwing knives and stars, hidden by the baggy top. He speaks fluent Urdu and Bengali, and that being so, he distracts customers away from Morgan, whom he treats like a lazy servant, cursing him in front of customers for his uselessness.

Both men are relentless and thirsty killers. Both men are rapists. Both men have done hard time for many years for their sins. Both are confirmed recidivists. Their confinement only made them hate the world all the more. They had met eight years ago when they'd been hired to do some wet work in Northern Ireland by the Provisional Irish Republican Army. They were part of a well-financed group that caused the Highland Bombing in February 1995. The two had befriended each other during the escapade, and a week later, they were bunked together at a cheap hotel in Dublin, waiting to be paid the last of their fees, when police surrounded the place and arrested them. They had only been hired as scapegoats. "Tips" were called in, pointing to Malik's ancestry and Saul's criminal record.

Arrest, trial and conviction were as quick and easy as blowing your nose. They ended up in Portlaoise Prison, situated on Dublin Road in county Laois, Ireland. Crime and their similar tortured pasts are their only commonalities.

Abandoned by their parents as children, each had been raised in an environment where only the meanest and most selfish people lived and survived. They were neglected and abused by dozens of adults. They learned early on that hating, stealing, hurting and running would be their only occupations for many years, never realizing it would blend into a lifetime. Tumbling through adolescence, they became hard and bitter men adding murder, rape and plunder to their resumes. They shared the isolation of prison.

They weren't friends by any means, but something bonds them; at Portlaoise, they quickly became a fearsome duo in the penitentiary yard. It was there they planned their escape, and after five years going over every possible scenario and its accompanying dangers or exposure, the solution found them instead. It became known around the pen that Morgan had money. His sister sent the maximum allowable each month. He didn't flash it around, but the guards knew about his loan sharking and some of them had even availed themselves of his services. So he was tight with a couple of the prison staff.

Guards Homer O'Donnell and Paddy Donagher, were up to their necks in debt and bemoaned the ways of their wanting wives, blaming them for their woes. They both had joined and failed many networking schemes, falling further into debt each time. They bought lottery tickets with every spare coin, promising they'd share any good fortune that befell them.

One Friday morning, Homer cornered Morgan in the laundry – where he worked – with a dire request for some much needed cash. "The wife is after me for a new coat, Morgan, and I can't shut her up. I need 100 Euros for a couple of weeks. Can you help me out, man?"

"Why can't you manage your fucking money, O'Donnell? I told you no already last week."

Morgan was adamant that he wasn't lending Homer any more money until he started to see some return. He had said no before, so Homer knew how stubborn Morgan could be.

"Keep your voice down, mate, this is nobody else's business but ours," Homer rebuked Saul's sass, reinforcing his command by slapping his club in his open palm. Saul paused in sorting clothes and eyed the truncheon, and then he looked Homer in the eyes. Homer backed off a bit. They both knew no amount of threats would work; Morgan would simply remind Homer of the money he's caught him stealing from the office petty cash when he'd been on housecleaning detail that evening. Homer claimed it was only ten Euros and he meant to return it. Nonetheless, Morgan skewered Homer's fear of discovery and will take advantage of it when he can.

"You know where you can stick that bat of yours, Homer. You're already in my books for 400 Euros and I haven't seen any cash for a couple of months. It's always next week with you. Now bugger off and go pester someone else." Morgan returned to his work. Homer skulked away, finishing his rounds, worrying what he was going to tell his wife.

A goblin called foreclosure came to vex Homer. He desperately went to Paddy with a plan: they'd hit Saul up for 50,000 Euros, 25 each; trade him a chance to escape. They'd arrange a work detail and maybe turn their eye. They often worked the same shifts and would sometimes accompany inmates to outside repairs. The cleanup gangs would be going out in the next few weeks, so it would be easy enough to make sure he was on one. The inmate would have to rough them up a bit to convince the administration that they had been jumped. It was risky business, but they were desperate. Homer wrapped up their plan with a certainty. "With another fifteen years to go in this hellhole, he'll jump at the chance."

Morgan did indeed jump at the chance; he had money on the outside. He'd get in contact with his sister. His one condition was that Malik be allowed to come, too. He needed a few weeks to get enough money together; someone on the outside would call, telling Homer where to get the cash: half now and the other half when they were out. Homer didn't like that at first but realized after lengthy negotiations that it was Morgan's way or no way. They shook on the deal, one of the criminals free to go home that night. Two weeks later, Homer received a call from the post office that a package had been sent to him but was addressed to general delivery. Would he like to pick it up? Getting in his car and retrieving the package assuaged any guilt he had been feeling previously. As soon as he returned to the car with the box, he tore it open. His greedy, beady eyes glistened at the sight of the stack of bills. His mind calculated which debts he'd pay first, but a new coat for his wife Aggie and a wee dram or two for the boys at the pub was top of his list.

Two days later Homer approached Morgan in the yard where he and Malik were lifting weights. "There's a work detail going out to clean up along the north wall tomorrow. You and Malik will be on it," he said.

He went on to explain that he and Paddy and one other guard would be watching the detail. There would be two other inmates as well. That was going to be a problem. Saul suggested two of the older inmates who had worked clean up before and who were too near to parole to run or get involved in anything fuzzy. They wouldn't talk for fear of being denied parole.

The next day, everything was going as planned. Homer sent the younger guard off for the water he had "forgotten." Homer and Paddy prepared themselves to be "overpowered," but they had made a fatal mistake. The money lender and the rag head beat the two guards to death, unchained themselves, knocked the two older prisoners unconscious, grabbed the guard's wallets and guns and ran.

Eventually they ran into Rizzato.

The Sicilian had been looking for hired guns. Word of mouth is an amazing concept; people talk and tell each other things. Carpenters know carpenters; sales people crow to each other; trucker's talk highways; lawyers compare cases; and criminals hear about other criminals. Gossip moves like radio waves in the underground world of immorality. About a year and a half ago, Rizzato had spread the word to trusted associates that he was looking for mercenaries. An opportunity had presented itself to mule several million dollars of uncut diamonds from Cote d'Ivoire to Liberia. It was the kind of a high risk-high escapade that Rizzato craved, but he had to steal them first.

For that he meant to recruit a small group of commandos, keep a few later on for security; he'd had too many close calls of late. Elias De Clerq, a Belgium arms dealer, had men available, but he wanted to meet the man "who would require such accomplices, who would rub shoulders with another cutthroat such as himself." They met in Amsterdam. Bartolo entered Holland with great difficulty; all of Europe was looking for him. It would almost have been better if he had stayed away. After an evening of sadistic pleasure arranged by De Clerq, Rizzato had a late night date with a .45-calibre bullet that cultivated a permanent furrow through his eyebrow, planting gristle and skin from his fragmented ear. Had it not been for his assailant being tripped up by the crazy kid in the car, the bullet would've found something more solid to dance with.

Drake Alexander had stepped into his life that night, almost ending it. Rizzato knew who he was.

He remembered with shivery pleasure raping Alexander's best friend's sister in Venezuela. Later after his men had had their way with the girls and they were dead, he had inspected the corpses, then sculpted the dead skin of their shoulders with a "Z", what he thought was a clever symbol. He remembers, the hair on his neck stood erect, goose bumps galloped, and psychic warnings flowed back then. He abandoned his crew to their fate at the camp he had established on a hidden cove in Mochima, Venezuela, and stole away with the hovercraft, heading out of the bay and avoiding Drake's approach from the village a few hours later. He had saved his own neck once more by the most fortunate of luck.

Nowadays, in fact ever since Amsterdam, Saul, Malik and other heavies were his shadows.

*

Against every warning from both Williston and Uday, Rafan returns to the city to pick up more clothes and his laptop. He had forgotten it there when he panicked upon finding the body in the trunk of his car last week. His computer contains urgent files he needs for work; he is getting bored in hiding and wants to catch up on his business. He figures he will be in and out in minutes. He'll be extremely glad when Drake arrives. As his *rikshawala* wheels him along the back streets of the rickshaw capitol of the world, he can see the Dhaka Sheraton over the rooftops, so he knows the market area is not far away. He had entered the city by bus but switched to the rickshaw to avoid many of the main thoroughfares where the human-powered taxis are banned. His cab is covered in red and yellow garnished hoops, the skinny rikshawala pedaling with muscled rhythm. People, noise and smells envelope him. He hides his nervous eyes behind a pair of Oakley's, glass and spheroids both brown and dark. A black baseball hat with a silver New York Yankees logo on its peak hides his short hair. A thin and neatly trimmed goatee frame crescent lips that forms a dreadful frown. He thinks of the dead body that was in the trunk of his car when he depressed the rubber button on his keyless remote to open it. The Jaguar's sculpted deck slowly rose, exposing the fractured carcass. He trembles still from the fright he had experienced. He had carried a box of files to place inside, but instead spilled them on the ground when the gaping trunk displayed its awful contents. What little blood had been left in the body had pooled around the man's head, looking like a burgundy pillow. The rest of his many, many injuries were crusted and ashen. Ugly tape covered his mouth. Rafan dwells upon the gross image even though he tries hard not to. He wants to force it from his dreams, force it to leave him alone; instead it loiters. He is jarred from his thoughts by a sudden jerk to the right as his rickshaw driver veers to miss a wayward car.

The excited hack yells in his native tongue at the offending lady that perhaps she might want to clean her glasses. This is not expressed in a polite manner. It is nothing unusual. Fifty to sixty thousand people visit the New Market area every day, someone is always loudly proclaiming their innocence or uttering threats, mostly with accompanying hand and finger gestures. Rafan feels secure amid the bustle, not knowing his naiveté will soon be bruised.

The day had started out overcast and smoggy, finally giving way to a tormented sun that heats the city. Rafan sits up to fan away the heat with his folded newspaper. Had he sat still the men might never have seen him. The vacillating wad of news catches Morgan's searching eye. The glasses and hat can't hide Rafan's lanky frame and Arab mien. Bunker, who is Rizzato's right hand man, had artfully gotten Rafan's name and description from Raheem, Malik's bigmouthed and traitorous cousin. Actually he had carved all the information he could from the screaming fool. After a little sniffing around, it was easy to find out where Bashara worked and lived. They had already trashed the man's apartment looking for valuables, thinking since they were going to kill him anyway, he wouldn't need them. Their cohort, Bunker who was familiar with the workings of many locks, breaking and entering being one of his professions, had stashed the body into the trunk easily enough. Opening a new lock was as creative as a musician humming a new tune; it's just a different talent. When he and Malik had wrecked the apartment, they had found a photo of Bashara and an older couple, probably parents. The man, they agreed, was just another rich fat fuck, but the woman looked interesting. They joked what they'd do with her if she were around, show her what a real man was like, their egos stoked by previous exploits.

Rafan signaled the driver," Thamun!" (Stop!) "Pull over by the building with the black glass on the front, by the *thaku,"* (the grandmothers). He alights from the taxi slipping the young man a five hundred taka note, which the driver hides in his leather pouch quite smartly, a smiling nod bespeaking his thanks. Rafan scans the crowd, his apartment just up the street. He is about 100 feet from his pursuers, oblivious to their intentions. He casually backs into the stall he has disembarked in front of, tugs and pulls at several rugs as if shopping. He wants to sneak a look around for anything different before he heads in. He gives it five minutes or so but can't detect any interference; no one is paying him any attention it seems. Just before he turns to cross the street, he gives a second glance up and down catching an odd merchant looking at him. Or he seems to be looking his way; maybe I'm just being paranoid Rafan thinks. The man looks out of place at a food cart. Moving around the rug stall he is in, he moves behind a tall rack that is weighted down with mats bright with solid and wavy patterns. Rafan can look toward the curious onlooker while being obscured from his view. The man seems to be going about his business, his partner yelling at him occasionally to get some help. It is almost lunch time and early eaters are pestering them for more rice that come from steaming pots, likely cooked earlier in the day. Rafan shuffles through some other rugs and watches them for another ten minutes. He is finally convinced they aren't interested in him. They are, however, just across from his place and it will be wise to be careful.

Morgan is unsure whether Rafan has seen him, so keeps up his charade while concentrating on his peripheral vision. He tells Malik in a heated whisper that he has spotted their quarry. Malik steps back from the hungry crowd, reaches down to check the case with his gun. He impatiently returns to the pleas for food and dishes out more rice to the patrons and verbal abuse to his helper, continuing their one act play.

Morgan misses Rafan crossing the street but picks him up when he notices the apartment doors opening. As he bends forward, he sees Rafan's back moving inside the entry. Rushing toward the building, he tears away the lungi and motions for Malik to follow. Running through this crazy traffic takes a brave man; foolish works also. In his hurry to get his hands on Rafan while he was still in his apartment, he runs in front of a gaggle of students from nearby Dhaka College on their bikes, knocking several over as they domino into one another. His foot has gone through the spokes of one of the rims as he leaped to avoid the boy he'd first felled and landed on the wheel of another rider. The tangled wires grip his sandaled foot as if it were a prize of some sort, impeding his advance. Angry moments go by in the de-tangling, the extra minutes maybe saving Rafan's life.

Rafan takes the stairs to the third floor, turns right and unlocks the first door he comes to, his apartment being the only one on the left. It is at the back of the building and affords a view of alleys and scattered buildings. When he opens the door and steps into the entryway, a foul odor accosts him causing him to gag. The air conditioner is off; giving what is surely spilled milk a warm spot to ferment in. He holds his nose as he steps into the living room, the smell is terrible but not as terrible as the scene that greets him with its mound of furniture and objects. The room looks like a giant has picked it up and shaken it. His new broom sticks out of the TV that looks as if it has been choked to death. Couches and chairs are upside down, torn. His teacup collection, many rare and of great value to other collectors, is a congregation of broken pottery. A small heap of pigmented shards lay in a corner, their compilation evidence of someone's sad take on fun. Rafan tries to grasp what is going on, what this wreckage means.

Suddenly he hears old Areebah's dog barking from the second floor, in the apartment just under his. It never barks. The noise stops mid-yelp just as quickly as it began. Areebah screams. Her yelps die just as quickly as her faithful companion's. Someone curses in English then speaks in hushed tones too low for Rafan to hear. Footsteps on her tiled floor are muffled by the closing of her door, but he doesn't hear it close. Terror almost consumes him. Rafan knows someone is coming for him, someone who might want to hurt him. They are too close for him to run, he thinks, before quickly realizing what he must do. He turns and shuts his apartment door, closing himself in, where they certainly want him.

When Morgan and Malik sneaked onto the second floor they run into Areebah, a humble septuagenarian, as she emerges from her apartment to take her wee Pekinese for a walk. The dog is well trained and knows to keep it's barking to a bare minimum, but a rash meeting with two rowdies trip its switch. It can smell the viciousness of these men; it barks in warning. It takes an aggressive stance toward the intruders. With a false sense of security the little dog growls with the same intensity as a pit bull. It rushes Malik, protective of Areebah. It rushes to its death.

With a hand quicker that seems possible, Malik shoves a gleaming blade through the dog's spinal cord right at the back of the head. The mutt dies instantly, the only reward for its tiny courage. Saul with equal reflexes grabs his gun from its concealed holster. He cuts short the old ladies scream with a silenced and centered shot to her head. He curses. "Why the fuck couldn't this old gal pick another time to take her dog for a shit." He and Malik quickly pull the dog and dead woman back into her apartment before anyone can see them. Most people are at work, but you never knew. Just as Morgan is closing his door leaving it slightly ajar, he hears a door upstairs close and running footsteps overhead.

Malik just shrugs at Morgan and says, "Stupid old woman, yeah." He isn't much for conversation; Morgan always makes fun of his English. He is constantly answering him back in Bengali, often telling him to fuck off in decorative ways. Morgan of course doesn't understand assuming from Malik's smile when he speaks that he is telling a joke or something.

"That stupid old woman probably warned him, but I think Bashara is still in his apartment. Let's go. We'll rush his place; go in low in case he has a weapon. Don't kill him; cripple him if you have to shoot or throw one of your knives. We need to talk to this idiot. I want to get this done and get back to the airfield with Bunker and Plum again. We got some strange shit happening out there Malik," Morgan ventures in a hoarse whisper.

At the top of the stairway, Saul creeps toward Rafan's door. The men stand on either side of the doorway. They can faintly hear something being smashed or wreaked inside. Morgan has his Walther in a two handed clinch, held tightly to his chest in readiness. Malik releases the catch on his case and withdraws a Glock 17, fastens a fitted silencer to it and attaches his custom laser light, set to pulsate, expediting acquisition of his target,. Malik likes to kill in style. Any spare money goes to his guns.

With his weapon ready, Morgan steps out to face the door and with a mighty shoulder he strikes the smooth outer skin. The helpless lock shatters and splinters the doorjamb. The door bangs open, with Malik diving in. He takes a prone position, the light from his gun pulsating for a target. Saul goes to one knee, his gun ready to blast anything that moves. Both men remain completely still for a few seconds, the silence is disturbing. They search the room for a sign of Rafan. Morgan is sweeping the room, his weapon leading his eye. Malik looks under the overturned furniture for movement. Gesturing to Malik to rise with him, Morgan slowly stands to search the shambles, soon noting there is no one in the living room. There are four more rooms to search; they know he has to be in one of them, they heard someone in here. Saul wonders if the man has a weapon. Assuming that Rafan is armed, Saul's movements are very cautious. He waves Malik to the archway that opens to the kitchen on their right. He creeps toward the opening. As he does, he gambles on his chances of being killed by Rafan. He gives himself good odds that he won't be this time around, guessing the guy is scared and hiding. He knows scared people can be strong though and not to be underestimated.

They search the kitchen, discovering an open window, the blinds at a forty-five degree angle, with bent and broken slats. Morgan sticks his head out the window, looks down into a slender alley, trashy and decorated with patched concrete. He believes that the twenty foot drop is possible, but it could just be a decoy. They check the bathroom and second bedroom easily, their open doors inviting them in. All that is left is the main bedroom with the door slightly ajar. They figure he has to be in there. They bolster their courage and rush through the door in much the same fashion as they had entered the apartment. Expecting an armed lunge or ringing pistol shot, the quiet is confounding. The mattress is tossed against one wall. The box spring, torn and shredded, rests askew on its perch. Dresser drawers have been thrown against the mahogany wainscoting, breaking several stiles and panels. Lamps have been smashed. Files and folders are strewn across the floor. The corners are littered with toiletries and small items. Saul realizes that Rafan is not here, not in the apartment. But it can't be.

"It's impossible, we heard him shut the door and then run through his apartment," shouts Morgan. He calls out to Malik, "Maybe he did jump; if he did, he probably hurt himself. He can't be far. You check around the outside of the building. Hurry!" he commands. Malik spins and races from the room, retrieving his gun case on the way out.

Morgan scans the room for any clue. He pulls at the moldings, but nothing gives. The paneling only comes to his waist; he can't imagine it would hide an adult. He flips over the box spring searching the floor for openings. He kicks a pile of rumpled T-shirts out of the way and stands with hands on hips, and asks himself, "Where the fuck did he go?" Then he thinks, "I'm in deep shit if I can't find this dickweed. I've got to think of some way to blame this on Malik."

Anxiety entwines him. His eyes happen upon a moon-shaped mirror shaped with seashells glued around its edge, resting on the wall by the corner. It is the only item still intact from the raping of the room. It's ugly. He steps closer and measures his profile in its silver glaze. He needs to shave, he thinks; his face is getting scruffy. He might not have a head to shave if he fails Bartolo. With abrupt anger he grabs the mirror with both hands and flings it into the corner with the least debris. It smashes on the paneled wood, eerie spikes of mirror tearing and cutting the polished finish. Some slivers stick in the wood offering a severed reflection of the chaos.

Morgan throws a few more things around not caring if anyone hears him and searches the place again, causing greater havoc, knowing that somehow the target has fooled them. It seems impossible that he could have evaded them so completely. He'll check for access to the roof. He should have thought of that before, he chides himself. Saul gives the apartment another fleeting look, then leaves to search the last floor and the roof, still considering that Bashara might have jumped, which doesn't seem likely. He calculates that if Bashara jumped and by luck, didn't bang himself up too much, then he'd had enough time, while they searched, to get back into the crowd, grab a rickshaw and be gone.

Already Morgan is preparing his dialogue for when he reports his failure. Bartolo had wanted to hear from them as soon as they grabbed him. He wanted to offer a little coaching when they apprehended Bashara. Well, that isn't going to happen today. Fuck it, Saul thought. He'd check upstairs and gather Malik later; he already knows that Rafan Bashara will get to live another day. Morgan formulates a plan. It is time to get to Bashara's family; his sister and her husband lived in Gulshan, an affluent district of Dhaka. Saul knows where they live. He had staked out their house for a couple of days, hoping to see Rafan, while Malik had watched the apartment. He had seen several children playing in front, so it was safe to assume that they had a child that an uncle would trade his life for. He'd run it by Rizzato. See what he thought.

*

Rafan Bashara sits bent over, cramps from the pitiful space compounding his discomfort. He heard the shattering of the glass as it hit the panel in front of him. He holds his breath, realizing his hunter is close by. He hears undistinguished shouting, but he catches the name Malik or something like that. He's been in his hideaway for over thirty minutes; he can see the luminous hands on his Tag Heuer as he calculates the time. That's all he can see. He sits in a rectangular space two feet wide, four feet long and three feet high, designed to hold sensitive files and rough diamonds, not a human being. His sweating hand grasps a remote, the only way to open and close the box, which is built on rails and hydraulic powered. Rafan had gotten the idea when he'd seen a travel trailer with a living room that slid in and out.

One of his uncle Uday's tenants is a diamond cutter who had taken a liking to Rafan, assisting him in setting up a small diamond export and import business. The cutter was retiring soon and wanted to pass on his contacts but had no heirs. Rafan's offices were in the same building, so he usually collected the rents personally. He struck up a friendship with the old Jew. They talked of many things, but mostly about their respective futures. The generous and lonely old heart shared his contacts in Israel and introduced his young friend to local cutters. Rafan set up a toy business, the first on his own, and could sell finished stones where he wished. Many times he brought diamonds home, so he needed a secure cache. Hence the box he is hiding in. On the outside of the building it is disguised by a disused chimney. Inside, the moldings were cleverly designed to hide its presence. Nothing short of electrical and hydraulic failure can open it.

When he had entered the apartment, he had run to the kitchen and opened the window, hoping they might think that he had jumped. Considering the consequences, he was not brave enough to jump twenty feet onto hard concrete. Can't run with broken legs, he had thought. He twisted the blinds to suggest a hurried escape, then rushed back to his bedroom and tore through the debris of his existence, searching for the remote that had been on his night table. The table itself was by the door; a couple of legs were broken. The items that had sat on it were strewn in the corner it had come from. The remote was in the pile. He grabbed it and cleared out the back right corner of the room so the drawer could slide out. He realized that if he could fit inside, the cleared corner might point to his presence or garner more attention to that area. He hastily chucked larger detritus from every corner into the center of the room and tossed some trinkets there instead.

Using the remote, he had opened the drawer, its hydraulic arms in no hurry at all. It extended into the room almost its full length. In it sat two file boxes and a paltry bag of finished diamonds. He grabbed the file boxes and flung them to the floor. The bag of stones he shoved in his pants. He heard them at the front door and panic overcame him. He hesitated, thinking he couldn't fit in the drawer. He couldn't decide which way to get in, feet first or head first. He heard the door smash open. He jumped in the drawer, forcing his ass towards the back, assumed a head to knee position and hit the remote. The drawer retreated, its silent rails sure and steady. With a burp of displaced stale air, the wall swallowed him.

Rafan waits twenty minutes after the last noise he hears. He is still too scared to get out, but his body is insisting on its release. He has serious cramps in his back and his neck. A charley horse in his left leg makes him want to scream. He needs to get out. He hits the remote and the drawer opens with a flash of light that stings his eyes. It moves several millimeters before stopping and then retreats back into the wall. Rafan pushes the open button again. Nothing.

Pressure sensors are built into the front panel in the event that the remote was displaced and the drawer needed to be closed; a gentle knee or fist to any part of the panel closed it and shut down the circuitry for a pre-set time: one hundred and twenty minutes. One of the glass shards is stuck in the front of the panel. It's about seven inches long and an inch wide and has jagged edges shaped like a lightning bolt, with dagger points. When Morgan had thrown the mirror, that shard had struck like an arrow. Gravity did the rest. The opposite end rested on the floor. When the door opened the two points dig in deeper and create a barrier. The pressure sensor picks up the resistance and does what it has been programmed to do: closes and shuts down the drawer.

Startled by his predicament, he dismally realizes he won't be able to try to open the drawer again for two hours. He is unsure if he can endure. Rafan almost pukes from the knowledge that nobody knows where he is. He's not going to get out on his own. He starts to weep.

Chapter 8

Earlier. Shah Jalal International Airport, Dhaka

Drake has changed on the plane so that he is wearing the best suit of clothes Jemina has packed: a pair of navy Dockers with a crisp white shirt. Matching burgundy belt and Florshiems with a reflective polish, highlights his business casual attire. After all, if anybody inquires, he's another North American businessman looking for cheap labor. A search of his bag, a cursory glance at his laptop, and he passes through customs with ease. He heads toward the arrivals area, where his war buddy will be waiting for him, along with whomever Uday has hired. Drake hopes that whoever he is, he can take care of himself. They aren't dealing with any pansies. He isn't worried about Dakin, who knows his way around tough guys.

He emerges into the waiting area, the crowd noisy and rude. Dozens of languages assail him. The sliding glass doors that provide an exit continually open and close. The odor of exhaust from waiting cars merges with scents of strange food and travelled bodies. Drake searches for his friend, finally spotting him near the car rental kiosks. He notices who he is talking to and smiles, thinking of Dakin's main weakness – a pretty girl. He's brave and strong but befuddled by a sultry smile. That's Dakin, 37 years old, single but not alone. Drake can appreciate the attention he lavishes on the lady, who's a little older than his usual interests but indeed attractive. He grins as he think that no matter how long they've been talking, Dakin already has her phone number.

Drake approaches the pair. The man is big. His Irish parents had donated the reddish blond hair, green eyes and firm jaw comes from the mother; the father has given him his rascally ways and quick temper. He had grown up in Spring Lake, North Carolina, in the shadow of Fort Bragg and knew from childhood he was going to be a soldier. He looked like a model for the Superman character inked in comics. The guy is crazy for fitness and does triathlons for fun. He wears a black golf shirt, the tight sleeves fondling his triceps and biceps. The shirt is tucked into a pair of camo pants, the kind he mostly wears, beige and brown desert design today. He has five or six pairs, all different designs devised by different services. He's a good guy, excellent soldier and fun to be around; he just wants to be liked.

The lady is exceptional, Drake concludes. She is tall and lissome. Her black EMC pants with useful side pockets do little to curtain her graceful shape. She has long brunette hair that is corralled and fed through the opening in the back of her black baseball hat. It cascades to her neck in a ponytail that reminds him of Beth. Blue eyes sparkle and laugh at something Dakin has said. A perky straight nose tops a disarming smile, and the slightest of dimples delight her face. She wears a coral short-sleeve shirt over a white tank top. Only one button is hiding the weapon Drake deduces she has holstered. He can see the outline of the strap under her blouse. He wonders if this could be the help Uday is sending.

Drake speaks up and jokes, "Mr. Rush, can't you leave the ladies alone for any decent length of time?" Dakin looks up at the familiar voice, and with a beefy smile replies, "Drake, so many lovely ladies and such little time, can you blame me for being distracted?" Then he presents the young woman.

"This is Mireille, isn't she irresistible"?

The question is rhetorical, just another opportunity to flatter the woman. He greets Drake with a "brothers" handshake and a one-armed hug. Both men are overt with their affection toward each other, comrades in arms, for life. They banter and tease each other in a mood suggesting that their separation has been brief.

The lady, still blushing from Dakin's compliment, watches the greeting with wary amusement. She envisions a friend she had like that, once. He's gone now and his absence still stings. She whips the thought away and concentrates on the two men acting like boys after winning a football game, high-fiving and back slapping. She envies their camaraderie. She considers that she will enjoy working with them. She lets them carry on for a few minutes then decides to butt in.

Speaking with a gentle authority, she extends a hand toward Drake, "Excuse me, my name is Mireille Lambert, those who have trouble with French call me Rae. You're the toughest guy on the planet, Mr. Alexander, according to Lothario here," she says, nodding toward Dakin. "Uday said you needed a guide and translator."

Drake shakes her hand, her grip firm and enthusiastic. They edge away from the crowd toward an emergency exit where they can talk. Before he speaks, he gauges her bearing. Drake is elated to see Dakin again. They'll be rallying the troops for another mission, the two other members of the team waiting for their call. Dealing with enlisted men and women, learning to trust and depend on one another; his gut has never let him down. He has a sensation that this woman is able, that she'll get the job done. He'll throw her a loop, see how she reacts.

"A guide and translator yes, but with all due respect, what I have planned involves some of the nastiest men alive, who will, no doubt, take us through Dhaka's depravity. We may have to prepare ourselves in minutes to travel anywhere in the world my adversary may lead us. These people do not forgive, and never forget. Are you qualified and eager for an adventure like this"? While Drake stares, her eyes never flutter or blink.

With a stance both erect and bold, she offers, "I spent 15 years in the Sûreté Nationale. As a rookie I was like all the rest but more ambitious than most. I had to beat up a few people, both physically and mentally, to get what I wanted. And not just bad people. I was the youngest female inspector for the Sub-directorate of Criminal Business. I'm very well trained, Mr. Alexander. For the last nine years my husband and I have built a very respectable investigation business. I've seen this city's perversity. There's nothing new you're going to uncover that I haven't seen before. In fact, I might know where the slime you're looking for is hiding. You can rest assured I won't let you down." She places one hand on her hip and with a coquettish grin adds, "I'm surprised you don't trust Uday's judgment, but then I would expect no less of an inquiry from what I've heard of you, Mr. Alexander." She is forever the diplomat.

Drake sees that she possesses more weapons than a gun; she is armed with feminine charm and steely grit. He gives her an understanding smile and says, "Okay. We can start by you calling me Drake. I do trust Uday, but I wanted to hear it from you"

He follows in fluent French, "I'm charmed by such a lovely name, Mireille", the last four letters rolled off his lips with a whispering ehhh! "But Rae's equally as appealing, so Rae it is. Welcome to our team. I see you and Dakin have already met. I need to warn you that unless you are discussing wars and weapons, don't believe anything this man tells you. He's a wonderful guy but doesn't take life too seriously."

Switching to English he says, "Do either of you have a vehicle? If not, I'll rent one. I have a stop to make and then we need to meet with Rafan. I'll fill you both in on the ride."

Rae said," I have my truck; we can use that for now, but please no bullet holes okay. I've got a beater at home for that kind of work."

Dakin reacts well to the truck part; he gets excited about trucks. He has half a dozen back in N.C.; three are mint and three await restoration. Rubbing his hands and flashing a smile, he says, "I'm starting to like you even better, Rae, but what's this you were saying about a husband? You never mentioned a husband earlier"? She ignores his remark, surprising them all with a gruff command, "The truck's this way and it would be good to know where we're headed." She takes the lead and waves them to come along. Dakin shrugs; he and Drake fist-bump then follow her into the crush.

As Rae leads them to the parking lot, Drake glances back at the airport building, admiring the architecture. Rhythmic columns rise up like glass stems to hold flat symmetrical slabs forming a vast roofline. Heavy arches echo across the facade. Drake thinks of it as Islam-modern. He prefers it to many others he's frequented. He had spent several months in Dhaka the first time he met Uday when he and Beth had been freewheeling years ago. He frowns at people's ignorance of Bangladesh. People remember the natural disasters, the famine, the widespread poverty and the political corruption. They miss the human equation, he thinks – the hard working people, filled with élan and hope; the bold, vibrant colors that adorn buildings and pedestrians alike. Money is migrating to

Dhaka and other major centers throughout the country. The poor from the rural areas follow the money. There is growth here. And so is Rizzato, he hopes.

Drake fills them in on what he knows at this point. Dakin, of course, had been with him when he tracked Rizzato after the girls were killed, so Drake places a file folder on the center console of the big Ford and tells Rae to give it a quick glance. He informs them that they will round up Rafan then split up briefly later, each with a list of things to do.

Rae wheels her black F-150 around the city at a frightful speed. Driving on the opposite side of the road is a bit freaky for Drake. The tuk-tuks are everywhere, painted garish and fierce colors. They gad about, burping exhaust. Rae gives them little regard. They dance on the streets in their own motorized way.

Rae says," I'm so sorry about your friend's sister, Drake. I want to help you find this man. So what we know for certain is that Rafan befriended someone who spoke of Rizzato; that man was then killed in a grotesque manner. And there are two other bodies that, as untouchables, nobody will care about. They might not even be missed. There's a similar mark on the bodies that ties them together; you encountered the same mark on the young women. That is definitely a starting point."

She looks over at Drake, who rides up front with her. He's thinking of her rundown. There is something about the mark that bothers him, what is it supposed to mean, some kind of symbol? This is something for Rae to work on, perhaps. Dakin on the other hand needs something solid to follow. Drake knows Rafan's information will give them more direction. Before he assigns any tasks, he wants to hear what the man has to say.

"What are you packing? I noticed the holster," he asks her.

"It's a leftover from my Sûreté days, a SIGp226. It's a good gun, well balanced, very accurate. I like it." Drake knows the gun; many law enforcement agencies use it. He still prefers the 1911; the cock-and-lock mechanism suits his style.

"How about you Dakin? Got a gun yet?"

"Oh yeah. I've been here a couple of days now. If you know where to look, you can always find a gun, right? You should've seen this guy, older than Buddha. He knew guns, man; he had about twenty of them for sale. I picked up a Smith & Wesson, a .45 semi-auto Chief's Special. It's a good gun. I picked up a slick ankle holster, too, and some clips. These guys are crooks though. Took me an hour to get him down to a reasonable price."

The crafty Irishman is busy taking in his surroundings from the backseat of the crew cab, eyes alert, always watching, checking for tails even though it's unlikely there will be any. Nobody knows their next step, not even him; but it was always better to know what's going on around you. If you don't, then when you're in battle, you could die. He looks toward Drake with a good feeling; he would do anything for that man. He'll always remember Drake and his Joint Task Force commandoes tearing into the mud hut where he was being held by Iraqi soldier wannabes, minutes away from losing his head. The machete was wavering in the air, ropes and arms forcing him down, his neck stretched and sweating. He can still hear the crashing of the door, Drake rushing in with his C7A1 assault rifle on full clip, cycling at 900 rounds a minute, almost taking the filthy executioner's arm off at the wrist. He had almost fainted from that moment of utter relief. So now when Drake calls, he comes running. He sits quiet for a moment, looking at Rae's eyes in the mirror. She watches the street with the attention this mania deserves. He's looking forward to getting to know this lady.

Rae drops Drake off at the Janata Bank, close to the National Stadium. Traffic isn't quite as bad here; just a mild panic. The building rises up brown and plain. He enters and briskly follows proper protocol, inquiry, presentation of ID, removing safety deposit box and finally being left alone. Soon he is sitting in a private room with a steel container the size of a shoebox on a Formica and steel table. The young man in the beige shirt and ugly tie who has assisted Drake gives him his key and leaves the room. Drake examines its contents, admiring Williston's resourcefulness. He withdraws the gun, checks the safety and notices the gun is loaded but no bullet is in the chamber. He loves the 1911. It is an older design but copied for over ninety years. Drake likes it because it's accurate, fast and delivers a wallop, more so than any other gun he's tried. It has a short trigger pull, so shooting is quicker. He tucks the gun into his rear waistband and tugs his shirt out over his pants. He'll be a little wrinkled, but so what, he thinks. He leaves the holster in the box.

He pulls out a stack of takas, the local currency and an American Express card that can be traced only to a numbered account. Knowing Williston, it will have been set up with a credit line of a million dollars; two million might take a phone call. There is a padded envelope with half a dozen untraceable phones. There are forged documents with Drake's likeness but a different name, passport included. The new identity comes with its own history, of course. He doubts he'll need them but they're terrific fakes. There are documents for Dakin, too. Drake stuffs everything into his overnight bag. He closes the box.

He's anxious to talk to Rafan and pick up Rizzato's trail. Drake has to admit he enjoys this work. A deeper want is hoping Rizzato puts up a fight. He feels guilty for placing himself in danger, his loved ones would have it different but his course is set.

He checks his bag once more, shifts the gun into a more comfortable position and summons his escort. The young man has been replaced by an older more dapper gentleman Drake perceives as someone of much greater authority. The man silently leads him, left and right, through the warren of offices to an exit. Ignoring the security guard there, the gentleman steers Drake around a metal detector and as far as the door. Inputting a code the door opens with ease. The alley in back is shaded by tall walls and is as discrete as bricks allow. Williston leaves nothing to chance if it is within his capabilities.

Drake crawls back into the truck and divides up the phones, two each; they take the time to memorize each other's numbers. Drake calls the number Uday had given him trying to reach Rafan. He identifies himself so that the lady who answers the phone would know it's okay to tell him where Rafan is. She told him that Rafan had left earlier and hasn't returned. She's worried because she doesn't know where he has gone or when he will be back. Drake decides to try Rafan's apartment and directs Rae there. They maneuver through traffic, finally reaching Azimpur Road. Rae parks the truck helter-skelter next to a cloth merchant who rants at the obstruction to his business. Can't they see that it is still lunchtime and he's busy? A quick glance tells the bunch his stall begs for a customer. Rae jumps out, charming the pants off the boisterous man, speaking his dialect, which softens him a bit but not enough. She has to part with 1,000 taka to leave the truck and have him watch it. It's more than the guy will make all week, and she promises they won't be long. Now they are best friends. The vendor drapes two cloths of magnificent color, yellow and red, over the rear fender of the ebony chariot, inviting the nosy onlookers into his shop. This appeal soon thins the crowd. The trio hustle up the street, Rafan's apartment just a few steps away.

The trio head up the stairs and pause at the third floor landing, Rafan's door is slightly ajar, jagged wood decorating the jamb. Drake puts up a fist and everyone freezes, listening. There are no sounds coming from within, but the culprits could still be inside. Drake as usual leads the group, all with guns drawn. They hug the wall and listen some more. A smell escapes from the room. Drake reaches out with the toe of his shoe and gives the door a gentle push. It is well balanced and swings open enough for him to get a look inside. He scans the entryway and is astonished by the jumble of belongings. He steps into the room and his team take up defensive positions, Dakin covering Drake's right out of habit and Rae instinctively covering his left.

Drake yells out, "Are you here Rafan?"

Rafan, aching and scared, hears someone. He is overcome with alleviation and starts to cry again. He yells out between sobs. He doesn't care who is out there. He'd rather be dead than stuck in here any longer.

`"I'm in here! Help! Help me!"

Drake hears a muted shout. It becomes a continuous sound and is coming from one of the rooms down the hall. Keeping their guard up, they scout the apartment. The voice is coming from the back bedroom. Once there, they realize it is coming from the back corner. The yelling is muffled and the words unclear. They can't miss the urgency behind it. The pressure sensitive panel is thick and tightly jointed.

Dakin drops back to cover the front door. Rae steps into the room and covers the hall. Drake clears away some glass and notices several thick shards stuck in the heavily grained wood. One of them, the longest, is pointing to the floor.

"Rafan, is that you?" Drake loudly exclaims, exploring the panel's trim for an entry. "It's Drake. Can you understand me?"

Rafan calms down, his throat is sore from yelling. It sounded like someone has said he's Drake. If that's true he'll be out soon. He bellows, "Yes, yes, yes, it's me, Rafan. I can't get out." He waits for a response; his cramped legs making the seconds seem like minutes.

Drake turns to Rae and says, "I can't make out what he's saying. I can't find a switch to open the wainscoting. Come have a look."

Rae inspects the wall, concentrating on the lower portion of the panel where the glass fragment forms a restrictive triangle. Taking a pair of fine leather gloves from a side pocket of her pants, she uses them to carefully pull on the glass shard and feels its resistance, both points embedded in wood. She motions to the floor and points out to Drake, "Enough pressure was exerted on the glass to push both ends into the wood but not enough to cause it to break. The panel is one piece top to bottom above the baseboard so it must slide out. There might be some kind of safety device that closes it with pressure. That might explain why the glass didn't break. If we rip the first stile from the corner off, we can probably tell how to gain access." She kicks away the glass saying, "I'll be right back." She hastens from the room and Drake hears her say something to Dakin on her way out.

He is interrupted by an explosion of words from inside the wall. Rafan is growing impatient.

Drake says, "If you can understand me Rafan, knock twice." More muttered pleas come from the wall. Drake talks to Rafan as if he can hear, to at least assure him they aren't abandoning him. A few minutes later, Rae comes back with a hefty pry bar from her truck. She says, "Stand back," and demolishes the moldings with fervor. Taking an overhead swing, she slams the teeth of the bar deep into the wood and pounds away at the top rail, the nails screeching as they are drawn from the studs.

Drake steps away from the flailing iron, watching Rae peel away the wood and tangled circuitry. Soon she is down to bare wall. She has exposed a hard rubber pad riveted to some type of backing plate. She continues to pry at the edges but nothing will give. Drake motions to her to stop. He can hear Rafan more clearly.

Rafan was listening to the commotion and the pounding on the wall before him. When the din fades he yells out for Drake calling his name, "Drake. Drake, is that you?"

Drake responds jubilantly. "Yes, Rafan, I can hear you better. How do we get you out?"

Rafan, now hoarse from calling, says," You have to cut the power in the basement; the lock is electronically shut down. Then you have to drain the hydraulic oil from the pump so it can be forced open. Did you get that?"

Drake holds his ear close to the edge of the metal box embedded in the wall and says, "Yes Rafan, we'll get you out right away. Where do we drain the pump?"

"There is an emergency tap behind the flush in the bathroom, close to the floor. Just open the valve. Go downstairs and cut the power, then you can pry it open," allows Rafan, anticipation of release overwhelming him.

Drake directs Rae to cover the front door and gets Dakin to go to the basement to find the electrical panel. He wants the electricity cut – to the whole building if necessary. He turns the room light on so he will know when the power has been severed. He runs to the bathroom to open the pump valve while Rae takes up her post at the door.

The toilet sits with its back against thebwall, behind a short barricade of glass bricks. It is in a cramped area, making the tap's access clumsy. Drake drops to his knees and reaches under the bowl. His fingers soon find the small metal tap with ribbed wings. He pauses, knowing the fluid will be under pressure. He withdraws his arm, searching for a towel. Grabbing one off the shower rod, he wraps it around his neck and face. A faint flicker of regret for his white shirt crosses his mind and decides to remove it first. He hastily pulls it over his head, reaches in and gives the tap a twist. The opening spews out a reddish liquid that goes up his arm and soaks the towel. He leaps away and a reddish piss shoots from behind the bowl. It gushes around the room, covering the floor and the walls. With another towel he wipes the greasy residue from his arm, shoulder and side. Chucking it aside, he rushes back to the bedroom. As he does, the light goes out.

Drake sweeps the pry bar from the floor and tackles the rubber pad at its edge, the drawer begins to give. Prying lower against the stiff edge, he opens the drawer enough to get both hands around the frame. Using the wall as a brace with his foot, he pulls the drawer slowly from its hangar.

Rafan is whimpering as he lifts his head; the drawer is moving. He croaks his hearty thanks with broken sobs. "Thank you, thank you, thank you, Drake. I'm going to kiss you when I get out. Thank you and thank you." Soon the bin is fully extended. Drake stands to help Rafan from his tomb.

With a painful effort Rafan straightens up like a leaf from its pod. His legs are wooden, two hours of cramps having petrified them. Drake shouts to Rae to come help him. When she comes into the room Drake commands, "Flip that mattress on to the floor, then give me a hand here."

The two of them pull Rafan's stiffened frame up and place him on the mattress. Moaning with blissful pain, he rocks his body in un-imprisoned ecstasy. Rae expertly massages his knotted muscles, his circulation responds to her practiced hands. Drake brings water from the kitchen, which Rafan attacks with relish. Drake and Rae administer to Rafan's woes totally unaware two fugitives are stalking the premises once more. There is no one watching the front door.

Morgan and Malik have searched the area around the apartment and several of the stalls, finding no trace of Bashara. They were doubling back to check the apartment again when passing below Rafan's open kitchen window they hear voices. They realize people are in the apartment. They jog to the front and enter the lobby. The stairs are clear, the place oddly vacant. They creep toward the third floor. Malik has his gun by his side, the aluminum case left at the bottom of the stairs. A Kohga ninja star spins from its center hole between his thumb and forefinger, its four points are razor sharp. He can't even pronounce *shuriken-jutsu* but he loves throwing these stars. He is quick and accurate.

Morgan has his gun out and leads them up the stairs. When they get half way to the third floor, they can hear people talking. They try to estimate how many. They can make out three distinct voices, one male and one female, not sure of the third. They approach stealthily. The stairs double back in a half circle and is open to the main lobby. A short wall 42 inches high provides a barrier and a handrail. They hug the wall as they approach the third floor landing. Halfway up the last flight of stairs, Morgan motions for Malik to wait, thinking about his approach. He doesn't know who was in there. He's considering backing off to wait until they come out. He knows his stolen cart will already have been re-stolen. Leaving a cart empty for fifteen or twenty minutes meant anybody bold enough could have it. They would have to hide somewhere in the crowd. As he thinks about trying to take them down outside, he realizes there are too many people around, too many escape routes. He might not get them all. Instead he makes a sign to Malik that they will storm the apartment shooting. The door is open, a few more steps and they will burst through spraying the room with lead. As Morgan ponders the disarray they'd left the room in, he plans the path they should take. Unknown to him or Malik, Dakin now has them in his sights.

Dakin had found the utility room and discovered an electrical panel for each apartment. None of them were numbered or named so he searched for the main switch. Finding it high and to the right of the electrical cabinet, he pulled the large handle and everything went dark. He waited a bit until his eyes adjusted. He knew his way out. The basement was well sealed and very little light entered. It reminded Dakin of his nights bound and gagged in a tiny Iraqi shed. His could not forget that fear, not the darkness or what the light might bring. One day, his captors draped a noose around his neck and tightened it several times, cutting off his airway. They taunted him for hours and toyed with his life. When they tired of their ridicule they kept him fettered and stuck in his undersized prison.

He disregards the disturbing memories and feels his way out, using his memory and the walls for guidance. Clearing the utility room, the light from bottom of the exit door creates a shadowy glow leading him back to the main floor. He is heading up from the first landing when he spies Morgan and Malik. It doesn't take a trained soldier to figure out what the guns indicate. They definitely aren't collecting for Red Cross. Both men looking up don't see him duck into the second floor hallway. Dakin can't see them from where he stands unless he steps out from his protective cover. He assumes they're after Rafan. They look like foot soldiers. He recognizes the breed. He has to warn Drake and Rae. He steps out into the hall yelling,

"Don't move, boys, and drop your toys!"

In case they don't understand English he waves the nose of the 45 he carries with the barest of pressure on the trigger. With his weapon in two hands, he lines up the sights of his weapon upon Morgan, keeping Malik in his peripheral vision. He never saw Malik's hand or the star until it strikes the back of his left hand, the needle point just missing the tendons and cutting through to the palm. His gun goes off. The unfocused shot tears a chunk of drywall from the corner of the wall just above Morgan's head. The blast of the gun is loud in the entryway. Both Morgan and Malik crouch down by the short wall. Dakin jumps back to the protection of the second floor hallway, around from the stairs.

Swearing out loud, he pulls a large handkerchief from a thigh pocket. He wraps the star and pulls it from his hand, tossing it to the floor before cloaking his bleeding hand. He applies pressure to the improvised bandage as he curses his impetuousness. Staying close to the wall he listens for movement, the throbbing gash rendering his left hand useless. The two men know he is injured. He moves to the apartment door behind him and knocks with the butt of the gun. After several seconds, with his patience already thin, he backs away from the door and with a terrific kick knocks the door from its hinges. He hunkers down in the doorway using it as a shield from the two men, checking his back that the occupant, if home, doesn't surprise him. The stench from the owner's unkempt rooms sallies out the doorway. A look of disgust creases his face as he reaches for one of the phones Drake has given him. He punches in the 1, speed-dialing Drake as he had programmed it.

Morgan and Malik are crouched behind the enclosed banister halfway up to the third floor, where it turns directions at the top of the U it forms. They're trapped. Morgan is impressed with Malik's throwing skill, hoping he's disabled the man below. Still, he isn't taking anything for granted. Morgan signals for Malik to wait. He wants to hear what the ones above are doing. He can only go either up or down and there is opposition on each end. Their cover is minimal. Disturbing images of prison life dog his consciousness, so no matter what happens in the next few moments he'll be clearing out of here, or he'll be dead. He gestures to Malik to be ready for an aggressive assault. Malik crouches down with his gun in a two handed grip, waiting for his partner's signal. It looks like there is going to be a shootout. Morgan is at his back and he thinks this is good. They might not always get along, but they work well together, two jailbirds eating the same worm. Malik eyes the downward stairs while Morgan covers the up side. He is surprised by a thundering crash from the hallway below where the man he hit with the star retreated to. The moaning from the apartment above has stopped.

Drake, alerted by the gunshot, forces a hush on Rafan and Rae. Rafan is sitting up on the flattened bed, feeling much better. The soreness, now numbness, is a by-product of his ordeal. It troubles his body to shrink down behind the mattress for cover. He is terribly frightened and is thinking he should have stayed home this day. He watches Drake, who moves to the hallway with Rae close behind. Drake has pulled his gun from his belt in response to the shot. He rushes out of the bedroom into the hallway as they cling to the wall. Waving Rae to the bathroom door they both draw a bead on the entrance, which is visible through the tangled furniture, the door slightly ajar. They can see where the third floor hallway meets the first step but not beyond. Anybody rushing toward them bearing arms would be going back downstairs with more urgency then their ascent, likely with a gut full of spent ammo. Drake hears shuffling from the stairway. Just then, one of Drake's phones ring. He flips it open and whispers, "Dakin, is that you? What's going on?"

Dakin, calmer now, speaks softly,

"Two targets, on the landing between the second and third floor. Definite thugs. These guys are armed Drake, one with what looks like a Glock and the other a semi-auto for sure, probably nine millimeter. It's likely that they were coming for Rafan. One bastard is good with those ninja stars. I unsuccessfully invited them to surrender, losing the use of my left hand. It hurts, but I'm okay. I'm behind cover and can watch their retreat if they come this way. I expect guns for glory exit here, Boss. They don't remind me of men who want to take up knitting". He can almost hear Drake thinking and asks, "What do you want to happen here, Boss?"

"We have an advantage that we both have cover and they're the ones stuck in the crossfire. Hang tight and if they come rushing your way try to wound them but don't make yourself a target. I wouldn't mind having a chat with one of them. I'll give them a few minutes. Rae can cover me and we can try to drive them back down and out. Somebody must have heard the shot and probably warned the police, so they're going to try something soon. I'm going........"

Their conversation is interrupted by a sudden outburst from the landing. A strident, raspy voice booms out. "Send out Bashara. Do it quickly and we may let you live. You have twenty seconds before we start shooting. Your time starts now!"

Drake pockets the phone, moving through the debris to kneel at the front door. Rae hurries behind him and positions herself just above Drake at the edge of the narrow entryway. She concentrates her sights about three to four feet from the floor on the stairway, aiming for a body shot; the largest mass of an oncoming aggressor. Drake knows Dakin will immediately be on the defensive. He realizes he has the upper hand when he shouts out, "I think your confidence is a little overblown, so I suggest you bring on your guns and forget about any plans you may have had for the evening." He goads them with an extra favor, "In these circumstances, I think you might want to lay down *your* weapons. *You* have twenty seconds, starting now!"

Morgan realizes the action is going to get hot. They aren't in the best position. Retreat is their only option. He isn't going back to prison. He checks the Walthers, the safety already off. Creeping over to Malik, he whispers, "We rush down, go through the hallway toward the other stairs shooting. I'll go first and you fire up when we run past, covering us. Once outside, we separate into the crowd and meet up at our ride. You get that, Malik?" To give himself a few more seconds he shouts up at Drake. "Hold your fire up there, give me a minute."

The Pakistani, silent as usual, gives a trademark shrug, the laser light pointing its pink needle at Morgan's foot who says "Be careful with that, *bonehead.* Trade me places." They scramble around until Morgan has one foot on the first down step and his knee on the landing. Morgan raises his hand, all five fingers outstretched. From behind him, Malik watches him fold one, then two fingers, knowing that in a few seconds his life could be over. He remembers a saying an old lady once told him, scolding him for his foolish ways of cheating and stealing. *"Oti chalaker galaye dori,"* she had offered Malik, meaning "every fox must pay his skin to the furrier." He whispers the same words to Morgan.

Morgan pauses on the last finger. Still concentrating on his next move, he acknowledges his co-conspirators adage. "So be it. And fuck 'em all, right Hajani?" Not waiting for an answer, because he'd heard it many times, he lunges for the second-floor landing with a roar. Reaching the second bottom step he leaps halfway across the landing and begins firing down the hallway.

Chapter 9   April 29 10:00am Cayman Islands

Bartolo Rizzato is leaning on the deck of his 6th floor suite at the Sheraton, compliments of Andrew Stratton, scrutinizing the beach with its early combers. He has just risen. He's wearing the complimentary white terry robe provided by the hotel, furry slippers, a fuzzy chin and nothing else. He looks like a q-tip swathed in paper towel, his skinny legs white as paper. He notices the morning breeze is scented with suntan lotion. Looking around he spies two sets of legs on a lower balcony on lounge chairs, obviously two gals catching early rays, although since he couldn't see the upper bodies it could be two guys with great gams, who knows these days. Anyway they're probably the source of the offensive odor, he assumes. The smell is sickly sweet. He can't understand why anyone would want to cook in the sun, getting red then brown of all colors. They look like a bunch of mulattos, he thinks, and probably most of them would look down on a real one. "Snobbish bastards," he squawks.

It's easy for Rizzato to work himself up. His temper is always simmering, a depressed flicker of a flame, like a pilot light. Trivial incidents and other matters can easily become combustible. His temperament had developed when he was young, of poor family and companionless. Bartolo was extremely homely as a child, of both face and frame. Gangly spindle-legs stretched to meet a bantam torso, a midget on stilts. His colorless eyes and absence of chin ruined any chance a face could have, it just didn't work. He was almost repulsive. Even the dweebs avoided him; worse still, his siblings ignored him.

That temperament landed him in a boy's prison at the age of 14, seven years in irreparable hell. What got him there happened on one spring day in the town of Scordia in the province of Catania, on the island of Sicily where he grew up. During the lunch break at school one day, a deceitful pudgy kid, a true bully named Veit Canelosi, taunted him while poking him with his butterball finger, calling him "due zampe mouse," a two legged mouse. It wasn't the name calling in itself that ignited Rizzato; his sensitivity to that annoyance had been hardened some time ago. That Veit did it in front of a brood of the prettiest and most popular girls in school and another seven or eight of their courtiers did. Each and every one of them laughed vigorously at Veit's smears and Bartolo's shame. A comely girl with bouncy sable curls, a sibylline model, stepped out of the crowd bending to pick up a smooth and hardened rock as big as her fist and threw it at Bartolommeo. It struck him on the ear with a piercing thud to the skull hurting both his head and ebbing tolerance. He abandoned his school bag and lunch pail to grab his painful ear. He reeled from the blow and almost fainted. The kids were still laughing.

A sheer terrible hollowness monopolized him. The idea that nobody – nobody – loved him emptied his soul. All he ever experienced were taunts; torment and always the torturous laughter. His emptiness became a repository for a barbarous spirit. Fuelled by a twisted enmity, he drove himself toward Veit and rammed his head into the harrier's flabby gut, knocking him to his ass. With a hand bloodied from the wound to his head, he grasped Veit's neck and all the pain from his lonely life turned into adrenalin. With an iron grip he choked the ignorant boy. The crowd, hushed by Rizzato's aggressive actions, gasped in collective disbelief as Veit's tongue waved and frothed from its scorning hole. He franticly pulled at Rizzato's hands. Panic seized his final heartbeats, his grip becoming feeble. And there in front of his audience, he completed his short life.

The kids stepped back as Bartolo looked toward them, his smile the scariest they would ever witness no matter how long each would live. Had they looked even closer before they all ran, they would have seen the wet and stained eruption around his crotch. The act of killing became like an aphrodisiac. It triggered the most hostile ejaculation and sharpened his every fiber. From that day on, the act of murder would fuel his lust.

He picked up the stone and threw it at the brats, causing the girls to shriek and the bunch to flee. He ran down the street the opposite way, his long legs fascinating him with the ground they could cover. He ran from the town and into the fields to the west. He ran to his private haven behind three large boulders exposed by the water's continuous journey through a deep-walled gully. Between two of the rocks and close to the ground was a constricted entrance to a small cave the size of a minivan. In the closest corner where light was visible during part of the day, was a bent and bandaged bird cage. Inside was a crested lark, tiny and common. An upright spike adorned its head, while dark greyish streaks clothed its back. It perked up and started a doleful whistle and various tweets when Rizzato forced his way in, the bird recognizing its feeder. Rizzato had had it since it was just a chick two years ago and he loved the bird. The bird loved him back, not caring how he looked. While feeding spiders to his chirping playmate, he told the bird of his dreadful deed and how much he enjoyed it. How much he relished the look on the faces of the ones who made fun of him. There was no shame, no sorrow, no guilt, just a lingering euphoria. He would be popular for a while now, he guessed, even if the attention was hate.

It wasn't long before the police found him, dogs smelling him out. He claimed self-defense but too many witnesses told of his guilt. He was charged with second degree murder and sentenced to ten years. He was tried as a juvenile and his sentence began at a prison for juveniles, serving the latter part of his sentence at the prison of Catania Piazza Lanza. While at the former institute, he was remorselessly defiled by two of the older inmates and one of the guards. His protestations were treated with disdain and disbelief, the three culprits covering each other.

After Rizzato was freed, he killed all three with his bare hands, each time a painful erection accompanied his atrocious act. Since those days, he trusted no one and hated everyone. The balance of his history was besmirched with criminal activity that allowed him to grow bold and moderately wealthy. Destroying somebody's life was like tossing a burnt match; it meant very, very little to him. His ruthlessness contributed to his coffers; unfortunately the cost to remain hidden and protected was a burden. Money bought him company, their acquiescence subject to his whims. And he had his birds.

Tucked away in the confines of an Embera village along the Rio Sambu in the Darien Gap of Panama sat an abode similar to what the natives lived in. It was a shelter built on stilts, open on the sides, braced and built of wood, somewhat larger than the rest. A grass thatched roof like a straight haired wig topped the simple outer walls that formed the structure. Inside this particular one hung four crafted cages, each housing one of four of the most spectacular bird species from Central America, each enclosure holding several. The cages were not modest, occupying a quarter of the domicile

Emerald tanagers of lime and yellow splendor, orange-crowned orioles of yellow and black with tangerine cap, rusty-margined flycatchers with yellow underpants and a pronounced white super cilium and the most striking of all, red male hepatic tanagers and their yellow mates were vying for the attention of an indigenous youth Rizzato supported, his parents both having been killed by a jaguar. The boy fed the birds and cleaned the cages; if he didn't, Papa, as he called Rizzato, would punish him. But if Papa was happy, Federico, the little one, would get many fine gifts.

Rizzato's early years of crime involved mainly drugs and the pipeline that spread throughout Central America. In his early twenties, he chanced upon a native youth of Panama who had been lured by urban life and disappointed by its indifference, soon becoming entangled in the macrocosm of narcotic wars. He, like many of the native people, had a Spanish name: Dimas. Rizzato and Dimas had shared a harrowing escape when one of the drug deals they were involved in was actually a sting operation by the Panamanian police. Perhaps for no other reason than Bartolo's frightened mien, Dimas led him from the raid. The two scared hoodlums fled back to Dimas' village to hide for several months, later parting ways. Several years later, with proceeds from his first major assassination, the mayor of Atlantic City no less, he returned. He brought medicine, generators, gas, cooking oils, food, sleeping mats and endless supplies. Dimas' family welcomed and protected him, honoring him by building him a home. He found a people who adored him, albeit with purchased comforts, and hid him from the world. There were also hundreds and hundreds of fascinating birds.

It was here that Rizzato fled from a disturbing and crazy world.

Only his demented sexual cravings and the crimes he committed to feed his purse took him away. From the minute the cayuca, a local watercraft, took him down the river to join his band of henchmen, the evil that claimed his soul would drive him to more cruelty.

Here he is today with his latest journey downriver from his home bringing him to the Cayman Islands. As he bats his shaded eyes at the luxury around him, he yearns for the cadence of the jungle. He lops across the deck, his bony fingers pushed into the robe pockets, returning to his bedroom to change.

Thinking of the pending meeting, he figures this will be his last escapade. He'll kill all the witnesses whether Stratton wants him to or not. He thinks about the crazy old fucker's scheme and guesses he means to kill himself anyway.

*

Stratton has the drapes drawn in his room, which is painted the same blue as the water. The lights are low, his mood sour. He sits on the edge of his bed, a damp towel around his neck, wishing he could stop drinking, especially drinking alone. He had postponed the meeting with Rizzato and Mado, putting it off until today. Yesterday had been good, he and Mado had located a plane. It was perfect; it didn't run but it was a crop duster and unregistered. It just needed a little fixing-up according to its owner.

He had made arrangements to meet with the two men last night for drinks and dinner, but once back at his room to freshen up; his kid's rings had ruined the night. While reaching for a different shirt, he had knocked his sports coat from its hanger, landing on the floor. When he bent to pick it up, he lifted it uncovering the two rings, which must have rolled from the pocket. A goldsmith had recently polished them and they beamed from the deep maroon carpet. A stray beam of light reflected from the shiny metal. The sense of having failed his children, having failed to keep them close, to save them, overwhelmed him. That's when he hit the scotch. He quickly knew that he would be useless that night, so he made his excuses and having rearranged his agenda, he settled in for an inebriated loneliness.

He hadn't spoken to his wife or Sophia for such a long time. They didn't know where he was. He wondered at himself for ignoring his living relatives, other than leaving them money, in return for his utter devotion to seeking retribution for his dead offspring. He knew that his life would never be the same again. The bottle grew empty, his acrimony grew sharper. Anger, sorrow, self-righteousness, indignation and belligerence sat around and played games with him, wearing him out. The liquor helped. He had woken up this morning around nine; face down on the kitchen floor. When he tried to move, absolutely everything hurt.

Crawling into the shower, he ran it as cold as he could stand it, then hot. As he sits on the bed now waiting for room service and the coffee it will bring, he dry swallows several ibuprofens to soften up the droning in his head. The last memory he has of the previous night is exclaiming that someone has to fight back against these cowards. It is going to be him, and his wrath will be much greater than anything they can imagine.

He's mentally going over what he wants to accomplish today when the phone rings, its shrill tone piercing his sensitive skull. He grabs it and chucks it on the bed to stop the ringing, not wanting to talk to anyone just now but the thump on the bed hits the talk button. He finally pays attention to the calling of his alias. "Mr.

Favors, are you there?" a foreign voice drones from the phone.

He picks up the receiver from among the pale blue sheets.

"This is Favors," Stratton replies.

A grating voice, conceitedly continental, announces, "It is I, Sir Reginald Whitecastle, at your service, Mr. Favors. Our confrere, Amado, has made me aware you have... business demands, shall we say, in Bangladesh, thinking that I may be of some assistance. As you may be aware, I was the British High Commissioner to Bangladesh for an unprecedented eleven years, so assuredly, Mr. Favors, I know the people well. I daresay though, I know the *right* people much better. Now, what can I do to earn this splendid retainer Senor Mendoza has sent me?"

Stratton dislikes these nose-in-the-air types. He doesn't have to see the caller to know he has leather patches on the elbows of his sport coat, an ascot maybe, something burgundy and cream paisley. Yuk, he thinks. He skips the how-do-you-dos and says, "My business needs are, land, buildings, import licenses, etcetera. I will need things done quite quickly and I need the authorities to ignore my doings, if you know what I mean, Mr. Whitecastle. To do this I would like the name, or names, of a government official who would be interested in a richer lifestyle. Not pen pushers please but...Oh, just a moment."

A waiter knocked and enters, pushing a polished blue-steel and teak dolly, the coffee pot bringing soothing stimulants. Stratton waves a generous tip at the young man and curtly dismisses him. This particular waiter has served Jack Favors numerous times during the winter season and is by now indifferent to his callousness. As usual, he gives him the one-fingered salute when he turns his back, pockets his tip and leaves. Neither spoke.

Stratton smartly pours the coffee, hot, black and wickedly strong, just as he likes it. Several gulps and a refill bring him back to Whitecastle. "As I was saying Mr. Whitecastle, I would appreciate someone that can make things happen in Bangladesh, especially in Dhaka and area. I can certainly make it worth their efforts. I'm on a very strict timeline. Perhaps your extensive service to the Queen has uncovered such a character?" Stratton had the phone nestled between neck and shoulder as he hops around trying to get his boxers on.

"Firstly, Mr. Favors, it is *Sir* Whitecastle, not Mr. I anticipate that my dealings with the likes of such adventurous men as you and Amado, Jack, will eventually strip me of my knighthood, if my gambling doesn't first. So until then I will indulge in the pleasantries it brings and Sir Reginald will do fine." Whitecastle pauses for effect as he delves his mental files even though a name had come to mind early in Favor's request: Aatish Tarafdar, a representative within the Finance Ministry. He controls hundreds of millions of dollars annually. His subordinates rarely if ever question his directives. An unquenchable thirst for women, song and drink, everything un-Muslim, especially gambling, and keeping it all secret with a little "baksheesh" costs money, a lot of money. His door is usually open to Sir Reginald, but the man detests Americans. Whitecastle hopes that an American with money to burn – literally, Amado had assured him – will perhaps quell his distaste.

"I assume, Jack, that your business dealings, as we refer to them, would not shine too brightly in the halls of the local courts. As to what they may be, they are of no concern to me, but I must inform you that should your activities conflict with my contact's interests, you will be a very, very sorry man. He controls the investigators assigned to his department, which enforce tax laws. The investigators are loyal to their liege and rumors suggest they can be very damaging to people he does not like. He and I have gambled and drunk together frequently and I can inform you the man has very little conscience and absolutely no morals. So be very careful Jack."

Whitecastle hesitates to name Tarafdar just yet deeming there may be more capital to be had with this contract. He should secure his position as a necessary conduit, become more valuable. He shifts the phone to his other ear and says,

"I understand these disposable cell phones are quite safe, but nonetheless it would be most advantageous to talk to you in person as absolute discretion is required. An audience is not always easy to obtain, sometimes taking several weeks. Are you free to pick up and go as soon as I arrange a meeting in Dhaka? It will have to be you alone, of course, as he will not accept a proxy?"

Stratton thinks about being in Bangladesh and relishes the idea. He wants to hate these people, these Muslims, face to face. His psychotic reasoning is that each one of them is responsible for killing his children.

"I'm eager to begin my project and can go immediately but we cannot wait several weeks. Can you possibly try for this coming week? Today is Thursday and I know it's late in Bangladesh, but perhaps you could announce our intentions by early tomorrow. Our retainer was quite generous, and was based upon your reputation Sir Reginald; however, I am able to sweeten the deal if you prove to be expedient. Could I hear back from you tomorrow?" It isn't a courtesy question but more of a command.

Whitecastle bristles at the authority in Favors voice but softens imagining the increased earnings he will gather. It gives him a chance to get out of London while he obtains more cash to cover his latest losses. The people he owes have little patience.

"That will be impossible, but I assure you I will do my best, Jack. I will call back when I have something and not before. There will be no reason to unless I have an appointment. Is there anything else?"

"I'd like to know your contact's name."

"I'll reveal his name soon enough." And with that statement, Whitecastle hangs up.

**

Two hours later Andrew is adjusting his Mont Blanc cufflinks, genuine granite from the mountain, garnished with stainless steel. He is fastening them to a charcoal silk shirt open at the neck and hanging loose over navy slacks, the colors matching his mood, dark and demanding. Stratton has contrived and schemed for the last several months; he's anxious to begin the next phase of his plan. The ground work has been laid, his two key players firmly in place, at his beck and call. Today is merely mechanics.

Stratton is satisfied with the plant in Durham as well as his lodgings there and will set up shop there for the near future. His foul mood last evening reminds him of his last bender in Durham. He has to get off this wagon, he decides. Get straight should be his mantra, concentrate on his mission to avenge his children. He wants to get back to North Carolina. He personally wants to look after the gas, the containerization, and shipping it to Bangladesh. As these thoughts occupy him, he realizes that then and only then, when he will wheel the repaired crop duster laden with the horrific gas, dispersing it into the sky through the nozzles situated on the wings, laying curse to the Muslim horde, will satisfaction and rest finally come to him, Scott and Sarah.

His inward ramblings are interrupted by the door bell, the crazy Sicilian he guesses. He places his laptop on the dining room table and powers it up before going to open the door. The sun is high, so the entryway is dark. Opening the door, the lights from the outer hallway cast a shadow, skinny and fedora bearing. Bartolommeo's beaming face is both scary and comical. It's those fucking eyes thought Stratton, who doesn't know what to do, laugh or get his gun.

Not bothering to wait for an invitation, Bartolo whizzes right in, his head crowned by a straw hat too big for his frame. It makes his head seem even larger, giving him a cartoonish, bad guy bearing. As Rizzato hustles around, looking for the liquor, Stratton scans the man's wardrobe and actually cringes. Rizzato wears a canary yellow golf shirt tucked into lawn green knee-length cargo shorts, beige knee-high polyester socks anchored by brown leather sandals. He's toting his ever present orange-and-black haversack.

Having found the bar, Rizzato is pouring himself a drink while complaining what he thinks is poor service from the staff— making derogatory references about the locals, along with a few swear words. Stratton stops listening, wondering how a man so devious, so clever, could possibly dress so horrendously. He knows he has to ignore the man's clothing in order to take him seriously. He has to trust Mado on this one.

"Can I prepare a drink for you Jack?" offers Bartolo, dropping ice into his own drink of dark rum.

"No, thank you, Bartolo, I treated myself last night and I'm not quite ready to indulge just yet; maybe later. Did you get a chance to visit any of the islands since you've been here?"

Bartolo ignores the question, figuring his private business is his own. He opens the drapes and light lays claim to the room. "What's with the dark anyway, Jack? You missing those kids of yours, shutting everything out?" he says, not caring if he hurts the man's feelings. "Let's get into the light, Jack. We got payback coming for those Islums, or is it Muslams?" He laughs at his own joke, then draws a serious face.

"I'm not much for chit-chat Jack, and as I recall, you want me in Dhaka by the weekend. So today being Thursday, things are tight. I have two people getting there tomorrow; my other two men are..." Bartolo pauses, removes his hat, the freshly shaved head is pale, and drops onto one of the several sofas placed around the living room. Thinking of the fat little bitch who had made fun of him at the restaurant last night and what his goons would be doing to her right now, a satisfied smile accompanies his next words, "...detained but will accompany me tomorrow. I'll have everyone set up at the safe house you're providing. With the info you've shared with me so far, I'd say we need to *fretta, fretta*. We will need to proceed quickly."

Stratton takes a seat across from Bartolo, bringing his notes and computer, which he sets up on the glass coffee table between them. He opens his personal humidor, which is sitting to the side next to where he set his laptop and offers Rizzato a cigar. Both men go through the ritual, whiffing and snipping, tasting and igniting. No *fretta, fretta* for the moment. The calming scent of the Fuente Opus X cigars fills the room. One of the most famous brands in the world, the cigars are wrapped in Rosado leaves grown in a tropical river valley on the Chateau de la Fuente plantation in the Dominican Republic. Stratton maintains a fresh supply wherever he is.

Inspecting the even ash on the tip of his cigar, Rizzato says, "Great cigar, Favors. Good draw and burn. I prefer the flavor of a Paul Garmirian myself, but these are damn good."

"Mado should be joining us soon," says Andrew, "but I wanted to discuss a more touchy subject that there is no need to expose Mado to. When we set foot in Bangladesh, Bartolo, I need the entire operation to run smoothly. I cannot accept any form of failure." He reaches over to the glass ashtray, tapping the elongated ash from his cigar, and with courage he doesn't feel, looks in Rizzato's eyes. They aren't kind. He continues, "So, I need you to cover our tracks. No one engaged in my mission is to speak of their involvement. No one except you, your minions and Mado must know of my goal. Nothing can stop me." His voice grows harsher, more severe for a moment. "Do you understand what I mean Rizzato?"

Bartolo blows a smoke ring into the air, soft blue and wavering and replies, "Better than you do, Jack. Do you think I want my ass fried? Apart from my good looks and organizational skills, I know why you hired me, Jack. You point them out; I'll do the eliminating. I have guys working for me who enjoy that. So don't worry, Jack, I understand." Rizzato's expression never changes as he discusses the extermination of souls unaware. They could have been talking about the dinner plans for all his casualness.

"Good. You must assure me Bartolo that Mado must never be endangered. He controls the money for my requests, and yours as well. He will be the key to your early retirement package. You can hide forever if you want. The first week of December, eight months from now, you give me two or three days alone with my plane and a clear runway, and you can be away with your wallet stuffed. We'll part company to court fate along our own paths."

The two concentrate on their smokes until a steady knock on the door interrupts their interlude. It is 1:08 and Mado is a few minutes late. When Andrew opens the door, Mado enters, apologizing for his tardiness.

Almost calling him Andrew, Mado notices a small cloud of smoke hovering in the living room and assumes Rizzato must already be here, so says instead, "Jack, my youngest child, Estelle, was not feeling well this morning and I attended her until my wife returned from her errands, so please forgive me for being late."

"That's all right Mado; you must look after your children while you have them," Andrew replies, wishing he had practiced what he preached. "Bartolo and I have been chatting and I wasn't watching the clock. If you care to join us in the other room, I'll get you a drink. I know of your fondness for good wine, and the hotel has a wonderful selection of reds. Would you care for a glass?"

"That would be fine, Jack," he says, his words polished by his island accent. His long frame is clad in khaki shorts and a blaring blue short sleeved shirt. He grins and nods his thanks. His eyes betray his contentment. He carries a worn hard-body briefcase. After shaking Andrew's hand, he goes into the living room.

Andrew proceeds to the bar to decant a 1988 bottle of Medoc, Reserve de la Comtesse from Pauillac in France, a petite ville, surrounded by the finest grouping of vineyards in all Bordeaux. He busies himself gathering a plate of hors d'oeuvres he had ordered earlier, listening to the two men greet each other. From what he can hear, Mado is being most congenial, of course. Rizzato, for a change, is being respectful. Something he misses causes much laughter. Andrew blushes briefly, wrongly imagining they are laughing at him. A sliver of conspiracy flashes through his head. He knows they have worked together before, but no, he tells himself, he's in control; they will do his bidding.

Andrew places the snacks on a side cart and tows it to within easy reach of all three men before serving the drinks. Rizzato informs him that he "doesn't partake of the grape unless it is Italian, which as any wine connoisseur should know produces some of the world's most delightful varietals." Stratton refills Rizzato's dark rum, adding a twist of lime and joins the men around the low table. They are now perched around the coffee table prepared to work, gathering notes, writing material, pens and pencils when Andrew says,

"Now that we're all together, we have a massive to-do list and I'd like to get at it, gentlemen. I've explained what I want to accomplish before the first week of December, the third to be exact, to both of you. It's imperative that we meet or beat that date. And I will make you both very wealthy men."

Andrew reaches into a trouser pocket and brings out the two rings. He toys with them a moment and then softly places them in the center of the table. "This is all I have left of my children. Help me punish their killers and my fortune is yours."

He looks at both men, each of them tacitly acknowledging their intent with a brief nod; only one of them familiar with the madness in Stratton's eyes.

He hands each man several sheets of paper stapled together. It is a list of tasks to be accomplished by autumn. For Mado, there is also an inventory of expenditures and authorizations. For Bartolo, there are documents to sign, topographical maps of the outer environs of Dhaka and Google Earth images of the same area. He addresses Rizzato, "Please sign the paper-clipped documents, Bartolo. They will make you the VP of Research and Acquisitions for Reactor Chemicals. You will have signing authority in regards to purchases arranged by Mado or yourself as well as for any emergencies that may occur. This will be a valuable cover for our operation. You will be opening a new branch in Dhaka to make our pesticides where labor is cheap. We'll never get to that point, but it will give us some legitimacy. Will you do that before you leave today, Bartolo?"

"Yeah, sure! I'm going to be a big shot, huh?" Bartolo says. He speed-reads the document as Andrew turns his attention to Mado. Bartolommeo may not be much to look at, but his brain is admirable, totally aware and calculating.

Andrew says to Mado. "He's leaving tomorrow so I want these papers signed and things happening in Dhaka ASAP okay? Cut through the red tape. Is the cash set up and the accounts?" referring to Bartolo's means while in Dhaka and that of his men.

"Yes, Jack, I've arranged everything and will inform Bartolo later. We need to talk about the plane; the sellers will only hold our bid until midnight tomorrow. Is there nothing closer? I mean, the Ukraine is somewhat removed from Dhaka."

"So true, Mado, but this one hasn't been in service for several years; nor has it been out of its hanger. It's an Air Tractor AT401, an exceptional crop duster. I've actually flown a plane very similar to it— not this model, but I'm quite comfortable piloting this aircraft. The engine needs work, but the vendor has assured me it is fit to fly. And they've agreed to get it to the Ganges Delta unassembled by the end of May. It just feels right, this is the one I want. It will be up to Bartolo to get it to an as-yet-undetermined area where it can be re-assembled, serviced and tested before its swan song. So please proceed."

Turning to Rizzato, Stratton says, and "I will be meeting with our contact in Dhaka in the near future. Until then, I need you and your men to find land for us, firm ground for a runway, somewhere hidden but accessible to the river within the area I marked on the map. We have seven months to clear and prepare the land. We need a warehouse in the city, isolated in some Industrial park if possible. We'll need a boat and…. Mado will run down the requirements I've listed Bartolo. For now, work out of the safe house; watch your comings and goings. If it becomes useless, we have others available. Be sure to keep your men in line, Bartolo. Remember, no loose ends. Now about the maps… "

The men fall into animated conversation, not always agreeing. They plot and concoct for the rest of the day, stopping only after the sun has set. They part company laden with chores and deathly deals. Stratton sees both men off, crosses the living room and ventures onto his deck. He reaches the edge to place his elbows on the rail. The evening is quiet but for a muted tune creeping through the night. Something *lento* by Vivaldi, one of his Seasons, he thinks. It caresses his senses and he dreams of flying low over the crowd, Muslims running, fleeing from the confusion he will bring. He has visions of making high looping banks, returning to spray again, over and over until he covers the crowd, killing some now, more shortly after, and many, many more in the future. He thinks hard and long, wondering whether he too might be a coward. He's planning a daring theatrical escapade, one where he would look down upon his quarry from the safety of his cockpit. It's the only way he imagines he can kill as many as possible, and with that last thought he shakes off his doubt and goes to pack his overnight bag. He's leaving for Dhaka tomorrow. He is looking forward to meeting the bastards.

Chapter 10   Azimpur Road, Dhaka

Yasmin Alam is the only occupant in Rafan's apartment building at this moment. Having called the police when she heard the gunshot, she cannot ignore the noise from the hallway while waiting for them to arrive. It's probably young men with too much time and not enough chores, likely high on *khat* she thinks. She goes to the door of her apartment and is just going to take a peek. She'd been in trouble before for being so nosy; this time trouble comes with a gun.

From the open door she slowly sticks out her cute, moppish head, just as Morgan's deadly barrage erupts from the stairway. His first bullet, wild and un-aimed, hits a cheap print, knocking it from the wall; the second chips the wood from the casing on her door just above her head. Splinter's spray her pretty face forcing her back inside where she runs to hide in her bedroom closet. She doesn't come out until the police arrive many minutes later.

Having fired off three or four rounds, Morgan clears the second floor landing, bounds down the stairs and bolts through the front door, losing himself in the crowd. He never looks back, certain Malik is close behind and will join him at the tuk-tuk he paid to be waiting. Unknown to Morgan, about the time he made it to the street, Malik Hajani is lying on the landing between the first and second floor, barely conscious and seriously wounded.

When Morgan reached the stairs to the first floor, Malik was about three seconds behind him. Enough time for Dakin to move from the safety of the doorway to try and acquire a target. Hajani is in the middle of the landing, scudding backwards firing his Glock at the upper level. With a spin he turns to follow his partner down the stairs; as he does, he detects movement down the hall and remembers *"whitey,"* who he'd thought was out of commission. He is bringing his weapon to bear upon the threat when that threat brings him down with a lucky shot. The bullet from the S&W .45 enters his ankle as Hajani is spinning, blasting the talus into dozens of bony fragments. One of those fragments severs the posterior tibial artery; others tear through skin and nerves. The brilliant pain lasts for only a short time. The wound ruins his equilibrium and he literally flies to the bottom of the stairs, hitting face first, then landing on his neck when something snaps. Still conscious, all he can feel are the abrasions on his face and what seems like a broken nose. He can hear excited voices up the stairs. He tries to get up and run, but his pooled flesh doesn't respond. Nothing below his neck works. He has absolutely no feeling. Malik Hajani has just received a life sentence to be served inside his own useless body. He lays there uncomprehending; blood spurting from his demolished ankle and dribbling from his nose. His last thought before he loses consciousness is that the *furrier* he spoke to Morgan about only minutes before has only taken part of his pelt. He wishes he'd taken it all.

When Hajani dives down the stairs, Dakin yells, "I hit him Drake. He's down, but I'm not sure if he's out. Hold tight until I take a look-see".

He trots down the hallway to the stairway kicking the busted frame aside. It skids across the floor out by the stairs. The disturbance doesn't bring any response so he slowly peers out around the corner. He sees the dark-skinned man crumpled on the floor at the foot of the stairs. Dakin can see the bleeding ankle. He calls to Drake, "One man is down. He's still bleeding, so I don't think he's dead. I'm gonna check him out."

As Dakin approaches the fallen man, he is aware of what might be a ruse so keeps his pistol ready in his good hand, the other held tightly to his stomach in its impromptu sheath. He's giving the man a kick on the foot when Drake and Rae reach the top of the steps, guns drawn, covering Dakin. If that body moves, it will not do so again.

Getting no response, Dakin was about to turn the body over when Rae cautions him, "Don't move him. Where he has fallen, he may have head trauma or a neck injury."

She tucks her gun back in her holster and races to the bottom of the stairs, pulling a yellow bandana from one of the side pockets on her pants. Ingrained confidence and years of command lead her to seize control of the situation. Sirens murmur, a ways off yet.

"We have to stem the bleeding from his ankle, check if his airway is good."

Seeing Rafan creeping down the upper stairs she calls out to him, "Rafan, come quickly, I need you to help here. Hurry! Dakin, trade me guns. Drake, you and Dakin get going. I'll say I took the shot."

She detects a shallow breath, a weak pulse and leaves the fallen man prone. She is applying the unfolded bandana to the ankle wound, putting pressure on it. Thank goodness he's out, she thinks, this would be very painful.

Drake is about to protest when she interrupts him, "I know most of the major players with the local police, I can handle this, and Rafan will back me up. He hired me to protect him after seeing his room trashed. They cornered us and I came out shooting; it was us or them. The other guy is gone in the crowd, but he might be waiting for this fellow. Dakin saw him, so go now; the police are getting closer. Here, Rafan, hold this bandage here." She shows him where to place his hand, then removes her sidearm, passing it to Dakin as she takes his proffered gun.

"Are you sure you want to do this, Rae? I mean, we are a team you know. It's self-defense." Dakin said, admiring her decisive thinking. He loves a dominant woman.

As she is securing a crude bandage to the criminal's nose, trying not to move him, she says to Dakin, "I do this for a living. My husband was a former police inspector who worked with many of these people. I can handle this much quicker alone. You're strangers here. Without the proper introductions this could tie you up for several days. You just arrived in country today; they won't bring out the welcome wagon."

Drake stands pensive, thinking her rationale makes sense. She chucks him the keys and with an insistent demand, says, "Go now! Take the truck and please… be careful. I'll call you on one of your cells as soon as I can. Now get out of here!"

She turns her back to the two men and calls for an ambulance on her own phone.

Rafan is nodding to Drake, agreeing with Rae. He says, "We'll talk when this is over Drake. I have much to tell you. And thank you so much to all of you for finding me." He humbly turns to his charge, holding the bandage to the foot.

Drake says, "Okay, Rae. I appreciate what you're doing. You two take it from here. ID this guy if you can. I want to see the two of you ASAP, okay; we'll be at the Westin." He turns to give Dakin the keys and adds, "Take Rae's gear. Run down and get the truck started. I'll be right along."

He pats Rafan on the shoulder saying, "It'll be good to talk, Rafan. Until we meet later. Refresh your memory of the night at the bar okay, especially what you heard of Rizzato. This may be one of his henchmen. Good work, gang."

He nods to Rae and rushes down the stairs.

Dakin has the pickup in front of the building, revved up, door open. A crowd is forming. When Drake has one foot in the door the big tires bite into the street and throws him back into the seat, the door slamming shut just as his other foot clears the opening. Dakin maneuvers into the crowd scattering the pedestrians. He doesn't have a clue where he's going, just away from the flashing lights behind him. He knows that some bystander will remember the truck to the police but they'll be invisible soon, at least he hopes so.

Drake says, "I suspect the man that was accompanying our downed attacker is mixed in with the locals by now. It would be very difficult to find him. Just follow the traffic until I get my bearings. We can keep busy until we hook up with Rae and Rafan tonight. I want to think about our next step. I have a gut feeling our assailant back there is part of Rizzato's crew. We might be closer to finding them than I had hoped." He's looking around inside the truck. "She must have a map in here."

Drake goes through the glove compartment and center console, finally locating several maps of Dhaka in the back door side pocket. He knows the Westin is on Gulshan Avenue in the Gulshan District. Once he has figured out where they are using the map, he directs Dakin to their destination. Once they arrive, Drake registers getting a suite, while Dakin goes off to collect his personal gear. Drake wants to change and have something to eat before they resume the chase.

*

Rae is fortunate that Inspector Bitan Chowdhury from Detective Branch South was next on the board and the only one available when the call came in of a shooting near New Market. Chowdhury and Taj, her husband, were both Sgts when they started with the Detective Branch and Criminal Intelligence. Their paths had crossed many times during their careers and they've remained friendly even after Taj left the force, on excellent terms, to begin his own investigation agency. Rae hasn't seen Bitan in a little over a year, not since Taj's funeral.

Chowdhury is a hardened but affable man, respected by his peers, envied by others. He has a weak spot for Taj's wife and accepts that what went down was as Mireille said it had, she has a witness even. He's thinking of the funny drawer in the bedroom as he went through the apartment after his team had finished up, the owner's adamant refusal to re-enter his bedroom is not so odd after the ordeal he went through.

He ran through the paper work; self-defense – they both told the same story. He sent out an APB with a description of the other culprit. It's just after 7 o'clock in the evening as he sits at his desk, which like his office is neat and functional, facing Rae, who stares back at him. She says, "Are we finished here now, Inspector?"

Chowdhury says, "Yes, Rae but I suspect there is more to your tale than you've revealed. In Taj's memory, I will accept this for now, but when we find out what this...", he stops for a moment to pick up a one paged report from his desk and reads, "Malik Hajani, very dangerous, wanted in Pakistan as well as India, is about, we will want to speak to you again."

He tosses the paper back on the desk, having read it more for her sake than anything he needs to remember. Taj had thrown many bad guys his way. He figures his wife can do the same. If she's on to something, this man's identity will help. He stands up, his lanky frame commanding. Rae rises to greet his serious expression. When he reaches to shake her hand, he whispers, "Keep me informed if you can. Taj would."

Rae grips his hand, not having any words that won't cause her to cry, missing her husband at this very moment so very much. She languishes at times, still. The fourteen months since Taj's death by a crazed adulterer has passed slowly. They could only assume from evidence that Taj had been subdued by the individual he was waiting for at his client's residence. The gentleman who had hired him had strongly suspected that his wife was having a liaison with his banker. She was home that afternoon and the servants had been dismissed. The banker did indeed show up. He discovered Taj prowling the premises, overpowered him, dragged him into the house and, using the owner's gun, killed Taj, his lover and himself in a murder-suicide. Taj was an innocent victim in the man's maniacal rampage.

Six months after her husband's death, Rae had returned to the only work she knew, the longing for her dead husband is controllable now. She had realized that she needed to keep living, keep working; being emotional over her missing husband would still be as frequent but less painful, eventually changing to peaceful memories. She was a night hawk at first, working evenings and nights, exhaustion rescuing her from days filled with memories of working with Taj at her side. Life became more tolerable with each day that passed.

She ignores her brief sorrow and knowing Chowdhury could perhaps be of some assistance in their search for Rizzato says, "Thank you, Bitan. I might nose around. I'll see what my client wants. I'll stay in touch."

She finds Rafan in the drab waiting room facing the front desk of the Detective Bureau South building. Seeing Rae, he hobbles to her side carrying a leather tan overnight bag that he had stuffed some personal items into before they had been escorted to the police station. He had to forget his computer he had originally went to retrieve, it'd been wrecked. Walking stooped over, his back still tormenting him, he greets Rae with uneasiness. Gripping her arm, he stays close as they exit the building. With Rafan close behind her, Rae scans the area from the shadows of the portico, looking for the unusual. Satisfied they are clear for now, she gives him a reassuring pat, urging him along.

"We're okay now, Rafan. Our stories meshed and your bouts of insomnia helped. That was good thinking or did you really have some lapses?"

Rafan replies, "I'm so scared Rae. I want to forget a lot of things, especially the dead bodies that seem to pile up around me. I cringe at every shadow. I always want to keep my back to the wall now. I want my normal life back, Rae. What am I going to do?"

"We'll get you a safe spot, Rafan, don't worry. You fill Drake in on what you know. After that I know a good place you can rest at while we run these people down. Men like Drake and Dakin, they're not quitters. Your uncle is extremely anxious to bring his daughter's killers to justice as well as keep you safe."

He remains glued to Rae as they jump into the waiting taxi that Chowdhury has summoned for them, as if close contact will keep him safe. He wants to trust Rae. Their taxi is a yellow one that by law has to have air conditioning; the black taxis do not. The dark taxies are often treated with exiguous care, if not totally neglected. Neither are they keen on tourists. Rae gives the driver the address for the Westin on Gulshan Avenue. She surprises the driver by speaking to him in Bengali, berating him for quoting such an outrageous amount for the ride. By the time they are on the Outer Circle Road, they have reached an agreement on the price that neither one is really happy with.

Rae sits back in the seat and says, "We'll meet with Drake. I called him earlier. He and Dakin had settled in but were following up a new lead and said he'd meet up with us at the hotel when he returns. Our names have been left at the front desk, and there'll be keys waiting for us. We both need to freshen up and I'm hungry. How about you?"

Rafan relaxes slightly at Rae's assurance and stares at the passing vista, his mind going back to the night he had met Raheem at the Pink Lady. The bar didn't have any signs, no flashing neon. Its facade was plain and grey like most of the adjoining buildings. The street had been quieter than normal. The only peculiarity to the building was a glossy forest green door that retained a brass plaque the size of a post card at eye level that read, "The Pink Lady." Then in smaller italic script, repeated in several languages, was written "Ring for service."

The area was avoided by most inhabitants of the city. The owners who profited from the overly inflated rents did not do any advertising. *Rent* included protection from the curious and the law. Several blocks were owned by corrupt government officials, with brothels, gambling dens, drug pits and bars scattered among its otherwise boring normalcy. The Pink Lady was one of them. As the name might suggest, it was a bar for gay men, very private for the Koran condemned homosexuality and sodomy. A gay Muslim had to be extremely careful. The Pink Lady's distinction was that *rough trade* gathered there. Rafan's went looking for a thuggish sex partner; a dominant masculine presence. That night he found such a man, Raheem Ahmedani. Rafan remembered the man's muscled body and tattooed neck. The conversation was probing and flirting until Raheem mentioned Rizzato, liquor loosening his tongue. He told Rafan of his boss, who he thought was unhinged. He suggested the man was a lunatic, always angry. Rafan knew who Rizzato was and had been shocked when he heard the name. Rafan tried to lure Raheem home, buying him drinks, stroking his ego, trying to get him to talk. As they wove their way toward Rafan's parked car, he was thinking he couldn't wait to tell his uncle

Now, as he skulks in the back seat of the taxi, he dreads the moment Uday will discover his predilection. He never meant to let his uncle down. The remainder of the ride is quiet, the day's events onerous.

*

After having his hand properly bandaged, Dakin left by taxi to retrieve his things. Drake is on the phone with Williston. He has explained the events at Rafan's apartment, and that Rafan and Rae were likely being questioned by the police. He also tells Williston how confidant he is with Uday's choice of translator.

"She speaks the local lingo fluently, knows the local police, I'd like to hear her story some time." There was clear appreciation in his voice.

Williston said, "Uday has used her services in the past when she was working with her husband, Taj Al-Khuri, who is now deceased. He thinks she's top notch. I ran background on her. She met Al-Khuri at a forensics conference in Brussels. Sounds like it was love at first sight. She was single; he was married with two kids. They developed a relationship, he abandoned his family. He and Mireille quit their respective careers. She moves from France to be with him in Dhaka, and they created their own agency, investigating whatever was offered to them. He served twelve years with the Metro Police there in Dhaka ending his job as an Inspector at Detective Bureau Headquarters. She too was a police officer, as you probably know, lots of commendations in her files. Both of them advanced young, good at what they do. I can imagine that's why their business did well. No surprise. He supported his kids, left them comfy with some of his life insurance."

Drake had seated himself at the writing desk in the corner of the living room as he listens to Williston. He searches the drawers for writing paraphernalia. Finding a pad of writing paper with the hotel logo and pencils in the right upper drawer he flips it onto the table and writes Taj Al-Khuri as item No. 1. No. 2 Who is the injured man at Rafan's apartment?

"Yeah, it almost sounds dull. She is in no way a dull person, Williston. She's very decisive and engaging. She'll be a big help".

He changed the subject by saying, "I've called in the rest of my troops. The Glass twins will be joining us in a couple of days. I think the man Dakin immobilized is linked to Rizzato, Williston. I can feel it. I suspect they are the people who left the body in Rafan's car. Now they're after him. I don't understand all the connections yet, but we'll see what we can piece together. I'll know more when I speak to Rae and Rafan. Dakin and I are going to track down a couple of leads. Is there anything else, Williston?"

Drake wrote down No. 3, bodies.

"Uday, of course, has many contacts within Dhaka. Right now we're concentrating on them to see whether they are hearing anything out of the ordinary. As we agreed, Drake, we need to talk often. I need updated info frequently so I can help on this end. I'll keep you alert to anything I think can be useful. Until then, stay tight, my friend. I know I don't have to tell you but I will anyway, don't be heroes!"

"Don't fret brother. I'm as cool and calm as a brook."

They both laugh at the old joke from when they were boys during the first summer Williston spent in New Brunswick after Drake had rescued him from his school yard aggressors. They had been sitting on a fallen log, a brook babbling beneath them, their fishing lines floating in the water, when Drake said that the brook was cool and calm. Williston with heroic adoration in his eyes said, "Just like you Drake!" Drake had blushed at the praise, disguising his pride with hilarity. He had laughed so much at the quip that he'd lost his balance and fallen in. Williston had erupted with mirth at Drake's sodden regalement until he too had lost his balance. His amusement had ended with a belly flop into the waist-deep water, his arms tangled in the fishing lines. The two lads gamboled the afternoon away, wet and frivolous. Since then the simile of cool and calm would remind them of carefree summer days.

"Oh, by the way, Drake, I heard from Beth yesterday. She worries about you. I tried to reassure her that you had your guys with you, with the addition of a very able assistant. Beth wasn't excited that it was a 'she.' I gave her a rundown of what we've been doing so far. She says she wants to join me here, see if she can help."

Williston knew Drake didn't want Beth involved in their capers. Drake had told him how she had promised him she would focus on her singing and the farm until he returned. He had asked Williston to back him up, convince her to stay put if she contacted him.

Drake asked, "What did you say?"

Williston said with a bit of trepidation, "Well... what could I say Drake? I reminded her of her commitments and how you felt. She insists she can't concentrate on anything while you may be in danger. Look, Drake, you know how much she loves you. She'll be better off here where I can keep her busy, keep an eye on her, you know?"

Williston shifts in his seat, uncomfortable awaiting Drake's infrequent temper, totally surprised when Drake replies, "Mmmm, that's a good idea. Yeah. Keep her on the ship, that's great. And please, Williston, no matter how hot things may get as we chase Rizzato, you keep her there. It's because I care so much that I don't want her endangered. I trust you, buddy. When is she getting there?"

Drake remembers their lovemaking just before he left and his manhood stirs. Flashes of Beth's naked form, her erotic depths, accelerate his pulse. He pushes the images aside as he hears

Williston saying, "... tomorrow. I gotta run Drake, Uday's on the other line. We'll be in touch."

Drake had been about to twist Williston's arm a little more to ensure he kept Beth with him, but is cut short when Williston disconnects.

Williston had never acquired a taste for physical struggle nor did he have the urge to place himself in danger, so he probed the world for intelligence from the comfort of his den, well removed from the battle ground. He is analytical and curious, good traits for an info gatherer. Past experience has shown Drake that Williston's fount runs deep.

*

Drake finishes his shower and while dressing, he hears Dakin's arrival, his vibrant hellos hard to miss. Pulling a black T-shirt over his chest he tucks it into black pants much like Rae's. Pockets, some visible, some not, are filled with instruments of his craft. As he pulls a pair of Merrill hiking boots from his bag, the scent of the food Dakin brought with him beckons to his rumbling stomach. Drake carries the boots to the living room and tosses them by the couch. Dakin's at the dining table adding sauerkraut to his bun.

"This is a spicy little chicken thing the locals make up; they were on the menu." As he munches he speaks with a full mouth, "What's up now, boss?"

Drake is already gnawing away as he walks back to the living room and retrieves a section of an English-language newspaper. The local news section features an article on two bodies found in a trench in the Tongi Industrial Park and the coincidence of another body found in a dumpster on Mirpur Road. Evidence suggests the murders are linked: the same mark was found on each body but police are withholding details of what that mark was. Inspector Abhijit Hasan is the investigating officer and was not available for comment. Circled below the article with a yellow hi-liter was the name of the reporter, Samuel Rhodes

"These are the guys you were telling me about, right?" Dakin asks after scanning the article and finishing his meal. Pushing his plate aside, he adds, "and what's the deal with this Rhodes guy?"

"As far as the bodies, it definitely sounds like them. The details Williston gave me were brief and there were no autopsies yet. The fact is that the authorities are suggesting a mark but keeping it from the public so that it will only be known to the perpetrators. The problem here is that we know about a mark. We can't compromise Williston's sources by exposing our knowledge of it just yet."

Drake finishes eating before tying up his boots, stands up and places his pistol in the top thigh pocket. The pocket is a reinforced pouch where his 1911 fits nicely, padded so it won't chafe his leg. A Velcro flap keeps it secure.
"As to the name, I know him. It's a little after 4 o'clock, so he's probably still at work. Let's go see him."

Getting up from his chair, Dakin shakes his head, thinking they are 10,000 miles from home and Drake knows the guy. Why is he surprised? Dude had been all over the world.

"Okay, let's do it. I tucked Rae's truck in the parking garage below and rented another vehicle. I just signed it to the room. It's in the outdoor parking lot."

The two men are taller than the locals, and although quite tanned, are definitely Caucasian. As such, they are conspicuous. At the hotel, where foreigners abound, they blend in just fine. But in the city, they will have to keep their heads down. They don't know who their enemies are yet. They hasten to their vehicle, a white Toyota Land Cruiser.

Drake says, "I called our pals, Isaac and Elijah; they'll be here tomorrow or the next day. That should round out our team and give us plenty of backup. Elijah can probably blend in here, the rascal is so dark." They both chuckle at their friend's disdain for winter white; being a sun worshipper, he stays tanned all year long. "He'll probably like it here. The heat's crazy."

Dakin says, "Damn, it's going to be great to see the guys. We haven't all been together since our last chase of this slime ball almost a year ago. I really appreciate you getting everyone together like this, Drake. I mean, shit, we all like the chase, the danger. So, how do you know this Sammy guy?"

The Toyota creeps along, the traffic piling up, the noise tremendous, cars, people, horns and whistles fills the air. The sturdiness of the air-conditioned cabin give them some relief from the sounds.

"Interestingly enough, he's a Canadian. I went to sailing school with him when I was about sixteen or so. He's from Toronto. His father owns a couple of dailies in Ontario, but his mother was from Shediac and they maintained her childhood home as a summer refuge. It was an old place when the mother passed away but sitting right on the water with ten acres attached to it. I remember when the government built the wharf nearby, the property quadrupled in value the moment they dumped the first load of fill. Anyway, we sailed together several times and have remained friends. He's a decent guy."

Drake shifts in the seat as Dakin is pulling in and out of traffic forgetting occasionally that the roads are British rules, driving on opposite lanes to what he's familiar with in America, making him a bit nervous. He continues, "I haven't seen him since we left for Iraq back in '90. When we landed in Riyadh, he was covering the build-up of there, and I still to this day don't know how he found me, but he looked me up. He was with the Canadian contingent so his pass helped him to get around. His main problem has always been women, other men's woman. It's like an obsession with him. He used to joke that his job kept him away from all the jealous husbands he collected. I expect that he, like Rae, followed someone here and decided to stay. I helped him once, so he owes me. I'm hoping he'll have more knowledge of the situation than what he wrote in his article."

"What makes you think Rizzato is around here Drake, is there something more than the mention of his name to Rafan"

Drake had read from the newspaper's masthead and gave him the address in the West Nakhalpar area. A drive that normally might have taken twenty minutes became a stop and go for over an hour because of the heavy traffic. It gives them time for Drake to share what his instincts are telling him with Dakin whose insights are to be respected.

"When I spoke to Williston last Saturday, we have Rizzato's name coinciding with a dead and tortured body and a mark cut into the skin. We've followed leads on Rizzato with less. When we found Amber and Sakeema, they had similar marks on them. All this time later, he resurfaces, or I should say the mark resurfaces.

Since the girls were killed in Venezuela, the mark has never shown up in any major killing or sexual crime since. Williston has a fabulous network with dozens of workers inside the law. Now, he digs up details on these three killings here in Dhaka. But the mark has shown up again. Now Dakin, I'm wondering why this man would leave an obvious sign. What is he up to? Is it a coincidence? Is he bragging? I'm not sure."

Drake winces and jerks toward the door as Dakin veers to miss a rickshaw that comes from a side street, pulling right in front of them, missing them by the width of the black scarf the occupant drops in fright. It catches upon the back bumper, fluttering like a trapped raven. The turbulence from a passing vehicle releases it from its restraint and it swirls away into the sky. It slips along the currents until a deft and callused hand snaps it from the air.

Drake was watching the black silk's journey when, directly behind the callused hand, he spots a beige Isuzu Sportivo several cars back. It wasn't the car that caught his eye, but the man in the passenger seat. From the description Dakin has given him, it could be the man from Rafan's. Then a jolt of recognition hit him: he has seen this man before.

Dakin was suggesting, "Maybe it's not…" when Drake interrupts him.

"Check out the passenger in the beige car twenty feet behind us, is that the man you saw?"

Dakin checks his mirror and say, "I can't really tell. I don't recognize the driver and I can't see the passenger. Does he have a big flat nose; dark but doesn't look Bangladeshi, lots of hair?"

"It could be. He's wearing a light brown or beige shirt, short sleeves. He seems to be staring at us and me. I first noticed the car about a half hour back when we were stuck at that major intersection but I didn't pay attention to it.

"Should I lose them?" Even in this nonsensical traffic, Dakin could be like a whippet unleashed if Drake gave him a nod, but instead Drake replies, "No, let him follow us. I've got an idea."

He pulled out the 1911, checks the clip, and replaces it in the outer pocket.

"There's an office compound just ahead and it should be the first driveway on the right. There seems to be a parking lot behind the building. Pull in there; if they follow try to corner them or ram them in the lot."

As they drive toward their stand, Chris and Drake give each other a knowing look. What their eyes say cannot be done with words. Only another paladin would know.

Chapter 11

Sept 29 2:45pm   North of Virgin Gorda Island

The *Drifter's Dream* is a Lurssen, just over 134 feet of sleek, virile yacht. Built in 1995, its owners – there have been only two – have kept it in pristine shape. It is luxuriously commodious, outfitted for eight guests with a crew of five. At fifteen million dollars, with a three hundred thousand renovations and retrofit, it is a spectacular craft. She often proves herself worthy in rough seas; well commanded, she responds like an alloyed shark. Darkened glass encircles the ship, defining the different levels. The aluminum hull is enameled so white it is chatoyant. Seen from afar, it gleams a single ray of light.

 Beth views the ship from the cockpit of an Alouette III helicopter; she and the pilot are coming at the *Drifter* with the sun at their back. A satisfied smile adorns her pretty face. Through the Plexiglas bubble, she surveys the ship, slipping through the waters all alone and its beam of light dazzling her. She's anxious to join Williston to be in touch with Drake. She shivers as she thinks of him remembering his undressing her before he left, their lovemaking, the arching of her back when she erupted with unending pleasure and how it never seemed to end.

She returns her concentration to the task at hand. She has convinced Williston that she can get to his ship on her own turning down his offer to make port at her nearest request. Beth doesn't want to take Williston's attention away from the current events that occupy their small world. She yearns for adventure, to take advantage of her skills, to test her will and her stamina. This was her father's doing: no sons. Beth was the youngest of a litter of girls and together they had often gone wilderness camping, where she'd learned survival skills and to how hunt using a gun and knife. When time allowed, and her father worked hard to ensure it did, they slipped on their packs with only the barest of essentials, no food. They roughed out the nights, sleeping bags only. They ate what they found, berries, greens, bugs and roots, or an animal they captured, roasted over blazing coals. Two days later they would watch the sunrise, pull out topographical maps, compasses and become oriented with their location. Zigzagging about 20 miles from where they entered the woods, two very fit people can cover a lot of territory, seriously getting themselves lost. They climbed the highest trees, found landmarks like towers, sharp rises or drops, lakes and rock formations until they had a bearing they were confident would return them to their car. Beth and her father didn't always find the exact spot they left their vehicle but always found the road it was on and a short walk would bring them back to the car.

All in all, Beth can handle herself adroitly and is an able companion. Her skills have been reinforced by Drake's experience and passion for the unknown, for what might lie around corners they had yet to turn. Beth challenged her days, to experience something normally mundane in a different way, do something new, like write a song or, if the opportunity arose, jump from a helicopter into a gulping sea.

Williston is leaning on the railing on the foredeck on the main level listening to the helicopter approach from the southwest. He soon sees it as it circles his ship. The sun makes his mane much paler while it gave his skin a fresher tone. Having spent much of his working years indoors, suited and cocooned, kept his skin lighter; the sea changed that. He loves his boat and the forever waters. He often reflects on his decision to pass the mantle to his loyal managers to free himself to hunt for Rizzato. And even now as he watches Beth step out on the foothold of the helicopter's open cargo door, he thinks that no matter the outcome of their efforts, he is never going back to the office. He's been thinking more and more of what would come after they catch Rizzato, there are other foul people wanted by the law. He likes the idea of spending his money to hunt them down. Before he turns his full attention to Beth's descent, he makes a mental note to talk to his companions about that when this is over.

Standing by the cargo door, her back to the beaten air, Beth checks her harness, the locking carabineer holding her in, the rope running through the pulley and its position. Satisfied that all is as it should be, she steps away from the hovering vessel. She is in lust over helicopters. Drake's friend and fellow soldier, Elijah, had taken her for her first helicopter ride, or as she called it her first helicopter rollercoaster ride. She had never imagined a 'copter could be in so many odd positions and still fly. The flight had scared her, but she fell in love with the aerodynamics and pilot skills that kept her hovering over gasping waterfalls before plunging towards the earth like a mechanical dew drop before coming low to the treetops below them. Other times they had lurked between canyon walls, been dropped upon mountain tops in the whitest powder and visited the remotest areas only accessible by helicopter. With all her adventures she had never rappelled from the sky like she is doing now. She had been trained by Drake and had rappelled on dry land with him and his buddies but never from a helicopter and never into water, so Beth being Beth, she decided to rappel into the water by Williston's boat.

She is about twenty feet over the water that is being disturbed by the downdraft. The *Drifter* is about a nautical mile away and slowing as it approaches the swinging girl. The old guy that owns the helicopter holds it steady with an experienced hand. Beth had dropped her waterproof bag prior to leaving the aircraft and she spins slightly over it. She signals to the pilot to advance a short way. When she is clear of the bag and in the apogee of her swing, she releases herself from her harness, plummeting to the sea. She hits the water like a human nail and goes deep. Her black neoprene wetsuit offers some buoyancy as she strokes the warm water with downward thrusts, propelling herself to the surface. As she clears the bubbly depths, the *Drifter* approaches cautiously. Crewmen snatch her floating bag with grappling hooks after having loosened a stout rope ladder over the side. Berkeley is at the helm and keeps the ship still as Beth swims to the rope. Grabbing the bottom rung she waves to the grey-haired pilot who has been watching her descent. He returns the wave and turns the helicopter in a graceful bow before departing the scene.

By the time Beth has climbed to the lowest deck aft, Williston and Isabella are near the gunwales, waiting to welcome her aboard. She jumps to the deck, removes her mask greeting her two friends with delight, saying, "How's that for an entrance?"

Although Williston reveres his long-time friend, he refrains from hugging his wet guest, but Isabella, her slender frame clad in a tangerine one piece bathing suit, rushes to Beth's side and, bussing both cheeks, says, "You're much braver than I am, Beth. I envy you terribly for your sense of adventure. We're so glad you decided to join us no matter how you choose to arrive. Which I must add is likely the most unique I've witnessed and I guess what I admire about you so much is that we never know what to expect."

As he passes her a towel Williston adds, "I agree with Isabella. Your approach is a bit unorthodox but it's such a pleasure to see you again. We've prepared a cabin for you, and I expect you might like to get out of that wet suit." He grins as he nods to the crew that had assisted her ingress as they ogle Beth, her neoprene suit fitting her like the peel on an apple. "It may get their attention back to their usual duties."

Beth has always been at ease with her body and coyly enjoys the effect she has on men. She says, "Actually, I can get rid of it right now." She slides the oversized zipper down her front, exposing a white and blue floral bikini. Peeling the rubber getup from her supple shape she gestures to a younger man, asking him, "Would you mind putting this somewhere to dry?" The novice deckhand beams at being singled out by this beauteous arrival and nervously approaches her to take the suit away. "Certainly, senorita," he stutters. He blushes as his hand comes into contact with Beth's and like a teenager full of hormones, he watches as she towels the moisture from her hair and he falls instantly in love.

After directing one of the crewmen to wipe down her bag and take it to her room, Isabella takes Beth by the arm to lead her to the foredeck where refreshments and finger food have been laid out. "Are you hungry" she asks, "or would you prefer just a drink?" They stroll along the passageway, giggling and chatting like the friends they are who haven't seen each other for several months.

Williston watches them as they walk away, basking in the feelings these two woman leave him in. He often ponders on the fact that next to his mother and the memory of Amber, they are *the* most important ladies in his life. There are other women he holds in high esteem and respect, but Isabella and Beth nurture him and form him, each with a different type of love – one a wife, the other a sister-like presence. He's thinking of how different they are, Isabella at least three inches taller, long curly flaxen locks jaunty about her shoulders while Beth's pageboy says business first. Isabella's figure is slim while Beth is more curvaceous. Both are gorgeous women. He smiles as he thinks about his decision to formally retire and chase bad guys, maybe he could spend more time with them in the future.

Williston ventures to the top deck to speak with Captain Bill, directing him to make way to San Juan to refuel and pick up fresh food. That will be at sea for an unknown amount of time for the present. Williston's mind blurs trying to imagine what could occur by then. He had worked that morning tracking down Hajani and his cousin Ahmedani, gathering what data he could. He has been able to identify the man Hajani was with.

All Williston's resources are not necessarily virtuous, many are thoroughly nefarious. He's been introduced to individuals whose computers are their encyclopedia of the world's information but one whose pages aren't in order. Hackers can find scads of information. Williston thinks of it as a wonderful talent and uses a young man that goes by "Rassor". The computer whiz has run down the request he'd made, serving it with a little gravy. Another trace had just been uncovered. Williston is anxious to share it with Beth and Isabella before Drake calls. The time difference of nine hours makes it almost midnight in Dhaka so it is likely that he will call anytime. After Rae had identified Hajani, Williston went to work. During their conversation that morning, Drake had said he would call again when he could.

As Williston is going down to the main deck, he sidesteps into the bedroom that has been made ready for Beth, checking her bag and the room in general. It smells like Lysol still, the staff has scrubbed it until it shined. As he views the room his eyes are arrested by a portrait that stands out among the many that adorn the far wall. The figure under the glass still troubles him. It's a side shot, from her right, which Amber always thought of as her "best side." Her dimples define her character, frolicsome and impetuous. Auburn hair with wisps of platinum graces her oval face. The one bright greenish eye you can see expresses delight, her smile agreeing. The graduation picture offered promise to her future and thankfulness for her accomplishments. Williston's eyes water as he regards his sister's poise. He misses her terrifically.

He takes the photo from the wall, meaning to hang it in his office. The 8 x 10 is which is framed in burnished wood, fits snugly under his arm. His feeling of sadness is replaced with stern determination to find the man who took her away. He figures they have some good leads. Hugging the photo to him, he leaves the room going to join the women on the patio off the main deck. He descends the outer stairway that leads to the patio from the second level. The smaller deck on the upper level juts out over the lower deck, providing a shadowed area to dine and relax. It is also where a bar is located. Sitting next to it is a wireless satellite communications console tuned into the main centre in his offices. At the far end of the deck, the ladies, each with a drink in hand, have flopped down on lush impermeable furniture amidst greenery arranged haphazardly about the afterdeck. The women cease their conversation at Williston's entrance. Both of them, recognizing Amber's likeness as the photo faces away from Williston, are moved to silence, so unexpected is the interruption.

Williston smiles at their glassy stares and says, "Relax ladies, I haven't flipped yet. I wanted to have Amber's picture in my office. I always remember when she graduated from high school and I love how she looks in this photo; it really shows off her jubilance and spunk. She'll probably be looking over my shoulder offering advice, as she did when we were younger."

He places the photo on the coffee table, turning his face to the wind. He inhales deeply, the atmosphere both pure and salty. "Now what have you two been gabbing about?"

Isabella says, "We were talking of Amber as you came in and that is what stunned us when you entered with her picture. The coincidence is eerie."

Beth agrees, "She`s half of the main reason we're all together right now, with Sakeema being the other. I was telling Isabella of the time Amber returned from university, bringing her new friend home for Thanksgiving. The first time we met Sakeema."

Beth rises and steps over to Williston, giving him a hug. ``Yeah Williston, you always like to surprise us, don`t you? Isabella told me the best surprise though; you're going to be a Daddy. I'm so excited for you two and jealous also. Did you tell Drake yet?"

Williston grins, then frowns, "No, I wanted to tell him when I saw him in Antigua, but we were wrapped up in our planning. I was thinking of him going off chasing dangerous men and it didn't seem like the right time. But it's a happy time for us, and I definitely want to share it with "Uncle Drake." I'm sure he'll be as glad as I am."

Isabella makes a drink for Williston while he and Beth talk about her baby, who is only nine weeks old. She'll be showing soon. She is sated with pleasure as she thinks of being a mother, having Williston's child. She steers a modest dolly of sandwiches and sweets toward the two friends and says, "Excuse me, Williston, but I know you haven't eaten since this morning, stuck there in your office. I've had Emmanuelle make up the small lobster rolls you like. And there's peanut butter and banana for you Beth, although I can't imagine anyone's favorite to be PB and fruit," she teases.

She picks up a plate of sandwiches, offering one to Beth.

"Williston was telling me about a new thread he unraveled just before you arrived, Beth. I didn't know Amber well having only met Williston a year before she died, but I do know how much she meant to all of you, how much you miss her. The more I hear about her, the more certain I am of how well we would have got along. I think I would have liked her very much. Can you tell Beth and me about what you have, Williston"?

Beth and Williston have selected some munchies and are arranging their seats around the table, both somber for a moment, thinking of Amber. The fog clears in Williston's head and he says, "You're right, Isabella, you would have loved her."

Taking a few bites and, table manners aside, he starts to tell them what he's discovered as he eats.

"And I do have some decent information. I tracked down Malik Hajani and Raheem Ahmedani, cousins through their mothers. Both Pakistani, both subjected to extreme poverty and left to fend for themselves while very young. Both with considerable rap sheets, wanted for questioning in a variety of crimes in several countries, mostly in Asia, but oddly enough Hajani was serving a sentence and escaped three years ago from a prison in Ireland. He and a man named Saul Morgan had been captured together and charged for their involvement in The Highlands Bombing in 1995. Then, in 2000, they killed two guards as well as an older inmate, who died several days later from a head wound, while escaping. They've been eluding the law ever since."

Williston finishes his third sandwich and wipes some mayonnaise from his lip with his napkin. He takes a drink of his water, gives a healthy burp, smiles and says, "Excuse me, girls, but that felt good. Anyway I think that Morgan is the man who was with Hajani in Dhaka from the description Rae gave me. We did a run on him, same story except he wasn't from a poor family, just one that didn't want him. Very vicious. Before Ireland, he did time in South Africa for aggravated sexual assault when he was only 17, raping and almost killing two white girls, both thirteen at the time. He, too, is wanted for questioning in a couple of unsolved cases. This is one very bad man."

Beth is listening raptly. There are things happening she isn't totally aware of yet. She wants to be in tune with their investigation. She presses Williston with a flurry of questions,

"Is there anything concrete tying these two to Rizzato? Is Ahmedani the man who confided in Rafan at the bar and is he the one found with the same mark the girls had? What of the other two bodies you mentioned? And what's Drake up to now? "

"Whoa, whoa, just give me one question at a time," Williston insists.

"First, yes to Ahmedani. Second, the two other bodies we're not sure of yet, other than from the police report that the mark being the only thing that joins them. More importantly, just over two years ago, Morgan were detained but not arrested in the Netherlands. He was found unconscious outside a brothel on Bloedsraat in Amsterdam. He was employed then as a 'manager' for a Belgium businessman, name of De Clerq, who we've come across before." At that thought he groans trying to imagine a company run by this man, villainy his only credentials.

"We ran De Clerq again, of course. One of his businesses moves some small arms, all legit. But it's a front; he's been a suspect in deals with African guerrillas and Somalia pirates for some time now. He's small time in the world's picture. His profits seem impressive though; his bio suggests he has a liking for Bentleys and rare works of art. Crazy juiced up natives, brigands and other assorted warlords pay handsomely for his weapons; nothing's been proven though."

He continues, "The first time they were able to officially charge De Clerq with, oddly enough, was aggravated sexual assault. Two young prostitutes were so badly beaten they had to be hospitalized. Their "boss" was badly beaten also but was able to flee and call the police. There were two assailants; both had already left the premises. They were able to identify De Clerq, thus his arrest. The other, the victims only saw his face briefly. Neither of the prostitutes could agree on his features, other than his face seemed misshapen. He had left earlier, perhaps an hour or more."

Procol Harem's "Whiter Shade of Pale" begins playing from the communications console announcing that a new email has arrived. Williston rises from the table, holding up a finger to ask the girls to wait one sec, and goes to the console to check. He's expecting a hit from Rassor, hoping it's him as he logs into the secure account. He feels a sudden shift as the diesels deep beneath him open up their throttles. He knows they are about 90 nautical miles from San Juan. Captain Bill will soon have the ship cruising at 20 knots, its prow cutting a pass through the swelling sea.

The new message is from Rassor, with an attachment bearing further details on De Clerq's arrest. His earlier reports had been vague regarding the arrest and he had asked Rassor for all the details he could acquire on the matter. Williston prints the document of three pages. At the bottom is a postscript. "Give me something hard man! I know I'm faster, but you could've found this in the newspapers. Ping me if you need me." It's signed "Rassor."

Williston gathers the sheets of paper while laughing at Rassor's penchant for self-praise. His reach is much greater than Williston's. The illegality of it bothers him some but not enough to stop using him as a tool in his efforts to find the thief who stole Amber's life.

"What is it, Williston?" Isabella asks. She had sat at the table in silence while Williston had related his findings. She's excited by the intrigue of their quest and you can see it in her eyes. Beth, too, sits up straighter.

Williston is walking back to the table scanning the pages. He grimaces while nodding his head as if the information is sweet. Sitting across from the girls he reaches for the writing pad on the far corner of the table, itemizing as he speaks, "Beth, the date of De Clerq's arrest is May 14, 2002."

"The same night Drake chased and lost Rizzato," she says. "And didn't you say Bloedsraat"?

"Yes, that's right."

Isabella interrupts them, "So, what does that mean?"

Williston turns his eyes to his wife and says, "The night Drake confronted Rizzato, he was emerging from a private brothel, the same S&M haunt that the injured girls came from, obviously some time before the police arrived. Rizzato's host must have been De Clerq. It never connected before. I think it's safe to assume that Rizzato, after fleeing, hired De Clerq's henchman."

Beth is following Williston's line of thinking. "Then Drake has already tangled with the men in Dhaka. Didn't he tell us about the bodyguard he took out on Bloedsraat? He left him unconscious."

She gets up from the table and exclaims, "These men from Dhaka were probably working for De Clerq in May 2002. Drake found and lost Rizzato that same night. After he was detained, Morgan was let go and disappeared. Until now."

She reaches across the table and grasps her dear friend's hand, giving it a squeeze. "He's there, Williston."

Chapter 12

May 27 2:44am Westminster, London

Sir Reginald Whitecastle steps out onto Victoria Street, 52 Victoria to be exact, where the Albert Tavern is situated. The night has grown still. Few people are about, most on their way home. The greenery hanging and growing from the second floor casts furtive shadows in the streetlight. He turns back and admires the brick building. It's his favorite watering hole, as it had been his father's and his grandfather's before that.

He had hosted a quaint gathering, three of his gambling creditors and their whores. Upon arrival, his guests had each been greeted with an ivory parchment envelope, Whitecastle's family crest embossed in gold foil in the upper left corner. Inside was the exact amount he owed to each person; with interest. They have called off their dogs. Whitecastle can stop hiding.

He had come into the money two days ago on Tuesday when he left the government offices in Dhaka. After introducing Andrew Stratton to Aatish Tarafdar at the Minister's side office where "unofficial business" took place, he had hastily left the building. Standing outside by a waiting yellow taxi was Mado. The door was open and in the seat Whitecastle noticed a briefcase. Mado invited him to check the case's contents and if he was satisfied, he could be on his way.

He did. With a wink and stupendous smile, he demanded, in Bengali, that the driver hurry to the airport. He waved at Mado, sat back and finally relaxed. He had enough money to get back on top, clear his debt and keep him living and gambling for another six months if he watched himself. During his flight back to London he formulated an evening of drinking and good food at his favorite bar, getting back in his peers' good graces.

Now, as he stands on the corner outside the tavern, he checks the street to the left and right and sees that they are gloomy in the shadows of the tall buildings that line the roadway, shadows that normally frighten him. Tonight, rather this morning, they are merely dark spots blending with the night. He is staying at The Victoria Hotel on Belgrave Road, and it's a short hike so even though it's late he decides to walk. He pays off the cabbie he had called earlier and sets out at a fine pace toward the Victoria. He has always enjoyed a brisk walk; unfortunately this would be his last.

From a recessed and darkened doorway, Dragoslav Popovic, watches Whitecastle start out on Victoria Street heading south. The giant Serb slithers from doorway to doorway, maintaining visual contact. Cautious, quiet movements belie the bruiser's bulk. Like all the Popovic men across the generations, Dragoslav is muscled and big-boned. At six and a half feet and two hundred eighty pounds of mass, it is unreasonable to expect one of such girth to move with such fluidity. War and fear have created a disturbing and intrepid personality.

Popovic was part of the Serbian Diaspora resulting from the dissolution of Yugoslavia and the Bosnian civil war. Wanted as a war criminal involved in the ethnic cleansing led by Slobodan Milosevic, Popovic assumed another identity, becoming one of the many refugees escaping the war-torn country, eventually landing and hiding in the Netherlands.

Killing comes easy to Popovic, a skill not found on resumes but one that leads to continuous work. Tonight's assignment has been ordered by Bartolommeo Rizzato. Popovic, better known as Bunker, is the most trusted of all Rizzato's team. Rizzato has confided in Dragoslav that he has to trust his workers and really can't trust any of them, they are criminals after all. This is the reason Dragoslav always serves as back-up on Rizzato's ops, following unaware men on their assignments, watching for slip-ups and protecting their backs. Popovic always works alone.

Bartolommeo Rizzato is one of only two people on the entire planet who knows that Dragoslav Popovic is really Dragoslava Zorana Vukovic, a woman; she herself is the other. Cursed with the stature of her brothers, father and uncles, Zorana is trapped in a man's body, even barbate. The only remnants of anything female are her vagina and her mind. Growing up, she looked like a drag queen, long hair and dresses looking odd and foreign to its bearer. When civil strife tore through her hometown, she ran away from home – and torment – at fifteen. She had changed genders, assuming the role of a man, something she has been mistaken for many times in the past. She became Dragoslav, a guerrilla fighter, and he learned how to kill.

Twenty meters behind Whitecastle, he moves in the darkness like a feral cat. He waits a moment as Whitecastle stops to stare in the lighted window of an art gallery. About fifty meters on he notices a section of road with two street lights burned out directly in his path. It will be good cover for the task he is about to perform. He leaves Whitecastle to his artful pause. Remaining in the shadow of the buildings, quiet as a falling leaf, he moves up the street beyond him. One of the large buildings along the unlighted section has wide concrete stairs leading to the lower levels. The protective baluster that protects the upper portion of the stairs is about two meters high and covered with posters, notices and such. It is an ideal spot for an ambush so he positions himself with his back to the inner wall, his right side closest to the street. The roadway is deserted except for the odd cab; there is no other traffic. He steals a glance back toward the man he is about to assassinate. Whitecastle has just dropped his gaze from the window and is walking toward him. He pulls himself rigid and waits.

All Sir Reginald feels after he steps past the stair wall is a rugged embrace that picks him right up off his feet. A strapping bicep grips tightly around his neck, cutting off his air, his voice and his chances. He doesn't even have time to struggle before the Serbian reaches up with his left hand, clamps onto his right ear for leverage, and gives his head a savage pull twisting his neck. The head rotates as far as the tendons and muscles in the neck will allow and the ear rips right off the skull. His body goes limp, suspended by Bunker's brawny arm. He drops him several steps below in the darkness. The ear is still in his hand and he throws it across the street, where it splatters against a wall before falling to the sidewalk. He laughs out loud at the thought of someone finding it. The laughter resonates through the hollow avenues and the few who hear it walk on a bit faster.

Dragging the body to the foot of the stairs, the blackness of the night screening his dreadful act, he drops him on his face. He stands aside, hidden in the dark, unmoving for over an hour.

When he deems enough time has passed with powerful hands he rips his jacket and shirt apart, exposing scrawny white shoulders. Standing over the body he removes a stiletto from its sheath. Using the sharp tip he scrawls a brutish Z on his upper right back.

Flipping over the body, he pulls it into a sitting position by the wall. The dead man will appear to be either drunk or asleep. He tucks a fake gambling chit in his inner sport coat pocket and steals the wallet. Since Rizzato had shared his attempt at crude art by signing a Z on the two girls in Venezuela, a story he found grossly amusing, Bunker copies his motif. Little does he realize that his artless devotion will lead to his own demise, not too far down the road.

Chapter 13   June 11, 2004 Buriganga River, Bangladesh

Stratton stands leaning against the jamb of the cabin doorway as the sampan navigates upriver. The pollution inundates his senses. The smell is horrible; all he can think of is unwashed socks. He watches the water slosh against the side, greenish froth joins a wash of adulterated water. Dozens and dozens and dozens of boats everywhere astonish him. Many, called Panshi, display resplendent temperate colors. He was told they were home to many a family, often for their whole lives. He knows Bangladesh to be a riverine country, with 400 or more, but had never realized how many people lived and worked on the rivers. Large cargo ships swim cautiously; the *dingis* of all sizes scud about, being a nuisance. The traffic is becoming worse as they near the port of Sadarghat. In port, it seems there isn't enough river for all the floating vessels.

Stratton wouldn't normally be asail with this crew, but when he visited with Rizzato for a progress report touring the site along the Bhola River where he and his men are camped out, Bartolo had suggested he accompany them to Sadarghat if he wanted to see a lot of "believers" in one place, it being one of the largest river ports in the world. Two things immediately compelled him to accept the invitation. He had read of Sadarghat when he was gleaning the Internet for large gatherings. When he discovered Bangladesh had one of the largest Muslim populations in the world, he also learned that they hosted, annually, one of the most immense congregations of Allah's followers. It didn't matter that millions of Muslims who were peaceful and wonderful people; to Andrew they were all guilty. His ignorance and hostility beclouds reality.

Therefore he read as much history as he could find, especially on the city of Dhaka and its surrounds. He first considered Sadarghat when he read that 30,000 people were in and out of the port every day, with thousands lining the streets on shore. He finally settled on Tongi because he discovered that 800,000 Muslims will be gathered there in December. Nevertheless he wanted to see the port in case he needs a back-up location.

Secondly, he would only be gone two days. He planned on meeting with Tarafdar on Monday. The man assigned to assist them has not being as co-operative as Stratton would like; there seems to be a problem with their land purchases. Some is government land and the deeds are being withheld with no explanation other than they will be forthcoming. That problem compounds others. Rizzato has workers waiting, sequestered on land they don't own yet. One of the properties was a bankruptcy, so is abandoned. As he muses over these speed bumps, he remembers his upcoming appointment with Honey Aviation, also on Monday, later in the day though. He plans to have one of their helicopters fly him over the land along the bend in the Turag River where the Muslim men will be in the first week of December. As he thinks about the upcoming event, a malicious frown takes over his face as he fathoms the terrifying revenge he will wield.

He canters to the loading area abaft of the boat; the light breeze created from the motion of the boat relieves his dampened forehead. He wears workman's coveralls like most of the crew – Morgan, Hajani and Plum – to hide their guns more than their bodies. He is grateful for the forbearance to remove his other clothes first. Even with only boxers underneath, the weighted heat and the humidity cause him to hate the natives even more.

He inspects the near empty hold, littered with detritus of previous ladings. It will soon be filled with lumber and plywood. Rizzato will also be purchasing power tools and a powerful generator. The property where his few men have already gathered need additional sleeping quarters for the extra crew he will be putting together as well as a makeshift hangar to assemble and hide the plane in. According to their earlier schedule, the properties were supposed to be in their hands by the end of May to coincide with the delivery of the plane, which is sitting in the hold of a Norwegian freighter that is destined to be dismantled at the Breakers shipyards in Chittagong on the Bay of Bengal.

The Chittagong Breakers totally astounded Stratton when he viewed it from the cabin cruiser Rizzato had leased. For ten miles of beach, over a hundred abandoned ships have given up their souls. Gigantic ocean-going cargo ships, luxury liners, tankers among others are waiting to be destroyed, by hand. When they went in closer they saw litter weighing hundreds of tons covering the beach. Sections of ships larger than four average houses lay askew, rusting and dying. Hulls, some with loading cranes rising eighty to a hundred feet in the air, are grounded in the mud. Many are partially demolished, skeletal. Men, made tiny by these metal monsters, toil among the remains like insects devouring an iron giant.

The shipyards are inhuman. Unfair as it seems, if the ships didn't come here, they might go to India or Pakistan, and so would the jobs. Exposure to toxic chemicals, oil, asbestos, heavy steel, noxious fumes, and backbreaking labor are rewarded by about a dollar and a half a day. With no steel-toed boots, some wear sandals, many bare feet. They are clothed only in grimy lungis and western style shirts, no hard hats, no overhead cranes, no safety inspectors, some don't even have lunchrooms. Their days are swollen with drudgery and work so dangerous it is nonsensical. Luring workers away with safe work and high wages is going to be easy for Stratton and Rizzato. It really doesn't matter what amount is promised, they will never return home anyway.

The plane is an Air Tractor and it rests in the guts of the forsaken ship. The huge transporter is still floating at anchor just shy of the beach. The ship is being prepared for its funeral; anything of value and use is being off-loaded. The aircraft will be removed that night into two large *balams* for shipping up the Bhola River, about 70 nautical miles away. It had left the Ukraine and arrived in Bangladesh unregistered and untraceable.

Rizzato has just gotten off the shortwave after speaking to the chandlers in Sadarghat, arranging for the loading of his material. He joins Stratton, aka Jack Favors, at the hold. His lumbering legs are clad in black leather pants. A black t-shirt covered by a black silk windbreaker and black boots make him look almost normal. Except for the silk, it might be considered *motorcycle chic.*

"What's on your mind Favors?"

"I was thinking about our plane, the deeds we require, the men we need, etc., etc. And I am intrigued by the design of this sampan you hired. These Asians are quite smart; it's a very practical design. She's over sixty-five feet and mostly hold. I'm certain it can carry a large load." He meets Rizzato's stare and asks, "What's on *your* mind, Bartolo?"

Rizzato says, "It's pronounced 'sum-parn' in English, not sam-pan. What I think is that you need to knock a few heads around and get the paperwork done. We need to get started on the runway. I can keep the few men I have now busy for the next couple of weeks, but until you give me the go-ahead, I can't round up enough men from Chittagong for the rest of the work. It's like we talked about last night: I want to stay ahead of schedule and fly the fuck outta here before you go sailing off into the blue."

Stratton tries not to be ruffled by Rizzato's brash manners. "I'm on it, Rizzato. Monday will see it cleared up. Get the wharf repaired and when the plane arrives, you get it ashore no matter what. And get the men working on the outbuildings. I'll get the deeds. Mado has made all the arrangements, and it's a done deal. We're farmers now," he adds lightly.

"Oh yeah, can you see me on a tractor out checking my fucking corn?" says Rizzato, smirking at the idea of himself as a farmer.

He turns and leans against the gunnels, his back to the water, and faces Stratton. "I think that pissant, Lucas or Locust, whatever his name is, is going to hit you for more payola. A little more grease for the wheel, if you know what I mean, Jack. If on Monday you find out I'm right, don't give into the little fuck. Tell him you have to think about it and I'll have Bunker pay him a visit. I can assure you he will be more...uh... synergetic to our needs. Yeah, that's what he'll be, synergetic." For a second, a rubbery smile, provoked by his *bon mot*, mottles his face. "You okay on that?"

Stratton nods at the suggestion while thinking of Rizzato's answer to every problem. Threatening at first, maybe breaking a few bones, and if they still didn't co-operate, maybe they just disappear. He admits his methods are effective – very dangerous, but effective.

"His name, actually, is Lokesh," Stratton gets his own jibe in. "I feel that you may be right. My plan was to meet with Tarafdar to insist that our liaison could be persuaded to be more compliant. I meant to remind him of the contribution we made to his numbered account in Bern. I'd balk at more fees. But now that you mention it, perhaps I will forestall my meeting with the Minister until after I meet with Lokesh. We may not have to get the Minister involved at all. It might even embarrass him if that were the case. If indeed this underling is looking for his share, his *baksheesh*, we'll try it your way Bartolo."

Their boat takes a sudden yaw to starboard directly into the path of a humongous freighter bearing down on them. Their boat is on a straight course toward the ship. If they collide, the sampan will crumple; the freighter might not even veer off course, like running over a small animal with your car.

Both men straighten up, glancing back in the cabin where Morgan is supposed to be at the helm only to see Plum, one of Rizzato's hired hands, on his back, her legs wrapped tightly around his midsection while she tries to claw his eyes out. Morgan has one hand on the wheel; the other is twisting Plum's hair, oblivious to where he is steering the boat. He lets go of the wheel altogether, grabbing her claws, trying to pry them off his face. He takes three powerful strides backwards, walloping Plum's back against the cabin wall. When she hits, Morgan's rugged body maintains its inertia, driving the wind from her lungs. She gives a high-pitched "Uuuunh!" Her limbs lose their grip and she falls to the deck, gasping.

Rizzato starts yelling, "What the fuck's going on with you two?

Can't you stay apart for two days and not be at each other's throats. Shit! Somebody take the damn wheel. Straighten this bitch out." His arms are flailing and his eyes bugged out, he is so angry.

Hajani had been forward when the ship gave a lurch. Seeing what is happening in the wheelhouse, he drops the ropes he was coiling and rushes to grab the wheel. The sampan is about 100 meters away from the colossus that has already consumed the sampans paltry shadow. Hajani has never been one for water, so has never commanded a boat before, but he reacts with keen perception. Cars are more his game. When he sees the ship, he quickly translates his driving skills to the problem. Glancing again to the beast before him, he sees his shortest route. He'll go hard right; there is no room to turn back left. He gives it more speed.

He cuts the wheel sharp to starboard, pushing the hand accelerator full forward. The motor falters for a second, gives a smoky belch, then with a deep bellow gives it everything it can. Hajani watches the front and with a deep sigh when he realizes they will miss the freighter by a few feet. They are coming clear of the ship when the prow wave hits their boat, giving it a hearty rock.

 Andrew is tossed to the deck, rolling about beside the hold he was clinging to in fright. He had been staring up at the looming ship waiting for impact. Rizzato had ran back to the door of the cabin and braced himself between the jambs. Hajani, his feet set firmly apart, acts like the seasoned sailor that he isn't, locks on the wheel, trying to straighten out the boat. Plum is still on her back on the cabin deck, one arm braced around a bench that is bolted to the floor. She is retching and still gasping.

Morgan is sitting on the other end of the bench by the wall, having been thrown there by the wave. He hit his head on a small shelf jutting out from the wall, which knocked him unconscious. The rocking of the boat causes enough momentum to lift his head on one crest and whack it against the wall on the next, giving it four or five good knocks before the sampan settles down. Plum's sharp nails have left racing stripes on his temples. Some are red and oozy with fresh blood, others are only welts.

Rizzato's face is contorted and the color of wine he is so mad. He swears awhile in Italian telling them their worthless, promiscuous mothers are to blame, that they should've rid themselves of both when they were babies. He yells, no, he screams, "You fools! You *fungul* idiots! You could have killed us."

Realizing he has no audience, he throws up his arms. "Merde", he swears.

He turns to Hajani, "Can you handle this thing for a short while Malik, because I can't and I don't know if Jack can. These two, *children*, are out service for a bit. So what do you say"?

Malik gives his usual nod, liking this feeling of control. He's usually just a helper; someone else is always in charge. He thinks he can do this, but he doesn't know where their destination is or what to do when they get there. But he can steer and he'll just keep avoiding boats, which are all over the spacious river.

"Yes, I can do this."

"Okay, keep it as straight as possible and slow down. We're ahead of schedule anyway so, just... don't hit anything."

When he erupted, Rizzato's temper was like magma, searing and scathing. Rizzato has calmed a little; his color is more of a rose shade. He is still extremely upset, so his features are still tense, still knotted. The crew have seen that look before, usually when he was about to kill someone. Both fists on his hip, he turns his attention to the other two in the wheelhouse. Plum is sitting up, breathing quick short breaths, holding her chest just above her bust. She, too, is pissed but looking at the floor.

Morgan stirs, groaning, his hand massaging his scalp. Finding several bumps on his head, he flinches when he accidently scratches them saying, "Oh man that stings. Feels like small hills. What did I hit?"

He sits forward and bends his head low when Rizzato walks over and cuffs his bruised scalp. Saul ducks in revolt, his hand reflexively going for his gun. He halts at the butt as he catches Rizzato looking down at him with a penetrating glare. A spooky image comes to mind. If anyone ever de-robed the specter of death in the black hood, the ghoul would have Rizzato's eyes. It seems as if he can see through you, *in you;* it's frightening. Morgan sits upright, forgets about the gun and his head, waiting for the wrath to come.

"What, you gonna shoot me, Saul? Go ahead, stupid. Kill us all while you're at it. You almost did anyway. From now on I want you to leave her alone. I'm stressing this Saul or you will be cut free of this team. I won't be responsible for you anymore. You've never had it so good, so stop screwing up."

Rizzato is interrupted by Plum who wants to add more fuel to Morgan's chastisement, "He called me a chink bitch; I'm not Chinese!"

"Shut up," spits Rizzato. "Same deal goes for you, get along or get out. Besides, why do you listen to what he says? He's a bigot, a black, Jewish bigot. He's got two things going for him for everybody to hate; you've only got one. He's jealous. And stop baiting him."

When Rizzato is done blasting them, he bows his head and takes several deep breaths. He doesn't need Andrew to see the disharmony in his crew. There is too much money at stake for any mess-ups. He needs to be in control and put an end to their spats. These are stone-hearted, ruthless people, so he has to be harder than them to control them.

Then to the pair, in a voice more calm but still definitive, he says, "This is the last time you two work together. From now on, Ms. Steele, you will be staying on the farm watching over the men with Raheem. Bunker can be our third man if we need somebody elsewhere. This is the last time you two, and I mean the *very* last time, you two will be quarrelling. I demand more co-operation."

He eyes the duo until they both drop their gaze in submission. He adds almost *sotto voce*, "I don't personally care if you don't want to be friends. The big "but" here is, we keep our shit together for five more months and I promise you, you'll have more money than you will ever need. So be nice."

He claps his hands and barks out some orders. "Morgan, take the wheel, get us into port. Steele, you and Hajani get the debris and the old pallets out of the hold. Make sure our ropes and tie downs are ready. I want to get our supplies aboard and scram. It's better we're not seen any more than we have to be." Then to all of them, he says, "Now don't bother me until we get to port."

With that final command he ventures slowly back out to join Stratton, who is standing fore of the boat in front of the hold caressing his left elbow. As Rizzato nears the man, he can hear him issuing invectives and steels himself for the tongue-lashing he is certain is to follow.

Andrew is pushing up his sleeve to inspect his swelling joint. When he had been knocked to the floor, all his weight had come down upon it, hammering it on the deck. The scowl on his face bespeaks his pain. He is muttering incoherently, lost for a moment in pure hatred, blaming the Muslims even for his elbow. His mental capacity is rotting.

This is the first hiccup, as it were; in what has been a very smooth operation so far, but it instills within Stratton a sense that things can go wrong. While he had been rolling on the floor grasping his elbow, the pain almost unbearable, an irrational fear had swept over him that he wouldn't complete his task. It is all that matters to him. Random flashes of his son, his youngest daughter, fan through his head. Then they are gone, as if a switch has been flipped. He had risen from the deck nursing his arm, some of his sanity still present.

Stratton regards Rizzato as he approaches and says in a surprisingly deceptive but reproachful voice, "This is not good. Not good at all. I'm only going to tell you this once, Bartolo. If there are any more disruptions, I'm casting *you* and your people adrift. I'm sure Mado can find me someone else to complete your duties. I want your word that this will be the last such occasion." He winces as he touched his elbow and angrily says, "And my damn elbow is broken"

Rizzato reaches into his back pocket and pulls out a stainless steel flask – it has some kind of crest etched on the side. He holds it out to Stratton and says, "Here, have some of this, but be careful. I made it myself. It's been distilled three times so it's almost pure. A couple of shots of that and you can forget your sore limb. Have three or four and you won't even know you have limbs."

He gives a rare chuckle, knowing it is so. He had learned how to make corn liquor when he was younger. The booze doesn't just have a kick. At 30 over proof it can wreck your brain. Before Stratton can reply Rizzato says, "Your elbow's not broken, Favors, you're still bending it. You just gave it a good smack. And yes, you definitely have my word that there will be no more incidents with my staff. These people aren't known for their patience or good manners, an unruly bunch to be sure, but they'll do what I say. I'll get this job done right for you." He uncaps the flask, extending it to Stratton, "Go ahead take a swig of this potion."

Stratton grabs the flask and without heeding Rizzato's advice, took a large draught of the liquid fire. The liquor not only blazes on the way down, it literally takes his breath away. The elbow momentarily forgotten, Stratton claws at his throat trying to stop the burning, trying to inhale. Rizzato is laughing, an odd sight in itself, and relishing Andrew's discomfort, "I warned you, Jack. That is powerful shit. You should be sipping it, you crazy bugger. Sit down there on that tool box for a minute. You'll be okay."

Stratton sits on the box, more like drops onto it. The booze rests in his stomach for several minutes before activating its numbing qualities. His voice is high and strained, "Whoa! That's dangerous."

Neither man say anything for a few moments; the crew are quiet except for Plum and Malik chit-chatting in the hold as they work. The river makes its own sounds: foreign voices in nearby boats, horns, the waters being displaced, and the crying of the gulls. The air is a smorgasbord of aromas and odours. The sampan sails carefully toward port, seesawing with the motion of the river. Anyone noticing their craft will see nothing untoward; no one would know it carries death merchants.

Stratton holds up the flask. "Fool that I am, here's to good days ahead," and takes another deep swig. Holding the flask out to Rizzato to take it away, he clenches his teeth as the alcohol does a repeat performance of delightful agony. He shivers as the liquid settles in. Knowing what to expect, he recovers from the second drink much more quickly. His skin prickles and his vision clears as the hooch's turbochargers kick in.

While he sits leaning against the gunnels, Rizzato fashions a makeshift sling for Stratton's left arm, relieving gravity's tug on the injured joint. While tying a knot at the back of his neck, Stratton asks him,

"Did you take care of Whitecastle?"

"Yeah, Bunker looked after that a couple of weeks ago. It didn't cause much of a stir. I'll spare you the details, but it's done. No traces of us left behind."

"Good. Oh man that feels so much better. Thanks for the bandage and the drink, Bartolo."

"You're welcome. I told you I'd look after you, Jack."

Stratton closes his eyes leaning back on the gunnels, using a life preserver for a headrest. A warm sensation courses through his body. Nerve endings and stress go AWOL. For a short time he will forget about revenge, forget about Muslims. A misty image of his family when they were young, when they were small children, engrosses him. Memories of innocent times before life became complicated lulls him away from reality. Coupled with the pendulum sway of the boat, he soon falls asleep.

Rizzato watches the man doze off. Unfeeling as he can be, he is nonplussed by the sapless smile. It precedes the empty tears that escape from Favors' curtained eyes. They leave sluggish trails on his cheeks as they creep down his face. Several drops cling to his jaw line like dew. Rizzato considers it an exceptionally sad sight.

He leaves Stratton to rest and fight his demons. While heading astern to speak with Morgan and organize their landing, he thinks, "This man is not so tough. He would never last in my world. He's soft. Without his money, he would have no power whatsoever. I'll be glad when this gig is over, when he and his enemies are finally wasted."

Chapter 14 September 29 5:36pm Dhaka

Drake spots the parking garage at the rear of the office building as Dakin bullies his way through the traffic, cutting several vehicles off as he swerves into the parking lot entrance. He says, "There's a garage in back off to our right, head to the top floor. I'll watch to see if they follow."

"Okay," was all Daiken said as reaches down to his ankle, removing Rae's gun from its holster. He places the Sig on the center console, close to his right hand. He notices the garage is emptying, probably people leaving work. There are no cars going in so he speeds along. Stopping for a ticket at the automated entryway, he removes the slip of paper and the gate slowly lifts. The Land Ranger penetrates the gloomy entrance, many lights are burnt out. The up ramp is to their immediate right and hugs the outer wall; cars are parked inward on the opposite side, at an angle. The outer walls are open, with huge concrete columns every twelve feet, giving some light to the dark interior. Steel rails line the ramp on its climb to keep cars from going over; many are rusted.

Drake is looking back as they enter and spies the Isuzu coming around the corner of the building towards the garage.

"Here they come. When you get to the top floor, use the truck to block off their path so they'll have to come in on foot. We'll take cover on each side of the top area if we can. Let's try to take them alive, Dakin."

"Okay." There's nothing else to say. His concentration is intense, he is going into battle. Catecholamine's are hormones that are released by nerve impulses; their receptors are all over his body. His heart rate, pulse, blood pressure, all goes up. His face flushes and invisible caterpillars crawl over his skin.

The Toyota reaches the top floor, which is open to the sky. A waist-high patterned concrete wall surrounds the roof. The exit ramp is directly across from them as they clear the entrance ramp. The building is about twenty five meters wide and thirty meters long, there is a twelve meter drop to the ground. There are about a dozen cars sprinkled about. The center parking lanes have cars nose-to-nose. The center and outside lanes are separated by a six- meter-wide right of way that circles the top floor. Stunted shadows creep along the roof as the sun lowers its arc to the west.

Dakin swings the big truck around so that the passenger side faces the entrance ramp. The bulk of the Land Cruiser blocks the ingress to the top floor. He turns off the ignition and pockets the keys. Swinging open the door, he grabs his gun jumping from the cab to take cover behind the farthest vehicles to the left. There is an old Mazda quarter-ton truck backed into a slot about eighteen meters away. On the near side of it is a shiny new Smart car, mostly window. It would be poor cover, but still a distraction. He crouches down in the truck bed, which is empty except for a spare tire. Standing the tire up, he uses it for a shield. He can glance through its center while keeping his head covered. He holds his gun steady with his right hand; the left has been dressed and lightly bandaged by the hotel doctor. On it, he wears a paintballer's glove with the finger tips missing. He wriggles the fingers, feeling lucky they all work.

Drake crawls over the console and gets out Dakin's door right behind him, running to the right toward a 1969 Chevy Impala parked nose out seven lanes back. It's black, festooned with several shades of primer where its owner has obviously made repairs, auto body camouflage. It's parked near a bantam Japanese import, which is crowded in on the other side by a light grey, not so new Beemer, facing in.

He crouches down at the rear of the Impala, behind the back tire. It is semi-cloaked in the early evening shadows. Behind a black car in a dark spot and in his black clothes he'll be hard to see. He checks the door of the car. It's unlocked. He closes it gently until he hears it click. He, Dakin and their vehicle form a V at the top floor, leaving anyone coming around the truck an open target.

He pulls out his gun, switching off the safety. He is using .45APC hollow point cartridges. Used in the M1911 with a 5 inch barrel, the shells are man stoppers. With nearly 500 foot/pounds of bullet energy and large diameter, it will leave a deep and lasting wound channel, lowering his targets blood pressure quickly. It is especially effective on humans.

Both men are crouched behind cover. They can hear the Isuzu as it approaches. The groan of the oncoming engine falters as it nears the obstruction at the entrance to the top floor becoming a purr as it idles. Drake and Dakin can hear a discussion behind their vehicle but it is not loud enough to discern what's being said, it was likely their pursuers debating as to their approach. The defenders align the sights of their weapons on the openings near the Toyota and wait.

Bunker has impatiently grabbed a parking stub from the machine as the Land Cruiser they are pursuing spirals towards the second floor just above them. He eases the SUV through the gate, pausing inside the wide doorway. Bunker looks over at Saul, who sits fuming in the passenger seat and says,

"We do this my way Morgan."

"Who made you the boss"? He asks. "Rizzato wanted me and Hajani to take out Bashara, find out if he spoke to anyone about him. I should be telling you what to do."

"So, where's Hajani now? Where's Bashara?" The sarcasm shuts Morgan up.

Bunker reaches into the back seat and grabs a hard body case. More to appease him than to protect him, the big Serb thrusts the case toward Morgan saying, "Put that pistol away and take this."

Saul opens the case to find a FAMAS bullpup, a French assault rifle. The bullpup has the action and magazine behind the trigger, built more into the stock of the gun closer to the shooter's face. It's a shorter, lighter assault weapon maintaining a long barrel. Unfortunately the shorter stock makes it more difficult to avoid barrel spray, making it a poor choice for long distance. Today, however, it will be deadly in a confined space.

Morgan's attitude changes as he clutches the rifle. Admiring its stubby design, he says, "I've never fired one like this. I'm more familiar with an M16, but I think I'll catch on quick enough. Ah, here's the safety." He flips the safety back and forth, puts the gun to his shoulder, aiming out the window. He adjusts his shoulder, his grip for a few seconds, leaving the safety on full auto.

Sitting taller in the seat, he places the butt of the gun between his thighs, holding the two grips at ready. He stares at the dimly lit entryway, grits his teeth and said, "Let's do it."

Bunker proceeds with caution, expecting an ambush at each level. Some patrons are leaving on the lower levels down the opposite ramp; there is no one behind them. They are approaching the top level when Bunker sees the Land Ranger blocking their path. He stops his vehicle and muses aloud to his partner. His first thought is that the people they are pursuing might be below, waiting for them to retreat or planning to attack them from the rear. The Ranger is about 40 feet away. He shoves the brakes tightly to the floor while depressing the accelerator also. The rear wheels are screaming, bleeding blue smoke. The ass of the SUV starts to swerve when the speedometer hits 40. He yells for Morgan to brace himself then releases the brakes. The vehicle shoots forward and is going 60 when it hits the Land Ranger. The four-wheel drive Sportivo sports an all-terrain push bar mounted on the front bumper. It catches the Land Ranger at the bottom of the passenger door, the towing hooks digging into the rocker panel. It lifts the passenger-side wheels several inches off the floor. It's like a furious elk digging pronged horns into its opponent's flank.

The door of the Land Ranger buckles like tissue. The tires on the driver's side bubble with the weight and screech as they slide along the concrete until they catch in an expansion joint. The Toyota pitches onto its side, crushing metal and glass, making a horrific noise. The stench of burnt rubber gives the sound more weight. Bunker is relentless and floors the Isuzu, its own tires proclaiming insanity. He bulldozes the whole mess for another twenty feet until the roof of the Toyota smashes into the Chevy Drake is crouching behind. The Chevy caroms into the import, the import into the BMW then everything stops as the rear of the 252i hits the back wall.

In the mere seconds before the Ranger hit the Chevy, Drake has scrambled to get away from crashing cars. When he saw they were still coming, he dived under the import and crabbed his way toward the beamer. The import struck the beamer just as Drake was half way through. As he was crawling, splayed out, the beamer started moving, centimeters over his head. The noise was deafening as metal strained and complained and tires howled. The rear of the beamer crunched into the side wall, with the front starting to cave in. The front tire of the beamer cut off Drake's escape route, but he managed to get out from under the car just as everything stopped. He rolls into a kneeling position, hidden behind the rear fender. He listens to the sudden stillness until he hears their voices. One he recognizes.

For a few seconds the only noise is glass still shattering and the hissing of steam being released from the Land Ranger's busted radiator. Morgan had braced his feet on the dash after laying the bullpup across his lap. He had been holding the overhead handle with one hand. He relaxes and sits forward, grasping the gun and resting his arms on his knees. Staring at the crashed cars he looked over at Bunker for a second.

"Fucking 'A', Bunk!"

Emotionless, Bunker demands, "Get out and get down, quickly."

Morgan opens the door just as Drake stands up from behind the rear end of the beamer, his weapon trained on the twosome. His dark eyes bear down on them through the sight of his gun. In a tone of one familiar with giving orders he shouts, "Don't make any sudden movements." He rapidly shoots a glance with his eyeballs to the right, where Dakin is, his .45 aimed directly at Bunker's head, and adds, "We have you covered. Let's see some hands. Now!"

Three seconds go by, no one moves. It only takes two seconds for Morgan to tighten his grip and make up his mind. While he kicks out the door he yells at Bunker to get down. He is already pointing the gun in Drake's direction. Morgan let go with a quick blast at Drake, right through the windshield. The window shatters camouflaging their movements. Drake gets two shots off that tear through the damaged glass before he ducks for cover. One of his shots goes straight breaking out the rear window before lodging itself in the cement wall. The other one comes so close to shattering Morgan's collar bone that the bullet leaves a trail mark on his shirt, burning the fabric on its way by.

Morgan flinches, not the least bit surprised by his good luck. He'd been in too many fire fights to be able to count his close calls. He propels himself from the cab, rushing to the front end, which is still locked into the undercarriage of the overturned Toyota. The tangled vehicles make for good cover. Bunker joins him, his movements strikingly fluid for someone of such mass. He has his weapon drawn, an M1911 more doctored and babied than Drake's. Bunker has spotted the man to his left blasting a couple of shots in Dakin's direction.

Dakin hasn't been as lucky as Morgan. One of the bullets from Bunker's pistol comes through the front windshield of the quarter ton, through the back wall of the cab. As it enters his thigh it's travelling 2,800 feet per second with over 2,500 foot pounds of energy. It doesn't stay but the damage it causes will – for a very long time. It pierces the thin cover near the femur and nicks healthy bone before tearing through the muscles. It never even slowed down as it flew off into the sky before arching down several miles away, killing a stray cat. Dakin falls flat on the truck bed, his weapon cart wheeling through the air, crashing into the back of the truck. His free hand joins his bandaged hand as he grasps his busted leg. He wants to scream; the pain is so intense. But even his muffled torment can be heard by the other three men. Two of them smile.

Drake's mind temporarily clouds with concern for his comrade. He calls out, "Dakin, are you all right?"

Dakin lets go a groan he can't hold. He doesn't want to give the bad guys any advantage. the voice that follows comes out grainy, as if he has sand in his vocal chords, "It's okay, it's okay."

Dakin concentrates on anything but the pain. Straining, sweat glistening his face, he sits up using the side of the truck bed for support and sits directly behind the tire he had placed there earlier. The Smart car sits there, still undamaged, but that would soon change. He removes his shirt and makes a crude bandage around the wound. Knotting it off, he reaches back for the gun and aims it toward the vacant Isuzu and waits.

In a heated husky whisper Bunker exclaims, "I think I hit him but he's obviously not out. If we can take one of them alive, it would be very good. You and I can cut him up, force him to tell us what he knows. You'd like that, wouldn't you?"

Morgan would never be accused of being sensitive, instead, what he feels is repulsion for the man who cherishes blood-letting.

"Fuck off, you sick animal. You're the one who likes that shit. I just want to kill them. Now, what are we doing"?

They are both in kneeling positions. Morgan has his back to the overturned vehicle, watching the up ramp. Bunker watches forward. He whispers his plan. People downstairs are screaming, reacting to the gunfire, rushing to get away. Drake is still crouched behind the Beamer. He changes positions. Almost ten or twelve feet to his right are two cars in the middle slots. He scurries across and ducks behind the rear wheel of the closest one. The down ramp is behind him. Several cars are scattered here and there. There are too many open spaces to make running desirable. Especially with Dakin injured. He knows his opponents have an automatic weapon and can only guess at what else. He is still about ten meters away from the smart car and the Mazda Dakin is in. Checking the front once more, he dashes for the rear of the small truck. Seeing Dakin in the back, sitting up by the tire Drake notices the anguish etched in his face. But like a true soldier he's facing his enemy.

He gave Drake thumbs up just as a smoke grenade lands under one of the cars Drake had been hiding behind. A pale blue ghost expands filling the upper deck. It shrouds the vehicles as there is no breeze to disturb its masking effect. Morgan lets go a blast from his gun. He can't see through the smoke and shoots low, the burst of bullets sprays chips of concrete as they ricochet off the floor. The line of fire sweeps randomly through the haze. It moves higher with each sweep. The next one can catch up to them. When the bullets are arching away from them, both Dakin and Drake aim at the muzzle fire visible through the vapor. Each man fires off a quick burst. Three of their bullets simultaneously find a target, rifling Morgan's upper body.

Morgan is standing on the hood of the Sportivo when he opens fire through the fog. The answering bullets permeate his flesh. He's located about two meters from the outer wall and at the same height. The shock of the bullets carries him through the air with his weapon still firing chewing up the Smart Car, showering Dakin with glass. Landing on top of the outer wall, most of his body hangs off the edge. He teeters there for a moment before his weight pulls him over. His body somersaults as it falls. When it makes contact with the concrete sidewalk below, it doesn't matter that his skull is crushed or that his back and other bones are broken, he was already dead by the time his body was airborne. His gun lands between his legs a second later, its muzzle pointed at his crotch. Its trigger is jammed and it riddles him with fire until the ammo is spent

Bunker had schemed with Morgan for him to spray the area after he tossed the smoke grenade. He would scan for shots to determine where they came from. He knows Morgan is fired up and crazy at this point. He also knows that if they survived this caper, he will have to kill him anyway. He's fucking up too much. Rizzato has told Bunker to use his discretion when he had given him this assignment. He told him to watch Morgan and to eliminate him if he endangers their mission.

Bunker means to escape – to get back to Rizzato and let him know what has happened. If no one comes back, Rizzato will be in danger and Bunker, or rather Zorana, secretly wants to protect him. Rizzato is the first man "she" didn't hate. As soon as smoke had filled the air, Morgan had started his barrage. Bunker bounded for the down ramp, running to the main entrance. A puzzled crowd is by the front halfway back from the opening to the front of the office building, the gunshots making them curious and some people naturally can't avert themselves from tragedy even though danger exists They watch Bunker descend the empty ramp. A Mahindra Scorpio stands vacant in the lot outside the building beside the crowd. The door is open with the motor running. The owner had been looking to park when she was flagged by the bystanders. She poses in the midst of the speculating bunch when Bunker runs from the garage, heading toward the vehicle. She sees his direction but not the gun at his side. She dashes toward her car. Bunker, seeing he won't make it there before her, stops, aims and squeezes the trigger. The bullet connects just behind the woman's ear, blasting a fist-sized hole out the opposite side of her skull. Her forward momentum coupled with the thrust of the bullet twists her in the air and throws her on her back. Her legs are bare and her pretty red dress is bunched up around her waist. Her lacy white panties seem too fancy for the occasion.

Bunker waves his pistol at the crowd. Those who don't run throw themselves to the ground. The Serb reaches the vehicle, steps over its owner, jumps in the cab shutting the door. Grinning to himself, he thinks, "The stupid bitch won't need this for the rest of the day." With that thought he reverses the Indian auto to flee from the scene, running over the dead woman's body.

Bunker remembers the shots, Morgan screaming when he was hit, his damaged body tumbling over the edge into the air. He heard the body hit the sidewalk, his favorite gun still firing, rueing the seven thousand dollars he had spent for it. He shakes his head, thinking about Rizzato's reaction.

**

Drake waits several minutes before moving. A slight breeze had ripened and is blowing the smoke away from them, ushering it off the roof. As the cars start to come into view, the outlines are blurry and shapes undefined. There is stillness until he hears a shot from below. Drake figures one of the thugs has gotten away and is clearing a path. Either he or Dakin hit the shooter, likely both of them. The short scream and the thud that followed, gun burst of four quick shots from below and then the silence tell of his demise.

Drake rises cautiously from his position and hurries to the truck. Dakin has shifted himself in the bed and is lying prone, semiconscious, covered in pellets of safety glass. The tourniquet has slowed the flow of blood, but he has lost too much. He will need help soon or he'll go into shock.

Unsure if anyone is still waiting for them to show themselves, Drake rushes the crushed vehicles, scrambling around cars for cover. The gas has dissipated enough now for him to make out the mangled mess. He shouts, "Throw out your weapons! Throw them out now!"

Nothing. Making his way around the Isuzu, he checks underneath for feet or legs on the other side. When he springs around to face whatever might be there, he finds the premises have been vacated. With his weapon raised and eyeing the entry ramp, he proceeds to the front wall, looking down on the crowd in the driveway. A small group are encircling what appears to be a dead body. Someone is pulling down the dress, while others seem to protest the touching of the body. They are all waving their hands and gesturing wildly, everyone talking together. Several people stand away from the bunch, talking on cell phones. He realizes the police, a newspaper and several spouses are all likely hearing about the dead woman.

He walks back to the side where the vehicles are crushed together and looks over the side. Morgan's wasted figure is grotesque and morose in its final pose. Death always affects Drake, most certainly when it is by his own hand. He always searches his heart in these moments. He feels deeply that this killing was justified, in absolute defense. He is certain that his foes are cruel and deadly men with the world well rid of them. This eeriness of the aftermath troubles him, touches his humanity.

Deep in thought he has a fleeting hallucination as he stares at the shape forty feet below him. It twists, floats, transforms into a naked young woman. The vision stirs seeming so real. Scars and burns and cuts start appearing all over her body, she squirms and yells without a voice, her body spasms, then dies. The anatomy, once luscious, begins to wither and shrink...

"Drake, Drake, help me," comes a desperate plea. It fractures Drake's trance and Morgan's body comes back into focus. He returns to where Dakin lies trembling, his blood pressure dangerously low.

"I'm c-c-c-old Drake."

There is a folded tarp in the cab of the truck. Drake pockets his gun, grabs the tarp. Unfolding it, he covers his ailing friend. Retrieving a discarded jacket from the cab, he places it under Dakin's head. Dakin closes his eyes, fatigue overcoming him. His breathing is shallow but regular.

Drake pulls his cell from his pocket and speed-dials Rae. She answers on the first ring,

"Drake, is that you?"

"Yes, Rae. Call an ambulance quickly. Do it on your way here. We're going to need your connections on this one. Dakin is down and he's failing fast. Tell them it's life and death and they need to hurry."

As she listens to the location Drake is describing, Rae's shoulder's drop when she thinks of what has happened to Dakin. She was starting to like his swagger. She stiffens and asks, "What about you Drake?"

"I'm fine. We got one of them, Rae. Unfortunately he's dead. Another one escaped. We're no farther ahead right now though. I'm hoping your connections and mine can give us some direction."

He checks on Dakin; his breathing is shallow but even. He is mumbling but his shivering has stopped.

"Is it self-defense Drake? Is it obvious?"

Drake looks back over his shoulder at the wrecks behind him and responds with some irony,

"Oh yeah, I think they'll see that we were attacked."

"We have no choice now; we're going to have to let the authorities know what we're doing. Bitan Chowdhury is a stickler for protocol, but he also has an open mind about police work," says Rae.

Drake brushes aside his longish forelock, running his hand through his hair. His clothes are filthy from slithering across the floor beneath cars. His face is smudged with an oily stain where his cheek has scuffed the pavement.

"Get here quickly, Rae, please, so we can take care of Dakin. We'll get him good care. Isaac and Elijah will be here tomorrow and they're able men."

She informs Drake she'll call for the ambulance and head over. After making the call she grabs the keys to her truck, which she had found earlier on the coffee table in Drake's room where she and Rafan were asked to wait. She says to Rafan, "Stay here. Don't open the door unless it's Drake or me. Keep it locked. We'll be back soon."

"Okay, I need to rest anyway. Is everything okay? You seem excited."

"There's a problem. Drake and Dakin are in a little bind and I'm going to assist them, that's all. Don't worry about anything."

Rafan settles back onto the couch, increasing the TV's volume as he watches some comedian make a fool of himself.

She checks the firearm Dakin traded with her before replacing it in the pocket of the dark grey cotton jacket she has purchased in one of the boutiques in the hotel lobby. She needed a cover and paid too much because of the store's "boutigue-ness" and its clientele. She dons the light windbreaker and heads out the door.

She speed walks through the lobby, through the parking lot, reaching her truck, which has been cooking in the sun since mid-afternoon. When she opens the door she is welcomed with a hot whiff of stale air. She ignites the engine and when the V-8 responds she put the AC on full. The cold air is circulating by the time she leaves the parking lot to head southwest to the address Drake gave her. She knows the building anyway. Her work often takes her to that area when she contracted government assignments.

She dials Inspector Chowdhury on the private cell number he had given her when he reminded her of Taj's previous assistance. It rings a dozen times with no answer. It's after 7 p.m. after all. As she shifts about in the traffic, she closes the phone, reopens it and hits redial. It rings seven times before a disgruntled voice barks over the line, "Chowdhury here and this better be good. I was at bat and doing quite well, so this disruption had better prove worthy."

Rae gulps before she speaks, "Inspector, its Mireille. I apologize for interrupting you, but it's urgent. You were right earlier today when you said I hadn't been up front with you. I was operating under client confidentiality, but this is becoming too big. My client is trying to find one of the world's deadliest men and bring him to justice…"

She is interrupted. "A vigilante, is that right?" She recognizes his distaste.

"No, no, Bitan. He's a finder like me, like Taj. We just want to locate him, turn him over to you. Nonetheless, there has been an incident. We need your help on this; this could be a terrific break for you, Chowdhury, if you're able to nab this man. Help us and the credit is all yours."

She waits, listening to the buzz of the cell phones. Chowdhury is thinking.

"Okay, no promises on my end though until I get the full picture. Is that a promise from you, Rae?"

"Yes, Bitan, I promise. I will inform my client of our agreement before you meet with him. One of our men is down."

"Are there any other bodies?" "Unfortunately, yes. One of the culprits that started the shootout is dead."

"Then, I expect it will be self-defense again, Rae?" asks Chowdhury with mockery in his voice.

"Of course, Bitan. We don't start fights."

"No of course not, Mireille, not you. Ha! I expect that if there have been gunshots, someone's called the police already so I'll contact the responding department and tell them I will be commanding the scene. Now what is the address?"

She gives it to him as well as her ETA before closing her phone. As she speeds along the streets, her mind wanders to the big American. His jocularity reminded her of Taj. When she met him at the airport this morning she had softened in the presence of his southern boy smile and for a swift moment thought of what it might be like to be wrapped in his strong arms, to have someone handsome and bold protecting her. Since Taj had died, she often considered that there would be no other man in her life.

This man, though, provokes her, causing stirrings that had been hibernating. When he found out she was a PI and going to work with them, he had asked for one of her business cards and she remembered his touch as he slid it from her palm. Her skin tingled at the memory. As she drives she thinks of the big blond, his curly locks dominating his forehead, green eyes sparkling with mischief and she prays that he will be all right.

Chapter 15   9:20pm Detective South Branch, Dhaka

Drake leans against the wall of Inspector Chowdhury's office and crosses his arms. He had been sitting in the same chair Mireille had occupied the day before, telling Chowdhury of the events of the last three years. He had been speaking for over an hour when he had gotten up to stretch half way through, his muscles taut from the day's action and frustration. He had paced about the office as he related the rest of his story before leaning back against the wall.

The Inspector had interrupted occasionally for clarification on some points of Drake's narrative but mostly sat unmoving, wrapped up in the details. Drake began by telling Chowdhury of finding Amber and Sakeema, who they were, the condition their bodies were found in. In those very first sentences, Bitan learnt a great deal about the stranger in his office. When Drake had been itemizing the girls' terrible wounds, he had choked up. Chowdhury, who had been listening while writing his own notes, had looked up at Drake when he had gone quiet. The man was looking him directly in the eyes, not downcast, not covert, and not ashamed. Chowdhury could tell the effort it was taking Drake not to blink. The inspector stared back only for a second, dropping his gaze out of respect. He continued to write when Drake speaks again, stops writing and drops his pencil. The notes can wait, he believes, and listens intently.

"So you see, Inspector, every trail we follow has always led us back to Central America, but it goes cold when you set foot on the isthmus. He could be in the Honduras, Belize, Panama, Guatemala, we don't know. All we know is that he's involved in something here in Dhaka. Men, we can safely assume work for him, are chasing one of the slain girls cousin's, who by the freakiest chance heard someone speak Rizzato's name."

"Why didn't you contact someone in our departments when you arrived"? He asks, his English precise, his accent euphonic.

"Well, as I told you earlier, law enforcement agencies have not been effective in finding Rizzato. It has always been an international screw-up, with arguments over jurisdiction. The girls were in Venezuela, so agents there are involved. The girls were foreigners, one American, one Saudi Arabian living in the U.S.A. on a student visa, so those countries are involved. Bartolommeo Rizzato is a wanted man in several countries, so when his name popped up, they all got involved. Now your people will be involved. Do I need to go on, Inspector? Can't you see the bureaucratic mess? We had originally planned to do this on our own. But Rae is right, it's important for us to stay on the right side of the law. I think we need to work together. I have good people with me and we can find him. Let us bring him in."

Chowdhury gives this idea some thought. He muses that Alexander is probably correct for he knows how red tape can slow down the process when multiple forces are involved. Goodness knows there are too few detectives now for all the investigations to be done.

The Inspector has seen a lot over the years, insensitivity, depravation, cruelty, lies, amongst many things. But his sense of honesty, of a man's personal honor has not curdled over the years. He looks up at Drake, who is leaning against the wall. His arms are crossed but his chin rests heavily on his chest, eyes closed, features sedate. Chowdhury wonders if it is fatigue or the peace that comes from a complete confession, a sharing of your burden that makes the man so calm.

He studies Alexander for a moment. The man reminds him of a steed, a quarter-horse in its prime. Perhaps it would be wise to allow this man his "private investigation." Chowdhury believes this man, believes in the depth of his furor and believes in Rae. He sifts through the documentation he's received on Drake. Honorable discharge, commendations, mostly for his leadership abilities and acts of bravery. Absolutely no criminal record, an abstract so clean it defies possibility. His only black mark was the string of speeding tickets he has accumulated over the last ten years. The man must always be in a hurry.

Chowdhury interrupts Drake's reverie.

"Mr. Alexander, sit for a moment."

Drake hesitates; he wants to get this interview over with, to keep searching for Rizzato, not to get comfortable.

"Please, what I want to tell you won't take long. It will better explain why I feel we should cooperate." He unsteepled his hands and waves Drake to a more comfortable chair in the corner, to the right of his desk.

Drake is encouraged by the word cooperate and sits in the chair, which is obviously the Inspector's thinking spot: pipes, tobacco, ashtray, reading glasses, a magnifying glass, all are within easy reach. Like the rest of the office, everything is neatly arranged and spotless.

Chowdhury leans back in his chair; the rocker strains from lack of lubricant and gave a shrill dissent. He points to a large photo hanging over the wooden filing cabinets that claim most of the wall to Drake's right. Drake has to lean forward to see it clearer. There are four men in yellow and green cricket uniforms, obviously celebrating some victory. The man on the far left – one arm around his fellow player, the other arm lifting a magnum of champagne, bubbles fizzing over the neck – is Chowdhury. The other three are similarly gleeful, which is evident in their ear-to-ear smiles and victorious hand gestures.

"The man on my immediate left is Taj Al-Khuri, who was Rae's husband. We were great game mates and quite possibly the closest I've ever came to having what you might consider a "best friend." Taj was a man I greatly admired but could never emulate. He wasn't much for rules, as I suspect you aren't either. But he was always a man of the law; he walked the line many times but never, not even once, stepped over. He couldn't be bought, couldn't be coerced and couldn't be stopped once his mind was made up. Had he been a... toady I think the British call it, he would have certainly outranked even me, at an earlier age, he was really quite clever and a damn good detective."

The Inspector twists in his chair, his imagination sending his words off on a tangent, "I still can't get over the senseless way he died, how some businessman got the best of him, Taj was so much smarter than that..." He only ponders the idea for a few seconds, "Alas, he is dead and we will never know those last moments of his fruitful life, but we do know he married a sensational woman who is just like him. They were a wonderful team, always in love, always together. Poor, poor Mireille. It took her a long time to get over the ordeal."

He pushes himself away from the desk, rolling on whispering wheels, and rises from his creaking chair. He grabs the chair back and rocks it each way twice, the spring creaking a bit. "I must oil that soon," he reminds himself. He reaches for Drake's sidearm, which is resting on the corner of his desk. He picks it up along with the half empty cartridge and gives it back to Drake.

"Now, what I want to say to you, Mr. Alexander is this: Taj and I had a bond, a bond of trust, both officially and personally. I doubt very much that I shall ever attain a comrade such as him again; if I do it will most likely be his widow. But I am not an easy man to get close to. However, I'm not made of stone either. It is because of these two that I will entrust you to do your 'private investigating.' I had a chat with Rae earlier today, as you know. I am also acquainted with Uday Saad, albeit not well enough to have been aware of his daughter's plight. The people you are associated with, I hold in high regard. Therefore, you are free to carry on".

Drake is relieved to be able to leave; he wants to get to the hospital to check on Dakin.

"Thank you Inspector and I..."

"But," said the Inspector, interrupting Drake. He walks over to the cabinets the picture hangs above and waves Drake over. When Drake joins him, he points to the man on the far right of the picture and says, "Tomorrow this man will join you, and he will be like flypaper. Are you familiar with flypaper, Mr. Alexander? Extremely sticky stuff, flypaper."

Chowdhury grins at his metaphor and doesn't wait for an answer.

"His name is Gurupada Bannerji, some people call him Pada. I am assigning this case to him. He or Rae will liaise with me, keeping me informed as to your progress. Is that clear?"

The scrunched eyebrows and heavy frown on Chowdhury's face indicate his seriousness; this is not a negotiable issue. Drake nevertheless makes an attempt to dissuade the inspector, "I don't think we need a babysitter, Inspector. Rae knows her way around. My men and I are familiar with each other and I'm not comfortable with adding an unknown to our efforts. You've seen what we are up against. I'm not sure a desk jockey is a good idea."

Chowdhury grunts and goes back to his desk, "I can assure you, Mr. Alexander that Mr. Bannerji is no desk jockey. He is one of the top three shooters on the police force, both with a pistol and a sniper rifle. He is a practitioner of Haidong Gumdo. He is an all-rounder in cricket, being an exceptional batsman and bowler. He can be brutal if necessary. And he is single, which means he will be able to assist you twenty-four hours a day. I can guarantee that if push comes to shove, Mr. Alexander, Bannerji will be a valuable asset. I also need to remind you that you are short one man at present, with your comrade – who would be in some trouble for carrying side arms without a permit were it not for Rae and me – is in hospital."

Chowdhury sits in his corner chair and reaches for his pipe. He speaks as he fills it and tamps the tobacco, "I'm going to insist on this Drake, or your investigation will come to a quick end. I also expect that you will stick to the investigating and leave the arresting to us. Of course, I anticipate you will need to defend yourself in certain situations, but I don't wish for you to provoke anyone. Don't endanger my people or yours."

He hesitates before lighting the pipe, then looks up at Drake, who is still standing beside the filing cabinets.

"I don't think there is anything else to discuss, Mr. Alexander. I have your cell number and Bannerji will be in touch with you in the morning. May I tell him you are an early riser?"

Drake realizes Chowdhury has the advantage and that submitting to his proposal will make searching for Rizzato much easier.

"Fine Inspector, I agree to your conditions and look forward to meeting Mr. Bannerji. I'm available anytime he or you need me. Thanks for your cooperation. If you could arrange for someone to drive me to the hospital, I would appreciate it."

"Go wait at the entrance and one of my men will escort you. Oh, and I trust you will see to the rental that was destroyed, as well as the other vehicles. I'm certain the rental company won't be pleased and I'd rather they didn't have to bother us over this matter.".

He places a match to the packed bowl of his pipe, sucking in the flame. Thin plumes of aromatic smoke move gently about the room. Drake recognizes Borkum Riff, the same brand his father had smoked, the one with the whiskey flavor. A calm comes over him, a reassurance of something familiar.

"I take full responsibility for the vehicles. I'll personally see that the rental people are compensated. Is there anything else Inspector? If not, I'll bid you a good evening."

Their eyes lock for a moment. There is mutual respect there.

"Good night then, Mr. Alexander. Go cautiously."

**

Drake enters the Square Hospital on Panthapath Road through the emergency entrance. It is a for-profit medical center rising sixteen handsome floors. A circular wall two or three rooms wide, the top half all bluish glass, fronts the modern building. The lower levels spread to the right and left of the tower, divided horizontally by stripes of similar glass. It's an engaging building.

Drake approaches the information personnel, whom he is happy to find speaks exceptional English, their accent beguiling him. He is informed that Mr. Dakin Rush is in surgery at this moment. They are uncertain how much longer he might be. They direct him to the fifth floor, which houses a surgical complex with eight operating theatres, an intensive care unit, recovery rooms, labs and a pharmacy. There is a small waiting room tucked in the northeast corner for family, that he has been invited to visit since he is Rush's only connection in Dhaka. He is also informed that a Ms. Lambert is there already.

Rae had been at Dakin's side until the doctors had removed her from the emergency room. She had tailgated his gurney right to the treatment station, pleading with the medical staff to save his leg, to save him.

Drake joins the bevy of staff and patients working their way to the elevators. The lobby is quite crowded even though it's late in the evening, after ten. All the elevators are used for freight and patient transfer so are quite large, semi-mirrored on the side walls. Images of the crowd repeat itself into infinity. The bell rings for the fifth floor and when the doors slide open Drake moves around the lady in front of him, exiting the cubicle. To his right is a polished reception area. Walls the color of lemons, with peach and light green accents, and furniture make it cheerful. If he didn't know better, Drake thinks, he might be in the executive offices of a cosmetic company, not a hospital.

The lady at the desk has no more info on Dakin beyond what he has learned downstairs: the patient is in theatre and if Drake chooses to wait, he will be advised of the outcome by the attending physician. She points out the waiting area returning to her duties. Drake strolls down the hallway a short distance. Clinical smells creep from closed doors that separate the operating rooms and labs from the reception area. An open door at the end of the hallway offers a room for waiting and worrying. Even the light gray walls look worried. Several people sit about, several pace the room; anxiety occupies all the empty spaces.

In the far right corner near the magazine rack, Rae sits shuffling through a thick journal. Her legs are crossed, the top one see-sawing her impatience. She senses Drake before she hears him, looking up to see him approach. She is touched by the look of concern in his face. She tosses the magazine on the Formica cube that serves as an end table, rising to give him a reassuring hug that things will be okay.

"Thank you, Rae, for staying with Dakin. Can you tell me what's happened?"

"Oh Drake, he was in such bad shape when they finally got him here. I was so worried. They stabilized him with IVs and blood transfusions. The doctor explained to me that they were going to patch him up. Dakin was lucky, the bullet just nicked the thigh bone or he would've been really messed up for a while. And that's all I know. How did it go with Chowdhury? I know we did the right thing, Drake, by being open with him."

"Yeah, you were right. The law has never been much help in the past, but hey, things change. Anyway, I'm glad to hear Dakin is going to be okay. I can't imagine him taking too long to heal properly, not that guy. He's too restless. We'll make sure he has the best care."

They are interrupted by a hush as a doctor, still in his scrubs, enters the room. One of the pacers and two of the sitters rush to greet him at the door. The three are shocked by the doctor's silence and somber face. At that moment, everyone in the room knows that whomever he was working on has not made it. The older woman of the trio begins sobbing and wailing. The young woman tries to comfort her. The older man grips them both and follows the doctor into the hallway. The ensuing silence lingers for a few seconds. Because the grief belongs to someone else, the room returns to its previous mood.

Drake gives Rae a nod toward the door and strides from the room. Silently she follows him to the elevator, up to the sixth floor cafeteria. Each grab a coffee, Drake adding a day old ham and cheese sandwich to the tray; he pays and they sit at an offside table. Sitting across from each other, Drake is unwrapping his late night snack as he asks, "By the way, do you know Gurupada Bannerji?"

"Pada! Yes, I do, although not really well. He was one of Taj's team members from his cricket days. They often worked together on the force, but we never socialized with him. Why do you ask?"

"He's going to be working with us. How does that go down with you?"

"I don't have a problem with it. Taj always said he was a good cop, a good detective. I know he's always playing with wooden swords in his spare time, practicing some martial art; he's won some awards I think. How do you feel about it?"

"If he's as able as Chowdhury claims and you vouch for him, that's good enough for me. I'll look forward to meeting him tomorrow, which is going to be a busy day for us. The other guys will be here, we meet Bannerji, recap and recon. My gut tells me we're close. We just need to consolidate our information and leads. Maybe you'd like to go home and get some rest? I can stick around here."

"No I'd like to stay if you don't mind. I like the man and I'd like to know how he's doing. If anyone needs some rest, it's you; it's been nonstop all day. Is it always this rough everywhere you go, Drake?"

Rae gives him a smile. Small lines appear at the outer edges of her eyes, like quotation marks stressing her pretty looks. Drake notices a different hue to her skin, more confidence in her gaze. He has seen this before when Dakin is involved. He cares for both of them enough that he feels he should warn her,

"*Il cassera ton coeur*, Mireille, "he says (he'll only break your heart).

They spend the next twenty minutes discussing the merits and pains of relationships. Rae explains to Drake how she feels, how she still feels about Taj. They talk about their own disappointments, their triumphs, life's trickery and the magic of happiness. He tells her of Beth, how knotted their connection is. They both agree there is never an easy way.

Rae leans back in her chair, concentrating on the empty coffee cup, at sea for a moment. She remembers Dakin smiling as she approached his hand sign at the airport and says, "It's after midnight so you should get going, I'll wait and call you in the morning, I really don't mind Drake," her voice becomes softer, more lush as she adds, "*J'aurais besoin d'un ami, maintenant, Drake. Je pense que je vais prendre une chance.*" I need a good friend now Drake, I'm going to take a chance."

Drake stands and stretches his long arms. "Okay, I understand, and yeah, it is late. I still want to speak to Williston, so I'm going to head out. Please call me as soon as you know anything about Dakin, no matter what time it is. But definitely call me around nine. We're going to keep digging, Rae, until we find this man. There's a lot to do."

He walks around the cafeteria table and gives Rae a pat on the shoulder on his way out, saying, "Don't ever say that I didn't warn you."

Chapter 16

Aug 23   8:30am 15kms upriver from Bhola, Bangladesh

Plum, Malik and Raheem are scouting the periphery of the land Rizzato has assigned them to. At the moment, they're following the shoreline of the Bhola River, which forms one of the boundaries. The operation has acquired about 200 acres of farmlands, several houses and scarce forest acreage along a sharp bend in the river before it flows southeast to the community of Bhola. The land in this section is thick with banyan and pulm, hizal and karamcha trees, housed in universal greens. They are about a mile from their base. The land fronts the river for several miles on each side of the wharf they have repaired and reinforced. A metal framed warehouse stands at the land's end. Graffiti and rust are competing for space on the siding. The storage shed has been neglected since the small group of farmers had dissolved their collective, abandoning the family-owned plots many years ago. The cities of Chittagong and Dhaka consume them, by the thousands.

They come to the dock. Plum waves the men off to take a break and walks out onto the landing. Hajani gives her a raised middle finger when she turns her back, reaching for his smokes with the other. He and Raheem join the two men who are replacing the most damaged and rusted metal siding on the warehouse. The hiss of the torch as it cuts through the oxidized rivets joins the concert of chatter and the banging of a hammer. The bouquet of burnt metal blending with the ammonia of the river gives the restless air an industrial perfume. For a moment, as Plum watches the water swell and flutter as it moves downriver, the smell reminds her of the Port of Los Angeles. She hates that port, she hates L.A.

She sits at the end of the wharf, her feet dangling over the edge with the water seven feet below her. Had she known how odd an attractive Japanese woman might look here in the Bangladesh countryside, sitting in the morning sun, she may have been more careful in the spot she choose to reminisce. Workboats ply the waterway, several of which move slowly up river toward Bhola. One of the boats that work regularly between Bhola and Dhaka makes the trip beyond this bend several times a week. The owner, a Chinese merchant named Bohai Xu, upon espying Plum lazing on the pier, comments to his first mate that there are many strangers in this area of late, especially the little Japanese girl he points to. He remarks that there is much activity at this old wharf and he is curious as to what is going on. He watches her until he loses sight of her when his boat moves around the bend. Plum is oblivious to the merchant's scrutiny as she gazes at the water, her memories catching up.

**

Plum, whose real name is *Ume*, a Japanese word for that delectable fruit, chose the English version after she married her second husband, Rudolph Steele. Her father, who had been a gardener, exclaimed upon seeing his newborn daughter that she was as pretty as a plum blossom and named her Ume. Her mother, a homemaker, died of tuberculosis when Plum was only five. As an only child growing up in the Boyle Heights district of

Los Angeles, east of Little Tokyo, she mixed with the Latinos populating the area while spending an inordinate amount of time in the Flats, one of the most impoverished areas of L.A. She learnt more about survival from the gutter kids than she did from her father.

With help from the neighbors, he tried to raise his rebellious daughter. But because he was self-employed, his days were long, often beginning at daybreak when he would load his spades, hoes, rakes and garden tools into the back of his patched-up Toyota, often ending only after dark. He usually got home tired and cranky, paying little attention to Plum other than to her basic needs.

The little girl, left mostly alone, avoided school as much as possible, often taking to the streets, following the small gangs the roamed about the neighbourhoods. Kids, similarly neglected, formed clusters, the smaller ones learning how to swear, to steal, to run, to lie. For some it was their only means of existence; for others like Plum, it was a fantasy, an escape from some lonely life.

The police brought her home one evening when she was twelve. She had been gone for two weeks. She had been caught stealing some fruit. She would be given this *one* chance. Before they left, the police made Mr. Ishikawa promise he would supervise his daughter better. If he didn't, he could lose her.

She was filthy, wearing a man's red and green plaid shirt over a stained pink T-shirt, khaki denim jeans with both knees ragged and torn, mud and garbage stained sneakers that were trying to be red. Her father was horrified, not only over her appearance but the fact that his daughter was the first Ishikawa to be brought home by the police. He would lose much face with his neighbors.

When the police left he shouted at her that she was worthless, ungrateful. He told her how hard he worked and that he only wanted her to be good. She shouted back that she was always alone, that he didn't care. They argued until he slapped her, hard, across her slender face. They had been standing in the kitchen and she staggered from the blow. Tripping on the leg of the butcher block, she fell backwards toward the stove, hitting her head on the oven handle. The sharp whack rendered her unconscious.

When she came to she was tied to a rollaway cot in the utility room of their basement. Her mouth had been taped shut. Lifting her aching head, she watched her father as he carried items from the room. Several hours later, when the room was bare, he brought in several large basins of hot water, soap, shampoo, towels and clean clothes, then food. Leaving it all on the floor near the door, he walked over to her and tore the tape from her mouth. She swore at him with hate and pain until he slapped her again, driving her tiny head sideways, almost twisting her neck. Amid her groans and sobbing tears, he told her,

"Here you will stay until you are good," he said, and nothing else. He reached over and untied one hand. Turning his back on his daughter, he left and locked the door.

The first time he raped her was two months later, when she turned thirteen. The fourth time he raped her, another three months later, she drove a rusty spike in his ear just as he closed his eyes – as he always did – when he came. He spasmed and jerked as she forced him from her body, tumbling him to the floor. He soon became still as she watched him die.

She stared at his corpse for a few moments, filled with hate. She left the basement finally, heading out to the tool shed. Inside by the lawnmower was a gerry-can half full of gasoline. She took it into the house and poured the gas on the furniture in the living room. She packed a modest backpack, searched the house for anything she could carry and sell.

While going through her father's closet, she pushed the clothing to the left and found a hidden shelf. On it was one of those large glass jars that restaurants or hospitals bought pickles in. Inside the bottle, wrapped in a chamois, was just over four thousand dollars. She stuffed the bill-laden cloth into her backpack.

Before she went back downstairs to throw blankets and chairs on the gas stained carpet, adding fuel to be sure it all burned, she added a picture of her mother to the bag she was carrying.

It was early, just before six a.m. She tore down a sheer from the living room windows and rolled it lengthwise like a cigarette, laying one end on the gas soaked rug tucked under one of the wooden chairs she had piled in the room. The other end was closer to the kitchen, away from the fumes. She gathered several layers of the fabric, isolating them from the other rolled layers. She cut a small hole in the layers and placed them over a candle in a short holder so that there was about three inches of candle above the fabric. Before leaving, she would light the candle. It would take about two hours for the candle to burn down enough to catch the flimsy curtain on fire. By then she planned to be as far away as possible.

She would've taken the truck, but she didn't know how to drive. Instead she set out on foot and slipped into the world. Her father was the first man she ever killed but would not be the last.

**

As her thoughts return to the present, Plum checks the Sampan as it wobbles by the pier. One of the carpenters has built a traditional roof over the hold of the boat not only to keep the elements away but for privacy as well. It reminds her of a covered wagon. She notices there were wooden pallets in the hold along with several grey, dirty tarps. She knows that Morgan and several of the workers had been here earlier removing the last of the lumber from their previous trip.

She had awoken around 7 a.m. that morning. After a quick shower, she had dressed in dark blue denim jeans, a white T-shirt and an army vest in which she kept her weapons and essentials; she is definitely not a purse person. She had headed out from the small farmhouse that the security staff occupied. When she came out into the yard, she scanned the area they had been working in for the last three to four weeks.

The river is about 100 meters to her right and ran east to west along the northern border. It isn't visible from the farm as trees separate the land and water. There are three dirt lanes coming and going from a central point in the yard, one twists along to the wharf about 400 meters away; the other goes directly to the fields that are lying fallow in the southern section. The third leads to the main road a quarter mile to the west.

There are several outbuildings that had been in disrepair but rejuvenated to accommodate the eighteen workers Rizzato has brought to work on the runway. She had been informed that many of them had been scavenged from somewhere called the Breakers; others were what Rizzato had called "untouchables," nobodies from Dhaka. They had all been given work boots and two pairs of denim coveralls, possessions they prized. From a distance they all look like clones, their only distinguishing features are the crazy-colored shirts they wore. A 24 x 24 foot canvas tent houses the cooks who prepare mounds of food. A shower has been set up in the vacated greenhouse. Most of the workers think they are on vacation; they're happy and they work hard.

A larger building of new wood forms a hangar that is almost complete, only the last set of large doors to be finished on the front. Inside is a dull red AT-502A, an Air Tractor crop duster that is being assembled from the crates they had carted in last month. The plane is facing the rear of the building, which faces the runway. The back of the fuselage is visible from the yard. There is no rudder on it yet; the elevators are slack without their cables attached, same as the ailerons and the flaps on the wings. The engine compartment is exposed, its metal clothing set aside. The turboprop engine is propped on an impromptu frame beside workbenches that litter the right side of the building. Several workers are already tinkering with it.

The beginning of the runway starts at the back of the building and runs south for about 400 feet. Several hundred feet of cleared forest stretches beyond the hard packed dirt that is being laid down for the aircraft. The workers are broken into several teams. The youngest and hardiest make up the group that is clearing the trees. The rest of the laborers toil with the mounds of dirt being dug up from a vacant pit situated not far from the other farm two miles down the main road, where Rizzato maintains his headquarters. Bunker, Morgan and Kovalenko, the Ukrainian mechanic in charge of the plane assemblage, stay there also.

Plum is in charge of this section, with Raheem and Hajani to do her bidding, which they of course resent. Their role is to keep an eye on the workers to make sure none escape. Eager to work, naïve and uneducated, the workers are very cooperative; they are well fed, clothed and paid, so there is no problem with runaways. They believe the story that was told to them when they were recruited. Their employer is part of a pipeline for illegal drugs destined for Europe. Most of them smoked cannabis and don't care. They have no idea they are in a prison, nor that there will never be any parole. Plum also has to patrol the perimeter to keep the nosy and unwanted out. So far it has only been a small group of local boys that have had to be escorted away two weeks ago. After breakfast she had rounded up the two Pakistanis and headed out for a patrol along the edge of the property.

The water below the wharf where she sits is constantly moving, rippling, hypnotizing, and it matches her melancholy mood. She's sad this morning, tired of being on the run. She is burdened that her brief life has been meaningless. During the last few months, in her own self-pity, she has actually considered suicide. Her life has been rough. She had prostituted herself when she was younger in order to stay alive. There were always lots of men around the port.

The only man she had cared about was the captain of the freighter that eventually took her away from a lonely life. He fell ridiculously in love with her when she was only eighteen, he forty-two, extricating her from a sordid existence by marrying her and installing her on his ship. She sailed the world with him for several years; it had been the only happiness she had known.

Pirates in the Gulf of Aden ended that fantasy. The crew were slaughtered, the freighter diverted and Ume became a whore once more. The Somalis abused her. It was on this ship that she killed her second man, then a third and fourth. Anything was a weapon for Plum, a fork, scissors, a board, whatever she could reach. She would scheme and when the opportunity came, she was overtaken by a killing frenzy. Her sudden fury would bewilder her opponents. She recognized and seized that moment to strike.

Many days had passed after they had stolen the ship, at least four she thought. For several hours now, the ship had slowed and finally stopped. She figured they were at anchor or in port. She knew they were not going to let her live. It didn't matter, she would rather drown than let these savages touch her again, she told herself. She had stolen a fork from her lunch tray earlier by distracting the young boy who brought her meals by fondling him. Now she grasped the utensil handle in her tiny fist, tines pointed away from her thumb at the bottom of her hand, four blunt stainless-steel stabbing tips. She raised her arm, brandishing her measly weapon and waited by the door for whoever would be bringing her supper shortly.

Ten minutes later, it was the one who called himself Korfa, the one she detested the most. His organ was huge and he always hurt her. He was a long, gangly man; her outstretched arm would just reach his neck. When he unlocked the door, the key in one hand, a food tray in the other, she launched herself at him. She brought her arm back for the most leverage and rushed him, striking out with the fork. The shock of a naked screaming banshee coming at him froze Korfa to the spot. The inch and a half dull points plunged through muscle and flesh, splitting the carotid artery of his neck with two piercing holes. Blood spurted with each beat.

He dropped the keys, tray and food, grasping at his neck. The fork was all bloody and his hands slipped over the shiny metal. As he staggered from fright, Ume grabbed the baton from the belt he always wore. With all the hostility she could muster, she swung it in into his exposed gut. The baton had a weighted end and she held it like a baseball bat when she swung. She hit him at the base of his ribcage, breaking three of the primary ribs, which pierced both of his lungs. The force of the blow jarred her skinny arms.

Korfa was in tremendous pain, he doubled over pawing at his chest, blood dripping from his neck, when she delivered the final blow. For one brief, brief moment, Ume saw all the men who had fucked her up in this one pathetic, panting creature. She sensed a justice to what she was doing. She raised the stick as high as her scrawny arms allowed and struck him in the back of his skull. The heavy end buried itself in his head, smashing his brain into puree. When he slammed into the floor, his head claimed her club and pulled it from her hands. She backed away, astonished by her fury, the dead man on the floor, and the club embedded in his head. She looked to the open door. She knew she would have to act quickly if she planned on escaping.

She took his jacket, his pants would never fit. She stole his sandals as well, for he had unusually small feet. She stared down at the corpse and spit on him, telling him he was the sorriest asshole she had ever met. She put her foot on his head and pulled the baton from his skull. It came away with a squish. She cleaned it off with his t-shirt before she left the room. Before she made it to the main deck at the front of the ship, she had killed two more men with the same weapon. Most of the crew were at supper, so few were about. When she glanced over the port side, she saw lights on the beach guessing them to be about 300 meters away.

She had no idea where she was or how many people were around, but she never hesitated. She chucked the jacket and the club to the deck, doffed the sandals and climbed up on the port side where the anchor chain exited the ship. She stood upon the rail, bent her boyish knees, pushed off with a girlish grunt and sliced through the air into the tropical waters eighteen feet below, mentally thanking her bastard father for the summer at the Y when she was eight.

She swam slowly, swimming in the direction of the lights but not directly towards them. There was shouting from the ship as the crew discovered the bodies. The resulting havoc aboard ship gave her more courage and perseverance. Forty-five minutes later, she sprawled naked upon the beach not far from Diba Al Hisn, an old fishing port within one of the seven emirates that comprise the United Arab Emirates. She was concealed by a moonless night.

She rested for several moments, shivering slightly from the dampness. She stared at the stars overhead, wishing she were that far away. Soon the need for warmth and clothing forced her to her feet. She stood upon the coarse sand of the beach, looking in all directions as she understood her predicament: she had no passport, she didn't know where she was, she was naked, and she was hungry. She only knew she couldn't head toward the lights, so she ran in the opposite directions until she came upon a fishing port. That was where she met Rudy Steel, who worked for Elias De Clerq.

**

The crackle of her radio brings Plum back to the waters of the Bhola. She lifts the mobile from its holster and says, "Plum here!"

Bunker tersely responds, "There's another one Plum, get rid of it," before he flicks off.

She curses to herself before saying to the water, "He's a sick motherfucker and we have to cover his tracks. What a bastard!"

She rises from the end of the pier yelling for the men, "Hey you guys get the Zodiac ready. We have work to do."

Hajani lights up and hastens to where the inflatable is moored. Motioning for Raheem to get the oars from the warehouse because the motor has been stalling lately, he tells him to hurry up. He knows Plum will want him at the helm after the adventure in Sadarghat. He climbs aboard and fiddles with the engine, checking the adjustments he made. Plum directs Raheem back to the warehouse for two of the cement blocks the crew has discarded from the old warehouse while she unravels lengths of used ropes they stored on the sampan.

Plum jumps in behind Hajani, who is in the driver's seat on the port side. She helps Raheem load the blocks, which have reddish mud caked around their openings. Raheem unties the rope holding the Zodiac to the wharf, and joins her in the second bench seat. The Pro 12-man is a red and white 17 footer boosted by a Yamaha ninety horsepower four stroke, great for patrolling the river and delivering small loads.

Raheem uses an oar to push them away from the wharf. When they float clear of the sampan, Hajani steers it out to the river and turns to Plum. "Where're we going?"

"Head downriver to the spot where we picked up that body about three weeks ago, by the tall pulm trees, and never mind the plum and pulm jokes. There's another body. I've been told to get rid of it" she tells them, mocking Bunker's bass-y Serbian accent.

"We do what we're told, right guys?"

Both men face her when they hear the disgust in her voice. They both know of her dislike for Rizzato's urges, the wasted lives. Her frenzy can be seen in her dilated pupils; they themselves couldn't care less.

Raheem, said, "Sure Plum, you know us. We're a team. We do whatever you tell us. So do you think it's another of Rizzato's playthings we're dumping?"

"I don't know and I don't care. I don't like this. Just get the blocks ready and be quiet."

Raheem starts to coil the rope through the muddied openings in the cement. He actually likes the slight Japanese girl, both exotic and American, not sexually for certain, as women hold no fascination for him in that regard. He's actually a bit scared of her and would be leery of hand-to-hand combat with her. He prefers her as an ally and is not put off by her briskness as Hajani often is.

They ride close to shore, the zodiac lifting its nose off the water as Hajani urges on the Yamaha. They cover the nautical mile downriver in less than ten minutes. As they approach the familiar landmarks on the port side, where a narrow path leads away from the river, Raheem removes a crudely folded ten by ten gray canvas tarpaulin from the boat's storage bin and places it on the floor in front of him and Plum. A rusty, dried-up blood stain in the lower left corner, just above the fold, gives testament to the cloth's morbid purpose. Plum remembers the young girl who had left her vital fluid there; she may have been thirteen or fourteen. In some odd way Plum is reminded of her stormy youth, the incident that had set her upon her current path of melancholy, with side streets of regret.

Raheem jumps from the Zodiac onto the edge of the river with one of the stern lines and pulls until the boat scrapes upon the hard-packed shore. Plum grabs the tarp and steps from the craft saying, "Give me a few minutes, guys. I'll signal when I need help."

Malik reminds her, "Plum, don't get too sentimental over these girls. They're homeless, nobody cares. Maybe she's better off. It's none of our business anyway."

"Getting rid of her is our business and I think this is senseless. We're working for a damn pervert. I'm telling you guys, when this job is done, I'm taking my cash and I'm disappearing, but for now let me show this... it's probably a child, a little bit of respect, even if it is too late."

She gives the two guys a nod, noticing they have softened somewhat when she had said child.

The beach is only six feet wide before it rises sharply for a little over four feet to the forest floor. A foot path winds from the rocky shore, extending through the tangled trees. Sixty feet from the water she comes to a meager clearing. Five elongated pulm trees form a half circle fenced by clinging shrubs; the other side is a mixture of bushes and young trees that shield the clearing from the river. The ground in the center is grassy and rock free. Several fallen logs form benches around the perimeter. A fire pit of broken bricks is to the extreme right of the opening and before it lays a small brown being. Plum walks over to the dead girl and stares at her wounded tender body. She doubts the girl had been dead for more than a couple of hours, left in the clearing by Bunker moments ago most likely.

Dried blood congeals around a stab wound on her back. From where it is located, just above the heart, Plum knows it would've killed her instantly. As she inspects the torso she notices the blood around her anus, eventually spotting the crude Z upon her slender shoulder. It is the same signature as the other body they had disposed of. When she had quizzed Bunker on its meaning, she had been told, in an extremely biting baritone to "mind her fucking business."

Plum stoops down and turns the head, studying the bruised face, trembling when she realizes the victim can't be more than twelve, probably less. Plum can be ruthless when she had to be and has only ever killed people who were trying to hurt her. She thinks it repulsive that Rizzato and Bunker kill for fun. Maybe even Morgan, too. She shakes her head to break her gaze, stands and spreads the tarp before the girl. At that very second, she experiences what she would later refer to as her epiphany. She regrets every sad moment of her life. She has grappled with pangs of guilt throughout her troubled life which she blames on her father. She decides she can be better than this, it might not be too late.

She rolls the tiny frame onto the tarpaulin and folds over the edges. The girl is only about four feet tall and the tarp is twice that. Plum folds the extra half over on top of the folds that encase the girl; she frowns when she sees that the body hardly makes a bulge. She rises to cross her arms as she concentrates on the shroud. It's quiet, the breeze has calmed, and no birds fly, as if the surrounding enclosure collectively gives a moment of silence. She gazes at the sky as she promises herself that by the New Year she will be gone, taking her money and going away, far away, throwing away the bad things in her life. With that resolve and plans already formulating, she yells out, "Raheem, come give me a hand here!"

She bends at one end of the gray cloth and tests the weight, stunned by how light it is.

Raheem comes running down the path and pauses when he sees Plum bent at the end of the tarp.

"Where is the body?"

"Believe it or not, she's inside. That's how small she is. Can you see how sick these fuckers are, Raheem?"

As he peers hard at Plum, his look speaks of the first kinship he has ever shown her, "I know Plum. I think it's sick, too. Morgan told me that this girl was from a family of the poorest of the poorest. They sold her for five U.S. dollars. They're sick too, Plum. Don't bust yourself up about it. It's Karma. And listen, we'll finish this gig in another couple of months and with 50 g's each, we can do whatever we want. And I have to remind you that anybody that would do that, to someone that never even hurt them, would fuck us over very badly if we were to get shaky on this."

Plum knows it's not good to be antagonistic. She understands that her freedom is coming after this caper, and she can last until then.

"You're right, Raheem. It's still a shame though. I don't care what they do after we're done here, but I hope we don't have to do this again, I hate it. Can you understand that?"

She doesn't wait for an answer; she nods at the opposite end of the canvas and says, "Grab the end and let's get this on the boat."

Raheem picks up his end with little effort, puts the rolled end under his arm, and leads the way back to the beach. When they leave the clearing, a raucous chorus erupts from the forest walls, local birds of all colors, all sizes, dive about their heads, screeching, shrilling as if exclaiming their indignation over the ritual below them. Some of them collide briefly and some feathers lose their grip to twirl about in the air. The birds express their displeasure for only a few moments before scattering at different altitudes. The churlish complaints put fear in the hearts of the two bearers and force them into a trot. Just before they break through to the beach Malik yells to them from the Zodiac, "Wait; go back. There's a boat coming."

He is standing on the shore ready to push off. The engine is pulled up as he pretends to tinker with it. His warning is too late and Raheem bursts from the tree line with one end of the bag in both arms. Plum's accomplice digs in his heels at the top of the rise but he's too close to the edge. He slides onto his ass, dropping the canvas wrap, and tumbles to the beach. Plum immediately arrests her movements and pulls the tarp back out of sight. The commotion is enough to catch the attention of the two local youths in a dingi they are paddling laboriously upstream. Dark floppy hair covers their heads making them look like two Asian shaggy dogs. Their naked chests gleam from the sun falling on their perspiration.

The boys have seen this boat before at the wharf and fantazise about owning it, planning which friends they would take for a ride. They see Raheem fall and burst out laughing, yelling at him to do it again. Raheem claims a bit of his pride by joining in on the laughter; soon Malik joins in, feigning his chortles. While the two boys never saw the tarp, Plum, Raheem and Malik have to assume they did. And that makes the boys a problem that will inevitably have to be dealt with. Watching the duo paddle away, Plum knows she has to tell Bunker, and that isn't going to be pleasant.

She curses, lamenting her bad luck.

They wait fifteen minutes before taking the body to the boat. After tucking it in, Raheem pushes them free of the sand out toward the channel before jumping in. The sun is high enough to blast away, heating up the earth. Plum helps Raheem tie a super tight loop around the layered edge of the canvas, both tugging and grunting until they are certain the knots will hold. Raheem ties the loose end of the six foot rope through the opening in the two cement blocks and ties another secure set of knots. He says, "The last time we did this we used four blocks, you sure this is enough Plum, how about you Malik?"

Plum tells him, "I guess she weighs about seventy pounds, another five pounds for the tarp, the blocks must weigh fifty pounds each, yeah, yeah, we're okay." She speaks to Malik, "Take us downriver to the next junction, away from any other boats, somewhere deep enough to sink this bundle. Okay?"

Malik replies in his usual way saying nothing. He's concentrating on the craft accelerating to half throttle. Malik is characteristically indifferent to their task, but he notes that the other two are acting differently. He supposes they had had an argument. He doesn't like Plum and resents her authority, so he doesn't care and joins the silence.

They cruise out for over ten nautical miles before they find a suitable space. The river is wide, over 500 meters. They are far away from any approaching boats. Malik turns the Zodiac upriver, idling the engine keeping the boat relatively calm. Plum picks up the oversized bricks and balances them on the side of the boat, careful not to puncture the plastic hide. The two men can't fail to see the tightened muscles along her arms, and both are suitably impressed.

"Grab the canvas, Raheem, and when I toss the rocks, you roll it out. Understand?"

"Yeah, I got it, just give me a second."

He reaches down for the center of the canvas and picks it up to rest it on the side toward the back of the boat, with Plum in the front. He holds the body with one hand and chucks the loose rope into the muddy river.

"Okay, whenever you're ready," he says.

Plum slides the stones slowly over the side and they start to sink rapidly, Raheem rolls the corpse-filled canvas into the water. They watch it sink for several seconds until the polluted waters consume it totally.

"Okay, let's head back, guys, and you two can finish patrolling the perimeter of the property. I have to tell Bunker about those kids. We'll meet back at the worker's farm at lunchtime."

Malik rammed the accelerator wide open. The craft rises in the front and blasts up the river. None of its occupants are aware of the mistake they had just made: when they had tied up the canvas holding the slain innocent, they had tied the rope so tight that no water could enter. The body is sealed into the soiled sac.

The first stage of human decomposition is *autolysis* or self-digestion; cells are destroyed by their own enzymes. The second stage is bloating. Bacteria in the gut break down body tissue, releasing gas that then accumulates in the intestines and that becomes trapped due to the early collapse of the small intestine.

The gases in this case will be sealed in the body, sealed in the bag. The back and forth movement of the tide will fray the rope on one of the blocks and become detached. The remaining block will not be heavy enough to keep the gas filled body down.

As fate would have it, it will be the weary Chinese man, Bohai Xu, who will find the floating canvas several days later.

Chapter 17   Sept 30   5:52am Dhaka

The pool at the Westin isn't "officially" open, but Drake has persuaded the night concierge that the solitude would be extremely beneficial to his frame of mind. He related the late night at hospital with his injured comrade, how a morning swim would help him think. The night manager explained that there were no lifeguards until 8:30; it would not be safe. In the end, it was a twenty dollar bill that gained him entrance. He's on his fifteenth lap, midway along the twenty meter pool. Wavelets follow him like spreading wings. His brawny figure severs the water sharply with steady even strokes.

The pool area is unlit save for two lamps at the deep end, a meter below the water line. The ripples above cast rhythmic shadows over the colored tiles festooning the walls. Geometric shapes, both western and Muslim repeat themselves around the ambit of the pool. The back end is cast in shadow – the windows along one side displaying the faltering night. The hiss of an air conditioner drones in the background, giving the early morning some white noise. The silence is interrupted softly each time Drake takes a breath. He takes quick gulps almost as regularly as the beating of his heart. Every muscle is working to propel him along the length of the pool. The ocean had been his playground most of his life; he'd been swimming since he was four.

He would swim 100 laps before he quit – two kilometers.

Rae had called him as she had left Dakin's room to tell him the operation has been successful. He is elated with Dakin's recovery. He ponders on his friend for a while but is soon concentrating on the information Williston has passed on to him when they spoke six hours ago. The possible link between De Clerq and Rizzato puzzles him, are they working in Dhaka together, and is it an arms deal? He can't make sense of it all.

Then there's the body in London, one of the nobility no less, with an identical mark on his shoulder as the one they are pursuing. A friend of Williston's brother Al, works in the police department in London and knowing from the brother's inquiries about the mark has brought it to their attention. It is being kept hush-hush as it was not known to most that Sir Richard Whitecastle had gambling problems, which police feel are related to the killing and the grisly signature. Rumors had often been circulated, but because of his exceptional reputation and record as an ambassador, they were dismissed as nonsense.

Williston's diggers have confirmed Whitecastle's debts. Drake doesn't understand how they do that but doesn't care either; he just wants to know every aspect concerning the dead man. The authorities suspect a local crime syndicate with a rep for gambling and prostitution. Unfortunately their leads all came to dead ends.

There has been no connection of the mark in London to any other homicides yet even though Whitecastle was killed back in May. Maybe the London police aren't looking for any association. Drake fears he will have to share that with Chowdhury, he really doesn't want others involved, but he knows they likely will be. And the man is being more than fair with him, plus Bannerji will be working with them. He is frustrated that with all the action of the last twenty-four hours, there still isn't any sign of Rizzato. He is desperately impatient; he wants to pick up the crook's trail as quickly as possible. He begins to plan his day, not knowing the chase is going to take him longer than he imagines.

Seventy-five laps later, he crawls from the tepid pool, water dripping from his lusty frame. His lower anatomy is shrink-wrapped in black neoprene trunks. Droplets slowly flow down his torso, defining the taut musculature. He reaches for the monogrammed bath towel he'd brought from his room and wipes himself down. He's standing near the darker end of the pool. The quiet seems thicker, and Drake is suddenly conscious of being alone. He looks up at the sky that is turning light gray; daytime shadows will soon be waking up to go about their daily haunt. Drake stares at the whirling clouds wondering if it will rain. He bemoans the unpredictability of the weather. In his dismay he mentally compares it to the unpredictability of their rival, if it was him that left the mark in London.

As he rubs the towel over his sopping head, he forgets about the bad guys for a bit and thinks about Beth. Memory of her voice torments him; it is lush like her embrace. He misses her more than he thought he would. He recalls her last sentence over and over: "...when you come back, and I know you will, safely, I want you to propose to me! I'll say yes of course. I think it's time you asked."

She didn't want him to object so before he left, she added, "There's no more discussing it."

Drake grins thinking of her brass, her confidence, the certainty of getting her way with most, but not always with Drake. The idea doesn't sound so bad, he thinks, but he reflects on his conversation with Luis before he left. He will always be in the face of peril. Can Beth accept that, and the danger it might bring to her as well. He'd have to contend with that after he captures Rizzato; he has enough going for now he tells himself.

Checking his Submariner, he sees that it is 7:20; he'll head up to his room, shower and dress. He's meeting the brothers Isaac and Elijah Glass in the lobby at 10:00. They are arriving at the airport around 9:00, travelling from Hawaii on a red eye. It's been some time since he has seen them and he's anxious to renew their friendship. They had been part of his troop with the Joint Task Force, the Canadian commandos. Their bond went beyond that of soldiers; they are tremendous friends. Dakin and the two of them, led by Drake, saw lots of action, much of it covert. During a joint American/Canadian mission, Isaac had been taken prisoner and held at the same camp as Dakin. They had been rescued at the same time. It was Drake and Elijah who led two other men against an onslaught of crazy armed bandits dressed in dirty blankets to save them. All four guys were thick as mud after that.

Both brothers are good men. Drake is grateful they both have careers they can escape from. Isaac is a cartoonist; his take on four guys in a heavy metal band that seem to tour forever is called The Granite Planet, with syndication in over 170 newspapers. He has six months worth of material banked, so he can be mobile when he has to and his pay will still come in. So when Drake calls, he comes.

Elijah co-owns a helicopter company with his Dad that service oil rigs and drilling facilities. They have contracts in Louisiana, Newfoundland and the Canadian Arctic. His northern-most base is above the Arctic Circle in Resolute Bay on Cornwallis Island. His sister, Natalie, efficiently runs the main office in Shilo, Manitoba, the town where they had grown up. Their father, a retired pilot from the Canadian Armed Forces, Colonel Benjamin Glass, manages Louisiana where he has retired, with Elijah managing their Canadian affairs. His staff is composed of highly skilled pilots and qualified managers. The company runs very smoothly while he is away.

Back in his room Drake is pulling a white t-shirt over his head when the buzzer rings at the door of his room. He's thinking it's probably room service with the breakfast he ordered when he got back from the pool. He had showered and shaved, glazed his underarms with Old Spice, tugged on some jeans, spoken with Bannerji and is planning on calling Rae, right after he eats. He opens the door turning his back to the waiter he's sure is standing in the hall with a wheeled service cart. Instead two figures burst through the door, both clad in charcoal cargo pants, burgundy tees and black hoods. Both are strapping men. One hit him at the knees with a fearsome grip while the other hits him at the back encircling Drake's heart thumping chest with a hug that doesn't allow his lungs to expand. The trio hit the floor, with the two men taking the brunt of the fall holding Drake away from the floor so as not to hurt him.

The hit had been so fast and well planned that Drake hadn't heard a thing or had any time to react, which is an extremely rare occurrence. He feels a moment of helplessness as the assailants maintain their tenacious clench and confusing silence. Drake's inability to breath overcomes his shock and he finally reacts. He isn't going to be taken easily. His arms are crushed to the side of his body but his wrists and hands are still movable. He grabs the man on his back by the testicles and squeezes with all his strength. A man's balls are extremely sensitive and unless protected can be damaged quite easily. The culprit gives a mighty scream and squeezes Drake's chest even harder, trying to force him to relinquish his grip. But the pain becomes too intense and he drops his arms to grab Drake's hand. Before he can release Drakes grip on his groin area, Drake elbows him in the solar plexus, driving the air from his lungs at the same time as he releases the man's nuts. The man backs off, not trying to defend himself, holding his throbbing crotch, gasping and moaning with a discomfort so complete only another man can appreciate it. Drake now turns his attention to the man holding his legs when all of a sudden the thug lets go and jumps to his feet in a boxing pose, no weapons Drake notices. The man bobs back and forth with the mysterious hood on his head and starts to laugh....

"You're still sharp, Drake...." And with that, he throws off his hood and Isaac Glass stands before Drake, laughing so hard tears of mirth roll down his reddened cheeks. He reaches over to the other body crouched by the entryway and pulls the mask off his brother. Elijah Glass is griping his aching crotch but manages a sad chuckle. Drake, shaken from what he thought was an attempt to capture him, gazes at the identical twins, finally realizing the whole ruckus is a joke. He yells at them, "You idiots, I could've had a gun. I could have shot one of you." He shakes his head at the two imps and with a half-hearted scowl adds, "Or if I was lucky, maybe both."

The two guys look at each other for a couple of seconds, faces straight and remorseful, then shrug simultaneously and start laughing again. Isaac says, "You should see your face boss. It almost looks like your mad..."

Drake straightens out his shirt as he turns his back to the men and heads to the kitchenette. He is muttering to himself. "Silly buggers, had me going there for a bit..." Then aloud, he says,

"Come in, you rascals and have some coffee. I know you boys like your mud, so grab a cup." The coffee's delicate aroma calls out to them.

He points to several mugs on the counter, grabs his own cup from where he'd left it when he answered the door and refills it. Taking it black, he moves to the table, pulls out a white wicker chair and sits.

"Other than your shenanigans, it's good to see you gentleman. It's been much too long since we've been together, eh guys?"

Elijah, still unable to take deep breaths, reaches over the table and takes Drake's outstretched hand gripping it tightly with both of his own. A smile as genuine and beaming as a sunrise splits his handsome face; his eyes, brown as walnut stain, express his pleasure at seeing Drake. Hair black, thick and wavy, combed straight back, gives his head a glossy lid but the sides are shorn like a rookie soldier. Like his brother, a strong chin with a trifling dent completes his persona.

"You're damn right, chief, too long. My gonads might not agree, but it's great to get back in gear man. I'm itching for some action. You did good to call us, Drake. We'll catch this worm this time; we're with you all the way."

He winks at Drake, gives his hand an extra squeeze, stands at attention offering a mock salute. Looking around the rooms, he asks, "Where's the can, big guy? I have to check these babies, make sure they're not as crushed as they feel."

He heads off in the direction Drake points to at the rear of the suite on the right. As Elijah makes his way down the hallway bow-legged, Drake watches him gently caressing his crotch, grinning at their antics.

Wondering where the other brother is, Drake hears the front door shut. A moment later Isaac comes into the kitchen wheeling a trolley covered with a venting stainless steel dish, trays of cheeses, several varieties of olives, croissants, and fruit as well as ewers of milk, orange juice and water wanting to have the beverages Drake had ordered earlier. He's pushing the cart with one hand while the other stuffs a buttered croissant in his mouth.

Drake is always amazed by how much the men look alike even though Isaac is a few inches taller and his wavy hair falls to a whisper above his shoulders, perpetually tucked behind his ears. The grins are the same, deep brown intelligent eyes are indistinguishable, both honorable and courageous men. Isaac is definitely the calmer of the two, married to a wonderful lady named Dia, two and a half children, actually two ruffian boys and a cat named Konanne that is almost treated better than the kids. He is always collected and foresighted in battle: a planner and an ambush man, very keen with explosives.

Both men are a bit bigger than average, both buff from serious exercise regimes, and both are soldiers before all else. Isaac will recon and ensnare but when immediate action is required due to rapid developing circumstances, Elijah will step in. The pair are close to a perfect team, they had completed dozens of two-man reconnaissance, covert and wet operations. Drake as their leader had been taken to task many times for the twins' unorthodox methods. Their high success rate always helps convince their superiors to overlook the twins' odd ways. They were warned each time that this was to be the last time. Until the next time. Wink, wink.

"I ordered additional food for when you guys arrived so there's lots. The steaming dish is my eggs, but help yourself. I'll have some fruit later," says Drake. He studies Isaac as he butters another croissant, the end of the first one protruding from his mouth resembling a baked larva.

"De fuud wash tebibble n de pane", he muttered from his full gob. He holds up two fingers in a V before filling one of the wineglasses on the cupboard with milk, meaning to give him a moment. He downs a huge draft of white coldness and gives a symphonic belch before saying, "Ohh man that's so good, forgive me for being a glutton, I was sooo hungry. I tell you, Drake, the food was so bad on the plane even the waste basket refused it. Yuch! Hey so, where's our other good buddy, Dakin?" The three are close friends and have always stayed in touch.

"He's detained for the moment; I'll explain more when Elijah gets back from checking his jewels. I tell you, Isaac, I seriously thought I was in trouble when you two fools burst in. It's a wonder I didn't yank his balls right off." He gives a quick snap with his wrist; the fist clenched around the imaginary sac, and gives it a yank. Isaac grasps his crotch with both hands before doubling over in fake pain. Each man roars in delight. A few minutes later Elijah returns, the merriment greeting him halfway. An embarrassed smirk invades his cheeks, but with a touch of camaraderie and good cheer, he heard what Drake said and doesn't mind being the cause of such obvious gaiety. He enters the kitchen, eyeballing the two men who now sit at the table facing Elijah.

"Go ahead, comrades, get your chuckles now while they're hot. But beware, you both know me well, and I always get the last laugh," he jokes.

"Anyway, enough about my lower anatomy. I heard you say something about Dakin being detained. What's going on?" Elijah fills a huge white mug that says "Welcome to the Westin," with coffee, adds a little sugar and sits facing Drake; to Isaac's right.

Drake holds his chin in his hand, disliking the telling of bad news, although there is good, too. Sitting forward he begins relating the events of the last 24 hours. Hearing all the details, they react with typical aplomb; there is a mission to be mounted. Drake told of the three aggressors: one in hospital with what looked like a broken neck, one dead, and a big one who has gotten away. He wraps the conversation up, notifying them that the team he has gathered will be meeting at 1:00 p.m., and asks that they be back from visiting Dakin by then.

The men leave for the Square Hospital, leaving Drake's room arguing over the meaning of the odd name, Square. They will hail one of the yellow cabs perched a short ways down the street. After they leave, Drake scoops up the cups and places them in the dishwasher, rinses and dries his hands. Going into the living room, he picks up the remote for the curtains from the wooden coffee table and opens them to the late morning rain. Roofs, buildings and streets are sheathed in gloomy wet. The rain is on again, off again, seemingly unending. It has been falling all through the night.

Drake is relieved that the better part of the day will be spent inside planning, perhaps with some action later this evening. The weather might be better by then, but he wonders if the humidity of the latent heat will be better than this cool but clammy dampness.

He reaches for the cordless phone lying on the couch and sinks into the luxurious cloth, a rich texture that feels like silk. He dials the number Rae has given him where she can be reached, the phone rings twice before she answers. "Salaam. Hello."

"Hello, Rae, it's Drake. I hope I haven't gotten you at an inconvenient time, but I gather you weren't far from the phone."

"I was waiting for your call. I know you're meeting the men you told me about so I don't want to interrupt, but I'm refueled and ready to get on with our investigation. I can explain Dakin's operation in more detail later, but he did want me to remind you to save the visits and get well hugs for later. Just catch the culprits is what he wanted me to tell you. What's next Drake?"

"I'd like you to meet us here at my suite as we planned."
"Sure Drake, I'll rouse Rafan and bring him along He's very scared and over-cautious, even with our protection, and is getting very clingy-clingy with me. He trusts me, so I don't want to let him down. We'll be there."

"That's great, Rae. And thanks for looking out for Dakin. I can't believe you have affection for that reprobate when you've only known him for just over one day. I don't understand you ladies sometimes."

"Perhaps, Mr. Alexander, you don't understand love." An admonishing second of silence, then,

"Au revoir."

The silence of the disconnection is soon interrupted with the questioning dial tone. Drake feels slightly insulted but knows she's probably right. He finds love confusing sometimes; it's as if his heart never made it past adolescence. He's a middle-aged puppy.

He longs for Beth, for with her he feels a completeness that is indescribable. He thinks its love; however, he curses his roving eye. He is enchanted by an inviting smile, flattered by a sensuous touch, suffers from a rapacious lust. Can he be faithful to Beth, he asks himself as he sits staring at the black sculptured obelisk in the center of the coffee table, the focal point of his concentration. The sculpture itself blurs into a dark eddying pool. He imagines the question swirling in its thrall, disappearing in the vortex before he can even answer. He shakes himself free of his romantic trance, tucks it into a mental file and marshals his thoughts to his presentation.

The ringing of the bell urges him from the sofa, likely the props he ordered have arrived. Drake approaches the doorway pensively, having learned from the twins to keep his guard up. He'd never make that mistake again, he muses. He checks the eyehole and it fish-eyes a young man clad in black and white hotel livery. He notices the large easel just behind him. Opening the door he holds it while the skinny lad hustles in the easel that conveniently has wheels as well as feet. He also carries a large writing pad. Another young man pushes in a dolly that holds a small portable photocopier. The lower shelf is cluttered with an assortment of writing utensils: pencils by the dozens, pens, felt tip markers of several colors, and writing tablets with the hotel logo gracing each page. The waiter returns to the hallway and wheels in a second cart that contains a variety of liquids, some alcoholic, on the lower shelf. The top holds glasses and munchies.

He watches them park the carts, entertained by the boys' teenage awkwardness. He passes out tips as he escorts them to the door before locking it.

Drake gathers his notes and his laptop. The hotel's Wi-Fi

connection is impeccable, which is extremely helpful. Some of the team enjoy accessing the web; himself, he's a bit awkward in cyberspace, but he's getting his balance in there, finding things faster.

At 12:59 p.m., the doorbell's chorus sounds once more, but over and over. Drake knows the twins are back, Elijah impatient with barred doors. He checks the eyehole again before he turns the knob. He can hear the chatter of the group and sees a distorted Rae waving at the door. He realizes they have all arrived at the same time, and knowing the twins everybody knows each other already. He swings the door wide and greets them all. Rafan is huddled in the center behind Rae. She stands next to a squat heavyset man just slightly taller than her. He sports a thick, groomed moustache and a gregarious smile. From the photo in Chowdhury's office, Drake knows him to be Gurupada Bannerji. Elijah leads them all into the suite and heads for the expansive living room. Rae quickly follows, urging Rafan along. Isaac as usual is bringing up the rear, checking the hallways and doors. Everyone is on alert.

"Everything looks clear, Drake. We didn't see anything unusual around the premises or inside," he says. He turns to secure the dead bolt in contradiction to what he has just suggested. "But let's be cautious, shall we?"

Drake follows the troops through the suite to where they are all gathered around the easel he has placed in the dining area that sits in a wide alcove to the right of the kitchenette. Six chairs are dispersed around the oak table opposite the chart. Rae is coaxing Rafan into the last seat on the left while assuring him she will sit beside him. She goes back to the cart to get drinks for them both. Isaac and Elijah are laughing at some slight Isaac has made and

Elijah is blushing so it must've been at his expense.

Drake says, "Get yourselves some refreshments, people. Grab writing pads, pens or pencils, whatever you like. My laptop is available over there."

He points to the left of the easel, behind Rafan, at the powerful Toshiba that sits open on a wooden side table that has the same blondish stain as the other furniture.

"I'd like to get started right away, folks. I'd also like to extend a welcome to the Glass brothers. I assume you met in the hallway but otherwise, starting with you Rae, please introduce yourself to the group."

Rae wears a fresh pair of her ever present work pants, black EMTs, but today she had added a black tank top, then her holster, covering both with an open orange cotton shirt that stops at her petite waist. Not looking at the men but at the cart as she selects several pencils and a pad, in a dulcet accent, she says,

"My name is Mireille Lambert, but please call me Rae. I'm a private investigator." She makes direct eye contact with each man, her gaze strong, confident and trusting. Then, as if passing the mantle, she looks to Bannerji and smiles.

"I am Gurupada Bannerji. I am a member of the South Branch Division. I served in Narcotics for thirteen years. Four years ago I transferred to Dangerous Crimes, mostly Homicide. My supervisor is Inspector Bitan Chowdhury. I am delighted to be working with you, and please, call me Pada." His grand moustache can't hide white even teeth when he offers them a sincere smile. There is a spark in his eye that suggests he is a very happy man.

"Isaac Glass. I'm a soldier, an artist, a romantic lost soul, but mostly a nice guy." He too eyes everyone if only for a second or two. His eyes express very little; he's a difficult read. He nods to his sibling.

"I'm Elijah." Pointing his thumb at Isaac, he goes on, "I'm his brother as you can probably tell, lucky him. I'm a pilot, I adore guns and I love chasing bad guys. I'm not usually a nice guy." He winks at his alter ego at some joke they share. He flashes each person a grin that speaks mostly of mischief. He turns his head to Rafan with a questioning stare.

Rafan has been mostly quiet and unresponsive to the bustle of the team. All eyes are upon him, waiting for his response. He seems deep in thought. He can be compromised by his secrets. He is filled with despair at how is life is changing. He had made up his mind last night that he wouldn't let this bring him down, so he lifts his chin looking around at the faces in the room. He sees compassion, friendliness, people who care. He feels a little ashamed of himself for being so selfish, worrying about his own feelings. He needs to help these people. His uncle would want that and he hasn't been disowned yet, he thinks, so with a small dose of courage, he says, "I am Rafan Bashara. I am the nephew of Uday Saad, a business partner of Mr. Williston Payne. I also am employed by my uncle as his property manager for his establishments in Bangladesh, mainly here in Dhaka." He swallows dryly, his Adam's apple bobbing. "I am also the person who heard of Rizzato's presence."

Rae pulls out the chair next to Rafan, setting her pads and pens upon the table. She gazes down at him with a big smile. She notices a slight change in his demeanor; he seems more forward, not so afraid. She hopes the gang will do their best to keep him safe until their quarry is captured or defeated, however it turns out. She's relieved to see him relax. She gives him a light punch on the shoulder and says, "And we're glad you did, Rafan and you'll be a tremendous help in catching him."

She passes a pad and two pencils to Rafan, who sits up a little straighter, sudden responsibility providing a little backbone. He returns Rae's gesture with his own unsure grin, then sits forward, jotting down the salient points of his recent escapade.

By now everyone is seated except Drake, who stands beside the easel facing the group. Rafan is to his right, then Rae. Elijah and Isaac are still fiddling with their pads and stuff. Drake is bringing the easel closer while the twins get settled. Elijah has brought the laptop to the table. Bannerji is holding a grey nylon portfolio. Everybody is soon attentive and reading the list Drake has itemized on the oversized pad. The white pad has lined tear off pages. In bold black marker, the first page reads,

1   The Z mark   i) The girls in Venezuela
     ii) Three bodies in Dhaka (Ahmedani)
     iii) Whitecastle in London???
2   Malik Hajani/Raheem Ahmedani/Saul Morgan/De Clerq
3   Rafan meeting Ahmedani, who claimed to work for Rizzato.
4   Relation of De Clerq & Rizzato. Arms?

From the end of the table, Drake picks up what looks like a chrome pen, tugs at its telescopic arms creating an eighteen inch pointer. He taps the sheet saying, "I made notes of the things we need to discuss. I leave the floor open for frank and earnest discussion. I want to hear any thoughts you have, no matter how insignificant they may seem. We have in our midst two very good detectives whose reputations precede them, Rae and Gurupada, so we'll be open to your ideas and what your experience can do for us."

He shifts his focus to the top item and taps the "Z" with the pointer.

"I'd really like to see where we can go with this first item. It intrigues me, and it's more or less what brings all these deaths together so far. I'm anxious to read the autopsies that Chowdhury sent us. Would you be so good as to go over those for us, Pada?"

Pada unzips his portfolio and withdraws four manila files. He straightens them up, one atop the others squarely upon the table. When he speaks, his Bangladeshi dialect mixes with his high school and university English, making his voice pleasingly concise. He clears his throat and says, "Before I comment on the autopsies, I want to bring forth a discovery I made early this morning. I did a wider sweep, country-wide actually, looking for references to marks of any kind whatsoever on assault victims, dead or alive. I was rewarded only moments before I rushed over. This is only a brief report, but I think you will agree that it certainly cries out to be studied."

He has an extra copy giving it to Drake. Then Bannerji begins to read from the file: "Victim is an unknown female, thirteen years old. Cause of death is a knife wound to the back, penetrating the heart. Death would have been instantaneous. There was sperm in her rectum and evidence of forced entry. She had been brutally tormented." He shakes his head as he thinks of the sadistic person who has done this. It is beyond belief, he deems.

"She was found along the banks of the Meghna River, which is south of here. The body was sealed in canvas, weighted down by a cement block. The weight was insufficient to hold her down with the expanding gases sealed in a tight canvas. She had been dead for some time when a river man, unknown, found the tarp tangled in the roots of a fallen tree. He left the tarp on the wharf in Barisal. An anonymous call was made to the police station there, informing police of where and how it was found. We have a vague description of the man and his boat. But what makes this case more interesting is the Z on her shoulder. Local police did not think it was significant in any way, but we know that it is. What do you make of this, Drake?"

Drake looks hard at Isaac and Elijah; they had been with him when he had found Amber and Sakeema. The autopsies of all three would likely read the same. The twins focus on Drake, and see the steel rising in his eyes, a hardness that possesses him, driving him, goading him. He grits his teeth, scrunches his brows and says with certainty, "That rat is here." He looks at all five of his compadres, and with a voice full of emotion continues, "I made a promise to Williston Payne. We'll find this man and crush him!"

Chapter 18   Sept 15 6:07 p.m. Cayman Islands

Sophia Stratton waits with newfound patience for Amado Herrera y Mendoza to leave his office building, as she knows he will sometime between 6:15 and 6:30 pm. She has been watching his every move outside of his office and home for the last two days. She sits at an outdoor table at a coffee shop called Nairobi's. It serves dozens of world coffees, but the roast from the owner's home country in Africa is the most popular. There are not many tourists about and the streets are early evening quiet. The only noise is the fusion of the few patrons' prattle and *Norah Jones* coming mildly from the sidewalk speakers. The sun is seeking the horizon in the west, stretching the afternoon shadows.

She had witnessed Mendoza stopping each day at this café for a steaming cup of what she assumes is coffee. She wonders if it's really the refreshment he wants or the teasing banter he shares with the man she assumes might be the owner who always takes the time to serve him personally. She is trying to gather her courage to confront Mendoza and has decided that very morning that today she will follow him the five blocks from the café to where he parked his car. She isn't sure how, but she's determined to get him to tell her where her father is.

She signals the waiter to refill her cup, pretending to glance at the magazine she has brought as a diversion. Her eyes remain peripherally on the front door of the building, watching for Mendoza. She's thinking of the day three weeks ago when she had found a yellow post-it note stuck under the seat cushion of the chair in her father's home office. She had been searching for anything that would tell her where he may have gone. She had spent the first six months of her father's absence ignoring the checks that show up each month in her account. The amount is substantial. She had spent the last six months looking for clues to his whereabouts. She worried over their last conversation and what her father may be up to. She had vowed to try to stop whatever he was planning before it was too late. She hounded his VPs, his personal assistant, other management of his businesses. They all said the same. He had ceded all power to the boards of directors and simply vanished. She remembered the checks; they came from her father's lawyers in Chicago. They didn't know anything other than a substantial amount of money had been entrusted to them for monthly payments to both her and her mother. The last contact they had had with Mr. Stratton was in November of last year, they insisted, and he had left no forwarding address. Their fees were to be deducted from the same monies.

The post-it note had two names, Amado Cayetano Herrera y Mendoza, and Jack Favors which seemed mundane compared to its neighbor. It had been folded in half when she found it, noting the crease along its fold, evidence that it had been opened and closed many times. She thought that was significant, that her father was either nervous or uncertain, often referring to its contents, neither of which sounded like him. She safely assumed it was her father that misplaced the note, as no one else used his office. He even did the cleaning himself rather than let strangers in there. When she found the note she remembered his eyes that last time she saw him, realizing then that she really didn't know this man, her father. She had seen a desperation then that was uncommon in the man, eyes with a fever that scared her. Now she thinks he is capable of anything.

Ten minutes later, at 6:25, she sees Mendoza exit the building and walk the two blocks to the cafe. As he enters the cafe he starts his usual joking with the short black man behind the counter. The front of the shop is made up of two large roll up doors and in good weather they are always raised. She has afforded herself a clear view of the cash area. As she watches him, he shifts his briefcase from one hand to the other as he searches his pockets for change. Pulling out a handful of coins, he holds them out to the laughing old man, who sifts through the money in Mendoza's palm until he collects enough for the coffee. Amado looks down as he put the coins back in his pocket and spots the pretty young blond girl staring at him. He pauses for a moment, flashing the Herrera smile, totally unaware of how involved he will be with this woman in only a few moments. He is momentarily mesmerized by the blueness of her eyes and how they match the V-necked T-shirt she wears and the turquoise agate that lies delicately at her open throat. He gives her a brief nod and with a remark that causes his server to give him a wave of dismissal, he grabs his coffee with his free hand and starts walking back to where his car is located in the municipal lot several blocks from the downtown area.

He hurries past the building his office is in turning right at the next street where she knows he will walk over one street and then north for two more. When he turns the corner she makes to follow, scurrying along out of his sight, going right in front of his building to come up behind him on the next street over. She is wearing beige cotton Capri's with blue and white running shoes so she can easily keep up. A brown leather purse the size of a brick hangs at her left side, with the strap crossing her body from where it rests on her opposite shoulder. She clutches the purse and turns it toward the front of her body, opening the closure that keeps it shut. Checking that the small canister of pepper spray is visible, she leaves the bag slightly open. Sophia is not much for weapons and intrigue but naively thinks that the can might protect her and emboldens her step. She removes the slip of paper with the names written on it to grasp it in her fist.

She sees Mendoza ahead just as he enters the parking lot. He waves to the attendant who never even stirs from his perch, and heads toward the black polished Porsche at the back of the lot. Amado is so proud of his car, a limited edition Carrera that he pays for the parking spots on either side of his so they remain empty reducing the chances of his car being dinged by someone parking too close. The lazy attendant is given twenty dollars a month to keep his eyes on it as well. As he unlocks the door he sees the young lady from the cafe approaching him from the main entrance. She is waving and calling to him. She never acknowledges the attendant, who sits up suddenly as the "fine piece," as he thinks of her, struts through his lot.

"Mr. Mendoza, may I speak to you please. I'll only take a moment."

He opens the car door as she approaches and places his briefcase in the car. He stands behind the opened door with the car at his back with both hands on top of the side window, his position proclaiming his sudden uneasiness. The girl looks familiar, yet he's certain he doesn't know her. Something about her alarms him, and when she is ten feet away from his car he says, "Stop. Stop where you are."

She halts her steps immediately, surprised by the firm tone of his voice. When she looks up she sees that the handsome face is more creased, more careful; caustic almost. She is momentarily speechless and suddenly very nervous, but she's a Stratton and determined to find her father. Her hand gently comes to rest on top of her purse. She responds with equal temperament, "See here. That is no tone to take with a stranger to your islands. I merely seek your assistance; I certainly do not intend you any harm."

"Nonetheless, I'm put off by your aggressiveness. Are you a cheated wife perhaps, many of you are revengeful when I defend your spouses. Unfortunately for you I almost always win. Maybe this is a matter for the courts or at the very least you could make an appointment to discuss this in a proper setting. Don't you think?"

His face softens somewhat, assuming he is correct in his estimate. She seems harmless. The deflation he witnesses in her spirit is not an acknowledgement of his guess but her realization that she is dealing with a chauvinist. She goes straight to the point, "Do you know Andrew Stratton, and if so, where is he? I'm Sophia, his daughter."

She sees his jaw drop, the question completely unexpected. Stratton never mentioned another daughter. Mado believed all the man's children are dead, but he notices the resemblance to Andrew, the chin and the lips. He doesn't like where this could go.

"I know of no such person. Now I must leave." He turns to get in the car when Sophia says,

"Wait, you paused too long. You do know him. Listen, I believe he is going to hurt a lot of innocent people from a conversation he and I had when my brother and sister were killed and I have to stop him. Please help me, I beg you."

Mado looks around and sees they are drawing attention to themselves. He tells her, "Quiet down, okay? You're wrong, I thought the name sounded familiar, but I am confident I don't know it."

A couple who came to reclaim their car noticed the young lady ranting loudly at a man. The girl gives them a frigid glare and they hasten to their auto. Turning back to Mado she says, "Senor Mendoza, I found this in my father's home office". She hands him the post-it-note. She looks at him directly, waiting for another lie. Mendoza unfolds the small yellow paper and read the two names registered therein. They both know it is unmistakably Andrew Stratton's scrawl. Weighing his words, he asks, "How did you find me?"

"That wasn't very difficult. I put your name in my favorite search engine and guess what? Your name is mentioned in the Island Barristers Association; there were several references to your involvement in some shady land deals in Florida two years ago though nothing was proven. You are an amateur golf champion, you have a membership at Grand Cayman Links; the information just doesn't seem to end. The name I have trouble with is Jack Favors. Perhaps you know him as well?"

She reaches out to snatch the post-it from his hands, watching his eyes. They are steady but unsure. She places the note back in her purse and carries on, "I don't understand why my father had to come so far to hire a lawyer. He has been dealing with Forsythe, Short and Henke for eons. The only thing I can surmise is that your services must be unique, Senor Mendoza. Off shore accounts and that sort of thing, like the shady land deals. Am I right?"

She has her fists on her hips, demanding an answer to her inquires. Her head is cocked to one side, a habit her mother finds annoying when Sophia knows she is right. Mendoza remains quiet, pondering his options. He knows Stratton would not welcome an interruption. He also knows the man is demented in his efforts, but the money, the money, he thinks. Like others involved in this charade, he's to collect the largest fee in his career, one he wouldn't have imagined a year ago. He can't allow her to stand in the way. Perhaps persuasion and reason will deter her, he hopes. He says, "I can't help you with Favors, but yes, I know your father. There is much at stake, Miss Stratton. Your father has sworn me to secrecy and I am being very well paid to follow his wishes. You are asking me to betray a client, to betray the trust between us."

"Humph "she groans, "how about betraying those innocents he intends to hurt. Will you spend the money he pays you with a clear conscience? He must have told you what he intends to do. When he told me of a plot to provoke a catastrophe upon the Muslim world, to use his wealth and power to make it happen, revenge for the slaughter of his children – my brother and sister – I thought he was foolish, but something snapped when the police showed him the fingers after they received them from Israel. Do you want to be part of that? If you're not willing to co-operate with me, then I think the local police will be interested in a missing persons claim when I give them the note I found."

She crosses her arms, raising her chin to defy him. This is the Andrew part of her.

Mendoza steps around from behind the door of the car and walks over to where she is standing. When he is about a meter away he stops. Looming over her, he points a finger, emphasizing his words with a menacing frown, "Be careful, young lady. You have no idea what you are up against here. What my clients do with their money or their time is not my business. I am only a finder, a passer of information, a manipulator of the laws of many lands. I introduce people. I handle trust accounts. But as I said, it is not my business and I do have a clear conscience. And that part about the police is not wise."

He reaches out to take her arm and says, "Come with me and I will arrange for you to leave the Island as soon as possible. It is best that you forget all about this. Come."

Sophia backs off and puts her hand in the open purse. She grips the pepper spray pushing it forward as if she has a gun inside; Mado backs off with raised hands. The attendant catches Mado's gesture. "Tell me now or you'll be sorry. I'm desperate. I won't let my father kill those people or him. I know he can he helped; I just need to find him. Don't make me use this. I'll take one of your knees first."

She prays he won't call her bluff when suddenly she feels a cold circular piece of metal jammed into the base of her skull and hears a sharp order not to move as much as a hair except to slowly remove her hand from her purse, or she will become headless. The attendant had been ogling Sophia when he saw her point what he thinks to be a gun at Mr. Mado. He doesn't care how good she looks, Mr. Mado is a good guy, rich too, he thinks. He had quietly snuck around and came from between parked cars behind her. He pulled a much used and battered pistol from his hip pocket. Gripping it with a shaky hand, he pushes it hard against her head. It is the only way he can keep his hand steady plus it will show her he means business. He has never used the gun before; it's more for flash with the gang he runs with at night.

He's only fifteen years old, and he borrows his bravado from them.

Sophia goes white. Now she's scared. She is dreadfully reminded of being alone. Only a handful of her co-workers know she is somewhere in the Caribbean. She had never expected this element to her rendezvous with Mendoza. She looks up at him now. The gun, the heat, the hot asphalt, the smell of her assailant's sweaty body, it all overwhelms her. She becomes dizzy. She lifts her hand from her purse very slowly.

"I'm going to be sick, shoot me or let me throw up," she says, and with that she doubles over and heaves. Brown, sour juice spews from her mouth, all of it old coffee. Her sudden movement causes the teenager to panic and he pulls the trigger. He's tall and was pointing the gun down at Sophia's neck, but when he fires the gun kicks, almost flying from his weak grasp, causing the bullet to go high. It's a hollow point and strikes Mado in the chest just above and to the left of the heart, piercing a lung. The mushroomed head of the bullet blows a section the size of a baseball from his back. The force of the impact propels him backwards until he hits the car door he left open. He slowly slithers to the ground. His impeccable white shirt bears an elongating blot, deep red and puckered in the center. His head rests upon the pavement with open astonished eyes as he gasps with each painful breath.

The adolescent stands mouth agape, as he watches Mado fall back with stricken disbelief. Seeing him hit the car door before coming to rest on the ground is too much for the boy. He yells out "Oh my sweet Lord, what have I done? I never meant to shoot anyone." He swears and rants that he didn't mean to do it; he was only helping Mr. Mado.

He grasps his head in his hands, one of them still holding the gun. He has momentarily forgotten about it until he bangs himself on the temple. He yelps and stares at the weapon as if it is alive. He screams with a terror so vile it sends tremors through Sophia. When the gun had exploded, she had leaped three feet to her left behind a vehicle, where she crouches on all fours, one knee bleeding. She slowly peeks around the bumper, glancing at Mado for a second until the sight repulses her causing her to look away. She turns slightly to see the kid screaming in some local patois she can't understand. She can see his eyes; they are bugged. The cords in his neck are taut, spittle flies from his lips, and tears streams down his cheeks as he raves incoherently.

Suddenly he stops. He slowly pivots from his spot, glancing around the parking lot. He's looking for her. She ducks back quickly, then turns and crawls to the rear of the car, her knee tormenting her. Worried that he will look under the cars, she props herself up on the bumper and pushes on the car ahead with her feet, holding herself off the tarmac. She listens to the shuffling of his feet, the moaning coming from Mado. She's tense with the trouble she has caused and scared for her life. It goes quiet again. After a few seconds she hears a heavy grunt and sees the gun cart wheeling through the air over her head. The sound of running feet precedes the clang of the gun hitting something metallic, probably another car. There is a stillness for several moments as Sophia waits, her legs are strong from training, and she could stay there for some time, but a slow, mournful murmur alerts her to Mado who is amazingly still alive, she realizes.

Dropping to the ground she looks under the car for the gunman's feet. When she doesn't see any, she slowly stands. It only takes her a moment to ascertain that the boy is gone. She rushes over to Mado. There are several bystanders now. She yells at one of them to call the police, an ambulance.

She is holding his jacket against the effervescence of his wound, trying to discern his low mumbling. She places her ear next to his mouth and hears him say, "...father," He turns away, coughing spume several times before adding, "Dhaka... watch out for Rizzato..." And then he dies.

Chapter 19   Sept 15 9:07am Dhaka

As Amado lay dying, Stratton is getting in the co-pilot's seat of a helicopter not much bigger than a mosquito, all glass. It's one of the scariest things he's ever flown in and he's a flier. He feels safer in the cockpit of a plane, a turtle in its shell. Each time he greets Honey at the private airport north on Tongi, and there have been two others, he does so with trepidation. She is an overbearing and boisterous woman, hailing him loudly when she sees him and hugs him as if they were old friends even though he's only flown with her twice. Her appeasing British charm, diction and femininity belie the crucial mind and deft limbs that create an awesome stick pilot.

Honey Aviation is owned by Miss Honey Bea. Leaving the Dhaka airport, his driver passed a splendid billboard - largest airport advertisement he had ever come across. It had a sharp yellow background, like a lemon. In the center, hovered a humungous bee facing a pinkish-mauve morning glory. The flower's supporting vine and foliage of appealing greens covered a narrow portion of the left side. The insect was well detailed, but instead of wings, it had a spinning rotor, like a helicopter's. Under the giant bug were the words, "Honey's Aviation" and a phone number. In smaller letters, but still over two feet high, were the words "Owner: H. Bea."

When Andrew first saw the ad, he was hooked. He knew he would be scouting the grounds where the Bishwa Ijtema would be taking place and preferred a helicopter for his survey. After seeing the billboard he knew he wanted to meet H. Bea. Now as he straps himself him in, he glances over at Honey, who is flipping various toggle switches, turning dials on the control panel without even looking at them, like a musician picking a familiar tune on their guitar. She's studying the sky and grimacing at the clouds on the eastern horizon.

"Bleeding weather can't make up its mind; if it gets windy, we don't want to be up in this corkscrew. But this is the best machine for looking around and that's what you're after now isn't it, luv?" she asks as she throws the last switch. The air-slicing blades overhead begin to turn.

Stratton remains quiet, concentrating on his safety harness. He's still apprehensive as he stares out the rounded Plexiglas. He knows she doesn't expect an answer. When she had gotten nosy on their first flight he had put her off by telling her he was interested in buying land and beyond that it there was nothing else for her to be concerned about. It didn't stop the chatty questioning. After he's fastened in, he studies the other helicopters parked around the field. They all have a black and yellow motif, and like her flying jacket, her signage, her truck, they are all ornamented with the lingering bee from the billboard. There are two Robinson R44s, a four-seater version of the R22 he's in and then there are the workhorses, a stripped down Sikorsky HH60 Pave Hawk for light to medium lift and a tandem-rotor Boeing Chinook, a colossal heavy lift chopper, one she has scavenged from the Royal Air Force, she'd told him. It's a Special Forces version, of which only eight were built. He tries to imagine Honey flying that behemoth when he turns to study her.

Her grayish blonde hair is tied in a bun. There's a pilot's slim headset on her head that fails to hold all the strands and several hang down her face making her appear younger than the 41 years she claims to be. He watches her as she brushes the strands behind her ear, where they stay briefly. Pouting lips hum an unfamiliar tune as she studies the gauges on the center console. Her actions are true, with a steady hand. Chunky arms maneuver around a massive breast and he wonders how she is so adept. He remembers when he had checked on her with the Bangladesh Airports Authority; the person assisting him concluded his query when he told *Mr. Favors* that the joke around the flying community was that Honey was so good she could sneak up on a humming bird. He was sold!

The two rotors are fusing into a solid transparent circle. The R22 is one of the most popular light helicopters in the world, often used by police forces for observation. The lightweight aircraft requires an experienced hand. It's known to have a teetering rotor and suffers from a higher than average rate of mishaps that never seems to dampen its popularity. He grips his hands tightly in his lap as Honey buzzes, "Hold on to your bippy, Mr. Favors, we're going up."

The Lycoming engine is at optimal revs and picks up the bird with a tractable lurch. Andrew's sphincter tightens. With both hands, he hangs on to the safety strap that hangs from the frame. His hunter green golf shirt darkens under the arms, as if he suffers from hidrosis, the sweat glands overreacting to the tension. He steals a quick look at Honey. Her look is one of concentration, strangely stoic, but the clear eyes are laughing. He sets his sights on the surroundings to cover his uncomfortable feelings as the ground recedes and the buildings grow smaller. He relaxes a little, letting go of the straps, more comfortable with this part of flying. The craft affords him a panorama of sights, a mixture of modern architecture, worn down shanties, clusters of homes, industrial buildings, clogged and vacant streets. And there is always a river.

"I'd like to look at that vacant land on the bend of the Turag River we flew over on out last trip before. I remember you saying it had been vacant for as long as you've been here," Andrew says.

"Well, luv, if you're lookin' to buy land, you'll be very disappointed to know that that land is permanently reserved for what the locals call the *Bishwa Ijtema*, the second largest gathering in the Muslim world after the Hajj. Just over three months from now, there will be over a million Muslims coming together to pray for peace. Isn't that touching now, dear?"

Andrew's eyes flare like a candle biting fresh wick. His pulse quickens. He believed that 800,000 Muslims would be in attendance. He never imagined that a million targets would be available. His skin prickles as he contemplates hundreds of thousands dying at his hands. His mouth goes dry as he stutters, "a...a... million, you said?" It seems beyond belief. He's confused for a moment. He is recalculating the quantity of gas he will be transporting and spraying, trying to digest the enormity of the killing field as Honey banks the helicopter to port, dropping to 250 meters and heading west, the buildings below them looking like penny matchboxes.

Honey takes a quick peek at Andrew. They aren't far apart as the seats in the R22 are close, close as two cards in a deck, the queen and a joker perhaps. She senses a heightened awareness from the man. She'd known enough of the opposite gender to recognize neurosis; he's acting different, and his eyes are glazed with what seems like obsessive delight. He makes her uncomfortable and she tells herself, "I'm not hugging this man anymore." She says to him, "Yes, a million, possibly more. They come from all over Bangladesh and many parts of the world! Are you all right?"

"What... Oh, sorry, I was just trying to imagine so many people in one place and it baffles me. How big is the area?"

"About five square kilometers."

Andrew overcomes his shock and grins like a multi-million-dollar lottery winner. His diabolical intentions just had more heft added to them. He was worried when he had seen the tents over a portion of the grounds on their last trip but hadn't looked close, too wary of drawing attention to his interest in the property. This outing today is intended to study the approaches and decide how he best can spray around the tenting, but he knows that the covers propped up by scrawny poles he had seen will never hide the multitude. He'll study the open area where he feels he'll be guaranteed success of coating many people with the gas he plans on using.

He tries to appear more casual and in control. With feigned interest he says, "With that many people attending, security must be an issue."

Honey says, "Well, yes it is, the authorities put extra efforts into the Ijtema because of the high profile it affords the city. There is usually helicopter surveillance, as well as ground troops stationed about the surrounding verge. There are normally over 7,000 law enforcement agents in attendance, but I understand the RAB, that's the Rapid Action Battalion, an elite anti-terrorist group, will be used as well this year."

With an irony he expects Honey will miss, he remarks, "That makes sense I guess. Nothing should interrupt a peace gathering."

They come about just past the area they had been discussing and approach the grounds from the west with the sun at their back. She follows the river for half a nautical mile swooping in low over the tented section. Andrew can see the rough poles that hold the swaying material aloft, about eight feet off the ground. From the air, the tents are different shades and textures. They provided a covering from the tormenting sun during the long days. There are no sides to the structures offering any form of protection from sun or rain. The organizers never dreamed of some madman spraying the crowd with toxic gas.

Honey hovers over the terrain for several minutes as Andrew scans the earth once more. She watches him for a moment. She has in fact detected the irony in his voice, the way it became husky when he said "peace." The short hairs at the base of her neck not only stand up, they shout for attention. He wiggles his ass into the seat, crosses his hands in his lap, looks at her and says, "I've seen enough; take me to the site you suggested this morning."

There is something about the man that bears watching, Honey thinks. It's a suspicion she has when she sees the meanness in his eyes. Next week, when she will be officiating at the Cricket tournament, she will mention him to her friend Chowdhury. And after today, she will be "too busy" to accommodate Mr. Favors anytime in the future.

It matters little to Stratton what she's thinking. He is in a dream state as he stares out the glass globe. The land is unfocused, his eyes taking a break. His mind is scrambling over other details as they finish their flight, each eager to be rid of the other. After they return he exits the field to find his limo waiting for him. The uniformed chauffeur hold his door with fervid friendliness. He instructs the man to take him to Banasree in the Rampura suburb. He will get out on Meradia Road where it ends at Road #4, explaining he wants to be picked up at that very spot at five o'clock, no later, no sooner.

When he has been dropped off, he watches the dark stretch limo barter for space with vehicles half its length, eventually fading into the cityscape. He waits a few moments to be sure the driver is well away. He looks up and down the street and across at the rising apartment buildings facing the street. He can smell the fumes of passing vehicles, aromas from the street vendors' wares, bodies both sweet and sour, a potpourri of humanity's incense. The unfamiliar city with its hated inhabitants makes him ill at ease so he heads west along Road #4 two blocks before turning left and going the next block to Road #5, where he finds Plot #660. A slate grey high rise stands before him, so new the landscaping is still being done. Several men are going about with shovels and rakes as he walks the short distance to the glass front door. Bold white numbers on the wall beside the door confirm the building to be 660 Road #5.

He has not been to the safe house, apartment 904 on the top floor, before. Rizzato and his men use it when they are in the city. It has been leased by Mado and registered to the parent company that also owns Reactor Chemicals in North Carolina, for their executives of course. Rizzato had explained to Stratton how to reach the apartment and had asked him to meet with him as soon as he was able. Andrew remembered being somewhat concerned as to the urgency in Rizzato's voice but he had been assured that it was just business, details.

Caution signs and a pleasant scent warn him of the presence of fresh paint. The entryway ends nine meters in. A chromed elevator waits in the center of a royal blue wall whose smoothness is interrupted only by a slim metallic directory to the right. Number 904 is near the bottom. Andrew glances at the name and sees the imaginary tenant's moniker, Pham A. Lee!

When he gets off the lift at the ninth floor, he turns to his immediate left and withdraws a brass-colored key from his pocket. It had been left at his hotel this morning by a courier. He places the key in the keyhole, gives the wood a light tap and unlocks the door, which opens to a small foyer. A soft bluish brume of cigar smoke greets him as he enters the apartment. He recognizes the aroma of the Nicaraguan tobacco. It might be San Cristobals; they had been his favorite for years until he discovered the Fuente brand. The plumes of smoke curl in the air like ghoulish fingers summoning him.

Off to the left is the long narrow living room where he finds Rizzato seated near the large bow window that occupies most of the wall. The beige linen curtains are pulled apart and one of the side windows had been cranked open. The oversized dark brown Laz-i-boy Rizzato sits in is extended out and polished black western boots are lifted off the floor, their pointed tips sticking up like mini-spires.

Another person, a huge hulk clad in a faded denim shirt and jeans sits on a green floral davenport across from Rizzato. Both men eye Andrew in somber silence until a crooked smile breaks Rizzato's ugly face as he says, "Welcome to our hacienda, Jack. Comfy little get away isn't it? Your friend Mado thinks of everything, doesn't he?" He raises his glass, which holds a dark and cloudy liquid, in mock toast. His guest, whom Andrew has never met, is drinking

Hunters malt beverage from the bottle.

Andrew says, "That's Mado all right. From what I can see the premises seem agreeable. I haven't heard any complaints from you for some time so I expect your quarters in the country are comparable? I plan on visiting shortly, and I intend to stay over for several days, but right now I'll join you gents in a drink so excuse me for a minute."

Andrew withdraws to the kitchenette which is down the hall and to the right. The room is painted a soft yellow. A portable bar has been set up. He inspects the room as he pours himself a Glenlivet. The label proclaims it to be 18 years old. He holds the old fashioned glass close to his face and inhales the rich nose from the propitious golden liquid and takes a short swig; the fluid is mellow and long winded. He returns to the room where the two men are waiting, still quiet. The large man is staring oddly at the wall in front of him remaining still except to take a quick drink. He pays no attention to Stratton, as if he'd never entered the room, barely even blinking. The man reminds Andrew of stone covered with skin or an oversized ventriloquist's dummy, waiting for Rizzato to place him on his knee. The idea causes him to smirk. "Are you going to introduce me to your robot here, Bartolo?"

The robot turns its articulated neck and shoots imaginary poison darts at Stratton, another man for Bunker to hate. Bunker sizes him up, realizing he could squish this man with one hand. He stands and steps over to Stratton, all 80 inches towering over him. He give him a warning – one is all he will need – and says in accented English, "I may work for you but you will never, never make fun of me again. Is that clear?"

He places a massive hand on Stratton's shoulder and gives it the gentlest of squeezes. Bunker can feel Stratton trembling. Leaving Stratton speechless, Bunker steps away to settle back into his spot and continues to stare at the opposite wall.

Rizzato had been watching this exchange with considerable exhilaration. He enjoys intimidation. He remembers his last two meetings with Favors since the boat incident. Jack had been after him to keep his men in line and was adamant that he should get rid of Morgan before he caused more trouble and maybe even the Japanese girl. He couldn't afford any screw ups, Stratton had lamented. It had been their only disagreement thus far in their plans. Rizzato had grown tired of the ranting and brought Bunker along to cow Favors. He's thinking, job done!

"Well, actually Jack you don't need to know who this is, only that he works for me and me only."

Andrew is angry, the residue of fear.

"There's no need for bullying. I know you people are tough, I know what you're up to. That's fine, then, you keep your people, but remember, Rizzato, this is my gig, my mission. I need this to succeed and I need you to understand my fears. That's all. Now, you asked to see me and I have a project for you, so let's get on with it. How are things progressing and what problems are you experiencing?"

While Andrew sits down in a matching recliner opposite him, Rizzato places his cigar in the ashtray on the side table and sits up straight in the chair, feet on the floor. Leaning forward until his elbows rests on his knees he says, "Well, the runway is coming along good. We're at 900 feet now and we should have the other 300 feet done by the end of next month. Remember, Jack, a lot of this work is done by hand. We have that one small dozer, the old tractor and cart, a lot is still done with wheelbarrows. Even though, we're still four weeks ahead of your schedule."

He shifts in his seat; his long legs stretched out, gives Bunker a quick look and says, "We have two problems, Jack. One is not a big deal; the other is more sensitive. Both are solvable. The first is the engine for the plane. The pump is defective in the radial compressor. Kovalenko can't get the parts he needs so they will have to be machined. Some of my men will have to get the compressor to Dhaka because it will be impossible to bring machining equipment here and we don't have the space anyway and if we want to keep as much as we can under wraps, Kovalenko says he can do it if he had the equipment. How do you want to handle this?"

Andrew takes another swallow of his drink and thinks for a moment before asking, "Why can't the parts be had?"

"I don't know Jack. I'm not a grease monkey, I'm just telling you what Kovalenko told me, maybe the engine is too old or we're in the wrong part of the world. He seems to know what he's doing, so I didn't question him on it."

"Okay, Bartolo, stay calm, I was just wondering. I know the engine is older but the Pratt & Whitney turboprop is very common, or at least that's what I was told. However, I think we can depend on Kovalenko, so have him compile a list of equipment he needs, get it to Mado, have it all delivered and set up at the warehouse you secured in the Industrial Park east of here. Make sure it's all done under Reactor Chemicals. Have this done no later than next week, Bartolo. No delays. Have a work detail take whatever components of the plane to Dhaka as necessary. How long do you think this'll take?"

"I'll be back at the ranch tomorrow and should have a list to Mado by noon our time. It'll be late evening for him and Friday so, probably two or three weeks should do it. After that there are only a few more nuts and bolts to tighten up, so you'll be able to get your practice runs in by the first of November. Does that suit you?"

Rizzato sits back in his chair tenting his fingers. Trying to remain calm he asks himself why his fuse was so short with Favors. He doesn't like the man, doesn't like working for him. He controls his temper and before Stratton can reply, he says, "And by that time I expect my services will no longer be required?"

Andrew is aware of Rizzato's dislike, unperturbed by it. He doesn't really care if Rizzato likes him or not just as long as the job gets done.

"And by that time, Rizzato, you and your…" he nods toward Bunker with disdain and continues, "…henchmen will be very well off. When the aircraft is running perfectly, when the runway is completed, when the isocyanate has been installed in the belly of the craft, when all "loose ends," as you call them, are taken care of, at that point in time you and your cadre can leave, not before."

Stratton polishes off his drink, sits the glass on the table and rises from his chair. A heavy frown creases his face. He stares at the two as if they were disobedient students and he the principal, "At that time, Mado will release the funds I promised you into the account we have arranged. When I say everything is ready, not before. And once more I'll remind you to keep your men in line. I know you're tired of my insistence, but I want no problems. Does that suit you?"

He gives them some time to think about what he had just said as he can see that Rizzato is at a low simmer. He wonders why the man is so quick to anger. Is the reason so deep rooted that it contributes to his violence. Stratton leaves the room to go to the bar to replenish his drink, the last one is just beginning to sand off the edges; a second one should polish things up.

When Andrew leaves the room, Rizzato says, sotto voce, "The damn money, huh, Bunk? I don't know why this fucker irks me so much, but I'll be glad to get rid of him. How about you?"

Bunker gives one downward nod. Whatever Rizzato wants.

Rizzato calls out to the kitchen, "Yeah, yeah, that's fine, Jack. Don't worry about my men; I'm as keen as you are on this baby going smooth. Bunker here will keep an eye on them; you can throw that concern in the trash. And speaking of trash, we have a more important issue that needs to be discussed. On your way back, bring us another drink, will you?"

Bartolo winks at Bunker, satisfied his sass saved him a little dignity from his kowtowing. And to boost his own morale, he forces a little air from his rectum in audible protest. Bunker groans, more or less his way of laughing. He likes it when the boss gets saucy.

Andrew returns with two drinks and a beer balanced in both hands. As soon as he turned down the hallway toward the living room, he smells something foul reeking from the room. It makes the air chunky and bluish. The smell is so bad, his eyes start to water. With both hands full he can't wipe them away and when he enters the room it looks as if he is crying. Both hoodlums in the living room, by now comfortable with the bouquet, glance up at Andrew when he enters and explode with laughter. Bunker's big body does a bogie on the couch while Rizzato's skinny frame shimmies in the chair, both guffawing.

Andrew sets the glasses down and wipes his eyes with one of the doilies he snatches from the coffee table that rests in the middle of the room. He doesn't find it amusing. The stench is still so rancid that he feels he might gag. Several minutes go by before the fermentation and chuckles fade. Andrew is standing by the end of the sofa, facing both men. He shakes his head at Rizzato as if to say, you fool. Rizzato doesn't catch it or doesn't care and says, "I was approached yesterday by Lokesh, Tarafdar's minion. He came to the ranch. That slime-ball is after more money. He says we need work permits for each of the men because we are a foreign company. I told him I needed to speak with you and that I would get back to him by the end of the week. He wanted the $20,000.00 right then, but I told him he'd have to wait. He didn't like that. I thought you had Tarafdar properly greased. Why is this weasel coming around?"

Andrew doesn't hesitate when he says, "Yes, Tarafdar has been very, very well compensated. I spoke with him only a few weeks ago and he was extremely pleased with our arrangement. Do you think this could be Lokesh digging around on his own?"

Rizzato said, "I think that's what we're looking at. I also think that we need to put an end to this sore before it festers into something worse."

Andrew distributes the drinks, the beer going to Bunker. He sips from the tumbler he holds, studying the faceted edges along the side of the crystal. As he turns the glass back and forth in his hand, rainbow slivers of reflected light tease his eyes. The idea of adding one more body to the pile doesn't bother him. What bothers him are his children, whom he always envisions at the bottom of the same mound of empty shells, so with no empathy for anybody else's loss but his own, he asks, "Can there be no traces left at all. Can he just disappear?"

Now Rizzato is excited. There's to be more killing. His enthusiasm is evident in the pitch of his voice, a sexual tension, when he says, "Oh, yeah. Bunker here's a fucking magician. When Bunk's done, even the man's shadow will be history. Consider it taken care of."

Andrew, totally in the dark in regard to his own warped psyche, considers the two men in the room wickedly demented; he wishes them gone and says, "Unless you have other matters, please drink up and leave. I'd like to be alone for a time."

Sitting in the same chair he earlier occupied, he watches Bunker and Rizzato finish their drinks. As they stand to leave, Rizzato reaches into the front zippered pocket on his backpack and takes out a San Cristobal Maestro and a lighter. Setting them on the coffee table he gives Stratton a brief nod and leaves.

Andrew stares at the cigar, for a quick moment it frightens him, reminding him of the brown dried fingers of his kids. The cigar band eerily resembles a ring. He goes to take another drink when he realizes his glass is empty. He visualizes the bottle of Glenlivet in the kitchen. Glancing at his watch, a Patek-Phillipe he realizes he still has over an hour to wait for his driver's return. He reaches for the cigar, rises with his glass. While heading towards a refill, he hopes he'll be able to walk up the street in an hour.

**

As soon as they leave the apartment building, Bunker and Rizzato jump in a Subaru wagon and head toward Bara Kathaldia, a suburb northeast of the city where flat and fertile land becomes more abundant. It is there on the edge of the city where buildings give way to farmland that Azul Lokesh owns a modest pony ranch. Bunker had followed Lokesh off and on for the last week. The government official maintains a lavish apartment in Gulshan, where his wife and two boys most always stay. Every second night he visits his small farm and relieves the groom who attends the animals while he is in the city. Bunker knows he will likely be here tonight, staying until morning and after 7 p.m., alone.

Bunker drives the twenty miles in silence, nodding only when Rizzato's interjections need reinforcement. Rizzato is gabbing about Lokesh, how he's no good, can't be trusted, lowlife, needs to be put away. All the time he is massaging his groin, his description of the anguish they'd bestow upon this traitor is rapturous telling. Bunker is jealous, irrationally impassioned by this solitary man. Several days after their first brief meeting, he had asked Bunker why he disguised himself. Bunker never said anything, only acknowledging what Rizzato knew with his silence. In his own maniacal way, Bunker yearns for him, adores him, imitates him and would die for him. He doesn't know how to tell him except with his loyalty.

They drove past Lokesh's ranch until the road swings sharply to the right. Bunker parks the car in a copse of trees about a quarter mile beyond Lokesh's farm. There is a pot holed road that is dusty and hard packed running behind the properties parallel to the main road. A neglected corner contains enough shorter growth that the all-wheel drive SUV rides over it with ease and is hidden from casual view. They wait until dusk, when they know that Lokesh will still be grooming the animals. There are five horses and he usually finishes just as darkness fell. The light is low, the last of the sun's rays hiding behind the cityscape on the western horizon, the shadows seeming endless. They have turned the interior light off so it won't shine when they open the door to get out. Rizzato's black boots snap a light twig when he steps down. The sound shoots through the stillness sounding to Rizzato like a sonic boom, but in reality, ten or so meters away the sound dissolves into the dark. It's loud enough to cause Bunker, with a warning sneer, to remind Rizzato to be careful.

Rizzato meets Bunker at the back of the vehicle as he's opening the rear hatch to retrieve a compound bow and a soft suede quiver of arrows that are tipped with Rage broadheads. Easing the hatch closed, he places the quiver behind his back within easy reach and straps the narrow leather band across his chest. He had bought the bow two months ago and had been practicing at the compound. He had always had a bow of one sort or another since he was a child, watching old black and white Westerns on TV with his father, always wanting to be the Indian. Bows fascinate him. He often hunted when possible with the bow, but had never killed a human with one. There is nothing fascinating about this kill for him, but Rizzato wants some drama knowing Bunker is a bow enthusiast. Rizzato insisted he take Lokesh out with the bow, with several arrows in fact, not just one. Most importantly he stressed, he wanted to watch. Bunker told him, "It'd be my pleasure."

They follow the crooked road until they are across the field from the plot that holds his barn. Through the line of trees that grow along the paths, they can see the open door to the barn. Lokesh is brushing the bay mare. They are about one hundred meters away; each field is about fifty meters wide ending at the road they are on which runs parallel to a narrow stream behind them. There is a pile of rotting lumber, a couple of old vehicles, one of them might have been a tractor, all forgotten, at the opposite edge of the field from where they stand directly in line with the barn. Bunker signs Rizzato to be very quiet, then with a swift wave to follow, crouches down until reaching an abandoned stack of wood. He sits at its edge, hidden from view, as he watches Rizzato crawling behind him. He surveys the grounds for anything odd. There is the occasional vehicle that passes by, but it's too dark for them to be seen from the road. The nearest neighbor is some distance away. Bunker watches Lokesh brush the haunches of the horse; the man's right side is fully exposed.

Confident he can't be seen, Bunker stands with back straight, raising the lethal curve. It's an exceptional bow, a Mathews Reezen. He loves how fast and light it is. He notched a Gold Tip Hunter Pro arrow cut to his specific length. Because he is so tall, he has an especially long draw length, 30½ inches, creating tremendous draw weight. Once the cam on the limb rolls over, the bow has a "let off" of about 65%, reducing the draw weight by the same percentage, he could hold it all night. He will wait for the precise moment. He lines up Lokesh's lanky body in his sight. It is only about 20 meters, he estimates, realizing he could easily kill him with one shot. The Rage broadhead will produce an inch and a half entry wound, slicing and severing everything in its pathway. He sights Lokesh just under his arm, thinking how simple it would be to just let fly a bolt that would destroy both lungs, most likely severing the aorta as it passed through. As he is imaging releasing the arrow, he thinks for a moment he will have to shoot true; he doesn't want to hurt the horse. He jiggles a little, laughing inside, ruining his aim. Refocusing he waits until Lokesh is facing him; when the man goes down he wants Lokesh to see his killer. Bunker wants to toy with him; He's thinking he might shoot him three of four times before he dies.

Rizzato has been watching Bunker set his arrow and draw the string taut. He stands in awe of the hulk who looks like a true warrior. There is very little light on them, just a powdering to define the edges. He tries to see the eyes, what's going on in them, because he knows Bunker enjoys killing. He hoped they might reflect what his own eyes must look like, but it's too dark to tell. He checks around the grounds quickly. Everything about them, except the open barn and one window in the house, is in blackness. The city, many miles away, causes the western sphere to glimmer scantily.

Bartolo looks back just as Lokesh turns to face them, walking around the horse, when Bunker's arrow strikes the man just under the right shoulder, passing through his living flesh, cutting muscle, arteries, veins, tendons and exiting a fraction of a second later before thudding into the back wall. The pain is defining.

Lokesh screams! The curry comb flies from his hand as he grasps his wounded shoulder. He staggers for several seconds when another shaft enters his inner left thigh missing the femur by the width of a pixel. The arrow's stainless steel blade is unbelievingly sharp. It pierces and hacks at anything along its route and in this case especially the femoral artery. Whether it is a blessing on not, he will soon bleed to death.

He falls to his knees right behind the reddish brown horse, his garments rubied from the flowing lava of his wounds. The pain he is experiencing is miniscule to the fear that squirms through, consuming him to the soul. He stares at the two approaching men; one huge, drawing another arrow, another tall and gawky, someone familiar, wielding a large hunting knife. He shivers with fright as he hollers for help. His shrieks startle the other horses and several break free. The mare behind him is pulling and bucking when she kicks her back hoofs out in terror, one of them striking Azul at the base of his skull, crushing it and killing him. The worn metal on the horse's hoof actually rescues him from pain more notorious than he had already experienced. His body topples forward from the impact, crashing to the ground. The mare tears free from her restraints and gallops after her stall mates. It becomes disturbingly quiet, and then somewhere far away, something wild and canine bellows into the gloom. It would've chilled ordinary men, but not the two executioners.

Bunker relaxes the tension on the string, lowering the bow as he stops in front of the corpse. He checks the rear exit wounds, nodding his head, satisfied with the arrows' destroying potency. He can see the bone and fractured scalp where the hoof had connected, nodding again in admiration at the killing shot. He is interrupted by Rizzato as he comes up from behind.

"Damn, I was hoping to cut him up a bit while he was still alive, see how loud he could really scream. Oh well, the rat's dead now. That dumb horse did us a favor; did him a favor for sure, right Bunk?"

Rizzato eyes Bunker and he just nods. Rizzato is reminded of Hajani. Real stingy with their words. He kicks some dirt at the body in disrespect and sniffs at the air. The tang of horse manure, made fresh by the animals' recent scare, emits a unpleasant scent. He wrinkles his nose and says, "Let's get this over with and get out of here as soon as we can. This place is giving me the creeps and you know I don't get spooked too easy. Gimme that contraption and grab the body. Let's get it to the car and get rid of it."

Rizzato takes the bow, finding it awkward and cumbersome. He fiddles with it for a moment to get a good grip. His eyes dilate in homage to the sleek executing tool. He holds it with respect. Bunker retrieves his arrows from the firm grip of the wooden stalls, passing them to Rizzato. He easily picks up the dead man, who is slight and at the moment, quite pliable. He carries the body in his arms and if anyone saw them, it would've looked caring almost, the sleeping man cradled in the giant's bulky arms. Any evidence of Azul Lokesh is going to be difficult to find.

Chapter 20

September 18 6:43am Bhola River, Bangladesh

Rizzato and Plum are on their makeshift wharf, whose old planks are interspersed with new lumber. The moorings are solid, sunk into concrete shafts that pierce the river bed. The monsoon season usually lasts from June to October, but this September is unusually dry while the temperature is cooling. The river is still high, obese from its gorging of the rains. It continues on to the Bay of Bengal, oblivious to the villagers and denizens living, working and plotting upon its banks.

They watch the sampan as it putters downriver toward the main flow, where it will push north to Dhaka. They can see Kovalenko in the wheelhouse while Raheem, Bunker, and three peasants, two they have taken on for muscle, the other, a waterman, to sail the boat back, are sitting or standing on the deck. Kovalenko had decided he could work more efficiently at the warehouse, so they are taking the aircraft's engine. Tarps cover the apparatus, which is nestled into the hold and secured to the pallets it rests on. In the next few days the power plant will be dismantled at the warehouse Mado has leased in the Tejgaon Industrial area, not far from the safe house. They have told Rizzato they expect to be back in a week to ten days.

"What do you think, Plum? Can Raheem be trusted to look after those ragamuffins? I can't have any loose ends with Favors running things in Dhaka. I know Raheem usually does what he's told and he's been after me for more responsibility – says he wants to be like me, the little ass-kisser. He's smart enough, but he does stupid things sometimes. They only have to deliver the engine to the warehouse and watch the place for a few days; he can't fuck that up, can he?"

"I don't know, Boss; he's a little too carefree sometimes for me, draws attention. I think Bunker or me, or that creep Morgan should go and keep an eye on him, watch his back, you know."

Rizzato's brow becomes shallow ruts. His washed-out eyes shutter momentarily as he rubs his nonexistent chin; the skin at the base of his neck prickles, the sensation is something intuitive, an inbred early warning system. It isn't strong, just cautionary. He's always paid attention to these premonitions in the past. He reflects on how many times they have saved his precious hide and he says, "Your words are wise, Plum; you surprise me when you think like I do. I need you here; the workers like you. Malik speaks their lingo, so you two do better here. Morgan's looking for those two boys you told us about. I think Bunker's the one for the job. Get him on your radio or cell phone for me."

"The cell phones have not been very reliable here Mr. Rizzato. I'll reach him on the radio."

Plum had been hoping to get away from the compound for a while; she wanted some alone time. Since she had disposed of the young girl's body, she had been formulating an exit plan. She isn't sure if she even wants the blood money anymore and yet she realizes she will need a cushion while she changes her ways. She's dreaming of a home, a good man, maybe children; after all she's only 28, she tells herself. She ruefully ignores these thoughts and paws at her hand held radio.

"Plum to Bunker, over."

Bunker's agitated deep voice replies,

"Yeah, Bunker here. What do you want Plum?"

"I don't want anything, Boss here needs to talk with you," she says passing the radio to Rizzato.

Knowing the other occupants in the sampan might overhear his conversation, Rizzato says,

"As soon as you make Sadarghat, Bunk, get private and call me at the house, use your cell, I have more detailed work for you. Out."

He doesn't wait for a reply. Plum follows Rizzato as he heads off the wharf toward the old metal warehouse at the edge of the river. She watches him from behind with loathing. For the briefest moment she thinks of shooting him in the back. They are alone, Bunker is on the boat and Morgan is gone. She could commandeer the Zodiac and be gone from this nightmare in minutes, but the realization that she will be alone again bothers her more. She dislikes the company she keeps, but being adrift on her own with little funds scares her mightily. Head bowed, she tells herself to be patient and follows Rizzato.

Raheem Ahmedani poses at the bow of the sampan watching the water below; a small wave preceding it like snow before a plough. Bunker is in the wheelhouse chatting Kovalenko up; two of the misfits are in the hold sitting on the slats that case the engine, smoking. The smell of their cheap, harsh tobacco flitters about the boat. As he gazes at the wash, his mind focuses not on the water but on the idea of being in the city alone.

Ahmedani is a sex addict, brutally addicted. His affliction is a dark secret unknown to most, even his cousin Hajani, mainly as a result of his attraction to other men. He is a very masculine man, blue collar attitude, who likes his partners tall, slim and manly. He had been a male prostitute for several years in Pakistan, catering to those who liked their sex rough, until he accidently killed one of his clients. With the assistance of another customer, he had fled to Europe and joined his cousin Hajani, working for De Clerq and eventually Rizzato. The waters he stared at blur as he conjures images of wrestling naked with another man, the phantasm accompanies him all the way to Dhaka.

Bunker on the other hand is thinking of what Rizzato wants. His thinking gets lost as the drone of a small freighter greets them at the mouth of the Bhola River. The sampan yields to the Padi, an elongated low slung transporter, its dark green sides buried deep in the murky channel like a giant pea pod challenging the river's forceful flow. Bunker and the crew turn to port and will follow the laden boat for several hours. One of the paeans they brought along, familiar with the river's mysteries, acts as pilot and guides Kovalenko to the surest routes. Sailing upriver is baffling to a non-native; the waterway is joined with many rivers; from large and bossy ones to tiny rills that spill out upon the shores almost everywhere. The many coves, small isles, river mouths, shimmering sunlight glazing the waters that are rife with river craft greet each sailor, novice or true tar, with a harmony of delights and frights. There are still river pirates, river hazards and careless boaters giving it a darker charm. Fields of crops and riverbanks crested with uncounted trees makes the river friendlier.

The crew is settled for the time it will take to get to Sadarghat. No one is speaking, each person occupied by their own concerns.

Their engine provides a little background disturbance, a duet with the splashing of waters perturbed by the boat's path, lulling them with its repetition. The silence of the crew is rich with gossip, rumours, threats, longings and ideas that swirl around their collective heads. Not one of them could imagine in their wildest moments the events of the next two weeks that will shape their futures, ending it for some.

It's dark when they arrive in Sadarghat. Kovalenko is an experienced boatman, having many of his own watery toys, but nothing prepares him for the turmoil and congestion that accosts him when he tries to dock the sampan. The evening is filled with streams of people upon the jetties, the business day still active even though the sun has long disappeared from the sky. All forms of craft ply the river, many unlit and heedless of whatever might be floating in its path; the scene is pure pandemonium. The berth Reactor Chemicals has rented is annoyingly occupied by a foreign vessel, three times the size of their sampan – the wharf's owner double dipping on fees. They are anchored to the rear of the ship. Bunker is arguing with someone on his cell phone, a disagreement that goes on for over twenty minutes. Finally with Bunker's threat to break both of the owner's knees if they weren't supplied a berth in the next ten minutes, a vacant docking becomes available half a nautical mile upriver. They pull anchor with Kovalenko giving their tinny horn several blasts in formal complaint.

Soon after, a red flashing light beckons them from an empty slot between a dirt-streaked white and green ferry and an iron clad coal freighter. People milling about the passenger ship make it look like a ghoulish anthill while the shanks of the work ship are decorated with multi-colored patches of primer, making it look like a gigantic mural by Booth. Kovalenko steers his bobbing craft adroitly between the behemoths. While they creep toward the wharf Raheem readies the ropes and when they are close enough he throws them to a waiting longshoreman. Kovalenko reverses the engine slightly then kills it, the momentum carrying it forward until it thumps against the tires hung to shield the pier. One of the workers drops an anchor from the rear as the men secure the ropes to the pylon on shore.

Raheem, having snapped out of his reverie when they near the river port, has taken command, setting the workers to get ready to off-load the engine. He sends Kovalenko to retrieve the truck they have hired. Unfolding the map that Bunker has given him he checks again on the location of the warehouse and safe house the company has rented. After reassuring himself on the directions, he climbs two iron rungs to the top of the wharf, the sampan being lower than the pier. He is confronted with workers slick with laboring sweat toiling among the many ships. Vendors, buyers, bystanders, hagglers, beggars and bosses gave the night a toiling chorus. Diesel fumes, body scents and aging detritus create a polluted blend.

Bunker climbs up behind him and over the din of the market abruptly says, "Raheem, I have an errand to run for Mr. Rizzato. When I return, please have the boat ready to sail back. Watch the men staying with you carefully." He lifts his broad chin toward the men in the hold adding, "Keep them busy and don't leave them alone. Get them to the safe house and back, get them fed. Our boss is giving you a chance here. Get this detail done right, could be a bonus. Follow Kovalenko on what he needs but when it comes to security, you're the decision maker. Kovalenko thinks seven to ten days on this. You call *me* with any problems. Don't bug Mr. Rizzato. Are we clear on all this?"

Raheem is eyeing the crowd and nodding his understanding. He says, "I'm on it, Bunk, don't worry. I can handle these workers. I'll keep a close eye on them. Kovalenko told me that they'll be busy helping him anyway. There's not going to be any problems"

He gives Bunker thumbs up, wanting to convince the big Serb he is capable of getting the work done, he has confidence. Looking into Bunker's eyes he gives him a grin.

"Anything else, Bunk?"

Bunker hands Raheem a set of keys, a twist tie knotted through their silver throats. From a back pocket he withdraws a folded envelope fat with taka notes. He says, "This is for gas money, food, that kind of stuff. The keys fit the apartment in Rampura, the warehouse and a Tata Safari. Use the SUV to get around, and no screwing up, Raheem. Drive careful, no speeding or stupid shit to cause accidents. Don't bring any attention to us. I'll be back in a week."

With that he turns from Ahmedani and joins the host of wharf people. His wide shoulders and lofty stature blaze a trail through the busy mob. He's a head higher than the people around him so Raheem can watch him progress until the crowd finally claims him. His attention is diverted by the honking of the horn from the truck Kovalenko has retrieved. Before he supervises the unloading, he eyeballs the sweating workers one more time. Their exposed muscles glisten in the night light and fuel his sinister lust.

Six days later Kovalenko is hovering over the disassembled compressor from the turbine. With calipers and machinist gauges, he is taking the dimensions of the last parts he needs to replace.

He's a shorter man encased in grey, grease-smeared coveralls. Totally bald, the last surviving locks around the base of his skull shorn each morning, his head shines from the overhead lights on his workbench. There is a four inch question mark tattooed on the back of his hairless dome. He's a gangster like all the rest, just from a different country. His best attribute is that he can fix a broken engine much like a veterinarian can treat a sick animal, its inner workings clear in his mind. He's a keen mechanic, psychopath on the side. He empathizes with nuts and bolts and metal shavings but humans bewilder him. He avoids crowds and human contact so the dense mass in the city makes him aggressive and snarly.

He is in a bad mood after having spent the morning tracing a short in the lathe they had purchased before having to rewire from the switch to the motor. He vented his anger by thrashing one of the workers for smoking in the shop; he hates tobacco smoke. Ahmedani broke it up but not before the serf was disabled, suffering a black eye and a missing tooth. It took all Hajani could do to stop the injured worker from calling the police for being assaulted. Then he wanted to go back to Chittagong, but Ahmedani reminded the man of the money he would be losing by leaving before he finished the project he was hired for. The man reflected that the money for this work was more than he would normally make in a year so he grudgingly conceded to Raheem's ministrations, vowing to stay until the end and to smoke outdoors from now on. Hajani knew if the man fled, he would have to kill him. His prickly skin flushed as he thought of Rizzato and his wrath if he messed up.

Raheem had never factored in Kovalenko's disagreeable attitude and ferocity when provoked. Language is a problem; hand signals and gestures, murdered English is how they all communicate when Raheem is busy. He has been continually called upon to split them apart. The worst was an argument when one of the worker's, the one Kovalenko nicknamed *Durnyy*, which is Ukrainian for stupid, dropped his end of the turbine casing on to the workbench almost knocking it to the floor. When Raheem had come from outdoors, Kovalenko was cuffing the worker with the back of his hand while threatening him with the pistol that usually rested in his toolbox. Kovalenko was yelling in Ukraine at the man, who was pleading his innocence in Bengali as they rollicked around the empty space in the back of the workshop acting like two of the Stooges. He had to calm the fiery machinist and bleeding native. He became a nursemaid to the three as well as a field medic.

He is seriously stressed. It is only the fear of Bunker and Rizzato that keeps him from seeking solace in drink and fierce sex. He remains restless every night in anticipation of the delights waiting for him when his nights are free, with cash in his pocket. His urges are so strong, he already planned what he would do if the situation arises; he would sneak out one night for a couple of hours. As he spent his days working with the men and guarding the premises, he watched for any opportunity to break away for a short time, but after six days, there had been none. On day seven, an idea comes to him as sudden as a sneeze. Kovalenko had been bitching about sharing the apartment with the two workers, their constant snoring and farting in the night, the faulty air conditioner that worked only sporadically. He was going on about putting a cot in the warehouse office. Raheem had put him off not wanting to separate the men. Bunker had been specific about keeping everyone together but hadn't warned Raheem of any problems with the Ukrainian. Raheem figures Kovalenko won't be roaming around the city, he is always complaining of the heat and the crowds and the relief he'll experience on returning home. His usual plaint is that he wants to get the job done and go gone. Raheem will arrange for Kovalenko to spend the nights at the workshop. All that remains was to find a secure way to leave the two peons at the apartment alone for several hours and he has an idea on how to accomplish that.

It is an early Saturday morning when he delivers the men to the warehouse and is heading to a small diner to pick up some bagels and have three thermoses filled with tea. While he is there, he procures a phone directory and makes several calls on his cell phone. When he returns, he parks the Safari directly in front of the office door, manhandles the food and drinks before rushing into the warehouse. They have all worked late last night so they are cleaning the work area before they start their day. *Durnyy* is sweeping the floor around the workbenches whistling an odd tune. Kovalenko is changing the grimy and used-up solvent in the cleaning basin while the other worker is cleaning the tools and arranging them in the tool chest as Kovalenko has shown him. The still air in the warehouse is already warming up, permeated with the robust scent of Varsol. Raheem approaches Kovalenko and says, "I've been thinking about your sleeping arrangements, Anton. What you suggest makes sense. I can see how hard you work; you're still at it at night when we all want to go home."

He starts the first of his lies when he adds, "Bunker's cool with you being here by yourself; you can keep an eye on things. Just remember that we're supposed to keep things hush-hush, so be careful of your comings and goings. I'll dig up a cot for you, some sheets and a pillow and after lunch you can take the car back to the safe house and pick up what you need. How's that sound?"

Kovalenko is totally agreeable with the plan. He pats Ahmedani on the back as a stream of Ukrainian dialogue erupts from his toothy grin. He finishes his rant with, "Spasybi! Velke spasybi!" Thanks! Many thanks! And in English says, "Sorry you will not be. I can work hard and much late, you will see."

With that he turns back to his work, filling the deep basin with fresh cleaner.

"Listen Anton, I'll be gone for an hour or so; *please*, be patient with the men. If you want to be away from them at night then don't create more headaches for me, okay"

Kovalenko has his back turned to Ahmedani pouring cleaner into the metal bowl. He gives the question mark a tip and says,

"Yeah, yeah, I know Raheem. I'll be good."

Raheem stares at the tattoo on the back of the man's head, realizing then that the reddish dot at the base of the punctuation mark is not a period but a teardrop of blood. He will wonder off and on throughout the day what that signifies. He will have to hurry to get his things done. As well as finding the cot and sleeping paraphernalia, he plans to stop at a drugstore and pick up some over-the-counter sleeping aid, hoping to dope the two workers later tonight. He jumps in the SUV, already cooking from the rising sun, contemplating his evening of indulgence.

Bunker is hidden across the street, in a building shaded from Ahmedani's view by large palm trees that border the property flanks. The building that shares the grounds with the trees is empty. A huge sign by the driveway declares the space vacant and for let. Large hand drawn digits form a phone number for anyone who might be interested. Bunker watches the Safari race off, tires spinning in the graveled yard proclaiming the driver's hurry. He knows Ahmedani will be lost in the traffic before he can get to his rented car to follow so decides to wait for him to return, thinking he could be on an errand for Kovalenko.

Bunker remembers the conversation he had with Rizzato after leaving the vicinity of the sampan about a week ago. He had found a quieter spot near a warehouse. He was a short ways north of a busy intersection that opened to a main thoroughfare that relieved the clogging of the piers when he had dialed his boss.

Rizzato had warned him of the feelings he was having, instructing him to rent a car, get a hotel room and shadow Raheem. He wanted him to watch him for a few days then get back to the base, which he did after he had tailed him for two days and was confident that he had things under control. He missed the ruckuses that ensued as a result of the close quarters. He had been in touch with Raheem by phone every day, never sensing any irregularities.

Rizzato on the other hand had not been reassured by Bunker's insistence that all was well. When he thought of the detachment in Dhaka, he was still experiencing an uneasiness that he heeded as a warning, sending Bunker back to check on Ahmedani, see if he was up to something, then to take over either way. He instructed Bunker to get the job finished and get back to the compound by the middle of next week latest. It would be ten days since they first left and he knew Stratton would be getting antsy.

Arriving in Dhaka only an hour ago, he observes the warehouse from across the street; checking the grounds. A ten foot lawn separates the building from the street. The facade is beige bricks touched up along their edges with brownish pollution. A patched up parking lot occupies the land to the right, extending twenty feet beyond the rear of the building. Remnants and trash from previous occupants are rusted and rotting behind the building. A galvanized metal fence surrounds three sides of the property supported by tall steel posts.

Just then one of the workers opens a large bay door facing the parking lot and pushes an oversized wheeled garbage receptacle to the back of the building, casually dumping it at the first vacant spot. The whole yard is an environmentalist's nightmare. As Bunker watches him, he is surprised to see the man kick at the garbage and then hurriedly retrieve something from the pile. He notices it is the worker with the big nose; he can see its outline from here. He thinks his name is Ari. The worker looks around as if sensing someone's presence. Bunker ducks a bit lower, losing sight of the man for a second but not before he sees him remove something from inside his coveralls. The Serb moves slightly away from the huge bole he is hiding behind and watches Ari as he chucks a wad of rags onto the pile. Looking around again before reaching for the handles on the bin, he wheels it back to the open door.

Bunker is puzzled by what he has witnessed and will be talking to Ahmedani about it. Right now he has other tasks to attend to. He leaves, meaning to return before the men finish for the day. He'll regret the trouble that her mistaken trust and Raheem's selfishness will bring.

It is just after 8 p.m. when Raheem escorts the two workers back to the safe house. The western sky is drowsy with blues and greys, soft pinks and burning reds as the sun goes into hiding. The colors swirl about like enormous silk scarves before mutating into twilight. All three men pause outside the apartment building, awed by the spectacular sunset. Raheem, anxious to get the men settled, hurries them on, balancing the two pizza boxes on his left arm, steam still rising from the lid of the top box. He had ground up the sleeping pills he had purchased at the warehouse, planning on spreading it over the pizza he will give the workers. They normally watch TV for a while and are abed by midnight, but tonight, they should be asleep by the time they finish eating. At that time, he will be able to get away for several hours.

After entering the apartment, Raheem takes the food to the kitchen and while the other men are changing from their work clothes, he spreads the crushed pills over one of the pizzas, leaving it on the table. He removes two pieces from the other box for himself before storing it in the refrigerator so the men will eat the one on the table first. They soon enter the kitchen and not having eaten since noon gorge on the food, pizza being a rare treat. There is twenty times the regular dosage diffused upon the pie so it isn't long before both men are asleep where they sit in the living room in front of the TV, their snoring attesting to the depth of their slumber.

Raheem changes quickly into clean, loose clothing. He removes a handful of taka notes from the envelope Bunker has given him. Stuffing the money into his pocket, he removes a slip of paper from his wallet before placing it on his dresser. He gazes at the scrawl on the note, remembering the young man who had given it to him. He was thinking of the first time the youth had served him at the deli he had frequented the past week, immediately recognizing his effeminate ways. He had flirted with him for several days before Raheem was comfortable enough to question him on entertainment venues for men of his proclivity. Yesterday the young man had passed Raheem the scrap of yellowish note paper he now holds with the words, 'The Pink Lady' scratched in the margin. Raheem refolds the paper to slip it into his back pocket as he is leaving the apartment; he doesn't notice that the paper actually falls to the floor, fluttering like the seed of a maple tree. The note wedges itself between the carpet and the baseboard of the entryway just to the right of the door. Ahmedani leaves the apartment and the note behind. In less than three hours he will be falling down drunk. In less than six, he will be dead.

Its 10:45 when Raheem jumps into the taxi he had called on his cell phone. The yellow cab is tearing down the vacant street, blue exhaust erupting from its tailpipe. The car swerves as it turns right on to the main thoroughfare, its back wheel catching the edge of the curb. The impact knocks off the hubcap and it rolls down the street like a sliver cookie. Bunker is entering the same street going in the opposite direction and veers from the racing cab, completely unaware of who occupies the front passenger seat. The hubcap rolls toward his Toyota, crashing into the driver's side before being crushed under the vehicle's oversized rear tire. Bunker pulls to the curb cursing the reckless driver. He steps from the car, inspecting the scratches the errant wheel covering has made along the rocker panel and bottom of the door.

As he observes the damage to the car, the worker called Ari is retching in the bathroom of the apartment. The powder Raheem had painted the food with doesn't digest as well as he had hoped. Instead it reacts unfavorably with Ari's digestive system, causing severe stomach cramps and nausea. His stomach rumbles as he belches into the toilet bowl, pepperoni and acidy bile fouling the porcelain throne. He reaches for a towel to wipe the scum from his lips, dizzy from the pill's adverse effects. He rests against the vanity as his head begins to clear. His eyes and mind are bleary from the heaving. Several moments go by before he staggers out of the bathroom. He was heading for his bedroom but in his delirium enters Raheem's bedroom instead. When he recognizes the pile of work clothes upon the floor as Ahmedani's he knows he is in the wrong room. The strangeness of the empty bed sobers him as he realizes that Raheem is not in the apartment. A quick search of the other rooms verifies that the two men are alone. He returns to the bathroom to wash his face. As he splashes the tepid water upon himself he winces from the bruises that the crazy mechanic has left upon his brow the day before yesterday. A sudden wave of homesickness overcomes him. Without Raheem to placate him, he seethes with anger and frustration. He knows he has to get back to Chittagong; he wants to go home.

He packs what little belongings he has into a worn blue duffel bag before going to wake his co-worker. He explains the situation, telling of his decision to flee now that they are alone. The worker they had all come to call Durnyy agrees to leave with him. The two men take their meagre collection of clothing and possessions and leave the apartment.

Bunker is coming up the street intending to pull into the parking lot of the apartment complex when he spies the two men crawling over the fence in the back. They are escaping under the floodlight that illuminates the parking spaces and he recognizes the man with the large nose that he had witnessed earlier at the warehouse. He decides the two men are trying to flee. Before they can see him, he cuts the lights of the car and coasts to a stop in front of the building. He shuts off his vehicle and hastens from the car. He runs to the rear of the building just as the second of the pair clears the fence. Creeping among the other cars until he can see through the gap between the wooden slats, he spots the men as they run between the houses that back the building they have been living in. Bunker sees them reach the other street. They pause in front of the house they had crept beside and seem to be arguing over the direction they should go, each man pointing and waving in opposite directions. He immediately goes into a defensive mode, climbs the fence and begins stalking the men as they take off down the street heading east.

Once again he is amazed at Rizzato's keen sense that something is awry. He is pissed off that some people have no sense of loyalty. While he trots behind the men, his anger blossoms into a full-blown rage. He will have to eliminate them. He closes in on the duo. An evil gleam takes over his usually staid countenance. He is relishing the notion of what he will soon be doing.

The two men hustle away until they come to the junction of streets that serve the Industrial area they have been working in for the last week. Ari explained to Durnyy he had stolen a cordless drill while he was taking out the garbage that morning and has hidden it in the bushes behind the workshop. He convinces him that they should retrieve it and sell it. The money they can probably get for it will feed both of their families for several weeks. Durnyy agrees to fetch the tool as they also needed money to hire a boat to take them back home. The only money they have is sixteen 1 taka coins Raheem had given them for spending money while they were in Dhaka. While that is equivalent to a week and a half's wages at the Breakers, it might not be enough to get them home.

A half hour later they finally reach the warehouse. The night is murky and moonless; burst and shattered street lights make the grounds indistinct. Blackness envelopes the rear of the warehouse and the two men stumble on debris while searching the bushes for the precious bounty. They are totally unaware of Bunker's presence as he approaches. He waits by the side of the building for his eyes to adjust to the absence of light. All that is visible are the shapes of the men as they scuffle about the back yard. The only other noises in the deserted industrial park are the rats and wild cats scurrying about the rotted garbage that has gathered at the rear of the adjacent buildings. A collection of wooden pallets lean against the back wall. Bunker scrunches his bulk into the shadows of the frames, scheming of taking the first one out with no noise so as to not alert his companion. He hates running, giving chase to startled quarry is not Bunker's forte; rather a hunter's patience dwells inside his heavy chest so he would wait.

Kneeling beside the barricade, his diligence is soon rewarded. The two men are having trouble finding the drill as Ari can't orient himself in the dark forgetting where he has stowed it. He is wandering toward the bushes at the back of the property while Durnyy is drifting toward the rear of the building looking for something else to steal. Bunker watches his approach. About ten feet away from him he stops on the tarmac in the night shadow of the large bay door. Bunker is bewildered at what the man is staring at; his silhouette is unmoving and remains so for many minutes. Then he realizes Durnyy is listening. He slows his breathing, willing his pulse to slow down. Bushes rustle in the distance, the search not yet successful.

Durnyy isn't listening per se but rather feels another presence. There is a strange aura about that disturbs him. It's weightier here at the edge of the building. His mother, his grandmother and her mother have all experienced the same form of what they gathered to be paranormal, like a sixth sense of another's presence. The kids of each generation joked of eyes in the back of their mothers' heads. But this eye is in their skin. Right now, tiny static-electricity sparks are going off inside his body. He has never been so scared.

He has every reason to be terrified when Bunker lunges from behind the pallets with a swiftness that would have made Nureyev proud. Fingers the size of thick rope clenches the man's throat, locking on like wolf's fangs. He squeezes, ending the man's ability to breath, to scream. He lifts him by the neck until his arms are fully extended to the sky. The dying man's hands beat at the mighty fists. His kicks are weak and ineffectual. Bunker holds him aloft as his body whips about like a dying fish. Lack of oxygen soon stops his heart and he melts in his killer's grip. He places the crumbled corpse noiselessly on the ground. The swishing of the search among the alder bushes at the rear of the property stop. Bunker drops to a crouch in the penumbra of the building and listens. An exuberant voice calls out. Ari has found the drill and is waving it in the air. He is coming towards Bunker.

In a husky whisper Ari calls out in his native tongue, "Durnyy, you fool, where are you? I found our ticket home. Let's get away from here."

No answers come from the night. With a hint of worry he says, "Tanvir, what are you doing? You and I..."

The words are cut off when Bunker stands up in front of him to ram her tremendous fist into his face, pulverizing nose cartilage, jaw bone and teeth all in one blow. The force of his swing knocks the man to the ground. A bloody gurgling shriek leaves his throat as Bunker drives his booted heel down upon the shattered face, driving shards of facial bone deep into the brain. Death arrives right away but he continues to stomp the battered skull until it is trampled pulp.

Stepping away from the grisly work he pants from his efforts. He takes deep breaths while looking around for any witnesses. He wants to cry out with a warrior's victorious yell, the smell of death clinging to the eventide. Instead he bends to pick up the dead man's feet, dragging him to the front of the warehouse. He deposits him behind the ragged shrubs that grow by the front of the building before going to retrieve the other body. After dumping the second corpse there as well, he runs back to where the car is. He brings it to the side and places the bodies in the trunk. Kovalenko is passed out inside the building from hard drink and never heard a thing.

While driving around the industrial park looking for a ditch, he removes the stiletto from the sheath at his waist, placing it on the front passenger seat. The polished razor tip glistens in the glare of the streetlights. Moments later he finds a littered channel cut around the edges of the park. He stops the car in the murkiness. Pulling the bodies from the car, he places them face down on the ground. He uses the point of the knife to carve a crude Z on the shoulder of each man before he heaves the carcasses into the tainted rut that is already slushy with debris.

It is 1:51 a.m. when Bunker drives away from the abandoned figures. He is extremely upset. When he goes looking for Raheem, he is telling himself that it doesn't matter what the Pakistani's reasoning is. His appetite for slaying has only been whetted.

Dark Side of a Promise

Chapter 21   3:05 a.m. Road #5, Dhaka

Bunker pulls the car into the parking lot at the safe house. He glances up at the ninth floor noting that the lights are on. He assumes Raheem is still there, probably drunk. His anger has dropped a notch but not enough to stop him from slapping the Pakistani around for his carelessness. He had been fuming when he left the Industrial Park. Rizzato is going to go ballistic when he finds out that the two workers had been left unsupervised, allowing them to get out on their own. The only security Bunker will have when he informs Rizzato is that the culprits have already been liquidated. He remains in the car for a moment with the windows rolled down.

The night air is warmer than usual, as lifeless as a pane of glass. So too is Bunker as still. He stares at the fence where the two men had clambered over only hours ago. He guesses that Raheem will not tbe found upstairs; if he is, he'll most likely be dead. He is calculating any danger that could exist; something unusual is happening. Sphinx-like, he waits for over thirty minutes. Satisfied nothing is amiss; he leaves the car to head for the ninth floor apartment.

He takes out the key to the flat, holding it cupped in his hand. He gives a sharp knock then reaches for the brass knob with his free hand. The door clicks open. Before swinging it inward he withdraws a P08 Parabellum from a holster inside his shirt. Manufactured in 1944 by Georg J. Luger, in mint condition it cost him $15,000.00.

It's his favorite weapon. Standing to the left of the entry, he gives the door a push with a triple E toe. There is enough energy to send the door banging against the inside wall. It's certain to alert anyone to his presence. He tarries a moment before entering; the rooms are silent. Cautiously he approaches each room throughout, finding them empty, no sign of either Kovalenko or Ahmedani other than a pile of clothing in one room. The closets and dressers are empty in the next two rooms also. He doesn't believe that anyone is at the warehouse; he has just come from there and it had been in total darkness. The Safari is in the parking lot. He's stumped. His head hangs for a minute as he stands in the deserted entryway. He realizes he has a problem. As much as he feels loyalty to Rizzato, he understands that his boss will flay him alive if he loses Kovalenko, his mechanic. Ahmedani they can dispose of if they have to. He hopes with a portion of his stone heart that it isn't the police that have them.

He begins to pace as he tries to decide his next step, guessing that he will have to tell Rizzato and have him send Malik and Morgan. He dreads making the call even though he had never let him down before. Rizzato will remind him that Stratton is going to be displeased if he learns of the missing men. He is standing by the door when he hears voices from the end of the hallway, someone coming home late. Treading lightly on the carpet he reaches over and soundlessly closes the door. As he turns to continue his circling, he catches sight of a piece of yellow paper the size of a book of penny matches stuck in the edge of the carpet. It contrasts with the white baseboard and he would've noticed it before because it has been behind the door.

He reaches down to pluck it from its refuge. Opening the fold he focuses on the three words that doesn't mean a thing to him as he can't read English. As a matter of fact, he can't read at all. The failing of his schooling is one more pin in his voodoo doll, one more sharp point to his inner despair. He hates the scratches on the paper. The eleven characters on the yellow paper he holds could have come from outer space for all he can tell. Self-pity sticks another long needle in him, impaling his decaying nerves. It electrifies his anger, forcing him into gear. He knows what he is going to do.

He leaves the building and jumps in his car. He speeds around the busiest streets until he spies a black taxi, the ones used by the locals. This one has a dented trunk that is held closed by a bright red bungee strap. It announces its presence with a ruptured muffler as it disgorges its occupants near an all-night market. Bunker approaches the car. He takes the note from his shirt pocket as well as a twenty dollar US note from his wallet, tucking the duo between two fingers.

The man in the driver's seat looks old enough to have met Allah personally; thinning grey hair caps a pale wrinkled visage. Bleary reddened eyes look up at the large person who is approaching him. He detests foreigners. He is thinking that one of them wanting something at this hour, is up to no good. He can never understand their gibberish, most of them too stupid to know his tongue, he often exclaimed to his friends. He doesn't want any trouble tonight he decides and floors the aged Volvo. Only three of the required four cylinders work properly and it hesitates as if it has dementia and is unsure what to do. The small engine evens out and the car gives a lurch. The ancient cabbie rumples his cheeks in a faint smile thinking he is clear of the *foreigner.*

Bunker is about ten feet away from the oncoming car. He waves the twenty dollar bill that is wedged between the first two fingers of his right hand and steps in front of the car. Only two wheels have functioning brakes, albeit with brake pads so badly worn they are down to the rivets that hold them together. The rivet heads are screeching as they dig into the metal brake drum when the driver stomps on his brakes, bringing the car to a sideways halt only a few inches from the human barrier. A dirge of foul language bursts from the frightened man, complaining of the stupid foreigner's stupid actions. He puts the vehicle in park and leans out the window saying in a mixture of Bengali and Pakistani, "What is the matter with you, are you stupid? You could have wrecked my car you big ape. What kind of manure do you eat, you swine, to make you so large? What..?"

The cabbie abruptly shuts up when he stares at the big person's eyes. They are dilated more than they should be. The grizzled hack stares into the deepest, darkest and emptiest pools ever; the inner corneas are misshapen and he imagines a skull where the pupil should have been. It makes him think of ice and a chill scurries along his backbone. Only when the Serb lowers his hand to the driver's eye level to flash the US money does he look away. The lure of money is stronger than the fright of the unknown. Apprehensively he takes the money offered to him and notices the yellow scrap of paper. He lays the twenty in his lap and opens the note. Unfortunately for Bunker, the man can't read English. But the old hand recognizes the scribbling. He knows where there is a small brass plaque with the same markings on it.

The old man peers up once more at the person who towers over him. He knows what the clientele do at The Pink Lady and is thinking he wouldn't want to be on the receiving end of this big lug's aggressive and impassioned energy. The man is standing there waiting; he doesn't say anything. The cabbie isn't sure what to do. He can use the money; his son is sick and his three grandchildren are hungry. He lifts the twenty from his lap and pointing at it, raises three fingers. He reaches over and curls one finger into his palm then lifts the twenty and points at the finger deducted from the three, then stresses the paired fingers left over.

The Serb nods taking forty more dollars from his wallet. As he hands over the money, the driver motions for Bunker to get in. Bunker shakes his head and pantomimes driving while pointing to his own car, waving him to go ahead. The driver again tips his head in understanding and relaxes as he realizes the hulk will not be in the car with him. He watches as Bunker goes back to his vehicle, folding himself in. He drives away slowly as Bunker turns to pull in behind him. Fifteen minutes later the cabbie slows and points to a dimly lit street that reeks of temptation. The black and dusty taxi speeds away, its rotted muffler making the only noise in the night.

Bunker parks his car behind a dumpster in a refuse-ridden alley two blocks away. Sticking to the shadows, he walks down the left side of the street where there are more dingy lights above or near the doors. Some are of such low wattage the glow they cast is only the size of a basketball, most often only to illuminate a name plate. He walks eight blocks before the street dead ends, a six floor office building standing in its path. None of the signage along the street looks like the marks on the paper.

He looks back the way he has come. He notices that a few people came from the odd entryway here and there along the street portion he can see from where he stands; their shoulders scrunched trying to distort their identity. Depravity and sin within its walls along with obscure illumination give the street an unpleasant pall. Bunker is crossing the roadway when a half a block from where he is a door bursts open and a disheveled man is literally tossed from the premises. Bunker is close enough to witness the man falter before falling. He lands on his shoulder, scraping it along the raw asphalt. The man is sodden with liquor, malodorous of cheap whiskey and beer. He ends up lying in a fetal position groaning from the torn skin on his upper arm. His back is to Bunker.

Bunker dashes ahead, ducking back into an unlit doorway near him. It doesn't conceal him totally but he doubts the drunk can see clearly in the condition he's in. The door opens once more, with another evictee being given the boot. This one is still standing but well into his cups. He is turning to face the doorman but is too late as the door slams shut. The man yells at the slab instead, "We just want one more dink...Ah, I mean drink!"

Rafan Bashara doubles over, snickering at his own raillery. His merriment is soon interrupted by the moaning of his cohort. He straightens up and staggers over to the prone body and says, "Look at the fucking mess you made of your arm, Raheem. You're going to bleed to death before I get you home. Come on. I'll help you up and we'll get my car, but we're going to have to walk a ways."

Bunker immediately goes all ears when he hears Raheem's name. He's fuming. He's about to step out and arm twist him back to the car when he is halted by the stranger's next remark.

"Come on you brute, you silly brute, you can tell me more about the asshole you said you work for – Rizzato wasn't it? Or something like that... yeah. And I can't remember where you said you were working. Anyway we can talk some more later."

Rafan gets Raheem hoisted up with an arm around his shoulders trying not to touch the wound. He straightens Raheem's shirt, tucking the torn part of the sleeve inside itself. He's trying to steer him up the street a couple of blocks where he thinks he left his car. He listens to the intoxicated man's blather, thinking he would normally take a cab but tonight is different. He concentrates on his good fortune and the most unlikely coincidence of hearing Rizzato's name, He remembered in the bar when Raheem was belittling his boss, calling him ugly and crazy. He realized where he had heard the name Bartolommeo Rizzato before. His heart had almost stopped when he grasped it was the man who had killed his cousin Sakeema and her friend Amber Payne. He's torn between wanting to detain the man to get more information from him or turn him over to the police. He had been trying to lag behind Raheem's drinking without provoking his curiosity, but they are both loaded and he knows he shouldn't be driving. But he wants to get him home as soon as he can. He's itching to call his uncle.

They venture up the center of the road reeling like a top at the end of its momentum, their slurred chatter dissipating in the gloom. Bunker stays well behind them, creeping along the doorways. The buildings that share the street are butted up against each other at staggered heights with no alleyways. Some have porticos; others have recessed openings that make tailing them quite easy. They are unaware of anyone paying attention to them. Bunker watches constantly until the two lushes turn a corner after several cross streets and disappear from his view. He hurries to the exit they have taken, sticking close to the buildings shielded by the murkiness they offer. He spots them in the front row of an almost vacant parking lot that is well lit. He slips into the rear entry of the first building on his right. The parking lot is across the street and the next lot down. Bunker can clearly see the tall skinny one wadding something that seems to be paper and Raheem is spread out on his back on the hood of the Mercedes. The Pakistani is a terrible looking hood ornament, he notes. Scanning the street up and down, Bunker sees no one about.

As he watches the stranger fumble in his pocket for his keys he takes out his gun, thinking to take out the newcomer first then torture Ahmedani to find out what stories he told and who he told them to. He's standing in a makeshift porch. Grey and weathered plywood cover the ten by ten stoop. There is a rough opening for a door that has never been installed and he steadies his pistol on the naked wood of the jack stud. Bunker's target is doing an inebriated waltz while he digs about in his pockets, it is difficult to draw a bead on him, but Bunker is patient. He eyes the post on the tip of the Luger's barrel centering it in the rear notch waiting for the dark man's head to be directly in front of the post. Just as Rafan's swaying noggin is on a trajectory that will bring him in the sights, Bunker is fantasizing of the hole the bullet will make on the other side of the man's head. His finger trigger tightens a fraction of an ounce.

Rafan is cursing and bobbing. It's good luck for him that he can hardly stand up. Weaving up and down and back and forth he shouts out, "Hurrah, I found the buggers."

He makes to grab his keys from under his wallet when his index finger hits the bright red panic button on the electronic fob. The Jaguar immediately comes alive, its horn blaring, lights flashing. It startles Bunker and only his slick nerve keeps his from shooting accidently. It startles others as well. The light comes on over his head. Someone is coming out to investigate the noise. Bunker hastens away in the opposite direction until he's back in the shadows but still in sight of the men. Hunkering down near a garbage bin he watches as the owner gets his key fob out pointing it at the car until he finally hits the right button and the furor stops. By this time there are several people checking the action, too many, thinks Bunker; he will have to follow the two men.

Raheem has slid from the hood and lays face down on the ground. The horn doesn't disturb his delirium. Rafan and one of the nosy bodies hurry to heft up his accomplice once more to shuffle him into the car. Rafan gets them away in a puff of blue smoke as the tires add another shriek to the night. The Jag isn't new but in exceptional condition except for the left taillight. It's always shorting out and the garage doesn't know why. Tonight is one of the nights it doesn't function properly and as such, will work to Bunker's advantage. The few times he loses them on the way to New Market, the missing taillight proves to be the clue in relocating them up and down the streets.

Rafan parks the car in one of the eight numbered slots at the rear of his building. There is another couple standing at a car door in slot number three, sneaking kisses in the early morning. Rafan recognizes the young man from the second floor, always with a different girl. He grunts at what he perceives as foolishness. Raheem is beginning to stir from the sudden lack of motion. Rafan elbows him and says, "C'mon big guy, give me a break here. Get it together and I'll help you inside."

Raheem is having nightmares of Bunker finding him away from the apartment. He is lost somewhere in alcoholic space trying to remember where he is and what time it is. The car door opens and Raheem almost falls out. Rafan catches the man pushing him back upright. He reaches down and grabs Raheem's feet placing them on the ground. With a worried voice Raheem says, "Thanks man, for... for looking after me. I'm kinda fucked up. Uh, I got to get going man; Bunker's going to be pissed and my shoulder is stinging."

"No, no, you can't go yet, Raheem. I'm going to fix that scrape and we're going to have fun. You promised me you were going to stay the night. I'll take you wherever you have to go tomorrow morning, c'mon man! Who's Bunker anyway?"

Raheem leans out of the car, his head in his hands; the picture of destitution.

"Never mind fella. Shit, I can't even remember your name. Is it Rabin? Oh no, I think I'm going to be sick."

"No, you idiot, its Rafan, Mr. Rafan Bashara. Don't puke here, hang on" And being a little facetious he says, "And I'm the General Manager of Saad Enterprises, Bangladesh, by the way. I'm very important."

He laughs and lifts Raheem under his good shoulder, helping him upright when Bunker catches up by foot to where he has seen Rafan park his car. He witnesses the man that Raheem has befriended trying to get Raheem out of the front passenger's seat. Thinking there is no one about, he decides to overtake the tall man and choke him and then deal with Raheem later. He is only one building away. Abruptly one of the parked cars starts up and is reversing into the alley he's in. He offers a malediction in his Slavic tongue at the interruptions he is encountering. He can see a young girl waving from the front seat of the moving car, so there could be others around. Ducking behind a parked car he cranes his neck around the bumper to get a better view.

The young man that had been giving his date mouth-to-mouth runs over to help Rafan with his burden. The two of them manage to wrestle Raheem up to the door. As Bunker creeps from the rear of the car, he reaches for his gun again. By the time he has it unholstered, the back door of the apartment building has shut with a slam. He runs over to the entryway and begins pulling at the locked door. Through the glass in the sidelight he can see the three men ascending the stairs along the opposite wall. As they approached the mid-floor landing, Rafan spies a giant moving away from the door. It's nobody he knows and forgets about it.

They get Raheem as far as the front hall of the flat, where they drop him on the floor. He has passed out on the way in and they had to drag him up the last flight of stairs. The young man turns down Rafan's offer to share a refreshment as a reward for his help, bidding them good evening and the peace of Allah. Rafan shuts the front door and gazes down at the man on the floor, thinking he really doesn't look so good anymore. Thank goodness he's sobering up, he reflects.

He has a foreboding that there is trouble coming. He might need somewhere else to stay. There is only one man he feels he can trust, his closest friend, Panji. He will call him right away and then he will call his uncle. He dials up his buddy, listening to twelve rings before a voice that sounds like a throat full of steel wool answers. He spends the next twenty minutes sprawled out on his bed relaying the details of the evening, not mentioning which bar. By the time they are finished their conversation, Rafan can't stay awake. He drops the phone on the floor, dropping off the rim of consciousness. When he wakes three hours later, Raheem is gone.

Ahmedani is in a slurred dream. He sees himself standing in front of a wall size mirror in an otherwise empty room. The whole room is stark white, there are no defining lines of floor, or wall, or ceiling, just a feeling of squareness. He isn't looking at the silver backed glass but down at his body. He is bare-chested and wears only a dull charcoal lungi. The copper skin of his bare feet fascinate him. He can focus on the hairs on the second joint of his toes, which seems to him to be of such clarity that he can count them. He wiggles his toes and espies the reflection of the moving toes in the mirror. He watches them for what seem like many minutes. He becomes frightened because the toes aren't his. He freezes.

With his heart trying to get out of his chest, he slowly scans upward at the image in the mirror. The lungi is the same color as his own but where it would have stopped on his true reflection it continues until it comes to fleshy handles that hang over the cloth like bread dough, tapering out to a scrawny caved-in hairless chest. He doesn't want to look at the face because he already knows who will be staring back at him. He moves his hand slightly instead and the likeness does the same. He watches goose flesh form all over his opposite's body. His heart is racing, pounding, his brow is wet and slick. Every second in his dream seems as a minute.

When he has enough courage he looks up at the face. What he feared the most becomes pitilessly real as he stares up at Rizzato's vacant grey eyes. Even though he feels his eye blink, the orbs in the mirror drill deeply into him, then with a maddening hiss a black slimy forked tongue ejects from the mouth, coming right out of the glass. Just before it strikes Raheem in the face he wakes with a heavy gasp. His heart is still speeding. His clothes are soaked with perspiration. He sits up and rubs his aching head, relief and agony are co-hosts to his awakening. He looks around, not having a clue where he is. Seeing a clock on the hallway wall he curses; it is very late.

Bunker had posted himself where he can see through the window of the back door of the apartment building. He had returned to his car and parked it lengthwise behind the dark green Jaguar. The adjoining building bestows its shadow upon it, hiding it from casual view. The back door on the driver's side is slightly ajar. He has removed several items from the trunk: a roll of duct tape, a pair of handcuffs and a police man's truncheon. The baton hangs from his belt, the handcuffs are open and in his shirt pocket. The duct tape is on the trunk of his car, missing a one-foot strip that is flattened and sticking to the thigh of his jeans. The glue on the tape will barely be blemished from resting on the denim and he knows it will be strong enough to do the job he requires.

He sees movement on the landing and just then Raheem comes into view. He rushes over to the left of the door knowing it swings in to the right. Flattening his mass along the wall as best as he can, Bunker unloosens the truncheon from his belt. Placing his right wrist through the leather loop on the end of the handle, he grasps it with a substantial mitt.

Raheem is almost running when he bursts from the door as if the monster in his dream is chasing him. He has no idea of the fate awaiting him on the other side. Cumulonimbus clouds, tall, vertical and dense, have formed in the night and the early morning is nebulous as is his fuddled head. He only notices the bulk standing in the shadows when it is much too late. Bunker steps up to the fleeing man and cracks the baton into the joint behind his knee. The impact adds to the force of his forward movement sending him sprawling to the ground with shooting pains raising hell up his leg. Before he can even cry out, Bunker straddles his upper body, and pulling the duct tape from his thigh, wraps it around his face, covering his mouth. Surprise, pain, fright and pounding claustrophobia crowd his brain and he blathers behind the tape like a child.

Before he can react, Bunker forces one of his arms behind the man's back to subdue him. Raheem's arm is almost wrenched from its shoulder socket with pain beyond what he can bear. He forces a muffled yell from his panicked lungs, tears and snot the evidence of his terror. Bunker tosses the baton in the back seat of the car, snatching the handcuffs from his pocket. He snaps one stainless steel circle closed upon a wrist. He barks into his ear, "You've been very bad, Raheem. Give me your other arm or I'll break this one off."

Raheem is gasping behind the barrier on his lips; breathing through his nose is becoming difficult. He moves his unfettered arm from beneath his body, swinging it around his back. Bunker handles it roughly, clasping it into the free handcuff. He releases the other arm and turns him over. Raheem's eyes are like light bulbs, fearfully swollen and bright.

"I'm going to help you up Ahmedani and you're going to get in the car. My gun is only seconds away, so be very careful of your actions and don't even think of running."

He nods his head in agreement. Muzzled pleas gain no sympathy from his captor. Bunker lifts him off the ground as if picking up a leaf. He guides him the twelve steps to the car, opens the rear door shoving him in. Climbing in behind he pulls the door quietly shut. Raheem sits crouched against the opposite door, his arms against the door frame with the handcuffs pushing against his lower back. Behind the tape he mouths, "Don't hurt me, Bunker. Don't hurt me, don't hurt me" over and over to no avail. The sounds are smothered, echoing and dying in his throat. Sitting up straighter, he hangs his head while forcing air through his nostrils, panting like a ridden horse, wailing.

"Shut up, you fool," says Bunker, reinforcing his command with an open-handed slap to the side of Raheem's head. Raheem careens back in the seat from the force of the slap. Before he can respond with a scream or more tears, the giant has his stiletto out pointing it tight under Raheem's chin. There's enough pressure on the point that it breaks the skin and any forward or sudden movement from Ahmedani will cause it to impale the skin at the floor of his mouth.

"I'm going to ask you a few questions and I'm only going to ask you once Raheem and if you want to see the sunrise, I expect your answers to be correct. Blink hard if you understand."

Raheem blinks so hard he may have bruised his lids.

"If you move or if I'm tired of listening to lies I'll drive the point of my stiletto through your mouth into your brain. You might not die right away, but you will certainly hope you were going to. So we're going to have one blink for yes and two for no. Things go right; we can get back to work. Is that clear Raheem?"

Another hard blink.

"I heard your new friend talking about our boss; I think you called him crazy. Did you tell anyone else Raheem?"

Two powerful blinks.

Bunker stares in the man's eyes. He can see Raheem is scared. He has experience with scared people and they often tell you what they think you want to hear. He changes hands with the stiletto, freeing his right. The point digs in a millimeter farther, almost lifting Raheem off the seat. He strains in the seat, trying to elongate his neck. With his free hand, Bunker removes another knife from his back pocket. There is nothing special about the folded pocket knife except its stainless serrated blade with tiny half-moon razors.

"I don't like your answer Raheem. Try again."

He flicks the blade out with his thumb and swipes the open blade across Raheem's rib cage in one motion. The serrations easily cut the cotton of the shirt while slicing the underlying skin open like soft rubber. The point of the knife etches its signature along the ribs bones and sternum. Small severed blood vessels erupt with a red pulsing flow. Raheem's pink muscle shirt is being decorated with human ink. He screams within.

Ahmedani blinks his teary eyes twice quickly, trying to mime his certainty that he didn't tell anyone else. The pain across his chest burns like a thousand candles dripping hot wax upon his skin. He knows he is going to die. He locks his brain in revolt thinking to bring his chin down and end the pain to come. Bunker senses the movement and releases the point microseconds before Raheem's attempt. He slams his huge fist into the face, propelling him against the far door. The eye he struck immediately begins to swell.

"I'm going to remove the tape from your mouth for one second, Raheem. I want to know the name of the man you were with and where Kovalenko is. I'll know if you're lying and it won't be pleasant for you. Believe me, it can get much worse than the position you are in right now."

Bunker tugs the tape edge at the back of Raheem's skull and with a forceful yank uncovers his mouth. Raheem is gasping with relief at finally being able to breathe through his mouth. Between gulps he says, "Rafan, the man's name is Rafan," he wheezes, "Rafan Bashara. Kovalenko is at the warehouse; he's sleeping there. Please Bunker let me go. I won't fuck up again, I promise. I…"

He pulls the tape tight and rewinds it around the head, shutting his pleas off. He feels for certain that Raheem hasn't lied. He knows he should kill him now, but before he does he will cut him some more, watching panic consume him from inside. His cutting knife slices across Raheem's face' opening up his cheek. He's screaming behind his mask, air and blood escaping from the severed cheek, begging with his eyes to be free.

Bunker tortures him for ten more minutes before he delivers the stroke that kills him. He moves from the vehicle, removing the blood-smeared latex gloves he wears turning them inside out before pocketing them and straightens out his clothes. Looking around he sees the new day beginning. Early workers are leaving their homes; garbage collectors are at the head of the street. He will have to be fast. He removes a small tool set from his front pocket and fiddles with the lock on the trunk of the Jaguar. He isn't as speedy as his teacher had been but there isn't a lock he can't pick. The trunk clicks open with a welcoming snap. He waits a few seconds, scanning the surrounding alley and windows to make sure he isn't being watched. Carrying the corpse from the car he places it in Rafan's trunk. Before he closes the lid, he once again removes his stiletto and scores a crude Z upon the shoulder of the dead body.

Turning towards the apartment building Bunker stares at the top floor. He knows he will have to get to Mr. Bashara before he can blab to anyone. He assumes he'll be sleeping all morning and that the surprise in his trunk should keep him quiet for a while. It's a chance he'll have to take. But first he has to get rid of the car he's driving, with its blood stained trunk and back seat, evidence of his killings. He's also thinking that later he will have to get to Kovalenko: find out how much longer the mechanic is going to be, if he needs help. After he will return to the ranch to relay the night's events to Rizzato in person, a task he dreads with all of his ruptured heart.

Chapter 22   Sept 29 Westin Hotel, Dhaka

Rafan had been relating his story to the group for over an hour with few interruptions. Rae recorded the highlights of his tale with her own form of shorthand but her pencil drops when Rafan is telling them of finding the body in his trunk,

"...and there were deep blood crusted cuts all over him, it must have been very painful when he was alive. I still see the body in my dreams...no, no, in my nightmares. It won't go away."

He hangs his head in his hands, elbows resting on the table. The circle sits in silence as Rafan deals with his demons. A huge teardrop wells from his eye lid to splash on the writing pad in front of him. He takes several deep breaths and says, "And the worst part of the whole night, the part that haunts my visions the most, is his face. The face still strapped with that filthy grey tape, the slash on his cheek with his eyes still open and dead...dead as the rest of him. It was terrible."

Rae passes him a napkin and Rafan dabs at his eyes, blows his nose, takes a drink from his water glass and says, "I immediately called my uncle, Uday, then I left for my friend Panji's parent's house and remained there until I arrived back in the city yesterday. And that's it, here we are."

He looks around the table, settling his eyes on Drake. Drake gives him a reassuring wink and his trademark grin saying, "Thanks, Rafan. I can appreciate how brave you've been in confiding aspects of your personal life. I want you to know – actually we all want you to know – your life is no one else's business but your own. That information doesn't leave the room. Everyone agree?"

They all respond with a positive gesture, Rafan is part of the team.

"Rest easy, Rafan, we'll keep you hidden, or maybe you could visit your uncle or Williston on the Drifter? You think about it, Rafan."

Rafan says, "Thank you to all of you. I feel safe in your company. If you would excuse me now, I would like to rest for a bit. Could I perhaps lie down Drake?"

"Certainly, Rafan. Okay, folks, let's take a ten-minute break. We'll go over the leads we have from Rafan, then I want to talk about the marks again."

They disperse to stretch their legs, visit the washroom and refill their drinks. Some are into the stronger fluids: the brothers open new beers and Rae opens a liter of white wine. Gurupada is still drinking water. Drake leads Rafan to a second bedroom that contains an ensuite; Drake pats him on the back before leaving him at the door. Drake looks over the others as he comes back to the dining room, Pada and Rae head to head. The twins, Drake knows, will be speculating about Rafan's comments in the childhood idioglossia only they can understand, which perplexes him to this day. He has a good team. All they have to do is find Rizzato now, figure out how they will deal with him later.

"All right, gang, let's get to work."

Everyone shuffles back to their respective chairs; Drake pulls up a seat to sit opposite them.

"I'd like to see you, Rae, work with Isaac; Eli can team up with Pada." Pointing at Rae and Pada with his pencil he says, "You two know the city, speak the language. Is that okay with everyone?"

Elijah, ever the teaser says, "Pada, be careful, trouble is attracted to my brother. Watch his back for him. I know he'll be watching yours. I guess I'm the lucky one, getting the prettiest of the bunch for a pard. Too bad guys."

A pinkish tinge shades Rae's complexion as she smiles inside at the openness of these North Americans. She thinks again of Dakin at the hospital, when she had been admiring his sleeping face before she left. She enjoys the way she feels when she thinks of him.

"Thank you, Elijah. I must warn you that when I pick up a scent, I don't let it go until I discover where it leads. You might not think you are so lucky if our days are long and often dangerous."

"I don't mind dangerous, Rae, that's what I've been trained for. As far as time goes, I'm ready for whatever is needed. "

He turns to Drake and said, "Ain't that right, Boss?"

"You bet, Elijah, and I appreciate it. So do Williston and Uday."

Drake rattles a few pages from his pad and says, "I've itemized some things we should be checking out from Rafan's story. He mentioned that the man with him, wait what was his name, again, Rae?"

"He has been identified as Raheem Ahmedani, a Pakistani."

"Right! So this Raheem mentioned Bhola. What does that mean to you, Pada?"

Gurupada has been mostly quiet up to this point, concentrating on the details he's been hearing. He's removed his jacket and the protruding gun from his shoulder holster makes him look more like a gangster than a cop. He says, "Well that could mean several things, Drake. One of Bangladesh's districts is Bhola, the largest island region encompassing over 3,000 square kilometers. The region is only accessible by boat and lies about 90 to 100 nautical miles south of Dhaka. We had a triple homicide there about a year and a half ago and I assisted in solving the case."

He smiles at Drake at this admission, not to brag but as a confirmation of his abilities.

"But there is also a community called Bhola, as well as the Bhola River, all within the region. It is a very large area with many rivers and waterways. People can and do hide out there for some time before being discovered. Because Ahmedani was not more specific, I suggest we start with the town. Do you have access to a river craft?"

Drake said, "Not at present, but I'll take care of that later. You tell me what kind of terrain we'll be navigating, what kind of boat we'll need. We can work it out in the morning. Do you know the area or do we need a guide?"

"I am familiar with the area so I can act as your guide. The bad guys will no doubt have access to boats if they are in that area. There are many type of boats and ships that ply those waterways, not sure what to be looking for."

Elijah says, "He also mentioned a warehouse here in the city. I think somebody should be tracing that as well."

Drake says, "That's a good point, Elijah. I have that on my list, too."

He makes a check mark on his page. Gurupada is shuffling some papers in his portfolio. In an excited voice he says, "Drake I know you wanted to get back to the mark later but I just had a revelation. I'm looking for that report on the young girl. Ah, here it is."

He pulls some stapled sheets from his case and leafs through to the second page. He says, "Yes, it's the Tentulia River where the boatman found the body."

He looks up at Drake continuing, "That's the western border of the Bhola District and the Bhola River flows into it. If the mark is relevant, then we have another reference to that area. I think that's very positive. I'm concerned about what Rae said earlier, though. Does this signify that the man we are looking for is doing it or could it be a copycat somehow?"

It was Rae who came to the conclusion that while the girls in 2001 had a similar Z as the other bodies they differ on some points. The latest rash of markings from London to Bangladesh is a different weapon, a different delivery. The Z's in Venezuela were done with a downward slash while the others had been done in an upward slash with a different cutting weapon, possibly a stiletto. She had suggested a copycat. That idea had been tossed about the group.

Drake says, "I believe Rizzato is behind it. Something is going down here in Bangladesh and he's part of it. Question is who is killing and marking these bodies, and why?"

Isaac says, "You know, Drake, I think we need to find whoever was following Rafan, and from there we'll get to Rizzato. I think we should be checking for cars, stolen or rented and the bar, see if anybody saw something unusual or different that night. And if the bar is as notorious as Rafan has suggested, perhaps you might want to send my brother. He's into things like that."

Elijah says, "Up yours Bro. I wouldn't want to ruin your fun." He gives Isaac a mock blow to the chin.

Drake grins at the twin's never-ending ribbing and says, "Regardless of sexual attraction gentleman, some of us will be checking the bar for sure. I think that with what Gurupada has just told us, we need to be working the Bhola area, starting with the community and river, you two can work on the car and the nightclub."

Rae speaks up, "Look here, Drake," she turns her pad toward Drake, pointing at two words she'd written in the center of the page. It was obvious they troubled Rae as there was a heavy lined rectangle around each word.

"I think we need to do some looking at the two words, I think one of them is a name or place. Rafan said Raheem had blurted it out when he had been mumbling incoherently, something that sounded like *Scranton* or *Stratton;* he couldn't be sure. Do you remember? Could this be important?"

Rae has made a vital connection; unfortunately the two words will remain an enigma for the crew for some time yet. Drake is nodding his head as he studies the words, other than noting Scranton is a city in Pennsylvania, neither word is familiar.

Pada suggests, "If we had more time or manpower we could study it more closely but I think our other leads are more substantial. I'm not suggesting we ignore them but remember the man was drunk. It could've been a dozen different words he mumbled. And we also need to consider that Rafan admitted that he also was quite intoxicated."

Drake agrees with Gurupada, "You're probably right, Pada, but I think I'll pass them on to Williston and see what he can make of them. He's the info guru. I think we can run with what leads we have, troops. I've got some information that Williston came up with on the culprits we've already connected with that I want to share with you before we get going. You can see what kind of people we are dealing with. We won't get a chance to talk to the other Pakistani in hospital, if ever, for at least three or four weeks I've been told."

Drake passes out copies he had made earlier and gives one to each person. The group discuss the criminals, tossing ideas around of De Clerq, his guns, the connections, the huge gangster that fled from the parking garage. They talk about Drake tracking Rizzato to Amsterdam. Conjecture, suggestions, sarcasm, bon mots and ideas bounced back and forth like ping pong opinions.

Drake is in tune with the healthy discussion that is revolving about the group but not in it. He's thinking about Amsterdam, of how close he had come to nabbing Rizzato, how close he had come to killing him. He recalls the man Morgan, large nose and swarthy skin, muscular. Drake had located the S&M brothel where his contact said he would find Rizzato. When he was casing the buildings on the same block, he saw a man standing sentry next building down, about fifteen feet from the entrance Drake was about to approach. He was crouched against the wall where the two buildings met. One jutted out in front of the other by three feet and it was in these shadows he was hiding. Drake at first could only make out the man's outline but could tell by his stance it was not someone casually waiting. The man seemed alert and relaxed, his head turning slowly and repetitively, sweeping the street and surrounding buildings

Drake had watched him for ten minutes or more before he

surmised it was Rizzato's bodyguard or worked for someone else that walked scared. Either way, Drake was going to have to take him out. Drake had circled the buildings from the rear until he was able to come up behind the guardian. He knew the man had the jutting wall to his back. Drake assumed the man felt protected and hidden by the wall and the obscurity it provided. He was able to creep right up to the outer wall without detection. Drake took him out with three swift kicks, the first to the face, specifically the mouth, shutting it up for a week or two. The man slammed into the wall at his back. He called out his surprise with an impassioned "Uuuunh!" The second kick followed in milliseconds and struck the man in the groin with a stiff upward whack. The third connected with his skull, rattling his brain, the sound was like thumping a champagne bucket filled with ice cubes. The kick turned something off and the man fell flat on his chest. He didn't get up.

At the time, Drake thought there'd been nothing personal; they were only doing their jobs. Ironically, it was the same man that put his friend Dakin in hospital. Drake reflects on the coincidence, how things might have played differently if he had had to kill the man back then. Would Dakin be okay, he wonders? Probably not, he tells himself. There is always going to be crime and the people that lurk within its hollows. Someone else could've been here to pull the same trigger. Who knows?

He glances at the twins, warming to their presence, feeling happy that they will be at his side when the going gets rough, as he feels it is sure to do. He always worries some about Isaac; thinking about the man's wife, Dia, and their kids. The man is a clever and courageous fighter and came of his own free will, a cautious schemer who counts on seeing his family again. Elijah, on the other hand is like an untamed mustang. He had been married to a native Canadian Mi'maq, a woman born of a warrior spirit, her ancestors feared and mighty men. She would never have thought to sway Elijah from his soldier's path for she too had been a serviceperson. They had met during Desert Storm. Along with him and his men, she had been in the somewhat smaller Canadian contingent of approximately 3,700 participants who had served in the Gulf War. She was a major and a rotary wing pilot in the Canadian military also. Drake knew them to be an awesome pair, normally inseparable but something difficult had passed between them, causing a split. Elijah has never spoken of it.

Along with Dakin, the men have shared tense and frightening moments, often whole days in armed struggle. Drake remembers times when all four had been quite literally back to back in combat. Every second of his life was in their trusted proficient hands, as each of theirs was in his. Leading men so loyal to your commands as to place themselves in mortal danger at your request is a difficult, stressful, and often painful calling. But Drake thrived on it. All his life he had wanted to lead men, take them to war with honor, protect home and country, whatever it took to be a soldier. Even now, he thinks, *I can't leave it alone*. He smiles to himself and the visions in his head fade. The din of the conversation brings him back to the present.

All four individuals are looking at him, Elijah with a smirk. Drake sits back in his chair and says,

"What... what's wrong?"

Rae says, "You looked a little odd there, Drake, when you were woolgathering. Your eyes were open, but you weren't seeing us. Hope it was a happy reflection. Its 5:20, I know it's late but I'd like to get looking for the warehouse. Elijah's anxious too, so we're going to head out. The bodies of the two unknowns with the same mark were found near the Tajgaon Industrial Area, maybe we can start there. When do you want to connect again?"

"Why don't we all plan on meeting here tomorrow night, say around eight?" Directing his next comment to Pada he says, "I'm going to get to work on that boat and I'll keep in mind your suggestion. So you can do as you wish tonight but I'd like to get going around 6 a.m. tomorrow. There's a breakfast bistro down stairs, I think it's called Mango's. Meet us there."

Gurupada stands and replaces his notes in his case and said, "Actually, Drake, I'm heading back to the station and will run down any reports of stolen or destroyed vehicles. Scrape up any info I can. I can do that easily at my office. I'll get whatever I find to Rae and a copy to you in the morning. It's been a pleasure to meet you all."

He reaches out and shakes the twins' hands. The two offer their own regards to Pada, with Elijah thumping him on the back and sending him off with a gaff, "If you're going to hang with Drake tomorrow, you better get lots of rest tonight. The silly bugger doesn't know how to stay away from trouble and I won't be around to protect him. We're depending on you my new friend."

Gurupada teases with equal jocularity saying, "When Drake sees how well I respond to emergencies or trouble as you call it, he will have no need for you two has-beens any longer."

Drake points at Elijah and says, "Touché! I don't think we'll have to worry too much about Gurupada. I hear he can take care of himself quite handily."

Pada takes the compliment in stride, joining Rae and Elijah at the door. As they leave the room Drake can hear Elijah laughing, probably regaling his tiny audience with one of his many war stories. Drake turns to Isaac, who is still sitting at the table scribbling on his notepad. He's humming a tune and Drake notices he's sketching a caricature of who might be Rizzato, at least what he thinks Rizzato looks like. Nobody really knows for sure. When he and Williston had been tracking him after Venezuela, they had been fascinated that such a terrible man had been arrested only once, when he was a juvenile. The last known photo of Rizzato's ugly mug was from the correctional institute in Sicily that was taken in 1973 when he was fourteen. Williston had hired Isaac, who was also a composite artist, one familiar with aging facial features, to render a sketch of what Rizzato would look like at 45 years old. They also had older copies of police sketches. Drake tries to conjure an image of the villain when he saw him in Amsterdam. He had recognized the man's profile from the other drawings; the likeness Isaac makes is uncannily similar.

Looking down at the drawing, Drake says, "What're you thinking about, Isaac?"

"This man intrigues me. Where does he hide? Where does he run to when he's not doing bad things? It's been, what, over a year since you had a hot trail on him?"

"More than a year actually. I always regret not calling you guys for help. I acted like a greenhorn, a rookie soldier. I tell you, Isaac, I never felt a rage as powerful as when I saw that man for the first time. I wanted to get my hands on him and beat him senseless for what he did to the girls. I rushed him too soon, he evaded me and took flight and I just frigging lost him."

Isaac stops doodling, throws his pencil on the table and looks up at Drake. He said, "Damn Drake, I would've felt the same way. I saw the girls remember, I saw what that prick and his men did to them, you and me and that fat bastard who told us where the bodies were. Between you and me, I think you killed that pig too quick."

"We don't kill for pleasure. I know I'm a fine one to talk right, Isaac? When I saw Rizzato I was experiencing the same madness I encountered when that piece of trash was relating what he had done to the white girl. He had no way of knowing I understood Spanish, and I can thank Luis for that. I stepped outside of the law, Isaac. Am I any better than them?"

Drake is not being humble, not feeling any great remorse; he feels that man and men like him who are the basest of all criminals do not deserve to live. He's studying Isaac's drawing. While Drake had been talking to him; Isaac had completed Rizzato's face and had added a gallows beneath him and the hangman's noose tightly about his neck. Isaac also gazes at the cartoon and says, "Way better, Drake, my man. You gave him a knife to defend himself, I wouldn't have. I feel the same way you do, Boss. One less piece of crap littering the streets, just like this buzzard here," he says pointing at the paper. "We're going to hunt this man down, Drake, and we're going to take him out. There have been enough dead bodies. The next one I'd like to see on the pile is his. I'm with you on this."

Drake gives him a nod and says, "Thanks, Isaac, you're a good friend. So, you must be getting hungry, huh?"

"Yeah, yeah I could use some grub. What are we up to anyway?"

'This morning I made some calls before you all arrived. You and I are going to meet an acquaintance of mine who is a foreign correspondent for the British *Daily News* here in Dhaka. His name is Sammy Rhodes and he agreed to meet us not far from here in, let me see, fifteen minutes. Time enough for us to walk over; we've been sitting all day."

Isaac rises from his seat while tucking his T-shirt in. Drake notices the small print that does a one liner across Isaac's shoulders. He leans in because the wording is small and faint against the other color until he can read it. It said: "If You Can Read This, Back Off, Or You Will Soon Be Hypnotized by My Shirt. If you're Already Hypnotized, Give Me Your Wallet, You're Girlfriend and All Your Passwords." Drake surprises Isaac as he starts to snicker close behind his back. Isaac says,

"What are you doing Drake?"

"Here's my wallet, that shirt is pretty crazy. Just like a lot of other colorful stuff you wear. But you can't have my girlfriend. C'mon, let's get going. Rafan is still sleeping and I've left him a note."

Isaac reaches for his light cotton jacket from the couch on the way out and says, "How is that luscious Beth anyway, you lucky dog? Are you going to marry that girl or what?"

Drake ignores the question, wondering why so many people are interested in him and Beth's relationship. The two men make their way from the hotel, venturing onto the streets among the usual horde. They walk along Gulshan Road, which runs through the heart of the Gulshan Thana. Traffic has thinned, there isn't as much blaring of horns or impatient voices. Sidewalks aren't sardined with people. The evening is cooler than usual, provoking Isaac to don his jacket. The men are quiet, introspective perhaps. A tuk-tuk of vivid orange and faded turquoise, flying flags of royal blue, is overtaking them. It belches a puff of blackened smoke as it passes the men. Smelly propane exhaust fumes join them for a ways.

Drake is explaining to Isaac some of the history of the Thana as he had heard it from Rae. It has been going more upscale since the early '90s. There are embassies in the area; lavish residential quarters are becoming the norm. The principality around the Gulshan Circle 2 is dominated by high rises and office buildings. Chic eating establishments are abundant.

They are meeting Rhodes at a newer restaurant called the Blue Neon Bistro that is owned by a friend of the reporter, on Madani Avenue, three blocks from the traffic circle #2. Rhodes had told Drake he will recognize it by the namesake faint blue neon that decorates the black marble facade. Rhodes promised him he would never experience lamb the same way anywhere else again. He had gone on and on about how the meat was roasted, how chefs expertly prepared the meat and smothered it in herbs and blue-ribbon sauce. They are consistently delicious he guarantees.

Once they arrive, they enter the foyer where to the right a maître'd attends the couple that have arrived just ahead of Drake and Isaac. Drake looks around, liking the dark gray walls adorned with huge black and white prints of famous people. The two in the entryway are classics of James Dean and Salvador Dali. Chrome and copper hints are used throughout in odd and clever ways. Off to the left is an archway through which he sees a small bandstand where two musicians are backing one of the most ravishing black women Drake has ever encountered. One man, who looks like a native, is playing a Gretsch hollow body; the other man is Oriental, with the heavy eyes and wide forehead of the Mongols. He's playing a timeworn doghouse bass. Drake recognizes the song as a more torpid version of Sade's, *No Ordinary Love*. The woman's voice is the most beautiful and delicate of the three instruments. It meets your ears with intimacy.

Isaac has approached the maître'd, introducing them as Mr. Rhodes' party. The host is a small man, dark sweeping hair and a pencil moustache. His manner speaks of sophistication. Isaac remarks that the man looks more like a banker or doctor than a head waiter. At the mention of Sammy's name, the maître d' stands straighter and with much flourish says, "Yes, yes, Mr. Alexander and Mr. Glass, I assume."

He moves from his station and adds, "Please, follow me, gentleman."

Leading them down the wide hallway that leads to the dining area, he turns to his right. They are greeted by open tables, semi-private booths, polished wood floors with ebony stain, multi-level sitting areas in the corners, each with their own electric fireplace and other pervasive enlargements like they saw in the entryway. Black and white, copper and chrome, retro modern furniture, subtle white and soft blue neon – it's very impressive. Drake says, "I feel like as if I'm in a Frank Miller story. Know him, Isaac?"

"Oh yeah, he's *tres* cool; my hero."

The maître d' leads them to one of the corner sections made private by two high back booths that face each other obliquely. The fireplace on the opposite wall is warmly waving its faux flames. Three colossal photos dominate the wall above the stirring hearth. Grayish monochromes of Elizabeth Taylor as Cleopatra, Ringo Starr from the Rubber Soul album and the famous Bangladeshi model and designer Bibi Russell are their silent guests for the evening. Each booth forms a semicircle and can hold six people comfortably. Seated to the left are Sam Rhodes and a striking redhead. Sammy jumps up from his seat and grasps Drake's hand in earnest. "How wonderful it is to see you again Drake. It's been some time now, much too long actually. I'm very pleased you got hold of me. Imagine meeting in Bangladesh of all places, eh Drake? Is there a war going on somewhere nearby I should know about or are you here to start one?"

Drake puts a hand on his host's shoulder and says, "No, no wars. I had no idea that you were in Bangladesh, I just read your story in the paper, the one about the corpses that bore an odd mark, which we're very interested in, but we can talk about that later, I hope. For now, please meet a good friend of mine."

He turns toward Isaac, who is slightly behind, and notices that he and the redhead are exchanging smiles.

"Ahem, Isaac this is a fellow sailor from my youth, Samuel Rhodes. Sammy this is Isaac Glass."

He looks to the fair and lovely lady, "And who is this interesting person?"

"This is *my* good friend, Samantha Treat. Sam, please meet Drake Alexander and Isaac Glass.

Handshakes all around and when Isaac clasps Ms. Treat's delicate fingers, he asks, "Sam and Sam?" He lifts one eyebrow in a questioning motion.

She replies with a happy voice and a charming British accent, "I prefer Sam and Sammy if you don't mind, he being Sammy of course."

""Well then Sam, please call me Isaac."

As the men take the seats proffered by Rhodes, the newspaperman is telling them that Samantha is an administrative assistant at the British High Commission here in Dhaka. The foursome spends the next hour or so over drinks catching up and getting to know each other. The conversation before dinner is light and frivolous, Samantha warming to her date's friends. Soft murmurs of conversation whir in the background before coalescing with the light jazz that trickles from the ceiling speakers. The ambiance created by low lights, burning candles, velvety fabrics and heady spirits promote stimulating and revealing conversation.

Drake is amused by the young lady, feisty and as sweet as candy. He admires her pale complexion that is salted with the lightest of freckles, warm hazel eyes that makes him think of spring. He likes that she is not naive but displays a shy intelligence. He is warmed by her stories of the tribulations and joys of being the youngest of four, the other three boys. She has never played with dolls, and she grew up in London but now has property in Southend-On-Sea back in England.

By eight o'clock the waiters are clearing away the last of the dinnerware and refilling their dessert glasses with more outstanding Canadian ice wine. Drake wants to turn the conversation to his original intent now that the meal is complete.

"Tell me Sam, by the freakiest of chances, do you know Aloysius Payne?"

"Interestingly enough, Drake, Mr. Payne is the lawyer for two of my brothers, Scott and Wellsford. They own half of the District of Kent", she exaggerates. "I barely know him but my brothers have been associated with him for …uhm, over a decade certainly. They speak quite fondly of him. How do you know Mr. Payne, Drake?"

"He's a childhood friend, Sam. His brother, Williston, is one of my close friends. It is actually because of their sister that we are here in Bangladesh." Both Drake and Isaac look knowingly at each other. Drake wonders how much he should tell a reporter but then tells himself Sammy already knows about the strange marks, not their relation. He directs his comment to Sammy,

"You remember, Sammy; when I called you I mentioned the reporting you did on the bodies found in the city that bore a mark on their shoulder. The police are withholding details of what it looked like but that there are similarities they were looking into?"

Sammy said, "Yes I do, Drake. What does that have to do with the Paynes' sister?"

"Three years ago, Amber Payne was murdered in Venezuela. She and her college friend Sakeema Saad were abducted in broad daylight when they had been out on a birding expedition in the Henri Pittier National Park on a Tuesday; we found their bodies five days later. The man responsible fled before we arrived. I've been hunting him ever since."

Rhodes is attentive now; he sits up and pulls a worn leather-bound notepad from his sport coat pocket. "I spoke with Inspector Chowdhury's office and I was informed the investigation was being carried out by his office but that's all he would tell me for now. I was reminded that it wasn't my business. What does all this have to do with the marks my contact informed me about? "

"Listen Rhodes, you can't report anything I tell you. If you can help us out, eventually I can give you the whole picture. I can identify the mark and where it originated – as far as we know, that is. The man we seek is here in Dhaka; rather, we believe he is here. We don't want anything to scare him away."

He closes his eyes for only seconds but a memory of Amber and Beth when they were teenagers, fills him with melancholy and he says with much sadness, " A similar mark was on the girls bodies as well, Sammy."

Sammy nods at his friend, the four are quiet, a moment of respect. Rhodes can see that the slain girl's memory troubles Drake.

"Okay then Drake, let's see what I have,"

He opens the notebook, rifling through several pages before finding his notes and relating what he had discovered so far about the two men and the odd marks found on their bodies. But he doesn't tell him everything. Not yet, he thinks. They talk about what they each know of the dead men, Rhodes impressed at the depth of Drake's knowledge. He hastily writes down the salient points of their talk. Drake surprises both Sam and Sammy by saying, "There's another death you should know about Sammy; it may help you with your investigation. I assume, Sam, you've heard of Sir Reginald Whitecastle?"

"Why yes," she replies with alacrity, "he was murdered this summer in London. The poor blighter was even missing an ear, terrible business. He was the High Commissioner to Bangladesh for many years, before my time of course, as I came here just after he had left. Is he involved in this? I've heard many rumors about him, but I believe there were some actual instances of misbehavior, after all he is a man."

She toasts the men with her demitasse, having changed to coffee. She isn't joking. Her enchanting mien challenges them. None of the men are laughing until Isaac says, "You've got a point there, Sam. I think you mentioned you worked with six or seven other ladies at the embassy and I'm sure you must be drowning in rumors. After all, you are women."

The jabs cause easy laughter. Drake says, "I think if either of you do some digging you will find that the police in London have information about a mark of sorts."

Drake checks his wrist for the time while stifling a yawn; his day has been long. The liquor is numbing him and he longs for rest. He notices Rhodes is distracted by the BlackBerry that vibrates on the table. As he picks it up, Drake says, "With that admission Rhodes, I think I must be off, busy day tomorrow. Let's stay in touch on this, okay Sammy."

He nudges Isaac who is sitting on the outside of the booth. Isaac slides out and stands aside as Drake makes an effort to slide over. He is stopped when Sammy says. "You might want to stick around for a few more minutes, Drake; I just got an email from my contact at the morgue."

He looks up from the Smartphone and says, "A piece of a human body was brought in an hour ago and it has a Zed cut into the skin. Is that what your mark is?"

Chapter 23

Sept 20 George Town, Cayman Islands

Stratton starts off from his hotel at a brisk pace, he's anxious to be at Mado's office when he shows up. He is frustrated that Amado has not responded to the cell phone number he told Andrew to use, it's the only one Stratton has. Nor has Mado returned any of his calls for the last several days. Stratton had been in North Carolina preparing the MCI for shipping, having a custom tank fabricated for transportation. He had been interrupted by Rizzato three days ago when the normal cash transfer Rizzato had requested had failed to arrive. After a dozen unanswered calls, he had started to believe that Amado Mendoza had stolen his money and fled, but that didn't make sense. No, Andrew thought, Amado Mendoza is already quite wealthy; something's wrong.

The morning is typical for September: temperature around 76 degrees, some cloud cover. He feels foolish that he hasn't brought an umbrella knowing that the Islands receive more rain than usual in September. Tucking his hands in his pockets he quickens his gait. For the past week Andrew had been involved in the logistics of getting the gas to Bangladesh. Dhaka is good he believes. He had spoken to Tarafdar, who was also bewildered by the absence of one of his chief operators, Lokesh. He apologized profusely to Andrew for the lack of support. He couldn't explain Lokesh's disappearance, only that he would personally look after Mr. Favor's requests. During the conversation, Stratton remembered thinking, *I don't know where he is either but I do know he isn't comin' back.* Tarafdar had assured him once more that all details for arrival, inspection, fares and taxes had been seen to. It was only a small matter upon arrival for the goods to be cleared.

Getting it ready for delivery had been more tasking than he had anticipated; and then there was trouble with the engine in Bhola, then Lokesh, and now this. He worries more as he gets closer to his goal, frantic over the operation going smoothly. He doesn't need any more headaches. Little did he know that a migraine is loitering just around the corner.

Andrew is twenty steps away from the imposing building when a burst of rain pelts him and everything else. The ten seconds it takes him to reach the protection of the portico over the main entrance sees him drenched. Standing in the entryway before the stairs to the second level, he shakes himself like a wet Lab, droplets sprinkling the floor tiles. He runs his hands through his hair, the excess water running down his neck. Globules of moisture cover his face, gravity causing them to flow like tears.

His clothes cling to him; he's thinking this must be what it feels like when you put your clothes on straight from the washing machine. He swears at his bad luck. It will be difficult to seem imposing when you are soggy. He hurries up the stairs, meaning to find a washroom where he can dry off some. As he gets to the head of the stairs, a curvaceous, stoutly lady comes through the nearest office door brandishing a hand towel.

"Oh! You poor dear! Here", she says, offering him the cloth, "Use this."

Andrew hesitates at her kindness, skeptical of her intent; he isn't used to people being nice. He notices her soft eyes as he reaches for the towel.

"Thank you." He rubs his face dry, his hands and his neck, the rough nap of the material brings color to his usual ashen pallor. Last, he runs it over his hair before handing the dampened towel back. As she is speaking to him, he admires her friendly expression, the beauty of her native skin, dark and lustrous. He is amused by her appearance, matronly yet exotic. It sparks his low spirit prompting a rare smile.

"... and when I saw you running in the rain, I knew you would be soaked. So, you're welcome."

She turns to go back to her work when Andrew impulsively asks her, "Forgive my boldness, but could I repay your kind gesture perhaps by buying you lunch? Somewhere close by so you wouldn't be late in returning?"

She stops to peer back, not really interested but flattered nonetheless. After all, at 50, offers for lunch are not frequent. He does seem to exude a certain charm; the wet hair makes him appear dashing, carefree. Maybe a coffee she thinks; he might be interesting.

"It's not necessary to repay me and I do have errands at noon..." she pauses as if to reconsider, noting the man's disappointment, so obvious in his eyes, "but I will let you buy me a coffee. Do you like coffee Mr...?"

Beaming, Andrew says, "Favors, Jack Favors. Please call me Jack. I actually love coffee. And you are?"

She thrusts out her hand saying, "Melinda Porter. How about Nairobi's, just across the street, at say...12:30 Jack? If you enjoy coffee, Nairobi's serve some of the best."

"Well, I'm not too familiar with the city, but if it's just across the street, an old duff like me should be able to find it. 12:30 sounds fine."

White and perfect teeth smile brightly at his self-mocking. She is even prettier when she smiles he thinks.

"Was running from the rain what brought you in here Jack or are you looking for someone in particular?"

"I have dealings with Senor Mendoza, and I've come to visit him."

Her smile quickly disappears. Surprise causes slight creases upon her brow and she blurts out,

"But Jack, Amado is dead; he was killed less than a week ago. His funeral was only yesterday."

Seeing the reaction on Andrew's face, the utter disbelief, the loss of words, she says, "Oh, I'm so sorry, Jack; I didn't mean to be so abrupt. I was just so surprised when you mentioned his name. We all liked him so very much and still can't believe he's gone."

Andrew's heart is working hard, his brain working harder; he can't fathom Amado being dead. He is vital to his plans, his goals. Questions deluge his psyche. He moves toward Melinda, grasping a forearm in each hand, and looks in her eyes, frightening her with the ferocity in his own. He speaks with a madness made evident by the urgency in his pleas and spittle in his speech. He isn't being reasonable by asking this stranger questions she can't possibly have answers for.

"What do you mean, dead? How...how is that possible? He can't be, we're not done. We've so much to do....Dhaka and my... my... my.... What am I going to do?"

He drops her arms. She starts to back off, scared now, rubbing where his fingertips have dug in, and knowing they will soon bruise. She stares at the vacant expression on his face. His color fades before her eyes; she detects anger about to erupt. She's nervous and she slowly eases backwards toward her office when suddenly a woman comes from an adjacent office into the hallway, heading away from them. Andrew calms down, protective of himself now, realizing he is scaring the woman, and says softly so as not to be overheard, "I'm sorry, forgive my rudeness. I'm just flabbergasted. How did this happen? Please tell me."

"I don't know. There was much speculation and talk of a young lady being involved, but I can't remember her name. Stratton or the likes. I don't know..."

She staggers back at the man's reaction to the name Stratton. His skin already white from stress and lack of sun goes cadaver pale. He reels from the news, almost falling downstairs. He can't believe what the woman is telling him. A young girl named Stratton; it could only be Sophia. The stress becomes too much and like a giant fist it squeezes his mind before breaking his maligned heart.

His hand goes to the pain in his chest, the other grabbing the railing at the head of the stairs for support. He leans back against the wall, one hand still gripping his shirt front, the other fumbling in his pants pocket until it produces a lighter-sized sprayer of nitroglycerine. He brings the container to his mouth, grips the cover between his teeth. He pulls the cover off the spray nozzle and spits it out. Lifting his head he sprays a quick blast under his tongue. The nitro immediately enters his bloodstream. It instantaneously opens the arteries so that his blood can flow more freely, easing the beating muscle.

He slides to the floor more from shock than relief – and from the pain. He knows he has to remain calm. He will give himself another pump in fifteen minutes and he should be okay. His doctor warned him this could happen someday due to his unhealthy eating and drinking habits coupled with the stress he so often had to deal with in his business. He is bewildered thinking why Sophia would be in the Islands, why she would kill Mado, it makes no sense.

Melinda reacts to Jack's stricken plight with empathy and concern. "Oh my goodness, are you all right? I'll call an ambulance, I'll call one right now…"

"No, no, Melinda, I'll be okay, just give me a few minutes. I'm just shocked. You gave me the fright of my life when you told me of Amado. I can't believe it."

The other woman is returning to her office when she notices Andrew sitting on the floor. She rushes over to offer her assistance. Melinda explains that Mr. Favors is reacting to the shocking news of Senor Mendoza's death and asks her to help get him to a chair. The other woman is taller than Melinda, younger and stronger. She is able to lift Andrew and, against his protests, the two women help him back to Melinda's office, where they prop him on one of the sofas in the waiting room.

By now a small contingent from the other offices on the second floor are gathered in front of Melinda's office. Commotions are rare in their usually imperturbable environment. He detests being the center of attention, but before Melinda is able to shoo the workers back to their domains, Andrew hears mention of a young man who had killed Mado and who had been apprehended just yesterday. There is a small amount of relief that it wasn't his daughter who had caused Mado's demise. He gives himself another spray from the atomizer and decides to wait ten more minutes. He is confused momentarily as to what he is going to do, but he knows he can't stay here much longer.

The people go back to their duties as the excitement dies down. There is no one else in Melinda's office, a real estate firm, he learns. He is welcome to rest as much as he needs. Melinda is fussing over him, offering him a damp cloth, a drink of cold water, when he asks her in a small voice, "What now, Melinda? What of Amado's clients – what will happen to their files?"

He is worried that the authorities will be searching Amado's office for any possible hints as to what had happened. He feels that his business with Amado will be legitimate under scrutiny – land acquisitions, offshore registrations, money transfers, nothing unusual – but he is still worried. There are likely several references to Dhaka. But it is access to the money that he has deposited with Mendoza that worries him. He curses under his breath.

Melinda says, "I don't know Jack. His office has been sealed. There have been so many people about, detectives, technicians, police officers; you'll have to speak to them…"

She stops in mid-thought and says, "But there is one person who could possibly help you, I know her to be an acquaintance of Senor Mendoza, a lawyer as well. When I met her they were working on some project together. Her name is Beatrice Bond.

She has an office in the Thompson Building off Main Street; it's not far from here. Let me call her and inquire if she can see you."

Andrew decides he has to rest and regroup. He will return to his suite, rethink his options.

"No, but thank you, Melinda. I do need to rest. My business can wait. Would you please give me her number and I'll arrange an appointment after I've composed myself."

He struggles up from the couch, leaving a wet outline of his torso on the fabric.

"I'm sorry, Melinda, for making such a mess of your morning. I really must go and I trust you will understand my not being able to partake of your kind company later. I do hope our paths cross again in the future. Would you mind calling a taxi for me?"

He gives her the slimmest of smiles, eyes downcast, seemingly abashed.

Relief overcomes her. While at first she had found him interesting, what she feels now is more like pity. She rubs her arms where he had handled her earlier, thinking she can understand his rash behavior, the shock of the news. He had spooked her when she'd seen his eyes: hollow and angry at the same time. She will remember them for a long time. She'll be glad to see him leave.

"That's okay, Jack, my mornings need a little excitement, but I'm happy these things don't happen very often. I'll write Ms. Bond's address and number for you.

She hastily writes on a sheet of her notepad, tears it off and hands it to Andrew. A tight lipped smile says goodbye. "Please take care of yourself."

An hour later, Andrew is sitting at the dining table in his suite. He has changed into olive dress slacks, a navy short sleeve shirt and polished brogues. He is strapping a Movado to his wrist. Staring at the face of the timepiece, he thinks how much he loves this watch – black face with no markings, the gold dimple at twelve o'clock. He admires it as he would a work of art. He turns his attention to the notepad before him. As he ponders deeply about his next steps, he doodles on the paper: arrows, window boxes, flowers.

When he finally lists the effects of Mado's sudden demise, he becomes a little more optimistic. The real snag is the money, the business operations for Reactor Chemical's, signing authorities. He then made a to-do list.

1. Money to Rizzato ASAP.
2. Beatrice Bond   a) Reactor Chem.
3. Sophia????
4. MCI

The acumen he had gained in board rooms lead to action and decisive direction. He still has more than enough money, so really the money tied up with Mado isn't as great a concern as he originally thought. The only issue is how to spread it around; he'll need a lawyer for that. He feels he is back in control; he preens about the suite like a peacock as he searches for the box of cell phones he had purchased. He finds it on the bar, removes one phone and a battery. Snapping the power source in place he opens the flip phone noting the number displayed inside. Then he makes five calls.

First he phones Rizzato, obtains the banking details on his end and informs him he will be in Dhaka with the shipment in four days. He notices Rizzato is much more obedient and quieter than usual. When he mentions it, Rizzato explains that everything is going so well he's bored.

His second call is to Ms. Bond's office. He describes his problem to the receptionist and is informed that there have been many other emergencies created by Senor Mendoza's untimely death, but she will see what she can do. She asks for his number, suggesting she will call back shortly.

His third call is to his wife, Janice, in Chicago. They are in the same time zone and it's almost noon, so he assumes she's home. She is actually outside at her pottery wheel, shaping a bowl and not the least bit interested in who might be calling. It will be another hour before she gets his message.

His fourth call is to the machine shop in Durham that is constructing the tank he will need to ship the gas. He reminds them he will be arriving in North Carolina the next morning and that it needs to be ready by the close of business tomorrow. They assure him it will be delivered to the plant in the Triangle by 4 p.m. This is the only phone call that has been reassuring.

His fifth call is to Allnite Airline Charters to book a business-class jet for the next several days. It needs to be a long-range aircraft, a Gulfstream preferably. He gives his name as Jack Favors. He informs them he wants to leave that day, around 6 p.m. They advise him that such a plane is available, thanking him profusely.

Placing the phone on the table, he goes to the bar. He thinks to reward himself for his determination by uncapping the new bottle of Lagavulin he brought with him. The smoky flavor lifts from the open neck impugning his willpower. The truth, Andrew muses, is that any reason is a good reason for a drink. He hasn't been drunk of late, but he's become partial to the buzz that accompanies him throughout each day. He'll nurse the precious fluid. The first long swallow is like a hammer in a pillow, pounding smooth.

The phone is set on vibrate as well as tone and it hums on the table as it gave a sharp old-fashioned ring. "Yes?" he commands.

The irritating voice of Bond's receptionist asks with equal rudeness, "Is this Mr. Favors?"

"Yes."

"Ms. Bond will see you at 2 p.m. She wanted me to tell you that she will only have fifteen minutes to spare as she is due in court at 2:40 and we're not sure how long that will take. Can you be here then?"

"Yes."

An impatient pause on the caller's end waits for the usual questions.

Andrew said, "Is there anything else?"

"No"

"Good day, then."

He can visualize where the offices are and knows it won't be more than ten minutes by limousine. Going to his bedroom he retrieves his wallet, passport and check book. While packing them into his worn valise, the phone starts dancing and singing again. He returns to the living room and answers it, this time the single greeting is relayed with more politeness.

"Yes"

A girlish voice much like his daughter Sara's but more mature, more sapient greets him, "Andrew, is that you? I didn't think you were still alive. I haven't heard from you for almost a year. Where are you? What are you doing?"

This is all asked out of sheer curiosity, she had stopped loving Andrew many years ago. She stayed because he was the father of her children, as poor at it as he was. Besides, she loved the life she and her children lived. She had been hoping he wouldn't call, but now that he has she felt she should tell him about Sophia. She started to ask more questions when he says,

"Janice, Janice, give me a minute, just one question at a time. Where I am and what I'm doing is irrelevant at this point. I need to know what is going on with Sophia. Is she there?"

"Of course not, the little fool is off looking for you. What are you up to, Andrew? She warned me that you wanted to hurt a lot of people over Scott and Sara. Andrew, you know that's crazy. Come back home, forget this madness. We'll work things out from here."

"How did she know how to find me?"

"Oh, so she did find you?" she asks with surprise, and then asks once more, "Where are you?"

"Never mind where I am, Janice. My children..." then he corrects himself, "our children were murdered, possibly tortured and you want me to do nothing?'

Condemnation is in his tone, he wants her to hurt the same as him, not to forgive and forget as she begged him to do.

"Yes, do something but something constructive, help these people somehow. Let the memory of our kids live through your forgiveness. Don't use your money to hurt people, Andrew. Give it up... Come home."

Her plea is honest; he can hear her sobbing on the phone. His mention of her babies – she still thinks of them as babies; to her they will never grow old – provokes a bitter melancholy. She says in broken speech with a crumpled heart, "I...I miss my children...I ache for them every waking minute. I know it is wrong but I too want to kill the horrible people that hurt them but we'll never know who it was. Until you called, I was at peace, Andrew, you bastard! The two of them are gone, for always, nothing you can do will change that. If you continue with your self-destruction, I'm through with you. Do you understand me?"

"We're never going to agree on this are we?" he asks, already knowing the answer.

"No, we're not..."

A huge gap follows; the silence at each end is monumental, the defining moment when each knows, with absolutely no doubt whatsoever, they will never see each other again. One mad with torment, the other tormented by the madness. Andrew slowly removes the phone from his ear and carefully shuts it. Janice Stratton hears the faint click then the dial tone. She gapes at the receiver in her hand, willing a happier voice to call out to her, tell her everything will be okay. Her hand weakens and the phone slips from her fingers. Huge teardrops make her vision blurry. She brings her hands to her face as if to hold back the flow, and yet a gush of agony streams from her silky greens.

She sinks to one of the dining room chairs beside her and cries for all the terrible things that pain her. Hurting for Scott and Sarah, hurting for not knowing where Sophia is, hurting for her lost and sick husband. Her thoughts turn to Muslims. What is he going to do? She sits up and removes a napkin from the ceramic holder on the table, wipes her eyes and blows her nose. Getting up with haste, she says out loud to her empty nest, "I have to talk to Pastor Buckingham."

Andrew also stares at his phone, but he with a cool glare. The instrument is the last link to a woman he knows he had lost many years ago. All connections to his wife are severed except for the checks that will arrive from an account that is likely to outlive her. Checking his watch, he sees that he has forty minutes before he can see Ms. Bond. He calls for a limo, finishes gathering his things, packs his black leather overnight bag and checks out. As he exits the hotel, the doorman opens the door of a long grey car and inquires, "Mr. Favors?"

Andrew nods and jumps in, informing the driver of where he wants to go. During the solitude of the ride, Stratton sits morosely in the back scheming. He focuses on the enormity of his attack to come. It is mind swelling, and as such crushes any empathy he might've experienced, any itch of regret.

The fifteen minutes Beatrice Bond grants Jack Favors was the best paid in legal history, at least on this Island, she guessed. Before he sat in the wing-backed chair she offered him, he placed fifteen one-thousand-dollar bills on her desk. He said with all the cockiness he could muster,

"If I hire you, I will be paying you for your confidentiality. I will pay you very handsomely. There are... shall we say some irregularities... to my actions, which will never concern you nor will they ever come to haunt you. If you're not interested, and I sincerely think you will be, the cash on your desk is yours anyway. Are you willing to hear my story?"

Beatrice Bond is a big woman, not very tall but plump. Glasses with a fine gold rim sit on the end of her pudgy nose. Her light brown beacons eye the strange man over the top; her mouth is puckered into a moue of concentration. Her auburn hair is spun into an Amish gyre pinned to the back of her head. Her skin is deep brown and beauteous. A wide strand of pink freshwater pearls graces her robust neck, the only adornment she wears. The battle grey business suit and white blouse she has on makes her appear authoritarian. She has been a lawyer for over twenty years and this is by far the most original approach. After five minutes of reckoning she says, "Meet me back her at 3:30. I should be finished by then."

Three days later Stratton is strapped into one of the jump seats in the foredeck of the Boeing 737 air freighter Reactor Chemicals has hired to transport the 600 gallons of methyl isocyanate from the factory in North Carolina to Dhaka. He's paranoid about the delivery of the gas to the point that he has vowed to accompany it everywhere it travels. When he had contracted the special tank built he had thought about the Air Tractor that is sitting along the Bhola River. He knows it has a capacity of 502 gallons. In his calculations, he has allowed the difference for spillage or possible evaporation; he judges he will have more than enough for his purposes.

He has been daydreaming as he watches the blanched mountains of cloud inch past the window. He is mesmerized that a mass so humongous is light enough that it floats so high in the sky. The pilot had told him earlier that they were flying at 32,000 feet; even at that, they fly through the odd cloud, reshaping and deforming it with the plane's turbulence. It is perhaps symbolic of the turbulence that storms through his being, an illusion that confuses right and wrong.

His dreams range from joy to sorrow, shopping through the catalogue of warped emotions that poison his reason. His imaginings center on the gas in the guts of the aircraft, the liquid that will soon be released upon his enemies. He considers all Muslims as enemies now. He is absorbed by the calamity he will create, the panic that will follow. He sits in a malicious trance until the pilot wakes him from his musings.

"Mr. Favors, we're experiencing a favorable tail wind. Our ETA should improve by about forty-five minutes. If you have to make any arrangements, you're welcome to use our satellite phone."

"Thank you Captain Forester, that won't be necessary. I have many tasks that will keep me occupied until my people arrive with their transport."

The pilot, a heavy pallid man with wisps of thin blondish hair covering his dome, passes Stratton a stapled packet of papers.

"This is a copy of our manifest, customs declaration and associated documents that you will need when we land. Our staff will handle the offloading. If there's anything else we can do for you, let us know. If you'd like, there are sandwiches in the small galley just aft of the main cabin if you get hungry. We still have another four hours until we arrive in Dhaka."

Stratton reaches down and unsnaps the safety belt and says, "Thank you Captain, I think I will have something to eat."

He rises from the uncomfortable position, rubbing his buttocks. Thinking they'd only been out of Oahu for just over an hour, he dreads four extra hours sitting in that torture pit as he thought of the lightly padded steel seat. Shaking his head he realizes he has paid an outrageous amount of money for the honor of that throne. He proceeds to the galley that is just outside the cockpit on the port side discovering the platter of sandwiches and sweets, a chrome thermos, cups and condiments waiting on the narrow counter. He pours himself a coffee before reaching in the pocket of his tan sport coat pulling out a tiny bottle of Advil. Dumping three of the tablets into his palm he stares at them for a moment, thinking of the three he had taken only two hours ago. He is sorely aware that every morning is now the same: headaches, hangovers, hot flashes, hurt. The pills rest in his hand like three guilty slugs. He shrugs as he tosses them into his mouth, washing them down with the steaming liquid almost scalding his throat.

Helping himself to one of the sandwiches he heads to the puny lavatory on the opposite side of the plane. He munches on the morsel as he enters and locks the door. He is undoing his zipper when he experiences a slight shiver. He sees his reflection in the mirror that hangs over the small sink to his right and bitter disappointment sinks in. He is ashamed at his appearance, unruly hair, baggy eye lids, whiskers grey and 48 hours long, wrinkled disheveled clothing. He remembers the days when 5:00 a.m. would find him shaven, groomed and garbed in the best his tailors had to offer. He marvels that it had it been such a short time ago. For the slightest of moments he feels sorry, asking himself what he has become. Sanity had only the briefest of moments to perhaps answer that question. Instead strands of something benign snakes through the mist in his mind like electrical charges reminding him of his lost children, of lost opportunities in their lives, his engagement of revenge.

The plane passes through a small burp in the air, sending a slight disturbance through the fuselage, enough to break the mood. Stratton finishes urinating, zips up, unlocks the door and retrieves his overnight bag. He returns immediately, locking himself in once more. Thirty minutes later he emerges polished from top to bottom, coiffed, shorn of stubble, fresh clothes, gleaming shoes; new man, same fiend. From the galley he takes several more sandwiches, another cup of coffee and returns to his cramped perch. Balancing the snack on his lap he watches the boring sky languidly go by.

Three hours and fifty-one minutes later they touch down at the Shah Jalal Airport. Freighters unload at what is called freight villages 2,000 yards beyond the main terminal. Tarafdar had made his agents aware that Favors was to be "accommodated," no searches were necessary and paperwork should be hastened. His minions were rewarded by generous bonuses on their pay checks.

The freight yards are chaotic. Twenty-four hour service is available to the many freighters coming and going. Most freighters carry garments and trinkets manufactured by the poorest of Bangladeshi, paid wages so low it barely covers daily subsistence. Stratton stands at the bottom of the plane's stairs, stretching as he inspects the wares that are being shuffled about, loading, unloading, storing. He remembers reading that forty percent of the population of Bangladesh work for less than a dollar a day. He wonders how many of them toil over the goods filling these warehouses.

He scrutinizes the worker's unloading the airplane, the men on the forklifts, the uniformed customs officers carrying their cardboard notepads, off-duty flight staff leaving as additional crews are coming to work. Any he expects to be Muslim, those with brown skin he reasons, he leers at with disdain because of his growing hate. While he waits for one of Rizzato's men, he is feeling good about how he has worked everything out. His mood is temporary, soon to be spoiled when Rizzato himself shows up. The news he will bring isn't good.

Chapter 24   Sept 20 Bhola River

Bunker sits in the back seat of the water taxi he has hired to return to the compound. Of the twelve seats available, he chooses the one farthest from the driver, whose incessant chatter in his own tongue and broken English scrapes at his consciousness like a nail file. The sampan still sits at the wharf where they had left it. He isn't comfortable with the controls of the boat or the ways of the water so had decided to hire a taxi boat to get him back so he could tell Rizzato what had taken place over the past three days. He's going to be pissed off.

Bunker is contemplating his movements over the last 24 hours, trying to determine if he has done everything possible both to track down Rafan Bashara and to accommodate Kovalenko, who is now wrapping up the repairs on his own. Finding him asleep at the warehouse yesterday morning, Bunker roused him with much banging upon the office door. The mechanic had chosen the farthest office to the rear of the building to create a temporary bedroom. Bunker guessed that had been one of the reasons Kovalenko hadn't heard any of the events that had occurred outside late at night when he had been stalking and killing the "loose ends" he'd caught fleeing two nights ago. The empty liquor bottles littering his new bedroom were probably a factor as well.

When he had searched the warehouse, he had studied the burly mechanic's room. He noticed first the unmade cot Raheem had provided Kovalenko that was shoved up against the far wall. Besides the bed, the only things there were an old TV sitting upon a battered desk next to a microwave. A second hand apartment refrigerator sitting on the floor beside a wooden chair complemented the decor. Another chair was hiding under his wardrobe, pants across the seat, shirts hugging the chair back. Ukrainian cozy, he thought

There had been nothing unusual inside the rest of the building; tools, machines, workbenches, parts, and dust were scattered about the main work area. He had looked carefully at the engine as Kovalenko explained the mechanics of what he was doing. The Ukrainian had been asking where Raheem and the dummies were. Bunker told him that they were needed back at the compound. They had left not long ago, he lied.

Kovalenko had said, "All da heavy work is done, anyway. I just need to install da compressor, put everything back together, dat's it. Done two days for sure. I can finish by myself, but not to take to da boat. You big guy, you help!"

Bunker remembered telling him that he would send a couple of strong guys to help, he was to wait for them as they had some errands to run and Kovalenko could pilot the boat back. After he left the warehouse, he went back to Rafan's apartment. He had stalked the building yesterday for sixteen straight hours and never saw sight of him. He assumed he had fled and was likely in hiding. He imagined him to be too scared to go to the police; he was hoping he was right.

The door at the rear of Bashara's apartment by the parking lot was always locked and rarely used. The front entrance had a vestibule with the interior door always locked as well. He rang several buzzers on the intercom panel until one of the lazy occupants electronically unlocked the door rather than inquire who was there. Bunker had read Rafan's name on the directory, noting which apartment was his. He climbed to the third floor. Drawing him sidearm he knocked on the door when he located the apartment. There was no answer, of course.

Bunker picked the lock and opened the door as easily as if he had a key and was in the apartment in record time. It didn't take long for him to ascertain that the place was empty. On the bedroom dresser he had found a photo of an older man and woman standing proudly behind a younger man dressed in graduation garb. Bunker assumed it was Rafan Bashara as there were other likenesses of the same young man with different individuals lining the hallway walls. He took the photo from the silver frame, leaving it empty on the bed. He left the apartment, leaving the door unlocked. If Rafan came back, he wanted him to know someone had been there.

His thoughts return to the present when the inboard diesel engine of the taxi boat is throttling down as the driver approaches the Bhola River. The driver inquires in scattered English where they are to go. Bunker moves to the front of the water taxi, guiding the verbose man to the wharf of the compound. The pier is deserted of people this morning. Only the Zodiac and the Cruise is tied up to it. There is no traffic on the river, which in itself is odd for a Monday. Normally at this time of the day there are several boats travelling up or down the river near this bend. Bunker takes advantage of the emptiness. To entice him from the boat he explains to the driver that he wants him to help with a small but heavy package that is needed back in Dhaka.

Together they secure the craft to the wharf and disembark. Bunker indicates that the package is in the metal warehouse at the end of the pier. He walks over and opens the heavy door with a key from the set he carries in his pocket. The driver is about five or six steps behind. When he enters the building, he immediately steps to one side so that the driver when he comes in he will be uncertain of Bunker's whereabouts. He removes the knife with the saw-like blade from his pocket. The driver enters and hesitates, looking around the building, waiting for his eyes to adjust to the darkness of the interior. As his head moves to the left, away from him, Bunker seizes that moment to reach out and clutch the man with his mammoth arms. One hand clamps around his head, covering his mouth, and before driver can react he plunges the knife deep in to the base of his skull. He shoves the knife in as far as possible, wriggling it into the brain. It takes less than five seconds for him to die; Bunker shivers when the body goes still. He clutches the dead frame closely for a moment before tossing it to the dusty floor. After Bunker wipes the greyish, reddish gore from the blade on the dead man's shirt, he removes the five hundred Yuan he had given him when they left Dhaka from the trouser pocket. "He won't need it," he says aloud.

He leaves the building, locking the door again and replacing the knife in the leather sheath attached to his belt. There are no vehicles about so he sets off on foot to the hangar compound. The dirt road twists several times through the woods before opening onto a fallow field on his left, overgrown with weeds and long grasses. On his right is a mango orchard. Light green heavy spheroids, full of cheek, are ripening on trees whose canopies are forty feet high. He enjoys the quiet, the sun shining down on him as he hurries up the road. Taking deep breaths through his nose, the smell of the aging fruit, of living and dying grasses, of still and heated air, probe his senses.

He concentrates on the calm for it is to be short-lived. He's sure Rizzato will go haywire when he relays the news. Bunker worries about an expression that Morgan was always sprouting. "They shoot the messenger." He doesn't think his boss will shoot him, but he'll keep his back to the wall just in case. He knows the man to be crazy and extremely deadly. He has been witness to his many moods, anger being the deadliest. When Rizzato becomes enraged over an issue, he is totally unpredictable.

Bunker remembers when he had first started working for him; he was acting as back up when he went to collect money from one of his dealers, the man who was next in the pipeline out of Panama City. He had been awed at the amount of illegal drugs Rizzato had access to: pounds of cocaine, kilos of hashish, tons of marijuana, acres of pills. The man's name was Philippe; he couldn't remember his last name. Rumor was that he was the largest mover of product for Rizzato, which explained why Rizzato put up with his rude manners and tiny brain.

To this day, he had no idea how Rizzato had found out that Philippe had been stealing product from him, a little here, a little there. They were to meet Philippe that day at the edge of the city; the address was a vacant house with a Private Sale sign in front. When they arrived they found the door unlocked. The inside showed evidence of remodeling started and interrupted. One wall was partially dismantled, loose studs stood in one corner, twisted and splintered, many still with nails protruding. Debris littered the floor. There were odds and ends of furniture forgotten in the rooms, covered with dust. In the center of the drab living room was a burgundy hard-body briefcase, so new that the brass from the clasps and corner trim was golden-colored mirror. It would hold the money; the briefcases, he had come to know, always held the cash, lots of cash.

Philippe was tall, thin and masculine. Rizzato had told Bunker he was half French, half Panamanian. He wore a rose-colored silk shirt, white cotton pants and a pair of cheap neon flip-flops on his feet. He was chatting on a cell phone in an unfamiliar language. He held up a finger to Rizzato to give him a moment before turning his back. That didn't sit well with Rizzato, who was already miffed. Probably five or six minutes went by and Rizzato was so angry you could almost see smoke coming from his ears. Philippe had been haggling on the phone, his free arm flailing the air like an upside down egg beater. He had his back to them as he stared out the grimy living room window.

Finally Rizzato had had enough. He walked over to where the two-by-four lumber sat, seized a piece about three feet long. It had several nails sticking through the opposite end from the one he was holding. Some of the nails were bent flat but there were two still projecting from the wood, their ends pointy and piercing. Walking up behind Philippe who was still ranting into the mouthpiece, he swung the broken wood with great effort. Bunker thought he was going to hit him on the head with the nailed end.

Instead the two-by-four struck the hand holding the phone, one of the nails going straight through the back. The momentum of the swing tore the nail from the hand with a gouging rip. The phone flew to the side wall and spilled its parts all over the floor. Philippe screamed, vilifying Rizzato with foreign curses. Beetling eyes proclaimed his fear. Rizzato was yelling in a strange tongue only he and Philippe could understand. While the injured man bayed, misery tinting his high pitched voice, Rizzato struck him over and over, breaking bones and driving the offending nails into his flesh. The final blow fifteen seconds later was across the forehead with the flat of the wood, sending the wrecked body to the floor. Philippe landed right beside the briefcase, matching burgundy liquid seeping from his wounds. Bunker remembers how much the two of them had enjoyed watching the man slowly die; it had taken more than thirty minutes. They had picked up the briefcase and let themselves out, locking the door behind them.

Bunker's head is clearing as he approaches the compound where the hangar is. He can see activity through the hangar's enormous doors. Plum is standing in front of the oversized tent berating one of the workers, her finger jabbing at his chest. Bunker likes the feisty little Jap; he doesn't care for many people but Plum is an exception. The tarps that form the tent walls are rolled up on the sides and front. Wooden picnic tables, perfectly aligned, fill the inside, serving as a mess for the men. Bunker figures lunch is over; two of the older workers are cleaning up the tables, piling dishes on trays. A man wearing a cook's stained apron is emptying the contents of a large pot into a smaller dish.

As Bunker draws near he watches Plum shoo the man off with a warning.

"Don't let me catch you sleeping again when you're supposed to be working. I'll send you home and you won't get any pay."

The middle-aged man bows before him while backing away. Grateful he will continue to work, he says, "Apni, apni...yes, yes, always work...no more sleep." He turns to sprint down the graveled road that passes the hangar on the right. His royal blue and yellow lungi is stained brown along the hem from working in the soil and hangs loosely at the top of a pair of dark steel toed boots. His scrawny back is bare, dark, glistening with perspiration and as Bunker watches him run he thinks of coffee pouring from the pot.

When Plum notices Bunker approaching, she turns towards him. Bunker says, "Do you know where the Boss is?"

"Hello to you too, Bunker. Nah, I haven't seen him today. He was here looking over the plane last night. Didn't even talk to me. I'm not important enough I guess. He and Morgan checked out the runway, had Malik talk to the men about..." here she inserts quotation marks with her fingers, "productivity, bonuses, some other shit I didn't catch cause I don't understand what they're saying anyway but Hajani told me later."

"A no would have been sufficient Plum. But hello to you, too. I shouldn't be so rude. I had some fuck-ups Plum and I can't think straight. Boss is going to be pissed."

Bunker shakes his head, stuck on that idea for a moment. He had never confided his doubts to Plum before, to anyone for that matter. Plum is surprised by the emotion on Bunker's face *and* by the apology. Neither is a common occurrence. The big ape, as she regards the Serbian, is always poker faced as well as commanding. Plum notices something different on the man's face, something almost female but that's impossible, she thinks.

Bunker sees the look of questioning concern on Plum's face. He wonders if his masquerade has just cracked with the slightest of fissures for a second. He stares at the woman and something profound from the abyss of his soul aches to be like Plum, to be thin, to be pretty, to be tough and still be a woman too. He looks down at his own bulk instead, lifted his weighty claws, visualizing the rough-cut nails as polished and bright red. That'll be the day he thinks, and stirs from his self-pity. He blurts out loud without thinking, "Fuck it, fuck it all."

Plum is distracted from the apparition of Bunker's true identity and steps back.

"Yeah' right Bunk, fuck it all. That's the right 'tude when we're dealing with the Boss. Like that old Doris Dame used to say, *what'll be, will be.*"

"What are you talking about Plum? You don't make sense sometimes. Never mind. You got any wheels here?"

"Yep, the Waggoner is over by the house. Here are the keys."

She pulls a worn leather fob from her pocket with a single key attached and chucks it to him. A fat hand clutches the key in midair. Without another word, Bunker turns and starts walking toward the house. Plum gazes at the broad back and asks, "What's Boss gonna be pissed about?"

Talking to the air if front of him Bunker says, "You'll find out soon enough Plum, but something for you to think about: Raheem ain't coming back."

Ten minutes later Bunker pulls up to the main house where Rizzato normally stays. There is a gray Nissan quarter-ton truck in the yard. He parks the big Jeep right in front of it. The yard is sun-baked dirt and scraggly grass. The house is a storey and a half, wearing a jacket of white patchy stucco, badly in need of paint and repair. Faded red shutters chaperon each window. The gable of the house contains a solitary window with one of its shutters askew, held with only one nail. Bunker glances up at the reflecting sun and sees Rizzato staring down at him. His scalp starts to itch. He knows something's wrong Bunker thinks. He can't remember ever being so nervous; a gentle sweat condenses on his brow.

The inside contradicts the exterior in that it is almost new and well laid out. It seemed as if the previous owners had just got started on renovations and when they finished the inside, they moved out. Bunker steps into a foyer that opens into a living room on the left; straight through, a short hallway brings you into a dining area; and to the right are a set of new wooden stairs.

From above Rizzato shouts out, "Bring that big bottle of Pepsi from the fridge with you, Bunk, and my cigars that are in the kitchen somewhere and c'mon up."

Bunker proceeds through the dining area into a small kitchen to retrieve the soft drink. As he is glancing around the cupboards for the cigars, he stops for a moment. His nerves and the midday heat do nothing to stop a sudden chill that braces his troubled mind. A grisly vision of him floating face down in the swirling river waters bursts through his skull and echoes there like a broken film clip. He feels things unraveling. He checks his gun. He is still wearing the navy short sleeved shirt, extra, extra large and the fabric hides the holstered weapon fastened snugly at his back. The two knives are within easy reach. Remembering Plum's agreement on all this bullshit, he tries to ease his nerves. What is coming is going to come anyway, so get it on.

He spots Rizzato's custom case, collects the cigars and the Pepsi and heads upstairs. The whole top floor is a maze of bedrooms. The window that held the frowning face earlier is to his left in the room facing the yard, the room that Rizzato and his birds use. A giant fan on a stand facing him blows cool air around the room.

On the right Rizzato is sitting at a chrome and smoked glass desk. He poses behind it in an elephant of a chair. He is skinny and occupies maybe a third of its girth. The extra black leather stands out from his shoulders like two bodyguards.

Rizzato is wearing a black tank that should've been a size or two bigger. Two heavy chains of gold hang around his slender neck and on his head he wears a black cotton kepi, the back flap flimsy and moving in the manufactured breeze. It is amusing in itself thinks Bunker but the factor that causes him to start laughing is that the room has obviously been designed for small children before because the short walls and the other gable end are wallpapered with Winnie the Pooh and all his friends. To Rizzato's left behind him on the wall is a life size image of Roo emptying a jar of honey. It looks like the kangaroo is dumping the amber syrup into Rizzato's lap.

"What the fuck you laughing at you big lug?"

If Rizzato had pointed the Luger that sat on his desk at Bunker and commanded him to stop, he would have had to shoot him. For the first time in too many years, Bunker enjoys a braying gut aching laugh. It lasts a minute or more and is fortified by the look on Rizzato's face who bears the amusement with his usual indifference, turning back to his PC. He had been visiting some S&M sites, and this one was about Japanese geishas tying knots and shit. He enjoys bondage but he expects to be the one doing the tying. As he shuts down the computer, he's thinking maybe he should ask Plum if she can tie knots. He stares at Bunker, who is standing bent over holding his stomach wiping tears away. He is down to an occasional squeak and starting to breathe normal.

Rizzato leans forward at his desk and steeples his fingers over the glass, "So, tell me the joke, you crazy Serbian."

"It's... It's the big yellow marsupial behind you, boss. He... He looks like he's going to douse you with honey... It's too fucking funny," he titters, and then sets his straight face, "Sorry, boss."

Rizzato swings his chair around and sees the animal on the wall. It is pouring honey down a little bear's throat. Ignoring the figures on the wall is easy; he really doesn't give a shit.

"Never mind, tell me what's going on and where Kovalenko is with that damn engine. That prick Stratton is on his way here, tomorrow in fact. That engine had better be here very soon, you get me Bunker."

Bunker collects himself, straightens to his full height and strides over to the desk. He wants to be close if something is going to go wrong. He can see Rizzato is already edgy.

"Kovalenko assured me this morning that he would be done today at the very latest. We can get it aboard the sampan and be back here sometime tomorrow."

That calms him down. "Good, good, tomorrow will be good. Stratton can live with that. We have to keep this fool happy, Bunk. Only three or four more weeks and we are gone. What's going on with Raheem and his two dummies? I keep getting a feeling that something's not right with him, my senses have been going batty since yesterday."

"You're right as usual, Boss. That's why I'm back, wanted to give you the bad news in person."

Rizzato stiffens a bit when he hears "bad news".

"It's that dickhead Ahmedani, isn't it? What did he do?"

"Well he left the two locals alone and they tried to hightail it. I was lucky enough to catch them in the act and they're...uh, no longer a threat. I dealt with that. Worse though is Raheem visited a bar. I found him quite by accident, but not before he opened his big mouth."

Bunker hesitates here, shifting into a more relaxed pose, what the military would call at ease. His hands clasped behind him back, close to his weapon if he needs it. He goes on, "He was arm in arm with some local guy when I heard him blabbing about working with us, namely you. I tried to take both of them out several times but to no avail. I finished Raheem in the morning but I got all the useful information I could before I sent him to his Allah. The other one I lost. I know who he is and where he lives, and I left a threat he will heed. I'll hunt him down."

Rizzato sits back and folds his arms over his chest. The silence is not what Bunker expected. He waits for an eruption; none comes. He remains loose but tense, not realizing his own worth. Rizzato isn't going to get ugly as he usually does, not with Bunker. He needs Bunker until the end; after that; well, he would wait until then before passing judgment on the big oaf. He says, "Sit down somewhere close Bunker, relax and get your hand away from your gun. I know you; you would've done everything you could. It's cool, Bunk, I'm not going to throw a tantrum like I usually do. Only real dumbasses get me going. Sit."

Bunker feels the tightness leave his body, relieved that he had been worrying for nothing. He drops his hands to his side as he looks for a place to sit.

"First tell me how you killed that rat, then go get Malik and

Morgan. They should both be at the hangar site. They should be keeping an eye on the workers and watching the grounds. We're so close and now this. Shit!"

After the recap, Bunker leaves. Soon Rizzato hears a car start. He watches the far window facing him for a while as he contemplates his options. He hears tearing of the gravel thinking Bunker has floored whichever vehicle he's driving. Soon a beige cloud of dust rises past the bottom of the window thinning as it ascends into the tight warm air. As he stares at the settling particles outside his eyes slowly glaze over. Rizzato's mind is churning the concerns, which problems are most serious, which ones that can wait to be dealt with. The two workers don't matter. They were nonentities to the whole job. Bunker just accelerated the inevitable anyway. They will make do with the ones they have left he calculates. After a few more minutes he relegates Raheem to the same dung heap. They can manage without him, he still has his four commandos and then with a smirk he realizes that there is him also. He regards himself as a killing machine, no soul, hard as stone. He enjoys that image.

But the other factor is a loose cannon. He glances down at the day timer spread out on his desk where he has scribbled the name, Rafan Bashara. He turns to his computer, starts it up again and within the next hour knows most of what he can about the man, except his underwear size. As he is writing down details on Bashara, Morgan comes up the stairs followed by Malik and Bunker.

Bunker has filled them in on what has taken place when they had driven over. It had taken him some time to locate the two men as they had been patrolling the perimeter like they did each afternoon. Morgan is all too aware of the man's impatience remaining mum as he confronts Rizzato; Malik as usual has nothing to say. Both men stand in front of the desk. Rizzato studies them for a moment sizing up his warriors. He shakes his head as he thinks of them as ugly fuckin' losers, especially that Morgan he tells himself, his black Jew. He shrugs at his own thoughts and says,

"I want you to go over everything with Bunker." He passes Morgan a sheet of paper, "Here's all the info on him I dug up. Find this asshole and bring him back here. I don't care how you do it, just do it and don't cause any more trouble. We'll find out if he told anybody else anything when I get my hands on him. I'll give you guys a lesson on making people talk that you haven't even been able to imagine. His work address, his home are all marked here. He has a sister here as well, married to some doctor; the addresses are there too if you need them."

He is interrupted when Morgan wants to ask him something,

"What if…"

"Shut up Morgan and listen. I'm only telling you this once, all of you. We are very close to becoming exceptionally rich men. Three, four weeks we're gone, you take your money and run and I couldn't care less where to. But for now, we keep things tight, real tight, puckered asshole tight. Take Malik with you and locate this man, Morgan. Bunker will take you guys out with the Cabin Cruiser and be bringing Kovalenko back with the Sampan. Remember where the boat will be tied up and don't come back unless you have Bashara. Do you understand Saul?"

Morgan squints below his hairy brows at his boss and gives him a nod.

"Then get outta here."

Rizzato is right about one thing only, the two goons are never returning.

Chapter 25   Sadarghat, Bangladesh

Bunker is at the bow when Malik coaxes their boat into their berth beside the sampan. Saul commented earlier that it was unlikely their berth would be occupied since Bunker had roughed up the dock master the last time they had arrived and had found their slip occupied by another boat. Morgan was choking his own throat, bugging his eyes out and gasping, portraying a man quacking in Bunker's grip. This caused Malik and Bunker to chortle at his playacting. When the two men heard Bunker laugh, they were caught off guard as the giant had never been given to laughter in their presence. That in itself would have been odd but his amusement was deep and resonant, almost eerie, an anomaly of his usual apathetic character. His peculiar behavior quieted the two men.

Morgan reluctantly moves to the bow beside Bunker, busying himself with the mooring ropes, uncoiling one from the pit of snaked piles at his feet. A beanstalk of a man with a droopy moustache and mondo ears is waiting to tie them up. Malik reverses the engines, and the boat begins to slow. He guides it skilfully between two larger boats that shadowed the smaller craft. The boat stops about ten feet from the dock, so Morgan throws the rope out to the longshoreman. The man seizes the line with deft hands, looping it around a crude, thick wooden post and pulls them closer to the pier. Malik joins the men at the bow.

Bunker says to them, "Okay, you two know what you have to do. Get into his apartment, check around the market, go to his office. Whatever you have to do, find him and detain him. Remember what Rizzato said, we want this man alive."

When he said this he faces them directly, putting his hands on his hips for emphasis. He is almost as wide as the two of them and at least ten inches taller. His eyes are icy and blank as he continues, "Malik, you do as Morgan tells you. I know this city is crazy but be careful. You two blend in pretty good so don't make any scenes; find him and subdue him when he's alone. I'm going to get Kovalenko, get him back on board with the engine. I thought I might need you two to help, but Kovalenko told me yesterday we can do it. I'm going to assume you'll find Bashara so I'll meet one of you mid-afternoon outside of his building in New Market."

He steps a little closer to Saul and taps him on the chest. "Don't fuck up, Morgan."

At that he returns to the cabin to grab the black case he has brought with him. He returns to the bow, heaving his great bulk up to the wharf, looking in each direction as if uncertain as to where he should go. Even at this late hour, hundreds of people mill about. The night lights from the buildings and the hanging bulbs that mark the boundaries of the wharf illuminate the crowd, casting crisscrossed shadows that makes Bunker look like a signpost above the shifting melee. Just as Malik and Saul come up behind him, he makes up his mind and heads left. He's planning to find a rickshaw to take him north out of the old city. He will then find a cab to drop her off near the warehouse to connect with Kovalenko

As unfeeling as he is, he pities any cyclist who has to haul his great weight to his destination, so he opts for the motorized version instead. He has picked up enough words to tell the man where he wants to go. He never hassles about the money, knowing he will likely pay much more than he should. Rizzato had chucked him some local currency telling him to share it with Morgan. He had split it up, but the remaining bills made a roll that bulged in his pocket. The bulge in the opposite pocket is of a much more deadly payout.

Morgan is shaking his head, trying to get his bearings among the groups that are departing the ferries. Diesel fumes filter through the night so he decides he'd have a smoke later. The stench of garbage floats from his right as the ship beside theirs is unloading its refuse into a large metal bin that squats on the trodden planks. He starts into the mob, waving to Malik. "C'mon, Hajani, let's get us one of those carts with all the spiffy colors. You can tell him where we need to go."

Malik nods in response and follows Morgan into the crowd. He's thinking of the boat and how he's going to buy one when he returns home. He dreams of spending days on the rivers. Had he decided then to bow out of this caper, he could have easily lost Saul and gone on with his tumultuous life.

They are shuffling through the people almost at a run and soon come to a side road that leads into, then out of Old Dhaka. Morgan confides in Malik that they will try Bashara's apartment before checking his workplace in the morning if he isn't at home tonight. Morgan is going over Bunker's instructions in his head, the directives flipping through his mind like a one armed bandit's spinning window. Malik rushes ahead to where several tuk-tuks sit waiting for a fare. Morgan watches them babble, Malik shaking his head when he holds out some money. After the hustle, they are hastened away by the young man clad in garish lime and brown clothes.

They soon stand at the main door of Rafan's apartment, backs against the stuccoed wall of the building, and watch the entrance for a short time. Malik is closest to the door, studying the lock. He recognizes the universal Yale, knowing it will be easy to pick. Turning to Saul he tugs at his partner's sleeve accompanied with his usual silent nod. Morgan isn't too worried about Hajani, he hasn't been stumped yet anywhere they needed to get in.

Morgan scans the shallow group that move along the road. He checks his Timex and sees that it is just after eleven o'clock. He is glad there are stalls still selling their wares. Many of the permanent stalls have painted and beaten doors pulled across their face. He leans toward Malik and says in a heavy whisper,

"No one seems to be paying attention to us, Hajani. Quick, get us inside."

The Pakistani sets the gun case he is carrying down after moving hurriedly to the door. He removes a collection of picks from the supple leather belt tucked under his shirt that holds his throwing stars and knives. Standing before the locked entryway, he closes his eyes and feels blindly for the two picks he will need. He tests himself occasionally and tries to do the simple ones with his eyes closed. This one proves even more eager to be released and he has them in the building in less than 90 seconds. The door on the third floor only takes him 60.

Inside the apartment, it is totally dark except for a moonbeam that enters through a kitchen window on their left. The greyish glow fades as Morgan approaches what he assumes are the bedrooms at the rear. There are three open doors. The first on the left past the kitchen proves to be a bathroom. The room on the right is very dark. Morgan waits for a moment, letting his eyes adjust to the blackness. He pokes his head around the doorjamb and makes out the silhouette of a bed. As his pupils dilate, he can make out an uneven bulge upon the mattress. Morgan's right hand grips his Walther as his raised left signals Malik an okay gesture. Turning his face sideways, he points two fingers at his eyes and then back toward the door. Malik recognizes the sign and backs slowly to the front door they had left slightly ajar, to stand sentry.

Morgan's sandals crush the thick fibers of the carpet as he creeps up to the bed. He remains still for a moment staring at the figure sprawled out before him. He can't hear any breathing, which bewilders him. He thinks the man isn't very big and imagines he can easily overpower him. He replaces his gun in its holster under his shirt, intending to grab the man by the head and muffle his cries with an open hand. He lunged for the bulge in the blanket. There is no resistance. Removing the blankets he digs his hand into two fluffy foam pillows. Realizing his mistake, he's relieved that Hajani has not seen him. He blushes in the darkness as he thinks of how he must look, sneaking up on bedding.

He glances back at the doorway, its opening painted in dim smoky reflections. He can discern a switch next to the door. He walks over and flips the plastic toggle, which powers a tall lamp in the left corner. He whistles at the luxuriousness of the room. The wood that decorates the lower wall is textured and manly. Works of art adorned the walls and shelves throughout the room, paintings, figurines and, oddly, many crosses. He sees the empty picture frame Bunker had left on the bed. Shifting his gaze to search the room, his eyes stop on the dresser in the corner along the wall opposite the bed. On top are at least twenty watches. Going closer he marvels at the timepieces, many are diamond enhanced. The one he takes a liking to is huge and multi-dialed. He has no idea of the value of watches, never considering them more than something to tell time with, but these ones look like jewelry.

He unfastens his Timex, the leather bracelet worn and cupped, tossing it on the dresser. He picks up the Breitling he fancies, fastening it to his wrist. He has no idea that it is an original Navitimer from 1952. To collectors around the world it would be priceless; to Morgan it's just a prettier way to tell the time. He leaves the room, shutting off the light, carefully checks that last room to find it empty and approaches Malik who waits by the front door. He whispers very softly, "The dickhead isn't here, Malik, but you should see the neat shit he has. Let's find a place to stay and come back early in the morning."

After they trashed the apartment, Malik follows Morgan out of the building and back to the rickshaw they had told to wait for them. The driver takes them to a small hotel that caters to foreigners. The building is dingy in the night but the interior is clean and brightly lit. They take a chamber with two beds, paying in cash. When asked to register Morgan wrote Donald Duck and Mickey Mouse on the sheet and a phony address in Johannesburg. Folding the book shut, the attendant doesn't even look beyond the Taka notes in Morgan's hand.

When they enter the room on the second level, each man flops onto a bed on top of the sheets. Sleep comes to Malik easily and he's out five minutes later. Morgan on the other hand gets back up and kills the light, returning to the bed and lying on his back with both hands tucked under his head. Streetlights give their quarters a diminished bloom. Morgan lies there alert, the coming day occupying his mind. He's trying to imagine what Rizzato has up his sleeve to make the man talk once they deliver him. Scenes of gruesome torture jump the fence instead of sheep and a half hour later he's under a sleepy spell.

The following morning the sun peeks in their window as soon as it tops the buildings next door and jabs Morgan. He stretches like a lazy feline waking up. He looks over at Malik curled up on the bed next to him before rousing himself to his feet. After using the washroom he shakes Malik until he stirs.

"Let's get going, Hajani, have a piss and get ready. We've got a big day ahead of us; let's go get something to eat."

Malik groans and breaks wind, shaking himself like a lazy old hound. A trip to the john wakes him up. Rejoining Morgan in the room they leave their latest sanctuary behind.

**

Six hours later Morgan is running through the crowd at New Market, tearing away from the shootout at the apartment. He dodges around the hodgepodge of people and rickshaws along the street, tripping over some, toppling others. He's trying to remember where he had left the waiting rickshaw, hoping to recognize the cherry red canopy topped by a frayed and yellowed flag. In his haste he never checked for Hajani, assuming he was not far behind. He finally stops to look quickly behind him, expecting to see Malik, but after a couple of minutes self-protection kicks in and he flees back into the crowd. As a result, he misses the alley to his right where his carriage is parked.

Bunker stands beside a grey Isuzu Sportivo. The hood is up, more for a distraction than any other purpose. He is just about to head over to Bashara's apartment to meet the men when he is distracted by a familiar figure ramming through the masses. He moves towards the runner. His substantial stature and the whiteness of his skin draw curious glances, but it is the wickedness in his scent that parts the crowds. He recognizes Morgan and curses to himself. If he's running away, something's amiss. He calls out, "Over here, you fool."

Morgan is stunned to hear Bunker's deep voice. He shoots a look to his left, where the sound came from, and spies the Serb right away. He has been running with his eyes on the crowd and the littered street in front of him. He would've run right past Bunker had he not called out his name.

Morgan trots up to Bunker and doubles over trying to catch his breath, winded from his retreat. Bunker's voice is angry and demands, "What did you screw up now, Morgan? Where's Hajani?"

Saul straightens up still taking deep breaths. "He should be close behind, man. I don't know. There were guns there, Bunk. This guy has some protection. We were pinned down and I was damn lucky to get out."

Bunker rubs his chin for a second, the heavy brows wrinkled in concentration.

"Get in," he tells Saul while closing the hood. He edges his vehicle through the congestion until he is only seven meters from Rafan's apartment and waits. It isn't long before two white men rush from the building towards the black truck parked across the street. As they scout the streets, Bunker and Saul duck down out of view.

"It's them, Bunk. The guy with the bandage on his hand is the one Malik struck with one of his stars. You should've seen it Bunk, the kid's real fast."

"Shut up," he says.

A few second later, he slowly lifts his head just in time to watch the truck take to the street in a crazy zigzag. He hears the sirens as they wail in the distance somewhere behind them. He realizes that the men he is about to follow might be strangely fleeing from the law. He follows the men. It is all he can do to keep the truck in view. They are far behind, but the truck is an uncommon sight on the streets. He dents a few fenders during their rush but manages to follow them undetected to the Westin Hotel, where the truck drives up to the main entrance. Bunker parks on the street behind a delivery van. He sees the men get out. The driver tosses the keys to a red-vested young man, joining his mate as they enter the hotel.

Bunker moves his vehicle to a more inconspicuous spot and keeps watch on the entrance from behind thick foliage that grows at the property's edge, lining the sidewalks by the street. By sitting upright, he can easily see the doors. The shrubs are high enough for him to hide behind. Never moving his eyes from the hotel he says, "Tell me what happened, Morgan. Don't leave anything out."

It is late afternoon. Three hours pass before the men emerge from the main door. Bunker watches them as they march across the tarmac. These are soldiers, he thinks. He knows the swagger; he knows the costume. Fatigues bloused into black boots, pockets full. They walk with the bearing of those who survived boot camp. He knows inside that these men are not to be taken for granted. He sees them enter the parking lot and is suddenly alert to the fact that they are walking in his direction. Crouching down he presses her finger to his lip as he motions to Morgan to be quiet. He withdraws his gun. His gut telling him to rush them now, but Bashara isn't with them and he hopes they will lead him to him. He waits.

Soon an engine starts directly beside them where the rentals are parked, the noise surprising them. Bunker cups both hands around the butt of his pistol, ready to raise it into a two fisted aim. The droning of the engine retreats, the vehicle backing away. Soon Bunker sees a Toyota SUV leave the parking lot occupied by the men. When they turn away, he waits a few seconds, starts his own truck and pulls out to follow them

At first, Bunker maintains a fair distance but his anxiousness takes them closer until they are only a few cars behind. The traffic is stop and go. The vehicle they are tailing swerves unexpectedly to avoid a rickshaw in front of it. He is momentarily distracted from the chase by a fluttering piece of black fabric as it stirs through the air. When he looks back at the truck, the man in the passenger seat is looking in his mirror, directly at them.

Suddenly the truck tears to the right and then another right heading toward a parking structure at the rear of an office building. Bunker realizes they have been spotted and urges his vehicle along. He watches the garage and sees the Toyota climb upward. It disappears behind the second floor supports and a short upper wall. Bunker understands they are being lured into the building but he hesitates for only a moment. He enters and after a brief argument digs out the black case from the rear seat, opens it and hands Morgan the bull pup. He stops when he sees the vehicle blocking the upper entrance. Morgan and Bunker rant for a few moments at what they should do. It didn't take long for Bunker to reach a decision. He stomps on the brakes with his great strength and depresses the accelerator. Screaming, burning rubber accompanies them to their fate.

After fleeing from the upper level of the parking garage, Bunker races toward the idling Scorpio. He is amused by the sudden stillness of the crowd as he shoots the woman running to her vehicle. Bunker is trying to adjust his seat when he runs over the previous owner's dead body. He isn't comfortable with driving on the right so tears out of the parking lot entering the street on the left hand side as he normally would only to face an oncoming truck blasting at his ignorance with a disapproving horn. He veers back into his lane, just missing the large van by inches.

He makes a jagged retreat along the street, dodging in and out of traffic. After several blocks he cuts across traffic at the first chance, turning onto a narrower two-way thoroughfare. There are fewer vehicles, more rickshaws, tuk-tuks, vendors, carts and a bevy of beggars. Bunker pulls the SUV to the curb in front of a dilapidated brick building, several windows boarded up with rough lumber. Along the front lower facade sits a dozen beggars, many offering the cheapest of trinkets for a "donation" to their meagre coffers. There are three ragged men on the right a ways from the other beggars. They all sit on their haunches, scruffy and deeply poor; all have bent and scarred tin soup cans with a few coins at their feet. They all have eyes that are similarly clouded with the whitish, filmy mire of blindness. They gab and argue in strange dialects, calling for alms to unseen benefactors when the noise from their neighbors increases calling for same.

It is to the skinniest of all three, the one in the middle, that Bunker walks to and chucks the keys to the stolen Scorpion in his cup. He pulls out his wad of notes, shoving a 10 Taka note into each of the three cups. Then, he reaches in his left pocket and withdraws a dozen or more coins. He throws the change to the sidewalk in front of the other needy souls. Frenzy erupts as the men and women tear at each other scrabbling for a scrap of salvation – a two taka coin can buy food.

To Bunker it's funny. He grunts as he walks away from the scene he created, amused by the desperate plight of Dhaka's forgotten populace. He disregards the bunch and hurries along. People will be looking for the car soon so he loops around for some distance to eventually return to a larger roadway where he hails a cab. Instructing the driver to the street of the safe house, he settles back in the rear seat, relaxing for the first time in many hours. He's grown weary of being angry at his men, not being able to depend on them. He nods his big head as he watches the crowds that seem to be growing thicker, nearing the time most people leave work for home he figures. Flipping open his cell phone, he sees that it is nearly 7 p.m. He thinks about calling Rizzato, but finds that unappealing.

Reaching into his shirt pocket, he removes a folded sheet of plain white paper. He unfolds the unlined page and stares at the letters, a mystery of lines and swirls. There are two names and an address circled on the bottom of the sheet. Bunker has the names memorized, Dr Ihtisham Thaku and his wife Medina, Rafan

Bashara's sister and her husband. The jumble of figures on the paper go fuzzy as they blur while he thinks about what he must do. He refolds the paper before returning it to his pocket. He crosses his big arms, two fence posts across the chest, deciding he will rest before going to their home. He tells himself he will find young Bashara and with him in hand, the boss will be more docile and receptive to the loss of his men. The rest of the trip to the safe house is consumed with ideas of how he will slay his captives after their usefulness has been fulfilled.

Chapter 26   Sept 23   Radisson Hotel, Dhaka

Sophia is relaxing on the plush sofa in her suite at the Radisson, the big green cushions engulfing her. She's tired, her feet ache, she's hungry, not having eaten all day, and she is deeply frustrated at not being able to find her father. She has just hung up the phone, having made reservations downstairs at Sublime, the hotel's fine dining restaurant. She had thought of eating out but she found the open cooking area she had seen when checking in interesting. She likes watching a chef prepare meals, the hustle of the waiters.

She made the reservation for 7:30, which allows her to rest for a while before changing. Reclining her head on the sofa back she reviews her movements of the last week. She knows she's no detective; finding her father is a lot more difficult than she anticipated it would be when she left the Cayman Islands. She couldn't and wouldn't imagine that Amado had been lying to her. He had said Dhaka during one of the last breathes of his life. The thought that nags her over and over is that perhaps it was his final joke, sending her to the other side of the world looking for Andrew Stratton who could actually be thousands of miles away plotting his terrible reprisal.

She had talked to her mother when she had returned to Chicago from the Islands, about the trauma of seeing a man die, the bedlam of the police station. Her mother had been sympathetic but remained indifferent to Andrew's actions, explaining that she only wanted to be left alone and to forget. Sophia realized she was on her own. Having no idea how long it might take her to find her father and stop his foolishness, she had arranged for a leave of absence from her work. Her boss, Chief Dave Sawhill of the Engine 34 Company out of Archer Heights, had been extremely accommodating, allowing her to take the four week absence she had requested. He reminded her that she still had a week's holiday left, as well as nine sick days she was entitled to. He suggested she use those up and if he hadn't heard from her after fourteen days, he'd submit her leave request with his approval.

She had been relieved that he hadn't pressed her for more details of why she needed the time. He took her at her word when she explained it was something personal. Their meeting ended with her having a sense of foreboding, the same spook that held sway when the klaxon of the fire bell called them to work. As she rose to leave his office, he walked her to the door. She still remembers his words, "You're one of the best firefighters I've got, Stratton. Make sure you come back."

Sophia had left Chicago on the 19th, arriving in Dhaka on the 21st because of the tremendous time difference and the layovers. Disembarking in the middle of the night when she arrived in Dhaka, she was not exposed to the splendors or the tumult of the city that greeted each new visitor during sunlight hours with its blaze of colors and its ritual cacophony.

She had settled into her suite at 3 a.m. After only four hours' sleep, she had headed out with no idea where she was going. She rented a Toyota Yaris. The concierge, a rotund smiling man, had kindly listed all the upscale hotels in the city, with addresses. Armed with her pocketbook full of local currency and copies of a photo of Andrew Stratton that was a year old, she headed out into a different and complicated world. She knew her father well enough to know that regardless of what he may be up to, he was unlikely to break old habits. He'd be travelling first class; after all, even if he wasn't at his desk any longer, he was still worth a considerable amount of money.

She had spent many hours yesterday as she had questioned everyone available at each hotel she visited – the desk people, the concierge, the waiters and waitresses at the lobby restaurants, anyone who could speak English. She had been asked to leave twice. She left a photo where she could at each hotel with an offer of a reward if he was sighted. If they would inform only her, she offered an extra four thousand Taka to keep it a secret. Today she had trod the sidewalks showing her father's picture at restaurants near the hotels and other high-end restaurants around the city to no avail. It was the only thing she could think of. If he was here, he had to eat.

She had had no idea how large the city was, how dense the population was, how busy the populace would be, how crazy the traffic, with vehicles on the opposite side of the road like the British. The brief history she had read on Dhaka emphasized the importance of the Buriganga River. When she had arrived, the first thing she did after registering at the hotel was to show the young man working the desk the photo of her father asking him if he knew the man. The agent informed her that he didn't recognize him. She asked if she should be searching hotels near the river. He told her that the closer you got to the river, the older Dhaka would become. Unless the man she sought had specific business on the river, it is unlikely he would venture there.

Wishing her detective skills were keener, she tried to imagine what her father might be planning. She remembered their last conversation. She had never seen him so defeated, so sullen as when they discussed her siblings' deaths. Soon their chat matured to an argument. She became annoyed with him as he bemoaned *his* loss, *his* missed opportunities, *his* neglect. On and on he went, and never a second of concern that she and her mother were scarred with the same pain.

He had talked about how groups all over the world killed at random, and killed and killed. When one cell of terrorists was destroyed or defeated, another was born. He had ideas he wanted to share with her, how he would use his fortune to extract a vengeance worthy of the Stratton's. She can still remember him ranting,

"...so Scott and Sarah would not have died in vain, we'll bring a terror so great to all Muslims, not just the ones that killed your brother and sister. A terror to end further terror, we'll fight back.... Please, Sophia, join me and we'll..."

She forces the awful thoughts away and shivers as she remembers her father's eyes that night. She had been afraid of him then, but not anymore, she told herself.

She tries to sit up straighter as she wiggles around on the sofa, holding her hands around her face. Her eyes are closed as she massages her temples, willing the dull ache in her skull to ebb. She is overwhelmed with her task. Forget the haystack she thinks, she feels like she has to find a needle in a whole stinking field. She rubs her eyes and checks her watch. With only twenty minutes until her reservation, she decides to get ready.

As she shifts in her seat to get up, her eyes fall upon the yellow post-it note she had found in her father's office. It's folded in quarters, the edges weary from refolds. Its contents are branded on her brain, but still she picks it up and unfolds it once more. Besides Amado's name, she had drawn a crude cross with tiny flowers at its base. But it isn't Amado's name she's interested in. Jack Favors. The words come off the page bursting with awareness. She thumps her forehead with the palm off her hand, saying out loud, "Jack Favors! Why didn't I think of it before? I can't find Andrew Stratton because he doesn't exist here. Damn!"

She scurries back to the entryway, snatching her purse from the side table. She's digging through one of the zippered sections on the side; keys, loose change and receipts are falling to the floor as she pulls out the folded sheet of paper with the list of hotels. She hastens to the living room again and lifts the cordless phone from the coffee table. Before she places it to her ear she punches in the 9, which took her directly to the restaurant. When they answered, she says, "Yes, this is Sofia Stratton, Room 404. Please cancel my reservation. Thank you."

The first number she dials is the Sheraton, because she knows her father favored their hotels when he travelled. When the receptionist answers she asks if there is a Jack Favors registered with them or if he has reservations. She is asked to hold while they check. Each second she waits seems unbearably long; her anxiety is tantamount to her impatience. Sophia is told that there is no one by that name registered or with a reservation. She doesn't even say thank you, she just severs the connection and moves down her list.

A half hour passes as she places a dozen calls, all with the same disgruntling results. She starts to lose hope as she stares at the last hotel on her list. It isn't because it's on the bottom of the list but that she can't pronounce it. Knowing her father, he would be unlikely to stay at a hotel he couldn't pronounce.

With great reluctance and a slither of hope, she dials the number for the Sonargaon Hotel, not realizing that it is a jewel in the Pan Pacific line. The operator is more pleasant than the previous respondents, even though she speaks with the musical lilt of Asian intonation.

"Can you please tell me if you have a Jack Favors registered there?"

"One moment, please."

Sophia doesn't have enough time to begin a new thought before the operator speaks, "I'm sorry, Mr. Favors isn't registered..."

She is interrupted by a soft moan from Sophia, whose disappointment is something solid on the line. The operator continues, "...but Mr. Favors has a reservation for tomorrow."

Chapter 27   Sept 30 Dhaka

Gurupada has arrived early for his rendezvous with Drake, finding a booth in the rear near the windows that face southeast. The pale lime and yellow decor is cheery and bright, spacious beige Naugahyde seating coax patrons to linger. The sun hasn't risen over the surrounding buildings yet and Pada takes pleasure in the silhouettes that forms black shapes and squares against the morning's marbled sky. Thanking the waitress for the coffee she served him, he turns back to view the pinkish swirls, white wisps and burning oranges that are smeared across a charcoal background. As Pada is studying the daybreak, he's thinking that the dawn defines his spirit. He feels the animation of a thirteen year old on his first date. He is anxious for Drake to arrive as he has important news to share with him.

He had been at the police station until one in the morning concentrating on stolen cars, related reports and recoveries, as well as abandoned vehicles. He had collected a bundle of information, spending several hours sorting out the irrelevant and the ridiculous. Before he left for the night, he checked the police force's intranet for yesterday's developments; an article with double asterisks caught his attention. It was a report of a dismembered body found on the edge of the city.

That alone would have been worthy of notice, but what really interested him was the identification of a mark on the shoulder of the torso. It was also remarkable in light of the details Drake had shared with him at their recent meeting and for that reason alone he had printed out the report, what little there was. On the bottom of the page was a file number for future reference and the names of the investigators assigned to the case.

He's thinking he will talk with Chowdhury as soon as possible about the file. His thoughts are interrupted by Drake and Isaac entering the restaurant. He waves an arm to attract them. He studies the two men as they approach; their bearing making him feel chunky. He feels he keeps himself in reasonable shape, but he's shorter, stockier; these men are tall, lean and well-muscled. They're dressed in black fatigues, black boots, only their T-shirts differ. Isaac's is tie-dyed purple, white and orange on a tan background; as lively as the grin on his face. Drake's is khaki and hugs his rigid frame. He likes these guys. He'd read their bios: decorated soldiers, successful businessmen. He admires them; he trusts them.

Greetings are exchanged as Isaac slides into the booth opposite Gurupada, Drake moving in next to him. A familiar, comfortable rapport develops among the three men right away. Anxious to share his news, Gurupada says, "Drake, wait until I tell you what I discovered late last night, I think it's connected to us."

"Is it about the dismantled body found yesterday?"

The look of disbelief, then disappointment and then disbelief again shutters Pada's face, causing a chuckle with Drake and Isaac.

"How... How did you know?"

Drake says, "I have a contact at the newspaper that has a contact that has a contact. You know how it is, Pada. You should see the look on your face; it's kind of funny."

"I was just surprised that you knew, Drake. After all, I am a police officer and the body was only found late yesterday afternoon. But then I have to remember that you're a private investigator and have experience with secrets."

Isaac says, "Yeah, Drake's uncanny; he's always full of surprises."

They discuss the body and what it could mean. Drake agrees with Pada that he should check with Chowdhury. They only had to link the mark on the body's shoulder to the other bodies with similar marks. Gurupada had checked with Forensics and had been told that they were still working the terrain where the body part was found, so it is too early to have anything substantial to work with. Drake decides to give it to Ray to see what she can come up with; she has Chowdhury backing her.

After their meal, the waitress clears the table, leaving the men to their discussion. Gurupada says, "We will have to start at Barisal; it is a river port on the Kirtonkhola, not far from Bhola. With a fast boat we can be there in four to five hours. I spoke to the Officer in Charge, Patwary, and we're to meet with him later this afternoon. We're starting there because that is where the mystery boat dumped the body of the girl. It was deposited on the wharf and an anonymous call informed the police where it was and where it had been found. There were fortunately several witnesses, so we'll be able to learn what he has."

Isaac asks, "Where did you say the body was found?"

Pada says, "On the Meghna River, not far from the mouth of the Bhola. Its assumed body gasses brought the tarp to the surface and that it floated near shore where it got caught in the roots of a dead tree. There was a cement block attached to the body, but it failed obviously. A passing boat seeing a tarp for the taking couldn't resist. They must have some conscience, though, as they could've just tossed it back in if they had wanted to and no one would've know the difference. If they were hoping not to get involved, they're in for a revelation. "

Isaac has been fidgeting in his seat. "Well lucky for us. I don't know about you guys but I'm anxious to get going. How about we hit the road, Drake, or I should say, hit the river."

"You're right Isaac, let's go."

Three and a half hours later, Drake is at the wheel of the blue and white Chris Craft he had purchased the night before. It skims the surface of the Meghna River like a greyhound on vitamins. Isaac is below deck going over the topographical maps that Gurupada had secured that morning, familiarizing himself with the rivers Pada has marked for transit. Gurupada is seated behind Drake on one of the upper cabin seats, perusing some of the reports he had amassed the previous night.

Drake is thinking about the broker who had allowed him to disturb his evening when he had explained that he needed a craft for early morning, the enticement being he would pay him on the spot, no haggling, if his price was fair. Drake had described what he was looking for and the dealer, a frumpy middle-aged man named Ezazul, had come up with a 1987 336 Amerosport, a 33 footer that was in exemplary condition considering its age. The most alluring aspect was that it was fast and available right now. Drake had been assured that the 7.4 Merc engine had just been rebuilt and was capable of 340 horsepower. If he had to move quickly, he was told, this boat would get him between two points with the agility of a sea snake.

He didn't even negotiate the $39,000.00 Canadian price tag so keen was he on the boat. Drake told the man to top up the tanks and passed him his American Express. The transaction was done in minutes and by 9 p.m. last night the deal was complete. The elated salesman, already mentally shopping with the extra profit he just made, ordered one of his worker's to fill the fuel tanks, bowing repeatedly to Drake, thanking him in several languages.

The three men have sailed at full speed once they had moved past the water traffic along Sadarghat earlier. The congestion thinned out several nautical miles from Dhaka. The three men had divided duties at the helm, but it was mostly Drake who steered them toward Barisal, with Gurupada navigating the river courses. About noon Gurupada calls out to Drake,

"Keep to your port side, Drake; stay off shore about 200 meters. The land on your left will sweep away toward the mouth of another river. Follow that but move to the center and stay at least 1000 meters from the shore, lots of shallow water to port. Continue on until you sight a large island on the starboard side, all flat land except for one stand of trees in its center then follow the waterway to the right of the island. That should be about fifteen, twenty minutes from now."

"Will do, Pada."

Drake is drinking in the country air. It isn't as pure, as unblemished, as the familiar breezes from the Atlantic, but it is refreshing nonetheless and keeps the moisture from his brow. The sun is slightly beyond its zenith scorching every surface it touches. The boat's engine hums as the crafted hull races along the rivers. He is drawing close to a small tanker that is wallowing, heavy laden, drifting with the tide. He swings the boat to starboard to overtake the ship and a thump is heard beneath him. He guesses that Isaac has toppled to the floor from the sudden swerve. He smiles, knowing he'd find out soon enough. Several men are at the stern of the ship and wave as they pass. Drake gives a full arm response and leaves the large floater behind.

They enter the busy port of Barisal, which is settled on a curve of the Kirtonkhola River. Drake is amused by all the traffic. It's not as bad as what he'd had to negotiate when they left Dhaka, but there are ferries everywhere, tankers, freighters, open and closed boats of every size and every shape, carrying coal, bricks, barrels of fuel, people, gravel, vegetables and fruit, bidi (local tobacco), tons of rice, other grains and more people. He finds the port much like Dhaka. Brilliant colors abound on the walls, the boats, the people dressed in gay and vibrant hues. He had been wrong in his previous thinking about this country, ignorant of the possibilities, of its people.

They find an area to dock the boat near the police cruiser that sits at a public wharf. The dock master informs them that they are able to leave their boat for a fee, but it cannot remain overnight. Gurupada assures him that dockage is only needed for a few hours. They will be on their way shortly. He then leads Drake and Isaac to a waiting taxi, telling the driver where they are destined. The taxi is a 1987 Chevrolet Caprice, a flat black whale of a car. How it made its way to the backwaters of Bangladesh would probably be an interesting tale, Drake imagines. The aged vehicle grinds its way around the city with its horn bellowing in the congested areas, eventually bringing them to a fairly new two-story structure. Like most of the buildings along the street, it has a stucco exterior, gritty white with royal blue trim. Pada pays the driver before escorting Drake and Isaac to the second level. It is mid-afternoon crazy along the hallways, with police officers, men and women, going about their daily fight against aggression. Loud muffled voices escape from some offices.

With Drake and Isaac waiting behind him, Gurupada checks in, showing his ID to the constable at the upper desk. He is told that OC Patwary isn't available as he has been called away on urgent business at the Metropolitan headquarters in Dhaka. When the constable manning the desk recognizes Gurupada' name, the young man's slender face splits into two rows of white shiny teeth, his smile so grand. Gurupada is still remembered for his work with CID in finding the Shoestring Killer last year. He is told they will meet with the head of the Criminal Investigation Division (CID) Barisal. The receptionist wheels a padded office chair, motioning for Pada to use it. To Drake and Isaac, he points at the bench that lines the opposite wall, telling them in English and Bengali that Inspector Kazi Ullah will only be a short while.

The bench sits uninvitingly before them, wrought iron and stiff orange cushions. Isaac walks over and plops onto it. In response, it wobbles from side to side for a few seconds. Drake gives it a skeptical glance and says, "No thanks. I think I'll stand over here by his highness." Pointing to Gurupada in his swivel chair, he says, "Looks like they think quite highly of you Pada!"

"Well I can assure you that not everybody does, but the younger men treat me with respect and frankly, Drake, I like it."

Gurupada swings the chair back and forth, his feet out like a small boy, a blushing tint darkening his light brown skin. To cover his modesty, he swings around to Isaac and says, "As you no doubt saw from the maps, our rivers number in the hundreds. Hundreds and hundreds of boats make their living on our waters, so narrowing down our possibilities will be a daunting task. Perhaps your presence will bring us good luck, huh? Did the maps give you any insight into our monumental undertaking, Isaac?"

"I'll bet that if this is where they dropped the body, then this isn't likely a normal port of call for them. He wouldn't want to be recognized, so he must work other ports in the area."

Drake says, "I expect you're right, Isaac. We can probably assume that he sails the Meghna often. It's a huge river; there could be many ports, I expect, but we'll find them."

Gurupada says, "We know that Ahmedani referred to Bhola, so we should do that river and town first, as we agreed, unless Inspector Ullah's information points us in another direction."

Drake says, "You worked with these people before, Gurupada, have you met the Inspector before?"

"Actually I haven't; he's new to the post. The gentleman that headed up CID last year has since retired and gone to live with his daughter in Los Angeles. Ullah is originally from the Khulna Thana and has been here since March of this year. I'm afraid he doesn't speak any English, so whatever questions you have, I will have to translate."

"Well, Pada I think you've been at this game long enough that I can trust you to ask the right questions. We just need as much info as you can get so we can track down whoever brought the body here. Whatever info is available about the mark, too. Would you prefer to talk to him alone?"

"That might be a good idea. I know Chowdhury has already been in touch with OC Patwary, so they will do what they can to oblige us. This office is responsible for a large area and they already have too much work here anyway, so even though I can vouch for you and you are welcome to help, you are still outsiders. Ullah will likely be more forthcoming if I speak to him by myself, if you don't mind?"

"Okay Pada. How about Isaac and I go grab a coffee and we'll meet you back at the boat in about an hour. Is that enough time for you?"

Gurupada gets up from his seat and while wheeling the chair back to the reception area, he speaks to the young man at the desk in Bengali.

"Is that small diner called Ferula still open?"

The agent replies with an eagerness that almost suggests he owns the place, "Oh yes, sir, and today they have the boti kabab and it's delicious. I had it for lunch."

Gurupada returns and says, "Go out the front door and turn right. Down the street about 100 meters, you will find a diner with the word Ferula written in English beneath the Bengali name. The signage is bright pink, so you can't miss it. The constable says their special today is a boti kabab; it's made from lamb and quite good. They serve a decent coffee also. It's a lot better than any fare you might find in the cafeteria downstairs. I'll meet you at the boat. "

Just then a robust man emerges from a door down the hall and calls out to Gurupada. Waving his arm for the officer to join him, he turns and goes back into his office.

"That's Ullah. I'll catch up to you soon Drake."

Gurupada waves them off and proceeds down the hallway. Drake says to Isaac, "C'mon, buddy, lets head out. I'm getting hungry and kabab sounds good."

The two men bid farewell to the constable and leave.

When they exit the building, the late afternoon sun is casting long shadows on their side of the street. A somnolent current of cooler air meets them at the doorway and follows them down the sidewalk. There are several eating establishments on the same block as the police station, with screen doors covering the entryways. Smells of curry and unfamiliar spices waft from the doorways, tempting passers-by with the eating pleasures within. By the time Drake and Isaac reach the Ferula diner, closeted in a grey building with large pink letters above the door, their stomachs are rumbling with anticipation. Isaac says, "If the food tastes as good as it smells, I think we're in for something pleasant, Drake."

Drake is thinking of Williston, wondering why he hasn't heard back from him yet and misses the comments his friend made. Isaac isn't waiting for an answer anyway and pushes through the glass door of the diner.

"Get out your credit card pal; we'll give it a workout. I'm hungrier than I thought"

The diner is well-lit; square tables with green-and-white checkered tablecloths line the walls on each side. They are partnered with four chairs each, and at this time of day, many of them are occupied. Sitar music rises softly above the prattle of the patrons. Several waiters mill about, some are delivering trays of steaming dishes to their charges while others clean vacated tables. Isaac surveys the scene and assuming Drake is still close behind, said, "There's a table on the right across from those three young ladies chatting in the back. How about that one?"

Checking for Drake's response, Isaac sees him still on the sidewalk with his cell phone to his ear. Isaac is alarmed by Drake's countenance as he stands outside listening to the caller. When he sees Drake respond with a four letter word he realizes something is wrong. He joins Drake outside.

"I can't believe that Elijah," Drake is saying. "We told him to stay put. Why would he take off now?"

Isaac solemnly waits for an indication of the trouble Drake is obviously upset about.

"His sister? "Drake asks, "What does she have to do with us?"

The answer to that question takes several moments as Elijah explains what has happened.

"Are you with Rae now Elijah?" Drake asks. He listens for a few moments before replying, "Okay, we'll be waiting for your call. Get back to us ASAP."

Drake slams the cell phone closed with a slap to its back and replaces it in the holder on his belt. He's looking at Isaac with a stare that passes right through him.

"What's going on Drake? What's happening?"

Drake says, "Rafan is missing. Rae and Elijah returned to the hotel this afternoon to work on the discoveries they made in regards to the warehouse and the car they were looking for. When Rae went to check on Rafan, the door to his room was wide open. When she looked through the suite, he was nowhere to be found. She did find a scrap of paper by the phone in the hallway. All that was written on it were the words, *my sister*. Right now we don't know what that means, just that he's gone."

Isaac said, "I remember us talking about his sister. Do you think the people we're chasing got to her?"

"It's possible" Drake says. "It's like we talked about, we don't know what Rizzato is up to or what his people are after, but we know that the man Rafan met at the bar is involved, but not how. I believe that someone is trying to reach Rafan to find out what he was told or to shut him up, neither situation would be pleasant for him."

Drake goes quiet, one hand on his hip, the other rubbing his stubbled chin. Isaac leaves him to his musings. He's seen Drake many times in this same pensive mode.

"Okay, here's what we're going to do, Isaac. Go grab us some take-out, something for Pada, too. Wait for him at the station, inform him of what's going on, and I'll meet you back at the boat. I need to talk to Williston. I'll use the satellite phone onboard. Pada should be done soon. Elijah and Rae are on their way to Rafan's sister's place and will call me as soon as they find out what's happening."

Isaac re-enters the diner, never questioning Drake's commands. Drake steps into the roadway, hailing one of the rickshaws idling across the street, several cyclists standing in a small cluster gossiping and smoking. When he catches their attention Drake points to the man in the red T-shirt and baggy shorts. His muscled calves suggest he will be hasty. The long limbed man drops his cigarette to the ground grinding it under a sandaled heel. He backs his three-wheeled buggy from the tight cluster of colored pedicabs, gesticulating with a waving hand for Drake to get on.

By now Drake has picked up enough Bengali to say, "Take me to the river, please."

The driver seats himself and swings the cab into the traffic without even looking back and pulling out in front of a Suzuki mini truck. A shriek of stalled rubber escorted by the peal of a high-pitched horn see them away. The driver waggles a fist out his window, bellowing something unintelligible. Nobody cares.

Drake settles in to the rhythm of the cyclist, the seat is as soft as a cotton marshmallow. Rafan's disappearance is an unexpected twist. It awakens an anxiety in Drake that he should have been more protective. He knows that Rizzato, ergo his men, are diabolical, their morality nonexistent. They will stop at nothing to fulfil their dreadful plans. Unless his team can act quickly, Rafan is likely in danger, as well as his sister and her family. He's expected to lead and yet he hasn't taken all precautions he should have. He's getting ahead of himself he thinks, better to wait for Rae or Elijah's call.

If something is indeed amiss with Rafan or his family, it's better to be prepared. It's possible he will need rapid transit, a helicopter most likely. He grins as he remembers the giant bee on the billboard at the airport and wishes he had written down the number, it's not as easy to remember as the name is. He reaches for his cell phone, punches in 411, the universal digits for directory and asks for the number for Honey Aviation. He dials and is greeted by a standard ``*please leave a message*`` recording, which he does. He's surprised the office is closed as it is just after one o'clock; he hopes they will call back soon. If he needs to be back in Dhaka in a hurry it will be quickest via chartered helicopter. On the remainder of his commute back to the boat, he calculates his manpower and how best to deploy them.

It's just a few minutes before three. Drake, Isaac and Pada have been scheming for the last ninety minutes. Drake has called Williston and flirted with Beth for a short time. The aviation company has called back and a helicopter chartered. Gurupada has gone over the information Ullah has shared with him.

They have a picture and a good description of the boat from witnesses. There are ten or more descriptions of the man in the bow of the boat that had laid the tarp on the wharf. Imaginations are creative and the culprit wears many masks. The only information they all concur on is that the man is Oriental, possibly Korean or Chinese, depending on whom you asked. One had even offered that he may be Mongolian. The other point they agree on was that the man is peg-legged and because of that, they all suggest he must be a pirate.

The young girl's body had been sent for autopsy and the mark on her shoulder had been photographed. The men talk about the significance of the mark in light of all the previous bodies and what they can possibly mean. They conclude that the murderer is leaving a trail, but they can't understand why.

Drake decides to have Isaac and Gurupada carry on up the Bhola River in search of the boat. He will accompany them if nothing is wrong back in Dhaka. In the event that Drake has to leave, either man can pilot the boat. He's telling them about Williston's discovery and is interrupted by his phone.

"Drake here."

No sound comes over the line for a moment, the silence is ominous. Finally in a voice both doleful and troubled, Rae says, "Oh Drake, it's horrible. They're dead Drake. I've never witnessed such depravity, such cold killing. And we can't find Rafan."

She can't continue, her despondency so penetrating. Drake hears her sniffling and soon the phone drops from her hand to hit something hard, a table or a desk.

"Rae, Rae, what's going on?" Drake asks. His body goes on full alert, muscles tense, mind clear.

Elijah comes on the line, "It's not good, Boss. All we found of Rafan is one of his running shoes in his sister's driveway. We found his sister tied to a kitchen chair in the living room. Her throat was cut; blood was everywhere. We think she was positioned there to witness what else they did."

Elijah hesitates, words seemed bulky and cumbersome. His emotions are feuding, anger and regret jousting with hate. Drake is stunned and waits with disbelief, guilt harrowing him.

"What of Ihtisham and the little girl?" He senses his friend's confusion. "C'mon Elijah get it together, what's going on? Did you call Chowdhury?"

"Yeah, yeah, I'm sorry, man. Ihtisham is with Chowdhury now. We called the Inspector as soon as we could and they called him. The police team is on site now. But the worst Drake is…"

Again Elijah pauses, his anger so great he is unable to talk, several deep breaths calms him but belligerence braces his words,

"She's the same age as my niece, Drake, and the bastards nailed her little hands to the wall."

Chapter 28   Sept 29 Meghna River Bangladesh

Rafan is in the hold of the Sampan, unconscious and badly bruised. His supine body lays close to the rack that holds the engine Kovalenko has repaired. His shirt is torn, one sleeve totally missing, revealing a fiery red needle mark. His jeans are scuffed and dirty as well as sodden from his nightmare. The odor from his body blends with the smell of burning engine oil, stagnant water, pitch, and bad tidings, a symphony of unlovely aromas. His head flops occasionally with the sway of the boat. His face has dried blood around the chin and upper lip.

It was only two hours ago he had entered his sister's house. He was welcomed by the bloody torso of his only sibling tied to a chair in the living room. He froze for a second, suffering intense alarm, fear clinching him. When he spied his niece, he started to scream. At that instant Bunker stepped out from behind the door and bashed his face with his beefy fist. The impact cut off the sound. In the same instant, the blow hurled Rafan's lanky body against a closet door. The impetus knocked the thin barrier off its track and both tumbled to the floor.

Bunker had slammed the front door shut, not worried about being seen. The property was surrounded by tall, well-trimmed hedges that hid the house from public gaze. He pulled Rafan to the entryway floor, ripping his sleeve off. He retrieved and opened a small black leather bag, reaching inside for a hypodermic. The needle is decorated from its previous work, sterility not being a priority with Bunker. He withdrew a small vial of clear fluid with the familiar rubber cap. Plunging the germ-laden tip through the membrane he drew off a quantity of the liquid. Pulling the needle out, his thumb tightened and the needle gave off a squirt. He dropped the bottle back in the bag and poked the needle into the muscle of his captive's exposed shoulder. Bunker slowly pushed the plunger down the glass tube, forcing enough Chloral Hydrate into Rafan's system to keep him out for eight to ten hours.

Three men stand in the cabin near the bow, all three staring ahead; none of them are speaking. Bunker towers over the other two, his hairy dome rubbing against the ceiling. He had told Kovalenko to take them to the compound; otherwise he doesn't answer when spoken to or invite any familiarity. He had called Rizzato when he spied Stratton waiting at the boat, hastily filling him in on what was going down. He cut off Rizzato's ranting after he told him of Malik and Morgan by informing him of Rafan's capture. He calmed immediately, telling Bunker to say nothing to Stratton about anything other than that Bashara was a stray worker that got out of line. Bunker did just that, said nothing.

Kovalenko is still stunned over the barbarity from what the Serb told him of how he had dealt with the woman and little girl. He had been privy to deadly crimes in the past but had never witnessed someone enjoying it so much. He concentrates on the river, trying to remember the way, but all he can really see is the cruel elation in those saucer-like eyes when Bunker told him how he slowly drew the knife across the woman's throat. He shivers again as the vision eats at him. He tries to clear his mind, thinking about the river, the engine, the stranger with them, anything other than those shocking circles. He reaches into his coveralls pocket, checking his sidearm. Its presence soothes him some. He decides he'll watch the big bugger; his work is almost done.

Stratton stands on the right of Kovalenko, incongruous in his sport coat and dress pants; his companions wear greasy or disheveled garments. His hands are joined behind his back as he gazes toward the water as well. He rocks on the tip of his toes as if he's nervous, but in reality Stratton is well pleased. He had spoken to Rizzato when he arrived in Dhaka and had learned the only issues left to deal with were the return of the plane engine and the completion of the runway. His tank of killing fuel is warehoused at the airport in Dhaka. It will be picked up by this boat tomorrow. He was put out at first that it couldn't accompany him on this trip, but he knows the engine has priority. He's somewhat unnerved by the body lying in the hold. When he had asked Rizzato's lieutenant who he was, he just shrugged saying, "a stupid worker," as if to suggest it was nothing unusual. Stratton will have Rizzato clarify the meaning of the unconscious man.

If Rafan would have awoken then and looked up at the backs of the three men, he would have found it a conflicting image. Kovalenko, a smallish wiry man in gray grease-stained overalls that completely encloses his torso stands in the middle, steering the boat, his polished dome with the black question mark inked on his skull making him the roughest looking. Bunker, clad in blue denim coveralls over one of the persistent blue short sleeved shirts he always wears, is to the shorter man's left, huge and foreboding. Stratton, on the right, is dressed for a dinner date, the only one with manicured nails. All of them are desperate; all of them are murderers; all of them have uncertain futures.

There are numerous water craft ahead and behind them, many

are long and skinny, skimming the surface of the river like needle bugs. None of the sampan's occupants are aware of the white and yellow water taxi that trails them several hundred yards to the rear containing Andrew Stratton's daughter. Nor have they paid any attention to the blue and white cruiser that has passed them earlier with Drake and his crew. The lone passenger of the water taxi will cause them a lot more problems in the immediate future than they will care for.

Sophia Stratton is sitting up front with the driver of the water taxi she has hired to follow her father down the river. The driver can speak some English but not enough to carry on a conversation, so the ride is mostly silent except for the thrumming of the motor and the pounding in her brain of what her father's odd behavior means. Afraid of where he is leading her, yet destined to stop his diabolical plans, she watches the dark boat that her father is on, her driver changing positions on the wide river following them. She remembers how astonished she was at the change in her father when she saw him at his hotel. He had been getting out of a limousine at the front door of the Sonargaon Hotel. She had been hiding in the valet's hut, having convinced the two young men, with crispy twenty-dollar bills and her feminine wiles that she was looking for her unfaithful husband.

When he had stepped from the vehicle, her father had straightened and stretched his back from the drive, smoothing out his jacket. His chin was held high, he seemed arrogant as usual but the face was wrinkled, pale and troubled. His hair was longer and whiter. His teeth and lips were different. She almost didn't recognize him but when he turned her way and scanned the ground about him she knew from the eyes that it was her father.

It didn't matter that they were a different color; they were still the ones that scrutinized her behavior when she was young and out of hand, or glowed when she did things he was proud of. The light was gone now; something sinister abided there instead. She had wanted to run to him, he was her father and she loved him; instead the blackness she saw in his eyes kept her away, she was scared of him. She was terribly confused, uncertain what to do. She had waited and watched and thought of dozens scenarios to stop her father, none seemed logical. When she saw him leaving the hotel again twenty minutes later, she decided to follow him.

She is startled when her driver, a whiskered, beak-nosed man, blurts out, "They turn, Lady, they turn. Bhola, they go Bhola River."

"Stay with them," she says, "not too close."

The driver moves his boat to the opposite side of a large fishing boat that is steering toward Bhola as well. They will be unnoticed there. They motor up the river for a short time until they see the Sampan slowing and moving toward shore ahead. Sophia gestures for her driver to move to the opposite side of the fishing boat, using it as a shield. As they pull toward the front of the boat they are hiding behind, they slow to the same pace, watching the Sampan move toward a short pier on her starboard side. About fifteen minutes later, they lose their view of the Sampan. She watches a slender woman on the wharf chuck ropes to them. A native man is wheeling a wagon close to the dock; another is pulling ropes from a metal shed. A man who looks like her father is jumping from the boat when she loses sight of it when her taxi follows the bend in the river.

When they are completely around the curve, she gestures to the diver to take her to shore. She has a small backpack by her side and when they butt up to the rough ground she reaches inside and pulls out a hundred American dollars, five twenties. She waves them in front of the man whose eyes follow their every sway. Using hand gestures and repeating words she makes him to understand to be in this very spot tomorrow at the same time. She stresses further that if she isn't there tomorrow, he should come back the next day. She then tears four bills in two, gives him four halves and a whole twenty before depositing the other halves in her pack.

She jumps from the boat, her boots landing in several inches of murky water. The bank is only about four feet high, which she scales easily. There is a thicket of shrubs that lines the levee that she scrabbles through until ten or twelve feet later it opens to a field of rutted soil which had been turned for seeding but never harrowed. It is neglected and overgrown with tall grasses.

She pauses at the edge of the bushes surveying the land before her. The field stretches back ending about 200 meters from where she is. Another stand of trees takes over from there obscuring the wharf. She can see an opening in the woods and hopes it's a path that will lead to her father so she heads across the field towards it. As she is walking she slings the backpack over her shoulders, shifting it until it is comfortable. Her mind is filled with possible scenarios of what she might find and what she will do when she confronts her father.

Kovalenko and Plum have dumped Rafan in the back of the golf cart they keep for transit while Bunker and Stratton have gone ahead to the compound. Then with the help of two workers they wrestle the plane's engine onto the wagon. They are using an ancient yellow forklift with a boom attached instead of forks. The boom consists of steel cables, hooks and pulleys. Kovalenko is coaxing the sputtering lifter backwards with the two workers balancing the ends of the engine to stop it from spinning. The smell of propane is thick and sickening. Plum is watching the men at work, pinching her nose to obliterate the odor. She is shouting directions to the men as they near the wagon. Soon the group is settling the engine onto the blocks on the bed of the wagon. Kovalenko kills the engine of the forklift, letting gravity lower the cable on the boom. He is about to make some snide remark to Plum, whom he covets with a lecher's lust, when they are interrupted by the snapping of a branch from the wooded area behind them. Everyone freezes.

So does Sophia. When she had spied the three men and the woman through the branches from thirty feet away, she moved from the path and crouched down behind a large tree to watch for a few moments. Her knee had landed on a twig lying under the detritus of the forest floor. She realizes that the workers have heard it also and panic crawls up her throat. She waits, not even breathing, until she sees the woman remove a revolver from her waistband and start toward her. Sophia hastily scans the area around her for a hiding spot. There are waist high scrub bushes on her right that surround the base of the scattered trees. Beyond that she can see a rubbish heap. She creeps stealthily on her hands and knees along the matted ground feeling first for errant branches with her hands.

Plum holds the revolver in front of her as she poses at the edge of the woods studying the forest floor from left to right. She looks in the opposite direction as Sophia moves toward the garbage pile.

Plum is questioning the noise she'd heard, some animal perhaps. But she has to be sure. She's taking no chances while she's stuck here, so she watches the wooded area carefully for any movement. Suddenly on her left in a bushy space beside the garbage dump they use, she sees a branch move. Only the one, something is there. Heading into the woods toward the movement she holds her raised weapon with both hands.

Sophia has unknowingly given herself away. She had tried to move like a snake but a shrub stalk caught briefly on the edge of her boot. Sophia spies a pile of rotting pallets. There are about ten stacked one upon the other with another four leaning against them. The leaners offer a small area for her to crawl into. It won't hide her completely, but it is the only protection she can find. With her heart racing, she slithers into the small opening. She waits. She can hear the shuffle of bushes as the woman with the gun comes closer.

Plum can see the hillock of debris and is about to wade through the bushes to inspect behind the pile when suddenly a chital, a spotted deer, barks its uncanny warning and breaks from the wood's edge just in front of her. With a trained response Plum sights the rufous coated deer and places a slug dead center into its brain. The small animal cartwheels onto the dirt path and skids to a dead stop. Sophia almost wets herself when she hears the shot, thinking she has been spotted until she hears the woman shouting.

"Hey, Kovalenko, here's our noise maker and supper to boot. Can you skin an animal?"

"Yeah, Plum, I can do this if you get this troubles engine back to hangar."

Kovalenko walks over to the dead animal and cuts its throat to bleed the meat. He waves to one of the workers to help him and they carry the animal to the warehouse beside the wharf. Bunker's dead taxi driver has already been removed and buried.

"I make you a hat, Plum?" he asks while laughing at Plum's face, which is scrunched up in disgust.

"Sure, Kovalenko, I need a hat for this hot weather; make it with ear flaps."

She replaces her gun into her waistband. Pointing to the other worker, she makes a driving motion to him, telling him to drive the tractor. She checks the tie downs on the wagon. Satisfied the engine is stable; she jumps onto the wagon to sit on the side with her legs hanging over. She lifts her chin to the young driver, indicating for him to get going. The man has pulled his lungi above his knees so that he can work the paddles. Plum is grinning at his skinny legs as they proceed up the dirt road. Kovalenko and the other helper run to catch up with the transport, jumping aboard alongside Plum. Sophia emerges from her hiding spot in time to witness the pretty Japanese girl, the smaller bald man and the obedient Bengali men pull away from the riverside. She waits until they are out of sight before following at a discrete distance.

When Plum and the men approach the compound Rizzato, Stratton and Bunker are standing inside the open hangar door. Rizzato has his arms across his skinny chest, scowling in the afternoon sun. He's wearing his black beret over his hairless dome and sweat trickles from the rim, making tiny rivulets down his temples. A white t-shirt, gold chains and black jeans clothe his body. The yellow cowboy boots he's wearing looks like two pointy lemons. He has a sidearm strapped to his thigh. The hangar is empty except for the airplane. The only movement is from the cooks in the open mess tent laying out the utensils for the evening meal.

When Bunker wheeled the electric cart up to the hangar earlier, Stratton jumped out before the vehicle came to a complete stop. Stratton didn't bother to say hello or anything, he went to inspect the plane. Both men are eager for different reasons: Stratton to wield his deadly apparatus, Rizzato to be done with this onerous task and back home with the Embera. After doing a circle around the plane he joins Rizzato and Bunker at the open door to watch the approaching engine. Neither man bothers with pleasantries. Stratton asks, "Things are going well?"

Rizzato replies, "Yeah, Jack, the plane will be ready in a couple of days and the runaway should be completed by the middle of next week. In about ten days you and I will be parting company. Is your precious cargo safe back in Dhaka?"

"It is and I need your men to return to Dhaka to transport the container back here as soon as you can."

Stratton questioningly points to Rafan that is sprawled unconscious in the rear compartment. Rizzato takes a few seconds before responding carefully choosing his next words. He doesn't want Stratton to be aware of the untangling of his crew or the demise of his men.

"That's one of our workers that decide to make a run for it Jack, tired of the working conditions I expect."

Rizzato gives a false chuckle to signify that it is nothing serious.

"I had Bunker detain him especially with you in mind so that you would see that we are keeping a tight rein on the workers as you requested. We want to have a little discussion with him and some gentle persuasion as to what he has been up to. Perhaps you would like to join us?"

"I think I'll pass on witnessing your games Bartolo but I'm not impressed that he was able to leave in the first place. And by the way, where are the rest of your stooges?"

"My men are busy Jack; they're not able to attend your arrival party."

He turns from Stratton, who is staring at Rizzato with obvious distaste and while pointing a thin finger at Rafan says to Bunker, "Lock that peasant in the shed by the house; we'll deal with him later. Get Kovalenko working on the installation. I need to talk to you in a few minutes."

Bunker nods and picks up Rafan's listless body from the golf cart. He hefts him over his shoulder like he's a sack of puffed wheat and carries him to his prison. Rizzato heads towards the hangar. He motions for Stratton to follow him and the men walk inside the large garage inspecting the plane together as they talk. Rizzato says, "Why am I not hearing from Amado? I still don't have the account number and whereabouts of the money you promised me. I'm getting a little nervous here, Jack. My time is almost done; I'm at the last of the funds you guys gave me to work with. I'm starting to wonder if I can trust you..." and here he stops his circling of the plane and swivels to look Stratton directly in the eyes, "...perhaps I should be using your real name now that we are alone, eh, Andrew? What's going on?"

Stratton stares at the beady eyes in Rizzato's ugly mug, the greyness empty and impossibly eerie. Before he answers he is relishing the thought that in less than two weeks the man will be out of his life. At this point he doesn't really care that the crazy man knows who he is, that has been established many months ago, so long as no one else knows. He's grinning inside when he says, "Amado's dead, Rizzato." He doesn't bother mentioning his daughter's involvement.

Rizzato's head bobs in startled response and his hand automatically moves to sidearm, as if the statement is a threat.

"What the fuck are you talking about, Stratton? Dead? What are you saying?"

"Relax Bartolo; get your hand off the gun. I'm going to reach inside my jacket pocket and I have a very pleasant gift for you."

His hand slowly reaches inside the left breast pocket and removes a leather bound note pad and his pen. Removing a scrap of paper, he hands it to Rizzato.

"Here is a copy of the deposit slip that was faxed to me. The bank has explicit instructions to release the funds we discussed to the bearer of a certain password, which I will give you when you're done here. You can then live the life of leisure you've always yammered about. Does that suit you Bartolo?"

Rizzato is reading the information on the paper as Stratton waits for a response. When he has memorized the details he balls up the paper and places it in his mouth. He stares balefully at Stratton as he chews the paper to a pulp. When it is wet and soggy he spits it to the ground at Stratton's feet and says, "That's fine, Jack, just fine."

He grinds the pulpy blob into the dirt with the heel of his boot, further obliterating the valuable information.

"Admire your toy here," he says pointing to the plane, "I've got to talk to Bunker for a minute, then get them organized to pick up your gas. Does Bunker have the details?"

"I gave him the manifest from the shippers and told him where it was but I don't know if he understood me, the big galoot doesn't talk much."

Andrew ignores Rizzato as he leaves the hangar. He places his right hand on the polished fuselage and lovingly strokes the frame as he circles the aircraft once more, inspecting the work that has been done, the new paint gleaming.

Rizzato meets Bunker half way across the dusty yard and the two of them go into the house. They are discussing the events of the past days. He listens intently to Bunker as he explains in detail what happened to his charges. They are sitting at the table in the kitchen each nursing a cold beer when the Serbian finishes his dialogue with a description of the man they saw. A stiff silence ensues before Rizzato rises from his chair and slams a fist onto the table. Bunker is undisturbed by Rizzato's fury, he's getting familiar with his tirades. He watches him as he rants and swears. After a few moments he stops his pacing.

"Okay Bunk, I understand what's going on. It's that cowboy Alexander again. We've got to be very, very careful from here on. That fucker is bent on payback for some fun I had a few years ago at the expense of his friend's sister and her Arabian cohort I told you about."

His eyes lose their focus for a moment as he remembers the torment he had subjected the two girls to at his river camp in

Venezuela when he was running cocaine into Brazil. There is a tingling in his abdomen as he recalls their screams from that fateful night. His thoughts are interrupted by an image of Drake Alexander, how he had escaped a small army in Venezuela led by the man as well as how close he had come to death in Amsterdam. He realizes then that death will be the only way to stop this man from pursuing him in the future. It might be something he and Bunker will undertake before he retreats to Panama.

"Okay, here's what we are going to do. As far as Ahmedani and Morgan and the two nothings you got rid of, it doesn't matter anymore. It's a task that needed to be done anyway. We aren't taking them with us. But Malik's a problem. I can watch the men here now. I'll tell them that in two weeks they are going home with a substantial bonus and that will keep them docile until you can kill them all when they're done."

When he mentions killing he looks into the killer's eyes. The face remains stoic but the eyes are telling.

"I want you to take as many men as you need to return to Dhaka with the Sampan. One of the cook's helpers can handle a boat and he knows the waters, take him too. Kovalenko stays and gets that damn plane ready. After the gas is on board, make sure the driver stays with the boat even if you have to drug him and tie him there, kill the rest and then find out if Malik is dead. If not, then eliminate him. After we're done here, we are going hunting for that bastard Alexander. You got all that, my friend?"

"Yes, Boss."

The Serb rises from the table and is shocked when Rizzato comes close to him and puts his arms around the big man. Rizzato is tall and gangly but is still dwarfed by Bunker. He plants a wet kiss on the thick lips and stands back.

Bunker doesn't know how to react. "Did you think I didn't know you were a woman, Dragoslava? I'm a lot sharper and smarter than a lot of people give me credit for. I'm hoping you're not a huge dyke; you kinda turn me on you know."

Rizzato flashes Bunker a genuine smile, his full lips blubbery and red. They stare at each other for a few moments, an unnatural lasciviousness emanating between them. Rizzato is turning to leave when he says, "Are you still a virgin Dragoslava?"

He stops at the door and looks back at this woman so bent on being a man. In one of the few times in their partnership, Bunker's wide face breaks with a satisfied grin. He eyes the skinny man up and down and nods yes. The two part with visions of a sexual encounter that can only be described as perverse.

As Rizzato and Bunker are leaving the house, Plum and her entourage are backing the wagon toward the hanger. He pats Bunker on the back and yells out for Stratton to join him in the gray Nissan. They take off in the small truck, the wheels creating a burst of brown dust that hangs in the air like a soiled cloud. Bunker approaches the hangar to speak with Kovalenko.

Sofia is hiding in the mango orchard, lying in the tall grasses. A low stone fence adjacent to the dirt lane separates the orchard from the yard. She has crawled as close as possible to the edge of the rocks while still remaining hidden from the buildings. She had removed a pair of small binoculars from her pack and has been watching her father as he inspected an airplane in the huge building. She watches him leave in a truck with an odd looking man with a gun strapped to his thigh; all the weapons are scaring her. Through the sandy fog kicked up by the spinning tires she sees a huge man walk over to the gang around the wagon. The Japanese woman that had almost found her is standing off to the side with arms crossed still staring at where the truck had been. She seems oblivious to the noises and motion behind her as the men carry the engine into the hangar. The biggest one totes one end alone while the bald man and two darker men carry the other end. Sophia watches the band of gangsters intently for the next half hour.

She has no idea where her father has gone, if he's coming back, or how long he might be. She is deep in meditation of what she should do and how silly she is being. She knows she is out of her element; she's only a firefighter she reminds herself. She asks herself tough questions as she waits.

"What evil is my father up to that he needs these kinds of people? What will I say to him when I see him? Will they hurt me?"

She has no answers. Lying in an overgrown field, halfway around the world, worrying about a father she loves, sorry for what he is becoming; it's a weighty burden to her slender and feminine shoulders. She feels helpless and alone.

Lowering the spy glasses from her face she drops them to the ground. She settles back behind the stubby wall and rubs her aching eyes. She feels sorry for herself but for only a short time, it isn't in her to be that way. She recognizes that she'll have to tell the police. She can't confront this bunch on her own. Her good sense tells her that they are doing something wrong or they wouldn't need guns. She decides to watch for another hour to get as much background as she can. It's getting late in the day. She will find a secluded area after dark and bunk down until her boat comes back tomorrow. Unfortunately for Sophia it isn't going to work out that way: as she put the binoculars back to her eyes, the sun reflects off of the lens.

Plum watched the departing truck, glad the men were leaving. She experiences an odd chill and crosses her arms as if her own caress can banish the thin icicle of doubt that stabs her. She yearns for the happiness she hopes awaits her after she flees this criminal existence to start a new life. And almost as if to give the unhappy girl a sign that her desires are true, the drowsy sun drops below its cloud cover to shoot thousands of sparkling rays across the land.

When she starts towards the field to bring the men back for chow, she sees a sudden flicker of reflected light from the edge of the orchard. She carries on towards the hangar as if nothing is amiss. Bunker is talking to Kovalenko, who is searching through his toolbox as Plum draws near to them.

"Hey, Bunk, follow me for a sec will you, it's important."

Bunker watches Plum as she strides deeper into the hangar towards the front of the plane. He follows her until they are alone. Plum faces Bunker and says, "I caught a reflection from the stone wall a moment ago. I think someone might be watching. I was going to go out to call in the workers. I'll head that way, but when I get past the hangar I'm going to head to the river and come back behind the orchard. Can you watch the front of the wall without really watching, if you know what I mean?"

"Sure. I'll go over on the other side of the plane; I should be able to watch from there. Be careful."

"Careful? Aw gee, Bunk, I didn't know you cared."

She gives the Serb a punch on the forearm, she can't reach the shoulder. The big guy seems different, still scary but a touch more human. She leaves the building, ignoring the stone wall as she heads toward the back of the hangar. Once she is out of sight of the yard, she sprints towards the river. It's about sixty meters through some tall trees and shrubs to the shore. Once there, she moves up the river, returns back towards the buildings. Plum likes the odd trees that line the riverbank; their leaves, too numerous to count, offers substantial coverage as she gently steps toward the orchard. When she reaches the edge of the tree line, she notices that she has gone past the wall by about twenty feet. She eyes the length of the stone structure but can only see the top two rows of rock and nothing else. Nothing moves.

She backs away from the edge of the field and cautiously tiptoes closer to the wall. She can see the row of stones from her path and eases back toward the clearing. As soon as she looks up the fence line, she sees the top of a head with a hand holding binoculars. The rest of the person's torso is hidden by the grass. Plum sinks to her hands and knees and crawls toward the intruder.

Sophia is still looking for the Japanese girl when a sharp command startles her, scaring her more than she has ever imagined possible.

"Don't move a muscle or you will be a dead woman."

Plum had crept up on the unwanted visitor, realizing as she got close that it is a woman. Plum had been so quiet she had gotten within four meters of the lady, withdrew her gun and stood up.

"Okay, okay, I don't mean any harm," said Sophia, who remains as still as dead leaves. "Can I put the binoculars down?"

"Drop them and stand up very slowly with your hands raised. Don't try anything stupid. I'm pointing a gun at you. I'll kill you if I have to. Understand?"

"Yes, yes, I, I...I understand." she stutters. She is wickedly frightened. She can't control her shaking as she tries to get up and keep her hands raised. "I'm very scared and I don't want to hurt anybody. Please don't hurt me. I just want to see my father."

Sophia is desperately trying to control her emotions.

"Your father? What do you mean, your father? Who are you?"

Sophia is so scared that she forgets about her father's alias.

"Andrew Stratton, the passenger in the truck that left a while ago? I'm Sophia, his daughter."

Plum holds her gun with both hands, aiming it at the woman's back thinking for a moment, she doesn't know anyone named Stratton. Then it clicks.

"You mean Mr. Favors?"

"Yes, He calls himself Jack, Jack Favors. Yes, that's him"

Plum is confused. With that confirmation Sophia starts to turn towards the other woman.

"Stay still I said. I don't care whose daughter you are. Don't even think about moving unless I tell you to."

Bunker has been watching the two women. He too draws a gun and starts walking toward them. The two workers, Kovalenko, the cooks, everyone had frozen when they saw Sophia stand up. Bunker looks around and says, "Go back to work, all of you."

Sophia spies the monster coming from the other side of the plane aiming a weapon at her also. Her previous fright seems trivial to the terror she feels right now. She will tell them the truth hoping her father will be back soon.

Plum tells her to put her arms down but to be still as the grass around her. The large man in front of her is menacing enough with his cold eyes but his silence is strange. Even though she is still scared she looks him straight in the eyes. She is still a Stratton and her father had taught her never to be cowed. She interrupts Plum's next question with a voice that is set and defiant, "I want to see my father and I want to see him right now"

Plum was about to step up to give her a slap to the head when she sees the swerving grey truck approaching them with twin billows of spitted sand and dust blooming in its trail. She says instead,

"Well you're about to get your wish. Here he comes now. Let me warn you, you stupid woman, the man he is with makes us look like Muppets. Be very careful what you say or do even if Jack Favors is your father. Bartolommeo Rizzato has a rare and sickening taste for beautiful women."

Sophia watches the oncoming vehicle with sudden apprehension that displaces her previous relief of her father's presence.

As the men in the truck get closer to the compound, their conversation ends abruptly when they catch sight of the showdown by the orchard. All they can see for a minute is an unarmed woman sandwiched between the two guns of Plum and Bunker.

"What do we have here now? This looks interesting", says Rizzato as he slams the brakes causing the truck to skid sideways before finally coming to a stop in the middle of the yard. The inevitable formation of dust particles follows. Rizzato jumps out, storming towards the group demanding an explanation. Stratton goes numb when he recognizes the intruder. He can't believe its Sophia. How could she have possibly found him he thinks? Soon a huge grin crosses his wide face. He assumes she has come to help him to take his revenge, to abet him in his final glory. He is consumed with happiness. Once again he has misread one of his children.

He leaps from the truck shouting, "Sophia, you've come to join me. How exciting!" He walks faster toward her with open arms and notices the guns again. "Put those weapons away you fools. It's my daughter, Sophia. You can all relax"

He meets her where she stands and embraces her with genuine warmth. They are both speechless at this act of love; she hasn't been in her father's arm since she was a babe. She slowly raises her arms and hugs him hard. He whispers in her ear as he holds her like a child he's just found, "I'm so happy you came, Sophia. Together you and I will rid this indecent world of hundreds, no... thousands of the people that stole your brother and sister from us. Yes, yes Sophia, together we can do it."

He grips her with more emotion, carried away with his malignant imagination. Sophia on the other hand understands that her father is even worse than the night he tried to persuade her many months ago to help him, she can tell by the dreadful look in his eyes. A penetrating distress swamps her; she knows now she is too late to save her father. She can hear the lunacy in his unpleasant voice. Her only ambition now is to stop his awful plans. She undoes her hug and pushes against his chest, propelling herself away from him. His smile fades and his eyes question her action.

"No", she yells, "No, Dad. I'm not here to help you; I'm here to stop you. You can't do this. Stop and come home with me."

They face each other, everyone still around them, even those that don't understand English. The blue in Sophia's eyes is steel as she stares at her father. She can detect that same set in his shoulders from when she was younger and he was about to scold her. And then his face gets ugly.

"Home with you? What kind of home do you think I have now, Sophia? How could you or your mother go on without getting back at these terrorists, these killers? How could I? I have the means Sophia; I have the power, the money. And I guarantee it will happen, I will have my revenge."

Now he stands before her with hands that are fisted. He towers over her, daring her to answer back. In his temper he regards her not as someone who cherishes him, not as a defenseless woman, not as an escape from his neurosis but as a splinter in his skin, a disturbance, a stumbling block to his kismet, an enemy. Nothing, he shouts in his mind, nothing will get in his way, not even his daughter. Sophia trembles in his presence, lacking even enough courage to back away. She loses all sense of normalcy, of any promise of saving her father when he says to someone, anyone, as he stares her down, "Chuck this asinine woman in with the other prisoner."

Chapter 29   Oct 1 Aboard Drifter's Dream

The Drifter is anchored off the Florida Keys, wavering in the clear teal waters. The temperature is 76 degrees Fahrenheit with the sun directly overhead pitching incandescence over the harbor. A slight breeze from the northeast cools the midday warmth. There is an unusual amount of traffic around the Keys; it being Friday, leading into the weekend. The Lurssen is bobbing easily to the wrinkles in the water made by passing boats. Williston is taking advantage of the favorable weather to sit out on the foredeck. He is going over the latest emails he has received from several of his sources regarding the words Stratton and Scranton that Drake had told him about. He's actually staring at the latest memo, not really reading it, lost in thought over the last conversation he had yesterday with his best friend. He drops the emails on the table in front of him and sits back with heavy thoughts.

Drake had called him from Barisal, a city in Bangladesh, where he was working with Isaac and a detective named Gurupada. Williston is concerned about Rafan's disappearance. He hasn't told the girls yet. He'd have to do that when they return, he reminds himself. Drake has been very hard on himself for not keeping a closer eye on his charge. Williston had to remind Drake that he had been forthcoming with Rafan of the reality and desperation of the people they are dealing with, telling him to stay put. After all, he told Drake, wouldn't you or I have done the same thing if our sister was being threatened?

What Williston is dreading is that Rafan might already be dead. He doesn't relish the idea of having to tell Uday if that becomes a certainty, it's tragic enough that Rafan's sister and niece have been brutally murdered. The calamity will only be compounded by Rafan's death. He knows that Uday still suffers from the absence of his eldest daughter; that misery will never go away. Williston is definitely able to empathize with the man because he shares a similar soreness. He trembles with the thought and forces it away.

He wipes his brow with the towel that is strewn across the chair beside him. He wears only wet plaid shorts and sandals with no shirt. His skin is smooth and bronzed by the rays of the sun. He had been working out in the gym in the belly of the ship earlier trying to think of other things for a short time. He has just come back from a quick dip off the platform at the stern. The salt water has dried on his skin and it feels sticky. He runs his hand through his curly mane and picks up the emails once more, wanting to reduce the information to something useful for when he talks to Drake again. Drake suggested he would call around midnight in Bangladesh, 3 p.m. in Florida. It strikes him then that Isabella and Beth had asked him to send the skiff back to shore for them around 2 p.m. Beth had been adamant that morning that she wanted to speak to Drake when he called. She has been ill for the last two mornings, and Isabella had insisted she visit a doctor. She seemed fine to Williston.

He has reduced the glut of possibilities the two names suggest to just a few by whittling out the key issues he considers relevant. He has already eliminated the word Scranton as there is nothing unusual about the name. There had been a mass of information with the name Stratton, ski hills, jewelry, photographers, a publishing house, real estate, construction equipment, and blogs. But Williston has spent much of his life dealing with intelligence and is adept at systematizing it. What had triggered an alert were the news articles of the death of Scott and Sarah Stratton in the Middle East last year. They were a brother and sister team of journalist and photographer, both award winners in their professions. He had instructed Rassor to concentrate on them, to find any threads that led to Bangladesh. Earlier this morning Rassor had forwarded a horde of information about Sarah and Scott, but more importantly, about their father.

Andrew Stratton is a noted Industrialist, a tyrannical raider and a multi-millionaire. Williston is aware of this man. Although they have never met, they do move in similar circles. What he didn't know is that the man has suddenly disappeared shortly after his children's death. Apparently the man had excused himself from all directorial boards, from company masts, appointing many of his VPs to assume command.

Williston had asked Rassor to get into any personal email accounts Andrew Stratton used. Rassor agreed he would attack the computers in Stratton's main office in Chicago and go from there. He rattled on a bit about his genius and finding Internet Providers, collocation, DSL, ADSL, broadband, their footprints and the difficulty he faced. Williston promised him a substantial fee if he would shut up and work fast.

Less than an hour ago, Rassor had contacted him again with the info from Stratton's personal computers at his home and office. Neither had been used for the past nine months but are loaded with goodies. He had also penetrated other family members' personal computers as well. Williston had made hard copies of Rassor's info. He narrowed down the items to those he thought were important and had written them down.

a) Wife Janice, nothing of interest on her computer.
b) One other daughter, Sophia, a firefighter in Chicago
c) Amado Mendoza – Lawyer, Cayman Islands ****
d) Only other children killed by Martyrs Brigade in Tel Aviv
e) Sophia Stratton tracked to Bangladesh via usual credit trail.
f) Mendoza recently killed; Sophia Stratton involved but not the doer.

He scribbles and scratches at the words, rearranging their importance. The lawyer part and his location pretty well bellows money. Williston is a lawyer, knew dozens both honest and bent. Whatever Stratton is up to, Williston's certain, Amado Mendoza is his ticket. He's confused about the lawyer's death, why Sophia Stratton is involved. She recently went to Bangladesh, suggesting it's possible her father is there. The only thing still tying the whole chase together is the mark left on the shoulders of the dead bodies, as on his sister. Unconsciously he scratches a large Z on the page. He traces it back and forth, faster and faster until the lead breaks. The pencil slips from his hand. He stares at the mark he had rendered until everything gels in his mind. He is beyond confidant that the man who had defiled and killed his sister is within Drake's grasp.

"Stratton's possibly setting the stage for a vendetta. It has to be! That's why Rizzato is in Bangladesh," he speaks aloud. "Whatever Stratton is doing, it's guaranteed to be hostile if Rizzato is in his company."

The other questions he asks himself: Why Bangladesh? Why not in Israel where his children have died if he's looking for payback? Where are they hiding now?

He rushes back to his office on the first deck, pulling out the desk chair to sit at the computer. He spends the next two hours poring over anything he can find on Bangladesh, its war for independence, its early beginnings in the 70s, its geography, its culture, its famous people, its politics, its major events. The one thing that intrigues him is the huge majority of Muslims. That has to be an issue for someone with vengeance in his heart.

He pauses asking himself "Am I any different?" He looks over at Amber's picture, but just for a moment. Yes, he thinks, it's different. He leaves it at that.

The alarm on his watch vibrates, reminding him of his wife. Williston shuts down the computer, stands up and stretches. He can't wait to share this with Drake. As he stares out the tinted Plexiglas, his thoughts turn to his friend. Good old Drake, he muses. He knows the man will do anything for him; but then he would too. Drake is his very closest friend. With that pleasing thought he leaves for the bridge to arrange transport for his ladies.

Beth and Isabella had caused quite a stir at the clinic, well mainly Beth. When the doctor had questioned her, he'd heard the list of symptoms suggesting the she was more than likely pregnant. That was the first time she started screaming. She was beyond happy. She'd been dreaming of this moment for so many years. Her excitement was so great that she continued her joyful outburst. The doctor was startled by her reaction and backed into a tray of medical utensils, which clattered to the floor.

Out in the waiting room was a rookie cop who had an

appointment with the same doctor. Upon hearing the scream, he was spooked like everyone else, automatically assuming something was wrong. He jumped out of his seat and unstrapped his gun. Of the five other people in the waiting area, two immediately sprawled on the floor, one fainted in her seat, one tore from the office, and Isabella followed the officer. The receptionist was surfing the net with headphones on so she just kept chewing her gum. Suddenly there was a crash in the examination room. The young cop overreacted, racing to the door and kicking it open, scaring both Beth and the doctor. Beth reacted with sudden regret at her verbal gushing, covering her mouth with both hands and turning bright red.

Order was restored soon enough, Beth apologetic, the doctor upset. The second time she shrieked was when the doctor confirmed her pregnancy. This time he was expecting it but was no less disturbed. He handed her the usual pamphlet on pregnancy before shooing her from his office. She dressed and rushed out to tell Isabella. They hugged and danced a short jig unique to new moms. They left the doctor's office laughing and especially proud. They decided to celebrate with decadent chocolate sundaes. They walked down the street arm in arm in search of a dairy bar. When the conversation turned to daddies, it stopped. Isabella knew what Beth was thinking and said, "When are you going to tell Drake?"

Beth didn't answer right away, wishing Drake was with her now. She would love to look in his eyes when she told him. She replied, "I'm not sure Isabella. I want to tell him right away. It's his baby too, but I worry it will distract him from his work. Is now the right time?"

She hugged her friend a little closer tightening the crook of their arms. Isabella studied her companion, feeling a bit sorry for her plight. She felt she was too biased to offer an opinion with Williston always by her side. But she knew Beth would expect her to be honest so she said, "I don't envy you, Beth, your man so far away. I don't know that I could ever give my love to a soldier to be one of the items he carries in his pack. I can see you love him and understand his ways. I think you should tell him", she paused for a moment before she spoke the words they were both thinking; "Sometimes soldiers don't come home."

"You're right Isabella, it's difficult. But I've known Drake since we were adolescents. He's doing what he's been made for. He would do it anyway, with or without my blessing, so I accept his role in life and cherish every minute we share. It's not a perfect situation, but I would never want to be without him."

She gave Isabella another short squeeze, smiled and said, "I'll tell him right away. Now let's find those sundaes."

They reached the edge of the town, where a bustling market separates them from the beach. Among the many kiosks in the market square, the one with the giant ice cream cone sitting on its roof is the one they head for. Finding a deserted table in the adjacent park the ladies dig into their treats, extra maraschinos on Beth's. Chocolate syrup, baby chatter and future plans occupy their time as they wait for transport back to the yacht. Their talk is eventually interrupted by one of Williston's crew members. He advises them where the Zodiac is docked and when they are ready he will return them to the Drifter.

When they approach the yacht, Williston is standing on the foredeck watching their approach. He waves to the girls. Taking the phone from his ear he points to it and then Beth. Beth knows that Drake is on the line. By the time the women disembark the rubber dinghy, climb aboard the boat and join Williston, he'd had enough time to tell Drake what he discovered and to listen of Drake's recent developments. It isn't all bad news: they found the car they were searching for as well as the warehouse. The worst news is that two more bodies have been discovered hidden at the back of the lot. Both are males, both bear the telling Z, both Bengali, both unidentified. When he sees the ladies nearing he says to Drake, "We have to find these people, Drake, and put an end to their killings. I'll call Uday then. Here's Beth."

He hands the flustered girl the phone. He can see she's excited. He eyes Isabella, who stands off toward the bar motioning him to join her. He hasn't seen his wife this jubilant for quite a while, her face is glowing and for lack of a better word, he thinks how healthy she looks.

"I miss you too, sweetie, sooooo much." Beth is saying. She listens until she starts to blush.

"Oh, Drake, don't tease me over the phone, you pervert." She notices Isabella and Williston both grinning at her coyness. Beth and Drake banter as lovers do for a few more moments. He doesn't mention Rafan; he'll leave that to Williston. After Drake finishes telling her what they are doing and is about to say goodbye, she blurts out, "Drake, I'm pregnant. We're going to have a baby." Then, with the thinnest of worry in her voice, she asks, "Is that okay?"

There isn't much silence to endure because Drake responds with an exuberance to match hers.

"That's wonderful, Beth. You can't begin to know how happy that makes me. We talked about this before, but life kind of got in the way. I'll come to you right now if you need me."

"No, Drake, finish what you're doing. For Amber and Sakeema, we have to finish this. But come back to me as soon as you can. I love you; no… we both love you."

She listens to the quiet on the line, their thoughts the same. Before she bids him farewell, she answers what is unspoken, "If anything happens to you, Drake, I'll always have a part of you."

Chapter 30   Oct 2   Dhaka

Officer in Charge Chowdhury stares at the occupants in his office. Rae and the one called Elijah, whom he has just met, are seated opposite him. Drake stands to his left leaning against the filing cabinets that line the wall. To the right are three other men standing near the closed door to his office. Even with the air conditioner chugging from the side window the room is over heated from the antagonism in the room. Bartolommeo Rizzato's resurfacing has created a flurry of international activity that has coalesced in Bangladesh much to Chowdhury's dismay. When Drake had informed the OC of his belief that Rizzato was involved in the criminal activities that brought him to Bangladesh, his office had sent alerts to the International Criminal Police Organization, better known as Interpol. It hadn't been long before interest had been generated due to Rizzato's alleged involvement in other crimes around the world.

The three individuals to the right are the most interested in any information they can acquire regarding Rizzato; Christopher Moar, a plain clothes Detective Inspector with Scotland Yard, for Rizzato's possible involvement in Sir Reginald Whitecastle's murder; Adam De Vasquez with the Venezuelan Directorate of Intelligence and Preventive Services, for Rizzato's alleged trafficking of women for sexual exploitation; and Mark Delong with the American DEA for Rizzato's alleged drug trafficking from Central America to the U.S.A. Chowdhury's comments are directed to these three specifically.

"At this point, gentlemen, I can assure you that my people are doing everything possible to find Mr. Rizzato. I appreciate the assistance you are offering. I will have portfolios created for you with the information we have gathered. Please leave your whereabouts with my assistant on your way out. Thank you."

Mr Moar is about to say, "I don't think that…" when Chowdhury interrupts him.

"As I said, Mr Moar, tell us where we can reach you on your way out. This is my turf, gentlemen, and things will be run my way. Thank you and good day."

Moar gave Chowdhury a scowl that suggests he isn't pleased but leaves the office anyway with the other law enforcement agents behind him. Chowdhury then turns to Rae.

"Okay Mireille, what's going on?"

Rae says, "We're all in shock over the disappearance of Rafan and the death of his family. We need to move quickly, Bitan. We need to know anything your team might have on the recent bodies from the Tejgaon Industrial Park as well as Sumita and her daughter, Dipika. Anything that can give us some direction."

Drake says, "I left Gurupada and Isaac last night, they were heading up the Bhola River today searching for the boat that dropped the girl's body at Barisal. There are several descriptions but we all know how vast the Meghna River is. I understand that after they comb the Barisal wharfs they're heading for two or three ports closer to Bhola and then on to the district town of Bhola. I think this is our best lead Inspector."

Drake shifts his weight to his other leg and adds, "Elijah and I are taking the chopper we chartered from Honey Aviation and will survey the same locations by air. We'll meet up with Isaac and Gurupada later."

Chowdhury directs his question to Elijah, who sits in front of him. "Have you met Honey, Elijah?"

"Oh, definitely. Very friendly woman, I thought there for a moment we must've been related. Good pilots out there though, and their equipment's in good shape."

"Yes, she can be a bit much sometimes, too huggy for me. She's one of our biggest supporters at the Cricket matches though, tremendous fan, very verbal. Anyway, I think it would be good if you could liaise with my men, Rae. I'll arrange it. I heard from Pada, Drake and I'm sure he'll find something for you, he's a good man.

"I agree," says Drake.

Chowdhury rises, Rae and Elijah ape him. "Sit, sit," he tells them, "I just need to stretch. So what else do you have?"

Mireille spends the next fifteen minutes going over her notes, telling Chowdhury of the vehicle they have found with Gurupada's assistance, the one they believe was used at Rafan's apartment. It had been towed into the police compound late last night and had been swept. Evidence found led them to the warehouse in Tejgaon. She tells him of finding the two bodies that the police are dealing with now, confirming that the same people are involved in the killings because of the mark left on the corpses.

They discuss the tools that were found in the warehouse, the reasons for such equipment, the bedding found in one of the offices, the victims left there, who are as yet unidentified, what their role could be. The results of their talk and estimations are that the car and warehouse had both outlived their usefulness and thus had been abandoned. There would be nothing more to go on unless forensics discovers something else. The conversations end. Everyone knows where they are going; hands are shook and Chowdhury's guests leave his office.

Rae drives the two men to the airfield. Elijah had called ahead and the Robinson R44 is waiting for them. Elijah had picked up Drake yesterday at the police station's helipad in Barisal with the R22, a two seater. On their return to Dhaka, Drake had asked Elijah to make arrangements for a larger chopper for today. Elijah told Drake there was a C35 Chinook available. They both had laughed at the overkill and decided a four seater would be adequate.

They reach the airfield that Honey Aviation flies out of. Elijah proceeds to the main office, which is at the front of a large hangar to go through the necessary paperwork. Drake and Rae wait in the parking lot, both lost in thought, comfortable in the silence. Ten minutes later Elijah comes out and his face is all red. A large breasted woman stands in the doorway, both hands on her hips. She is saying something to Elijah before giving out a laugh. She looks over at Drake and Rae, giving them a wave. She watches Elijah trot along the tarmac for a few seconds, obviously interested in his butt, before returning to her office.

Elijah motions to Drake and Rae to follow him with their vehicle as he walks over to the helicopter. It's majestic in its glossy blackness, the queen of all mechanical dragonflies. Just aft of the

Plexiglas painted on the glossy finish is the hovering Bee, as bright a yellow as the call letters on its tail. He is met at the chopper by a short, bearded young man. He greets Elijah with obvious good will. The two speak for a few minutes before going through a quick check and the start up. Rae drives up to the aircraft. When she stops Drake gets out going to open the rear cabin door. Out of the back deck of the truck, Drake removes two canvas black bags, putting then in the space where one of the back seats has been removed. Returning to the truck he lifts out a large coil of climbing rope. He tosses that in the back of the chopper before closing the door.

The window of the truck is down on Rae's side and she leans out to talk to Drake briefly before leaving to return to the city center for her meeting with the detectives that Chowdhury has arranged.

"I saw Dakin this morning and he's getting out of hospital later today. I told him I would help him get settled. If you need anything, get me on my cell."

"I feel bad that I haven't had more time to be with my friend, Rae, so I'm glad that you're able to help him. I spoke to him on the phone yesterday briefly and he sounded in good spirits. He mentioned something about setting up a temporary camp here in Bangladesh; did you have anything to do with that," Drake asks with a sly grin.

She smiles and says, "It's possible." Before she motors away she adds, "Happy hunting, Drake."

Drake gets in on the left side of the helicopter; Elijah is in the pilot's seat. He straps on his seat belt as Elijah starts the rotors spinning. Drake says to his partner, "Let's go find this boat, Elijah. I have a strong feeling it'll lead us to our quarry."

Four hours later Isaac and Gurupada are slowly approaching the district town of Bhola. The river has narrowed considerably, but boats are still plentiful. The two men had scoured Barisal in the early morning, coming up with no evidence that the mystery man was known there. They had visited two other river ports with no success. They had remarked that each time the greetings were becoming more unfriendly. It was almost as if the river people were being warned of their approach as well as their nosy questions. Gurupada suggested to Isaac that rumors and gossip have always flown rapidly amongst the rural people that live on and by the waters. Now with cell phones it's harder to sneak up on people.

They have maneuvered up river until they approach a bridge that marks the beginning of the town center. Positioned just before the bridge there is a rickety walkway jutting out into the river where two other boats are tied up. They park the Chris Craft there and head up toward the street that follows the river. It widens out for a stretch to facilitate the offloading of boats. There are several single open boats with heavy loads, four more bunched up halfway down and several more in a knot beyond that. At the first boat, they come up to the man that looks to be the owner. Gurupada asks him several questions in Bengali. The scraggly man remains mute, shaking his head in a negative gesture. He's barely listening as he watches the men unload his boat. When Gurupada shows him his identification, the man becomes rattled and insists Gurupada search his boat or leave him alone, he's too busy for talk.

The next two sailors are slightly more co-operative but uninformative. Neither know nor will admit to knowing about the boat they are looking for. They are nearing the cluster of four boats, all small freighters. One is very much like the boat from the description they have. Gurupada advances upon a group of workers standing in a semi-circle across the street in front of an open-doored warehouse. The building is in better condition than its two closest neighbors, the smell of fresh paint lingers. Two of the men's clothing is smeared with the same colors. To the right of the men is bamboo staging that is being used to reach the upper walls. A roller taped onto an extended handle leans against the staging, bright yellow tears dripping from its edge.

The men are smoking and gabbing, obviously on break. With Isaac solidly at his back, Gurupada interrupts the men and says in Bengali while pointing at the freighter by the wharf, "Excuse me, do any of you recognize that boat and know who owns it?"

There is a chilly silence present. The men all look at the man directly across from Pada. He is bigger than the average Bengali. Shallow cheeks and a droopy moustache shadow his upper lip. His eyes are bloodshot and a half burnt cigarette protrudes from his thin lips. He looks directly at Gurupada and remains stock still.

The man does indeed know the boat and Bohai Xu as well. He knows Xu to be gnarly and disagreeable most times, but he pays his workers well and always keeps his word. The man also knows that Xu sticks his nose up at the authorities at times and carries small amounts of cannabis from port to port. Xu always joked "so he could retire someday and get off the damn river." The stranger eyeballs the other man, who he assumes to be an American, and thinks that this questioning can only mean trouble.

He says to Gurupada, "Why do you look for this man? Is he in trouble?"

"No, not in trouble. We need to ask a few questions. We're looking for someone and he might know where that person is."

The man, who the rest defer to, looks to each of the men with the slightest of nods before studying Gurupada for a bit longer. There are four other workers, and with the subtlest of moves, they start to surround the two strangers. Isaac sees immediately what is happening, removing his hands from his pockets and assuming a more defensive stance. He checks quickly for weapons, not seeing any. This doesn't look like a street gang, he thinks. He missed the knives the two on his right are carrying in the band of their lungis, short, sharp and damaging. The men are hard workers, muscled from their chores. They aren't warriors in any sense, but they are skilled at survival. The man in the middle steps back from the group. He crosses his arms nodding heavily. The men on his right, the painters, quickly confront Isaac while the two on his left rush toward Gurupada.

Isaac takes the first man that approaches him low at the calves with astonishing speed. Gripping both legs in an arm vice, he lifts the wiry man right off the ground. The man is swinging his arms trying to maintain some balance when Isaac throws the body into his partner behind him. The second man doesn't have time to avoid the human projectile, catching the flipped man in his open arms. The force of the impact forces them both to the ground. The man lying underneath lets out a painful grunt when he hits the ground, the weight of his partner driving the wind from his lungs.

Isaac never gives them a chance to recover. Before the man on top can right himself from his cushion, Isaac kicks him between the legs. The man groans and grabs at his crotch, rolling around on the ground. The one underneath is still trying to get his breath back when Isaac stands over him and slams his fist into the man's nose. The noise of crushing bone and gristle can be heard all the way to the wharf. Blood explodes from his nostrils. He yells out in pain-laden gibberish that makes him sound like a cartoon duck. He scuffles to his feet and, holding his hands to his bleeding face, takes off running down the street. The man on the ground is lying face down with both hands caressing his balls when Isaac walks over and places a headlock on him that soon renders him unconscious.

Gurupada sees the men on his right advancing more slowly than the ones after Isaac. They have pulled short stabbing knives from their waistband while they circle the cop. Gurupada surprises them by rushing the man in the middle that has stood back to watch knocking him to the ground with a shoulder to the solar plexus. Stepping over the body he grabs the stick that had the roller taped to its end. He turns back just in time to see the man closest to him with his knife held high in a striking position. Gurupada propels the paint roller into the man's open mouth with enough force that it snaps the man's head back, halting his mad approach. The tape tears away and the roller falls to the ground. The man is spitting, swallowing and gagging on paint. His cheeks are smeared with a shade of lemon that matches his mustard-colored T-shirt.

Gurupada changes the position of the stick into a two handed sword. Crouching low as he swings the heavy wood that connects with the second man across the shins. The forward leg receives most of the blow, breaking both the tibia and fibula into several pieces. The energy from the man's advance is decidedly impeded and he flies forward right over Gurupada's crouched form. The knife he had been wielding tumbles from his hand. He lands face first on the gritty dirt road, which scrapes the soft skin of his cheek and forehead, removing the first layer of skin like sand paper. It also knocks him unconscious.

The man that Gurupada had initially knocked to the ground, the one that started the whole fracas, has righted himself while watching the two strangers decimate his companions in mere seconds. He now faces both Isaac and Gurupada alone, one on each side. As big as he is, he's a coward and starts to beg for salvation. With Pada swinging the heavy stick in threatening slices and Isaac in a boxer's stance, they close in on the scared man, intending to teach him a lesson, when from the open door a burly individual with one wooden leg and long grey hair yells out for them to stop.

The man has a wide face, bushy eyebrows and heavy slanted eyes. He is thick-chested and wears a light cotton shirt that hangs over dark, short legged pants. Both of his lower appendages are exposed. One hairy leg is shod with a worn leather sandal; the other is greyish wood that tapers and is capped at the bottom with shiny scuffed metal. With hands on his hips, he addresses them in a language that is a mixture of Bengali, Chinese and English.

"What do you seek and why do you bother these men?"

Gurupada and Isaac step back from their antagonists. The one with the paint on his face has fled inside the warehouse looking for succor from the foul taste in his mouth. Two others lay dreaming in the dirt. Gurupada chucks his weapon at the feet of the only man standing. "We didn't come looking for turmoil; we were only defending ourselves from this gang's aggression. I could arrest them for assault if I chose to"

Pointing once more to the boat that attracted their attention in the first place, he says, "We're looking for the owner of that boat. Is it yours?"

The man doesn't respond right away and instead says to the coward, "Get those men off the ground and into the warehouse. Tend to their wounds."

Then he says to Gurupada, "And what if it is? Who are you and what do you want?"

Gurupada shows the man his ID and explains that they only want some information. If they could ask a few questions, the man that owns the boat will be free to move on as he has done no wrong. Gurupada waits for the man to reply already knowing they have found the right person.

Bohai Xu senses the Bangladeshi cop isn't hiding any other motive. "I am the owner of that boat."

The cop and the merchant speak there in the yard for over half an hour with Isaac standing guard. Xu explains that he had sighted the grey tarp floating at the edge of the river, stuck to a tree root. He could see that it was folded. He went to retrieve it, bringing it on board. He and his mate had been surprised by the weight until they discovered the cement block tied to the end. There had been a length of frayed rope dangling from the block. He assumed that there may have been other blocks tied but the motion of the river had cut them away.

They had cut the ropes that had bound the tarp to discover a horrid reek and a dead young girl. She was still bloated from the gases of death. He admits he had been tempted to throw the corpse back into its liquid grave. He tells them that he has a daughter back in China and decided that the authorities should know about this poor girl. That is why he dumped the body in Barisal and left the scene as quickly as possible. He made an anonymous call to the police to tell them where he had found it and where he'd left it. He had chosen Barisal because it was a river port he rarely sailed to.

The last question Gurupada asks him is, "In your travels of late, have you noticed anything unusual, anything odd besides this dead girl?"

The question triggers an image of a young woman dawdling on the end of a wharf, looking both sad and lonely.

"Well yes, now that you say "odd," I did see a young Japanese girl not long ago sitting on a rebuilt wharf some distance from here and I remarked to my mate that there were many strange things going on."

"Can you show us where this was?"

"I do not have time to show you, but I can tell you because if you came by the river, you would have seen it yourself."

Xu explains where he had seen Plum. Gurupada informs the man that he will need to know where he can be reached if they have more questions. They talk for a few more minutes. Gurupada shakes the man's big hand before Xu turns away, limping back into the warehouse.

As Pada is explaining the good news to Isaac, Isaac's phone rings. When he answers, he is distracted by the whomp-whomp of turning rotors from a helicopter overhead. The bird is black and glistens like the feathers of a large raven. He says into the mouth piece, "Yeah?"

Drake answers, "I can see your crazy ass from here, Isaac. What are you two up to? Are you having any luck?"

Isaac realizes that the whirlybird overhead contains Drake and most likely his brother. Before he answers, he watches the aircraft turn about before hovering directly overhead. "I can see you guys too. That's a good-looking bird. I'm going to let Pada explain what's going on."

He passes the phone to the cop and watches the surrounding area for any threats.

Pada relates to Drake what they have found out and explains where the wharf is. They decide that Drake and Elijah will scout the area from the air. Drake warns Gurupada not to go aground yet as they don't want to scare anyone off if they are this close. If they spot anything suspicious from the air, they can check it out tonight under the cover of darkness.

"You and Isaac head back to Barisal and we'll coordinate our next move from there. Pass the area slowly, look for anything telling."

Before Gurupada can hang up, Isaac says, "Wait, I want to talk to Drake." He takes the phone from Pada. "What's going on with Rafan?"

"It's bad, Isaac. His sister and niece were murdered and they abducted Rafan from what we can tell. There's more bodies too, Isaac. Rae's working with the other detectives on that angle."

Isaac responds with acid in his voice, "The bastards, let's find these creeps and put them away, Drake."

"You got that right, my friend. We'll get them, Isaac. Oh and by the way, our pal Daiken is out of hospital today and recovering. Stay cool, buddy, and we'll talk soon."

Pada and Isaac watch the helicopter disappear into the horizon and return to their boat. They chat about what they have discovered. They pretend to ignore the wharf Xu has told them about as they sail past in case anyone is watching the river traffic, noting that it is vacant of human activity. Gurupada comments on the Zodiac and cabin cruiser tied up there. Isaac watches the shore closely and notices a path that leads up from the river a kilometer or so below the wharf. He files the image and is already visualizing a stealthy approach from the river to find what is hidden in the trees.

Drake and Elijah make a low level pass over the area they have discovered, trying not to bring any attention to them. When Elijah flies over the hangar compound, Drake sees a huge man enter what looks like a big garage, his photographic memory calls up the image of the person leaving the parking garage where Daiken had been injured. He says, "This is it Elijah, head for Barisal."

Chapter 31   Oct 2 near the Bhola River

Stratton is walking the back fields of the farmhouse where Rizzato is bunked down. He's thinking he might remain here until the project is completed. After the workers have finished the runway, he knows Rizzato and his people will be eliminating them, dumping their bodies in a huge hole yet to be dug. Rizzato has told him that is a week or more away. Once the engine has been installed, he will take the aircraft out for a test flight. If everything is satisfactory, the gas will be loaded, the fuel tanks replenished, the plane covered with tarps to stand ready.

When everything is done, Stratton will make a phone call delivering a new password to Rizzato's account and he and his team can depart. At that point, he will select the day with favorable weather, a slight breeze to carry his poisonous fumes over as many targets as possible and he will exact his revenge over Sadarghat with as many sweeps as possible, either until his tank is empty or he's knocked from the sky.

During his walk, he visualizes his trip. He will leave here flying as low as possible to avoid being detected. Once he approaches the river port, he will fly even lower; and when the congestion of people is great enough, he will release the methyl isocyanate upon the filthy hordes that have killed his children. While he is gloating over these evils thoughts, he is interrupted by the swirling sound of helicopter rotors. He looks up as it sails overhead, low enough for him to recognize the black and yellow design. He ducks under some trees that line the edge of the field. He feels exposed and a ripple of panic surges through his shattered brain.

Andrew Stratton is psychotic. The only rationale that exists is his selfish need for satisfaction, his egocentric need for vengeance. It was when he'd had his own daughter thrown in the grubby and heated confines of their makeshift prison that reasoning became impossible. Everything beyond that has no meaning. Even his personal hygiene suffers. He shaves and bathes sporadically. He eats very little and he drinks too much, trying to bolster his confidence. He is agitated, wanting to rant and rave at anyone who will listen to his hate, his passion for retribution. But there is no one now except Rizzato, who tells him to shut up, to keep his madness to himself.

The helicopter has passed without slowing down, skirting the sky well beyond the property when Stratton moves away from his cover. He runs the short distance to the house where Rizzato is holed up. He has a sudden urge to plea with Bartolo to move things along. He knows he will find him tending his birds, he can't understand the man's fascination with them. Covering the distance in several minutes, he enters the house through the back door. It opens into a kitchen area that is cluttered. The sink is full of unwashed dishes; the counter is decorated with birdseed that has escaped from the torn bag resting on it. A metal and Formica-covered table with three mismatched chairs has newspapers piled in the center, and a mop stands sentry in one corner.

Stratton shakes his head at the mess, calling out, "Are you upstairs, Bartolo?"

Rizzato's hoarse voice answers. "Yeah. What's up, Jack?"

Stratton moves to the stairway heading to the second floor.

"Is there any way we can move things forward so that we could be done here before the end of the week? I want to be airborne by next Saturday morning, early."

Rizzato meets Stratton at the head of the stairs having come from the last bedroom in the back which he occupies with his birds.

"Jack, I told you already that we will be done here by next week, I don't know if it will be Saturday, or Friday or Sunday. You keep insisting that you need over 1200 feet of runway. You know we had some rain lately and the end of the runway is right at the irrigation pond, which still needs to be filled. All we have is that old dozer, an older tractor and a half assed wagon. If it's that important to you I'll have Plum get the men to put in a little more effort. Besides I thought you were only going to fly that damn thing in December. If that's still the case, we are way ahead of schedule. Getting out of here earlier would suit me fine; I'm getting tired of this sweating hellhole."

"I've changed my mind. I want to take those crazy zealots out right away; I'd do it today if I could."

Stratton is wearing his impatience like a suit that doesn't fit. He's at the head of the stairway staring at Rizzato. The men are quiet for a few moments; the only sounds the twittering of the birds in their cage. Stratton glances toward the back bedroom and says, "Noisy little buggers aren't they. How can you stand that racket all the time? I'm thankful I'm sleeping downstairs. Plus they stink."

Rizzato too looks back at where he keeps the cage and says, "Never mind about my babies, Jack. These little darlings are leaving with me as soon as this caper is done and not before, so think about something else and mind your business."

Rizzato gets closer to Stratton Taking him by the forearm, guiding him back downstairs.

"C'mon, let's go outside for a minute and talk there."

They leave the house. The sun is lower and there is some shade to sit in where an old picnic table sits crookedly by the river side of the house.

"Grab a seat, Jack, and hang on a second."

Rizzato returns to the house, coming back with two cigars, two empty glasses and a bottle of Crown Royal. The smokes and the drinks are common soothers for the men, as different as they are. He sits across the weathered wood from Stratton and offers him one of the half coronas. He pours each of them two fingers of the Canadian whiskey. Rizzato slugs the first drink back like its water, gives a slight shiver and refills his glass. The men perform the ritual of lighting cigars and are eagerly puffing when Rizzato says, "I have a full night ahead of me. I want to spend a little quality time with that Bashara character and my power tools, see who he talked to and find out who we might have to track down. I also have to deal with your wayward daughter. On top of that, I have to get your work done and now you want it done ASAP. What's up with you anyway?"

Rizzato doesn't really need an answer to that last question; he can see the deterioration in the man already. He notices of how ill-kempt the man has become, how he's unravelling, He's also thinking of how much he dislikes Jack Favors or Andrew Stratton, whatever he wants to call himself, but he constantly reminds himself of the money that is waiting. As he watches Stratton relish his smoke and savor his drink, obviously thinking of his reply, Rizzato is concentrating on the villa in Venezuela he craves. He loves the jungle and his Embera friends, but he's growing tired of the seclusion. When he's done here, he already has an escape route planned back to Panama. Travelling is difficult for him, but he has his hooks into a daredevil pilot that he keeps supplied with all the cocaine the man can handle. He will be flying out with Bunker and Plum soon. He'll ditch Kovalenko as well as the other rowdies they have hired along with the workers when time is up.

Stratton says, "Good cigar, Bartolo." He sits forward and the wooden seat creaks. Waving the cigar about for emphasis, he continues.

"Here's what's up. I'm getting edgy waiting. You know what I'm planning and that's why we're here in Bangladesh. But things aren't going well. First there's Sophia. She's crazy"

As Stratton takes another draw on the half corona, he's thinking of taking his daughter with him when he flies over Dhaka. Rizzato is thinking it's the man in front of him that's crazy, not the daughter.

"Secondly, I get the feeling we are being watched."

He tells Rizzato about the helicopter.

"Thirdly, I don't think you're being up front about your men. Where are the two Pakistanis and that sadistic South African you hired? The only muscle you have left around here is the big Serb, the Japanese girl, that bald headed mechanic with the weird tattoo on his head and the three thugs that don't seem to have names or any brains."

Rizzato remains quiet, gulping down the rye, smoking his cigar. His answer to Stratton's queries is silence. He knows if he gets into an argument with this man, he will be tempted to blow his head off with the .45 strapped to his thigh.

Stratton is pouring another drink when he says, "Listen, Rizzato, none of that really matters anymore, anyway. I'm just being paranoid. I don't want to wait any longer, so here's how things are going to go from now on if you want to get out of here with your money. I want the runway done by next Friday. I want you to get rid of Bashara – no torture, just get rid of him. I want your people to dig a huge hole by Friday and fill it with those workers, buried deep. Friday night when that's complete, I'll make a phone call and give you the new password; you get the money I promised you. I don't care where you go or what else you do after that."

Rizzato doesn't answer Stratton. He continues to stare at the man with his colorless eyes. After a few moments of silence, he just nods to Stratton, agreeing with everything.

"Drink up, Jack" He offers his half-filled glass to Stratton in a toast and adds, "Why don't you go back to Dhaka with Bunker? Go back to the Pan Pacific where I can find you if I need you? They're leaving here soon. One of our workers is from these parts and knows the waterways very well. We'll get the gas here tomorrow. Kovalenko has assured me that the aircraft will be ready by Monday. He tells me that once he has the engine running and every bolt tightened up, then the plane will do what you want. You don't need to try it out, which is a bad idea anyway. Let's keep it under cover until you're ready to go. We'll have the gas installed by Monday night. I guarantee that the runway will be done by the end of the week. You meet me here on Friday around midnight. I'll be the only one around and then once you give me the password, I'll be gone. I give you my word on all this."

Stratton lifts his eyebrows in question and says, "Your word? When you're gone, what good will your word be then?"

Rizzato bestows upon Stratton one of his weird grins saying, "You don't have a lot of choice do you, Jack?"

The men sit in solitude for a while, each chewing on the cud of their words. Stratton mulls over going to Dhaka. Two more drinks are poured and the cigars butted before Stratton agrees, "Okay Bartolo."

Rising from the wooden table somewhat unsteadily Stratton leaves to pack a few items before leaving for the hangar compound. Rizzato's eyes frost over before he says, "What about your daughter?"

Stratton pauses again and gazes up at the sky. He rubs his hands together as if he's nervous and says, "I was going to take her with me on Saturday, but I've changed my mind."

He looks Rizzato in the eyes and says, "Do what you want with her."

Rizzato watches Stratton retreat to the house. He lights another cigar and waits until Stratton returns with his carryall, gets in the Wagoner and leaves for the other farm. While he smokes, he thinks of Bashara and the Stratton girl, becoming submerged with evil gladness at the possibilities of what he will do with his captives. Reaching for his walkie-talkie he calls Plum.

"Yeah boss?"

"Jack is on his way over there and will be leaving with Bunker and the men. Go to the wharf and make sure they're away. Around eight-thirty, I want you to take that woman in the shed and tie her upstairs in the house over there; gag her, too. Use the back bedroom and just make sure she can't escape. Then I want you to bring Bashara here in the truck that Jack will leave behind. When you bring him, Plum, make sure the chainsaw is gassed up and bring it too. Very early tomorrow morning there will be a couple more bodies for you to get rid of. One of them will be in pieces so bring plastic bags."

Plum waits in silence, thinking how demented the man on the other end of the line is. It takes considerable effort for her not to tell him off. She is so angry she's afraid to say anything.

"Are you still there, Plum?"

"Yeah boss, I'm here. I'm on it."

Rizzato can sense a change with Plum, but he doesn't worry about it. She's been on edge lately and he attributes it to her being stuck here with all the men. He never questions her loyalty because De Clerq has vouched for her as one of his best people. Besides, he has promised her a lot of money and he knows she needs it. Not a saver, that one.

"I know you don't like these details, but don't worry, I won't ask you to watch."

With a short laugh that sounds more like coughing to Plum, he adds, "I'll see you around nine tonight Plum, don't be late."

Cutting the connection Rizzato rejoins his feathered soul mates. When he enters the bedroom, the bright blue birds come alive.

They are devoted to their master. Rizzato spoils them with attention and food. Searching around the room he spots the carrying cage in the corner of the bedroom. Everything is ready for when he will flee from the confines of his temporary residence. He'll call his pilot telling him where to be Friday after midnight. From Chittagong he and his birds will become cargo and all flown to Latin America via the Philippines. As he feeds his angels and tinkles their bells, he's thinking of the beautiful woman that will be tied in the bedroom later and the delights that will follow. At least it will be delightful for him.

Plum had seen Bunker, the hired thug named Oppermann and their pilot leave in the sampan. She is walking back from the wharf mentally preparing herself for the task before her. Her remorsefulness is much deeper tonight knowing she will be delivering two innocent people to painful and inopportune deaths. She can't even begin to imagine how Rizzato might use the chainsaw on their captive. She forces the thoughts away, focusing on the pretty girl she has to tie in the bedroom. She feels the most sorrow for her. She has been witness to the horrors Rizzato imposes on the female flesh with his deviant ways. She shudders as she asks herself, "Is this all there is to my existence?"

"No," she says aloud to the night, "I can't do this anymore."

She has almost reached the compound, which is quiet now except for the men around the bunkhouse at the back of the buildings. They are yakking in their strange tongue. She can still smell the spices in the air from the evening meal. That's something else she is getting tired of, the constant taste and scent of curry powder. She keeps busy until it is time to do as Rizzato asked.

Later on she checks her watch. The dots just above the numbers are luminous and she can see that it is close to eight thirty. She stops in the yard off to the side of the house. She has to think. She remains completely still as one of the hired men Bunker has brought in last week walks around the yard checking for anything odd on the grounds. She doesn't care much for either him or the other gangster, wondering where Bunker found them. She regards them as something you'd scoop out of a pond of dead water. The man strolls past her, not even noticing her in the darkness. It's then that she comes up with a plan. She steps out of the shadow and calls out to him, "Hey, Adzic."

The man jumps at seeing Plum. He says in rotten English, "Fuck, Plum, you scare me. Don't do no more"

His bulk is menacing, but Plum says with the most seductive of voices, "Where's Gourab?" meaning the other hired gun.

"With men in bunker house."

The man softens some. Like a lot of stupid men, he thinks mainly with his penis, yearning to toy with this oriental woman who barely speaks to him. He is grinning, thinking that maybe she has realized how irresistible he is.

"Listen, I need you to do me a favor. I have to take the two prisoners over to Rizzato. I have to take them to the wharf and then motor over there with the Zodiac. It's been very quiet here for a long time, but we are expecting some trouble from some of the workers; they don't like the guns. Forget about the grounds and concentrate on them."

At this she winks at the Serb as if to suggest there could be more intimacy to follow.

"If you can keep them quiet and an eye on Gourab, I'd appreciate it. I'll make it up to you later tonight"

The Serb can hardly contain his excitement at the chance that this tiny woman would be so kind to him. He blusters and reddens as he bows to Plum. "Yes, good lady, this will I do."

He marches toward the bunkhouse and when he is out of sight, Plum runs to the shed beside the hangar that holds their prisoners. She removes the lock from the door with her keys. Digging a small Maglite from one of her pockets, she opens the door. The two creatures turn their heads away from the light. The shed has been shrouded in the black of the night and it takes several moments for their eyes to adjust. Rafan and Sophia are surprised to see the Japanese girl. They are both bound at the ankles, with their hands manacled in front of them. Their mouths are covered with grey tape. Rafan's is damp with the snot from his nose and the tears from his eyes. His hair is disheveled and askew. The tears have made streaks through the dirt on his cheek. The swelling has gone down on his face, but a portrait of Bunker's brutality is still painted with a yellowish bruise on the side of his face. One of his eyes is still partially shut. He quivers slightly, his fear undiminished.

The woman, on the other hand, is quiet, no tears and no runny nose. There is an air of resignation about her that seems to control her emotions. Soft blue eyes blink in the illumination of the small light, looking up at Plum, begging. Plum studies the two for a minute. She hopes that what she is about to do will work. She says to them, "Do either of you have large amounts of money? By large, I mean over two hundred thousand dollars, because that's what it's going to take to buy your way out of here. I need the money. I know you won't understand it just now, but

I'm sick of running from the law and more than anything I need you both on my side."

Both of the captive's vigorously nod their heads, the man with more tears, and the woman with more eyeful pleading, both with more hope.

Plum lets them know what they are in for if they aren't keen on her plan. They continue to shake their heads in a yes gesture as she speaks. She explains what she wants them to do, to trust her because they have very little time, very little choice. The keep nodding until their necks are sore. Eagerness covers their fear. Plum unties the ropes at their ankles. She tells them she will remove the tape and hand holds later, after they are certain no one can see them.

"Okay, then, get to your feet and when we leave the building there is a road straight ahead that leads to the wharf. Keep walking as fast as you can, but not like you're running from me. When we get in the woods, I'll let you free. Please don't do anything foolish. If you do, I'll be as dead as you will be."

The three of them set off down the road, both Sophia and Rafan wobbly from sitting in a cramped position most of the day. As soon as they are in the woods and far enough away from the compound, Plum reaches in a side pocket to remove a small tarnished key. She halts the duo to undo their handcuffs. Both of them rip the tape from their mouths gasping in big gulps of night air through their mouths. Plum chucks both sets of handcuffs deep into the woods. She reaches into one of her side pockets and gives Rafan a handkerchief to wipe his face. Sophia is rubbing her wrists when she asks, "Why are you doing this?"

"I'll explain it all later. We have to get going because Rizzato will be looking for us very soon. Now grab your friend there, he doesn't look good, and let's hustle to the wharf."

Rafan is shaking with relief, with hate, with sorrow and regret at the way his life has changed so dramatically. He can't talk, his burden is so great. He prayed to Allah as he never had before. He lets the strange women lead him away. Sophia is smothered in reflections: her captivity, the mocking of the huge man that teased them through the day, the decadence and sickness of her father, the sadness that he doesn't love her anymore and all she wanted to do is save him. She walks down the road in front of the Japanese girl with a heavy and disturbing silence. Guiding the ravished man beside her as best she can, his legs are weary and he drifts as if he hasn't a care in the world, but she knows better. Like her he is still scared. Sophia looks back at the woman who is looking back at the road they are walking on, checking for something.

"What's your name?" Sophia asks.

"My name is Ume, but I like the English version much better, so you can call me Plum."

"My name is Sophia. Thank you, Plum. Your name is as pretty as you are."

Plum dons a shy grin and waves them on. Sophia looks to the man she is leading, trying to get his mind on something other than what's eating at him, "And you, what's your name?"

When Rafan doesn't answer she shakes his arm a little and repeats her question, "What's your name?"

He stares at her with a distressed countenance and blabbers in his native Saudi tongue. She interrupts him by saying, "Never mind. Let's concentrate on getting out of here."

They reach the wharf fifteen minutes later. Plum steers them toward the Zodiac, telling them to wait for a minute. Running to the small outbuilding she opens the door. There is still a strong scent from the rotting corpse that Bunker had left there several days ago. It had well roasted from the heat of the day when she had gotten rid of it yesterday. The foul odor hits her and she heaves up her supper of noodles and chicken. She pulls up her T-shirt to wipe her mouth and then uses it to cover her nose as she reaches inside the door to the hook where the keys to the Zodiac are normally kept. She can't feel them and with more boldness than she thought she had, she enters the building, shines her light to see that the hook is bare. The keys are missing.

"Damn, damn, what am I going to do?"

She hasn't imagined in her hasty plans that the keys wouldn't be there. They are always there. Panic grips her, squeezing like a boa constrictor. She turns from the building and stares at the silhouettes in the boat. Now their lives are in her hands and she doesn't know what to do. In this flash of weakness, she almost loses her composure. She wants away from all this so much. Not knowing her next move, she walks slowly to the Zodiac. She checks her watch to see that it is a few minutes before nine. Rizzato will soon be calling her on the walkie talkie, wondering where she is. She removes the communicator from her belt and throws it into the river.

She hurries over to the boat. She tells the two people waiting for her about the missing key. Her shoulders fall in defeat and Sophia feels pity for the woman. So secure and sure one minute and beaten the next. Sophia also knows that Plum is in danger by the possible consequences of her action. The three are as quiet as the stars that shine above when Sophia is struck with a simple revelation. She blurts out, "Plum, I have transport coming for me tomorrow in the afternoon. I made arrangements for the man that brought me here to pick me up either today or tomorrow. It's not far from here. Let's go. We can hide there."

Now Sophia is in charge. The two women prop up Rafan between them and they scurry down the path to the open field that Sophia had traversed yesterday. She leads them across the uneven terrain to the spot roughly about where she had come ashore. As they are more or less dragging Rafan through the scrub bush that lines the river, they are quieted by movement on the shore. They duck and pull Rafan down with them. They wait in scared stillness until Sophia whispers to her new friend, "Wait here with him."

Creeping to the shoreline she scans the river's edge. The moon had been full less than a week ago and the waning orb emits sufficient light, enough that she is able to see the most wondrous sight she has ever seen. The man that had brought her here is camped asleep in the taxi, which is bobbing in the moving tide. It was the motion of the craft they had seen. Sophia slides to the bottom of the river bank and runs over to the boat. She gently stirs the driver and he greets her with the greatest of smiles. He starts jabbering in Bengali until Sophia motions him to be quiet. She indicates to him to wait and goes back to find Plum and Rafan.

"C'mon Plum, let's get this man in the water taxi and get outta here."

They guide Rafan to the boat, getting him stowed in the back seat.

Plum jumps in beside him and Sophia sits in the front beside the driver. Sophia says, "Take us back to Dhaka."

The four individuals sit in silence as the craft starts down the Bhola River. Rafan is like a slate wiped clean; his mind will never be the same. Sophia is angry, her head busy with the things she needs to do to try and save her father. Plum is anxious and nervous, hoping she can trust this woman in front of her. The driver is indifferent, still thinking of the money.

None of them have a clue that they will never make dry land in Dhaka

Chapter 32   Oct 03 1:49am   Bhola River

Drake and Gurupada are paddling up river toward the area that Drake and Elijah had spotted earlier in the day. Both men are dressed in black; their faces are darkened with theatrical shadow makeup, the whites of their eyes making them look like apparitions. Both men wear a small pack, black with dark plastic buckles, strapped to their back. There is no possibility of any reflected light coming from either man. They are staying close to shore, dipping their paddles in total silence as they propel themselves toward the foot path Isaac had told them about. Trees along the riverside hang over and hide them like hushed helpers. Additional cover is provided by co-operating clouds that are scattered in the sky, blanking out the partial moon.

Their inflatable boat, painted as dark as its occupants, is one Gurupada has secured from the Barisal Police Station. They had towed it behind the Chris Craft, which is stationed about a half a kilometer downriver where the Glass twins wait. Both Isaac and Elijah had volunteered for the scouting mission but Gurupada had insisted he accompany Drake. His logic was that he is a police officer and if anything goes amiss, his authority will protect them. They're plan is to reach the path, go ashore and reconnoiter the property for any evidence that Rafan or Rizzato are present.

Drake raises a hand and Pada stops paddling. The boat floats to a standstill. They are close enough to the shore to hold the boat steady in the tidal movement. Drake whispers, "If we've timed it properly, we should be very close to the path Isaac saw. Let's go ashore here."

The men push on the river bottom with their paddles, moving their transport sideways until the bottom scrapes on the rough ground. Drake noiselessly steps from the boat into water that is up to his ankles and pulls it ashore. Pada joins him and the two men tug at the craft until it is resting on dry land. The bank where they're standing is about two meters high, shouldered with vegetation. They find a large rock, securing a rope that is attached to the front of the boat to the stone. They tread soundlessly up river with Drake in the lead. After about ten to twelve meters they can see an opening in the trees. They scramble up the levee, and following the footpath, they soon come to a clearing. Tall timber guards a cleared circle.

The forest emits a scent of the greenness surrounding them. The aroma of death that had shared the very spot they stand upon was absorbed by the verdure of the wooded area. The men wait for a few moments, their eyes adjusting to the shadows that loiter about them. They can see an opening that parallels the river. Drake signals Pada to follow as he heads off into the mouth of the passage. They sneak along the path as quietly as moth's wings until they come to an open field. They crouch at the edge of the woods.

From where they kneel they can see the outline of several buildings, one quite large about 300 meters away. To the left of the structures they see a formation of trees that suggests an orchard. Drake removes the pack from his shoulders, unsnapping the catches. He takes out a pair of night vision binoculars. They are Generation 1 light intensifiers from ATN Corp. They will amplify the available light several thousand times. The only thing he doesn't like about them is the slight high pitched hum they give off when turned on.

He switches them on, placing them to his eyes. The view is a greenish hue of the buildings with blurry edges. There is another building beyond the larger one that looks like a house. To the right is a longer building sitting in front of a small greenhouse with busted windows in the rear. As Drake scans the area in front of him and to his right he sees a graveled section that looks like a raised roadway. He is about to pass the binoculars to Pada when he sees someone move around the large building walking toward the rear. The person seems of no significance except for the firearm he carries in his grip, a rifle of some sort. The sentry stands still for a moment obviously looking around the grounds. When the individual props his gun along the side of the building and tugs at the front of his trousers, it becomes clear to Drake that the man has stopped to relieve himself.

He removes the binoculars from his face and passes them to Pada. He crouches even lower as he says, "There's someone at the end of the large building Pada, take a look."

Pada is looking through the binocular lens when he says, "I see him Drake, looks like he's taking a piss."

Gurupada ignores the man while he examines the terrain checking the layout of the field before them and the position of the buildings when all of a sudden there is a flare where the man is standing. He quickly takes the binoculars from his face. Drake says, "The man just lit a cigarette."

Pada and Drake squat where they are and wait as the man finishes his smoke. They're discussing their approach to the buildings to get a better look. It's obvious that there is something hidden or protected here or there wouldn't be guards posted. They want more evidence that these are the men they're looking for.

Unknown to them Rizzato is waking up from a fitful sleep about a kilometer south of their position at the same time as they are watching the guard. Rizzato is restless that night and sharply aware of the mess he is in. When Plum couldn't be reached over the walkie-talkie earlier, he sensed immediately something was asunder. He had stormed down the roadway to discover that Plum had abducted the prisoners, fleeing the premises. Adzic had explained to him what Plum had instructed him to do. Rizzato sent the Serbian to the wharf to check if the Zodiac was gone. Adzic had taken the golf cart and within fifteen minutes was back, reporting to Rizzato that the boat was still tied to the pier. There was no evidence of the trio.

Rizzato had raged at his hired men for their stupidity. He ranted and chucked debris from the prison shanty as if he could uncover the culprits that might be hiding like insects. He soon realized there was nothing he could do until Bunker returned and even then there might be too much damage done. He had taken the truck back to his farmhouse, instantly preparing for his departure. It was getting too risky to stay here any longer. He decided that as soon as Bunker returned he'd leave Kovalenko and the rest of his men to their own fate while he and Bunker would return to Dhaka. Once they visited Stratton, they would force him to forward the password, kill him, and then get out of Dodge.

All night he had tossed and turned. He sits up on his bed throwing the flimsy sheet aside aware that something is wrong. Even his birds are frenzied and fly about their cage in an agitated manner. He gets dressed, grabs his gun from the nightstand and goes outdoors to check the premises. He leaves through the back door as quietly as possible and sweeps the area with eyes accustomed to darkness and danger. He paces around the house for twenty minutes before he is satisfied there is nothing unusual about the evening. The tingling he feels as a warning sign is still going on though; there is something happening at the hangar he realizes. He jumps in the Isuzu and heads there.

Drake watches the man by the large building until he finishes his smoke, picks up his rifle and walks back toward the front of the structure. He repacks the binoculars and says, "Let's stay along the edge of the field Pada until we reach what looks like an orchard. There seems to be a short fence or other structure there we can hide behind."

Gurupada nods his agreement. The men are crouched low, creeping toward the fruit grove when lights appear in the driveway to their right. The glare bounces up and down and sways left to right as Rizzato steers the truck toward the farmhouse. They are only halfway across the field when the vehicle enters the yard. They flatten themselves amongst the weeds and tall grass just seconds before the light sweeps the area they are traversing. They are kissing the ground and there is little they can see. The slightest of breezes touches the tops of the longest straws offering little to disguise their movement. The light comes to a rest just above them. If they move even slightly they will disturb the grasses and give themselves away. The two men are barely breathing they are so still.

Rizzato puts the truck in neutral and jumps from the cab. Just then Adzic comes from behind the longer building that houses the workers, joining his boss in the yard beside the truck. The Serb is nervous around Rizzato having witnessed the man's fury earlier when he had discovered the missing prisoners and seeing the gun, remains silent. Rizzato says, "Have you been scouting the grounds tonight Adzic? Have you seen anything unusual?"

"Yes I have and no boss, nothing unusual. What's wrong?"

"I don't know. I just get the feeling that something is not right here. My sixth sense has never let me down before."

"Your six cents?" asks the Serb.

Rizzato looks at the man as if he has two heads and shakes his own head asking himself, "Where did Bunker find these idiots?"

"Never mind, take the cart and go to the wharf. Keep the lights off and when you are almost there, sneak down and see if anything is wrong."

"Yes, boss."

Just then the Isuzu comes alive, giving way to gravity to start rolling down the slight incline toward the orchard on its own. Rizzato sees the truck moving, jumps back in the cab and puts it in park, kills the lights and gets back out. Adzic is still standing in the yard with a look of befuddlement on his brow.

"Well, get going, you idiot. Go check out the wharf like I told you."

The man leaves in the cart, its electric motor a low hum in the darkness. Rizzato poses in the yard slowly looking over the terrain with beady gray eyes. It takes a few moments for his night vision to return and even then there is so little light that he remains still for many minutes with arms akimbo staring down the roadway that leads to the pier. He's surprised that his entrance hasn't yet roused the workers. As he waits for Adzic to return, he listens.

As soon as the light has been killed, both Drake and Gurupada raise their heads enough to remain unnoticed but high enough to be able to see two men standing in the yard beside a small truck. They watch as one of them hurries to a smaller vehicle that looks like a golf cart and drives down another roadway to their left. Drake surmises it has an electric motor as there is no noise accompanying it. They watch until the small vehicle disappears into the tree line. Suddenly the breeze stiffens for a brief moment, causing the grains to sway. Drake says *sotto voce*, "Now, Pada! Let's move to the low wall about ten meters to your left."

The cop is slithering on his stomach as slowly and quietly as a worm, with Drake close behind him. When they reach the stone wall, Drake removes the binoculars from his pack once more. He crawls forward a few feet and is able to see toward the yard. He can see the silhouette of the tall man. Whoever he is, he appears to be looking right at them. Slowly Drake raises the binoculars to his eyes and switches on the night vision. The hum startles him, it sounds as loud as the buzzing of a hundred bees in the darkness. The man he sees hears it too and looks right toward them. Drake immediately switches off the night vision. The binoculars have remained on long enough for Drake to see who the man is.

Rizzato's hearing is keen; he heard a hum that lasted less than five seconds. He attributes it to the insects that feed in the night. Nonetheless, the hairs on his neck perk up and he moves behind the truck. He searches the fields where he can see, but nothing moves. The night seems to stop breathing. He is thinking that when the guard returns, he will have him walk the open grounds to be sure.

Drake had dropped the binoculars. He automatically reaches for the gun in his waistband. Just then a light appears upstairs in the main house. Gurupada sees what he is doing and places his hand over Drake's. He can feel the heavy pulse in Drakes fingers; he can feel the anger as it throbs like his racing heart. He cautions the man by his side because he knows it isn't fright that is making him tremble.

"Wait, Drake, we don't know how many men are here, how much fire power they may have. What did you see?"

Drake reluctantly releases the grip on his gun, slowing his breathing while cursing a hasty urge to kill the man. He knows Pada is right. He remembers his impetuosity in Amsterdam. It is only Rizzato that makes him this way.

"It's him Pada; the man in the yard is the one we are after, the one we've been chasing for the last three years. I want to take him out right now, wound him and have you arrest him, but I know you're right"

"Drake, we can't stay here. Let's move down to the edge of the trees behind us and find a better spot where we can see what's going on. We have all night and all day tomorrow if we need it."

The two men move stealthily to the grove of trees and shrubs behind them, crabbing their way into the foliage. Once they are screened from the yard they moved into a suitable viewing position and wait.

Rizzato is joined by Gourab, who has come from the main house still buckling his belt. They are also joined by several of the workers that have been disturbed by the lights. Rizzato instructs the Bangladeshi to calm the men, get them back to the bunkhouse and settled in while keeping an eye out for anything odd.

As he waits in the yard, Rizzato listens to his inner musings about leaving the scene. He thinks about getting in the Zodiac and fleeing but he decides he's just being overly cautious. The whole caper is making him edgy; Stratton is getting on his nerves. He's also thinking of the man named Alexander and wondering where he is. He's certain that he can't remain here much longer. The gas and Andrew Stratton's madness are secondary to his own well-being. He whips out one of his throw away phones and dials the one he had given Bunker before he left. Even in the middle of the night, Bunker answers on the first ring.

"Bunker, something's not kosher. You and I need to get out of here as soon as we can. Where are you now?"

There is a moments' silence on the line, interrupted by the slightest static, before Bunker answers, "We're about six, seven hours away."

"Do you know if Stratton's at the Pan Pacific?"

"Yes, he told me that's where he would be."

"Good, carry on."

He flips his phone shut, turns to meet Gourab, who is approaching him from the bunkhouse.

"I think you need to talk to the workers, Mr. Rizzato. They are asking too many questions for me"

As Rizzato nears the bunkhouse, he pulls a stuffed wallet from his rear pocket, removing a handful of taka notes and American twenties from it.

"I know what will make these losers happy, Gourab, watch this."

The men go to the bunkhouse and the Bangladeshi translates Rizzato's words about what a great job they are doing and how they will all be returning home by the end of the week. He talks about bonuses while passing the money in his hand freely about the room. He grins as he passes it out, knowing he will be taking it from their dead bodies in the very near future.

When Rizzato leaves the bunkhouse, he sees Adzic coming back from the wharf. He waves to Gourab to follow him and meets the scruffy Serb down by the orchard. They are seven to eight meters away from where Drake and Gurupada lay hiding close enough to hear the following conversation.

"Did you see anything, Adzic?" Rizzato says.

"Nothing boss. All is okay."

'Okay, listen up. Bunker will be back at about eight o'clock or so. I want both of you to patrol these premises and keep a sharp eye out for anything different. As soon as my other men get back, I want those workers in the field. That's up to you, Gourab. You can get some rest later. Adzic, you work with Kovalenko and Bunker to get their cargo here and then you too can catch some shuteye.

Call me if you think anything, and I mean *anything*, is wrong. I'll be back after lunch."

Both men nod their heads in acknowledgment. Gourab follows Rizzato back to the truck as Adzic parks the cart. The two men take off behind the hangar to do a circuit of the perimeter. As Rizzato is turning the truck around, he says, "Adzic, check the river side too."

The Serbian nods. Rizzato drives off into the darkness.

Gurupada whispers, "Well that tells us what we want to know. I think we can safely assume that there are at least three of four more men besides this bunch. We don't know how many are in that building that seems like a bunkhouse or if they have guns, it might be a bit much for just the two of us. I think we should be cautious here, Drake. We get help on this and arrest all of them. Do you agree?"

"I think you're right. We don't know where Rizzato went and we heard him say he would be back after lunch. Let's go round up our people and make a plan to get back here and wait for him.

They scoot through the remaining wooded area until they are back on the shore. They follow the river back to their boat. Untying the transport they push it out a little before getting in. They maneuver downriver to where the twins wait. During the twenty minutes it takes, Drake tells Gurupada what he learned about Andrew Stratton from Williston and that Chowdhury has been informed. Williston also emailed an image of Stratton to the Inspector's office. Williston guessed that it was possible the two men are working together and that Stratton might be the reason Rizzato is in Bangladesh.

Chapter 33   Oct 03   6:33Am   Meghna River

Bunker is sitting on the bench in the cabin of the sampan, his bulk incongruous with the smallness of the hut. The sun is low in the sky to their left, the fiery ball still behind the treetops, the shattered rays emphasizing the breadth of the mighty river. Even though he has sailed this route several times, he is unfamiliar with the variances of the waters and the surrounding land. Sailing at night is hazardous and much slower than he had hoped. The man that is guiding them is often uncertain of the route in the darkness, so they have stayed on the Meghna moving slowly and as close to the port shore as is safely possible. Bunker had installed powerful spotlights on the boat, the heavy beams penetrating the duskiness.

Kovalenko is steering the sampan as usual, arguing with the man leading them back to Bhola. If Bunker wasn't occupied by the desperation of Rizzato's call in the night he might have found their conversation comedic. The Bangladeshi doesn't speak much English and Kovalenko's grasp of the language not being much better, so whenever the mechanic asked for directions or made any other comment, the man in the lungi would just say, "Straight, go straight."

Kovalenko says, "Bunker, are you sure this guy knows where we go? If my thoughts are good we should go east soon."

"He got us to Dhaka and back yesterday and quickly as well, so do as he says."

The Bangladeshi must have understood some of what they were talking about as he says, "Turn soon, not now, soon."

Kovalenko is grumbling in his own tongue, not happy with such vague instructions. They settle back into a quietude that seems compulsory but uncomfortable. Bunker turns his jumbled thoughts to the tank in the hold, the flat-red circular top visible from where he sits. He is thinking that it signifies the end of their time here in Bangladesh and will be glad to leave. The heat is stifling at times, the language is odd. His moods are tied to Rizzato's and senses the danger of lingering much longer. Images and ideas roil about his head like air bubbles escaping from boiling liquid. He never usually thinks much about tomorrow.

Bunker has never had a relationship with anyone that cared about him before and yet Rizzato suggests there could be something between them. The woman inside him thinks of her dead father, the only person that has ever shown her any kindness or love. Excited exclamations from their Bangladeshi guide cut the silence of his thoughts. He is pointing to their left at a boat that is wallowing in the water about a half a kilometer from them,

"Look, look," he is saying.

They can see a man standing on the bow of a smaller craft that Bunker recognizes as a water taxi, similar to the one he had used only days before. The man on the boat is waving a red cloth over his head trying to catch their attention. Bunker says, "Never mind them, Kovalenko. We don't have time for this."

The Bangladeshi doesn't understand what Bunker is saying and continues to explain in his mother tongue that the people in the boat are in trouble and they should go help. Bunker quiets him by saying, "Shut up."

As the sampan nears the stranded craft, the occupants are becoming more distinguishable. The three men can see someone, possibly a woman, trying to stop the man from waving his makeshift flag. Suddenly Kovalenko, whose eyesight is eerily keen, blurts out, "Bunker that's Plum."

When Plum, Sophia and Rafan had left the shore where they met up with Sophia's arranged transport, the man had told them he would be unable to navigate in the dark; they would have to either go to Bhola or tie up somewhere for the night. They had decided to move downriver to where the Bhola River joins other waters. They tied up under a bridge that spanned the waterway and waited until dawn before moving on. Rafan had been as docile as a drugged mouse spending the night sleeping. The two women, both stressed with their present situation, talked the night away, becoming familiar with and consoling each other. The driver was in a state of happy delirium having received the second halves of the twenty dollar bills from Sophia and he too slept until Sophia roused him awake when the pitch of night started to give way to the greyness of morning.

They had followed the winding river to its mouth where it joined the Meghna just as the drabness gave way to the redness of the sun's rising. Spots of morning fog like dusty wisps hung over the river. It was here that the boat's engine began to cough and gag as if it had lungs. It gave a final gasp before losing power. The driver scolded the boat like he might a small child. He checked the fuel tank to discover it was more than half full. He tried the ignition several times to no avail. He realized then that his problem was likely mechanical and explained that they would have to flag a passing boat to get towed to the nearest port. They soon realized that the traffic on the river was almost nonexistent. The few boats that saw the red rag he had dug from under his seat were not interested in giving them aid. The tide was coming in, with the river pushing them closer to shore. While they were discussing what they might do, a dark-sided sampan came into view less than half a kilometer away. The driver stepped out onto the bow of his stricken boat and waved the red flag. As the sampan came out of the fog, Plum recognized it and rushed to stop the man's actions.

"Stop." She says to the driver. She reaches for his arm to cease his waving. The man looks at her oddly, questioning her with unbelieving eyes. She is looking at him but says to all three of her companions,

"Those men are very bad and extremely dangerous."

The driver either isn't listening or doesn't want to believe her. He untangles himself from her grip and continues to sway the rag above his head. Soon a bullet from Bunker's weapon hits the man in the forehead and tosses him from the boat. Plum follows the body over board as she yells out,
"Over the side, you two, get behind the boat."

Sophia dives into the murky water beside Plum. Rafan panics and instead of seeking refuge with the women, sits up straight instead. He may as well have red and white concentric circles painted on his body as a flying slug tears through his chest dead center. It passes through his heart, ending the muscle's heightened beat and its owner's young life.

Bunker had recognized the patrons of the taxi and had whipped his Glock from the waistband holster. He started shooting and yelled for Kovalenko to steer toward the crippled boat. The first shot found its mark, stopping the red flag from attracting anyone else. He aimed for Plum next, but the woman moved too swiftly, jumping into the river. Bunker continued to spray the boat with random shots.

The man Bunker had searched for last week, the one that started all the problems, offered himself as an easy target by sitting up straight. He thanked him with a bullet to his chest. His arms fly in the air as his lifeless body falls from the seat. To Bunker, it looked as if he were waving goodbye.

Plum has dug her gun from her waistband as she jumped from the boat, gripping it tightly so as not to lose it to the river. She paddles toward the front of the boat and in the V where the nose rises from the water, she returns fire. Kovalenko had been steering the sampan towards them when a bullet breaks through the rough wood of the cabin, missing him by the slightest margin, but splinters from the shattered wood catch him in the face. One of the slivers, about an inch long and as sharp as a tailor's needle, strikes him in the eye. It misses the pupil by millimeters, piercing the glossy orb; the eyeball stopping it from entering his brain. He brays in sudden pain and lets go of the wheel. His hands go to his head as he tries to pull the tiny spear from its lodging.

The boat swings suddenly to starboard when Kovalenko falls against the wheel. The Bangladeshi falls toward Bunker, knocking him aside. It is only that sudden motion that saves the huge man from the bullet that would've taken his life. Instead it hits the little brown man in the shoulder, jerking him to the opposite side of the boat. The sampan is heading for the smaller boat at full throttle with no one at the wheel, no one visible in the cabin for

Plum to aim at. Just moments before impact, she yells to Sophia, who is huddled by the boat, to watch out. Plum strokes away from the rushing boat with all her strength, losing her gun in the effort. Sophia only makes it a few feet when the sampan bashes the small boat to a zillion pieces. One of the spars that held the canvas top flies through the air, striking her on the head. She loses consciousness and starts to sink.

Bunker was trying to right himself when the sampan hit the water taxi. It knocked him to the floor once more. The crunching of fiberglass sounds like screeching under the bow of the heavy boat. The sampan passes over the smaller boat, creating a blanket of flotsam bobbing in its wake. Bunker rises and grabs the wheel as he pulls back the stick, shutting down the fuel supply. He reverses the engine and opens the throttle once more but it's too late. The sampan beaches itself upon the riverbank. The reversing engine churns the green water but can't pull the big boat free. Bunker shuts it down turning his attention to the women in the river.

Plum had swum free of the oncoming boat and avoided injury. As she watches the sampan hit the shore she calls out for Sophia. The young woman is nowhere to be seen. The water around Plum is littered with pieces of the water taxi. The rear of the boat is the only large fragment left and it floats nose down, the engine stuck up in the air. Rafan is caught between the back seats; only his lower torso is visible. Plum is swimming through the debris when she spies a woman's hand just above the surface of the water about ten feet away. The hand slips below the surface just before she reaches it. Plum takes a deep breath and dives. Her eyes are open in the putrid water, but she can't see anything. She propels herself toward the bottom until she literally bumps into Sophia's flaccid body. Plum grasps a piece of clothing and hauls the girl to the surface.

Bunker turns just in time to see Plum dive in. He rushes to the back of the sampan with his gun in both hands, waiting for her to resurface. If Plum has a weapon in her hand when she comes back up, Bunker decides to shoot her. As much as he enjoys killing, he will be sorry to take the Japanese girl's life. There had been something about the young woman's independence that had pleased Bunker. The skin of the river erupts when Plum breaks through. Bunker watches as she is pulling the limp body of the other young woman toward the shore. Bunker says, "Give it up Plum, she's probably dead."

Plum is beyond caring about her future at this point. There is a need within her to do something right, something good. As she pulls Sophia's head out of the water, she pushes toward the river bank and she shouts out, "Fuck you Bunker. Shoot me if you want. I'm not letting her go."

Plum reaches the side of the river, towing Sophia behind her. She drops the unconscious woman on her back and begins performing CPR. She has never had any formal training in first aid but had seen the act on TV. Sophia has only been under for a short time and had not been breathing when she went down, so there is very little water in her lungs. Plum's efforts are soon rewarded as Sophia responds with short gasping watery breaths. She chokes as she expels dingy fluid from her throat.

Bunker has been watching the rescue with unusual interest, trying to understand why Plum is here in the first place. When he had spotted her in the boat he had known something was wrong. Now he realizes why Rizzato had been so upset when he had last spoken to him. He watches as Sophia gags on water. Plum turns the woman on her side to get the fluid from her lungs.

Bunker says, "What are you doing here Plum? Why are you with these people?"

Plum looks up to the big Serb and doesn't answer right away. She is still trying to comfort Sophia who coughs and sputters. Both women are sodden, their hair hanging down and their damp clothes clinging to their bodies.

"I was trying to get away from the trash that commands us, Bunker; I can't be part of this filth any longer. If you're going to shoot us do it now, you big fool!"

"Why would I do that, Plum, after all your hard work in saving that poor girl? No, I think I'll bring you back to that...trash as you call him and let him decide your fate. I can assure you Plum; it's not likely to be pleasant; but then who knows, maybe he'll forgive you."

At this last remark, Bunker chortles before scowling at the two.

"Get your friend on her feet, Plum, and get your asses in the boat or I *will* shoot you both where you sit."

Sophia says with rapid gasps, "No, we can't leave Rafan. We need to bring him back."

She is struggling with Plum when Bunker shoots at the dirt at her feet. The women stop, shocked by the closeness of the bullet.

"Never mind him, ladies. That thing will soon sink and like the other sap in the water, he'll soon be food."

Kovalenko has removed the splinter by holding his eyeball with one finger as he pulled the wooden shaft out, hoping the eye wouldn't come out of the socket. Kovalenko has scars all over his body and is familiar with pain, toughened by a life of rough despair. He is continuously thankful that his injuries haven't killed him yet. Even though he can't see from his damaged eye, he reasons that he still has another. He removes a greasy rag from his back pocket and a semi-clean handkerchief from his coveralls. He wads the hankie with the cleanest part upon his eye and ties it tightly to his head with the rag as a bandana to hold it in place.

The Bangladeshi is lying on the floor gripping his bleeding shoulder with his good hand, trying to muffle his frightened moans. He's more afraid than he's ever been, tears flowing from his terrified brown eyes. He looks up to see both men staring at him, the giant with a gun still pointed at the shore, the mechanic with a rag around his skinny bald head. He watches as Kovalenko looks back at the big man. He sees the big man nod at the mechanic. He watches in sudden fearfulness as the man with the weird mark on the back of his head removes a gun from his baggy coveralls. For a few seconds he remembers his mother and father, both beggars. The blast of Kovalenko's gun is the last sound he hears above his screaming pleas for mercy.

Kovalenko replaces the gun in his coveralls before reaching down for the murdered man. He drags the skinny body out of the cabin toward the rear of the boat. As he does so, he tells Bunker that they will have to wait for the tide to lift them off the edge of the shore before they can depart. He checks to be sure there is no one in the vicinity as he lifts the man over the side. The bag of bones hits the water with an indifferent splash; the man's lifeless body face down in the water. It slowly sinks to meet its brethren on the bottom. Soon the two dead men will be bloated and nibbled at, trying to float. As irony would have it, Bohai Xu will be the first to spot one of them and the first, but not last, to ignore them.

Bunker is at the front of the boat with his gun pointed at the two women. He is watching Plum help her companion stand, slipping and sliding along the muddy shore. When they are close to the sampan he says, "You should have stuck it out, Plum; you would've been a very rich girl. As much as you may dislike our boss, he wouldn't let us down."

Bunker is soon to find out that what he believes will turn out to be a lie.

While Bunker extols Rizzato's virtues to the women in the boat, Rizzato is sitting on the edge of his bed panting and sweating, his heart pounding in his chest. His bald head is dull and throbbing, his eyes are still unfocused. He is clothed in only a pair of grey baggy boxers. He sits on the bed with his hands at his sides propping his tired, ashen and skinny body up. His head hangs down, with his eyes teary. He isn't usually awake this early, but something dreadful nags at him.

He had been dreaming of the Embera Indians in Panama where he had been in hiding. They were holding him in the air on their bronzed shoulders like a returning hero, a victorious champion. They were carrying him toward a huge cauldron set over a fierce fire that Rizzato imagined held a celebratory meal. As the crowd carried him closer to the boiling pot, they were ululating with huge smiles upon their brown faces, the women began tossing flowers at him. He was ecstatic with the adoration being bestowed upon him. Soon the large kettle was being surrounded by strange apparitions that were naked and dancing around the pot. He recognized most of them as people he had murdered in the past. Leading them was Viet Canelosi, the fat boy he choked when he was only fourteen, the first human he had ever killed. Following him were the girls from Venezuela, their bodies bleeding and scarred from the torment he had subjected them to. Behind them was the young girl he tortured only last week. More and more of his victims appeared from the dust of the stamping feet.

Suddenly his jubilation turned to fear as the brawny men carrying him tightened their grip upon his body. It was then that he realized they were going to throw him into the boiling water. He began struggling, kicking, yelling for mercy. The men lifted him even higher as they neared the heavy boiler. He looked around at the crowd trying to find Bunker as he screamed her real name.

"Dragoslava, Dragoslava, help me, help me please..."

The cheering from the crowd turned to a heavy chant to kill him. The faces of the woman, young men and children in the crowd turned to masks of absolute horror; fangs, bleeding eyes, horns from their heads, suppurating sores with green and yellow pus dotted their bodies. Still the men lifted him higher. They neared the edge of the steaming vat; the heat from the boiling liquid and the burning fire was intense. Then they threw him in. He awoke with a terrified scream just before he hit the scalding fluid.

As he sits on the bed, his heart calming down, he feels tremendous relief that it had only been a dream. It had seemed so real; he thinks. It is then that he realizes something is wrong. He knows he has to leave – right now. Forget Bunker; forget this project. He urges himself to get dressed, get going now. Within forty-five minutes he is washed, dressed, packed, his birds in their carrying case and in the Isuzu truck. He decides he will drive to Dhaka, even knowing it will take twelve to fifteen hours because of the many ferries he needs to take. He will call Andrew at his hotel and explain that he has terrific news to share with him, for him to await his arrival. Once there he will force Stratton to pay him and then he will be gone.

While he speeds from the farmhouse, he calls his pilot, the man that will sneak him back into Panama, telling him to be in Dhaka in twenty-four hours. Hurrying away, his warped and uncivilized mind is churning with unmade decisions, the foremost is whether he should kill Andrew Stratton or let him live.

Chapter 34   Oct 03 6:33 am   Barisal

The rotors hum in circular harmony as the chopper lifts its skids from the ground. As the helicopter rises several feet above the roof of the police station, Elijah changes the pitch of the spinning blades and the machine sprints into the atmosphere. Drake is strapped into the seat beside him and is checking his weapon. He's thinking how much he loves the one-nine. Earlier this morning he cleaned and serviced the gun, doing the chore by rote as his mind went over the images of the compound they are about to assault.

Through the night he and his team had spent several hours discussing their approach. There are many things they don't know. Drake is most puzzled by the sudden appearance of the man he wants most: why had Rizzato arrived in a quarter ton truck? They had shuffled a deck of ideas: Where was he coming from? Did he not stay with his men? And if not, where would he be? What operation did he have going? Where did Stratton fit in this?

On and on the questions went. Theories flew. The discussed the men at the site, the layout of the buildings, the geography. One image in Drake's keen memory had troubled him – the one he had based a part of his plan on. There was a house about a kilometre and a half beyond their target that Drake had seen from the air when they had surveyed the area yesterday. He also remembered a small pickup that had sat in the yard. He was certain that the house would contain Bartolommeo Rizzato. And a plan developed.

He reminded his team of his promise to Williston, the main reason they were all here. He had said to them, "We saw Rizzato there around 2:00 a.m.; we can't wait. We all agreed that he can't be far. Instinct tells me that if he's not there, then he's at the house to the south. Rae will come with me to check it out. Here's what we're going to do."

By 5:30 that morning Elijah was ferrying Gurupada and Isaac to the town of Bhola where they would pick up the Chris Craft. They were to cruise down the Bhola River, anchoring five hundred and fifty meters upriver from their objective. They would cross flat fields at water's edge until they reached the area where a wooded section hemmed in the buildings going south. The wharf would be to their right and covered by a narrow growth of trees. They had decided the men should hike farther east of there through the trees for coverage. They would take up a position at woods' edge where they could watch the site from the rear as well as the driveway.

Isaac and Gurupada are nestled in a slight depression at the edge of the field shielded by scraggly shrubs. The rear of the old green house is about thirty meters away to their left. There is a building directly in front of it. They can see men milling about in front of a large tent that is in front of a newer, much bigger building to the left of that. The roadway is twelve meters to the same side. They crawled up behind the foliage and can see where the roadway curves away; they are able to see anyone approach for over five hundred meters. It is an excellent vantage point. When they are securing their position they are distracted by the smell of the morning meal: fish and rice. They will wait for Drake's signal before approaching the premises.

While Pada's stomach grumbles its emptiness, Drake is sitting in the chopper adjusting his headset, identical to the one the rest of his team is wearing. They can communicate with each other within a four hundred meter range.

When they are flying over the Meghna he twists around slightly to speak to Rae in the back seat,

"How you feeling, Rae?"

"I hate flying, Drake, but I'm okay."

She stares at the back of Drake's head, not wanting to see the ground so far below. She rubs her hands together, the palms damp with anxiety.

Drake bends his head just a bit more, speaking as quietly as the engine will let him, "You don't have to do this you know."

She doesn't hesitate, "Yes I do. I've seen what these people are capable of; it has to stop. More importantly, Dakin told me about how you two discovered your friend's sister, he told me how you saved his life, how much you mean to him. Now he means a lot to me, Drake. I know he wants to be here, so I want to finish this. For him."

Drake nods his head, smiling inside. He notices the grin on Elijah's face. Both men are aware of Dakin's fondness for the ladies. Drake remembers Elijah's comment earlier when Rae was out of earshot that at least this woman has a brain, that Rae is not the kind of person to be taken advantage of. They had both agreed on that. Drake is staring through the bubble as the helicopter approaches land. They're crossing a large island that splits the river about ten kilometers away from their objective. Square and rectangular plots of farmland lay undisturbed beneath them.

Drake is concentrating on his next move. He and Rae will get off the chopper about a kilometer from the house that spooked him, which should be far enough not to catch anyone's attention. Elijah will set down in a gravel pit two kilometers beyond the house and await their call. Drake and Rae will scout the house assuming that Rizzato is there. If he is, Drake is certain the man will be armed. The uncertainty of who might be with him leaves Drake a bit edgy. Rae has insisted on backing him up; and he has come to trust her. Together they will check it out, and take Rizzato if he's there, preferably alive. They will then link up with Isaac and Pada to take the rest of Rizzato's henchmen. Drake's last thought before the helicopter begins its descent is that if they have to kill Rizzato, so be it.

Elijah keeps the chopper hovering about two meters off the ground at the edge of the forest that separates the house from the fields and the wide glen in front of it. Both Rae and Drake unbuckle and jump to the ground. Drake waves Elijah off and motions for Rae to follow him. They set off through the woods in the direction of the farmhouse. The field is damp with morning dew, droplets forming on the pair's polished boots. Once they enter the wooded area, a flurry of birds scatter from their trail, the rush of their wings hissing in the air.

Fifteen minutes later they are at the edge of the woods with the house visible across an overgrown field. The two crouch down studying the structure while watching for any movement. The house is a story and a half, the inside rooms upstairs would have slanted walls. The front of the building is to his left facing a yard of brown dirt. A slight breeze comes from the west and it teases an open door. No windows grace the side that he can see. Only a portion of the back yard is visible. Drake says softly into his headset, "The truck is gone and the front door is open, it doesn't look promising, Rae. I want you to move to the right and follow the tree line until you are in position behind the house. Find an area where you can see what's going on. There's a drainage ditch that follows the field to my left; it curves around to where the field ends at the front yard. I'm going to follow that until I can get a closer look. Let me know when you're in position."

Without a word Rae steals away, moving through the trees as fluidly as a startled doe. Drake drops to his stomach to crawl on elbows and knees toward the house. The ditch is filled with debris and unpleasant growth; his movement is slow as he wiggles around or over obstacles. He can't see the house but it makes its presence known by the tapping of the loose front door against the jamb, the breeze toying with it. Ten minutes later the ditch levels off. He is still four meters from where it begins by the front yard, still deep enough that he can't be seen. He slowly raises his head where the grass is thicker along the trench.

He is on the opposite side of the building from where another building sits halfway between him and the house. A crooked wooden table rests ungracefully off to his right. Flakes of paint peel away from the stucco siding on the small outbuilding making garish pink curls. The siding on the main dwelling looks worn and elderly, having lost its color years ago. There are three medium-sized un-curtained windows spaced evenly across the side, their glass smudged with dust. Doorsteps of rough wood grace the front and back of the house.

He watches, nothing moves. He says into his mike, "What do you see, Rae?"

"A closed back door, a window to the left of the door, some junk in the yard. When the front door opens I can see inside what looks like a hallway. No movement."

"Can you see the shed?"

"Yes"

"Is it to your right?"

"Affirmative"

"I'm just to the right of the shed. I'm going to make a dash for the side, you cover me. On five."

After five seconds, Drake rises from his position; sinuous strong legs propel him to the protection of the structure. He leans with his back to the outer wall, his weapon chest level in both hands.

"I see you, Drake. Still nothing."

Drake doesn't respond right away. He is fine tuned to danger, but he doesn't feel it here. He can now see tire tracks leaving the yard, they don't look old. An odd sensation of disappointment engulfs him when he realizes the house is empty. He isn't clairvoyant; he just knows it is. He steps away from the protection of the shed, heading for the front door with his weapon cocked.

"There's no one here, Rae. I'm going in the house. Cover the driveway."

He walks slowly to the front door, footsteps creating small puffs of dust. As he approaches the entry, the breeze abates. As if the dwelling has nothing to hide, the door swings open, inviting him in. He steps beyond the threshold, to stand in the downstairs entryway. There is a living room on his left, a hallway leading to what looks like the kitchen straight ahead, a broken window visible on the far wall. To his right is a set of stairs that rises two thirds of the way up the wall before turning left to finish its ascent. The warmed up air is unpleasant – the scent of soiled food, unwashed dishes, dust and emptiness. He pulls the mouth piece away from his lips, cupping the microphone in his hand and says,

"You bastard, Rizzato, you're gone again. But I know you were here. I can feel it in my gut. I'm coming for you."

Rae has moved to the front of the house and stands with her back to the door, watching the road. She can hear Drake's grumbling from inside; it sounds like cursing. He must be very angry, she thinks. She seeks to console him, "He's probably at the other location, Drake. Let's go get him."

"Hang on for a minute, Rae, I want to check upstairs."

He takes the steps two at a time and is soon in a short hallway with a bedroom on each side. One of them has a strange aroma emanating from its open doorway. A familiar odor. His sister had many pets, and what he smells is bird feces. He checks the other room first to find it littered with clothing, an unmade bed and not much else. The air is close upstairs, swelling in the trapped heat; causing him to sweat. He slowly enters the other room to find several large cages under the window, perches and seed dishes confirming that it has been a home for birds. There is another messy bed with articles of clothing thrown about the room, some on the bed and some on the floor. It suggests somebody has packed in a hurry, travelling light. Drake walks over to the cages reaching over them to open the window.

He turns from the window, returning his gun to its holster. With his arms folded he surveys the room once more, slowly. A wind-up clock rests on a plywood-and-cement- block night stand. It ticks faintly. As he studies the walls and floor for any evidence of Rizzato, something that will justify his feeling he'd been there, a sharp gust of warm air blows through the open glass, stirring the seed caps, the bells and the feathers in the cage. One feather weaves its way upward on an errant draft until it hovers over Drake's head. It floats for a fraction of a second before spinning downward in a blue and gold swirl. During its descent, it brushes Drake's check tenderly as it passes by his face. Drake eyes the bright plumage, watching until it spins into his open hand.

He marvels at its brightness, the fine separation of colors along the feather, royal blue turning to gold then deep orange as the shaft thickens near the bottom. It makes him think of his sister Glory, how much she loves birds. His thoughts return to his mission and he moves to toss the feather away. Something makes him clamp his fist over it instead. He reaches around to unzip his back pocket to remove a small notepad. Between the middle pages, he places the plumage flat, thinking he will show it to Glory.

While descending the stairs, he adjusts his mouthpiece. "Okay, team, Rizzato's not here. He could be at the other house. Is there a small grey truck in the yard, Isaac?"

Waiting for his friend's reply, he waves to Rae to follow him and heads through the field toward the compound where Isaac and Pada are stationed.

"Negative on the truck. There are a dozen or so men with

wheelbarrows and shovels working on a road of some sort four hundred meters from us, there is someone sitting on a bulldozer but it isn't running right now. There are two locals in what looks like a mess tent. We have three aggressors: two appear native, both armed. One is with the field workers. He's carrying a long gun. The other's a Caucasian. They seem to be organizing the men. Right now they're eating. The workers don't seem threatened by the display of weapons."

Gurupada adds, "I can get closer, Drake, see into the other buildings as well as the yard. Isaac can keep an eye on the driveway. You okay with that?"

"Okay, be careful. We'll be coming through a narrow copse of trees that borders the road they're building. There is a short stone wall by the orchard in front of the buildings. We'll be in place there within fifteen minutes."

Drake can see the river from where he and Rae are walking. They see shiny glimpses of water as leaves stir and sunshine reflects. They cross the field, entering a wooded area sandwiched between the runway and the river. The foliage is thick here. As they near the end of the runway, they can hear the chatter of men at work, the shovels scooping dirt, rakes smoothing the rocky soil. Drake motions Rae to be still. He sneaks through the woods until he is able to see the men. There is a lanky brown-skinned man sitting propped up in the shade of an old tractor, his gun is leaning against the front wheel beside him. He growls at and sometimes laughs with the other men.

Drake goes back to Rae telling her what he saw. He instructs her to stay hidden in the woods to keep an eye on the men and await his word. Had they been watching the river, they would have witnessed the passing of the sampan with its two prisoners and the extra guns it is bringing. The boat will dock just as Drake crawls along the stone fence.

Gurupada looks into the windows of the house and reports that there doesn't seem to be anyone else inside. He informs them the two men with weapons are sitting at a table under the tent talking as the cooks clean the mess. He is positioned to the left of the building in front of the greenhouse, crouched down in the weeds. He tells Drake he has a bead on the Caucasian. Drake acknowledges the information as he crawls into place.

"Isaac, can you see the other man?"

"I can see him clearly through the crosshairs of my scope."

"Okay gang, we wait. I want to see Rizzato before we move."

Isaac, Gurupada and Rae click their head set in response, settling in.

CHAPTER 35 Oct 3   8:35am

Bunker helps tie up the sampan after Kovalenko guides it to the wharf. The two captives sit bound on the cabin floor, where Bunker is able to keep an eye on them. Their hands are tied behind their backs and they are gagged. Bunker tosses the end of the rope on the planks and says, "Okay, Kovalenko, let's get the tank on the wagon."

He raises his chin to where the men had left the wagon at the end of the wharf. A tractor is parked beside it, with a pole sticking from its front, a rusty pulley hanging from the end of the pole. It's a better tool for handling the container than the forklift. Kovalenko jumps up on the seat, pulls the accelerator open and turns the key. The engine turns over sluggishly, with a mellow whine. Soon the motor gives off a belch of black smoke. Because the vehicle has a busted muffler, it roars. The noise startles the two women who are tied to each other. It startles the men at the compound, none more so than the ones in hiding. Pada is the first to ask, "What's that?"

Drake says, "Stay cool, people. We've got company."

Drake is at the stone wall that he and Gurupada were at the night before and sees both armed men in the tent rise from their seats. The white man is pointing at the wharf, motioning for the other man to go there. Drake scurries backwards, low by the wall, until he is back in the cover of the trees. He says, "I'm going to follow him. It could be Rizzato. Isaac, move toward the river the way you two came in, toward the wharf. We'll see what's going on. Pada, stay on whitey. Watch your man and be careful, Rae."

Drake waits until he hears three clicks before moving stealthily through the trees that separates the orchard from the water. He remembers the terrain from his flyover and knows the woods follow the river right up to the wharf. He inspects the ground closely where he walks while sneaking looks at his quarry.

Gurupada sees Adzic reach in his pocket for a cell phone. As he talks, his demeanor changes; he loses his cockiness.

Bunker is on the other end, saying, "Didn't Rizzato tell you to get rid of those men in the field? Haven't you spoken to him this morning?"

The man is apologetic, explaining he hasn't seen Rizzato or heard from him since he burst in on them in the middle of the night. They had been patrolling the ground until early morning and had found nothing amiss.

Bunker thinks back to the last conversation with Rizzato and remembers distinctly that he was going to have the workers eliminated this morning and then Bunker was to eliminate the eliminators. The two of them were supposed to head for Dhaka to get the money from Favors intending to leave this sweltering overheated country together. Now that he thinks about it, there should have been a plane on the river, the one to take him and Rizzato away. A troubling sensation embraces him. "What if he left without me?" He shakes his big head, remembering how he had last looked at *her*. "No, no, he wouldn't do that."

He interrupts the ranting of the other Serb and says angrily, "Get on it now. Go to the field; take the cooks too and do them all. Dump them in the hole at the end of the runway then meet me back at the hangar."

He closes the phone and pockets it, turning his attention to Kovalenko and the tractor that is easing along the wharf toward the sampan's hold.

Gurupada is suddenly alert as the man in the tent removes the phone from his ear quickly. Pada watched him listen briefly before flipping the phone closed. He hurries over to the two men washing dishes and yells something at them in a language Gurupada doesn't recognize. Both of the aproned men react with confusion. When they don't respond to whatever he told them, he bashes the shorter man in the face with the butt of his weapon, knocking him to the ground. He quickly points the gun at the other man and motions for him to start walking toward the field. The man is trembling, stunned into silence. He understands what the thug means and with his hands in the air shuffles toward the roadway. The ruffian transfers the gun to his other hand and points it at the back of the walking man. With his other hand, he reaches for a hunting knife sheathed at his waist. He kneels at the fallen man's side and is about to plunge the gleaming blade through the man's chest.

Pada had been watching the man's movements and realizes what the Serb is about to do. As the man unsheathes his knife, Gurupada reacts like the police officer he is. He fires his gun. The bullet obliterated the Serb's two middle fingers, causing him to drop the knife as he howls in pain. He tries to use his gun, which is in his left hand; in his panic he fires toward the house, where he thinks the shot has come from. Gurupada still has the man in his sights. Bullets strike the siding over his head as he fires again. His next bullet tears through the man's chest puncturing a lung. The cook who had been in the yard drops his hands and runs.

Gourab, the brown-skinned man with his back against the tractor, was dozing off when the first shot is fired. He is shaken from his laziness; his arms fly about and he knocks his rifle to the ground. Jumping up he looks toward the main buildings. The workers stand with their tools in their hands. When more shots ring out Gourab sees one of the cooks running around the building, his apron flapping like a white cape. The workers take this as the bad sign that it is, drop their tools and dart for the main road. Gourab scrambles for his gun. He picks it up, brings the barrel to his shoulder and aims at one of the running men. Before he can pull the trigger, Rae drops him with a bullet to the back of the knee.

Drake is at the wharf when the shots ring out. He had emerged from the woods behind a metal building, listening to the tractor engine groaning in front of him. The engine dies as suddenly as the shots began. Drake hears a deep voice say, "Never mind, Kovalenko. The boys at the farm are getting rid of some witnesses. We're almost done here. We'll be leaving soon. Now get that tank on the trailer."

Drake squats by the building and says in a worried whisper, "Pada, Rae, talk to me."

Gurupada answers, "One of the guards was going to kill one the workers. I stopped him. Things are a little chaotic here as I can see the workers dispersing through the back field, but my man is out.

Rae says, "My man's down, too. He was going to shoot the unarmed men in the back as they ran. I'll try and round up those men."

"Okay Rae, get those men under control. Pada get your man secured and then get down here. I don't know how many there are yet. Isaac?"

"I'm positioned across from a metal building and can see a skinny guy on a tractor lifting some kind of tank off the boat. A huge man is helping him position it on a trailer. The dark skinned man that just came down from the house to help is on my left."

""I'm behind the building, Isaac. I can't see anything; the foliage is too thick. I need to move. What's in front of the building?"

"It's kinda buried in the trees. The men are on your left about ten meters in front. The one on the tractor has his back to me. The dark one has his back to you and the bigger one has his right side to you on the other side of the wagon. I can't hear them talking over the motor noise. They have the tank in place and are untying the chains. They'll have to turn the tractor around to hook it up to the wagon. What do you want me to do?"

"Do you see Rizzato?"

"No, unless he's on the boat. I don't see anybody else, Drake."

"Shit, where is that bugger? I saw him here last night, only six, seven hours ago."

Isaac listens to Drake's rhetoric, remaining silent.

"We need to talk to these guys. Do you see guns?"

"Yeah, the big one has a bulge under the arm. The dark one has an older rifle, but it's leaning against the trailer. I don't know about the man on the tractor but I'd guess it's safe to say yes. He has coveralls on and there are lots of pockets."

"Pada, where are you?"

"I'm coming down the roadway. I can see the bend of the road and the tractor turning around."

"I'm going to move up river more and come up behind them. Give me three minutes and when I give you the word, I want each of you to step out with your guns on each of the men. Isaac, you take the man on the tractor. Pada, you take the dark-skinned man. I'll move up on the big one."

Both men signal they understand. Drake moves easily to the riverbank. Pushing some brush aside he climbs a short distance to the shoreline. The wharf is only six meters away. He is bent down using the ground as a shield. Maneuvering to the foot of the wharf he climbs slowly up the side. He sees that the men are still positioned as Isaac has described them. The dark man is strapping the tank to the trailer. The large man is standing with his arms crossed, watching while the man on the tractor backs it toward the trailer, looking behind him as he does.

Drake prepares to lunge and says, "Now."

Isaac steps out of the woods in front of Kovalenko and yells for him to "Freeze." Gurupada, who has snuck up to the front of the tin warehouse, steps out at Drake's command and points his weapon at the young man's head, yelling the same command. Drake sprints the three steps to the big man's side and thrusts his gun into his ribs.

"Don't move or I'll put a bullet through your heart."

Isaac closes in on the tractor with his gun trained on the thin man, reaches over and turns off the key. The silence that follows the churning of the engine seems just as loud. Before anything else can be said Bunker thrusts her mighty elbow into Drake's face with a rapidity and mobility that he will talk about for many years. As agile as he is, he can't sidestep the Serbian's hard edged forearm. He is knocked over and his gun falls from his hand. Bunker swings around with the momentum of her defense reaching for the weapon under her arm. From the corner of his eye, Isaac sees Drake go down; he steps to his right and fires at Bunker. One of his bullets tears a chunk of flesh from his right thigh The wound only pushes Bunker more quickly onto the boat. He dives onto the deck. The impact of the weathered wood sends his gun flying to the opposite side of the boat while dozens of splinters enter his face and shoulder as he skids along the boards.

Kovalenko takes advantage of Isaac's distraction, pulls his gun from his pocket. He fires randomly toward the man shooting at Bunker. One of his slugs catches Isaac in the lower back. Another slug grazes his scalp. He topples to the ground in pain. Gurupada, in response, puts a bullet in Kovalenko's head. The Ukrainian topples from the tractor, landing face down on the ground. The odd question mark on the back of his head never seemed more appropriate. The other thug grabs his rifle and swings it up toward Gurupada. He is much too slow for the experienced police officer and Pada shoots him in the leg. They man goes down, moaning loudly. Pada rushes forward and kicks the rifle away. He looks over at Drake, who is by then rushing toward the sampan, gun in hand. He is yelling for the big man to come out. Gurupada turns his attention to Isaac who lies bleeding.

Drake is frothing with anger for allowing himself to be knocked about in such a fashion. He stands on the gunnels and waves his gun back and forth. Suddenly, a figure appears in the cabin window. He swings his weapon toward it, but doesn't fire. It's a woman, gagged, with a gun pointed at her head. Her hair is plastered to her head and frightened blue eyes stare hard at him. He trains his weapon on the big arm with the gun.

Bunker rises slowly. He holds another woman, bound and gagged, in front of him, one arm strangling her tightly about the neck. This woman is Japanese. There is no fear in her eyes, just pure hate. Bunker says, "You must be Mr. Alexander, am I correct?"

Drake has positioned his gun, aiming directly at the big man's head.

"You're correct. And who might you be?"

"Oh it doesn't matter who I am. What's important here is that I have a shield and you have fuck all. Now, what's going to happen is that you are going to throw your gun overboard, then move away from the boat. I will leave with my guests. I suggest you act quickly, while I'm in the mood to let these poor girls live."

"I don't believe you; and I don't even know these women. I think you know who is going to die here so don't make any false moves. There are two other guns trained on you."

He places his mouth closer to the microphone and says, "Are you listening, Gurupada?"

Gurupada has tended Isaac as best he can and then moves behind the tractor. He could only see along the side of the boat where Drake is as the other side is facing the water. He yells out a bluff. "I have a bead on him, Drake. Tell him not to move."

Bunker gives an evil grin and says, "I can kill both women within seconds – no, a fraction of a second. One bullet and one broken neck. I don't care what happens to me. But do you want to be responsible for these two? If not, get off the boat."

"Tell me where Rizzato is and I'll think about it."

Now the Serbian laughs out loud, "Rizzato? You'll never find him. He's gone. I must admit I'm very disappointed, I was hoping to leave with him. No, you won't find Rizzato."

His bulk sags a little. He is actually filled with sadness with what he knows to be true. Rizzato is gone and he has left Bunker behind. He keeps his eyes trained on the man in front of him as he pushes the barrel of the gun against Sophia's head, motioning her to move to the far wall. Bunker moves behind Sophia, the gun still stuck in the woman's ear. Plum is crushed in the gargantuan arm, her feet off the ground. She is squirming against Bunker's grasp, almost unable to breath. Gurupada has used the quiet to move toward the front of the boat, thinking he can remain unseen. Bunker notices the motion. Using Plum as a shield he twists about with an unexpected flurry and fires at Gurupada, hitting him in the chest. Drake fires too, hitting the ox in the shoulder.

The bullet grazes Bunker's shoulder clipping the collar bone on the way through. His thigh is weak from the wound he received earlier and the impact of the slug knocks him backwards. He makes an ugly grimace as pain shoots through his body. As he starts to fall back, Sophia breaks free and rushes through the cabin door. Drake can't get off another shot without hitting the moving girl but as Bunker is falling he lets go of his grip on Plum as he raises his gun toward Drake. Both weapons fire at the same time. Bunker's bullet grazes Drake's bicep. His gun flies in the river. Bunker's gun drops from his hand as he falls to the floor.

Drake rises quickly from the deck where he landed, the women tearing past him for the wharf. He ignores the pain in his arm and dives through the open door. Landing on the Serb he pounds the man with both fists. Each blow holds the explosive force of all his anger, the anger of losing Rizzato, the anger of all the needless deaths. To Bunker, the blows feels like beestings. He shoots out a huge fist hitting Drake on the side of his head. The blow knocks him up against the cabin wall. Bunker lashes out to kick him, but Drake sees the blow coming. As he rolls away, Bunker gets up and faces him. Drake moves into an offensive position.

He plants his left foot solid on the floor and prepares for a *maegeri*. He waits for his opponent to come to him. He has his arms up, prepared for the attack he is sure is coming. Bunker means to move in and overwhelm his antagonist. He hollers a Serbian obscenity and with his good fist raised, rushes at Drake. Drake lashes out with a thrusting front kick aimed for the stomach. Acting with practiced speed he strikes the huge warrior just above the solar plexus. He can feel and hear several of the lower ribs crack. Bunker doubles over as his breath whooshes out, one of his hands going to the pain where a rib punctured his lower lung. Aiming for the large face, Drake quickly strikes him in the mouth with his fist. Such a strike should've rocked a normal person; instead, Bunker seethes with anger. He shakes his large head, spits out a couple of teeth, blood and saliva flying from his face. Before Drake can move away, he charges him, enfolding him with mighty arms and squeezes.

The pain in Drake's chest is monumental and he can't breathe. His arms are pinned tight to his body and his ribs will soon break. Bunker roars into his face, his breathe hot and sour. Drake uses his forehead to butt him directly on the nose. The pain must be excruciating but still the man clings to him, squeezing even harder. Again and again he rams his head into the nose. Finally it hurts too much and Bunker drops him to the floor, grabbing at his bloody face. He backs away from his opponent, trying to see him through teary eyes. Drake moves into position to deliver a *mawashi-geri*, hoping to strike the hulk in the nose again. Bunker is standing in front of the door inside the cabin. He is about to rush Drake when his right knee comes up to execute the roundhouse kick. He puts all his weight behind the kick, connecting with the behemoth's solid jaw. He hit him with such force that the deep tread from his boot leaves an imprint on Bunker's chin and propels him backwards out the cabin door. There is nothing to hold him back. He cartwheels from the blow until the back of his legs hit the short wall of the hold. The heavy bulk flies through the air and he lands on the floor of the hold with a heavy whomp. His shrieks die suddenly in the cruel morning heat.

Drake hurries to the hold and looks in. The huge body is lying on the debris-laden bottom of the boat; a long metal bolt that had been affixed to the wood to hold down the tank is sticking through the chest. The eyes are open but Drake knows the man is dead.

He can hear cries of agony behind him. He runs from the boat. Rae has arrived at the scene after rounding up the workers and is administering to Isaac's wounds with what little supplies she has. She yells out to Drake as he bends over Gurupada.

"He's alive Drake but just barely. He has a stomach wound and there's blood on his scalp. He needs a hospital ASAP. What about Pada?"

Drake crouches over the moaning man who has red froth

dribbling onto his chin. Pada has been shot close to the right side of his body. It appears to Drake that the bullet has pierced the lung. Drake reaches down to pull a section of Pada's shirt to place it over the sucking wound. He and Rae both ignore the whining of the dark-skinned man.

Drake calls Elijah telling him to hurry; they need to get his brother and the other men to a hospital. Elijah is already airborne hovering above the action a few seconds away. He lands in the barren field just above the wharf. With the large blades still whirring, he removes two of the three seats from the aircraft. Drake and Rae cart first Isaac, then Pada to the chopper. Rae explains to Drake quickly that the white man has died from his wounds and some of the workers are watching the other thug. Drake tells her to go with the chopper and come back as soon as she can. He will phone ahead to the Barisal police station that they were coming in and give them Elijah's frequency to offer directions to the closest hospital. He'll clean up here.

The chopper lifts off while drake says a short prayer that his men will be okay. Daikin is already out of action; now two more men are down. He realizes that all the worrying won't change anything. Looking up to the sky for a moment he thinks of Rizzato. Disappointment cloaks his soul. He knows he can't let it get him down; he tells himself he will hunt the man until he finds him. He remembers the two women from the boat.

Chapter 36   Oct 3 8:15pm   30 kms from Dhaka

Rizzato has been driving for fourteen hours. He's unruly, edgy, hot and frustrated. There's a road map rumpled on the seat next to him, which probably caused him more delay than it provided benefit. He had only been able to obtain one in the local language and every time he stopped to consult it he grew angry. There are several drained cans of cola on the floor, empty chip bags, sandwich bags and chocolate bar wrappers, too. Both windows are down and he's still sweating from the intense heat. The fan isn't working on the small truck, compounding Rizzato's irritation. He had just received a call from the pilot taking him back to Panama telling him that he wouldn't be in Dhaka until the evening of the fifth. Rizzato argued and threatened to no avail; he was told several times he would have to live with it or find another pilot. Finally Rizzato gave in; he knew there was no other option.

He is still a good distance from Dhaka by his best calculations. He is crossing the Meghna Bridge as it enters Panam City. The large sign that announces the city's entrance causes a calm to flow over him. He sees it as an omen of better things to come because the name reminds him of Panama. He relaxes somewhat as he follows the highway, knowing that he will be dealing with Stratton soon. He decides to stop calling the man Jack Favors as it is just bullshit.

During the many lonely hours on the road, he had day dreamed of packing things up and saying goodbye to the Embera that had befriended him many years ago. He can see himself in a villa on

Isla de Fajardo in Venezuela, overlooking the Orinoco River and the city of Puerto Ordaz. He realizes it could be risky in that country; after all, he and his men had killed two female students and been involved in the kidnappings of other young girls. He wonders how Alexander had found him in Bangladesh. He figures that he will have to take on a new identity, but that's fine with him. He thinks he would like to be a Spaniard; he can speak Spanish, so why not? He'd have some surgery done. As he thinks about this, he looks at himself in the mirror and contemplates a new chin. These ideas occupy him until he enters Dhaka.

He stops at the edge of the sprawling city to put enough gasoline in the truck to get him into the city center, when he calls Stratton. The phone continues to ring with no answer. Rizzato has a moment of panic before closing the phone. He is afraid Stratton might have abandoned his hopes, overcome with the trials involved. If that's the case, he knows he's fucked. The only resources he has are buried near his hut in The Darien Gap thousands of miles away. He won't even be able to pay his pilot and the man will want to be paid up front. Just then his phone rings. Rizzato snaps open the phone,

"Yeah, is that you, Stratton?"

A tired voice on the other end says, "You mean Favors don't you? I don't know any Stratton."

"Never mind that crap, Andrew. I've been on to your game a long time. This is Rizzato."

"Oh sorry Bartolo, I didn't recognize your voice, it's usually much squeakier. I was sleeping and was awoken by the ringing."

"Listen, I've got good news for you."

"That's a relief. I was having a terrible nightmare. I'd been caught before I could have my vengeance. I can use some good news about now. What is it?"

"I'm in the city and I'd like to talk to you in person. We can get the money details out of the way and you can fly wherever the fuck you want."

"Wait now, Bartolo; I want to see if everything is okay before I dish out more cash. That was the deal, don't you remember. Once I'm satisfied that you and your men have accomplished everything we set out to do and that the men have …uh, been taken care of, you'll get your money."

"Yeah, yeah Andy, you and I can take that chopper you hired yesterday to check things out, then it can ferry me back to the city while you fly off into the wild blue yonder.

"Don't call me Andy!"

"Whatever. Are you still at the Pan Pacific?"

Stratton is hesitant to give Rizzato his whereabouts. He feels secure in his new nest. He had moved as soon as he returned to the city, extremely nervous now that he is so close. He doesn't want anyone to know his whereabouts. He had been up all night going over his approach and how he would spray as much of the populace as he could. He has decided to fly over the city around noon when the river and wharfs are the most heavily populated.

At random times, his memories trip him up: images of his wife and of his children when they were small. He's confused when this happens because he can't remember his wife's name anymore. The horror he is to unveil directs his every thought, every action.

"Are you still there, Stratton? What's going on?"

"Sorry, sorry, no Rizzato I'm not at the Pan anymore. I'm at the Golden Gate Hotel, 28 Mirpur Road, room 110. When will you be here?"

"I'll be there in an hour or so."

With that he hangs up. Stratton stares at his phone, not surprised by the man's rudeness. He shrugs his shoulders, deciding to get cleaned up and get something to eat. He hasn't had a bite all day.

Rizzato pockets his phone and checks the traffic on the divided street. Even this late in the evening, the traffic is thick. He surveys the street more closely, saying out loud to himself, "These are crazy people, driving on the wrong side of the streets. They're as bad as the bloody English. They're major litterbugs, too. The only thing I like about this place is the wild colors."

While he is heading back to the truck, he changes his mind about driving. He returns to the kiosk that houses the attendants at the gas bar to ask for a taxi. Rizzato is surprised how many people actually speak some English and is relieved that it is so. He remembers some of the history he has read about this country, how there had been some British involvement many years ago. He tells the man at the cash register to find a driver that speaks English, also telling him he will be back in fifteen minutes.

Jumping into the truck he drives about three hundred meters down the street until he finds an empty spot to park the Isuzu. He removes a screwdriver from the dash, leaving it open, which he uses to remove the registration plate, all the while wishing Amado

Mendoza was still alive with his ability to fix things. At least he doesn't have to worry about the fee for connecting him with Stratton. Leaving the keys in the truck he hopes someone will steal it. It will never be reported, so anyone is welcome to it.

He grabs the registration from the glove box, his bag and the bird cage and returns to the station. As he walks back, he tosses the plates behind a stone fence that fronts a small park. When he arrives at the kiosk, there is a newer yellow taxi waiting for him, a Toyota Corolla. The man behind the wheel is clean shaven with two huge teeth in the middle of his smile. He greets Rizzato with a mixed vocabulary, but Bartolo cautions him with a raised finger, suggesting he should wait. He buys a bottle of water from the attendant and gives some to his birds; he coos and baby talks to them as they drink. When he is satisfied that they are comfortable, he refills their seed dish, wipes the sweat from his forehead and enters the coolness of the air conditioned taxi.

An hour and twenty minutes later he is knocking on Stratton's door. The concierge had given him a hard time over bringing the birds in, but a twenty dollar bill found favor with him and he personally delivered them to the room Rizzato had registered for. He didn't register as Bartolo Rizzato; he never travels under that name. Phony passports, credit cards and various ID are easy to obtain for anyone with the right connections. Once more he mentally thanks Amado Mendoza. While he had been in Bangladesh, he had been known as Viet Canelosi. He relishes the irony when he uses the fake IDs.

There is no answer at Stratton's door. The beige walls of the hallway seem to close in on him as another moment of panic hits him. He begins to rap on the wood much harder when a voice behind him says, "Don't knock it down, Bartolo."

Stratton is walking toward him with his room key spinning on one finger. There is a lopsided grin on his face, but the eyes are dull and weary looking. Rizzato thinks he looks like Bella Lugosi and wants to call him Igor. Both men are tense with their own worries, their own anxieties; the air around them almost sizzles. Rizzato steps back, waiting while Stratton unlocks the door. Stratton speaks toward the room as he enters, "Come in, Bartolo, and we'll have a drink. We can go out on the deck and have a smoke. I bought some Cohibas. I understand they were Fidel Castro's favorites when he smoked, so if they're good enough for him they should do for us, don't you think?"

Rizzato enters the room three steps behind Stratton, removing a beavertail sap from his backpack as the man speaks. The sap has a flat profile as opposed to the cylindrical one of the blackjack. It is a leather-covered lead rod with a spring handle meant to stun or render an opponent unconscious. It doesn't break bones as easily as its cousin. He takes two quick steps toward Stratton striking him on the rear of the right thigh. It stings with the ferocity of a 220 volt electrical charge. Stratton drops to his knees. Before he can yell out from the pain, Rizzato cuffs him on the side of the head, knocking him to the floor. It looks like he's dead.

Rizzato is experienced enough with the deadly weapon to know that Stratton is merely unconscious. He will be coming to soon enough. Rizzato lifts the man and dumps him on the blue flowered couch. He stares at him for a few moments, feeling contempt. He pulls several plastic ties from his bag and straps Stratton's hands together, then ties them to his belt. Then he binds his feet. He scans the room for a gag spying one of Stratton's handkerchiefs on the foot of the rumpled bed. Balling it up Rizzato pries open the man's mouth and stuffs it in. Satisfied with his work, he looks around the room until he sees the bottle of Glenfarclas 25-year-old single malt scotch on the rosewood night table by the bed. It poses beside several glasses wrapped in tissue and a small cylinder with a spray nozzle stands beside them. Unwrapping one of the plastic drinking vessels, he fills it half full, not bothering with ice or water. He tosses back two inches of molten fluid, clenching his teeth at the liquor's delicious bite. He refills the glass, snatches the bottle up, finds the cigars in the drawer of the small night table and returns to the living area, where he sits on the big chair across from the incapacitated man.

Andrew Stratton, aka Jack Favors, opens his eyes to find light green walls spinning about him. His head and leg are burning with purple agony. He feels the soggy cloth in his mouth. He automatically tries to bring his hands to his face to remove the obstruction but even though he can bend his elbows the hands are tied to something, leaving him unable to grasp the cloth to take it away. He feels a wash of consternation overtake him. He has no idea where he is or why he is in this situation. The event only heightens the steady decay of his sanity.

The walls and ceiling are slowing but unfocused as his mind races to find an anchor. The watery film in his eyes and the foggy film in his brain start to clear. Just then Rizzato's ugly face hovers over him. He watches the man take a huge handgun and screw a silencer to the end of the barrel. He watches as Rizzato presses the cold steel tightly to his forehead and with his other hand brandishes a cell phone. Stratton's heart begins to pound with the fear of impending death. His only thoughts are of the termination of his revenge. He begins to sweat and a steady gripping pain forms in his chest. He tries to sit up but Rizzato presses the gun much harder, forcing him back.

"Okay Andy, here's how things are going to play. I'm going to remove the gag and we are going to talk. We're going to talk about a phone call that you guaranteed me. The good news I promised you is that everything you wanted for your fantasy of killing Muslims is in place. If you're a good boy, we will both leave here with our original plans intact. If anything varies from that path, I will kill you. If you understand me, blink your eyes a thousand times."

With that last comment Rizzato laughs out loud at his wit, places the phone on the coffee table and pulls the rag from Stratton's mouth. Stratton gasps with labored breaths and speaks with a hoarse whisper,

"Rizzato you rotten fuck, get that vaporizer from the dresser, the one by the liquor bottle and spray it under my tongue. I have angina and if you don't hurry, I could have a heart attack and you won't get a fucking thing."

Rizzato is perturbed at this change in the procedure he's formulated while watching Stratton. He hesitates for a moment until Stratton scrunches his face as agonizing pain enters his chest. Andrew squeezes out the words in a groan, "Hurry, it hurts so much."

Rizzato sweeps the gun away and races for the small bottle he had seen on the dresser. The cap is already off and he can see the nozzle and slanted finger indentation where he has to press. He swiftly brings it to the couch and points it at Andrew, not having a clue where it is supposed to go.

"Under my tongue, quick."

Stratton opens his mouth and lifts his tongue. Rizzato places the inhalant near Stratton's mouth and gives it a spurt. He backs off to see if it works.

The nitroglycerine soon opens the arteries and the pain slowly subsides. Both men wait; Stratton with his eyes closed and panting, Rizzato with eyes bugged out and hardly breathing. He's never witnessed anyone have a heart attack before. Stratton's breathing soon grows easier. Stratton mumbles, "Another hit. Same place; not quite so much"

Rizzato bends down offering Stratton another burst of relief. He is still speechless from the spectacle of near death. He wishes he didn't need the money, he would've enjoyed watching a heart attack victim die. Not trusting the man on the couch he wonders if it is all an act to catch him off guard, but he realizes that doesn't make any sense. He will keep a close eye on Stratton, nonetheless.

"If this is an act, Andy, you had better be careful. If you try anything weird, I'll end your useless life right now. I enjoy my freedom more than I'll enjoy your money."

"Yeah, sure Rizzato. You didn't have to do this; we could've talked. If you say everything is in place then I can deal with that. Now untie me so I can get up. I'd like to sit if you don't mind. My chest still hurts."

"I'll help you sit up, but remember the gun is loaded and the safety is off."

Holding the gun in his right hand, he reaches down and pulls Stratton upright. He picks up the cell phone from the end of the couch where he had thrown it.

"What's the number you need to call?"

Stratton looks at Rizzato with eyes that blaze. He doesn't like not being in control. He understands he is in a very awkward position with the crazy man pointing a gun at him. He knows Rizzato well enough to know that he will indeed kill him if he withholds the money at this point. It doesn't matter, he decides; he's done with his money one way or another. Where he is heading, he won't need much; maybe none at all.

"Get the notepad from my briefcase; it's on the floor on the other side of the bed."

"That's okay, I have one right here."

Rizzato pulls a scrap of paper and a pen from the backpack that roosts at his feet, never taking his eyes or the gun off Stratton. He bends down, one knee on the floor, and places the paper on the coffee table.

"Okay, what is the phone number, the password, the account number and bank?"

Stratton recites from memory, "The Bank Frey and Company, Bahnhofstrasse, Zurich, the phone number is 410442043300. The account number is 7762177. Ask for Mr. Zubreggin. How do I know that when I give you the password you won't kill me?"

"I thought about that to be truthful, Andrew, but I know how bad you want this and I'm looking forward to reading about you in the international news. Now what's the password?"

Stratton only pauses for a few seconds before replying, "BlueblaZes1960, the first b and the z are uppercase.

Rizzato packs the pen and paper in his bag, picks it up. Slowly backing towards the door, he says,

"Keep your mouth shut, give me ten minutes and I'll send someone to release you. You might want to make up a story as to why you are in this predicament or else the cops will be here with many questions. Hasta la Vista, baby!"

Rizzato leaves, shutting the door behind him. He strolls casually down the hallway, looking like a man on holidays. He slings his pack over his shoulder, the orange an ugly companion to his red golf shirt. He was a little concerned about staying in the same hotel as Stratton, but then he's conscious of the fact that Andrew would have no idea who Viet Canelosi is. He grins, feeling he'll be safe for two more days.

Arriving at his room he drops his bag on the floor. He disrobes as he struts across the living room, leaving a trail of clothes like a ten-year-old. He will take a shower first before using one of his disposable cell phones to call the front desk about Stratton. He'll pretend he's a brother-in-law or something of that nature and let the person he speaks to in on the joke they've played as a result of Mr. Favor's stag party. He hopes the sap at the front desk knows what a stag party is.

Fifteen minutes later Rizzato plops down on the couch that is the same color as Stratton's with the TV remote in one hand, a cell phone in the other. As he flips through the channels, he calls the front desk. After taking care of Stratton, he phones his pilot. The last time they had talked the man gave him a number to call at midnight in Madagascar, Mananara Avaratra to be exact, The call is actually forty minutes late. That's okay Rizzato thinks, Robert van Geest hardly ever sleeps. The two men talk for some time. Van Geest tells Rizzato that getting him back to Panama is no big deal so long as he has a week to ten days to kill. There are enough countries that the rogue pilot has contacts in where a little baksheesh will cause the customs people to overlook certain peculiarities. He tells Rizzato he will need ten thousand dollars and lots of patience and yes he can bring the damn birds.

Rizzato dons a purple silk robe; he looks like a fresh bruise. He settles on a rerun of *Three's Company* and then calls room service to order a cheese omelet, a pot of black coffee and a bottle of their best scotch.

Chapter 37   Oct 3 Noon   Bhola River Compound

Drake returned to the wharf area to help one of the Bangladeshis from the farm bandage up the miscreant with the bullet hole in his thigh, dressing the wound temporarily with makeshift bandages, placing him in the golf cart the man has arrived in. He also has the young man bandage his wounded arm. Drake had no need to bind the prisoner who is delirious. They also put Kovalenko's body in the back of the cart. This was all done with nods and hand gestures as neither speak the other's language, they wouldn't have been able to understand each other anyway. The Bangladeshi looks at Drake with sadness as if to ask if this is all necessary; the local man will only find out much later how he too could've been dead had Drake and his team not showed up. The man offers Drake a seat in the cart but Drake just shakes his head signaling that he wants to talk with the women.

Drake sees the girls huddled on the sampan, looking into the hold. They have been able to rid themselves of their bonds, he notices. He wants to find out about Rafan. Drake has the eeriest feeling that he won't like the answer. He is experiencing a moment of trepidation, certain that he has let Uday and Williston down again. When he had been a professional soldier leading other men, he had a difficult time dealing with the loss of any of his people, knowing full well that it happens. He clears his head; it never gets easy he thinks. He squeezes his fists together wishing Rizzato was in his grip.

He walks along the wharf until he is able to step into the sampan.

As he does so, he notices the Zodiac tied up at the end of the wharf. It waltzes to the music of the tide. The women are quiet as he approaches them. He studies the two briefly, guessing both are in their twenties. They differ not only in their race, but in that their eyes tell different stories. Earlier he had identified the iron in the Oriental woman's eyes; he had seen it before in professional soldiers, men and woman who deal in death. The softness is gone. The other one has pale blue eyes that seem to be undecided as to whether they are still innocent. He sees that the two women are of similar stature except for the toned musculature of the Caucasian. Other than the disarray of their garments, he has to admit, they are both very good looking women.

When he nears them he hears the Oriental woman say, "I think he's a woman."

The ladies are so intent on their own thoughts that they don't hear Drake approach. He says, "What makes you say that?"

The two women turn to face him. Rather than answering his question, Sophia steps forward and offers her hand and a gracious smile saying. "Thank you for saving us. I know mere words aren't enough but I mean it wholeheartedly. My name is Sophia Stratton."

While he shakes her hand, the other woman moves forward to offer her own delicate hand. "Yes, that goes for me, too. We would've been very bad off if you had not come along as you did. My name is Ume but I prefer Plum."

Drake bows slightly to her and says in near perfect Japanese, *"Ume wa, ryohono gengo de, hijo ni kereina namaedesu."* ("Ume is a very pretty name, in both languages.")

"*Anata wa hijo ni yoku nihongo o hanasu*" ("You speak Japanese very well"), she answers.

Drake switches to English. "My name is Drake, Drake Alexander. My girlfriend and I lived in Japan for thirteen months and languages are a hobby of mine, but I must admit I would be hard put to carry on a conversation."

Plum just nods her head. Both women wait for Drake to continue.

He drops his gaze toward the bulk in the hold saying, "What makes you think that monster is a woman. He looks like a very big, ugly man to me."

Plum replies as Sophia looks down in the hold again.

"There was something in the eyes once. I don't know how to explain it; it was just a feeling I had."

"You know him?" Drake says.

"Yes, unfortunately, and before you judge me I hope you will listen to what I have to say."

She doesn't wait for an answer but jumps into the hold. She walks over to the supine body, shooing flies that are gathering and feasting on the blood. She bends and places her hand on Bunker's crotch feeling the smoothness and cleft of the vagina. She looks up at Drake and Sophia saying, "I knew it." After a rueful silence, she continues, "She was truly a monster, but what are we going to do about her?"

"My team member's will be back soon and I expect that the police will be along shortly. For now the corpse should stay there."

Sophia breaks her silence. "What of your own men? Will they be alright?

"Gurupada, the Bangladeshi, will be fine. My friend Isaac, I don't know. It's a stomach wound. He's tough though and I believe, I want to believe, that he'll be okay. We'll just have to wait. Now why don't you two ladies accompany me back to the main building so we can check on things and perhaps you can explain what you know about what is going on. I also need to know if either you have heard of or seen a man named Rafan Bashara?"

Plum crawls up out of the hold to stand near Sophia. The women look at each other and their looks confirm Drake's earlier feeling. The silence is telling and Drake's voice is almost a hush when he asks, "Do you know where the body is?"

They both nod yes. Sophia has tears in her eyes and motions that she can't speak right now. Plum puts her arm around Sophia and says, "C'mon. Let's get out of here and I'll tell you what I know, Sophia can tell you her story afterwards."

Drake follows them onto the wharf toward the path that leads to the old farm house. They walk slowly, Drake and Sophia enraptured by Plum's tale. She explains how she had met Rizzato, how she became entangled in the world of crime with De Clerq, the arms dealer, through her former husband. She tells them of bringing the plane in from the Bengal Bay in pieces, of Kovalenko coming on board. She tells them about the men she has been working with: Morgan, Ahmedani, Hajani and Bunker, of the three thugs who had been brought on board recently, the ones his team had killed or captured that morning. She tells him about the workers, where they came from, what had been promised to them, their role in the building of the hangar. She tells them of Rizzato's evil.

Drake interjects here, admitting he's aware of the man's deceit, vilification and cruelty. He relates why he is involved, of Williston's sister and her friend, Sakeema, who was also Rafan's cousin. He shares the details of their unsuccessful hunt for Rizzato as well as what he knows of the latest batch of criminals, of his team's role in subduing them. He tells them about Rafan.

"If it had not been for Rafan, we would not have been able to pursue Rizzato here."

Drake feels a ton of pressure upon him. He knows that by now Uday will have gotten word of Rafan's sister and niece, the news of Rafan, too, will be a heavy burden. He says to the women, "Rafan's sister and niece were killed. The only fortunate thing is that their parents are both deceased, but their uncle Uday, Sakeema's father and a dear friend of mine and Williston's, will be crushed to lose more of his family to this evil man. But I still don't know why Rizzato was here. What was he doing?"

Sophia speaks for the first time. "It's because of my father, Andrew Stratton."

The three of them are walking past the orchard with the yard in sight when Drake halts at that comment. Sophia carries the shame of her father upon herself.

"He came to kill as many Muslims as he can. He wants revenge for the death of my brother and sister at the hands of the Martyrs Brigade last year. It drove him crazy. I couldn't believe what he was doing. At first I imagined it was only a temporary, impulsive reaction. But then he disappeared. I couldn't live with myself if I didn't try to stop him. I found a scrap of paper in his study with two names on it and I decided to pursue them. I was lucky to discover his trail but I still don't know what he intends to do or what has been going on here. I only know that my father abandoned me."

Sophia starts to cry, tears laden with sorrow. Both Drake and Plum have no words just then. Sophia wipes her eyes with the hem of her shirt and says, "Regardless of what happens or has happened, Mr. Alexander, you must do everything you can to help Plum. She saved me and Rafan from what she says could've been a horrific death. You must do all you can to help her."

Drake says, "I don't know what to say ladies. I know the police will be here soon."

He turns to Plum and asks, "How bad is it Plum? What things have you done?"

"I've done bad things Drake; I've hurt people, but only in self-defense. I've lived in other criminal's shadows, I've been a prostitute. I've never been arrested, and I don't know if I'm wanted anywhere. But I've never been as sorry as I have been in the last weeks. I need to straighten my life out. I just don't know how."

Drake stares at the woman, who looks directly in his eyes. He can read the truth. He feels something odd, a feeling his father had described years ago when they had talked of bringing the Piscontes to Canada, of saving the family from an uncertain future. He doesn't need to think about this.

"Okay Plum. I'll do what I can. When the police arrive you two won't be here. We'll talk more later, okay?"

Both women shake their heads, understanding, sensing the man's goodness.

"Now, let's get things under control here and then I want you to take me to Rafan."

Drake leaves the women beside the orchard to head towards the hangar. He finds twelve men, only one of whom can speak some English. The man shows him where they have put the dead thug Adzic inside the greenhouse, covered with a dirty tarp. The other two men had their wounds dressed and are softened by painkillers that has been part of a kit that Bunker had given the men to tend to any injuries they might've sustained while building the hangar and runway. One of the Bangladeshi has an inkling of first aid from his employment at the Breakers, where he had been assigned to tend to sick workers and help if accidents occurred. The rest of the men stand around not understanding what is going on, some are complaining, others are wondering about their future and of the money they had been promised. While not chaotic, the moment is one of confusion.

Drake does all he can to reassure the men that they will be returning to their homes and he personally will see to their compensation. He asks only that they comply with the police and have patience. Once the situation is stable, he tells the man that is translating for him to keep the men around while they wait for the authorities and that he and the women are going to retrieve the body of a dead friend. He crosses the yard to the women and the three return to the wharf. During the walk, he promises Plum he will help her and assures Sophia they will try to find her father.

At the river Drake hotwires the Zodiac to head downriver to where the girls said Rafan and two more bodies can be found. During the trip they see the chopper overhead, recognizing the black and yellow body. Drake removes his phone and calls Rae.

"What's the story, Rae?"

"Thankfully they are going to be okay. We were able to land in the hospital parking lot and they were both rushed into surgery. The doctor attending them did quick examinations and informed us that while the injuries are serious it was fortunate that they were quickly brought in. Isaac's wounds are critical but the doctor assured us he will recover. We're over the yard now and Elijah is going to set this bird down."

Rae pauses as the helicopter approaches the buildings.

"Inspector Ullah and one of his men are inbound with us. He has another team on the way by water. I've already spoken to Chowdhury and informed him of what went down. We're good here. The APB on Rizzato has been updated. What do you want us to do?"

Drake explains what he is doing and asks her and Elijah to wait for them, to help Ullah anyway they can. "Did you or Elijah mention the two women in the boat?"

"We didn't say anything about them specifically as it didn't seem pertinent to the questions we were being asked. We only mentioned that there were innocents involved. I had considered them as such. Was I correct?"

"Yes. Thanks, Rae. I'll explain it all later, but it's best not to say anything. I have more information on Stratton and he may yet lead us to Rizzato. This is not over. I'll see you in a couple of hours. If Ullah asks for me, tell him I went to retrieve Rafan's body."

Rae is very sad and upset about Rafan's demise. His dependency upon her of late makes the information much more difficult. She warily replies, "Okay."

Plum guides Drake to the Meghna, to where the water taxi had failed. They soon see what is left of it has floated close to shore. It has lost some buoyancy and is now laying on its side, with the bottom of the boat facing them as they approach. Drake guides the Zodiac around the battered shell and sees Rafan's torso. The head and shoulders are still in the water but he can see the bullet wound in the chest. The legs are tangled in the lower supports for the seats, the body scraping against the gunwale, the face obscured by the unclean river.

Drake toys with the accelerator, keeping the craft as steady as possible. Plum is at the rear of the Zodiac. Drake maneuvers it close enough for her to reach over and grab the wreckage. He slips the gear into neutral as Plum pulls them closer. As their boat gently nudges against the other, Drake shut off the engine, changing places with Sophia, who moves to the front. Drake says more to himself than his audience, "Poor bugger. He goes to a bar one night and two weeks later he's dead. It doesn't make any sense."

The women remain quiet; they have nothing to add. Drake bends toward the body to lift it by its shoulders so its head will come out of the water. As he does so he says to Sophia, "Can you grab his legs after I lift him so we can untangle his corpse? He's not going to look very nice, Sophia. Can you do this?"

"I'm a firefighter Drake. There is nothing sadder or more grotesque than a burnt body. I've seen several, so I doubt he will look much worse."

She moves beside Plum and waits for Drake to lift Rafan. They soon free the tangled body, easing it onto the floor of the Zodiac.

The face is fleshy, bluish, bloated and nibbled at. As he motors away, they scout the immediate area for any sign of the other two bodies. After fifteen minutes of searching, Drake heads back to the wharf.

The return trip consists of the revving of the engine, the sloshing of the water as it smacks against the hull, but not of any conversation. The sameness of the waterway and the land it cleaves is hypnotic, leaving the three to concentrate on their own mental dilemmas. The ladies thoughts are of their yesterdays and unsure tomorrows, both hoping that Drake will bring them salvation. They remain deep in thought until Drake approaches a bridge that crosses the Bhola River where he asks the women to disembark and wait for him.

While Drake is returning to the wharf he is thinking about Rafan, Amber, his men Dakin, Isaac and Gurupada. He is remorseful that such bad things happened. But his hunt for Rizzato has to continue. He can't let these incidents divert him from his goal. As he gets closer to the wharf, his ideas are shaping. He decides he will help Sophia find Stratton; find out what the man is up to. He could still lead them to Rizzato. He also wants to check out the plane Plum has told him about. And he knows he will help Plum; he'll get Williston working on it.

Inspector Ullah's people that had come by water had entered the Bhola River just as Drake had approached the battered taxi. Now when he nears the jetty, a police cruiser is tied up to the wharf beside the Sampan. He motors up to the opposite side of the wharf, shutting down the engine to let the Zodiac float. He neatly lassoes the post at the end of the wharf. He tugs at the rope hand over hand along the wharf, pulling the boat closer to shore. After he secures it, he climbs onto the planks. He can see Ullah, another man with one rubber-gloved hand in the air, and Rae in the hold of the Sampan. They stop and look up at Drake's approach. Ullah says something to Rae before she scampers up onto the wharf to meet Drake. She says in a low voice, "Where are the women?"

"I dropped them at a bridge not far from the mouth of the river. We can pick them up later. So what's Ullah saying?"

"He's not happy and he holds you responsible for Gurupada's injuries. He doesn't agree with "private investigators" doing what his people should be doing. One of those jurisdictional jealousies."

Drake rubs his chin, looking over at the men.

"I talked to Chowdhury. Gurupada was conscious and stable enough to talk to him briefly. We're all clear. The men we captured here are severe criminals, and he's looking good at Interpol. By the way, did you know that the man in the boat is not a man?"

"Yeah. Plum figured that out."

"Anyway, Ullah still wants to have a chat with you. What of Rafan?"

Drake turned toward the Zodiac, points and says, "He's in there, Rae."

She moves to go to the Zodiac to confirm it herself but Drake reaches out his arm and stops her.

"You don't want to see him, Rae, it's very unpleasant. Remember him from before. It'll be easier."

There is something to Drake's words that makes her pause. She doesn't want to believe that the man is gone; she wanted to see the body to be sure. She looks at Drake with stubborn eyes before she yields to his advice. Drake breaks the bond by saying, "It's best if Ullah's people take the body. I'll talk to Ullah before we head back to pick up the girls and sniff out Stratton's trail. I can probably use your help on that, Rae."

She grasps his upper arm. "I'll help anyway I can. I'll stay and help Ullah for a while and go in with them in their chopper. I'll get in touch with you later and Elijah can pick me up in Barisal. Sound okay?"

"Great. Thanks, Rae."

Drake joins the Inspector in the Sampan, Rae directly behind him. Handshakes are exchanged. Ullah's English is very limited but Rae is able to translate, confirming Gurupada's statement of events. The group move from the sampan as Ullah's men remove Bunker's body from the boat, taking three of them to lift her hefty bulk. Drake and Rae share what they know of the situation until Ullah is satisfied with what he hears. They agree that Rizzato could likely still be in Bangladesh as well as the man Stratton. The Inspector tells Drake he will post two men at this site for a few days. He is taking the wounded men back to Barisal and will advise Chowdhury of any pertinent information he might gather from them as well as results from his forensic team. The conversation ends with more handshakes.

Drake leaves Rae to walk back to the main buildings, where Elijah will be waiting by the helicopter. He wants to pick up the women and get back to Dhaka but first he wants to check the buildings. As he approaches the yard, he can see the group of local workers that are gathered in a circle around one of Ullah's men. Several are talking at once, gesturing with their hands. Drake expects they are dismayed by the sudden turn of events, looking to be paid one of their priorities. Drake has told Ullah of his decision to compensate the men. He knows that whatever their anguish is about, it is nothing compared to what their fates may have been. He avoids the group going directly to the large building that houses the airplane.

The buildings have been taped off with the universal yellow crime tape, all except the hangar. One of the large doors facing the yard is open. A portion of the bright red plane is visible. The building is crudely built, obviously meant only as a temporary structure. He enters through the open door, admiring the plane's lines. He doesn't recognize the make but can see that it's a crop duster from the spray nozzles lining the wings. It is a one-seater with a long nose. He rubs his hand along the fuselage, puzzled as to why it is here, as to what Stratton's and Rizzato's intentions were. Then he remembers the large tank on the wagon by the wharf. He hasn't paid much attention to it but he suspects that it has something to do with the men's plan. He will mention it to Ullah and Chowdhury.

The lighting is low, so he steps back and opens the other door, letting in the bright sunlight. Elijah joins him beside the plane.

"What do you think is going on here, Drake?"

"I'm not sure yet Elijah but there are a couple of ladies waiting for us not far from here that can perhaps shed more light on things. One of them told me the plane arrived in pieces and was assembled inside this hangar."

Drake turns to face his friend. "Do you remember when we talked about Andrew Stratton?"

"Yes"

"Well his daughter, oddly enough, is one of the women waiting for us. She told me that she had come here to try and stop him from some crazy vendetta. There's a large tank that was being unloaded at the wharf when we took down the criminals. I expect that and the fact that this aircraft is a crop duster is part of some diabolical scheme."

Drake looks around the workspace, noting that all the tools are neatly arranged in an open toolbox. The workbenches are cleared of debris.

"It looks like whatever was being done to the plane is finished. Everything seems to be put away and in order. No sign of any work in progress considering we disturbed the people here in early morning."

Elijah says, "I can't believe we got this close and Rizzato's not around. He has an uncanny ability to disappear. What's next?"

"I want you to take me back to Dhaka, but first we need to make a quick stop for two passengers. I have information that Stratton is in Dhaka, so it's possible Rizzato is hiding there, too. Later you will need to return to Barisal and pick up Rae. So let's go."

Elijah follows Drake back to the chopper. Several of the locals are inspecting the black and yellow bird. Drake goes over to the police officer, asking him to tell Inspector Ullah of the tank. He also asks the man to remind the workers of his offer to pay them. He gives the man an email address for Williston also informing him Williston would wire the funds directly to Inspector Ullah's office. The men can be put up in Barisal at his expense until they are paid. Any transportation required will be looked after as well.

Several minutes later, he climbs into the front passenger seat as Elijah prepares the helicopter. The men standing around the yard back off as the whirling rotors create dust eddies. It soon lifts off, heading out over the buildings. Drake tells Elijah to head south-southwest to the coordinates he has mapped on his GPS. The women should be waiting for him at the foot of a road bridge. He says, "There's a cluster of trees and an open field where we can do a quick set down to pick up the ladies."

"What's the story on these gals, Drake?"

"As I said, one of them is Sophia Stratton; the other is one of Rizzato's cohorts but something provoked her to try and save both Rafan and Ms. Stratton. I don't know all the details yet, Elijah. All I can tell you at this point is that for some odd reason I trust the woman. I can sense true remorse. I'm hoping she can help us find Rizzato. She's Japanese and her name is Plum."

He looks over at his pilot giving him a wink. "At another time, you'd be in for a treat; both are single and terrific looking to boot."

Elijah just grins at Drake's perpetual matchmaking and asks, "What of Rafan?"

Drake looks Elijah in the eyes and shakes his head in a negative gesture. Elijah is smart enough to know that Drake doesn't want to talk about it and says, "That's too bad. I liked the man. I can see a bridge. Is that the one? Should I to set down on the left or right?"

Drake is glad for the distraction taking his tormented thoughts away from Rafan. They are about 30 meters off the ground and can see the women at the end of the bridge by the side of the road.

"Go to your left. Can you see them?"

"Yeah, I can. I'll drop on the flat area close to the road."

Elijah pilots the chopper to the open field, setting it down as gently as a newborn. He cuts the acceleration to slow the rotors. The tall grass flattens in the wash of the turbulence. The women are running toward the craft along the slope of the roadway where it rises to meet the bridge deck. Drake reaches back and opens the rear passenger door of the four seater. Sophia is the first to reach them and climbs into the helicopter. She looks at Elijah and offers him a nod of thanks. Elijah is barely aware of Sophia as he has his eyes riveted on Plum. Her hair is no longer tied up; it flows about her head like a black ribbon. He gawks at her as her slender body glides through the long grass. She climbs into the copter as Sophia is buckling herself into the seat Elijah has replaced.

Plum steps onto the metal skid, grabbing the door for balance. As she looks into the cockpit she gazes into the pilot's eyes, which are locked on hers. Elijah softens his curious stare with the widest of smiles. It causes Plum to stop momentarily as she returns the warmth he projects with her own sensual grin. That moment of wonderment, the blossoming of awe, will be the first of many sweet moments they will share over the ensuing years.

Elijah remains speechless in Plum's presence as he listens to Drake question the women. He waits patiently as the three formulate a plan. All Elijah can think of during the entire trip back to Dhaka are Plum's dark, exotic eyes.

Chapter 38   Oct 3 5:45pm Dhaka

Drake, Elijah, Sophia and Plum had arrived in Dhaka forty minutes ago. They left the chopper at Honey Aviation, asking that it be serviced, fuelled and made ready for another flight later. As Drake speaks to Williston, Sophia sits in the living room of Drake's suite drying her hair. She has just come from the shower wrapped in an oversized terry-cloth robe with the Westin "W" emblazoned on the chest. They had stopped at Sophia's hotel to pick up her things, including her passport and identification. They had also stopped enroute to the hotel for new clothes for Plum as she had brought nothing with her. Plum had preceded Sophia to the delights of hot water and new clothing. She had accepted Elijah's invitation to have dinner with him and they are downstairs. Drake had watched her leave dressed in a white lace blouse over a lavender granny dress and sandals. He had commented to Sophia on the transformation of Plum's physical appearance as well as her demeanor when she had pirouetted about the living room in her new skirt. She had left the room in a blushing flurry.

Drake is sitting on a stool in the kitchenette. He has just finished telling Williston what they had found along the Bhola River and what has transpired since their last conversation. He is saying, "I don't know, Williston. We'd seen him on the premises only hours before we raided the site, but he wasn't anywhere to be found. I searched all the buildings. There was another house about a kilometer away, but it was empty. One of the bedrooms looked like it had been vacated only a short time before. There's a small grey truck that is missing, but he could be anywhere. I don't know how, but he always seems to sense our presence. It's like trying to track down a ghost."

Drake listens intently to his friend. He's scribbling on a note pad as he considers his friends words.

"Well I did find a feather. That could mean he has birds with him." A thought strikes him like a hammer

The feather! A memory from the camp in Venezuela arises deep from the recesses of his retentive mind. When he and his men had scoured the camp, there had been cages there, too, with the birds still in them. He had watched Elijah open the doors and set them all free. He remembered that there had been over a dozen, all vividly colored.

"Now that I think of it Williston, there were birds in Venezuela also. Obviously Rizzato has a thing for them. Listen my friend; I'm sending the feather to my sister at her office at the University of New Brunswick. Call her now and tell her its coming. Get her to identify it; maybe it can tell us something"

Drake gives Williston his sister's number.

"Right now we're going to search for Andrew Stratton or Jack Favors, as he calls himself. He might have other aliases. We don't know. Sophia, his daughter I told you about, is certain he's still here. She believes he's still bent on his act of vengeance. There was no evidence of him at the compound on the Bhola, but she knows he was staying in Dhaka. Plum said he returned with some of Rizzato's henchmen. Inspector Ullah's men have an ABP on him and promised to inform Chowdhury if they came upon him."

Drake is interrupted by Williston.

"Uhm... well Plum is another story Williston. I'll tell you later, but now that we are talking about her, I need you to get her new ID, a passport, a driver's license and anything else she'll need. And can you arrange a photographer to come take her photo and get the documents to us here as soon as you can.... Trust me on this, Williston."

Drake and Williston talk for another half hour, during which time Elijah and Plum return from the restaurant. Sophia has changed and joins them all in the kitchenette.

Drake is aware of the nine hour difference and finishes his conversation by saying,

"No, don't wake her up. I'll talk to her later. Tell her I love her and to take care of our baby. And you, too, Williston, take care of your family. Can you imagine, we're going to be dads? Unreal isn't it? Yeah you too, buddy. Later!"

He plunks the phone down on the counter to face the threesome staring at him.

"What's this about being a Dad?" Elijah asks.

Drake tells them about Beth and Isabella. He blushes at their good wishes and soon turns the conversation back to their mission. Sophia has a photo of her father and he is going to have copies made for Chowdhury and his men, and he'll fax one to Ullah in Barisal. Sophia suggested that they fax the photo to all the hotels her father might hold up in. She explains her father's irrational behavior, adding that she doubts he will relinquish his need for luxurious surroundings even as his madness eats away at him.

They all agree that will be the best way to start. Rae had called telling them that Ullah had more questions and she wanted to be picked up in the morning instead of tonight.

Drake shares his desire with Elijah to talk to Dakin. He knows that Rae had taken him to her apartment and had arranged for nurses to attend him round the clock. So he decides to call him before they all leave. Both Drake and Elijah take turns teasing and soothing their buddies' conscience. They tell him what they are doing, what has happened, and assure him that they will all be together soon. They tell him about Isaac. Buddy and soldier talk occupy the three men for fifteen minutes or so. Drake meets with the concierge and arranges to have an envelope with the feather in it sent overnight to Canada advising him that there is chartered aircraft waiting for the envelope. He emphasizes how important it is that the package be there within the next half hour. Returning to join the ladies in his hotel room, he plans his next steps.

The next morning, Elijah takes a taxi to Honey Aviation. Twenty minutes after he left Drake's phone rings. He recognizes the number. "What's up, Elijah?"

There is urgency in Elijah's voice when he speaks. "You're not going to believe this, Boss, but Honey asked me where I was headed and when I told her Bhola, she wanted to know what was going on down there. Turns out an American she's been ferrying around lately left about forty minutes ago heading to the same area. When I asked her who it was she told me his name is Jack Favors."

Drake hesitates for only a second. "Wait for us Elijah; we're coming too. See if you can find out exactly where he went. I'll bet its back to the compound. Won't he be in for a surprise?"

Chapter 39

Oct 4 7:22am. Aboard Chopper B9V37

Stratton ignores the pilot's chatter, mesmerized instead by the chatter of the rotors as he concentrates on his atrocious plans. His thoughts momentarily return to the night before, when Rizzato had knocked him unconscious, rendering him helpless upon the sofa. Having wrestled with his bonds after Rizzato left him; his mind had focused on his dark plot. His mental state made him claustrophobic, and he had tried not to panic, knowing the anxiety could lead to heart failure. Eventually a bellhop had entered his room to free him from his ties. While he did so, he laughed at the foolishness of men and their stunts. Andrew had remained silent as he rubbed his wrists where the bonds had dug into the soft skin. He weakly rose to his feet, removing his wallet as he did. He had placed a 1000 Taka note in the man's hand as he led him to the door.

Today, his wrists still have red marks where the plastic had chafed his skin and he unconsciously rubs them again as he watches the river speed past below. His contemplation returns to the task at hand. He will be back at the compound shortly, uncertain of what he is going to find. He wants to believe Rizzato's parting confirmation that everything is prepared. He cares nothing for the money he has handed over to the Italian as long as the plane is ready. He wants to have faith that his vengeful plotting is not in jeopardy. He had been warned in the beginning that Rizzato was only a tool. Amado had assured him that man's greed would keep him on track. All he cares about at this point is the safekeeping and reliability of the airplane, nothing else, not even the future. As he thinks about it, he realizes that he may not even have a future. He has no idea what he will do after he kills the people he thinks of as his enemies, his children's enemies, his family's enemies.

He asks the pilot how much longer it will be before they're at their destination.

The man flying the helicopter is a young Bangladeshi, his enthusiasm and smile as crisp as the Honey Aviation logo on his black short-sleeved shirt. He informs Stratton that they will be over the Bhola River in less than half an hour. The man checks the coordinates he has written on his clipboard, which sits between the two men on the cockpit floor. Their destination will only be another five minutes after they reach the river. He asks, "Where shall I set down, Mr. Favors?"

Stratton is demented but not stupid. He's not willing to rush straight into a situation he isn't sure of. He will have the pilot do a flyover first.

"When we arrive, I'd like to do a quick flyby before we set down. My men are building a runway and I would like to check on its progress from the air."

Silence prevails in the cabin for the next twenty minutes. A black and grey duffel bag rests at Stratton's feet. It contains his wallet, his notepad, a GPS unit, a disposable cell phone, mini binoculars and a Glock 17 semi-automatic. The handgun had been delivered to his room this afternoon. He had wanted the security of a firearm but hadn't wanted to go through the same process as he had in Panama. When he approached the concierge in his hotel the man had expressed shock and dismay that such a gentleman as Mr. Favors would come to him with such a request. Stratton had been extremely nervous in his attempt to seek some form of protection but did so knowing that everything and every man had a price. As the concierge was suggesting that the police would be suspect of such a petition, Andrew slipped an envelope onto the man's desk. The concierge picked it up slowly and opened the unsealed flap. The wad of green bills nested inside interrupted the man's dialogue. He had lowered the envelope to waist level out of sight of the front desk and rubbed his thumb along the edges of the bills. He counted twenty fifties. He had looked Stratton in the eyes and after ten seconds slipped the envelope into his jacket pocket. The gun had been delivered two hours later.

The chopper dips to 200 meters as it follows the curve of the river where the mouth of the Bhola yawns. The pilot says, "We are only a few minutes from the coordinates you have given me Mr. Favors. How shall I proceed?"

Stratton directs the man to where the Bhola River turns sharply to the right before heading on to the community of Bhola. He points out the concentration of buildings where Rizzato and his men had been assembling the plane. He points out the runway in the foreground saying,

"Go in low over that group of buildings; the runway is in the back.
"

He unzips the bag at his feet removing the small binoculars. As the helicopter approaches the farm he can see the sampan, the cruiser and Zodiac still tied to the wharf. The door to the metal shed is open, the forklift is idle, nothing moves. He's checking for any sign of people. He never notices the red tank that he had worked so hard to get to Bangladesh sitting, abandoned, on the road that leads to the farmhouse. Ullah's men had moved the tractor and wagon out of the way and it sat obscured by trees. The helicopter is moving slowly toward the buildings. Stratton has his eyes trained on the hangar when he notices the yellow tape cordoning the buildings. He curses to himself. He has no way of knowing what happened here yesterday, but he knows without a doubt that the police were involved. As his helicopter passes over the hangar, he witnesses two men walking from the rear of the runway. They are the only people he can see. He realizes he will have to be careful. He will have to find out what is going on without exposing himself. He becomes nervous, sweat beading on his forehead.

For a moment, he can't think straight. He is flustered and angry, scared and uncertain. Desperation is like a carving knife slicing off thin layers of lucidness. He is lost in the conundrum until the pilot repeats his request more loudly,

"Mr. Favors, Mr. Favors, where do I let you down?"

The pilot is shocked by the paleness of his passenger, the sweating brow. He can see the eyes blinking rapidly, watches one of the man's hands grip his chest while the other reaches into his duffel bag. Stratton removes his nitroglycerine from the bag and gives himself a shot under his tongue. He knows what is happening and his mind screams, "No, no, I can't have a heart attack now! I'm so close!"

He gasps for breath, forcing himself to remain calm. He directs the pilot by hand gestures to the house Rizzato and Bunker had been staying at. He has to get on the ground and get to the plane. He concentrates on flipping the switch in the aircraft that will release a ton of gas from the nozzles beneath the wings. He concentrates on the agonizing pain he will bring to his children's killers while trying to forget the pain that grips his broken, twisted heart.

"Are you okay, Mr. Favors? You don't look well," says the pilot as he guides the helicopter over the far tree line. Looking the man in the eyes he sees that they are glazed over. The man is ashen-skinned; air bubbles escape from the corner of his lips. It reminds the startled aviator of the occupants at the mental institution two streets from where he grew up. Suddenly Stratton sits up and begins pointing to a house to their starboard side.

"Over there," he says.

The pilot drops down toward the house, levelling off ten meters above the driveway. He hovers while waiting for instructions, not wanting to look at the man. Stratton is looking down at the dust that circles about, born from the wash of the rotors. He sees the front door swinging;, the house looks deserted and the whole scene adds to his melancholy. For only a second, the dusty swirls formed an image of his son, a mirage of filial failings. The illusion sparks his psyche; the troubled man regains control.

"Set me down in the yard, then leave."

Stratton gets ready, grabbing his bag, stuffing his canister and binoculars back in. The medication will give him some time. The soreness in his chest reminds him he has little of that left. He forces his mind to fight on; he wills his body to finish his task. Only then will he be satisfied. As the chopper touches down, the pilot decreases the acceleration to an acceptable level and Stratton jumps out. As soon as the pilot sees him step off the skids, he revs the strong engine and lifts away. Stratton bends under the wind stream, his bag in one hand as he trots towards the house. He can see one end of the yellow tape waving foolishly about the air, its opposite end anchored to the side wall. Crime tape. He'll have to be careful. He hopes the two men he had seen are the only ones around. He hasn't seen any other activity.

Entering the house, he remembers his conversations with Rizzato. *I won't miss him*, Stratton thinks, remembering how he had always disliked the man as well as the big goon he kept at his side. *I won't miss any of them.* That idea causes him to focus on the plane. He looks around as he stands in the hallway, ironically in the same spot Drake had stood yesterday. There is nothing here of any value to him. It's messier than usual, but he attributes that to the police having been there. He does a final sweep before opening his bag. He is holding only one handle and as he unzips the top, something heavy falls to the floor.

"Just what I was looking for, my steely friend."

He re-zips the bag as he bends down to pick up the gun. As his hand closes around the handle, a voice calls out in Bangladeshi, "Leave the gun on the floor and stand slowly."

Stratton doesn't need to understand what the person said; there is authority in the tone. He swears to himself for being so reckless. He remains absolutely still as the shock of the voice settles. But he doesn't let go of the gun.

One of the police officers that had been left behind paid close attention to the helicopter that flew overhead. It was similar to the one the Canadians had been in. When he saw it dip down to the other house, he told his partner the private investigators had returned and he was going to see what they wanted.

He had proceeded down the runway on the golf cart, leaving it at the edge of the wooded area that separated the two properties. As he came through the trees on foot, he saw Stratton jump from the helicopter. He saw him well enough to know he wasn't one of the people he'd seen yesterday and he was immediately suspicious. He had crept silently toward the house when the chopper lifted off. Moving slowly, he watched from the edge of the front door while the man opened the bag he is carrying, and he saw the gun hit the floor. Prahbat Mantasir has been a police officer for ten years; a pistol means trouble. When the man reached down to pick up the gun, Mantasir had drawn his weapon and called out.

Now he sees the man hesitate and not let go of the gun. He feels a brief moment of panic as he speaks no English. He rushes forward, meaning to kick the gun away from the man. The policeman yells out a flurry of words Stratton can't comprehend, but in Stratton's peripheral vision he sees the man coming toward him. He grips the gun, flips the barrel toward the oncoming officer and fires. The slug shatters the man's kneecap. He is thrown to the floor from the force of the blow, his gun flying into the living room. His painful yells stir Stratton, who grabs his bag and runs.

Out the front door, into the yard, around the small shed he rushes. Into the bushes at the back of the house he disappears, blending into the wooded area near the river. He runs until his heart starts complaining. He's thankful for the nitro he's injected earlier. He stops by a clump of jackfruit tress leaning against one of the bigger ones, trying to slow his breathing. He has to rest for a moment. Reaching inside his bag once more to retrieve his blaster, he gives himself another puff. He drops the bag to the forest floor, resting his palms on his knees. He decides to wait five minutes before trying to get to the plane. Remembering that he'd seen two men earlier, he worries about that also.

Sadhan Sengupta, the other police officer from Barisal, heard the gunshot. It came from the direction of the other farmhouse. He knew Prahbat had gone there and tries calling him on his radio. There is no response. He is about forty pounds heavier than any cop should be, slower than most. He breaks into a half-hearted trot, thankful he doesn't smoke. He arrives to the other house to find his partner in dire pain. At that very moment, Stratton is opening the hangar doors that faces the crude runway.

Drake is sitting in the cockpit with Elijah as the helicopter approaches the wide turns of the waterway below them. They are streaming across land, the mouth of the Bhola only minutes away. Sophia and Plum are sitting in the back. They have been quiet most of the trip. Sophia still hopes she can save her father. She is concentrating on what she will say to him, how to stop his terrible plans. She isn't listening to the conversation in the front or to the noise from their transport; instead she listens to her heartbeat, which suggests she try to use the love she has left for her father, for his tortured soul. It is the only weapon she possesses.

Drake is pointing toward the far horizon, punctuated with scattered clouds. A black dot comes out of the sunshine moving steadily away from them, heading west.

"There's his chopper. It's coming from the east, where the compound is. We don't know if he's still on the helicopter, but we'll check along the Bhola first. Crank this thing up, Elijah"

"It's already cranked up, Boss. Be patient."

Drake scowls at Elijah, but only until Elijah hits him with the Glass grin. He turns his head a bit and says, "I know we talked about it, Sophia, but can you remember anything about where your father might plan to strike. If he's already airborne, unless we make visual contact, we won't be able to find him."

Sophia is moved from her thoughts and responds, "No. I'm really sorry I can't be more help. I wish I could be."

Drake sees the remorse in her eyes and says, "That's okay, Sophia, we'll find him"

And then to Elijah, "As soon as we arrive, set us down in the front yard beside the orchard. Some of Inspector Ullah's men should be there. We'll check with them. We should be there in five."

Stratton has been considering his good luck at reaching the hangar undetected, not having encountered the second police officer. It is likely that the other man has gone in search of his friend if he heard the gunshot. After he rolled the large doors open, the sun streams into the building. Dust motes swirl through the air as the breeze enters to caress the bright red body of the aircraft. Stratton pauses for a few seconds admiring the polished surface, thankful that Kovalenko had taken such good care of the assembly and refit. Stratton is soon sitting in the Air Tractor going through the start-up procedures when he hears a helicopter approach. At first he thinks it will pass over the building, but then he hears the noise of the rotors remain constant. He urgently begins to flip switches, setting the choke and priming the engine. He doesn't have time to check if the tanks are full, instead he will have to count on Rizzato's word that everything is ready to go. There is no reason or time to believe otherwise.

The engine starts on the first attempt, giving off a healthy vibration. Stratton is anxious to get moving, not bothering to allow the engine to warm up. He knows he will have to be careful as he rolls the plane from the hangar. The doors, which are on heavy overhead rollers, move laterally when opened to provide a fifty-two foot exit. The wing span is forty eight feet. Once on the runway he'll stop, accelerate the engine to max speed and then be off. He feels a brief moment of glee, thinking he is finally going to be airborne to carry out his mission. As he gently moves the aircraft out the door, his mirth turns sour as he espies Sophia running around the edge of the hangar yelling for him to stop. He is flabbergasted; he'd forgotten all about her. His fevered mind sees her only as an obstacle, not as his only living child.

Sophia is only ten meters away. Stratton keeps the airplane moving until he is at the head of the runway. He needs just a few minutes to rev the plane to full power. He had removed the pistol from his bag earlier putting it in his jacket pocket. Slipping the gun out, he aims away from his daughter and fires several shots. Sophia stops suddenly as the bullets kick up dirt just to her left. She is stunned, glued to the spot by her father's crazed reaction. She is frightened and unsure. She assumes his madness is overwhelming him. He doesn't recognize her.

She yells out, "Stop this craziness Dad. It's me, Sophia. Come with me and we'll find the people that took Scott and Sarah away from us, all of us, you and me and Mom. Please Dad!" she begs.

Her father is impervious to her pleas. He cuts out most of her ranting by thrusting the accelerator to fuller power. All he recognizes are the words Scott and Sarah, sparks that inflame him to action. He releases the brake, giving the aircraft its head. Sophia is dispirited, but only for a moment. She gathers her inner strength, the Stratton grit she demonstrated at work, and runs toward the plane. Its bright red nose is pointed down the runway and with a burst of power it starts to roll. As the plane begins to move Sophia steps up onto one of the three struts that hold the spray line in place, grabs the door handle and pulls it open.

The thrust of the plane puts her off balance and she reaches in for the first handhold she can see, her father's seat belt. She is yelling over the engine noise for him to stop. All of her weight pulls Stratton back in the seat, disrupting his concentration; the plane weaves to the right. He quickly compensates the direction and elbows Sophia in the chest. The jerk of the plane combined with the force of her father's blow causes her to lose her grasp on the seat belt. She falls face first onto the wing. The door of the cockpit slams shut. The airplane is picking up speed and there is nothing for Sophia to hold on to. She starts to slide off the wing. As she does, she sees the struts that sweep back from the wing to hold the spray line. She lets herself slide onto two of them, one at her chest and the other just at her knees. Only the pipe that carries the fluid to the nozzles keeps her from falling off. She grips tightly to the strut, realizing she is in a precarious and deadly position.

Drake has come around the corner of the hangar just as Sophia falls onto the wing. He gasps as he sees her sliding off the wing. The plane is moving fast enough that the third wheel, in the back, comes clear of the ground. He sees Sophia come to rest on the struts below the wing. Drake experiences a second of relief even as he realizes what he has to do. He hastens back to the helicopter.

Stratton is a seasoned flyer but not the most skilled. The plane's contrary ways coupled with the unwelcomed intrusion of his daughter requires all his concentration. He disregards the extra weight upon his wing, watching the trees at the end of the runway fast approaching. He's hoping he'll be moving fast enough to get the plane off the ground by the time he reaches them. He keeps stealing glances at the toggle switch that will release the gas. In his imagination, it is the most brilliant, largest button on the dash. He can flip it without having to look for it. He reads the speedometer, smirks and pulls back the yoke. The plane leaves the graveled surface, lifting ungracefully into the sky.

The force of the oncoming air is trying to tear Sophia from her perch. She has wrapped one of her legs around the one inch pipe at the end of the strut. The thin metal struts are digging in to her shins and just above her breasts. She has a perilous grip on the strut. She doesn't know if the struts will be able to support her full weight for long but she's okay for now. She will have to get up on the wing if she is to save herself and stop her father; unfortunately there is nothing she can see to grab on to.

The plane veers northwest as Stratton turns toward Dhaka. The helicopter rises over the hangar. The black and Plexiglas chopper gives chase. Elijah points the nose toward the rising plane, accelerating to catch up. The R44 is not quite as fast as the Air Tractor but Stratton cruises low to the ground and not at full speed. Drake is at the back door, watching the squirming body on the strut, knowing they will soon overtake the small plane. He uncoils the rope he had brought, putting one end around a U-bolt connected to the floor, tying it quickly and securely. He straps on a safety harness used for rappelling. He slips the ten meter length of rope through the silver brake attached to the harness with a locking carbineer. Plum stays out of the way, speechless

"Get me about ten feet over the wing, where I can reach Sophia. Once I have her secured, you'll have to set us down before we can pursue Stratton and try to force him down."

Elijah gives Drake a wave of acknowledgment, keeping his eyes on the fleeing craft. He is only about 300 meters away and 20 meters or so above the plane. He follows it until it levels off over the tree line. He approaches the shaky plane until he is directly above it. He has to watch closely in case Stratton tries to gain altitude while keeping Drake over the wing. His hands and feet work as one to match the speed and direction of the plane below him. Drake opens the rear door. A blast of wind slams it against the chopper body, holding it tightly out of the way. He throws the loose end of the rope out and it falls, uncoiling like an overburdened spring. It straightens and sways in the turbulence. It dangles three meters away from Sophia and two meters too far to the right. Drake steps out onto the skid with his back to the air. He hollers out directions to Elijah. The helicopter moves into position and Drake drops into the void. He lets the rope slide freely but under control as it slithers through the brake. He drops ten meters in two seconds before stopping just above and behind Sophia. He can see her clearly as she stares at him with huge eyes. He speaks directly to Elijah through his headset, guiding him closer. As soon as he is near enough he ties off the brake with one hand. As he reaches out to grab Sophia, the plane suddenly dips as it comes over the Meghna River.

Stratton had been watching the rescue attempt but thinks Drake is trying to board the aircraft. His determination is so acute, he's already forgotten about Sophia. When the river came into view, his original plan to follow the course of the waterway until he reached Sadarghat overtakes any other thought. He drops the plane to fifty meters, urging its powerful engine onward. His tenseness is evident in the way he grips the yoke, sitting forward, keeping it close to his body.

Drake prompts Elijah to follow. Soon he is in a similar position, but this time Sophia is more alert. She has one arm outstretched toward Drake as Elijah skilfully closes the gap. As soon as they connect, Drake's strong arm reaches out for Sophia. Their hands clasp tightly about each other's wrist. When Drake's firm fingers set into her skin, she lets go of the strut and falls toward the ground. In the few seconds of free-fall, she tightens her hand, reaches up with her other one and clings to her rescuer, both scared and relieved. Drake alerts Elijah of his success and soon feels the sway of the helicopter as it moves away from the plane. He looks around the mighty river for the closest shore. He sees flat land to his left just as he feels the chopper head that way. He looks down into Sophia's grateful eyes. He can sense a variety of emotions. He calls out, "We can still catch him, Sophia. Just hang on a few more minutes."

She nods her understanding but there is little hope in her look.

Stratton is aware of the sudden absence of the extra weight as Sophia drops from the plane. He watches them move away feeling triumphant in some odd way. He turns his thoughts forward, paying attention to his flight. He never looks back. A feeling of freedom fills him, thinking himself finally clear. He looks again at the toggle switch, experiencing calmness. He flies on as images of Scott and Sarah flash in his mind, alternating with pictures of screaming Muslims as the gas showers them from the sky.

Elijah hovers over the edge of the river as he settles the chopper closer to the ground. The swaying bodies below swing lightly as he keeps the machine steady. Sophia's feet soon touch solid ground. She releases her handhold as she stares up at Drake. She feels the relief she can see in his eyes. Soon he is standing beside her. Releasing the rope from his harness, the two step away briefly as the helicopter moves aside to settle lightly in the field at the water's edge. The struts are only touching the long grass when Plum begins pulling in the loose rope. Drake and Sophia rush to the chopper to climb aboard. As soon as the doors slam shut, Drake instructs Elijah to follow Stratton.

Fifteen minutes later, the helicopter come into view above Stratton, ripping his peacefulness to shreds. He swears at them, waving one fist in the air. It's an ineffectual gesture and he soon stops, realizing how foolish he is. He watches the helicopter slow and descend until it was a huge blemish in the air just above him. He veers left then right, but the helicopter pilot matches his every move, sticking with him as if they are attached. He pulls his pistol from his pocket and begins shooting at the helicopter through the roof of his plane. The three slugs that are in the magazine tear through the flimsy skin. One of them flies unimpeded through the atmosphere but two find the body of the helicopter. Both ram into the engine, going completely through the cast aluminum alloy head. One lodges itself in a combustion chamber exploding one of the pistons upon impact; the other breaks the rocker-shaft bearing support of the engine.

The helicopter falters as it struggles to keep going on its other pistons but pieces from the shattered chamber rip the engine's guts out. Elijah reacts with adroit urgency, moving the helicopter as close to shore and as low as possible before it goes down. Fifteen meters above the waterline, the engine fails completely and the chopper plummets to the river with a gigantic, heaving splash. It rolls sideways, its rotors beating the water until they shatter. The momentum of the rotors causes the chopper to stay above water long enough for its occupants to free themselves and jump into the river. As the helicopter slowly overturns, the foursome swim the 100 meters to shore. By the time they reach dry land, Stratton's red aircraft is disappearing around one of the river's many curves.

Stratton saw the helicopter swerve away as he shot his last three bullets. He turned around to look and saw it plunge into the river. He laughs in gruesome chortles. He's feeling victorious but realizes he still has an hour before he can release his deadly potion. He relaxes, breathing deeply to control his errant heart. He knows his mission will soon be over and then he will escape until he can land or there is no fuel left for him to fly any further. He hopes to live long enough to read about the horror he is delivering. With a satisfied sigh, he settles into the long flight.

It is late morning when Stratton reaches the edges of the mighty river port of Sadarghat. He guesses he is about five minutes away from the main concentration of people where the ferries usually tie up. He lifts the plane until he is at the right altitude for his plans. He wants to spray the largest swath possible with each pass without being so high that the gas will be diluted by the polluted air. He keeps one finger on the toggle switch; the tip itches to flip it up. "Not now," he says out loud. "Wait," he says over and over.

Soon the river is filled with ships and boats, large and small. People swarm the riverbanks, working, living, and breathing. He speaks out, "Enjoy your final minutes you murdering bastards. This is for Scott and Sarah."

He pauses for just a brief moment before flipping the switch. He wants to experience the deep satisfaction of finally being able to pull the trigger, so to speak. None of the preparation, neither the trouble nor the planning has prepared him for this very second. There is no sense of right or wrong, no concern over whether the people below him are innocent or not. There is only the intense pleasure of knowing that somebody will pay for taking his children away. His smile is malicious and ugly as he toggles the switch.

Nothing happens. Stratton is stunned. He flips the switch again and again as he curses. He swears at the mechanic, at Rizzato, as if it is all their fault. He has no inkling of how Drake and his men have saved the innocent souls below him. Their raid came just as the methyl isocyanate was to be loaded into the plane. Stratton flicks the switch back and forth in disbelief until his finger hurts.

The startling realization that it isn't going to work crushes him. He screams in anguish. He begins to sob with heaving breaths and his heart starts to beat rapidly. The anxiety he is experiencing closes off his plaque-filled arteries. An intolerable pain storms his upper body. Letting go of the yoke with one hand, he paws at his chest. Using his other hand, he reaches into his pocket to grasp the two gold rings he always carries with him. He squeezes them until the sharp edges cut into his skin. His vision blurs as the aircraft dives toward the water unhindered by control. He knows it is over and he holds the rings even tighter as the plane smashes into a group of small boats close to the shore, killing three local men and one woman as well as himself.

Chapter 40

11:06am   Somewhere on the Meghna River

Elijah is the last to come to shore. While climbing up along the muddy bank he can see Drake and the two women beside a roadway that cuts through a small village several kilometers to their left, heading through flat fields to the right. A group of children are running towards them with a few adults walking behind. The downing of a helicopter is probably not a usual occurrence here, he imagines. Excitement will be reaching an all-time high along the riverbank. He turns his gaze back at the helicopter. Where it crashed, the water is only about two meters deep and the chopper is lying on its side. Half of it is submerged. The only things visible are part of the Plexiglas bubble, one skid and a yellow bee. One rotor sticks up in the air, bent and twisted – the only one that hasn't broken off. Elijah stares at it, wondering if there was any way he could have saved it. He shrugs and turns toward the trio watching him from the road. As he approaches them he says, "That was close, eh, Boss?"

Drake is brushing wet hair out of his eyes and says, "Thanks to your great skills Elijah. We could've been a lot worse off. We're in a remote part of the country, so I don't really know how well off we are. As soon as I can get to a phone that's not wet we have to get a hold of Chowdhury."

He turns his attention to the women, who are wearing T-shirts; both are damp, showing off their svelte figures. They had also been wearing khaki vests similar to those used by fisherman, with numerous snap pockets. They hang from a stunted shrub, drying off. Plum is crouched down on one of the wide flat rocks that line the edge of the road, pouring water from one of her boots. Sophia is seated on another, her feet in the shallow ditch, head in her hands and elbows on her knees. She is staring at a point far off across the river, nothing in focus. She feels she might never see her father again, but there are no more tears, only a terrific sorrow.

Drake sits on the river bank close to the women.

"How are you ladies doing, still shaken?"

Plum nods her head at Drake, still a tad shook up from the scare she got as the chopper plunged into the water, "I'm glad I decided to change before we left, can you imagine me in a lace top and long skirt now?"

The men just grin at her humor and Elijah says, "I love to imagine you in a wet skirt." Plum blushes at the compliment while pouring water from her other boot.

Sophia straightens up saying, "I'm tired of going swimming with my clothes on.``

 Plum is shaking her head in agreement as Sophia continues, ``When I get back to Chicago, I never want to fly again either, I can tell you. But what will we do about my father, Drake?"

"We'll have to let Chowdhury deal with it, Sophia. We've done all we can. I'm going to look after that right now so you wait here. I can speak a little of the local language, at least enough to get to a phone, I hope. I'll be right back."

With that he rises to his feet and brushes the mud from the seat of his jeans as he starts toward the village the people are approaching from. He ignores the excited and inquisitive children as he meets them and continues on until he can speak to one of the elderly men behind them. After a few words and a few chuckles from the man at Drake's attempt to speak Bengali, the grey haired man understands the hand sign for a phone. He points back to a long aerial rising from the roofs in the center of the village. Drake thanks the man before hastening into the community. "Dahn no bhad"

Entering the cluster of buildings along the river street, he sees that most are lean-tos, made from salvaged metal and wood. Some are painted but most are silvered from the burdensome sun. It is obviously a fishing village Drake realizes with the many boats floating near or pulled up on the shore. He keeps going toward the aerial several streets away from the river. Children playing stop to stare, other bystanders chatter while pointing. He soon arrives at the building that the aerial is attached to and discovers that the better built structure is a school and a post office, and a general store, too. He finds the person in charge, a tall slender man with a greying moustache and a hundred wrinkles, who is conveniently also the ham operator. The man's English is passable, understanding Drake's inquiries. He had seen the helicopter come down and expresses concern. Once Drake confirmed that everyone is okay, he has the man patch him through to Inspector Chowdhury's office in Dhaka. The gentleman excuses himself, leaving Drake to his conversation. It has been almost an hour and a half since they ditched the helicopter.

Minutes later, after Drake had describes the plane, Chowdhury is not surprised. Drake hesitates before saying, in a voice filled with disbelief, "Are you sure it's him?"

"Drake, come now, how many bright red crop dusters fly the rivers to Dhaka? It has to be. I can see the carnage now on my monitor. I'm getting photographs directly from Sadarghat. There are other casualties, it's very messy. I must say, Drake, I am glad this is over. I expect, and to be truthful I hope that your man Rizzato is long gone. I have men looking for him, but I think from what we know of him, he's running to wherever he hides. You should perhaps take your people and move on now."

"Well, Inspector, I'm hoping to look around a little, see if I can find a trail."

"You know Drake, it was because of my utmost respect for Mireille and her deceased husband that I let you have free rein here, but now it's time to let us handle it. I will give you until tomorrow at noon, almost twenty four hours, to pick up another trail."

There is a silence between the two men. Drake knows the man is right. Rizzato is gone; he should leave and meet Williston. He has a brief stirring as he thought of seeing Beth again, pregnant with his child.

"I appreciate all that you've done for me. I intend to see Gurupada before I leave. He's a good, brave man and it's been an honor to work with him. So, farewell then, Inspector Chowdhury, and thank you again."

"Before you go, Drake, let me mention that it wasn't just because Rae vouched for you that I came to trust you. You are a good man, brave as well. I warn you though, don't let this nemesis you face become an obsession until you deem yourself above the law. You will never be. Find him? Yes! After that, you can always call on me, anytime, from anywhere. You understand?"

"Yes I do, Inspector. Now, could you have Honey send another chopper to those coordinates I gave you earlier? But don't tell her about our bird yet, just that there's been a malfunction. I'll explain when I get back."

"Humph, your dead duck you mean!" Chowdhury grunts into the phone, "You are a rascal aren't you. Goodbye!"

Drake puts the receiver back in its holder, his mind drifting. He wants to tell Sophia in the most sensitive way he can. She's going to be upset and feeling guilty most likely he thinks. He feels sorry for her, on top of everything she's been through, to have her father turn his back on her. He remembers how wonderful his own father had been when a thought strikes him, *how would his Dad have reacted if his two children had been taken away from him by an unknown murderer?* He's uncertain how to answer that but he knows his father would want revenge also, but not this way and heads back to the chopper.

In the solace of the walk back to join his compatriots, he tosses thoughts and ideas around in his head. Where to go from here: talk to Williston, tell Sophia of her father, get Isaac and Dakin back home, find Rizzato, Glory and the feather... Each issue weighs heavily on him, but as he gets closer to the small group, he decides that Sophia is the first item he has to deal with and the rest will fall in line.

He sees Elijah along the shore, pointing at the helicopter, with a group of kids surrounding him. Likely he will be regaling them with anecdotes even though they probably can't understand him; Elijah enjoys young people. The men he had passed and spoken with are in another knot by the water, seemingly all talking at once, pointing and gesturing toward the downed craft. The two women are by themselves, standing on the side of the dirt roadway. Sophia moves behind Plum to help her tie back her hair. She looks up to see Drake as he approaches them. She slips some kind of loop around Plum's ponytail and starts walking toward him.

They join each other in silence, the one hundred meters seems like a long empty corridor. Sophia stops a short distance from Drake and says, ``Well?``

"Your father's plane crashed a short while ago in Dhaka at the river port they call Sadarghat. The authorities are on site now. It's a real mess, Sophia. Chowdhury said there was no way he could have survived. I'm sorry."

Sophia doesn't respond but continues to look Drake in the eyes as hers start to moisten. She knew deep within that this would happen. Her feelings of loss are even more profound than when her siblings had died, and yet there is nothing she can say. There is nothing Drake can say either. He watches her for a moment as she deals with the dire news until finally she hangs her head. He hesitates for a moment, realizing how terribly alone she must feel at this moment. He takes the two steps that separate them and holds her in his arms. At first she stiffens but soon she melds into his embrace, thankful for the support. She shakes with sobs. As he comforts her, he sees that Elijah has joined Plum watching him. Shortly Sophia breaks away from Drake and says, "Thank you. I'd like to be alone for a while. I'm just going for a walk."

She drifts down to the shore, heading toward the village. She doesn't go far until she reaches an overturned boat that is rotting. She perches herself on the edge closest to the water to stare out at the river. Drake heads back to tell Elijah and Plum what he has found out.

For the next hour, they discuss what they will do when the chopper picks them up. Drake asks Elijah if he could arrange for Isaac and Dakin to get home. He tells them that after he speaks to Williston, he will head back to wherever Williston might be. The hunt for Rizzato isn't over, he informs them, just temporarily stalled. Plum has been standing next to Elijah, holding his hand but not listening to them; her mind is on her new friend and how alone she must feel. It brings back distant memories of when she was young and her mother had died, leaving her alone. She leaves the two men to join Sophia, where they remain until the helicopter arrives.

Three hours later they are back at Honey Aviation, having gone to Barisal to pick up Rae first. They had dropped in to see Gurupada, who was recovering nicely, feeling well enough to be teasing the nurses when they joined him. They found Isaac alert and getting antsy. He explains to his brother that he has been in touch with his wife, Dia, and that she will be joining him as soon as she can get here. She will be looking after the details of getting him back home.

Rae has a friend waiting for her when they arrive and leave as soon as they touch down. She explains to Drake how things had gone down with Ullah on the flight back. She leaves to join Dakin back at her apartment. When Drake reminds her that they can help her get Dakin back home, she tells him not to bother, she has everything already arranged, they shouldn't worry about it.

Drake goes to the office to inform Honey of what has transpired, of how he will look after the downed aircraft. Plum, Sophia and Elijah go to the Land Rover Drake had left in the parking lot, a mini furnace sitting in the sun. Elijah opens the doors and rolls down the windows, letting the interior cool off. The three retreat to the shade of one of the open doors of the large hangar. Sophia is thinking of the arrangements she should be making. She has decided she will wait until she returns to tell her mother. She will ask Drake to introduce her to the people who can help her find out if her father's remains were recovered, so she can return them to Chicago. She knows that however much time and money it requires, she is prepared to give him a final resting place close to home.

Elijah and Plum are discussing her future.

"Do you still want me to go with you, Isaac?"

"Plum, from the minute I saw you, I knew that I wanted you to be part of my future. I'll do all I can to help you. And there's Drake and Williston too, I know they want to help. Would you like that?"

Plum reaches up, putting her arms around Isaac saying, "Yes Elijah, for as long as you'll have me."

She kisses him with a contained passion that almost embarrasses Sophia, but she's happy for Plum. She had broken up with her boyfriend, Aaron, several months ago when she had told him she wanted to go after her father. He had been worried; concerned for her safety and she had refused his offer of assistance, explaining that this was something she needed to do on her own. He had misunderstood, thinking he personally was being rejected, and had stormed from her apartment in anger. When she returns she will need him more than ever, she realizes. She hopes she can make it up to him.

The three of them are brought back to the present when they see Drake coming out of the office with Honey. They are obviously saying goodbye when, much to Drake's chagrin, Honey wraps her thick arms around him before sending him off with a pat on the ass.

Elijah laughs and says, "I don't remember seeing Drake blush before, but I can see him change colors from here."

Drake heads toward the Land Rover, waving at them to join him. When they come closer he can see the grins on their faces and says, "I know what you're all laughing at. Let's get back to the hotel. Elijah, you'll be free to make your way back home. Plum, your papers should be at the hotel when we get there. You'll need a current photo, but Williston will have probably sent instructions regarding that."

Soon Drake is alone in his room. He had handed Plum the package that had been waiting for him with her new identity. She and Elijah had left to follow Williston's instructions. Sophia has cleaned up, changed and taken a taxi to Chowdhury's office. Drake takes a quick shower to get the stickiness from the river off his body and changes into more casual clothing. He grabs a beer from the refrigerator, the phone from the kitchen counter, and a rare cigarette from his pack before going out on the deck to sit in one of the patio chairs. He sets his beer on the small wicker table and dials his friend. As the phone buzzes, he lights his smoke. Williston answers on the third ring.

"Williston, it's me. Whoa, slow down friend, what are you so excited about?"

He puts his feet up on the table next to his beer and inhales a puff as he listens to Williston.

"Yes, I am smoking. Mind your business and don't tell Beth. Now what were you saying about Glory? Did she get the feather?"

Williston is speaking rapidly, and so loudly that Drake has to move the phone away from his ear, the words spilling out of the earpiece. "Yes, she got it early this morning. We've had a real stroke of luck, at least I hope so. Do you remember how the trail on Rizzato always seemed to go cold in Central America?" He doesn't wait for an answer and continues, "Well Glory phoned me this afternoon. I told her I'd try to get a hold of you, which I've been doing with no luck. Where's your phone by the way?"

"Oh, it got a little wet but I'll tell you about that some other time. Go on."

"Well she identified the feather. The feather is from a very rare species only found in one location in the world, Panama."

Drake straightens up in his seat, removing his feet from the table. Nothing has ever led them to Panama before. After Amsterdam they had tracked him to Nicaragua through an arms deal, a trail that had turned sour on them when they lost his scent in Managua. Panama now makes sense.

"Panama has lots of places he could get lost. Where do we start?"

"I can't explain it as well as Glory. She's waiting for a conference call from us, so hang on and I'll get her in on the conversation."

Drake butts his cigarette in his empty beer can and listens to the silence. Soon his sister is talking.

"Hello, big brother."

"Hi Glory, it's sure good to talk to you. Forgive my rudeness, but what can you tell me about the feather?"

"I know how important this is so I worked all day on it. Believe me there are over ten thousand species of birds and if you think about the proverbial needle in the haystack, you'll get an idea what I was going through. I actually have Williston to thank for leading me to Central America. The Society of Canadian Ornithologists directory lists members' specialties. So I checked for anyone with knowledge on Central America and I got lucky."

There's a pause as she moved the phone from one ear to the other, causing Drake and Williston to ask simultaneously, "Well?"

"Hang on while I get my notes."

"Okay, now, the list had a Dr. Cornelius Branscombe, who is a full professor of Wildlife Biology and the Director of Avian Science at the Macdonald campus of McGill University in Montreal. I was able to reach him and explain the situation. I emailed him a photo and all the data I had gathered on the feather and guess what?"

Drake said, "Don't make us guess"

"Oh, be patient, Drake, because this is good. He was able to identify it in mere minutes. He said it definitely comes from Panama."

"How can he be so certain?"

"Because he discovered it"

"He discovered it? How could that be?"

"Well he spent sixteen months in Panama living among the Embera Indians, cataloguing birds as part of a grant he received from National Geographic. There are several species he is credited with and had the honor of naming them. This one is of the *Passeriformes* order, *Motacillidae* family. It's called *antus cornellia*, or more familiarly the blue pipit. While not as rare as the Maria Vega, they are indeed scarce. Isn't that neat?"

Drake says, "That's terrific, Glory, but was he more specific about their location?"

"Yes, they live in a rain forest in the Darien Gap."

"The Darien Gap?" asks Drake. Williston interrupts, "Thanks, Glory. Now listen, Drake, Dr. Branscombe has agreed to meet with you tomorrow. He is leaving in the morning for a conference in Liverpool and will be arriving around 3 p.m. their time. He said if you can get there, he will have all the pertinent information and maps for you. He can only give you a short time as the conference starts at 6 p.m. and he's one of the guest speakers. I have a jet waiting for you at the airport in Dhaka. This is it Drake, I can feel it. We'll catch that bastard this time, you and me."

"You and me?"

"Yes, as soon as Glory told me Panama, I told Bill to head for the Panama Canal under full steam. We'll be in Panama City three days from now, on Thursday. Go see Branscombe, do whatever else you need to do, and get to Panama City. Get back to me where I can find you in the city. By the time we meet up, everything will be in place to get us to the Gap."

"Where are Beth and Isabella?"

"I sent them home from Havana when I found out we were going after Rizzato. Don't worry, everybody is fine. They didn't want to go, but when I reminded them of their condition, well they were a bit more compliant. Your girlfriend has been walking on clouds by the way, very excited."

"To be honest, I am, too, Williston"

Glory interrupts the conversation, "What do mean by 'their condition'?"

"Good news, Sis, Williston and I are going to be dads in the New Year. Anyway, thanks Glory, you did great work. I'm looking forward to seeing you when this is over. We'll all get together soon."

"Congratulations, you guys, that's wonderful. I'm going to hold you to that promise, Drake. And please, you two, be very careful. I love you both. Bye."

The connection is broken and Williston says, "Sweet gal. Okay, Drake, I've got a ton of work to do so let's get on with it. I'll see you in Panama. Oh, and don't bother bringing any weapons. I'll have all the firepower we'll need in case Rizzato doesn't give up easy."

Drake is quick to pick up the sarcasm in Williston's statement.

"He's not the type to give up, Williston."

"I know. Aren't we lucky?"

Chapter 41

Oct 9 7:23pm   Sambu River, Panama

It has been raining since Rizzato arrived in Panama City yesterday just before noon, two days earlier than his pilot had foreseen. His jubilant mood upon arriving, with a briefcase full of money, his beloved birds and his travelled backpack, is slowly deteriorating. Tonight the sky is filled with continuous grey clouds that spilled their contents in unrelenting heavy drops. He's soaked to the skin even though he wears a hooded khaki poncho. This month is the worst of the rainy season but he isn't prepared for the excessive moisture; it isn't that that bothers him the most. It's the crocodile that follows fifty feet behind his dugout. It's one of the few things that Rizzato is deathly afraid of.

He slows the small engine that powers his dugout, not recognizing this part of the river. He idles against the sluggish flow of the water, looking for something familiar. Five minutes ago when he had looked back at his wake, off to his left he'd seen the reptilian slitted eyes just above the water, the nostrils round and wet preceding them. A little farther back were the ripples from the spines on his hide. What frightens Rizzato the most is that the predator is bigger than him.

He tries to ignore the menace, concentrating on not overturning the boat while looking for some recognition of his surroundings. He travels upriver another thirty meters before he realizes he has taken the wrong fork. He'll have to turn around. He cuts the engine and grabs his paddle. As the dugout slows, giving in to the river's opposing force, he uses the paddle to make the front of the boat slowly swing downriver. Soon he is face to face with the hungry beast. Rizzato has a sickening smirk on his face as he stares at the bulbous eyes and guns the small engine, pointing the dugout at them. He hopes he will hit it. The croc is smarter than Rizzato thinks and submerges gliding smoothly under the oncoming boat. Not hearing a scrape, Rizzato is sorely disappointed

Twenty minutes later he keeps to his left as he guides the dugout into the other fork. It is narrower and less used. The remotest Embera village where he has been hiding is still an hour away. Darkness is close; the evening is enveloped in a grey that matches the sky. The hum of the tiny engine compounds the patter of the rain; disturbing to his present state of mind. An urge to turn around and quit this rural hideaway nags at him as he ventures toward his hut. The feeling is strong now. He knows he should heed its warning; he's felt it many times before. He really has no choice but to continue onward, he thinks, but this will be the last trip. He won't even stay the night; he'll get what he came for, take his other birds, and give the chief some cash to remind him that Rizzato has never been there and leave.

The rain slows to a drizzle when he is about fifteen minutes away. He has slowed his boat, apprehensive about what he might find. He is trying to convince himself that everyone will be inside sheltered from the rain. He's glad he is arriving in these conditions, perfect to get in and out without being seen. A small figure that bursts from the trees lining the shore startles him. It hisses a slurry of words at him, a patois of English, Embera and Italian.

"Papa, Papa, over here, come to me, quickly."

Rizzato recognizes the strange language only he and one other share and the mellow tenor of the Little One. He reverses the engine, steering the boat close to shore. As soon as he reaches the riverbank, the brown skinned boy jumps into the dugout. It rocks slightly as he pulls himself in, giving Rizzato an abrupt fright. He's thinking of the crocodiles that live in these waters. When the boy plops down on the seat in front of Rizzato, he points to a spot downriver where a large tree has fallen into the water, suggesting he anchor the boat there. Once there, the Little One tells Rizzato that there is no one at the village.

He explains that he had gone fishing with boys from another village yesterday and stayed overnight. He had come home late this afternoon to find his village deserted. He is all apologetic to Rizzato that he hasn't fed the birds for two days; with that on his mind, when he returned, he had raced to Papa's hut, but there were two strange men standing outside. He didn't know what to do, too frightened of the men to stay, so he hid by the riverside waiting for someone to come. He figured the villagers would return and they would have to come by the river. He finishes his story, saying, "And the birds were very scared Papa; they were making a lot of noise."

Rizzato is dumbstruck. It is unimaginable that over seventy people would just disappear. The idea is absurd. Who could the two men possibly be? "What did they look like, Little One?"

"They look like the tourists only more..." he pauses, searching for the right words, "harder. They are dressed different than the tourists, many pockets on their clothes."

Police, Rizzato thinks. They have finally found him, but why just two? His ego is insulted because a small army hadn't been sent to capture him. Most tourists are American or European so they aren't locals. The boy keeps talking until Rizzato tells him to be quiet. The Little One has seen this look on Papa's face before, so immediately stops. Rizzato has a strong feeling that he should turn the boat around and leave, but he can't. His mind drifts to a packet wrapped in oiled cloth tightly draped inside a sealed plastic freezer bag. It is buried at the base of the large wild cashew tree twenty meters north-north west from the back right corner of his hut. There are three account books, a worn and tattered photo of his mother and more important, a dog eared journal bound in black matte leather. It is a catalogue of a few happy moments of his life, a list of people indebted to him, important underworld contacts and, dearest to him, all the birds he has owned in his lifetime. He reveres his feather friends, always finding peace in their presence, finding the comfort of something that loves him. Rizzato is a cruel, evil man and such sentimentality seems uncharacteristic. He tries to imagine existing without it, but it is the only real treasure he owns, a cache of the only things in life that has made him happy. He has to have it. His need is strong enough that he would kill for it.

He motions the boy from the boat as he says, "Stay here, Little One; stay as quiet and unmoving as a small mouse. I'll be back for you soon. Take the birds with you."

The boy would normally have protested, but he can see in Papa's eyes that he isn't to be disobeyed. He jumps from the boat, landing on shore with the cage clutched in his arms. As soon as he steps away, Rizzato moves the craft slowly upriver. The modest community is a fifteen minute walk from the river along the main path. But he knows of another entrance that the boy had shown him once, a dirt trail used only by the children not far above the regular walkway. It leads to a clearing north of the main entrance and he will be able to see his hut from the tree line. He proceeds stealthily until he is near the main entrance. He turns off his engine as the dugout nears the shore. By now it is almost dark. He disembarks and pulls the boat to the riverbank with the rope attached to the front, tying it to one of the tree limbs jutting out over the water. Shouldering his pack he heads along the shore until he reaches the second path. He removes his weapon from the top pocket of the bag and treads cautiously toward the village.

*

Drake had arrived in Panama City two days earlier, meeting Williston on the Drifter, which was berthed in St. Andrews Bay at the city marina. The men had spent the balance of the day preparing for a showdown Williston was certain was going to happen. Drake was not as confident as his friend, suggesting that Rizzato could be anywhere. Williston couldn't explain why he felt as he did but assured Drake that the man they were after would likely return here, if not to stay then at least to regroup or plan his next caper. He reminded Drake that, at present, this was the only trail they had. At the very least, this was an opportunity to comb Rizzato's nest for clues.

They had pored over the maps Drake had received from Dr. Branscombe as well as the man's information relating to the curious, warm and innocent natives. He had explained that many of the Embera villages were exposed to tourists in the summer season but mainly along the Chagres River. Where they were headed, the natives were a mix of two tribes, Embera and Wounaan, often referred to as the Choco. He had warned Drake that although friendly, they were leery of men travelling alone. He had given Drake a beautifully carved figure of an armadillo that hung from a leather string. It had been given him when he left his camp for the last time. Dr. Branscombe told Drake that when he arrived at the village he was to seek out the "Jaibana," the spiritual man whose name was Antonio. Drake was expecting a much different name for a native, but Branscombe told him that while many Embera had indigenous names, often of wild animals, they also used Spanish or English names as well. All the months he had spent in the rainforest with them, he never knew Antonio's native name. He went on to tell Drake that when he made contact with him, he was to show the Jaibana the carving and tell him that Dr. Branscombe only lent it to him and that he would return it safely. It would be a talisman that the men bearing the gift were to be trusted.

Williston's contacts provided them with transportation, packs, food, ponchos, knives and other weapons. They had headed out late yesterday afternoon until they reached a guest house far up the Sambu River where they had stayed the night as guests of the burly German owner and his native wife. That morning they had been provided with a motorized dugout and given further directions to the isolated village. Hans, the owner, reinforced Dr. Branscombe's earlier warning that they would find a group of people living much as they had as when Columbus discovered the area over five hundred years ago. The experience would be both shocking and inspiring.

The men had slowly motored up the river, Williston lost in thoughts of his deceased sister, the driving force behind this mission; Drake alert and cautious, watching the shore for any signs of danger. It continued to rain off and on, the men impervious to the dampness. The forest along the river was lush with rich scents of rotting vegetation and soggy earth. By mid-afternoon they were about thirty meters from the coordinates Dr. Branscombe had given them for the entrance to the village. He had told them that the opening would be visible as it was about ten meters wide at the river and there would be as many as a dozen dugouts pulled up to the shore. Williston was the first to see the canoes, warning Drake that they were near. Drake moved the dugout to the shore, where Williston got out and pulled the boat in. After tying up their craft, they shouldered their packs after removing their weapons and moved guardedly along the riverbank.

Williston took the lead with Drake bringing up the rear five meters back. They arrived to find the village quiet, with few people about in the rain. Most villagers were inside and unaware of the men's presence. Two men were carving a dugout from the trunk of a huge tree under a thatched canopy at the edge of the village. Drake motioned for Williston to hide his weapon but watch his back as he walks slowly through the trees coming up behind the men surprising them with a hearty "Hola". The men dropped their utensils in fear to back away from the approaching stranger. Drake spoke Spanish to them asking if there were any other foreigners in their camp. They didn't reply but continued to shake their head no. The men spoke very little English but understood enough of Drake`s Spanish so that when he asked for the Jaibana, one of them ran off to fetch the person known as Antonio.

Soon an older man wrapped in only a colorful loin cloth and beautifully detailed markings on his body came to them. His face and arms were dark from the dyes used by the tribe to ward off insects. Straight black hair covered his elderly head. When he neared the strangers he told them there were no foreigners about. Drake pulled the carving from the top of his pack and offered it to the shaman. Both he and Williston hide their guns in side pockets. The man took the polished carving in his hands, studied it carefully and said, "I've seen this before; it was a gift to a very dear friend."

"Yes, I know," said Drake, "And I will be returning it to Dr. Branscombe when we are finished visiting with you. He spoke also of your friendship. He wanted us to tell you he thinks of you and your people often and sends his fondest greetings."

The man returned the carving to Drake asking, "What brings you to our village?"

At this point Williston stepped forward to show him two pictures. The first was a photo of Amber. As Williston told the man of his little sister, of her hopes and dreams and of how she met her demise, Drake translated.

The man was holding the picture of Amber as Drake spoke and politely asked what she had to do with them. Before Drake could reply, Williston handed him the second photo he was holding, which was actually a photo of the sketch Isaac had made of Rizzato. Drake said, "This is the man that killed her and we've come to arrest him."

Antonio stepped back in astonishment when he recognized the man in the photo. After a moment studying the likeness, he said, "But this is the man that has brought us many comforts, medicine and protection from the Colombians that sometimes raid our villages. I have witnessed his anger but cannot believe that he would do this horrible thing. And he has been gone for many months, I don't know when he will return or even if he will."

Antonio wrestled with the idea of his benefactor being a criminal. After many moments of consideration, he told Drake and Williston of his relationship with Branscombe, how they had become brothers, how they had hunted for the different birds that the Doctor had come to see. He told them of the bond that had grown between them and the many times he had thought of and missed his good friend. He spoke of how he wanted to help the strangers because they came from Dr. Cornelius, as he called him. He finally admitted that of the two white men that had brought succor to the village in the past, Dr. Cornelius had been the most faithful. He said, "I don't know how I can help you other than showing you his hut."

Antonio led Drake and Williston to a larger shelter slightly away from the village center, isolated by surrounding palms for privacy. At the front of the hut, which stood on stilted beams, was a log with rough steps carved on one face. The steps that were cut into the log were pointing toward the ground. As Antonio righted the log so that the men could enter the refuge, he explained that the log was always turned when the occupants were absent or sleeping so that animals could not gain entry. As soon as Drake and Williston entered the hut they knew they had found Rizzato's hideaway. To both men, the feeling was akin to finding their way out of a complicated and bizarre maze. They admired the many colorful birds in ornate cages, remarking on the man's fascination with them. They stood in the center of the large room, scanning the sparse furnishings until Williston said, "This place gives me the creeps, Drake. I have a sense of foreboding, of corruption. Let's get out of here."

Williston immediately set his plan in motion to have the people leave the village for several days while they waited, hoping

Rizzato would show up. If after four days the man they were seeking did not appear, he promised Antonio they would leave. He passed the spiritual leader a heavy bundle of American money, currency that was legal tender in Panama along with the local Balboa coins. Antonio stared at the mass of bills and bag of coins he was being offered not having seen so much money at one time. He knew immediately what such funds could mean to his people. He assured Williston that he would speak with Melecio, his brother that was also the chief.

Within an hour Drake and Williston stood in the center of the village watching the people gather a few belongings. Antonio told Williston that Melecio would be taking half the village inland to the community's summer village while he and a few other men would accompany most of the women and children downriver to a neighboring village where they would be welcomed. Antonio informed Williston that he was saddened to know of Rizzato's cruelty but was relieved that the man would be gone from their village. He also told Drake and Williston that he would be bringing his people back in three days regardless of the outcome of their visit. If Rizzato had not shown up by then, they must leave and let the Embera deal with the imposter. Drake and Williston reluctantly agreed.

Rizzato had missed the convoy moving downriver by less than an hour. He had paid no heed to the conglomeration of extra dugouts at the previous village.

Soon darkness settled over the camp. Both Drake and Williston had scouted the area, checking for any possibility of surprises. The men are silent as they watch and wait in a vacant hut directly in line with Rizzato's. The rain has finally cleared, leaving a hazy mist to shroud the camp. It heightens the eeriness of the dusk. They listen to the silence of the forest around them interrupted by water dripping from the eaves of the thatch. Williston is the first to speak.

"I don't get the feeling that Rizzato will be showing up tonight, so I'm going to check his belongings once more."

"We can't be too careful, Williston. I'm going to do another survey of the village and edge down to the water to see if there's anything out of the ordinary. Keep your weapon handy; you know how slippery this crazy man can be."

Both men move away from their refuge, Williston going across the clearing to enter Rizzato's hut while Drake walks toward the main entrance, watching for any sign of motion. On the parallel trail above Drake, Rizzato eases stealthily in the opposite direction. By the time Drake reaches the river, Rizzato is standing at the base of a group of large ficus trees. He can see someone in his hut. The man is setting a lantern on the window ledge and Rizzato can make out some of his features: longish light brown hair, scrunched brow, pursed lips. He sees the man looking down at something in the back corner and knows it is a woven basket full of what Rizzato calls his "morbid mementoes." Items he has stolen and kept from his slain victims, mostly women. He grins as he thinks of some of the items in the basket, wondering what a psychologist might make of his collection. He quickly forgets about them as he spies the huge tree where he had hidden his packet. He doubts he could recover it without the man seeing him. Other than removing his poncho, he stays completely motionless while considering his options. While doing so, he looks around the village trying to see the man's accomplice.

Drake is at the river's edge watching the lazy flow, scanning the river in both directions. There is very little light, but his eyes are adjusted to the darkness. He listens to the natural sounds of the forest and water. The blanket of clouds overhead is breaking up like tattered remnants of raw cotton with wispy edges. A full moon casts a bluish light on the land and suddenly Drake sees something he might've otherwise missed, a set of footprints. He knows that the Embera were all barefoot or wore sandals of smooth leather. These prints are not lugged like the boots he and Williston wear but were dented at the heel like a wedged platform and pointed at the toes. They look like a print cowboy boots would make. He noticed that they go beyond the opening of the main passage. He follows the indents not where they are going but where they are coming from until he finds a dugout haphazardly tethered to a palm tree. He switches directions to follow them urgently.

Williston set his weapon on the window ledge in front of him and is sorting through a basket of items perched on a small stool in the back corner of the building, marveling at the collection of objects and noting that they are mostly feminine. He picks up the first item he sees, a tube of lipstick, holding it in his left hand. He moves the curiosities about, uncovering an eclectic jumble; a curling iron, a dangly silver earring, a happy-face pin, a small red leather coin purse, a scratched and broken pink cell phone. As he digs deeper he spies an item at the bottom that both startles and chills him. He reaches in to clutch the shiny gold object, bringing it out to inspect it more closely. He immediately recognizes the heart shaped pendant with sixteen small sapphires set around the edge. He had given it to his sister Amber when she turned sixteen. He is shocked. Goose bumps flesh his arms and neck; tears well up from his very soul, and he sighs a cry of despair. The pendant burns in his hand as he squeezes it hard, not in loneliness but in deep, violent anger that soon turns to a terrifying hatred.

Williston is about to turn to leave, to find Drake and show him what he's found, when from behind him a grating voice seethes at him to unhand whatever he found and turn around slowly or be killed where he stands.

Williston ignores the command, knowing full well who is issuing the warning. An abhorrence so profound gushes through his body as he says, "I know who you are, you bastard, and if you don't shoot me now, when I turn around I'm going to kill *you* with my bare hands."

Rizzato laughs out loud at the foolishness of the man in front of him and says, "I don't think so, amigo. I'm the one with the gun pointed at the back of your head. You make one rash move and you're as good as gone. I'm going to kill you anyway; I just want to see your face before I waste your useless life."

Then with a cold commanding insistence he shouts, "Turn around, now!"

Williston slowly turns toward Rizzato. All the years hunting this fugitive are culminating at this very second. He isn't afraid to die, but he knows with a certainty that he will take Rizzato with him. When he faces Rizzato, his arms held out from his body he says, "One way or another, Rizzato, you will never see another sunrise as a free men."

The two men stand less than four meters apart, staring deep into each other's eyes. Williston is surprised at the man that confronts him. He had expected a more fearsome individual. What he sees is a tall, ugly, ungainly man. He reminds Williston of the stick figures he used to doodle when he was a boy. Rizzato's face is a V poked with colorless eyes. It is as misshapen as his body, a gruesome caricature of a human and Williston finds it easy to hate him even more.

Rizzato gazes at the man before him, noticing the cold eyes filled with disgust. The man is shorter than him but solidly built. He sees repugnance cloud the man's features, anger in his clutched hands. He says, "You're not a cop, are you? Who are you and what are you doing in my home?"

"No, I'm not a policeman, just the brother of a woman you brutally molested and killed."

Rizzato replies with a casualness that stupefies Williston, "That doesn't tell me much. I've molested more than a few silly bitches in my life. What makes your sister so special? She's just another piece of fluff I've already forgotten about."

Williston can't imagine it is be possible to detest the man any more than he does, but his last statement drives him beyond reason. Williston is no longer interested in arresting this man, only of killing him. Since he can't be sure that Drake will return soon enough to help him, he has to act on his own.

"Do you remember Venezuela almost three years ago? That was my sister Amber and her friend Sakeema, two innocents that should still be alive today."

As Williston says this he opens his right hand, slowly exposing the pendant he had found. Rizzato takes his eyes off the man for a second, his vision drawn to the burnished gold. Williston seizes the moment. He is still holding the tube of lipstick in his left fist.

He flicks it with his wrist at the same time as he dives toward the man. The projectile hits Rizzato in the upper lip, splitting it against his teeth. The gun fires. Williston is only a meter away with his arms stretched toward Rizzato. The 60 grain slug tears a layer of skin off his right bicep. Williston is so pumped on adrenaline he doesn't feel it. He rams his elbow of his injured arm towards Rizzato's Adam's apple just as Drake had taught him but he is off guard from the bullet wound not incapacitating him. Rizzato backpedals while gagging and clutching at his throat, and pulls the trigger again.

Williston has kept up the forward momentum and grabs Rizzato's gun hand just as the weapon fired. Seizing Rizzato's wrist with his other hand, he swings his back to the man intending to throw him over his hip and slam him onto the floor. But as Rizzato flies over Williston's hip, he reaches out blindly and grasps a fistful of Williston' hair. The pain of hair being torn from his scalp causes Williston to tumble to the floor on top of his foe. His shoulder drops into the pit of Rizzato's diaphragm, forcing the air out of his lungs. More hate fuels Williston's strength and he squeezes the man's wrist until he feels and hears a bone break. Rizzato screams as his wrist is crushed and the gun scatters uselessly across the floor.

Rizzato is not a trained fighter – he's a street thug, dirty and mean. Still gasping while writhing in pain, his defence mechanism remains intact. He draws back his free fist and strikes Williston in the kidneys, several times. Williston arches from the blow, losing his grip on his enemy's wrist while agony climbs up his spine. Rizzato takes advantage of the brief respite to use his free leg to push Williston off his body and away from the gun. Williston falls forward on his face but quickly scrambles to his feet. He turns to face Rizzato, who is pushing himself up from the floor with his good hand. The two men are once more facing each other. Williston is almost blinded by animosity. Both men eye the gun that is teetering on the front edge of the veranda; the slightest jar will tilt it to the ground.

Rizzato has his back to the cages, oblivious to the nervous cries of the birds. Williston is at the opposite side of the hut, glaring at him with his teeth gritted. Rizzato knows he has to kill this man before his partner shows up. In his present condition, unarmed, he recognizes that he will be no match for two men. He reaches up to the top of the center cage, where the Little One keeps his skinning knife. He finds it quickly, much to his relief, closing his left fist firmly around the shaft. He holds the blade in the killing position he had been trained for. It hurts to talk as he taunts his quarry, "Where's your partner now you loser?" He lunges toward his target. The sight of Williston pulling a knife from a side pocket on his trousers stalls Rizzato for a mere second. Williston sidesteps Rizzato, pulling his knife from its sheath. He throws the worn leather at the man and lunges with his own blade. The men parry their weapons, Rizzato's striking Williston across the face opening a wound along his jaw. Williston is hurt and being backed into the corner as he tries to defend himself from Rizzato's cutting blade. Rizzato strikes Williston in the stomach with a lucky kick. Williston falls to the floor losing his weapon. He strikes his head on the wooden floor and is briefly dazed. Rizzato raises his knife to strike.

Drake has followed the footprints to the camouflaged path. The low hanging foliage, overgrown roots and narrowness of the trail slows him down and he is still minutes from the center when he hears the first gunshot. He shouts out Williston's name and races for the huts. He swears at himself for leaving his friend behind; he has already lost too many people. He will never forgive himself if something happens to Williston. Even with the moonlight, the shadows from the living canopy above make navigating the path difficult. The path roof is low and he stumbles several times over protruding roots, slowing his advance. Wet branches slap at him like protesting arms, spraying droplets in his face. He tries to keep his eyes on the footpath while separating the foliage as he runs. Many of the surrounding trees have small firm leaves that he can barely discern in the darkness. Just as he sees the glow at the end of the trail, the slivered edge of one leaf, sharp as the edge of a sheet of paper, slices across his left eyeball. It hurts and cuts his vision in half but it doesn't slow him down.

He bursts into the clearing directly across from Rizzato's hut - twenty meters away. Through the bird cages in front of the window, he can see a man raise something shiny – a knife? – Above his head. The man is too thin to be Williston; it has to be Rizzato. Unable to focus well Drake raises his gun and fires several shots at the man. The bullets ricochet through the wire cages, killing several birds. But one slug finds its mark, grazing Rizzato's scalp. An eerie screech escapes from his wounded face. The glittering metal flies from his fist and he dives through the open doorway away from Drake's approach. Drake runs toward the hut, worried that he can't see Williston.

Rizzato knows he is in mortal danger as he runs toward the wild cashew tree where he has hid his stash. His wrist is useless and his head is bleeding, both in exquisite pain. His survival instinct tells him to run, to get to his dugout, to flee, but first he has to retrieve his packet. He needs to dig up his pouch, then get to the river. He has another way to get to his dugout, without going back through the village. He arrives at the base of the tree as clouds move in to obscure the moon; he hopes that the cover of darkness will keep him safe long enough for him to dig up his packet and run.

Drake enters the Rizzato's hut to find Williston on the floor. There is blood on his neck from a wound on his jaw. Blood has colored the side of Williston's t-shirt. Drake stares at his friend for several seconds. Williston's eyes are open. He groans and tries to sit up, rubbing the back of his head. When his vision begins to clear he sees his buddy bending to help him sit. With a voice full of hurt, he says, "Never mind me, go after him Drake, after Rizzato, we can't let the miserable prick get away."

"You need help."

"Fuck that, I can take care of these wounds. Remember the promise you made: catch him or kill him."

He pushes Drake away as he sits up straighter. Drake looks around quickly for something to bind his friend's wounds. He spots a pillow on the cot in the corner and Williston's knife by one of the bed legs. He pulls the case from the pillow, grabs the knife and passes both to his friend. He looks out in the direction Rizzato had jumped but sees no sign of him. Then in the moonlight he sees movement near a large tree some distance from the hut. He isn't sure if it is human or animal but he jumps to the ground to pursue whatever it is.

Rizzato has dug desperately in the dirt with his uninjured hand, unable to find the plastic. He keeps one eye on the hut as he searches. He gives himself one more minute to find his cache and flee. In a few seconds, he uncovers the dirty pouch. He holds it firmly to his side and runs, cutting across the wooded area on one of many paths, knowing this one will take him to the main trail that leads to the river. He never looks back as he rushes through the water laden forest. His mind is focused on his dugout, the attaché case full of money in the boat, the Little One and the only birds he will be able to take with him. Although he has been using these paths for years, the dark night obscures the forest. As a result, he doesn't see the huge branch that has fallen off a rotting Spanish cedar. As his foot catches a branch, he trips. He careens through the air, landing on his crushed wrist. Unable to hold back his agony, he bellows into the night.

Drake has lost Rizzato. When he reaches the base of the tree, he is able to see where Rizzato had been digging. He isn't sure which direction the man has run, but he knows the villain will be headed toward the river. He decides to backtrack through the village. As he turned to head that way, he hears a cry of anguish directly in front of him. He can discern an opening in the trees from whence the sound came. Holding his weapon ready, he speeds off in that direction.

Rizzato scrambles to his feet, the pain almost unbearable. He had dropped his packet when he tried to break his fall. He searches the ground frantically until he feels the damp plastic. He is losing precious time. He picks up the sack and hustles again but can hear someone in close pursuit. He sees a huge panama tree with a forked trunk where the path he is on joins the larger one. He knows he isn't far from the river and wills his legs to hurry.

While running Drake scans the ground for obstacles and is lucky to see the branch Rizzato missed. He jumps over the debris and is soon at the junction of the trails. He stops for a second, looking toward the river, and see's Rizzato running twenty meters in front of him, a moving shadow. He raises his gun and fires several shots, more to warn the escaping man than to hit him. It's too dark to properly aim. He is hoping to take him alive. Rizzato doesn't return fire and Drake thinks it possible Rizzato doesn't have a gun. Suddenly the man veers to the right, out of sight. Drake can see the moon's reflection on the moving water ahead of him. Rizzato is heading down river. Drake runs with a greater urgency, without caution.

Rizzato almost wet himself as the bullets dug up the dirt at his feet. He feels panic, not knowing if he will reach his dugout. He sees another craft pulled up on the shore and is tempted to use it. But his mind is wrapped up in his need for the possessions in his boat. If he is to get to them, he knows he will have to slow his opponent down. He grabs an oar from the nearby boat and hides behind a cedrela tree. He clutches his packet between his injured forearm and chest. When he sees the man chasing him run toward the shore, he steps out and swings the paddle one-handed with every ounce of energy he possesses, striking Drake in the midriff.

The wind is driven from Drake's lungs as the flat of the oar strikes him. Staggering back from the blow, he sees the face of the man he had been chasing for the last three years. With strength from deep inside, he overcomes the pain and breathlessness and charges at his opponent. Rizzato, panicking, can't believe the man is still coming. He weakly swings the oar again, but Drake deflects the blow and knocks the oar from Rizzato's hand. He steps closer and rams his fist into Rizzato's stomach. The package flies from under Rizzato's arm and lands in the water. A vision of Amber surfaces in Drake's mind as he continues to pound away at the man. Strikes to the face and the body keep Rizzato off balance as he grunts with each blow. Drake slams the man with an uppercut that connects under the chin forcing Rizzato into the water, bleeding and quivering with pain.

Across the narrow river an alligator, submerged in the murky water and hidden by dark shadows, has patiently watched and waited. When Rizzato falls into the water, the hungry amphibian smells blood. Sharp teeth lines its elongated snout. It glides through the water to bite upon a lower limb in its vice-like jaws, ripping it off. Rizzato screams with such terror that Drake shudders. Drake moves toward the river, thinking to pull the man from a cruel and horrifying death. But Williston, who has followed as quickly as he could, shoots out a hand seizing his friend by the arm.

"Leave him, Drake; it's what the bastard deserves."

Drake is frozen by the vindictiveness in Williston's eyes but realizes his friend is right. There should be no mercy for the merciless man that thrashes in the water before them, begging for help. The two men watch as the gruesome beast lifts its head from the water, Rizzato's leg clamped in its jaws. Then, it raises itself up, drops the severed limb, crashes upon its wailing victim and bites down on Rizzato's shoulder. With unimaginable strength, it pulls the screaming man under. The river roils where Rizzato's twisting body has submerged but soon settles as water fills his lungs and he drowns.

Drake and Williston stand fixed upon the sand as the water calms. The giant reptile floats down the river underwater with his prey and the night becomes silent.

Chapter 42

Nov 7 2:20pm Aboard the Drifter's Dream, Antigua

Williston is putting Amber's graduation photo back in its rightful place in the spare bedroom aboard his yacht. He had sneaked away from the gang gathered up on deck, feeling slightly melancholy over his sister's absence. He had gone to retrieve the photo from his office, meaning to restore it to its original position. When he hangs the picture carefully on the brass hook on the wall, he hangs the polished pendant he had found with a new chain on a corner of the frame. Backing away from the wall to study the photo he espies his profile in the mirror above the dresser. He regards the three inch scar along his jaw, still red even though the stitches have been removed over two weeks ago. He grins as he remembers the day he and Isabella had visited the doctor to have the wounds he had brought back from Panama checked. He is feeling a bit down about the scar but he soon perks when he remembers Isabella telling him how rakish it makes him look, more manly she joked, more lovable. He returns his gaze to the photo for a while longer before he speaks to it.

"May your soul rest now, Amber, that the evil man is gone. I love you and miss you terribly."

He wants to take a few moments before he rejoins everyone on deck. He sits on the edge of the bed, staring out the window. The sea is as blue as a December birthstone, as still and seamless as a bolt of vibrant-hued silk. He is rubbing his bicep where the bullet had penetrated and his mind sweeps back to the ending of their quest. He remembers Drake dressing his wounds, getting him in the dugout before going back to the huts to collect their packs. When he'd returned, he'd guided them back to the German's cozy Inn, where they had radioed Bill aboard the Drifter to tell him where they could be found. The trip down river had been made in silence, both men feeling oddly empty now that their journey was complete. Yet there was satisfaction in knowing that the man they had pursued would commit no more crimes, kill no more people and break no more hearts. There really had been little to say. Drake had accompanied Williston to Panama, where he'd had had his wounds treated. They had parted ways there. Williston headed home to Antigua aboard the Drifter; Drake caught a flight back to New Brunswick to see Beth. They men hadn't said goodbye as such, but before Drake had boarded his plane, the men had embraced each other like dear friends do. Williston had asked Drake when he would see him again and Drake had replied, "I've got a stop to make in Boston, to see my uncle. I want to check on the business and see if I can find a gift for my love, something to celebrate our new family. Why don't you get the team together in about a month's time and we can plan for our next caper, find some bad guys to catch, as you suggested. Do you still want to do that, Williston?"

Williston looked his best friend in the eye and gave his tacit agreement. He really hated to see his pal leave but knew they would meet soon again.

"Yeah, let's do that, Drake. Let's rid the globe of some of the rot that's turning it sour. How about we all meet up at my place in Antiqua the first or second week of November?"

"Perfect, I'll see you then. Take care, buddy."

As Drake headed for the gate. Williston's handsome face broke with a lopsided grin as he called out,

"When are you going to marry that girl?"

Drake stopped, looked back, gave Williston a crooked grin and said, "None of your business."

Then he disappeared into the departing crowd. Williston had returned to his wife and together they had flown to Saudi Arabia to extend their condolences to Uday. They had stayed for only a short time. Although Uday had greeted them with genuine warmth, it was obvious the recent deaths in Bangladesh was a heavy burden making their stay uncomfortable. After Williston had told Uday the story of Rizzato's death in a private moment, he and Isabella had returned to Antigua.

Williston turns his thoughts to the people he has gathered here, the ones that have helped him in his search for Rizzato. His first thought is of his good friend, Dakin, the man that worships their friend Drake as much as he himself does. He hadn't seen the burly Irishman since he had left for Bangladesh to help Drake. The man walks with crutches but is as robust as ever. He knows that Dakin has pushed himself relentlessly during his physiotherapy. He's a bull and will soon be as strong as ever.

He has met the lovely Mireille, who has accompanied Dakin. Drake had spoken of her with admiration. Williston liked her immediately. She was certainly in the same category of beautiful women that Dakin usually surrounded himself with but is much smarter and brighter than his previous companions. He hopes she can talk him out of those ugly camouflage pants he always wears. Today, he sports black and khaki jungle pattern shorts with his ever present black sleeveless T-shirt. Rae, as everyone calls her, is wearing a royal blue and purple tankini that gives her luscious curves definition. He had chuckled when Isabella had caught him ogling the woman, chastising him playfully for being so smitten, reminding him he is a married man with a child on the way.

And then there are the Glass twins. Isaac, completely recovered from his ordeal in Bangladesh, escorted by his lovely wife, Dia. He had always warmed to Dia because she reminded him of Amber, the same playful twinkle in her eyes, the same awe she regarded life with. The only disappointing moment of their visit was when Dia and Isaac had confided to Williston and Drake that their most recent caper would be his last. Dia envied the strength that Isabella and Beth displayed, but she was through worrying about the man she loved. With his latest injury, she had pleaded with Isaac to stop rushing off to save the world. She had told Drake and Williston that they treasured the men's friendship, and it was because of that friendship that she was asking them to heed their wishes. They both agreed they would.

Isaac told them that the comic book he had been working on has been accepted for publication, advances have been paid and he will be extremely busy working on upcoming issues. His work is unique in that he is both the writer and the illustrator. Like his syndicated cartoon, the Granite Planet, the comic is about four members of a rock band with super powers. It is to be a tribute to his favorite group: Earth, Wind and Fire.

With a wry grin Williston ponders upon Elijah, the crafty, gutsy pilot – the joker in the crowd. The man is always a delight to be with, always up, always positive. He had regaled the group with anecdotes of the challenges of keeping man and machine working and content. The only indication of the twins' blood ties are the same face – the same eyes, the same nose and chin – they share.

Otherwise they're as different as salt and pepper. Williston is fond of both men, counting himself fortunate to be their ally.

And then there is Plum. A shy modest young woman, the most sensuous oriental lady he's ever met. He can see how much she cares for Elijah, how much she enjoys being with him. Last night after much urging from Elijah, she had shared the bare facts of her troubled past. She had been hesitant at first, but as Elijah had explained, she owed his friends, her friends now, a proper explanation of how she came to be involved with Rizzato, of how she had decided to turn her life around. She had kept nothing back, wanting her new family to know everything that had led her to them. At the end of her mini biography, the women were all misty eyed. A few of the men, too. In the silence that followed, each person had embraced her, welcoming her into their group. Williston had told her that even though her new identity would be Sakura Watanabe, the first her mother's name, the second the last name of her favorite actor, she will always be Plum to them.

He thinks about Drake's sister, Glory, and her fiancé Stephane. He had always accused her of being the serious one in the family, the bookworm, always off studying her birds. In reality she could be as feisty as her brother but much more charming. Although he had never met Drake's mother, his father had often told them that Glory was the image of his wife. Her boyfriend is new to the crew, but so far he has fit right in, the men all joking that he seems a nice guy even though he is a lawyer.

His mind drifts to Drake and Beth, the two people outside of his immediate family he loves the most. The man stands amongst them with an air of authority, an oak that will never bend, a man who will give his life for those he loves, a man who quite simply cares. There isn't a day they've spent together that Drake doesn't remind Williston of his father. They look a lot alike. He knows that with Drake at his side, there is nothing they can't accomplish, an awesome sense of unity. With Beth, the man is complete, even if Williston has to remind him occasionally.

Sweet, sweet Beth with her ever present smile is the first girl he fell in love with when he was a boy. He has never confided that to anyone, but his heart holds a special place only for her. She is unique, warm, kind and talented, with a voice as beautiful as she is. But he had learned that Drake was the only boy she ever cared for. He smiles now as he realizes that is the way it has always been and always will be. He is truly happy for them.

And lastly, of course, he reflects upon the jewel of his life, his wife Isabella. He is thinking of when they met, of how he had been concentrating on putting a cassette in the player of his car and had rear-ended her vehicle at a stop light. She had been fierce, utterly beautiful in her anger. He is thinking of the early days of their relationship, getting to know each other, when a voice soft as linen interrupts him, "What are you thinking about lover?"

Williston looks up to see his gorgeous wife standing in the open doorway. Her wavy hair is tied back with a clip, her eyes shining, the swell of her stomach blossoming where their child is growing. He says, "You, my love. I was thinking of you and how lucky I am."

Isabella smiles and moves toward him. He rises to embrace her, nestling his face in the graceful curve of her neck. "I love you," he whispers, "and I will forever."

She squeezes him as hard as she can and whispers back, "Me too."

She disengages herself from his loving hug, takes his hand and says, "C'mon. Drake has an announcement and he wants you to be there. Do you know what's going on?"

"I think so, but we'll soon see."

Williston follows his wife to the upper aft deck, where the gang is gathered in a close group. The women are seated on the leather couches – Dia and Rae on the right, Glory and Plum on the left, Beth in the center. A collection of brilliant and beautiful women. The men are standing in a knot to the left, beside the port gunwale a few feet from the couch, cold beers in hand. All except for Dakin, who is drinking daiquiris and sitting in a deck chair. Drake is standing in front of everyone with his back to Williston and Isabella as they approach. Dakin points toward Williston, saying to Drake, "Here's our gracious host now, Drake. So, what's this important announcement?"

"Be patient, Dakin, you'll soon know."

Drake turns to Williston and says, "Have a seat you two."

Isabella joins the women on the couch, sitting next to Plum, while Williston joins the men.

Drake looks around at the bunch; his dark brown eyes are full of emotion and says, "I'm very pleased that you're all here. You are the dearest friends that I have and the dearest friends any man could ask for. Each and every one of you have a special place in my heart and, if you all don't know it by now, I will always be here for each of you, whenever you need me, wherever you are."

He waits for a moment because deep down Drake truly means it and the words bring a tender moment to his heart. He eyes each individual as he pauses, the men nodding back at him in confirmation that they feel the same way. The women are all smiling: Dia, the most sentimental, with watery eyes; Rae and Plum with profound respect; Isabella blushing with modesty, and Beth flushed with pride. As he scans the small crowd, he continues, "But one of you is more precious than the air I breathe, more valuable than anything I possess, more perfect than anything our wonderful Lord has created and cherished more than my fondest memories."

Elijah calls out, "Is it me, Drake?"

Amongst the laughter Drake replies, "No, I'm afraid not. I expect you all know it's the love of my life, Beth."

All eyes turn toward Beth, putting her on the spot, as she blushes and beams at Drake's confession. While the girls are oohing over such sentimentality, Drake pulls a small black velvet bag from his front pocket. It is the size of a business card, cinched at the top with a pink silk ribbon. He lifts the small pouch in the air and the group quiets down. He walks the three steps to the couch, kneels before Beth, presents the pouch and says, "Beth Stone, will you be my wife?"

The men all hoot and hurrah, while the woman excitedly tell her to open the bag. Beth accepts the gift with her eyes locked on Drake's. If love were manifested by arrows, there would have been thousands shooting from her eyes. A hush permeates the crowd, except for the shuffling of the men's feet as they crowd around the couch. The women all lean forward to watch Beth and gauge her reaction. She unties the pretty ribbon and it falls to her lap. She draws open the top of the bag and reaches in with two fingers. She clasps the ring inside and removes it with baited breath. She holds the ring aloft and a collective gasp goes through the crowd. An extremely rare, one carat, natural pink diamond in a platinum Tiffany setting glistens in the sunlight. It casts a hundred miniature prisms from its flawless facets. With tears in her eyes, she slips the ring on the third finger of her left hand. Looking at the handsome man kneeling before her, she says simply, "Yes."

More whoops and jests emanate from the men as they pat Drake on the back. Williston pulls the man to his feet and hugs him briefly saying, "It's about time, you dog. Congratulations, my friend."

The women all hug Beth, exclaiming at the beauty and simplicity of the engagement ring. Williston goes to the bar and reaches inside the temperature controlled cooler to pull out several bottles of Dom Perignon and Veuve Clicquot. He pops the corks, adds champagne flutes to a tray and carries it back to the gathering. Setting down the tray he pours everyone a tall cold glass and lifts his own.

"I propose a toast to our friends. May your lives together be fruitful, full of love, babies and friendship."

Beth stands going to Drake's, holding him tight, her head on his chest, as everyone drinks to their long life together. She speaks loudly enough for all of their friends to hear.

"I love you, Drake Alexander."

Williston wheels the portable bar to the middle of the lounge area, shouting to the crowd to drink up, the party is only beginning. He goes to the console near the bar and fiddles with the computer until he finds the song he feels is appropriate for the moment. Hitting the select button, JJ Cale's romantic love song *Magnolia* croons from the speakers. He calls out, "I know this is Drake and Beth's favorite song, so let's give it a listen."

As JJ"s soft voice whispers from the stereo, telling them about "the best he ever had," the women joined their respective mates and sway to the tune as Drake and Beth waltz in a tight embrace before them. Soon all the couples are caught up in the beauty of the song and quietly dance with them, everyone high on the feeling of love. The song ends too soon but jumps right into Eric Clapton's version of *Cocaine*, and the party is well away.

An hour or so later Williston tells his captain, Bill, to make for shore so that the crew can join in the merriment. The ship comes about to head west.

A cell phone begins chirping like a lark. Drake and Beth recognize it as his phone and look at each other with a puzzled frown. Only a handful of people know the number and they wonder who it could be. Drake goes to the console where he had left it earlier in the day, picks it up and moves with Beth toward the stern where he will be able to hear better. With Beth listening, he concentrates on the voice on the other end, his smile turns to a frown. He listens for several more moments before he says, "I'm sure everything is okay. Don't worry. I'll fly out tomorrow and find out what's going on."

He closes the phone and turns to Beth.

"That was Jemina. She just heard from Miguel. He's in some kind of trouble. He told Jemina he's in a safe place but can't come home. He needs help and asked for me. Let's not tell the gang yet what's going on. I won't be able to get out of here until tomorrow. Of course, I'll tell Williston and I'll get ready to leave later tonight."

"Okay Drake. He's in Mexico isn't he? Doesn't he have a parish there?"

""No, he accepted a new parish in Peru, his home country, and moved there a month and a half ago. You know how much the Piscontes mean to me, so I want to help. I'm sure whatever it is can be cleared up in no time."

"Of course Drake."

Drake puts his arm around his bride-to-be and they stroll back to the party. When they reach the group that are dancing and cavorting on the deck, Drake pulls Williston aside and tells him the news. He offers to go with him but Drake kindly refuses. He says to his friend, "Let's keep this to ourselves for now. You know what the guys are like, I mention trouble and they will all want to come along. I'll find out what's going on first."

"Okay, but before you go back to the party, I want you to know that no matter what goes down, we're all here for you. You know that, right? All of them, except Isaac and Stephane, of course, have vowed to join us in our quest of the world's bad guys."

Drake nods in confirmation and thanks Williston. Williston punches him on the shoulder and winks before heading back to join the revelry. Drake focuses on his friends. He basks in the warmth of these people that mean so much to him. He reflects on the vows each person has given, the words each man and woman has expressed, thankful for them all. He knows they will follow him wherever he goes, through whatever toil and struggle he encounters. He feels empowered, tenacious and enriched. He is ready to take on the world.

Epilogue

Oct 9 midnight Sambu River, Panama

The Little One, whose real name is Federico, sits in Papa's dugout clutching a dripping piece of plastic. The boy had come upriver and climbed into the empty dugout after seeing the two strangers leave. The time had seemed like days as he waited for Papa to come and get him. As he remains in the craft, he watches the water as it flows, little ripples from dead branches disturbing the otherwise smooth surface. He is mesmerized by the moonlight as it dapples the tiny wavelets. About an hour ago something shiny had floated on the surface close to shore. It was spinning and sometimes its edges caught on a stone or branch by the riverbank. The glow from the moon gave it life as it bobbed in the water. He watched it as it floated closer. When it bumped into the side of the boat, he reached down to pick it up and recognized the package Papa had shown him last summer before he left.

Rizzato had explained to Little One what it contained. It had been the happiest day in the boy's life. Papa had shared his stories about the few times he had been happy while growing up. He had talked about his birds and how much he loved them. When he was telling his tales, he kept glancing at the crinkled photo of the woman he said was his mother. He had never heard Papa talk so much. They had spent the afternoon going over every detail. At the end of the day he showed Federico the account books, explaining the huge amount of money each held. He even had the boy memorize the passwords in case Papa left and never returned. The young boy had cried at the idea that Papa might never come back until Rizzato assured him he would always come back for his Little One.

The boy is confused and unsure what his finding the packet means. He holds it tight to his chest, praying that Papa is okay, but he wonders where he is. Why hasn't he returned to get him? For no explainable reason the small boy shivers in the night, feeling alone. Each sound in the woods frightens him now; even the ones he knows are only small night animals. He sits hunched over the packet, the bird cage at his feet along with the shiny metal case Papa has left in the dugout. It is late in the night, the moon almost hiding behind the trees on the opposite shore when Federico starts to doze off. Just before his troubled mind tips over into slumber, something taps the side of the boat. He cautiously looks over the side, thinking to see a young croc or one of the caiman that habituate the waters. Instead a blue waterlogged cowboy boot swirls in a small eddy next to the dugout. The boy shouts out painfully as he recognizes one of Papa's special boots. He drops the packet and reaches for the sodden shoe, almost tipping the boat. He pulls the damp leather aboard and starts to cry. At that moment he is certain that Papa will never return. He knows without a doubt that if he finds his Papa, he will be dead. But if he has died in the water then he will have been eaten by the terrible beasts that live in the river.

He holds the boot and wails in the night, rocking his skinny body back and forth. He is alone again; he cries out to his god, asking why he keeps taking the people that care for him. It is something he is too immature to understand. After his tears and grief subside, he considers what he will do. While lost deep in thought, his eyes rest on the metal case at the back of the boat. He reaches for the case, pulls it onto his lap and tries to open it, but it's locked. He sets it back on the floor and picks up the packet again. He lays down in the bottom of the boat and cries himself to sleep.

The sun pokes its nose over the shiny wet trees and a thin ray hits him in the face, waking him to an unusually sunny day. The boy rubs his eyes, staring at the packet he has in his hand. Tragic memories of the discoveries he'd made in the night come back. His sorrow is replaced with anger as he remembers the two men. He sees the shiny case once more and decides he has to know what is inside. He can see the little wheels with numbers that spin when he touches them. He is an innocent boy but also quite smart. He guesses that the numbers are the key to unlock the case. He tries different combinations starting with 0000, and then 1111 but soon realizes that it will not be that simple. He figures the numbers would be something easy for Papa to remember. Suddenly he thinks about the games the two had played when Papa was teaching him the names of the numbers in Italian and English. Federico would have to think of a number from one to ten and Papa would guess which one. He would always start the game with the number nine because he liked it so much until he figured out that Papa knew he was going to do that. One day Papa asked him why he always picked that number and he told him because it was his favorite, he liked the sound of the word nine in English. Then he said his next favorite was five. Papa said that five was also a number he liked very much but that his favorite was one. Federico thinks that maybe he needs a nine and two fives and a one. He tries various combinations until he dials 9515 and, much to his surprise, the latch pops open.

He slowly lifts the lid and gasps at all the money it contains. He stares at it for many minutes. He is moved from his trance when he realizes it is all his now. Like a flare igniting in the sky an idea comes to him, he knows what he must do. He places the case on the floor of the dugout to untie the rope holding the boat fast. It starts to float downriver as he tugs at the cord to start the engine like Papa has shown him. His young mind churns with ideas as he decides to head to the big city where Papa took him last year, where he had to wear long pants, a new shirt and stiff shoes. He will hide his money and start a new life. He knows he is only a boy of eleven, but he is smart enough to survive.

As the boat moves toward the Pacific Ocean, the boy's wonderment turns to anger as he concentrates on the faces of the men who had sailed away in the night. He guesses that they have killed his Papa and made him to be alone. By the time the young man reaches the mouth of the Sambu River, he has dedicated his small being to finding the two men. He swears he will one day take their families away. Just as they have taken his.

Allan Hudson lives in the seaside community of Cocagne, New Brunswick, Canada with his wife Gloria. The surrounding waters, the outlying island and the cheerful people he surrounds himself with are all an inspiration for his many stories. His short story, The Ship Breakers, received honorable mention at the Kyle Douglas Memorial contest. This is his first novel.

A collection of his short stories will soon be available in both digital format and hard copy. He is presently working on his second novel, The Wall of War.

Please visit his website for more information and especially for more entertainment.

www.allanhudson.ca

Made in the USA
Charleston, SC
13 November 2015